DAVID O. MCKAY LIBRARY

P9-DVD-915

DATE DUE

OCT 25 2011

JUL 19 2011

Demco

PROPERTY OF:
DAVID O. McKAY LIBRARY
BYU-IDAHO
REXBURG ID 83460-040

BEYOND THE LIMIT

BEYOND THE LIMIT

The Dream of Sofya Kovalevskaya

JOAN SPICCI

A TOM DOHERTY ASSOCIATES BOOK
NEW YORK

This is a work of fiction. All the characters and events portrayed in this novel are either fictitious or are used fictitiously.

BEYOND THE LIMIT: THE DREAM OF SOFYA KOVALEVSKAYA

Copyright © 2002 by Joan Spicci

All rights reserved, including the right to reproduce this book, or portions thereof, in any form.

This book is printed on acid-free paper.

Edited by James Frenkel

Book design by Jane Adele Regina

A Forge Book
Published by Tom Doherty Associates, LLC
175 Fifth Avenue
New York, NY 10010

www.tor.com

Forge® is a registered trademark of Tom Doherty Associates, LLC.

Library of Congress Cataloging-in-Publication Data

Spicci, Joan.
    Beyond the limit : the dream of Sofya Kovalevskaya / Joan Spicci.—1st ed.
        p. cm.
    "A Tom Doherty Associates book."
    ISBN: 0-765-30233-0 (acid-free paper)
        1. Kovalevskaëi, S. V. (Sof§'i Vasil§'vna), 1850–1891—Fiction. 2. Kovalevskiæ, Vladimir Onufrievich, 1842–1883—Marriage—Fiction. 3. Russia—History—1801–1917—Fiction. 4. Women mathematicians—Fiction. I. Title.

    PS3619.P648 B49 2002
    813'.6—dc21

                                                                    2002024363

First Edition: August 2002

Printed in the United States of America

0 9 8 7 6 5 4 3 2 1

To Sofya,
and all the unheralded women, past, present, and future,
who struggle in pursuit of an education

To Fred,
and all the unheralded men, past, present, and future,
who assist them

ACKNOWLEDGMENTS

The author is indebted to E. T. Bell's *Men of Mathematics* whose mention of Kovalevskaya first sparked her interest in the remarkable woman. Roger Cooke and P. Ia. Kochina's expositions of Kovalevskaya's mathematical work were invaluable. Most especially, thanks are due to Ann Hibner Koblitz for her masterly biography of Kovalevskaya and her untiring scholarship on Russian women pioneers of learning. The author is in great admiration of Koblitz's personal efforts to advance the opportunities of women mathematicians from underdeveloped countries. Ms. Koblitz has been most gracious and generous in offering encouragement during the author's long pursuit of an understanding of Kovalevskaya.

As with any historical work, numerous sources were referenced.

For Russian material, thanks are due to Laura Metzler, librarian, and to Oriental Research Partners for locating sources. And thanks to Ivana Černá for assistance in translation.

Special thanks and gratitude to my husband, Fred, for his expert advice, encouragement, patience, and emotional support. Thanks to the Saberhagen Grant for providing the author with the financial freedom to work on this project.

Any oversights and errors are the responsibility of the author.

PROLOGUE

Winter 1865 ❧ *Petersburg, Russia*

Through the double-paned window of her aunt's sitting room, Sofya watched the servant girl descend the front stairs. The small, slight figure hesitated a moment, pulling at her scarf until her nose and mouth were covered. Head lowered, she hurried along the freshly swept walk. On both sides of the walk new snow sparkled brilliantly in the late morning sun that offered light but no warmth.

A shiver went through Sofya, as surely as if she, not the servant, were facing the biting cold wind that whipped across the frozen river and down the streets of Vasilievsky Island.

With that servant girl go my chances for a happy future, Sofya thought mournfully.

This time Anyuta had gone too far with her defiance of parental authority.

Punishment might well be exile from their aunt's house and from Petersburg.

Just a few days ago, Sofya would have welcomed being sent back to their country home. Winters at Palibino were her time of freedom. Freedom to slide down the banisters without Mother's lectures on unfeminine behavior. Freedom to listen to Father's conversations with his male friends on politics, science, and mathematics. Freedom to explore the universe contained in Father's library. The winters had been lonely without her older sister, but that loneliness had been bearable.

That was before she had met *him*.

Last September, at Sofya's name day celebration, Mother announced that in the coming winter season, Sofya, now a young woman of fifteen summers, must be introduced to the culture of the capital, to balls, to the theater, to the young men of her own class.

Sofya had no desire for Petersburg society or for the inevitable unfavorable comparisons that would be whispered regarding her and her older sister. Sofya considered an appeal to her father for just one more winter at Palibino, but before she had found the right opportunity, a change occurred.

As far back as Sofya could remember, she had admired and envied her beautiful, spirited older sister. And Anyuta had treated her as a tagalong annoyance. Then, once Mother had decided that Sofya would come to Petersburg, Anyuta's attitude suddenly changed. She began to talk to Sofya as a friend, almost as an equal. Sofya reveled in the change, even though she suspected Anyuta was mainly interested in securing a loyal ally in the city. Anyuta wanted to be a new woman and Petersburg was the center of the new women's world.

Now, since Sofya had met *him*, the man who might soon appear, she had much more to lose than the tolerating attentions of her older sister. To be near this man would be to know freedom without loneliness. With a man like him, in a place like Petersburg, her life could be a Beethoven sonata.

Sofya turned from the window and glared at her sister. They were alone in the room, and for that matter, in the house. The few servants, perhaps suspecting some indiscretion, were keeping well out of sight. A special sale on party dress material had been announced in the morning paper, and Aunt Sofya had gone out shopping, taking Mother with her. No sooner had the women departed than daring Anyuta had sent the servant girl with a message summoning Fedor Mikhailovich Dostoevsky.

"Anyuta, Father forbade you to see Dostoevsky alone. If he finds out you invited him here . . ."

"I won't be alone with Fedor. You'll be here."

"To be precise, Father said you were not to see Dostoevsky unless Mother was present."

"You really must stop worrying about Father or you will never know life, my little one." With catlike grace Anyuta flung herself into a chair. Sofya watched as a smile spread from her eyes to her lips. " 'Father says, Father says!' " Anyuta lowered her voice to imitate Father's deep tones. "Dostoevsky is in poor health. Dostoevsky is a widower. Dostoevsky struggles to support his dead wife's grown, good-for-nothing son. Dostoevsky is in the filthy business of journalism, and he's not making any money. And on top of that, he was a convict. Altogether, an unsuitable companion!"

Anyuta again changed her voice, this time to imitate Mother whispering. "I have heard that Dostoevsky was seen in all the gambling dens in Europe with the daughter of a wealthy merchant."

Sofya laughed at Anyuta's accurate impersonations. Anyuta was never intimidated by Mother or Father.

Anyuta continued now in her own voice. "He was seen in the spa at

Baden-Baden with Polina Prokofevna Suslova. Everyone knows about that." Anyuta's eyes twinkled. "He's the most interesting man I've ever known. *And*, he's published my short story in his journal. I will meet with him!"

"Remember the last time Dostoevsky was here . . ."

The smile left Anyuta's pretty face. "Yes, my dear little sister, I remember." Her voice turned angry. "I remember how Mama flustered him with her silly questions and senseless talk of the weather. You don't talk to a sensitive man like Dostoevsky that way. And Aunt Sofya! She kept making excuses to come into the room just to look at the man. He must have felt like a creature in the zoological gardens, being gawked at by Sunday visitors. Now I have a chance for friendship with this extraordinary man, and I won't let it be destroyed. And I don't want him to think my whole family is scatterbrained."

Anyuta's eyes were shining mischievously. She stood up and walked nervously about the room. She picked up a trifle of pottery from a table, traced its glazed surface with her fingers, then replaced it. "I must talk with him where we can be free of Mother and Aunt Sofya."

"Mother will send you back to Palibino, if she hears about it."

Anyuta shook her head and spoke slowly, as if to a child. "Sofya, Mother will not send me back to Palibino. She wants me to stay in Petersburg and find a husband. I'm twenty-two years old and unattached. I'm being displayed, Sofya. The custom is very old-fashioned and most disgusting."

Anyuta smoothed her dress as she spoke. Then she daringly unbuttoned the top button on the bodice.

Sofya looked at her with envy. Anyuta's thick blond hair and flawless fair complexion made her a classic beauty. Her fine features reminded Sofya of a porcelain doll. Today the older sister was wearing a blue poplin dress trimmed in blue silk. A narrow blue belt with a delicate silver clasp accented her tiny waist. Anyuta refused to wear a bustle. Progressive young women often protested against such decorations, and anyway, on Anyuta's tall, slim figure the soft folds of the dress in a natural shape were more attractive.

Sofya glanced down at her own attire; a knee-length, dark blue, cotton-bibbed jumper with a blue striped blouse. The dark cotton stockings she wore no longer clung neatly to her legs, but sagged loosely at the ankles and calves. The color of her dress did not flatter her dark complexion and unruly, wavy dark hair. She was sure the outfit made her look short and chubby. Unbuttoning the top button of her blouse would have been useless. Sofya was painfully aware that she had nothing to show with a *décolletage*. Had she known Dostoevsky was coming, she would never have worn this childish jumper. Now it was too late to change.

Anyuta smoothed her hair with her hand and turned around slowly. "Do you see any strings or lint?"

"You look very elegant," Sofya assured her.

Satisfied, Anyuta sat down on the divan and began to flip through the pages of the weekly literary journal. Sofya sat at the opposite end of the divan with her legs tucked under her.

Anyuta spoke defiantly, but quietly, as if she were bolstering her own courage. "I want to see Fedor Mikhailovich. I will see him, away from Mother's prying eyes." Anyuta flipped the pages of the magazine. "Mother and Father's rules can be opposed." She looked at Sofya. "You've opposed them. You have courage and fortitude. But you haven't yet developed cunning. Your attacks are too direct. Watch me and learn, little sister."

Sofya felt admiration, mixing with apprehension that in this case Anyuta might have miscalculated the power of parental authority. On several occasions, she had watched Anyuta's plans, strong on initiative and weak on strategy, go awry. Still, being a partner in a forbidden enterprise, especially one involving *him*, was exciting. Anyuta trusted her as an accomplice in this bid for independence and freedom.

Within half an hour, marked by the slow ticking clock in the next room, someone knocked at the door.

Before answering, Anyuta looked around the room nervously. Then she waved her hand toward the piano. "Sofya, play something for us. Set a proper, cultured mood. Something by Beethoven. Dostoevsky loves Beethoven."

Sofya hurried to the piano, anxious to please their guest.

Sofya heard the door open, and then the warmth of her idol's voice. She did not even turn to look as Anyuta showed Dostoevsky into the adjoining room.

DOSTOEVSKY, IN THE NEXT ROOM, was whispering something in Anyuta's ear, and Anyuta was giggling now. Sofya at the piano, nerves tight with the strain of trying to listen to her older sister while executing a particularly difficult musical phrase, could feel the *Pathétique* breaking all to pieces in her fingers. Murmuring prayers and forbidden curses under her breath, Sofya stared at the music and tried to find the magnificent patterns of Beethoven once again.

Soon, laughter came from that next room. Sofya paused in her playing and stared at the silent keys, her fingers idle for the moment. She had completed the first movement of the sonata. Her fingers ached. She waited for applause, some sign of appreciation. None came.

What could be occupying her audience? Might it be only in her imagination that her sister and the famous writer were sitting close together in there? Close enough to exchange whispers inaudible a room away?

The white door to the next room stood open and now from beyond it there was only silence. Sofya arose and went quietly to the door. Neither the kerosene lamps nor the candles had been lighted in the small sitting room beyond, though only a pale glow of daylight came in through the frosty windows. The dark red wallpaper with its maroon vertical stripes, the matching velvet of the divan, the darkly painted floor all contributed to the dimness.

Anyuta was seated on the divan, her left profile turned in her sister's direction. Her face was most flatteringly silhouetted. The afternoon's fading light was at her back.

Dostoevsky, seated an arm's length away, leaned toward her. His hand, with fingers spread, pressed on the cushion that separated them.

Anyuta looked down at Dostoevsky's hand. She slowly fingered the velvet edged cushion that separated them. Her lips were turned up slightly in a half smile. With difficulty Sofya controlled a wave of jealousy. She had seen Anyuta use this exact expression and pose when flirting with other suitors.

Dostoevsky's left hand reached out and enclosed Anyuta's.

The pale light was focused on Fedor Mikhailovich, who looked sickly and tired today, worse than when Sofya had seen him last. His brown tweed suit coat hung from his shoulders as if it were a size too large. The black trousers draped too loosely over boots that did not match his jacket. His linen shirt was clean, but too shiny at cuffs and collar, much too worn for proper fashion. His whole appearance was disheveled, clothes wrinkled as if he'd slept in them. His unkempt reddish hair and beard were turning grayer by the month.

Dostoevsky was speaking. "Anyuta, I read your sensitive nature in your stories, and in the letters we have exchanged." He stuttered for a moment and went on, "I had hoped your letters would be filled with warmth. Letters of a Tatyana to an Onegin. I dreamed . . ."

Anyuta looked at him with a full smile. His face grew redder as he added: "Of course, letters like that can only have been written by a Pushkin."

Sofya thought he was talking too quickly, almost as if he were afraid of what might happen if he stopped. When he paused for Anyuta's reply, he bit his lower lip. His fingers nervously pulled at the hairs of his sparse beard.

Anyuta answered in a laughing tone, that sounded to Sofya like an imitation of innocence. "I too love Pushkin, but one thing puzzles me. Sometimes he writes with such admiration of his heroine's feet. I am at a loss. Can it be that a woman's feet are so very attractive to a man?"

Now Anyuta stared at her own feet, crossing and uncrossing them rhythmically.

Anyuta was wearing her blue velvet embroidered house shoes, without any stockings. A trace of bare ankle was visible even to Sofya.

Dostoevsky's gaze became fixed on the shifting feet, while he continued to talk more nervously and excitedly than before. "I am sure that the great master knew very well the nature of a man in love."

Dostoevsky's face was now very red.

"We will speak of something else." Anyuta slowly pulled her hand away from Dostoevsky's. She sat more rigidly, folded her hands in her lap. The action appeared to make Dostoevsky's discomfort even greater. There was silence. Then at last Anyuta continued, "Tell me about your business. The journal is doing well?"

In a moment Fedor Mikhailovich, much more at ease, was telling Anyuta of his efforts to organize the next issue of his journal, *Epoch*.

Anyuta appeared to listen attentively to her companion's outpouring of difficulties, now and then interrupting with comforting or encouraging words.

Sofya, stung by the fact that her efforts at the piano had been ignored, was standing boldly in the doorway, hands on her hips. Surely the couple must be aware of her presence.

But they seemed to have eyes only for each other. "Anya," Dostoevsky said, breaking a pause in the conversation. "I'm very glad you asked me to come. I was afraid that you would never want to see me again. After our last meeting, I was sure you thought me a raving madman, unfit for a proper woman's society."

Still he had not turned his gaze toward the doorway. Sofya wondered if he really did not see her.

"Nothing of the kind, Fedor," Anyuta assured him sweetly.

"Oh, but you must have! I couldn't, I really couldn't, speak sense in front of your mother and your aunt." Nervously his hands played with the edge of his coat, then passed over his knees in a rubbing motion. "I know this happens to me. I become tongue-tied and stupid whenever I'm with people who make me uncomfortable. In my discomfort I begin to talk about things that are totally inappropriate to the situation. I can't stop myself. I talk and talk. Finally, I feel the people around me are totally disconcerted and want only for me to leave. That's what happened that night with your family." He paused and folded his hands together almost as in prayer. "Please forgive me."

His speech completely wiped out Sofya's jealousy. She wanted to shout her forgiveness, her understanding, to take his hands and hold them to her cheek. She would confess that she too had felt the sting of social ineptitude. But he wouldn't even look at her. She remained at the doorway, hands now limp at her sides, and watched.

Slowly Anyuta lifted her chin. It seemed to her sister that she was drawing out her actions like the heroine in some melodramatic play. Didn't Dostoevsky see how she was playing with his emotions? Of course Anyuta could know nothing of the discomfort Dostoevsky had expressed. Sofya had never, ever, seen her older sister uncomfortable in any social situation.

At last Anyuta glanced toward the doorway, briefly acknowledging Sofya's presence. Blushing with embarrassment at the possibility of being thought an eavesdropper, Sofya edged back a little into the room where the piano waited.

Meanwhile their visitor, looking as awkward as a raw youth, still had not glanced in Sofya's direction. He grasped Anyuta's hand again, and for a moment Sofya wondered if he was going to kiss it, not formally as he had done on entering the apartment, but with an unrestrained passion. Sofya's eyes widened expectantly.

Anyuta stood up quickly. Dostoevsky was still grasping her hand and staring at her, his eyes blazing. He seemed on the brink of some great declaration.

"Fedor Mikhailovich, we are not alone!" Anyuta reprimanded him. "My sister is present."

Sofya felt the blood rushing to her cheeks. She wanted to hide, or perhaps even to cry. Would the great man now consider her a spy?

Dostoevsky's eyes turned toward her, at first blankly, as if he had forgotten who she was. Then they began to twinkle in a gentle, childlike way. Sofya sensed that again they shared a common feeling.

He stood up, brought his heels together and bowed slightly in her direction. "I thank you for the lovely piano music." The words sounded perfectly sincere. There was no mockery, no condescending to her youth. Again Sofya felt herself blushing, this time with pleasure.

Anyuta came to stand behind her sister, placing her hands on Sofya's shoulders. "Fedor Mikhailovich, on your last visit you encountered some of the older women of our clan. Their frivolous talk made you uneasy. I will demonstrate to you that the younger women of this clan are not foolish." Anyuta's voice carried a hint of playful mockery. "For myself, I have already offered you my work as an author."

"But I didn't mean . . ." Dostoevsky started, but Anyuta interrupted.

"I am not unique. I am not an oddity. Others of my sex and generation are engaged in serious endeavors. I present to you another woman"—she laughed at her own theatrics—"well, a very *young* woman, of the clan Korvin-Krukovskaya. Fedor Mikhailovich, my young sister writes verses!" Anyuta's eyes were glowing, her face flushed; she was beautiful. "Let me get the poems for you." Then the older sister, her skirts swirling, disappeared from the room.

Sofya, in agony as to whether she should protest or not, looked to Fedor. His eyes were not on her. The man of experience was staring after Anya; it was a hungry, almost hopeless look.

Will any man ever look at me like that? Let alone a noble, wise, sensitive man like this one . . .

Fedor Mikhailovich continued to look right past her, through the doorway where beautiful Anyuta had disappeared.

Sofya felt herself growing very warm all over. She had written the verses only to amuse herself while playing in the halls at Palibino. She was proud of them, but she knew they were only a beginner's attempt.

Anyuta returned, walking calmly, unhurried now. Silently she handed Sofya's notebook to the visitor. Anyuta and Dostoevsky's eyes met and lingered.

Anyuta moved about the room, lighting lamps. The increased light and the smell of kerosene drove the last wisps of magical romance from the room.

Dostoevsky took out a pair of steel-rimmed reading glasses and put them on. Then, slowly turning pages, he read out loud the titles of her poems.

" 'The Bedouin's Address to His Horse'—'The Sensations of the Fisherman as He Dives for Pearls'—'The Fountain Jet.' Well, let us see what we have here." Then, moving nearer a lamp where the light was stronger, he read quickly and silently to himself.

For a moment or two after he had finished reading Fedor Mikhailovich was still. Then he raised his eyes to Sofya—it was almost as if he were looking at her for the first time. "But this is very, very good. You show great promise."

Sofya had to harden herself against a wave of faintness. What ought she to say? "Thank you." In her own ears her voice sounded foolish.

"Some day, you too may be a published writer like your sister. But you must work at it very hard. Just as your sister will." And Dostoevsky's gaze returned lovingly—yes, that was the word—to Anyuta.

Anyuta had seated herself on the divan again. Noticing Sofya's deep blush, Anyuta mischievously chose to prolong her sister's discomfort. "Sofya's also very good at the sciences. Her tutor is very much impressed with her quickness at mathematics, though Mother thinks Sofya's already absorbed quite enough geometry and so on for a woman."

With a frown and a shake of the head, Fedor Mikhailovich demonstrated his scorn for such an illiberal attitude. Doubtless, thought Sofya, his reaction would have been stronger had it not been directed at Mother.

With a playful laugh Anyuta continued: "The two of us share a room while we're staying here in Petersburg. And late at night, when Sofya thinks no one is looking, she brings out a secret book and reads it by the light of the icon lamp. You'll never guess what she's reading."

Sofya was mortified. This time her sister had really gone too far. Sofya had been flattered to support a point in her sister's argument. Now Anyuta, sensing she was in complete control of the situation, was letting her playful nature take over. Sofya knew and dreaded that teasing tone in Anyuta's voice. "Please! Anya!"

Anyuta was not to be put off. "Guess, Fedor!"

Fedor Mikhailovich looked uncomfortable. But he was under Anyuta's spell, he could not refuse. "A romance by George Sand?"

"No! Guess again!"

He looked surprised at the failure of that first guess. Sofya could see him thinking: *But what else is a young girl likely to want to read?*

"Guess again!" Anyuta insisted in a playful way.

Taking up Anyuta's teasing tone, he answered, "How about Herzen's *The Bell*—or one of the other forbidden progressive journals her older sister hides away?"

"Anya, you promised not to tell!" Sofya tried again to stop her sister.

Anyuta ignored Sofya's entreaty. "No! You'll never guess it. She's reading an *algebra book* she's sneaked from our father's library!"

An angry pounding was beginning in Sofya's head. She had been betrayed. In a moment of confidence, Sofya had tried to explain to her sister her fascination with algebra. Just as words and images of poetry opened a room in her soul, so too the symbols and logic of mathematics opened a similar room. Anyuta's complete lack of understanding and her cruel laughter left Sofya with the feeling that her attraction to mathematics was unnatural. And now Anyuta was laughing again.

After a moment of silence infinitely painful to Sofya, Fedor Mikhailovich responded, "Such talent." His eyes moved slowly from her face to her feet, then back to her face. "And such a pretty girl."

Sofya was looking straight into his eyes, and for a moment there was a distance in his look, an utter lack of comprehension, that chilled her heart. Even he, who was educated as an engineer, did not understand her feelings for mathematics.

Then he must have seen her pain for his eyes softened, he rallied. "You know that you have extraordinary gypsy eyes?" he said just above a whisper.

Was it possible that he really thought her pretty? Her pain vanished. Sofya felt her cheeks warming to a blush. She longed to say something clever, something that would keep his eyes on her.

He must have interpreted her silence as a conclusion. He turned toward Anyuta who was seated on the divan. Sofya watched as Anyuta captured his complete attention. Sofya remained in the room, her presence unrecognized. Once more she watched Fedor Mikhailovich with silent admiration.

"Your demonstration of talented young people reminds me of an incident that occurred on my way here today." He was talking almost to himself as much as to Anyuta. "What a varied group you young people are."

"Whatever are you referring to?" Anyuta asked with a joking tone in her voice, a little blush coming to her cheeks.

"As I was rushing here from my office, I saw a young boy, a newspaper seller, about the same age as your sister. Poor fellow had no overcoat and was clutching his light jacket closely to his body. The boy possessed a natural spirit of friendliness mixed with the subservience so common in our lower classes. The young salesman called out a synopsis of the day's stories.

"A brassy young man dressed in the smart uniform of the Tsar's Corps des Pages, a young man no older than our paper seller, complained loudly that the paper was, indeed, yesterday's paper and not the latest morning issue. Our paper seller was thrown into confusion. Clearly this seller of papers could not read.

"The page in his sparkling uniform was laughing.

"The paper seller rushed off in despair, eyes so clouded with tears that he collided with me. Our eyes met. I saw the look of the humiliated, the trapped. The eyes of a prisoner. A look I have seen all too often."

For a moment the room was still.

Sofya and Anyuta were waiting for Dostoevsky's next words. None came.

"Prison must have been unbearable for you." Anyuta was trying to bring her visitor out of his trancelike state.

"Had it not been for the kindness of one aristocratic woman, a Decembrist's wife, I would have lost my senses." Dostoevsky was thoughtful, then continued, "When I stepped from the train and looked around at the vast bleak horizon of the Siberian landscape, when my mind raced forward to the years I would have to spend in desolation, this woman came up to me. With a smile, she handed me a book, the Bible."

"She said nothing to you?" Anyuta asked.

"Only that she would pray for me, as she did for all prisoners," Dostoevsky continued. "During the first year of my imprisonment, I was allowed no books, other than that Bible. I would have lost my mind had I not had that book. It will always be my most cherished possession. A reminder that I was a prisoner, that I was saved from madness by a stranger's kindness. And that without the law and hope offered in that Book, all is lost."

Sofya's eyes were wide with fascination as she asked, "Did you meet any murderers?"

"The politicals, like myself, were in the same dormitory with the civil criminals. Yes, I came to know many murderers, rapists, thieves, arsonists. I came to know how they think and what they feel. Prison is so . . ." He broke off suddenly. "But I had not meant to torment two lovely young ladies with such horrors. The Tsar's page was a prisoner of his training and class, the paper boy a prisoner of his illiteracy. And here in this very privileged house I find two more young people who have had in their eyes, from time to time this afternoon, the look of prisoners. I believe I have guessed what caused this look in each of you."

"You certainly must tell us what you have guessed about us," Anyuta said, with a slight tease in her voice. Only Sofya recognized that there was also dread in her sister's voice.

Sofya silently prayed that Dostoevsky would not go on with his revelation. She felt a chill of fear for her sister and for herself. The man had the power to look into souls.

Dostoevsky looked at Anyuta and then briefly at Sofya. "My dear young ladies, these truths must be discovered, not uncovered."

"Now you are teasing us," Anyuta laughed.

Conversation was interrupted by sounds in the hall. A servant's voice, a door opening. Moments later, Mother came rushing into the room, still wearing her sable coat and hat. Unruly packages threatened to escape from her arms. She gasped and came to a halt as she took in the scene. Sofya could see shock, disapproval, and even a little fear written on her face: *Good God, he's come. And there was no proper chaperone! Dear God, don't let Vasily Vasilievich find out!*

Taking advantage of the need to exchange a few words with the servants who came to help with her packages and outdoor clothing, she turned her back to the girls and their visitor. When she faced them she was calm.

Elizaveta Fedorovna Korvin-Krukovskaya was impeccably dressed, as always. She was still very attractive at forty-five years of age, and aware of her attractiveness. On entering the sitting room she had been in a delightful mood. She loved Petersburg, the shopping, the social life . . . But in the next moment, upon encountering her unexpected visitor, she had become perplexed and indecisive, an attitude her daughters had seen many times. Sofya had long ago decided that Mother was more alarmed by the prospect of her husband scolding her than she was by Anyuta's sometimes indiscreet behavior.

Anyuta put her arm around her mother's waist. "Isn't it wonderful? Fedor Mikhailovich was in the neighborhood and impulsively decided to drop in to see us. We've been having the most enlightening discussion." Mother looked at Anyuta's smiling face, then at Sofya. Sofya did not contradict her sister. Sofya quickly glanced at the visitor to see if he would give them away. But he was looking at Anyuta. His eyes were glowing and he seemed to be suppressing a laugh.

Surrounded by smiling faces and Anyuta's warm hugs, Mother's anger was soon defused.

Mother greeted Fedor Mikhailovich quite civilly, and apologized for not being at home when he had called. Bowing slightly, he returned the greeting.

Elizaveta Fedorovna motioned them all back into the sitting room, where she ordered the servant to bring hot tea and sweets. Mother was soon steering the conversation. Sofya watched, not completely free of contempt, as Mother performed the part of the proper social hostess.

"Is your journal doing well, Fedor Mikhailovich?" Mother asked in an innocent voice, as she poured the tea.

Sofya and Anyuta exchanged worried glances. This could be a point of friction.

"Financially, the journal is barely surviving," Dostoevsky commented. "But money and I have never had a good relationship. On the other side, the stories and comments in the journal are worth the reading. A woman of your sensitivities and love for Petersburg and Russia could only approve of our discussions of social issues. In this month's issue I have included my story, 'The Crocodile.' The story is written in a humorous and fantastic style."

"Fedor Mikhailovich, I do not concern myself with politics or social commentaries or fantasy, however amusingly presented. I am interested in charity work and the arts, especially music."

Sofya heard Anyuta gasp with horror at Mother's response. But Dostoevsky had evidently decided that on this occasion Mother's views were better left unchallenged. He countered them with a compliment. "Your daughter, Sofya, has inherited your musical abilities. She has been most pleasantly displaying her skill for us."

Mother was flattered. "Sofya has a natural talent for the piano, but I'm afraid she doesn't practice as she should."

Sofya blushed at the reprimand. She watched Dostoevsky's face for his reaction. Did he think less of her because of this? She thought she saw him give a quick wink of understanding and reassurance in her direction.

"Sofya has her mind on other interests. Interests she will certainly need to develop." Dostoevsky was soothing. He continued, "All arts must be developed. I strongly urge you to encourage your daughter Anna in the development of her literary talents. She has shown quite a flair."

"My daughter's literary efforts must remain only a hobby for her."

"Mother!" Anyuta burst in. Her face was red with anger.

"The decision to develop their talents is theirs," Dostoevsky paused, "and yours and your husband's. They are also quite lovely ladies. Another quality they have inherited from their mother."

That answer was to Mother's liking. Anyuta was also soothed, although Sofya suspected that Anyuta and Mother would exchange some unpleasant words when the visitor was gone.

An hour later, they were all accompanying Fedor Mikhailovich to the door. He had bowed to Anyuta and Sofya, his eyes lingering rather longer on Anyuta.

Mother offered her hand to the visitor. "Fedor Mikhailovich, I hope you will visit us again soon." Sofya and Anyuta looked on in amazement.

Dostoevsky took her hand and kissed it politely. "The company of cultured women is always delightful." He arranged a woolen scarf around his neck, then pulled his beard out over the cloth. Then he tugged a woolen cap, whose color did not match the scarf, low over the crown of his balding head.

Mother hesitated for a moment as she observed with puzzlement, tempered with warmth, the man's eccentric appearance. Gentle teasing came into her voice, "Dostoevsky, you are a most brilliant and interesting man. But you really must find a woman to see to your wardrobe!"

Dostoevsky's eyes twinkled. He was not at all offended. "I intend to do that, madame." He bowed again to each of the ladies, his eyes again lingering on Anyuta.

The door closed. Dostoevsky was gone.

Elizaveta Fedorovna turned to her daughters. The smile disappeared from her face. She motioned Anyuta and Sofya back into the living room.

"Well, girls," she began. She was struggling to make her words sound firm and authoritarian. "You allowed yourselves to be put in a rather compromising position this afternoon by entertaining a male caller when there was no suitable chaperone."

"Mother, there was nothing else to do," Anyuta pleaded. "We only wanted to maintain the gracious reputation of our family." Her tone suggested that a sob might be imminent.

Mother paced the room nervously, apparently struggling to maintain an attitude of indignation and parental outrage.

Sofya knew that Anyuta could easily defuse her mother's resolve by forcing an emotional scene complete with sobs, tears and accusations of not being understood or loved. Sofya and Anyuta exchanged looks. Sofya saw that this time, Anyuta had decided not to create such a scene.

"We are guests in your aunt's house. You are to respect the proprieties of the Schubert home. Furthermore, if even a hint of this indiscretion were to reach your father at Palibino, he would order us all back to the country."

Sofya and Anyuta submitted silently to the scolding, aware that Mother's admonitions were largely a result of her own dread of returning to Father's watchful eye and to the loneliness of the country.

AFTER THAT MEETING, Dostoevsky was frequently a guest in the apartment.

On one such evening Anyuta, Sofya, and Mother sat and listened in wonder as Dostoevsky related a scene from a book he was planning.

Mother's eyes were shining and her skin had just a faint flush. With skepticism, Sofya acknowledged the impressions of her senses. She saw a certain subtle flirtation in Mother's attitude toward the visitor.

The observation forced her to think about certain facts she knew already. Dostoevsky was forty-four years old. One year younger than Mother! Twice as old as Anyuta! Almost three times older than herself! These were mathematically true relationships. Of course it was possible to argue that this was only a numerical result that had no meaning without a physical interpretation. Just as the negative roots of quadratic equations sometimes had to be disregarded, so this mathematical result must be somehow irrelevant to the practical problem.

"Sofya," Mother's voice was calling, "Whatever are you thinking of? I've asked you three times to pass the sugar."

"Sorry, Mama." Sofya passed the silver container, meanwhile silently scolding herself. How could she have let herself be so absorbed in calculations when *he* was here?

Fedor Mikhailovich's gentle smile at her seemed to say that he understood how much of a temptation one's own thoughts could be.

Then, turning his gaze from Sofya to Mother and then to Anyuta, he continued to relate a scene that he hoped to use in some future book. "The landowner in my story, up to the time of this scene, has shown a fatherly concern for the ten-year-old daughter of his cook. The girl is quite lovely and shows talent as a singer. The landowner has allowed the girl to sit in on the reading lessons given by his son's tutor."

The storyteller sat back in his chair, and his gaze went far away. "One evening this wealthy landowner, after a night of drunkenness and debauchery, returns home and instead of going to his room, decides to go down to the kitchen quarters. There the ten-year-old is asleep near the fireplace. The old man's eyes are glowing, he is excessively warm, from drink, from the heat of the fire. A forbidden thought comes to his mind. A thought so heinous that at first he is repulsed. But the thought keeps returning. There is no one else in the room but the girl. And, despite all the pleas of his conscience, he is drawn to the evil deed. He is the master of this house. She is his property. So go the arguments of his crippled mind. And then, this landowner, this man who believes he is the master, the only law on his property, decides to break the law of God. To take advantage of . . ."

"Fedor Mikhailovich, please! Not in front of my daughters!" Elizaveta Fedorovna, whose dismay had been growing, at last interrupted.

With a start, Dostoevsky rejoined his dinner companions. For a moment he seemed not to know where he was. Stuttering an apology, he blushed, and ran a hand nervously through his thinning hair.

His reaction touched Mother, who redirected the conversation. "Speaking of young children, there will be a benefit performance for the city orphanage this weekend. I have an extra ticket. Perhaps you would attend, Fedor Mikhailovich." All trace of anger had left Mother's voice.

He accepted the invitation. Sofya listened with tender admiration as Dostoevsky spoke of his visits to the city's unfortunate orphans.

IN HER SECRET DAYDREAMS, Sofya loved to pretend that she had been with Fedor Mikhailovich in exile in Siberia. In the great self-sacrificing tradition of the wives of the Decembrists, the revolutionaries of 1825, she had followed Fedor into exile. The wretched Siberian natives honored her as an angel of mercy. Her days were spent in doctoring and teaching. She pictured herself working beside Fedor, suffering with him for some great though vaguely defined cause, having much to do with honor and loyalty to friends. He was a man who would never betray his friends.

SOFYA AND ANYUTA WERE DOTED on by their spinster aunt. Excursions to one of Petersburg's museums, libraries, or schools of higher learning was her joy. Frequently Aunt Sofya reminded the girls that their maternal grandfather and great-grandfather had been respected scientists, remembered for their respective contributions to astronomy and geology. They had been good men, and they had stayed away from politics.

When the sisters were alone, Sofya confessed that she loved Aunt Sofya's stories of the old days.

Anyuta groaned, "I don't want to hear history, I want to live it! I want to shape the future world." Anyuta continued in the manner of an instructor, "Have you noticed that when Mother and Aunt Sofya are together they speak in hushed whispers about a handsome military widower or a shy middle-aged professor? In a word, Mother and Aunt Sofya behave like foolish schoolgirls. Thank goodness you and I have better things to talk about than men."

Sofya hesitantly asked, "Do you talk about men with your women friends when I'm not around?"

"Not very often. I wouldn't at all if I could meet some interesting people of my own age. Unfortunately, almost everyone we know is the son or daughter of one of Mother and Father's friends." Anyuta smiled in a way that meant she had a secret. "Still, little sister, some of these young people are beginning to think critically and to whisper their discontent."

"You do more than whisper your discontent, Anyuta," Sofya noted with admiration, "You do manage to make friends outside of Mother and Father's circle. At Palibino you managed a friendship with Semevsky, and then with Filippovich. They were both modern men."

Anyuta raised her chin, and in her sister's eyes took on something of the expression of a general reviewing conquests. "Yes, on a few occasions I have been able to break the parental guard." After a momentary hesitation she added, "Still, Semevsky was sent packing by Father in no uncertain manner. And poor Aleksei Filippovich, his own father disowned him and forced him out of our district!"

"Aleksei pronounced his 'o's very strongly," Sofya recalled, imitating the country accent precisely, making her sister laugh. "He sounds just like a priest."

"Aleksei acquired that accent from his father, and his training in the seminary just reinforced old habits. He can't seem to escape that part of his background, although his thoughts are freed." Anyuta sighed. "He wasn't at all polished, but he had a wonderful mind. He introduced me to Herzen's weekly newspaper, *The Bell*." Anyuta became less defensive. "Anyway, who cares if he spoke with an accent." She laughed. "And who cares if his fingernails were always disgustingly dirty."

"No reason to care, since you're not going to marry him," Sofya observed. "We'll never see either of them again at Palibino."

"Small loss. But neither Father nor Mother nor Aunt Sofya nor any other force is going to separate me from Dostoevsky."

THE VISIT TO PETERSBURG would last only a few months. The three Kovin-Krukovskaya ladies would have to return to Palibino before the April thaw made the country roads impassable. Aunt Sofya planned a large party in honor of her winter guests, and Elizaveta Fedorovna was given full rein in ordering all the arrangements exactly as she liked.

Elizaveta Fedorovna invited some military friends and comrades of her husband, some of Grandfather Schubert's old friends from the university, some distant relatives, and a few old friends from Elizaveta's maiden days. Anyuta suggested a few names from among the sons and daughters of Mother's friends—and calmly added the name of Fedor Mikhailovich Dostoevsky. Mother made no objections.

As the time drew near, Elizaveta worried about the success of the party. The apartment in the Schubert house, though large, was unfortunately not well designed to hold large gatherings, consisting as it did of a series of small, cell-like rooms. Most of the rooms were lined with shelves crowded with curios, and tables holding prized vases and other memorabilia collected by the very busy aunt.

Would the guests move from room to room in a congenial flow? Would the gathering of diverse people find subjects of mutual interest, or would there be long, awkward silences? Would a respectable number of invitations be accepted?

Elizaveta Fedorovna was especially pleased when André Ivanovich Kosich, a distant cousin on Elizaveta's side of the family, was the first to return his acceptance. André Ivanovich was about the same age as Anyuta. His military career was advancing at a steady pace, and already he held an honorable position as an aide on the General Staff. If anyone had asked, Elizaveta would have described the young man as very well favored, very handsome, and possessed of impeccably good manners and charm.

In the last year, young Kosich had visited Palibino several times. He came to ask Vasily Vasilievich's advice on career matters. On these occasions André Ivanovich had stayed longer than absolutely necessary, spending much of the time with his attractive cousin. And last fall, Anyuta had been allowed to make a special trip to Petersburg, to accompany the young officer to a military ball. At that time, Mother and Father had made it subtly known to Anyuta that they were very pleased the young man was showing a definite, though of course respectful, interest.

To Elizaveta's delight, in the next few days, almost all of the invited guests returned acceptance cards. The apartment would be filled to capacity.

ON THE EVENING OF THE PARTY, the energies of the four women were concentrated on their appearance. Each wore a new dress. Each fussed with makeup and hair styling.

Looking into the glass, Sofya admired her new dress of dark green silk sewn especially for this occasion by Aunt Sofya's favorite Petersburg dressmaker. This was Sofya's first evening gown, and like Anyuta, Sofya had insisted on not wearing a bustle. The loose folds of the skirt made a swishing noise as she walked. The short sleeves and low-cut bodice of the dress were trimmed with coy ruffles. With Anyuta's help, Sofya rouged her lips and penciled her eyebrows. Her self-willed chestnut curls had been coaxed into an orderly pattern. The face that smiled back at her from the mirror was a little unfamiliar. Sofya thought it a pretty face, though certainly not beautiful like Anyuta's.

Mother entered the girls' room to conduct a final inspection. She fluffed the bodice ruffle of Sofya's dress and gave Anyuta's hair one last touch with the comb. Then Mother noticed an errant string of green thread hanging loosely from Sofya's left sleeve. In a voice made too loud by nervousness, Mother demanded a pair of scissors. After a moment of frantic search, the tool was found. Mother cut the offending string. "I hope that's the last. Turn around once more, Sofya, let me look carefully. Yes. That's the last."

Aunt Sofya entered. Noticing Sofya's uneasiness, she gave the girl a hug and lavished compliments on her grown-up appearance. Aunt Sofya also presented gifts: for Anyuta, a pair of diamond earrings, for Sofya an emerald necklace with a single stone surrounded by silver filigree. The girls, dazzled, thanked their aunt. "Put them on. Put them on," the older woman insisted.

The appointed time had come. Four magnificently dressed women received the arriving guests. Numerous candles were burning in all the rooms, giving unwanted heat as well as a welcome flickering light. Two waiters in white shirts and formal coats walked about, offering fruit, sweets, and *perogie*, finger-sized meat and fruit pies. Tea, wine and iced vodka were available at a sideboard.

Sofya sat in one of the rooms near the entrance hall, nervously touching the stone of her necklace. Beside her was Nicholas Ivanovich Kosich, the younger brother of André Ivanovich. The young man looked quite dashing in his uniform. Nicholas Ivanovich told her he was an artillery man. "In the regiment your father once commanded," he added with pride. Sofya listened as he spoke boastfully of the advanced mathematics he had mastered to calculate trajectories. Sofya did her best to appear impressed. Had this distant cousin of hers stopped talking long enough, she would have told him that she had read about the techniques he was describing, and thought them rather simple. But he offered no such opportunity.

Just then Sofya saw Dostoevsky enter the next room. In an evident attempt to fit into the society he expected at the party, Fedor Mikhailovich had put on a black evening coat, but the garment was ill-fitting, and not at all flattering to his spare figure. His thinning red hair refused to submit to order and stood in disarray. Sofya's heart ached for him.

Dostoevsky's eyes were intently searching strangers' faces. He looked very nervous.

Smiling warmly, Mother approached him. While paying minimum attention to Nicholas Ivanovich, Sofya's mind and eye followed Dostoevsky. Mother was introducing him to some of the other guests. In discomfort and an apparently agitated state, he was only grunting monosyllables at them. To Sofya his response sounded more like a growl than a greeting. Sofya wanted to go to him, to put him at ease. But now Nicholas Ivanovich was asking her questions and she had to allow herself to be distracted.

Soon Sofya's companion was again absorbed in his own narration and Sofya could let her eyes search the nearby rooms for her Dostoevsky. Mother was introducing him to André Ivanovich, who had been speaking with Anyuta. Dostoevsky's eyes were focused on Anyuta and André Ivanovich. It would have been impossible for him not to notice what a strikingly good-looking couple Anyuta and André formed. Or that he himself was being introduced to his antithesis. André was a handsome, composed young officer dashingly dressed in his guard's uniform with tight white pants showing his long, muscular limbs and a perfectly tailored green military jacket with silver epaulets accentuating his strong shoulders.

Without apparent explanation, Dostoevsky took Anyuta by the hand and led her to an unoccupied divan where he appeared to start an earnest and private discussion. For a moment Mother, André Ivanovich, and, from the next room, Sofya, watched with surprise.

Sofya thought that she saw the young officer flush slightly, but in a moment his good manners prevailed and he turned his attention to Mother.

Sofya had to know what was happening. She interrupted her companion's monologue in the sweetest tone she could manage. "Could we adjourn to the other room? I'd like some refreshment."

The young man immediately rose. Suddenly unsure of himself, he profusely apologized for not anticipating her need. She smiled sweetly, and let her glance drop. She would imitate the silly mannerisms she had seen her sister use, if they would get her where she wanted to go. The young man responded, and they were soon in the other room.

Sofya's hands surrounded a cool glass of punch. Her companion had again begun a monologue, for which Sofya was grateful, because she needed only to nod her head occasionally. Her eyes, her ears, and her mind were free to absorb the scene unfolding.

Mother was now chatting with a retired officer, one of Father's friends. The man kept staring at Mother through his monocle and commenting in a fatherly—and yet not so fatherly—way: "Oh, such beauty! And your daughters, how beautiful they are. But my dear, you are more beautiful even than your daughters. Yes, even than your daughters!"

Mother flushed with pride, she let her glance drop. Sofya sighed; Mother was certainly a master of party mannerisms. As the man reached for Mother's hand, Mother stepped back just a little. Sofya heard Elizaveta Fedorovna gently excuse herself, pleading a need to speak with her daughter Anya.

Walking to the divan, Mother scolded gently. "Anya, dear, you're forgetting your other guests. I'm sure Fedor Mikhailovich does not want to occupy you in a *tête-à-tête* for the entire evening."

Anyuta started to rise.

"Anochka, please, another minute," said Fedor Mikhailovich, grasping her hand again. He leaned his body against Anyuta's to whisper into her ear.

Mother, watching, was turning pale. Sofya could hardly believe her ears. Here, in front of all these people, Dostoevsky had addressed her sister, a grown woman, with a name of endearment that indicated a strong degree of intimacy.

"Fedor Mikhailovich, please, do not forget yourself!" Anyuta scolded.

Dostoevsky flushed with embarrassment. Clearly the words had just slipped from his mouth. He rose to his feet. In a disturbingly loud voice he stuttered, "Anna Vasilievna, please, another minute!"

At that moment, Sofya's companion stopped his monologue and looked in the direction of the loud voice. With a few half-thought-out questions, Sofya reengaged her companion's monologue, while she continued her observation.

André Ivanovich evidently was also observing the situation. He strode up to the trio, his face expressing determination, his body conveying the image of a charging knight. Mother, Anya, and Dostoevsky were looking one to the other in a potentially explosive silence when André Ivanovich joined them, positioning his body between Anyuta and Dostoevsky.

Forcefully, strengthened by the factor of surprise, he engaged Dostoevsky.

"Fedor Mikhailovich," André Ivanovich began, fixing his eyes on Dostoevsky, "I have become embroiled in a discussion that demands the insight of someone of age and experience. Won't you join our group?" André motioned vaguely to an adjoining room.

"What could warrant such a rude interruption?" Dostoevsky demanded.

"A matter of literature." André Ivanovich reached for Dostoevsky's arm, evidently to lead him away. Dostoevsky recoiled.

"Talk to him, Fedor Mikhailovich," Anyuta urged, as she moved to Dostoevsky's side. Her voice conveyed sarcasm as she added, "I'd like to hear what questions of literature an officer might have."

Dostoevsky silently examined the young officer, then turned to Mother, whose cold expression offered no support. She moved closer to André, and placed her hand lightly on the young man's arm, unmistakably announcing her preference and allegiance. Dostoevsky's face grew red. Mother didn't flinch. Her eyes reflected the ferocity of a she-bear defending her cub.

"I overheard some of your discussion. I've read the volume in question." Dostoevsky barely moved his lips as he replied to André. "I understand it has been quite popular in Petersburg's German society. What of value can anyone expect from a German? All Germans are pigheaded, thinking only their way is right. They are corrupting the purity of Russia." Dostoevsky pronounced the word "German" in a distinctly condescending, condemning manner.

Kosich's temper flared. "Sir, I am of German ancestry. I understand your remarks as an insult to myself and my family. If that was your intent, sir, I would be obliged to defend my honor."

Mother gasped. Her hand dropped from Kosich's arm. "Kosich, you're being much too rash!" Her look of firm, self-satisfied resolve had melted to fear at the suggestion of a duel.

Anyuta took Dostoevsky by the arm. "I'm sure Fedor Mikhailovich meant no insult to our cousin or to our family."

Dostoevsky's face had become very red. Sofya could see beads of perspiration forming on his forehead, but his eyes were still blazing. "Pardon, I meant no insult." Dostoevsky directed his apology to Anyuta, then to Mother, and, only after an agonizing pause, to Kosich.

Sofya's escort had made a step toward Kosich, as if in support of his brother. Sofya caught his arm, holding him back from the encounter.

Nervously Anyuta responded, "Your apology is accepted by all of us, I'm sure. Now, let us discuss this book like the civilized, cultured individuals we all pride ourselves on being. Or let us talk about something else."

Dostoevsky and Kosich glared at each other once more. Mother stammered, desperately attempting to salvage the conversation. "There is something of value in the Lutheran ideals mentioned in the book you cited. Many theologians have argued strongly for the necessity of individual Bible reading."

"The great Lutheran theologian, Johann Ernst Schubert, argued just this point." Kosich, staring at Dostoevsky, spoke with pride. "He was Elizaveta Fedorovna's great-grandfather."

"I know of the Schuberts," Dostoevsky responded curtly. "You don't have to drag all your ancestors into this discussion." With an air of having put aside a tiresome, nagging child, Dostoevsky turned toward Mother. He could contain his rage no longer. "Madame! Do Russian society women care about the Bible or about Christ? They know Christ taught: 'Wives, be subject to your husbands—husbands, love your wives.' Russian mothers know this, and still engage in the most crass, materialistic matchmaking for their daughters." Dostoevsky's fiery look went to André.

Before anyone had seized the chance to interrupt him, Dostoevsky continued, waving his arms in his anger: "Arranging marriages on the basis of property, money, position—never thinking of their daughters' or the suitors' welfare, inclinations, attractions."

Dostoevsky's left arm had struck a large vase on a nearby table. The urn tottered for a moment and then fell, to shatter with a loud noise upon the polished parquet floor.

For the space of two or three heartbeats the room was totally silent. Elizaveta Fedorovna stared at Fedor Mikhailovich. A tear had escaped and was running down her cheek, carrying with it a light blue trail of eye rouge.

"Excuse me, gentlemen." Elizaveta Fedorovna's voice quavered only slightly. "I will return in a moment." She started to walk from the room, then turned back. "Anya, I need your help."

Anyuta followed her.

A maid began fussing over the pieces of the destroyed urn.

Too late, Dostoevsky realized how harshly he had spoken. He began to apologize, too abjectly, to the stunned guests who had gathered around for the accident.

André Ivanovich turned without a word and walked away. His younger brother, who had been accompanying Sofya, went to Kosich, giving him the comfort of approving words. Guests who had been staring at the scene resumed their conversations a touch more loudly than before.

Dostoevsky sat on the divan, leaning forward, hiding his face from the world with his hands. Silently, Sofya sat next to him. She wanted to take his hand, to tell him his outburst was forgiven, that she understood his struggle to control his feelings. But she was too shy to touch him, or say anything. Soon the writer left the apartment, saying goodbye to no one.

THAT EVENING, as Sofya and Anyuta were preparing for sleep, Anyuta confessed that Dostoevsky had gravely disappointed her. The man was completely without social grace.

Sofya defended her friend. "Some people have a right and maybe even a duty to behave without inhibition, especially if they're upholding their beliefs. Dostoevsky was only stating what he believes is the truth."

"He could have done so with more grace," Anyuta insisted.

Anyuta tucked the down covers close around herself, then yawned and said goodnight. Sofya put out the lamp. She looked across at her sister. Anyuta just did not understand Dostoevsky.

FIVE DAYS ELAPSED before Mother allowed Fedor Mikhailovich to reappear at the Schubert house.

For a week he had visited almost every day. Sometimes, Anyuta refused to postpone other activities in order to entertain him. At those times, Dostoevsky would talk with Sofya, who convinced herself that Dostoevsky enjoyed their meetings more than the times he spent with the indifferent Anyuta.

One evening, Anyuta and Sofya were alone in the apartment. Anyuta sat at one end of the divan embroidering, as Sofya sat at the other end, reading aloud from a collection of Pushkin. Unexpectedly, Dostoevsky arrived.

"Where were you last night?" he blurted out angrily, confronting Anyuta.

"I was at a ball," she answered shortly, not looking up from her embroidery.

"I suppose André Ivanovich was there?"

"Yes, as were many others."

"You danced with him? A waltz, I suppose. Or was it a Polish polka?"

Now Anyuta did put down her needlework. "Fedor Mikhailovich, there's no reason why I shouldn't enjoy myself in the few days I have left in Petersburg."

"You are a silly, frivolous little girl. Not a woman." Head lowered, he paced the length of the room. Looking up, his eyes caught Sofya's as she watched him, an open book in her lap. "I'm sure Sofya Vasilievna will not conduct herself so when she's grown. She'll be a beauty with brains!"

Sofya was confused. Dostoevsky thought her a beauty, but this violent outburst of jealousy must mean that he cared only for Anyuta. A silent, furious, angry jealousy toward Anyuta was taking over Sofya's mind, a violence of emotion that rivaled Dostoevsky's outburst.

Anyuta was glaring back at Dostoevsky. "Attending an occasional ball does not make me frivolous!"

Fedor Mikhailovich stopped.

Sofya looked at her sister. Anyuta was standing. She was almost as tall as Dostoevsky. Her hands were on her hips, and she leaned forward a little from the waist, putting her body in a defiant position directly in front of his. A fire of angry indignation blazed from Anyuta's eyes. Gradually Dostoevsky's face changed from raw jealousy to calculated indignation. He took a half step back and raised the shield of agitated ranting that he frequently hid behind.

His speech was slow at first, each syllable carefully pronounced. "Perhaps it's better that you are frivolous." When Anyuta didn't reply, he continued at an accelerating rate. "Better frivolous than one of the new women, the 'Women of the Sixties,' as they call themselves. I've heard rumors about their deplorable actions! Women of good family who have left their homes and are living in apartments with girls from the country. The new women think they can help the freed serfs become integrated into city life, or some such notion. These young women of the gentry even take jobs in factories to associate with the working women. These so-called new women don't believe in God, marriage, or the fatherly love of the Tsar for his people. They despise all established institutions. You know what happens when belief in authority fails? Tragedy. Look at America. One deranged individual driven by a cause has just assassinated Lincoln! That's what happens when righteous individuals put themselves above the law." He paused for a moment, his mind obviously retreating to some distant refuge. More calmly he continued, "The women are called 'nihilists.' Turgenev invented the term to describe one of his ridiculous characters."

Anyuta interrupted. Her reply was loud and defiant. "I've read Turgenev's novel, *Fathers and Children*. The book distorts modern views. But what else should a reader expect from an old man writing about young ideas?"

Dostoevsky glared at her. Clearly he had taken offense.

Anyuta continued, "I think the women of whom you speak so scornfully are saints! They put their beliefs into action. They're not just talking about reforms, philosophizing about goodness. How can you be so blind as to not see this? How can you confine your love of humanity to paper?"

Dostoevsky grew pale. He swayed slightly. He sat down in the chair across from the divan.

Anyuta was still looking at him accusingly.

Dostoevsky put his hands to his head. The room was silent. Sofya rushed to Dostoevsky's side. Timidly she placed her hand on his. He pushed her hand away firmly, without looking at her.

He raised his head to stare at Anyuta. His eyes were blazing. He had been wounded. "You say such things to me? I've spent my time among the 'unhappy ones.' Thank God, not for any such naive ideas as these. I'll yield one point; perhaps it's not the women who are to blame. It's the fault of men. The university men who offer the women help and support, who tutor them to prepare them for entrance into foreign universities. The young men are using the women as part of their movement to westernize Russia, to bringing about some kind of social revolution. They'll all end up as 'unhappy ones' in Siberia, mark my words!"

Anyuta turned and resumed her position on the divan. Forcing a calm attitude, she took up her embroidery before replying, "Has your Siberian experience made you afraid of action?"

Staring at the calm Anyuta, he appeared to struggle to control his anger. In a softer tone he continued, "These ridiculous notions of what some call social action will lead to nothing but unhappiness. And the notion that science will save man is utterly naive! Art, literature, music! These are the only means of human redemption!"

Sofya couldn't hold back. Her voice trembled, but she said firmly, "Science will save man, just as much as literature and art."

Dostoevsky turned toward her. Again, for a moment, she had the impression that he had utterly forgotten who she was. Suddenly she had to fight back tears.

"An educated young woman, like her sister, she is ready to defend her ideals." Dostoevsky's voice sounded condescending.

Sofya's hopes were crumbling.

Anyuta's response was as pointed as the embroidery needle she continued to wield so deftly. "You are a man of the world. You have known the charms of more than one educated woman. It's no use your sitting there and telling us otherwise."

"Anya!" Dostoevsky said sharply. "The girl is little more than a child. Watch what you say."

Sofya blushed with humiliation. He thought her a child! Now there was no holding back the tears.

Dostoevsky's agitation dissolved as he saw that she was hurt. "Sofya, forgive me. Your sister and I are the ones who are behaving like unruly children." He stood up. His large hand gently lifted her chin. He was looking only at her. "I believe all our moods would be improved by some music. Would you play Beethoven's *Sonata Pathétique* for us?"

He put his arm around her shoulder. He led her to the room with the piano. She didn't want to play, but she couldn't refuse him.

As she sat down he placed one of his hands on her shoulder. In a whisper, he added, "Play only the second movement."

It was hard to focus her tear-clouded eyes properly on the notes, but she began to play, forcing herself to concentrate. Soon the calming tones of the movement were touching her heart. The regular rhythms of her left hand, the tender passion of the notes, magically soothed her hurt. She played for him.

As Sofya coaxed the last chords of the second movement from the piano, she felt great satisfaction. Never before had she played so well and with so much feeling.

She hesitated—should she continue with the third movement? Would the heightened intensity of that section bring back uncomfortable feelings for herself and for the one who most concerned her, Fedor Mikhailovich? She waited for him to give her direction.

The room was totally silent behind her. Fedor Mikhailovich must have been awed, totally enraptured by her music.

She turned around. She was alone.

Faint voices were coming from the next room. Getting to her feet, Sofya moved quietly to the doorway. There were Anyuta and Fedor Mikhailovich on the divan, almost as on that other visit, when she had also played for him. The aging writer was red-faced and flustered, and as Sofya watched he raised Anyuta's hand to his lips and kissed it repeatedly. He was speaking quickly and with great earnestness, but so softly that Sofya could not hear the words. Seeing his attitude, the look on his face, there was no need to hear. Sofya realized that he was declaring his love for Anyuta. His passionate love!

And Anyuta was unresponsive! Her face was calm, her eyes turned coyly down. She allowed him to pour out his soul to her, as if all his love were no more than her due. At that moment, Sofya felt like Lazarus at the gate, begging for a drop of water, while in the next room, her sister was satiated at the banquet. Sofya again felt the violence of jealousy. She hated her sister! Hated her beauty, her charm, her composure.

She had allowed herself to believe in unattainable happiness. What a fool she had been! She tried to swallow, but couldn't. She sobbed, but no one heard.

She turned and ran for the welcome darkness of her bedroom, illuminated only by the flickering red light of the icon lamp in one corner. Falling on the bed, she abandoned herself to tears.

It might have been an hour later when Anyuta entered the room and lit the oil lamp. Her voice was calm. "Sofya, have you been weeping all this time? You just disappeared after playing that lovely piece. Fedor Mikhailovich wanted to congratulate you."

"Don't pretend you wanted me with you," Sofya blurted out, her words half-muffled by the pillow. "I heard you and Dostoevsky. I saw!"

For a while the room was silent except for Sofya's sobs.

"Sonechka." Anyuta hardly ever called her by the endearing form of her name. Sofya turned over. Her sister's face was not angry.

"Sonechka, this is ridiculous. You're fifteen, he's forty-four! What kind of nonsense have you been imagining for yourself?" Anyuta's voice was just above a whisper.

"I love Fedor. Now you'll have him."

"So, you overheard his proposal." Anyuta touched Sofya's hand. "Dear little sister, don't be jealous. I'm very flattered by Fedor's request, but I haven't given him an answer."

"You haven't?"

"No. Sofya?" Anyuta's eyes were searching, there was no look of condescension, no more of the taunting attitude of the big sister. "Sofya, I must talk to someone. Tonight, especially, I must tell someone what I'm feeling. Be my friend."

Sofya stared at her sister for a long time. Hadn't Anyuta heard anything she, Sofya, had said? Was Anyuta so tied into her own feelings that she could ignore a cry of pain?

Sofya sighed as she realized that Anyuta could not see the pain in front of her. For all her beauty, talent, intelligence, and charm, Anyuta could not sense what was happening in another soul. Envy fell away, and Sofya felt a rush of love—love that was no longer childish, blind admiration—toward her sister. *How strange, only a minute ago I thought I hated her. Now, I find she is very, very dear to me.*

"Sonechka, I like Fedor very, very much." Then using the very words that had been in Sofya's mind, Anyuta said, "It's as if he sees my soul."

Anyuta continued, "There are many things in Fedor's life I'm not sure I'm ready to cope with. Our views on politics and religion are totally different. And Fedor demands and deserves utter devotion. I can't give that."

Sofya asked softly, "Do you love him?"

Anyuta hesitated. Then softly she answered, "No. I don't love him." She paused again, "But that's not why I'm not going to marry him. I know what I want from marriage. Companionship in freedom."

Anyuta's tone became lighter. "Someday I'll find someone who shares my thoughts, my goals, my beliefs. Then maybe I'll marry." After a moment she added, laughing, "Maybe neither of us will ever marry. We'll live together. We might live the rest of our lives in this very house."

Anyuta leaned over to her sister. For a long while they held each other. Then, silently, the girls undressed and put out the lamp.

CHAPTER ONE

1868 ๏ Petersburg

Sofya hurried along the half-familiar streets of Petersburg. Most of her remembered life had been spent in the countryside, where she had been accompanied on most of her walks by a boy with a long, sturdy stick to chase away stray dogs, sometimes a shotgun in case of bears. Here, her escort was a servant girl, insisted on by mother, who carried no stick, and the only creatures likely to cause problems moved on two legs. Sofya wondered if there would ever be a time and place where she might walk about freely by herself.

Sofya was returning from the district along the quay. She loved the mighty Neva. Each day she'd watched as winter winds cast their spell over the great river, transforming energetic waves into a motionless field of icy humps and crystal castles. She had stayed near the powerful forces longer than she'd intended. She was expected at home.

Her father's decision to move the family to Petersburg had come several months ago. Sofya's mother was a Schubert, and the Korvin-Krukovskys' townhouse was part of the Schubert House, a block-long building in a fashionable section of Vasilievsky Island, quite close to St. Petersburg University and the Academy of Sciences. For generations the Schubert family had counted astronomers, geodesists, theologians and masters of Oriental languages among their number. Thus, their home was near the people and institutions they loved.

Passing the University brought Sofya thoughts of her Grandfather Schubert, a geodesist, cartographer, and member of the St. Petersburg Academy of Sciences, who had died only two years ago. Great-grandpa had been an astronomer, run an observatory, and published books on his science.

Sofya hurried past the great, gray stone buildings of the University. No matter how hard she studied, she could never be admitted as a student. She was a woman.

She had resolved years ago that she was going to study, university admission or no. If she didn't hurry, she'd be late for her favorite lesson.

๏

IN ONE OF THE SMALL, cozy rooms sometimes used for afternoon tea, at a table large enough for a samovar as well as books and papers, Sofya and her mathematics tutor, Aleksander Nikolayevich Strannoliubsky, were sitting across from each other. The tutor's head was bent down, his eyes fixed on the paper on which he was composing problems for her next assignment.

Sofya's mind was tired, but still alert after more than two hours of solving problems. She felt this way at the close of each session. For several minutes, she would feel haunted by alternating feelings of accomplishment and disappointment. At this point in each session, she had to take herself in hand, force herself to stop thinking of the problems and to come back to the world of books and tables and people. Focusing on the presence of Aleksander Nikolayevich helped her return.

She studied the young man's features, as she did at every session. His face was pleasant, the features well proportioned and symmetrical. He had a deep cleft in his chin, not unlike her own dimpled chin. His hair was always rumpled—she liked that. He wore round, steel-framed glasses that made his eyes appear very small. He was probably a few years older than Anyuta. His clothes were immaculately clean but not at all stylish. She was sure he had worn this same jacket to each of their weekly sessions for the past six months.

At the end of each of these examinations, Sofya came to the conclusion that she liked her tutor very much. He was patient and thorough in his explanations, lavish with his praise. She wasn't accustomed to such encouragement and sometimes wondered if it could be entirely sincere.

The swishing sound of a skirt turned Sofya's attention to the doorway, where Mother stood looking into the room. For a moment Sofya met her gaze, then lowered her eyes to the papers still spread out before her. When she looked up again a moment later, Mother was gone.

Sofya sighed aloud.

Strannoliubsky looked up questioningly.

"The spy came by again," she said softly, trying to sound clever and carefree to cover her embarrassment.

"Your mother has a right and duty to supervise your lessons, Sofya." The tutor's voice was gentle and his smile understanding.

"She knows nothing of mathematics," Sofya said with a touch of sarcasm.

Strannoliubsky ignored her remarks. But a moment later he looked up again. "Almost finished," he said.

That was the signal agreed upon between them for Sofya to put away her papers and pour them each a glass of steaming tea. Sofya watched the vapor rising from the glasses with their silver holders. She made a little wager with herself, that within a second or two of the exact moment when the steam stopped rising, the tutor would finish writing. She had noticed this little coincidence at one of their sessions several months ago, and thought it quite uncanny how often it was repeated.

Just as the last visible vapors disappeared, Strannoliubsky looked up. He dropped his pen, reached for his tea, added two cubes of sugar, and sipped. "I've given you a few more problems where you'll need to calculate the derivatives. These are a little more challenging than the ones I gave you last time. I've no doubt you'll handle them just as deftly."

Sofya raised her own glass of tea to her lips, hoping to somewhat cover her proud blush.

Strannoliubsky continued, "You're catching on to this work incredibly quickly. Most students need several months before they feel so comfortable with differential calculus. I don't really believe I can take all the credit. I have the feeling you've seen some of this before, particularly derivatives and the concept of infinitesimals."

Sofya laughed shyly. "I saw the notation of calculus years ago."

"Really? Where?"

"On the wall in my nursery."

Strannoliubsky blinked at her, as if he suspected a joke. But already he had come to know his student too well to disbelieve on first impulse. "Really?" he repeated at last, with a tentative smile. He sat back in his chair, folded his arms and said, "There must be a story behind that comment."

She nodded her head. "When we first moved to Palibino, I was about eight years old. Mother hadn't ordered quite enough new wallpaper for all the rooms. So when it came to the playroom, there was a definite shortage. To get one more room's worth from Petersburg, five hundred versts away, would have taken forever and was simply not worth the trouble. So Mother had the walls covered with papers from Father's old chest in the attic. The papers were comprised mainly of the lectures of Ostrogradsky on differential and integral calculus, delivered during my father's student days."

Sofya and her tutor shared a laugh. Then she warned: "Don't mention this to Mother. She'd be upset if anyone else knew she hadn't decorated everything in perfect style."

Strannoliubsky's smile gradually faded to a serious expression. "Do you seriously mean that you taught yourself mathematics from this wallpaper?" He leaned forward, one elbow on the table.

"A little, anyway. I was just mesmerized by the strange symbols. I'd stare at them for hours, trying to figure out which page came first, which next, and so on. Naturally it was quite beyond me, but still I loved to try to penetrate the secret code."

"And no one ever explained any of this mathematics to you?" Strannoliubsky asked. "There were never any teachers?"

"I had three teachers while we lived at Palibino," Sofya said. Memories came flooding back. "No, I should say four. I can't leave out the old woman servant who first cared for me, taught me to do sums, and told me old fairy tales. Then came a string of governesses. First a pretty Frenchwoman, who taught French and Russian literature. She was very easily distracted and neither Anyuta nor I did much studying. After her, a formidable Englishwoman. By this time Anyuta was old enough to stop taking lessons, so I had the undivided attention of a very stern, rigid, and demanding Miss Smith. Her specialties were French, English, and religion. I was quite good at French and religion, but never could master English. Perhaps because I disliked Miss Smith."

"None of these people sounds the proper guide for a mathematical child like yourself. Didn't your parents notice your talent?"

"Father must have had some notion that I needed something different. He frequently caught me trying to read his books on science. He never scolded me very severely for this transgression, but still—it was discouraged." She paused. "One summer Father heard that a very respected, licensed resident tutor was between assignments. The man was highly recommended, and I suspect that Father wanted to have him on hand to prepare my little brother, Fedya, for the academy. But Fedya was only eight when Father hired the man. So that the tutor would not be totally idle, he was assigned to work with me for a few years."

"Who was that tutor?"

"Joseph Ignatievich Malevich," Sofya said with indifference. Another authority who had not been particularly to her liking. "He taught history, literature, science, and mathematics."

"I have heard of the man. One of my colleagues at the university was trained by him."

"Malevich drilled me extensively in algebra and both plane and solid geometry. But he was no friend of mine." She didn't want to sound too bitter. "Not like you." To break an awkward silence, she added quickly, "Oh, Malevich was all right. But I remember once he brought me to tears, because he insisted on my reproducing the geometry proofs exactly as in the text. I was so proud of my own way of doing the proofs, but Malevich only scoffed at them. I finally got the courage to show one of my proofs to Father. Father approved of my trying to do things my own way, and my proofs were correct!"

"I'm sure they were," Aleksander Nikolayevich agreed.

"Anyway, Father had a talk with Malevich. After that, my teacher was more understanding. Father liked Malevich. In the evenings, they would play cards. It was no drawback that Malevich made an excellent card partner for Father. Even now that he's no longer tutoring me or Fedya, Malevich comes to the house and visits and plays cards."

"I understand," Strannoliubsky said. "I know Malevich. He couldn't have been the one to help you with calculus. He doesn't know calculus."

"You're right. My calculus helper was another, not a teacher in the usual sense. A very dear and wonderful man, my Uncle Peter. Father's older brother."

"Ah, Peter Vasilievich Korvin-Krukovsky. I've seen him at all the popular science lectures here in Petersburg. An old man, gray hair, tall, thin, a kind of sad look about him?"

"That's Uncle Peter." Sofya smiled. "He's a darling. The paragraphs on limits and infinitely small quantities began to make some sense after I'd had a few talks with Uncle Peter. He came to visit us often, and he'd stay for weeks. He liked to talk to me about the ideas he'd read in popular science magazines. We'd have long sessions. I don't think that anyone else in the family paid much attention to him. He lives here in Petersburg. I get to see him much more often now. He taught me chess."

"Perhaps we can play someday." Strannoliubsky was patting his lips with the linen napkin. He pushed aside his tea, a few dark leaves stuck to the side of the glass. "You are a fascinating girl," he murmured.

Again Sofya felt herself blushing. "More tea?" she asked.

He handed her the glass. "When my friends and I were running the free school for women, back in my student days," he continued, "I met many aspiring young women scholars. But none of them could match you for mental quickness, and the sheer delight you take in such matters. You are going to pursue your studies at a foreign university, aren't you?"

"I'd love to do that." Sofya handed him the refilled glass. "I hope this doesn't disappoint you, but I don't want to study mathematics, at least not exclusively."

He shook his head. "No, you're quite right. Combine the mathematics with other sciences, maybe physics. You have a tutor for physics now, don't you?"

"Yes. I have a tutor for physics. I like physics." Sofya paused. "But I hope to study biology. I'd really like to become a doctor."

Strannoliubsky was surprised. "Very noble, very meaningful." There was no sarcasm in his words.

"Sometimes I daydream about the future. I'd set up a clinic in Siberia to help political prisoners." She flushed, thinking how foolish that must sound. "We know Dostoevsky. He made me realize the horror of conditions for the 'unhappy ones.' In my dream, my sister is with me, writing her fiction. Perhaps some other women would join us, my cousin Zhanna and her cousin Julia. Anyuta knows a number of serious women. We'd set up our own little commune. I imagine four of us, together, devoting our lives to healing and educating."

Then she reacted to what she imagined her tutor must be thinking. "Don't tease me. I know it's only a daydream but it might happen."

"It might," Strannoliubsky's face was serious. "But first, you will all need an education."

"Yes. If our fathers could only be persuaded of that!" Sofya's tone expressed her exasperation.

Strannoliubsky hesitated, then continued at a lowered modulation. "There are a few women who have gotten advanced educations. You and your sister are perhaps acquainted with Maria Aleksandrovna Bokova? She is doing medical work here in Petersburg."

"Anyuta has met her. I haven't. Father knows her father." Sofya pushed her glass of tea aside. "Ages ago, before I was born, our fathers served together in the Balkans. They've been friends ever since. Unfortunately, Father's bravery doesn't extend to a struggle against traditions or he'd allow his daughters a proper education."

"Sofya!"

She felt her face grow warm. She shouldn't have said that, not even to Strannoliubsky. She felt, just a little, like a traitor.

She glanced at the doorway. Mother wasn't there, thank goodness.

The tutor looked that way as well. "There is another woman, Nadezhda Prokofevna Suslova, who also works in medicine. You may know Nadezhda through Dostoevsky. He was a close friend of Nadezhda's sister."

"Again, Anya has met both sisters. I have not," Sofya confessed shyly, "My sister's circle of friends has a much larger radius than mine."

Strannoliubsky ignored her discomfort, and looked again at the empty doorway before continuing. "The ground has been broken by these women. They have succeeded academically. I have no doubt that you could be just as successful. But of course you will need to go abroad, to some foreign university."

"I know," said Sofya. For a moment she was cautiously silent. She was thinking that perhaps she could broach a subject about which she and Anyuta had recently talked a great deal.

The tutor was staring at her. "Women are accepted in some of the universities in Germany and Switzerland."

"Travel demands a passport. A single woman can only obtain a passport with her father's consent. A married woman must have her husband's consent." Sofya felt her face becoming very warm. There was no sense in stopping now; the opportunity for such a discussion might not come again. She plunged ahead. "Sometimes a husband gives consent when the father would not. Sometimes, a woman can find a very special man to be her husband."

Sofya and Anyuta had whispered together about the rumors that serious young women were entering make-believe marriages, with husbands in name only. Anyuta was tired of being tied to Father and Mother. She was almost twenty-five years old, and wanted to study abroad. Anyuta said she envied the women who had made such arrangements.

Perhaps Strannoliubsky could help. His expression was neutral, and he seemed to be waiting to hear more.

Sofya proceeded carefully. "I have heard that Bokova's husband helped her, when her father refused. I'm sure if Anya or even one of my cousins had such a husband, I could convince my parents to allow me to travel under the supervision of the married girl."

Sofya had heard the rumor that the Bokov marriage had begun as one "of convenience." Surely Strannoliubsky had heard those same rumors. It was even whispered among the university students that the Bokov marriage was the model for the marriage in Chernyshevsky's controversial and immensely popular novel *What Is To Be Done?*

Anyuta had mentioned to Sofya that she thought Strannoliubsky himself might even be interested in "liberating" a girl. Sofya had laughed at the idea.

Now Sofya looked at his face carefully, hoping for some clue. At the moment the young tutor was avoiding her gaze, frowning thoughtfully, with nothing to say.

Sofya glanced at the empty doorway one more time. Then, drawing in her breath, she proceeded boldly. "Aleksander Nikolayevich, would you be willing to meet with a group of women to discuss some ideas relating to the necessity of foreign travel for women? We could perhaps meet in the privacy of your study." She took another deep breath. But she wasn't going to let her eyes fall from his until he had answered one way or the other.

He frowned some more, and sighed. "Yes, I'm willing to take part in such a discussion. It might, in fact, be a very good thing."

Sofya smiled broadly. She pressed her advantage. "When?"

"Tell your friends I will be able to receive them next Wednesday at two."

"Wonderful! Thank you, thank you," she burst out uncontrollably, happy at her victory. She could see that Strannoliubsky was not at all elated. In fact, she thought his face had taken a particularly dark look. He was again avoiding her eye contact.

After some moments of silence, he looked toward the doorway, which was occupied again. "I'm leaving in a moment, Elizaveta Fedorovna," he said to Mother. "I'm assigning next week's work."

Mother smiled, in what appeared to Sofya to be her usual absent-minded, unknowing mode. She left the doorway.

Sofya watched as Strannoliubsky put some of her papers into his book. He tried to resume his businesslike manner, but Sofya could feel the strain behind each thought, each word.

He offered her the hand-written problems. "For next week, I want you to review the material on trigonometric identities, and try solving these problems using differentials."

Sofya nodded.

He continued speaking as they walked toward the door. "You've a good grasp of plane trigonometry. Next time, I'll show you some extensions of those concepts to a sphere. Your physics tutor will appreciate your getting a grip on spherical trigonometry."

Sofya nodded. She thought he was trying too hard to sound official.

When he had put on his coat and hat, he looked into her eyes very intently, and, she thought, somewhat sadly. "Until our next meeting."

"Until our next meeting." She smiled at him.

GENERAL VASILY VASILIEVICH KORVIN-KRUKOVSKY felt well satisfied, speeding through the streets of Petersburg to his club in an open *droshky* pulled by his magnificent gray Orlov mare, her long tail flying. Old Kolya, bedecked in a fashionable uniform, drove the carriage swiftly, expertly weaving in and out of the heavy evening traffic. Vasily smiled with pleasure as his carriage passed several others. Kolya had lost none of his skills while at Palibino. Two years had passed since Vasily had been in the capital. Now, the capital was to be his home.

Elizaveta, who had grown discontented in the country, was overjoyed to be again in "proper" society. And for once, the children seemed almost happy. Fedya looked forward to enrolling in the academy. The girls were busy with their studies and with a new social life. *It's only natural*, he thought, *my girls need to be with young people. They need to meet proper men, to choose husbands.* Husbands, what a problem that was turning into!

Perplexed, Vasily leaned forward. "Kolya, how are you managing your daughters?"

"They're both settled back in the village, sir. When they started getting a little wild and frisky, I harnessed 'em with some good, strong men. The older, she's due soon."

"Good for you, Kolya." Vasily sat back. If only it could be possible to arrange his own daughters' futures as easily. For the last five years, he had been chasing away unsuitable suitors from his Anya. Surely, his elegant Anya couldn't have been attracted to any of the rascals she'd been seeing. There had been that Filippovich, the uncouth son of the village priest. Then Semevsky, the penniless ex-pupil of Sofya's tutor. And then, right here in Petersburg, that persistent, socially inept ex-convict, Dostoevsky. He had been the worst of the lot.

When Vasily heard of the goings-on, the girls and Elizaveta had been packed off for a long stay in Germany with relatives. When they returned to Palibino, Anya was still writing to the man. Vasily flatly refused her request that Dostoevsky be allowed to visit. The enforced separation worked. Dostoevsky, clearly on the prowl for a woman, had married another young girl. Still Anya kept contact with him. Whatever was wrong with his daughter?

Vasily always struggled with his spoiled, strong-willed Anya, and now the trouble was spreading to his little Sofya. Just last summer, one poor specimen of a suitor, obviously suffering the lingering effects of excessive drink and completely without funds, had asked permission to visit with Sofya! What a ridiculous scene that had been. His Sofya with this lout! Impossible! He'd been shown the door.

Clearly his girls, otherwise so bright and clever, were incapable of choosing men. First, he'd find a husband for Anya, then in two years or so, for Sofya. After all, as their father, it was his duty to insure their futures.

Kolya pulled back on the reins and the *droshky* stopped abruptly. "We're at the club, sir."

"So, we are." Vasily roused himself and dismounted. "Don't wait for me. I'll take a taxi. I may be very late. I hope. And Kolya, I'm leaving all my family worries right here in the carriage. Take them away."

"As you say, sir," Kolya laughed. "Have a good evening, sir. May luck be with you!"

WITH A SHRUG, hoping to shake off his chronic worries about his family, Vasily entered the paneled foyer of his club.

He was going to enjoy himself. He had planned and executed a successful retreat from a boring evening at home. The piano music, supplied by his wife Elizaveta, and polite conversation, supplied by her adored younger brother, a paper warrior with the Ministry of War, and other equally boring characters from the Schubert circle of academics, were not to Vasily's liking.

Since moving to the city, such strategic withdrawals had become something of a specialty with him, he mused as he pulled off his gloves. What was novel was that Elizaveta had accepted tonight's announced disappearance without moodiness or a crying scene. Perhaps she had finally accepted that such masculine elements as camaraderie, cards, gambling, and rough talk were a necessary part of his life. A vision of Elizaveta with her hurt-little-girl look flashed before his mind. Well, they'd only been married twenty-five years. She would learn.

"Good to see you again, General," the attendant said softly, his head bowed respectfully.

"All the old crowd here tonight?" Vasily asked as he handed over the gloves, hat, and cape of his uniform to the old man.

"Yes, sir," the servant replied, knowing immediately which individuals were meant. "They've been asking for you. I believe they're settling at table seven."

With a quick motion, Vasily smoothed down his hair, then walked toward the rumble of male voices. His eyes teared a little as he scanned the smoke-filled room. At each of the eight small tables sat three or four men, many in military uniforms. Jackets were on the backs of chairs. A typical player sat with an ashtray to his left, a large tumbler of wine or vodka to his right. In this room, the game would be whist.

As always, when Vasily began a night of gambling, he felt a welcome flush of excitement. He loved this place and the others like it, the exclusively male clubs. In Petersburg, the two most renowned were the English Club for cards and other forms of gambling, the Chess Club for intellectual stimulation and liberal political discussions. Tonight he was definitely in the mood for the less subtle atmosphere of the English Club.

Here was where the real-life warriors, soldiers, and statesmen met. Vasily felt at home among these men, career leaders like himself, who had served their country well and honorably through many difficult times. As a boy of seventeen searching for adventure, Vasily had signed into the army as a cadet. Fifty years later he was still a warrior. Despite his age, he considered himself strong, healthy and clever. He played games the way he played at life, with cunning, intelligence and passion.

"Over here, Vasily! We need one more to start the next round."

Turning toward the call, Vasily recognized Evreinov, who had served on Vasily's staff in Moscow when Vasily had commanded that city's artillery and arsenal. When the regiment was transferred to Kaluga, Evreinov had managed to remain stationed in Moscow. Somehow the man had risen to the rank of general. Vasily attributed this good fortune to toadying at court. Unfortunately, Evreinov was a relative of Elizaveta's and could not be ignored.

Also at the table were Obruchev and Armfeldt, two generals more to Vasily's liking. Vasily had served with Obruchev in the Balkans during the Turkish war, from '28 to '30. Each had earned the prestigious Order of St. Ann for valor. Armfeldt, married to one of Elizaveta's numerous cousins, possessed a sharp tongue and a firm spirit bordering on stubbornness. He was definitely not a toady.

Vasily pulled back the empty chair, took off his uniform jacket and ceremonially hung it on the chair's back. Only after sitting down did he nod a greeting to the assembled men.

"We're just choosing partners," Armfeldt said. Each man picked a card from the deck, turned it face up, and passed the deck.

"Looks like you and I are partners, Evreinov," Vasily noted as he showed the card he had chosen. "Low card deals." He passed the deck to Obruchev.

As the cards were dealt, Vasily put his money on the table, then looked across at his partner. "I wasn't expecting to see you in Petersburg." Evreinov was on active duty, his latest assignment as executive officer at Peterhof, the Tsar's palace outside Petersburg.

"Business," Evreinov answered. "Should be in town several months, perhaps the whole winter. I might add, I wasn't expecting to see you here. I heard you had retired to the country."

"You'll see a lot of me, so you'd best sharpen your game." Vasily's tone was a challenge. Then, as if remembering that they were to be partners for the round, he added in a friendlier tone, "I've moved the family into town for the school year. I'll pay a visit to Palibino every month or so, just to check on the overseer."

Everyone's attention was fixed as Obruchev dealt the last card, face up, a two of hearts. Hearts would be trump. Each man picked up his cards.

As they concentrated, a fifth man, Perovsky, approached the table. "Mind if I watch?" he asked, pulling up a chair between Vasily and Armfeldt. "All the tables seem to be filled just now."

Looking up briefly from their cards and grunting, the four communicated that they had no objections. Perovsky lit a cigar. The smoke had a peculiarly unpleasant aroma, too sweet for Vasily's liking.

"There's been another disturbance in the students' quarter near the university," Perovsky informed them. It sounded like the fact did not particularly displease him.

A weary, muted groan came from the others.

"This time the law students took to demonstrating outside the provost's quarters. They claim they only want to organize private groups to help each other financially. The Tsar is rightly suspicious."

"It started way back in '61," Obruchev commented. "Now, disturbances are almost expected as part of the university life."

"My men took care of this bunch. There'll be some very sore heads tomorrow, and more students in Siberia next semester." Perovsky's tone and manner expressed a pleasure that made Vasily uncomfortable. Cruelty was one mark of General Perovsky. Inefficiency was another.

"Ever since that unfortunate incident in '66, you've come down rather heavily on every sign of unrest, Perovsky," Vasily said. "After all, they're only young people, feeling a bit too energetic. They'll fall into line as they get older."

"After '66, gentlemen, I view every sign of rebellion most seriously indeed. And so should you. I have no tolerance for anyone who questions our leaders, whether the leader be a university provost, or . . ." Perovsky didn't need to finish his statement. He had been governor-general of Petersburg in '66 when a young student had failed in an amateurish assassination attempt upon the royal person of Tsar Aleksander. Perovsky had been promptly demoted to maintaining order at the schools and universities. Now he was struggling by every possible means to work his way back into the Tsar's good graces.

Vasily roughly adjusted his chair, so he was nearer to Obruchev than to Perovsky. Every man at the table was uncomfortable. They all had children teaching at or attending one of the city's schools. They all worried that their own offspring might someday be involved in one of these student disturbances.

Vasily turned his attention to his cards. His hand was good. Seven high trumps, three losing diamonds, two losing clubs and one high spade. With any help from Evreinov, they should be able to take the hand and win quite a few rubles.

But Obruchev, frowning, his thoughts perhaps still elsewhere, hadn't led the first card.

Vasily, having decided on his strategy of play, studied the faces of his fellow players. They were all older men. Careers and fortunes had been won and lost and sometimes won again. They were all worried about their families now, especially their children. A wave of unrest, an epidemic of sorts, had taken over the young people of Petersburg and Moscow. The young, being young, longed for impossible freedoms.

Obruchev at last, forcefully, put down on the table the card for the opening play.

Obruchev had already lost control of his children. His son was in Siberia, exiled for distributing illegal political pamphlets. Vasily remembered the boy, an officer with real leadership potential. Obruchev's daughter Maria had married the most skilled, and most politically radical, physician in Petersburg, Peter Ivanovich Bokov. Bokov had escorted Maria to Switzerland, where she had received a medical education. Now, back in Petersburg, Maria was treating diseases of the eye, while proclaiming some very unorthodox views on women's place in society, views which might land her in Siberia as well. *Perhaps*, Vasily told himself, *it's just that strong men have strong children. But a child's strengths must be developed and channeled.*

Obruchev played a high diamond. Vasily and Armfeldt followed with lower diamonds. Evreinov took the trick with an ace.

"Petersburg's no place for young people these days." Armfeldt spoke with his eyes fixed on his cards. "Too many dangerous ideas, too many pitfalls for the young. If I were you, Vasily, I would have stayed in the country. Palibino's a far safer place for a family these days. But I imagine your beautiful wife talked you into the move."

Silently, they waited for Evreinov's play. Presently the card was thrown down.

Vasily said, "We're here for young Fedor. I want him to join the Military Academy. But he's not quite ready to leave the family, so I brought the family here." Vasily disliked Armfeldt's talking about Elizaveta. Old jealousies surfaced easily for Vasily. Elizaveta had been Armfeldt's first choice among the Schubert girls. Thank God, she had turned him down.

"Keep an eye on your son," Evreinov said. "Even the very young are being drawn into trouble with these free-thinking ideas."

"What a man won't do for the son and heir of his old age!" Armfeldt continued his needling. Armfeldt was considerably younger than Vasily, and his remarks were not without barbs.

Vasily didn't respond. He stared at his cards, remembering. He had been fifty-three years old when Fedor, his and Elizaveta's fourth child, was born. Fedor was Vasily's second son; the first had died at the age of two. After that loss, there were bad years for the family.

Vasily had begun to drink and gamble heavily. That reckless life continued for three years. He'd lost all his reserves and had notes out for much more. Then Elizaveta was expecting their third child. What would they do for money? The situation came down to selling either Palibino or Elizaveta's jewels. The jewels were sold. The very next day the child had been born. There was little rejoicing. The family jewels were gone. The third child was not a son.

Elizaveta became seriously despondent, so much that Vasily had feared for her health. She was really little more than a child herself. Eventually he had straightened out their finances and tried to be more attentive to her and the girls.

In three years, Elizaveta was again pregnant. Fedor was born, a strong, healthy son. God had smiled on them. Vasily was not going to lose this son to some ridiculous cause. He was not going to let his son be sent to Siberia. He was going to watch fiercely over his child.

"Vasily! It's your play!" Evreinov said sharply. "Damn it, pay attention and we might win this hand."

Vasily threw down a trump.

With a knowing look, Armfeldt added: "I'd say Vasily didn't come to Petersburg only for his son." He turned to Vasily. "Your girls are of marrying age and the best prospects are in Petersburg. I have a daughter of the same age." Turning to Perovsky he continued, "That's why you're here, isn't it, Perovsky? Trying to get rid of the women?"

The four card players laughed.

Good-naturedly, Perovsky joined them. Then with a serious sigh he muttered, "I wish I could free myself of all the women in my family." The others played as Perovsky talked on. "I should never have married again after my Nina died, bless her soul. But with the girls to be raised—" he paused. Vasily and the others were looking questioningly at Perovsky. It was odd, hearing this hard, cruel man talk so sweetly about his first wife. Perovsky's face abruptly reverted to its usual cold stare. Vaguely embarrassed, the players continued to play.

"Be firm with your wife. Beat out those radical ideas that are poisoning your girls," Evreinov advised.

"I am trying! But threats and heavy-handedness are useless with this woman." Perovsky rubbed his stubble beard. "I'm weakening. I've agreed to let the girls enroll in the new high school for women that's to open this year. At least I should never have to bring my troops against a girls' school."

"Are your daughters campaigning to enroll in the new high school, Vasily?" Obruchev asked. "It might be good to let them study here, then they won't be tempted to go abroad, like my Maria."

"The high school's not for my girls. I've made other arrangements. Anya's at Smolny Institute. Sofya is studying with tutors, until she's ready for Smolny."

Vasily could tell from the respectful silence, and the direct looks of the others at the table, that they were impressed.

"Smolny accepts only the most well-bred and highest of aristocratic ladies," Armfeldt said, more to himself than to the group. "There won't be any disturbances there."

"Yes, that's right." Vasily said firmly. "Anya will complete their two-year program in foreign languages. She expresses certain radical ideas, but she obeys her papa," he added proudly.

"Do any of you gentlemen object if we play cards? I thought that was the official purpose of this gathering." This was Obruchev, speaking past the cigar in the corner of his mouth.

The others accepted the rebuke, and play proceeded for several rounds with a minimum of conversation. The subject of still-unmarried daughters, though, once it had been raised, was not so easily forgotten. Vasily looked at Evreinov, now frowning thoughtfully at his cards. Evreinov had real problems. His young Zhanna, just about Anyuta's age, had caught the eye of the Grand Duke Nikolai Nikolayevich, cousin to the Tsar himself. Marriage in such a case was of course out of the question;

and what was a girl's father to do then? Thank heavens, that was not Vasily's problem.

Someone grunted Vasily's name, reminding him that it was his turn to play. He stared at his cards, getting his mind back into the game, before he made a play.

This was the seventh round of play. The partners who took this trick would be able to score. It was time to play his ace of hearts. The trick was taken.

Vasily studied his hand before playing the lead card. As the card dropped from his hand, Armfeldt quickly trumped it. Then, as if to trump Vasily's previous bragging he remarked, "Your Anya's at Smolny, but tell us about the younger girl. Isn't it true you've hired Stranno-liubsky as her tutor? Strannoliubsky has a reputation for free thinking."

"True. I employ Strannoliubsky. Rebel or not, he's the best mathematics tutor in Petersburg. My Sofya must have the best, her gift is profound," Vasily answered.

"But what good is mathematics to a young girl headed for Smolny Institute? I'll not let my Natalia have a mathematics tutor, no matter how much she begs. And she does beg." Armfeldt laughed a little as he finished speaking.

Vasily responded firmly in a tone intended to end Armfeldt's teasing. "Sofya will have the training she needs. Considering the unrest of our university students, the fact that she cannot hope to go to a university for her training is a blessing. I'll see she is kept challenged. And kept at home."

Vasily could clearly remember the day four years ago when Tyrtov, his neighbor at Palibino and professor of physics at Petersburg University, and old Lavrov, the mathematics and philosophy professor from the Artillery Academy, had happened to drop in at the country house. After dinner, Sofya had cornered Tyrtov and started talking to him about specific chapters in his new physics text. While her father listened, almost in disbelief, Tyrtov had patiently asked the girl questions to find out how much of the book she'd really understood. Tyrtov knew she hadn't had any training in trigonometry. He was very much impressed with her explanation of how she had managed to guess at the meanings; for example, determining what was meant by the sine of an angle, by examining arcs. The method worked fairly accurately for the small angles in Tyrtov's chapter on optics.

After talking to Sofya, the professor had absolutely insisted, had practically twisted Vasily's arm, to get him to consent to science and mathematics lessons for Sofya. Calling her the "new Pascal," and more.

Armfeldt took the trick. Half laughing he continued, "If our daughters do become scientists, how will we ever marry them off?"

"Oh, such problems!" Perovsky teased, "Beautiful, intelligent children are the price you've both had to pay for marrying into the Schubert family."

"Sofya's talents come from the Krukovsky family," Vasily snapped.

Fearing further unpleasantness, and annoyed at the turn of conversation, Obruchev commanded, "Gentlemen, please! Play cards."

Playing in silence, Vasily and Evreinov won the hand. Eight tricks were theirs. At the end of the round, Vasily pushed back his chair. "Perovsky, play my hand."

"Leaving so soon?" Armfeldt asked.

"I came here to get away from family pressures. I see there's no refuge for me here tonight. I'm moving on to the Chess Club. Perovsky, keep my share of the winnings."

CHAPTER TWO

1868 ⚬✧⚬ *The Search*

On Wednesday afternoon, Sofya, Anyuta and Cousin Zhanna set out for Strannoliubsky's apartment. For January, the day was not cold, morning fog had vanished and the air was clear. People were outdoors enjoying the gentle winter sunlight. By four o'clock darkness would again hold the city.

The women had decided their secret meeting was less likely to draw attention if they simply walked to the apartment.

Promptly at two o'clock, the women arrived at the building in which Strannoliubsky lived. They gave his name to the doorman, then proceeded to his apartment. Anyuta knocked at the door.

HEARING A KNOCK, Strannoliubsky nervously looked around the small room that was his study by day and his sleeping room by night. Yes, everything was presentable for receiving young ladies. From the day he had made arrangements with Sofya, he had been having second thoughts about the wisdom of this meeting. He would have to carefully weigh every word he said.

He opened the door, and smiled when he recognized Sofya.

Sofya made the introductions, presenting first her sister as spokeswoman for the trio, then her cousin, Anna Mikhailovna Evreinova, called Zhanna.

Strannoliubsky motioned them to chairs drawn around his desk. During the discussion that followed, he noticed that Sofya for the most part kept her eyes down and said nothing. From time to time, Zhanna would clarify one of Anyuta's ideas, but Anyuta was clearly in charge of the women's side of the proceedings. She quickly confirmed that all the women were interested in advanced study and pursuing their careers. Unfortunately, their families were not supportive.

With that much established, the conversation stalled briefly; an awkward and difficult stage had been reached.

"Aleksander Nikolayevich, would you, personally, be willing to free one of us to study?" Anyuta finally asked him bluntly.

He had known this question must be coming, but still he felt a shock at the directness. The problem was out in the open. He couldn't look at Sofya when he answered, although he knew she was staring at him. He kept his eyes on Anyuta. "You mean by 'marrying,' but not really marrying." He hardly heard his own voice.

"Yes, of course that's what I mean. By marrying one of us you would free all of us." Anyuta glanced calmly around at her solemn companions. "We are sure our families would allow the remaining women to visit and travel abroad under the chaperonage of the married woman."

My God, he thought, *they're planning a virginal harem for some unlucky man*. How indiscreet of Anya to speak so openly! What if she'd spoken this bluntly to others less trustworthy than himself? Surely the women realized that fictitious marriages were considered by the government as sacrilege, and were punishable as a criminal offense. Both parties to such a union could end up in jail.

He turned toward Sofya. Her steady, unblinking eyes confirmed for him that this boldness was her doing. The young one had a way of speaking exactly what was on her mind, and must have suggested this approach to her sister. Openness and directness were charming qualities that he admired in Sofya, and in fact were a hallmark of young liberated women in general. But in this situation the naive approach threatened to get Sofya and her friends into serious trouble.

Without answering, he got up and walked to the window. The room behind him was silent. After some moments in which he tried to finalize the composition of his answer, he turned back to the three faces anxiously staring at him. "I am willing, as you must know from my past, to do what I can to help serious young women acquire an education." He saw confident smiles come to the young faces. He sat down again, before continuing. "But I cannot marry this way. I feel it's not the road for me. In time I hope to find a true partner, an equal with whom to share my life." There was something unnerving about being alone with all these young, dedicated women who were gazing at him steadily, and by the time he finished he felt himself blushing, as if he had been forced into some immoral revelation.

"I quite understand. I hope you aren't offended by our inquiry," Anyuta said proudly.

"On the contrary!" Strannoliubsky shook his head violently. "I am most honored. But I just don't feel this is the right road for me. Perhaps not for you either. Please, think it over carefully." And at the same time he was thinking that a way, some way, must be found for Sofya Vasilievna, at least, to continue her studies. She was really astoundingly gifted, serious and hardworking. Her sister's ambitions were harder for him to understand. It didn't seem impossible that Anya should be able to become a writer without advanced study or travel abroad. Still, he argued with himself, every woman had a right to demand freedom from her parents at some time. The women were right to be outraged, and something must be done for them.

"We've decided that we will arrange a marriage somehow, with someone," Anyuta informed him firmly.

Strannoliubsky sighed. "Well then, let me try to help you. I will do what I can, asking discreetly among my male friends, not all of whom share my hopes for romantic love. But utmost secrecy must be maintained. Please, do not approach anyone else in the blunt way you have approached me."

Anyuta smiled at him. "We won't. We understand the difficulties."

"I hope so." He waited a moment before continuing. "Anna Vasilievna, you are acquainted with Maria Aleksandrovna Bokova."

"I am."

"Then why not let Bokova do this for you? She knows how to go about delicate matters in a way least likely to arouse suspicions."

A FEW DAYS LATER, Anyuta arranged a tea at home, carefully setting the time on an afternoon when Mother was certain to be out shopping and Father would be at the English Club. Anyuta and Sofya were fairly confident that for several hours they would not be disturbed.

Zhanna arrived early. She had told her parents she would be shopping.

Sofya intended to remain at her sister's side. She would not miss this meeting for anything in the world. Since she had been the initiator of the Strannoliubsky meeting, she had the right to be present at the follow-up meeting. Anyuta reluctantly agreed.

Maria Aleksandrovna Bokova was to report whatever she had been able to learn about prospective candidates at the afternoon tea.

When the maid showed Maria into the sitting room, Anyuta and Zhanna rushed to greet her. Sofya rose from her chair, but didn't join in the rushed greeting. Her attitude, enforced by what Anyuta had admonished her, was to be that of a quiet observer.

Anyuta motioned Maria to a place at the table. Zhanna resumed her own seat. No one said a word. Anyuta closed the door to the room, waited a moment, opened the door again, looked out, then closed the door again.

"I want to be sure the maid is not listening at the door. My checking will keep her at a distance," Anyuta whispered as she joined the others.

Maria Aleksandrovna, as expected, took command of the meeting.

"Good afternoon Zhanna, Anya." Maria smiled at Sofya. "And who is this?"

"Maria Aleksandrovna Bokova, let me introduce my young sister and dear companion, Sofya Vasilievna Korvin-Krukovskaya," Anyuta said with mock formality. Anyuta poured tea, serving Maria first. As she passed the sugar to the guest, Anyuta continued, "Sofya's usually with me. She's almost my shadow."

"So, you're Strannoliubsky's little *protégée*," Maria said in a kindly but admiring tone as she nodded toward Sofya. "He speaks highly of you. In fact, he's mentioned you so often to Peter and me, it seems I do know you."

Sofya could feel herself blushing at the praise. She had meant to keep quiet during the whole meeting, but here she was already in direct conversation with the guest. Maria was so friendly and attractive that Sofya found her shyness vanishing as she replied, "I very much enjoy studying with Strannoliubsky. I'm very interested in the sciences. I'd like to be a physician."

"Well, that's a worthy ambition." Maria smiled at her warmly. "If half of what Strannoliubsky tells us is true, there is no doubt you're good enough. You'd be welcomed as a colleague." Maria hesitated a moment, "As a matter of fact, I just read an article in a medical journal that might appeal to both your mathematical and medical interests. The article deals with correlating field data on environmental conditions to the incidence of disease. I'll have Strannoliubsky bring the journal to you."

"I'm very interested in seeing the article," Sofya responded immediately. "Thank you."

"Excuse us, ladies." Maria directed her gaze to Anyuta and Zhanna. "Sofya and I have digressed into science."

Maria's eyes turned once more to Sofya, carefully scrutinizing her. "Strannoliubsky tells me you are seventeen, but you appear younger."

"I turned eighteen two weeks ago," Sofya answered firmly.

"Looking young is not a drawback. You've wonderful dancing dark eyes and a pretty face. Quite charming." Maria added, "With your intellectual talents, you'll have quite a formidable array of tools with which to achieve your goals. And you might well need all of those tools."

Sofya began to feel uneasy about again diverting the conversation. She was relieved when Maria turned her attention to Zhanna. "Zhanna, I hear you've managed to learn Latin and Greek. I'm impressed. Preparation for your law studies?"

"Yes. Those private lessons I weaseled out of my old tutor should give me an edge when I study abroad." Zhanna was steering the conversation back to the topic of possible liberators.

With an air of solemnity and triumph, Maria announced: "Ladies, let us get down to business. I have a lead on a man who could be the one you are looking for!"

"Oh how wonderful!" the three others all exclaimed at once. "Tell us about him. What's he like?"

Maria was obviously enjoying the dramatic moment.

"First, he's a friend of a friend, so my information is somewhat second hand and there's a possibility that it may be inaccurate."

"All right, all right, but tell us!"

"Well, Peter and I are very good friends with Ivan Mikhailovich Sechenov, a physiology professor at the University and a trustworthy man. Sechenov heard of your search—though not your names, of course— through Peter and me. He described your situation to his trusted friend, Vladimir Onufrievich Kovalevsky. It appears Kovalevsky is willing to investigate the possibility of being a liberator for Anya. Naturally enough, he wishes to meet Anya first."

There was another brief outburst of comment. When it had died away Maria continued. "During the meeting Kovalevsky would certainly like to discuss the details of your future plans. And you, Anya, will have a chance to discuss any matters of concern for you before committing yourself further. Kovalevsky will give me his final decision after this meeting. Of course, after the meeting you may decide not to proceed, Anya."

Sofya could no longer contain her excitement. She jumped from her chair and hugged Anyuta. Zhanna must have felt the same electric jolt. She was also at Anyuta's side hugging first Anyuta, then Sofya. They'd succeeded!

Anyuta recovered herself and told the others to settle down.

Sofya and Zhanna returned to their chairs. Sofya turned to Maria; she was smiling. Sofya looked at Anyuta. Anyuta's face was flushed and she was nervously folding and unfolding her hands, but she was in control.

Coolly Anyuta said, "I can't imagine what would keep me from agreeing. After all, we're not going to live together for any extended period of time."

"You will certainly have to share an apartment for a time," Maria cautioned. "Remember, the marriage must seem authentic to your family or there could be grave consequences for both you and Vladimir. It is vitally important for all of you to be discreet." Here their counselor paused for emphasis, looking directly into each girl's eyes.

"Yes, yes, we know that," Anyuta said, so impatiently that Maria looked worried.

"Well, but what is he like?" Zhanna asked impatiently.

"In his favor are these points. He's only twenty-six years old, a reasonable age to marry someone your age." Maria looked toward Anyuta. "Second, he's a landowner, albeit a minor one, in your own province of Vitebsk. His mother and father are dead and Vladimir and his brother share the profits from the estate. A very small sum, I'm afraid, but it's something. Third, he's educated and very intelligent. He took a degree in law and graduated with honors, although because of some misunderstanding with the bureaucracy he no longer practices. His brother is a well-respected biologist studying in Europe."

Anyuta couldn't help interrupting. "Yes, and no doubt Father will be pleased he's a landowner from Vitebsk. And that he has a profession."

Sofya didn't dare say a word, but her elbows were on the table, her hands cupped under her chin, and her eyes were wide with excitement.

Maria was about to continue when Anyuta again interrupted: "Is he able to conduct himself amiably with the older generation? Four years ago my father rejected a potential suitor who could not control his tongue."

Maria sighed. "I've met Kovalevsky. He is outspoken at times. But he is a man of the world. He can deal effectively with people from all levels of society." Maria smiled. "He can be quite charming when he wants to be."

Maria resumed her formal, detached attitude and continued, as if reading a resume for a prospective employer.

"He derives some income from a small publishing firm he owns and operates. He publishes textbooks and popularizations of the sciences. He's very good at languages and does many translations himself. This business has done very well in the past. The workload was often so heavy that he hired additional translators. From time to time, Sechenov and I helped with these translations. Unfortunately, currently the business is not making much money and Kovalevsky appears to be heavily in debt." Maria sighed. "I must caution you, the prospect of a wealthy marriage may be as much a motivating factor in his accepting the position of liberator as his dedication to the cause. I happen to know that a few years back Kovalevsky was approached by another young lady with a similar request, and flatly refused her."

Now Anyuta's voice betrayed concern. "On what grounds?"

"I don't know."

"Are you sure he's sincere in his support for women's equality? He doesn't view this as an opportunity for lechery, do you suppose? If so, I want no part of a marriage ceremony with this man."

Anyuta and Zhanna exchanged worried glances. Sofya knew they had heard of several fictitious marriages where this had occurred, to the girl's horror. Sofya's joy turned to concern. Anyuta would be at particular risk because of her beauty.

"Vladimir's support for women's rights can't be questioned," Maria insisted firmly. "At the university, he and his brother were active in the movement. After graduation, Kovalevsky obtained a leave of absence from his government job and went to England to further his study of law, and while he was there he lived with Herzen himself, and Herzen's family."

Maria's audience, all well acquainted with the illustrious Aleksander Ivanovich Herzen, the exiled socialist and editor of *The Bell*, were suitably impressed.

She continued: "In England he was a tutor for Herzen's daughter, Olga. Herzen liked him so much, he introduced him to other sympathetic émigrés. What better endorsement could anyone have?"

There was a murmur of agreement.

Maria continued: "On Herzen's recommendation, Kovalevsky left England and participated briefly in the Polish rebellion of '63. I understand that at Lvov he distinguished himself with a very dashing rescue of a wounded friend, a freedom fighter. Then Kovalevsky, at great personal risk, hid his friend from the Tsar's troops."

"Some men from our area joined that rebellion," Sofya said softly. She was remembering a certain friend of hers, a neighbor boy who had written a touching romantic verse in her notebook just before he left for the fighting. Sofya had never heard of him again, and assumed he had been either killed or exiled.

"The Poles won't be kept down for long," Maria commented with sympathy and confidence. Then she continued: "When Kovalevsky returned to Russia, he joined the movement again. He supplied legal advice and helped set up programs of education and employment cooperatives for poor working women. That's where he met Evgenia Egorovna Mikhaelis. She was writing articles in support of women workers. Evgenia is a close friend of Herzen. Undoubtedly Herzen recommended Kovalevsky to her. She looks on Kovalevsky as a son. And in fact, Kovalevsky was once engaged to Evgenia's daughter, Masha."

"What broke up the engagement?" Anyuta asked.

"Well, as I remember the story, Masha's family were very pleased with him, and all seemed settled. However, just two hours before the wedding ceremony took place, Masha announced she would not be able to go through with the wedding."

"Why ever not?"

"Of course no one but Masha and Vladimir know the real story. But some say the problem went back to when the pair of them were arrested a few months earlier. That was at Chernyshevsky's mock execution, where Chernyshevsky was publicly stripped of his nobility. My husband and I were present. I'm sure you all know that story."

Sofya and the others nodded. Everyone knew of the novelist's trial and exile, and the romantic tale of how a woman had thrown a bouquet into the cart carrying him back to his prison cell in chains. The woman, along with several others in the crowd, had been arrested.

"After they were released from prison, Vladimir and Masha were seen arguing frequently and violently. Only they know the real nature of these arguments." Maria Aleksandrovna Bokova stopped to sip her tea, then proceeded. "The first petition for Vladimir to act as a liberator came at this very awkward time. Only a few weeks after the broken engagement.

"Shortly after this unpleasant string of events, Vladimir left the country and joined Garibaldi's army in Italy. You may have read some of his newspaper reports concerning conditions in Garibaldi's camp."

No one answered. Sofya knew that neither she nor Anyuta had followed the happenings in Italy. From the blank look on Zhanna's face, she had not read the articles either. Maria graciously overlooked their lack of knowledge of current socialist events, and continued, "Masha and Vladimir are still on friendly terms, but she definitely will never marry him. As far as I know, Vladimir has not been involved with another woman.

"It would seem to me that, from Vladimir's point of view, now is a perfect time for him to serve the women's cause as liberator. I'm told he's soured on romance, but at the same time he's very sensitive and chivalrous. He was hurt very badly by the Masha affair, and probably he wishes to protect himself against another disastrous romance. And, on a more prosaic level, he is in need of aid for his publishing business."

"He'll be very well protected indeed against any romance involving me," Anyuta said coldly. "When can we meet him?"

Maria considered. "Can you all come to my place, one week from today, say at eight in the evening? I'll have several other guests. Your meeting with Kovalevsky will appear casual and unplanned. Kovalevsky can contact me with his decision by the following Friday. I'll relay his position to you the next day, if that can be arranged." The matchmaker seemed to be following a detailed plan.

"Yes," Anyuta responded. "We'll meet here."

"It's settled, then," Zhanna said.

Sofya was staring into space, trying to digest all she'd heard about this man who was to be her future brother-in-law.

"Sofya, you be sure to come to the gathering at my place. I really do want Peter to meet you. Anya, you'll make sure she comes?" Maria had risen and was bustling about, putting on her cloak. "I must be going. I'll see you all Wednesday, a week."

WHEN MARIA ALEKSANDROVNA WAS GONE, the girls burst at once into excited talk. Soon Anyuta insisted that Sofya and Zhanna calm themselves. Mother would be home within the half-hour. Anyuta called for the tea things to be cleared away; another servant was sent to fetch a taxi for Zhanna. Mother must not suspect anything. Anyuta sat on the divan and picked up a magazine. Before beginning to read, she motioned toward the piano, "Sofya, Mother will be pleased when she hears you practicing."

The spirited measures of her favorite folk song, "Troika Running," greeted Mother's arrival. From the entry she joined her clear soprano to the notes: "Going, going, going to him. Going to my love."

SOFYA SIGHED WITH RELIEF as she climbed into the carriage and took the place beside Anyuta. Somehow Anyuta had done it. She'd managed to get Mother and Father to allow both of them to go out on Wednesday evening. A little deception had been involved, but not much. They would indeed visit the Perovskaya sisters, just as Anyuta had told mother. What Anyuta had not told Mother was that the visit would be brief. The rest of the evening would be spent at the Bokovs'.

Kolya, the aged carriage driver, turned his head to look back at them before giving the horses the signal to start. He gave a little wink to Anyuta. Like most of the household servants, Kolya was devoted to Anyuta and would never give away her secret. And a visit to the daughters of Father's friends was hardly scandalous—nothing to set the devoted servants gossiping.

The horses trotted away. Sofya and her sister snuggled under the wool blanket. Anyuta leaned close before speaking, so as to be heard above the wind. "Our plan is progressing well. I'm only sorry Zhanna won't be meeting us."

Sofya had expected Zhanna to meet them at the Bokovs'.

Anyuta continued, "I received a note from her just before we left. Up to the last minute, she had hoped to find a way of joining us, but she must accompany her parents to an aunt's birthday party." Anyuta hesitated, then lowered her voice so that Sofya could barely catch the words. "Zhanna's worried. The Grand Duke Nikolai Nikolayevich will be present. He asked her father specifically if she would attend. Zhanna's father considered the Duke's remark as nothing short of a royal summons. Zhanna's pleading that she would have to spend the evening fending off the Grand Duke's advances drew sympathy from her mother, but her father still insisted that she attend, that she not offend the Grand Duke, and that she conduct herself as a lady! Our Zhanna will have a very delicate mission!"

Sofya snuggled more closely into the blanket. She thought of poor Zhanna, pursued by the lecherous Grand Duke. Sofya was grateful that she was not as beautiful as Zhanna. She would never be subjected to such a degrading experience. But Anyuta might be.

ANYUTA AND SOFYA ARRIVED AT the Bokovs' at nine o'clock, to find the party well underway. A young man, a student to judge from his dress and age, answered the door and showed them to a room where they were to put their things. From the marbled entrance, the fine furnishings, and the obviously large number of rooms in the apartment, Sofya concluded that the Bokovs were not struggling for funds. The servants must have been dismissed for the evening.

The new arrivals removed their coats and threw them into the common heap on the bed, and placed their overshoes next to several dozen others on the floor. After straightening their dresses and hair, Anyuta and Sofya followed the party sounds toward a large room filled with young people. The simple appearance of the guests was in marked contrast to the elegant surroundings.

Sofya noticed that many of the guests were wearing some version of the informal uniform affected by members of the radical movement. For the women this meant simple dark dresses with white collars and cuffs, and for some of the more daring, blue-tinted, round, steel-rimmed eyeglasses. For the men, the fashion ran to peasant-style shirts and high boots. A few men wore their hair at shoulder length, while the majority of the women had theirs bobbed above the shoulder.

She and Anyuta had dressed plainly for the evening, suspecting that the company would be largely students. Sofya looked at her sister. Anyuta could not help appearing elegant even in the plainest of dresses. Her long, thick, beautiful blond hair was worn tied back with a cotton ribbon, in the style of the girls from the Smolny Institute. Even in this simple fashion, her hair formed a glorious decoration. Anyuta had not been able to bring herself to bob her hair, not even for the cause.

For once, in this particular company, Sofya felt that her own always slightly disheveled look fit in much better than Anyuta's natural elegance. Sofya disliked spending her time grooming, and her bobbed hair had curled naturally, and for the most part, stayed in place.

The young man who had met them at the door again approached. "Your first time at the Bokovs' Wednesday night gathering?"

"Yes," Anyuta answered, her eyes searching the room.

Sofya stayed back a little and said nothing, although the young man was now looking directly at her.

The youth continued, "Most of us are students of Doctor Bokov or

Professor Sechenov. We're science people. The women are private students, or frequenters of Bokov's public lectures. The men are from the university. I'm studying physics." He waited a moment, but Anyuta only nodded without much interest. He continued, "Occasionally a professor shows up, or a writer, or some other progressive friend of the hosts." Again he paused, waiting for some recognition from Anyuta. "Are you students?"

Anyuta did not bother to answer. "Excuse me, perhaps we can talk later," she murmured, and walked past the man toward the area where Maria Bokova was talking.

Sofya followed.

Maria must have seen their approach, because she broke off the conversation she was having with two men.

Maria took Anyuta by the hands and greeted her warmly. Turning to the men she said, "Gentlemen, the outstanding Korvin-Krukovskaya sisters. But where is the third woman, Anya? I believe you call her Zhanna."

Briefly Anyuta made apologies.

"Unfortunate, most unfortunate," nodded Maria. "I understand your efforts are coming none too soon. Let us get started."

Maria turned and introduced the men. Sofya guessed the first, Dr. Peter Ivanovich Bokov, Maria's husband, to be in his early thirties. His high cheekbones showed just a hint of the Russian peasant's Mongol features, offset by large, pale blue eyes and light brown hair. His manner was quiet and gentle. Sofya found him most attractive.

The second was Ivan Mikhailovich Sechenov, professor of physiology, a slightly older man. His black mustache and small black beard were flecked with gray. His face was flatter than Bokov's and pock-marked. Still, his eyes were fascinating and his presence commanding.

Standing one on each side of Maria, the men nodded to Anyuta and Sofya. Unlike the men to whom Sofya had been formally introduced at home, Sechenov and Bokov gently shook hands with the ladies. In this company, there was to be no courtly kissing of the hand. Women were treated with equality.

"The guest I wanted so much for you to meet has not yet arrived. For the time being, I'll entrust you to the care of Professor Sechenov," Maria said. "I'm sure he will be delighted to see to your comfort. Peter and I must return to our other guests. We'll talk again soon." Maria and her husband stepped away.

Sechenov brought the sisters tea to drink, then showed them to some chairs in the living room, a little apart from the others. Sounding just a little awkward, he started talking about the classes he taught at the university.

Sofya sat as quietly as a mouse. But she didn't feel calm, or quiet inside. She was quite exhilarated at being out from under the watchful eye of the older generation. She'd never before been to a party where there were no supervising old people. She had spotted Strannoliubsky drinking tea with another young man. His presence was somehow reassuring. She was among her kind of people.

Sofya noticed that several times Anyuta had started tapping her left foot gently, then as if catching herself in this unconscious habit, she would bring her knees tightly together and hold them with her hands.

Sechenov was smiling at her. Perhaps he too had noticed Anyuta's nervousness. From the expression on his face and his glowing eyes, Sofya knew that he had come under the spell of her older sister's beauty. He went into detail describing his classes and kept repeating how sorry he was that there were no women in them. He had read Anyuta's published stories, "Mikhail" and "The Son," and was impressed. He hoped she would write more soon.

Anyuta was warming to the flattery of the charming Sechenov. She began explaining the plot of her next story. Sechenov's eyes never left Anyuta's face. Sofya continued her silent watch.

Sechenov suddenly straightened in his chair. Anyuta stopped talking. Following the direction of Sechenov's gaze, Sofya saw Maria and Peter Bokov approaching, bringing with them a young man.

The man was tall and lean, but strong looking, with reddish hair, a high forehead and deep blue eyes. Sofya decided at once that he was definitely not handsome, although to be fair she could not quite say he was ugly.

His appearance was slightly disheveled. He was not wearing a peasant shirt. This man wore a linen shirt of the design favored by businessmen, but the stiff collar had been removed, the sleeves rolled up to the elbows, and the top few buttons were undone. The customary jacket worn over this type of shirt had been abandoned. His trousers were loose fitting and shiny from wear, his shoes lacked polish.

Something about him suggested an intensity. Perhaps it was his darting eyes, or his giant hands that went nervously to smooth his hair as he approached.

Maria quickly performed the introductions. As Sofya had expected, the newcomer was Vladimir Onufrievich Kovalevsky, their prospective liberator. After a moment, Maria, Sechenov, and Peter excused themselves and moved away.

A lull followed. Vladimir stood staring at Anyuta.

Anyuta looked at him with anticipation.

Then the young man came to himself with a slight start. "Please, excuse my rudeness. It's just that you remind me very much of someone." Vladimir pulled up a chair and leaned forward, sitting on the edge.

"We haven't much time to get to know each other, so I'm going to be rather blunt in asking you what you see as your future. If you were free, of course. Others have told me about you, but I'd like to hear you speak about yourself." He flushed, his face almost matching the unusual shade of red of his hair. "Our position is a little unusual."

Anyuta's eyebrows came together in a look of puzzlement. In a moment she had recovered her composure. "Your approach is most direct, Vladimir."

Sofya watched a look of cold control come to her sister's face. If this man had expected his unadorned remarks to be met with equal openness from Anyuta, he had badly misjudged Anyuta. Had he more properly started their discussion with remarks about some popular literary work or current play, he would have learned more about Anyuta's thinking than with this blunt approach. Why couldn't this fellow have been more like Sechenov? Anyuta had talked much more naturally with Sechenov than to this abrupt stranger.

"I'm a writer," Anyuta began slowly. She sat stiffly in her chair, hands folded in her lap. She looked coldly into Vladimir's eyes as she replied. "I've had several short stories published during the past few years. I'm a firm believer in universal equality, as I'm sure you are. I believe our current social order is destined to disappear. I believe that by my words and actions I can hasten that disappearance." Anyuta lowered her voice to make this last comment, despite the generally sympathetic attitude of the people around her. "I'm now studying languages at Smolny, but I hope and dream of being able to continue my studies and my writing in an atmosphere of freedom, in a place where words will kindle real change. It's the atmosphere of Paris that I have particularly in mind."

Vladimir nodded. He sat leaning forward in his chair with arms folded, gazing at Anyuta intently.

Anyuta flushed slightly under his continued inspection. "And now, sir, will you be as straightforward as I have been, and tell me about yourself, without reservations?"

Vladimir sat back and stretched his long legs in front of him. Again, he ran his hand through his hair. He delayed answering for a time, as if he were organizing his speech carefully. He glanced at Sofya. Sofya quickly lowered her eyes. She had been caught staring. When she looked up a second later, he had turned his gaze back to Anyuta.

"I'm a lawyer, who does not practice law. I'm a publisher, who is allowed to publish very little. My latest book has been confiscated by the censors, causing me much financial difficulty. I'm also expert at languages—I hope I need not be falsely modest, as our time to know each other is short.

"I also believe in universal equality, and"—here his voice too dropped almost to a whisper—"in the building of a new and better society."

His voice rose again. "I have seen both war and what is called civil unrest, and I have no more taste for either. From now on I intend to leave literature, publishing, and social turmoil to other people. I have read widely in the sciences. My hope is to become financially and emotionally free to devote myself completely to study in the biological sciences. I am convinced that our salvation lies in the sciences, if it is possible to find it anywhere."

There ensued a somewhat awkward lull in the conversation. Both must have realized how stiff the exchange had been. True, each had found out something new about the other. But Sofya did not like the awkwardness that threatened to persist between them. Vladimir and Anyuta were looking at each other critically. Sofya felt she had to try to save the situation. Their prospect of freedom could not be jeopardized by this somewhat poor beginning.

Sofya broke the silence, hoping to put the others a little more at ease. "Vladimir, you say you want to devote yourself to the biological sciences. Have you determined on some precise subject in that field?"

Vladimir turned his head, his eyes were widened in a look of mild surprise. Then he smiled at Sofya faintly.

"Well, I'm very interested in the work being done by an Englishman, Charles Darwin. Have you heard of him?"

"Certainly," Sofya answered. She smiled back, but she couldn't hide the note of indignation. How could he think any educated woman didn't know about Darwin?

He paused, his face betraying his disbelief in her answer. Then he continued, "I was fortunate enough to meet Darwin when I was in England, and I believe his theory of evolution is the most revolutionary idea of this century. In fact I have published Darwin's *Origin of Species* in Russian translation. It was not very well received, but in time people will get used to his ideas."

Sofya was nodding. "I've read that book."

"Have you indeed?"

"Yes," she said firmly. "Like you, I'm interested in the biological sciences, but from a more practical side." Sofya found it easy talking to Vladimir.

"You're really that much interested in science?" He shifted in the chair to face her more directly. "You seem so young."

"My sister is eighteen," Anyuta said. "She's studied quite a bit in the sciences."

Vladimir's gaze didn't leave Sofya's face. His voice took on a gently teasing overtone. "Really! Eighteen. And studied the sciences."

"I'm planning on being a doctor. I feel I can be most useful to society as a doctor, don't you agree?"

"Tell me, where did you study all these things?" Vladimir asked with a smile, ignoring her previous question. His smile had warmth, it was not only teasing. Sofya smiled in return, almost as if they shared a secret.

"Strannoliubsky's been my tutor in mathematics, I also have a private tutor in physics. So far I've only been able to study biology from books. Occasionally Strannoliubsky drifts to other subjects, and we discuss politics, economics or literature."

Anyuta, moving her head nervously, was looking impatient, and Sofya hastily changed the subject to something that could include Anyuta. "But you must tell me, us, about your experiences in Poland and in Italy. How very exciting! Were you a real freedom fighter?"

Vladimir looked at both of them, then laughed sourly. "Along with a few thousand others, I suppose I was a 'freedom fighter.' Not that it accomplished a great deal."

Anyuta leaned forward in her chair. With a tone of honest inquiry mixed with just a hint of mild sarcasm she asked, "You consider fighting for freedom not accomplishing anything?"

Vladimir refused to take up her challenge. He couldn't speak freely, because the three of them were no longer alone.

The young man who had met them at the door was now standing near Anyuta. He was not in her line of sight, but Vladimir looked at him as at an intruder. The young man was not shaken. Nodding to Sofya and Vladimir, and placing himself in front of Anyuta, he began, "You promised me a few minutes of your company. If now is not too improper a time, I'd like to take you up on that promise."

Anyuta rose from her chair. "We were having something of a serious discussion, but I'm sure my companions wouldn't mind if I took a few minutes to share some tea with you. But we have not been introduced."

"Vladimir, you heard the lady. Introduce us," the young man demanded.

Without getting up from his chair, Vladimir reluctantly complied. "Anna Vasilievna Korvin-Krukovskaya, I present Sergei Aleksandrovich Lamansky,"

"Thank you, Vladimir Onufrievich." Lamansky, putting on a comic expression, nodded toward the seated Vladimir. "I know how hard it is for you to part with even one of your two beautiful companions. But you will feel better for having overcome your selfish nature."

Vladimir stared after the departing couple. Turning to Sofya, he commented, "Lamansky seems to have pleased your sister. I suppose it was inevitable that I would not be able to spend the whole time talking with her. She is quite a beautiful woman and much in demand at parties, I suspect."

"Anya is very serious about some things." Sofya thought she must make every effort to put her sister in a favorable light with the prospective liberator.

"I'm sure." Vladimir followed the distant Anyuta with his gaze. Then he turned his attention back to Sofya. "Perhaps I can learn more about her from you?"

But the conversation, as it developed, had little to do with Anyuta. In a moment Vladimir and Sofya had begun exchanging stories on a variety of subjects, everything from living in the countryside of Vitebsk to attempted uses for electricity, the future of the gas engine, and the weather in England.

Sofya was having a delightful time.

When Anyuta rejoined them, without Lamansky, Sofya felt an unexpected disappointment. The conversation again turned to literature and politics. Vladimir's cold and formal manner had returned with Anyuta. Tonight, Sofya would learn little more about the mysterious Kovalevsky.

IN THE CARRIAGE on the way home, the sisters huddled together under a blanket, their whispers forming small clouds in the cold night air.

"Well Anyuta, what do you think of Vladimir?" Sofya asked excitedly. "I think he'd be an absolutely wonderful brother."

Anyuta hesitated. "He reminded me a little of Dostoevsky. Intelligent, nervous, high-strung, impractical, disillusioned."

Sofya was quiet, her enthusiasm dampened by her sister's remark.

Anyuta continued, "Those faults might be overlooked in a genius, but I didn't see any sign of genius in Vladimir Onufrievich Kovalevsky."

"That's not fair," Sofya said. "He hasn't found his true field yet. Perhaps his genius will be revealed in science."

"Perhaps," Anyuta conceded. "You'd think he'd want to serve the cause with the powers he's already developed, his publishing and legal skills."

"He has served the cause. Here at home, freedom fighting in Poland, and reporting from the Italian war zone. Now he wants to help the cause through science. Why, he's a rescuing knight, ready to save a lady in distress, ready to sacrifice himself for another. For you!" Sofya argued. "And that touch of sadness about him. Don't you find that intriguing?"

"Perhaps, a little. I wish I knew him better and could be sure that the touch of sadness isn't a sign of some inner character weakness." Anyuta pondered. "I think he may have lost his will to change society. He's interested only in helping some chosen individual. To me that's passive and cowardly."

"Cowardly? Passive?" Sofya whispered to herself in disbelief.

"Someday he may well need as much single-minded dedication from a woman as he now proclaims himself ready to give," Anyuta continued unemotionally.

Sofya knew a growing disappointment. "Then—about the marriage?"

Her older sister shrugged. "Oh, I expect he'll do for that."

THE DAYS FOLLOWING the party passed slowly. Mother and Father must have noticed that something was wrong with their girls, who were sometimes almost ecstatically happy and sometimes uncontrollably willful. Anyuta, particularly, was either hugging and kissing her parents as if she were about to depart on some long journey, or arguing vehemently with them about the smallest details of family life. Mother, when her quiet questions were fended off, could only hope that whatever was bothering the girls would soon pass. Father's patience was definitely wearing thin.

On Saturday, the plan called for Maria Bokova to verify the agreement between Vladimir and Anyuta. From that point on, it had been decided, Maria would leave all further marriage arrangements to the couple.

At the appointed time on Saturday, Maria entered the tea room of the Korvin-Krukovskys, where Anyuta and Sofya were awaiting her. Their parents were out. Zhanna had decided not to be present at this meeting, which after all was only a formality.

Once again the servants had all been sent out. When Maria was invited to sit down, she appeared not to hear and continued walking nervously around the room.

"What is it?" Anyuta demanded. "I suppose that Vladimir Onufrievich has changed his mind?"

Maria came to a stop and answered directly. "He is willing to enter the fictitious marriage. But there is one point on which he has drawn back from his original offer—at least as I understood it—and on which he refuses to negotiate."

"I knew there would be something. But what can it be?" Anyuta flared up. "Surely he is familiar with all the usual terms of such an agreement. Surely he understands that physical intimacy is to play no part—is that it, Maria?"

Maria blinked at her. "No. In fact it is nothing like that."

Anyuta's anger faded to puzzlement. "Then what?"

"Just this. Vladimir believes the original offer was for him to marry one of three women. Zhanna was not able to meet with him. Anya, you, of course, were the most obvious choice, being older and quite frankly more determined."

"Well?"

"Well. It's just that—" She paused again, and her gaze turned toward Sofya. "He now insists that the partner be Sofya."

CHAPTER THREE

1868 ⚬ *The Liberator*

Half an hour later, Maria was still explaining as best she could. "Vladimir insists that Sofya is the scientist among your group of young ladies, and he will sacrifice his personal life for nothing less than science. I don't know why he didn't make his beliefs known before. I'm sorry, this must be quite exasperating for you."

Anyuta made a sound between a sigh and a groan. "We'll just have to find another liberator, that's all." The words were firm and steady, but Anyuta's lower lip was quivering slightly. Her little sister could see she had been wounded by this unexpected turn of events.

Sofya, on her part, was astounded. How could Vladimir prefer her to Anyuta as a bride, even a fictitious one? In the light of all her previous experience it just didn't make sense.

She cleared her throat. "Wait, Anyuta. Let's not reject him just yet. We've had a lot of trouble finding a suitable liberator, let's not throw this one away."

"I agree," said Maria, looking from one sister to the other. "Vladimir realized that his decision might require some new thinking on your part. You are to give him your final answer on Monday at the Izmailovsky Cathedral." Maria looked sternly at each sister. "You—both of you—are to send a single representative to the Cathedral, at three o'clock. Vladimir will meet whomever you send in the back of the church. This will provide you with privacy for a discussion—there's rarely anyone there at that time of day."

"I suppose we can do that," Anyuta admitted.

"Good. I'm sorry about this difficulty, just when it seemed that everything might be settled. But arranging a fictitious marriage is never as easy as it seems it ought to be." Maria sighed. "As I well know."

After warning the sisters again of the need for secrecy, no matter what decision they reached, the broker departed.

When she was gone, Sofya found herself silently marshaling arguments in favor of the new situation, though she thought she had better wait for a more favorable time to present them.

FOR THE REMAINDER OF SATURDAY and most of Sunday, Anyuta stayed in her room. Several times Sofya knocked on her door and was admitted, only to be sent away almost immediately on the pretext that Anyuta was totally engrossed in her writing.

Just before retiring on Sunday, Anyuta came to Sofya's room. The story she had been working on was finished. Would Sofya read it?

Sofya settled on a rug before the fireplace with the sheaf of pages and began to read. Anyuta settled in the armchair facing the fire.

Sofya read slowly. She paused only once to look up at her sister. Anyuta's gaze was fixed on the fire. Sofya continued reading. Only when the last words had been read and the pages slowly and neatly restacked, did Sofya speak. "Anyuta, it's so sad and so beautiful!"

"I'm very happy with it. I believe I was able to make a serious social statement while telling a good story."

"Oh, yes," Sofya affirmed. "The poor heroine losing her student lover because she insists on acting 'in accordance with convention.' Then her slow unhappy death. The reader feels all the injustice and senselessness of the loss, because you make the heroine so very lovable. And the style is so . . . so lyrical. This is certainly your best writing. You must show this to Dostoevsky."

Anyuta showed no surprise at Sofya's lavish praise. "I hope I can get it published. Father's forbidden me to send out more stories."

"You must publish," Sofya exclaimed. Then, seeing a possible opening for approaching the larger problem, she continued cautiously, "You must have the freedom to work. Anyuta, you can have that freedom, if we accept Vladimir's terms."

Sofya moved closer to Anyuta. Putting her head on Anyuta's lap and staring into the fire, avoiding Anyuta's gaze, Sofya gave her argument as rationally as she could. "As I see the problem, there are two variables in an equation that equals our freedom, a liberator variable and a wife variable. By his own definition, Vladimir is a liberator. For the present, he is the only value in the liberator domain. He must be substituted in the equation for the liberator variable. For the wife variable, there is a domain of four women. The choice of Vladimir has determined that the wife variable will be me. But our system from the beginning has had an immutable axiom. That axiom is that we women are all going to be in this together. Each of us has pledged that if she achieved her freedom the others would come with her. So this superficial substitution of one value for another from the domain of the wife variable will have no effect."

"Clearly, this makes some kind of sense to you." Anyuta smoothed Sofya's hair gently, and smiled tenderly. "Perhaps your beloved mathematical reasoning has oversimplified a very complex relationship? Perhaps one of the older 'variables,' as you call us, could handle the complications more deftly."

"You mustn't try to shield me, Anyuta, just because I'm younger." Sofya looked into her sister's eyes. "I can handle this situation."

Anyuta hesitated. "I suppose there is the possibility that Vladimir will prove useful in pleading our case to other liberators. His friend, Sechenov, impressed me as a distinct possibility."

"You think the safest plan is for each of us to have our own liberator. I really don't see that as necessary."

Anyuta kissed her on the forehead. "Well, we certainly cannot waste a liberator, any liberator. We must pursue all our options."

❧

A QUARTER OF AN HOUR before the appointed time, Vladimir was waiting at the back of the cathedral, a dim and otherwise deserted place. The last few days he'd thought of little but his decision to be Sofya's liberator, and now he found himself anxious to hear her answer.

There had been moments as he thought the situation over when it seemed not to matter which woman he liberated. Didn't all women have the right to freedom? Perhaps the true reason for his reluctance to marry the older sister was simply that she had reminded him too much of Masha, both physically and intellectually. Was it possible that he was still reacting to that old wound, trying to shield himself from the pain of involvement with a beautiful, impetuous, emotional woman?

No, those were not his reasons. Was he absolutely sure? He ran his hand through his hair and continued pacing. If the liberation was accomplished, did it really matter what his reasons were?

As luck would have it, his back was turned when Sofya entered, so quietly that he did not hear her. When he turned around Sofya was approaching him cautiously, as if she were not absolutely sure that the man in front of her was the one she'd come to meet. Outside, the sun was failing behind clouds, dimming the high window. Inside, only distant icon lamps illuminated the church. He took a few steps to meet her, and stood looking down questioningly into her large, expressive eyes.

She whispered, with nervous formality, "Vladimir Onufrievich Kovalevsky?"

"Yes, it's me, Sofya Vasilievna. It's as dark as superstition in here." He looked around to be sure they were still alone. They kept their voices low.

She began hesitantly. "My sister and I were very unsettled by your offer."

"I hope you received it in the spirit in which it was intended. Did Bokova explain my reasons? But never mind, whether she did or not, I will naturally do so for myself." To his surprise Vladimir found the palms of his hands were starting to perspire. Why was this young girl's answer so important to him? Surely other young women, potential scientists, would welcome his services if this one declined.

"Maria did explain," Sofya assured him. "But I would like to hear directly from you anything you have to say."

"Then I'll speak plainly." He drew a deep breath. "I look at your sister, and I see—a good woman, yes, of course. But—there are a thousand others like her, a million rather, and they all want freedom and change.

Of course they all should have the right to study in Heidelberg or in Paris if they wish to do so. But—" And he raised a hand, to forestall an objection Sofya had not yet voiced. "But, she is bent on change by destruction. By means of words, in her case, but still I have had enough of destruction. In the end it will make very little difference to the history of Russia, or the world, if these women study abroad or not.

"Whereas in your case, we have someone capable of real achievements in science—and I've verified your abilities with Strannoliubsky. I think that one such person can make a very important difference in the world. To help such a person I am prepared to make certain sacrifices."

There was a silence. "I—I am honored," Sofya got out finally. "But you understand that the plan calls for three or four women to be freed by this one marriage. That is, those who remain single can travel abroad with the married one and her—"

"I understand, yes," Vladimir interrupted brusquely. "I also understand that plans, even those of revolutionary and liberated women, have a way of going wrong. In fact it has been my experience that they are very likely to do so. But, whoever actually becomes my wife will be under my legal protection. To that person, to her alone, I can promise the chance to go abroad."

So, Vladimir and Anyuta both thought acquiring individual liberators was the safest course. Well, they were being overly cautious. She cleared her throat and said: "After considerable thought, we've agreed to accept your offer."

Vladimir could feel himself assailed by a strange mixture of feelings. "I'm glad. I have good feelings about this arrangement."

"There are conditions of the agreement which must be perfectly clear," Sofya proceeded hesitantly, her eyes downcast in an embarrassed way.

"Sofya, I understand. Our marriage will be in name only." He paused. "I wonder if *you* understand completely?"

"Of course I do," she snapped.

"Perhaps. For me to give up the prospect of someday having a real marriage is one thing. I have . . . I have some experience of the world. I know what I'm doing. But for a young girl like you, innocent, a fictitious marriage may someday present a problem. You may encounter someone else, someone who comes to mean a great deal to you. Understand that under Russian law divorces are nearly impossible to obtain."

She nodded promptly.

"Annulments too are a long and ugly process. Sofya, are you sure you want to give up the chance of personal happiness?"

"I've made my decision. Work is my happiness, it will be my husband and my children. Vladimir, help me. That's what I'm asking."

Vladimir stood gazing at her, still wondering if she understood. The more he talked to Sofya, the more he was convinced that she was completely inexperienced with men. She'd probably never been close to a man, never been held, perhaps never kissed. How could she realize what she was giving up?

"Vladimir, believe me, I know what I am doing," she repeated, as if she had been somehow reading his thoughts.

"Then I'll help you," he said at last. "In every way possible. At all times and in all things, I promise to put your desires and ambitions ahead of my own."

Sofya put out her small right hand, and he enfolded it in his. "Vladimir, I promise I'll devote myself to study. I'll make you proud, and happy for what you've done," she said sincerely.

He said quietly "I'm sure you will."

"If I can ever help you," she hesitated, "with your career, either financially or personally, know you have the unrestrained support of your most grateful friend."

He nodded his acceptance.

FOR A TIME, they walked back and forth in the huge dim space. Vladimir's boots dully hammered the old stone floor. He watched with fascination as a mischievous smile turned Sofya's lips up slightly. Her dark eyes, focused on his face, gave the impression of shining in the gloom.

She murmured, "We've agreed on what we want and expect. Now we must devise a plan for getting it."

"Very true," Vladimir responded softly, as he lightly touched her elbow to guide her step. Without taking her eyes from his face, she moved closer to him, just avoiding the pillar to her right.

She said, "Our main problem, as I see it, is getting my father's consent to the marriage. I've come up with a plan. See what you think of it."

Vladimir smiled. "Go ahead." He was thinking that once this young lady made a decision, she was ready to take charge.

Sofya turned her gaze from him, they walked a few paces in silence, turned and started back. Then she spoke in a steady, urgent tone. "You must pretend you've never met me. You'll be introduced to the family on Thursday night when Father and Mother hold their usual open house for friends. You must plan a glowing introduction by the son of a general, or some other well-respected person—you know someone who'll qualify, don't you?" Before Vladimir could do more than nod she continued: "Once Father's met you, and talked to you, you can lead the conversation to his children. He loves to brag about us. You'll announce that you also are a student of science and would like to be allowed to talk to me about your studies. He'll probably agree to this. It's up to you to see he does. Be charming. I'll be there. You might speak to me a little about some area of study, but not too intensely. As you leave, I'll mention to Father that we've agreed to a study session on Friday, say, to compare textbooks.

"If this works, you will come to the house on Friday afternoon. We'll start to have frequent study sessions. After a month or so we convince Father that our studying together has led to a deeper relationship. What do you think?"

Vladimir, almost laughing, spread his hands helplessly. "I think you've thought this out quite carefully. I'm ready to try as you suggest. I haven't an alternate plan."

"Can you make the arrangements for an introduction by next Thursday? I don't want to waste a minute."

"Yes, I have the contacts."

"Is there some joke I've missed?"

"No, no. It's just that I thought you were timid and straightforward. Whereas the truth is you've a knack for concocting plots and intrigue." He laughed openly, the sound echoing in the empty church. He liked this playfulness in her. The shy girl was coming to life. The little theatricals with her father and others might be amusing.

Hailing a cab for Sofya outside the church and helping her in, he was impressed again with how young she seemed and how small she was. Like a delicate bird, but resourceful and capable of adapting and surviving. Yes, she'd be his 'little sparrow.' As they said goodbye, she smiled in the same charmingly mischievous way she had in the church. He liked that smile even more in the daylight.

As he watched the cab pull away, all of his doubts about insisting that Sofya be the woman that he befriend vanished. He knew himself well enough to know that he badly needed a friend with her strength of character. Sofya had offered friendship, along with the possibility of enough relief from his money problems to allow him to begin a career in science. Today, they had both made a very good bargain.

THE INTRODUCTION AT THE PARTY and the subsequent study sessions took place just as Sofya had planned. Twice a week for several hours at a time, Vladimir Onufrievich showed up at the Korvin-Krukovskys'.

The study sessions quickly became a serious business, when Sofya discovered glaring gaps in Vladimir's knowledge of science. If he was sincere about a new career, she'd have to take him in hand. He wasn't ready for university-level work. His readings in popular science had to be supplemented with a disciplined study of mathematics, physics, and chemistry.

With good humor, he had pointed out that her education also had gaps, primarily in political and economic theory. He gave her books and pamphlets to read, which she kept secret from her parents, but shared with her sister.

When Father was home, the couple purposely laughed and joked more loudly, carefully staying away from political conversations. Now and then Father would walk past the room and glance in through the open door. Sofya, aware of his observation, made a special effort to lean closer to Vladimir or to let her hand rest on his arm.

Inevitably Father took notice of Sofya's actions.

"Sofya. I want to see you," he ordered, then turned and walked into the hallway.

As Sofya stood to follow him, Vladimir whispered, "Hold your tongue or you'll ruin everything."

"I know what I'm doing," she whispered back. As she left the study, she closed the door. Father was standing stiffly a few steps away, his arms crossed over his chest.

"Well, Sofya, if you want this gentleman to continue visiting you, you will have to learn to behave in a more ladylike manner."

"What do you mean, Father?" Sofya feigned offense.

"You know what I mean. You're not to take his hand, or to hold his arm. If you're studying, you should sit across from him. There's no need for the closeness I see every time I pass."

"But he's a friend. I can't completely avoid touching him."

"He is here as a fellow student." Father's voice had the sound of a command as he continued. "I won't have you flirting."

Sofya flushed with embarrassment. She wanted to remind Father that she was eighteen and a little flirting was natural. But remembering Vladimir's caution, she only bit her lip and said, "Yes, Father."

There was an uncomfortable silence. She felt his eyes searching her face. Then he continued in a softer tone, "If the young man wants to court you, he should make his intentions known and present himself honestly to your mother and me."

"Yes, Father." Softly Sofya continued, "Vladimir has asked me to join him at a concert this Friday. We were going to ask your permission."

She met Father's stare with her best pleading look. "Please, may I accompany him?"

Father hesitated, then with an exasperated sigh responded, "All right. But you behave yourself." He turned and walked away.

Sofya returned to the study, smiling to herself.

THE STUDY SESSIONS, the social outings, and the General's watchfulness continued for several weeks. One particular clear, crisp evening, the General and his wife were walking along the embankment overlooking the Neva. The river was frozen now, her raging temper suspended until spring.

For a long time the General was quiet. "Liza, what do you think of Sofya and that Kovalevsky fellow?"

"Sofya enjoys his company," Liza answered as she reached for her husband's arm. A patch of ice had made her slip. "He's bright and witty. Sofya values intellect.

"I like him." she continued, "I think he's a very nice young man. Sofya hasn't had a real beau, not like Anyuta. She's enjoying the attention."

"Do you think she acts a little strangely with him?"

"How do you mean?"

"Flirting, but stiff. I'm not sure how to explain. A tension perhaps is missing, or perhaps false, in her behavior with the man."

"Vasily, really!" Liza looked at him. "Anyuta tells me Sofya likes him quite a bit. You know how close the girls are. If there was any trifling going on, Anyuta would know. And Anyuta would tell me.

"Sofya just lacks a little grace. She's always been awkward socially. Don't worry so. The young men will come and go. Sofya will be more experienced and charming when her real time for courting comes."

"I suppose you're right." The General wasn't really reassured. But for the time being he allowed his fears to rest.

VLADIMIR, AFTER TWO MONTHS OF "COURTING," still found himself in awe of this young girl. She had captivated his literary friends, his academic friends, even his associates in the publishing business. Everyone was congratulating him on his good fortune in finding such a beautiful, charming young companion. His closer friends mentioned how happy they were to see him finally emerging from his gloomy moods.

Only on the darkest and coldest nights, tossing alone and sleepless in his bed, did he acknowledge the growing suspicion that his happiness was being bought at too dear a price. Not for himself, but for her. He repeated again and again that this was an equitable contract, entered into freely and knowingly by both parties. Still, a vague sense of dishonor shadowed his happiness.

One evening, returning from a party in a rented open carriage, Vladimir leaned back, stretched his long legs, slumped and rested his head on the back of the seat.

"Look at those stars, Sofya. Isn't the sky wonderful!" he exclaimed.

Sofya looked at him instead. "You look as contented as old Ursa Major up there."

"At this moment, I am," he said, not taking his eyes off the impressive expanse. "I'm surrounded by beauty. And spring is almost here."

"Yes, spring is almost here," Sofya agreed thoughtfully. "We have to move on with our plans, Vladimir."

Vladimir sat up straight, his gaze fixed on Sofya.

"In a few weeks Father will be getting ready to move the family back to the country for the summer."

"And nothing is settled."

"Exactly." She sighed. "I want to start attending classes in the fall."

"I'll talk to your father tomorrow." Vladimir no longer felt content.

THE NEXT DAY, after visiting with Sofya as usual, Vladimir asked the General for a word in private. Vasily Vasilievich protested that he didn't have time, as he was meeting a business associate.

"Please sir, I assure you, the matter is important," Vladimir insisted. "I will not take much of your time."

The General sighed, looked at his watch. "Then I must send a message to the Club saying I'll be late for the meeting. Wait for me in the study."

Vladimir entered the small, neat room whose walls were lined with books. There was only enough space for a desk, two chairs, and a small divan. Vladimir stood in front of the desk. He ran his finger under his shirt collar, loosening the material slightly. The room was stuffy and overheated.

In a few moments the General joined him, closing the door. The tall, thin, gray-haired man was behind his desk in a few long strides. Without acknowledging Vladimir's presence, the General sat down, moved some papers on the desk, and then almost as an afterthought motioned Vladimir to sit.

"I prefer to stand, sir." Vladimir came right to the point. "Sir, I want to marry your daughter, Sofya Vasilievna."

"Sofya is too young," the General snapped. There was a pause. Vladimir's silence pointed out the obvious: that many women married at eighteen.

The General continued, "She's not mature enough, not experienced enough to know her own mind or feelings."

Vladimir insisted. "I believe this marriage is very much what Sofya wants. And it is what I want."

"You both may want it, young man." The General's remark was one of undisguised contempt. "But I am responsible for my daughter's happiness. I must be practical. Before I will begin to entertain your proposal with any seriousness, you're going to have to convince me that you are able to provide for my daughter's well being."

Vladimir explained that he owned a small estate in the Vitebsk region, and derived some money from that. The General shook his head doubtfully, knowing very well that a small, poorly managed estate in a swampy region of Vitebsk wasn't much of a financial blessing.

Vladimir continued, describing his publishing business in optimistic terms, going into detail on how much profit he expected to make when his next book was published. Vasily Vasilievich countered that publishing was a business where considerable expenses came before uncertain profits.

Vladimir persisted. "In a year or so, my publishing business will be firmly established. The wave of public interest in science is increasing."

The General looked at him doubtingly, and maintained a stony silence.

Vladimir tried another approach. "I did quite well in my university studies. I might return to the law, sir. Or state service." This was a deception. Vladimir knew he never could, nor would go back to that kind of life.

Finally, grudgingly, the General yielded. But not entirely.

"Well, young man, I see you're persistent." The General paused. In a quiet voice he continued, "I'm going to ask one more question. The answer you give to me is not as important as the answer you give to yourself. So examine your mind and heart before you answer." There was a silence, then: "Do you love my Sofya?"

Vladimir flushed, then answered, "Yes sir, very much." What else could he possibly have said?

The General was closely watching Vladimir's face.

"Then I'm sure you will agree that I am being fair to both of you when I do not refuse your request, but merely postpone my decision. Perhaps in a year or two, you will ask again."

"But sir—" Vladimir struggled to press his case.

"No, don't try to argue with me. You may continue seeing Sofya, while we are in Petersburg. You may write to her this summer when we are in the country." The General stood, resting his knuckles on the desk, he leaned forward and locked his gaze on Vladimir.

"But there is to be no further talk of marriage at this time." After a moment, the General motioned for Vladimir to leave.

Vladimir bowed silently. Nothing was to be gained by trying to push the matter now.

ANYUTA, MORE BEAUTIFUL THAN EVER, rosy and flushed from the cold, arrived home just as Father was showing Vladimir out. Vladimir greeted her with restrained politeness, "Good afternoon, Anna Vasilievna."

Anyuta acknowledged his presence with a slight nod. For a moment their eyes met. So Anyuta had not forgiven him for choosing Sofya. Her look, one he expected she reserved for roaches and other creeping creatures, told him that she considered him not much of a loss, even as a fictitious husband.

She turned quickly to greet her father, and asked for Sofya.

"Your sister is in her room, or so I think. Anyuta, please tell her that I wish to see her immediately in my study."

The General was frowning and rubbing his head as he curtly gestured a final goodbye to Vladimir.

BURSTING INTO SOFYA'S ROOM, Anyuta closed the door and perched on the edge of the settee, demanding in a whisper to know what had happened.

Sofya did not stop pacing the room to reply. "I don't know. They talked, of course, Vladimir and Father, alone in the study. Vladimir was to ask for my hand. They didn't come hurrying joyously to get me afterward, so it can't have been a complete success. I'm to meet Vladimir tomorrow afternoon in the cathedral. No doubt I'll find out then."

"I think you'll find out sooner. Father wants to see you right away."

"Anyuta! For goodness sake, why didn't you say so when you came in?" Sofya started for the door.

Anyuta reached out and touched Sofya's arm. "Sofya. Before you go, there's something I've just learned that I must tell you."

"Well?" Sofya sat down nervously on the edge of the settee.

"I've seen Bokova, she's been talking to Strannoliubsky. He was present recently when Vladimir received a letter from an old acquaintance of his—more than an acquaintance, actually his former fiancée, Masha Mikhaelis!"

Sofya searched her sister's face. "Are you sure?"

"As I said, Strannoliubsky told Maria Bokova and Maria told me. Now, what do you make of that? Vladimir's evidently corresponding with his old flame, just before asking Father for your hand. Seems strange to me. Nothing's going wrong with our plan, is it? Vladimir did ask for your hand?"

"He said that was the reason he was meeting with Father," Sofya snapped back at her sister. "He wouldn't deceive me." Sofya met Anyuta's stare for a moment, then turned her eyes away from her sister's searching gaze.

Anyuta continued, "Of course I suppose Vladimir and Masha may be only contemplating some kind of an affair, which would be none of our business under the circumstances."

"Contemplating an affair? What do you mean? That's impossible. Impossible." Sofya was stunned. She turned and placed a hand to her mouth as if to cough, unwilling to let her sister witness the flush she felt rising to her face.

Anyuta laughed. "Sofya, child, people do have them, you know. As a bride in name only, you won't have much grounds for jealousy."

Sofya's hand dropped to her lap.

"Why Sofya, you're flushed. You are jealous. Jealous!" Anyuta made it an accusation. "What childish possessiveness. It must stop. Grow up!"

"I'm angry," Sofya snapped.

"With whom? Over what? If you're right, and he's not going to back out on us with regard to the wedding ceremony, then this piece of news is not important. His personal arrangements are his own concern."

Sofya was silent. Her hands closed tightly about the sides of the settee, so that she felt a painful pressure on the tips of her fingers and against her palms. She welcomed the pain as a momentary relief from doubt, hurt, and anger.

"You're jealous." Anyuta's voice drew her back. "I know you too well for you to deceive me. I've seen your jealousy too many times, over too many petty things. It's a dangerous weakness in you, Sofya. This time you must keep that emotion in close check or you'll be the one to ruin our plans. You'll chase him off." Anyuta paused, then with an inflection expressing concern and sympathy, "Has he started romancing you?"

"Don't be ridiculous! You know the agreement. We both are abiding by the terms of the agreement."

"Good!" Anyuta nodded. "You're sure he's given no indication of wanting to back out?"

"No, he's not going to back out. Don't worry, our plan will work. We'll be free by fall." Sofya arose, looked sternly at Anyuta, then left the room. The door closed loudly behind her. The plan was working. Wasn't it? She must trust.

Hurrying to see Father, she struggled with a turmoil of new thoughts. If Vladimir was still writing to Masha—what did that mean? Perhaps he had changed his mind. But no, Vladimir wouldn't do that, he'd have said something to her. He wouldn't just betray her. Would he?

Sofya stood before the door of Father's study, her hand poised for a moment on the handle. She tried desperately to bring her emotions under control. She was jealous. Jealous, before she had become any kind of bride at all. She must push such unreasonable emotions out of her heart and mind. She needed all her calm and wits. Taking a deep breath, she pushed the handle, and entered the close, oppressive atmosphere of Father's study.

VASILY VASILIEVICH, looking up from his desk, motioned Sofya to the chair directly in front of him. A family crisis like this right before a big business deal was enough to drive a strong man to despair.

"Vladimir has asked to marry you," he informed her directly. "Of course, you knew of his action?"

His daughter sat rigid. A barely noticeable sigh escaped her lips. Her facial muscles seemed to relax a little. Her eyes remained fixed upon him. "Vladimir and I have spoken about our future together."

"You gave no indication of this to your Mother or me." The General heard his own statement quavering between a reprimand and an accusation of disloyalty.

Sofya sat silent and motionless, but he sensed that this was only a surface calm. Her attentive eyes searched him disturbingly. He was reminded of the look he had seen in the eyes of defiant prisoners about to undergo interrogation. Such a look from his daughter, in the present circumstances, unnerved him. He must be gentle. He could not be an interrogating general now. Not with his Sofya.

"Well, no matter now." He recovered his composure. "Do you love this man?"

For a moment the room was completely silent. The General waited and watched. There were small beads of perspiration forming on his daughter's upper lip. In all their disagreements and misunderstandings, she had never lied to him. He must trust that she would not lie to herself.

"Vladimir and I are very happy together. We both want very much to get married."

He could not allow her to evade giving a direct reply. He repeated, "Do you love him?"

"Yes." This time her response came out quickly and firmly. Her eyes stayed locked with his. Still, he felt that Sofya was fighting some inner tension. He hoped that her tension was the result of some feeling she had toward his parental authority. He hoped it had nothing to do with her feelings for the man she was talking of marrying.

He accepted her answer. "I've told Vladimir the engagement must wait a year or two. You both need more time to evaluate your feelings and position. You're only eighteen. And there's another concern. Your sister isn't married yet. Because you're so much younger than she, your marrying first would be a social embarrassment for her. In respect for her sensitivities, you can delay your plans a little while."

"But . . ." Sofya tried to argue.

"Nothing more now." He knew he sounded harsh. He hadn't meant to be harsh. Rising, he walked around the desk to Sofya, took her by the shoulders and kissed her gently. "Tomorrow we'll have more time to talk. I'm late for a meeting with Uncle Briullov." Pulling out his watch, he added, "I'm very late. There's a good deal of money at stake."

Almost at the door, he turned back briefly. "I want you to promise me to think this over very carefully. You are young. You still have plenty of time to make decisions about marriage."

He really loved his little Sofya and wanted her to be happy. And somehow, he couldn't rid himself of the nagging feeling something was not quite right for his daughter in her relationship with this Kovalevsky. He must spend time with Sofya, find out what she was thinking and feeling. But now, he must attend to this business deal.

❦

JUST BEFORE FATHER LEFT the house Sofya overheard him telling Mother what had happened, and insisting that all discussion on the subject of the proposed marriage wait for his return. At the last moment Father turned to Mother. "If all goes well at the business meeting, Elizaveta, we'll have a grand celebration dinner party on Friday."

Sofya returned to her room, grateful that Anyuta was not waiting for her. Alone she sat on the edge of her bed. Obtaining Father's immediate consent was going to be a problem. She thought over Father's words. Why had Father asked her if she loved Vladimir? She could not remember Father ever saying anything to suggest that he thought of love as being important in arranging a marriage. Money and position were his concerns, not love. She had been stunned by his unexpected question. Why had he insisted on so direct an answer?

And why had the question been so hard to answer? Here in the quiet of her room, all alone with her own heart and mind, she knew she had not lied. In justification to her committed agreement, she whispered silently to herself: *I do love Vladimir, just like a brother.*

Why had Anyuta upset her with doubts about Vladimir, just before the meeting with Father? Sofya allowed a sob to escape, then another. She couldn't stop the tears.

NEXT AFTERNOON, Sofya met Vladimir once more in the back of the cathedral. Brooding over Anyuta's revelation had strained her nerves, already frayed by Father's disappointing reaction. As she approached the meeting she was angry. Vladimir was scarcely able to finish greeting her before she accosted him with a question.

"Are you happy that Father won't announce our engagement?" She struggled to keep her voice low.

The smile of greeting disappeared from his face. "What do you mean?"

"I mean only that you're still able to change your mind. You don't have to go through with this, you know. If an attachment persists between you and Masha, just say so. Perhaps you're hoping she'll have you back. You wish to give her one more try before you're tied to a loveless relationship."

Now Vladimir looked reassuringly puzzled, not at all guilty. "Sofya, this is madness. Whatever gave you the idea that I wanted to rekindle my former relationship with Masha? That's all over."

"Too bad for you. Evidently you thought you'd write her one more love letter to change her mind."

"Ah, now I begin to understand. You've heard somehow of an exchange of letters." Vladimir looked around. A monk had come into the rear of the cathedral and was standing, as if deep in prayer, ten or twelve paces away. Forcefully, Vladimir took Sofya by her elbow and led her toward the front of the cathedral. Sofya hurried along, trying to keep up, needing two steps for each of his long strides. Abruptly he turned to his right, pushing her along with him.

"What are you doing?" she whispered angrily.

"Finding us a better place to talk," he whispered back, as he led her behind a beautifully frescoed pillar depicting scenes from the opening verses of Genesis. The broad pillar hid a small alcove. A simple wooden bench rested against one frescoed wall, a silver plaque dominated the wall opposite. High on the middle wall was a slim window which admitted just enough light to illuminate the alcove. Under the window was another fresco, rich in dark greens and deep reds, depicting some saint Sofya did not recognize. Most likely it was the patron of the man buried behind the silver plaque.

A strong smell, a mixture of dampness, earth and generations of humanity, permeated the area. Sofya was about to turn back to the relatively fresh air of the main church, when Vladimir took her by the shoulders and pushed her gently to a sitting position on the bench. "Sit," he commanded. He sat next to her.

"Listen. The fact is that I've written to Masha's mother, Evgenia Egorovna, and had a letter from her in return. Evgenia is my dear friend, and her daughter also my friend if it comes to that. Would you like to hear what I wrote?"

Sofya was flushed with anger, feeling herself almost out of control, knowing the reaction was unreasonable, and hating herself for it. In an effort to master her feelings, she remained silent.

Vladimir continued, "I wrote asking if Evgenia would take you in. I was going to suggest that you leave your father's house and go to the Mikhaelis'. They'd shelter you until your father agreed to an education abroad. Then you wouldn't have to get involved in a loveless marriage. I was trying to offer you an alternate plan, one that would not cost you so dearly. I am trying to do what's best for you."

She could only shake her head at him, not understanding.

Reaching for her hand, which had been clutching the edge of the bench, he said, "I care for you, Sofya. Deeply." Then, embarrassed, but not releasing her hand, he added, "This arrangement of ours is not necessary. Evgenia's agreed to offer you whatever help you need, whenever you're ready."

Sofya pulled her hand away from Vladimir's, and sprang to her feet. She fought back the overwhelming urge to cry. He, the only man who had ever preferred her to Anyuta, was rejecting her, in a kind way, but still a rejection. Unable to voice or explain this feeling, her mind struggled frantically for a sound reason why the plan he had just suggested would not work. "You don't understand my father, if you think my going to Evgenia would move him to allow me to go abroad. And what of Anyuta, and the others we could help? What of your hope for a new future in science? I have no intention of deserting my fellow captives, or you."

"Very well. Very well. We'll follow the original plan." Vladimir again urged her to be seated next to him. "I wanted you to have another choice—besides marrying a man you don't love."

Sofya felt somewhat comforted. Calmer now, more in control, she resumed her seat. But her anger wasn't totally gone. Vladimir hadn't really answered her questions about his feelings for Masha.

When he next spoke it was as if he were reading her thoughts. "I'm going to tell you about my break with Masha. I'd hoped the past could be forgotten, but I see from your reaction that that's impossible."

Vladimir hesitated before he continued. Reacting perhaps to the stuffiness of the alcove, perhaps to his own nervousness, he unbuttoned the collar of his shirt. Leaning forward, not looking at her but at his clenched hands, "Masha and I were deeply in love. Then it happened that, several months before we were to be married, we attended the trial and sentencing of the writer Nikolai Gavrilovich Chernyshevsky."

"I've heard the story," Sofya whispered. She too was staring at his hands.

"Almost everyone has. I've heard three or four different versions myself, but what I am giving you is the truth." He looked up, his face grimmer than she had ever seen it.

"When Chernyshevsky was put in a cart to be hauled off to prison, Masha threw a bouquet of flowers. Other women were also throwing flowers, but Masha's landed conspicuously right in the prisoner's lap.

"The police started arresting people." Vladimir turned his eyes away from Sofya. "One grabbed Masha and started to drag her away. I couldn't stand the sight, and I tried to strike him." His hands came together violently, then turned palms up, separate and empty. "The gesture was foolish and worthless. Masha and I were both arrested and taken to the House of Detention."

Sofya, her anger gone, had fallen silent. She moved closer to Vladimir and placed her hand on his arm. He was now the one having trouble controlling his emotions as he went on. "Naturally we were separated. I had no idea how she was being treated. The officer who questioned me several hours after my arrest, hinted that women in custody were not always treated honorably. They even were 'forgotten' sometimes. Each woman was kept alone in a small, dark, cold cell, he said. It might be months, years, before things were straightened out. He asked me, did I want that to happen to Masha?

"I had no doubt that the officer was not exaggerating. Horror stories told by prisoners are common."

"I know," Sofya breathed.

"Then my interrogator offered me a deal. Masha would be treated leniently—if I would cooperate with the police to some extent in the future."

"Oh," she whispered, unable to hide the horror and fear in her voice.

"He didn't want much, he said. Perhaps I could keep them informed of student movements, pass on whatever information I thought might be helpful to them. Nothing too demanding. Just a word now and then.

"I refused, as I knew Masha would have wanted me to do." Vladimir was now gazing at Sofya with a pleading, demanding expression. "I swear that I refused."

"I believe you," she answered firmly.

"And then, as I was preparing myself to face the punishment for my refusal, the punishment I knew would certainly come—the officers let me go. Masha they kept. What an ingenious punishment! As soon as I reappeared among my friends, they were suspicious as to why I had been released so soon. And the things that I imagined were happening to Masha were more painful to me than physical torture." Vladimir nervously readjusted his position on the bench. Again his eyes turned from Sofya.

Staring vacantly ahead at the silver plaque, he continued, "Fortunately Masha suffered no serious harm. A week later her father was able to arrange her release, with the stipulation that she return to their country home for one year. Her father mentioned our intention to marry. The officer insisted she could not return even for a wedding. We'd have to have a country wedding.

"But from the day we were arrested, nothing was ever the same between us. For a time I feared that she too suspected me, because I had been released so quickly. In the weeks that followed, Masha and I quarreled frequently. I told her I could never again stand to see her arrested, never again live with the fear that she was being tortured. As my wife she would have to stop provoking arrests. What if she had been pregnant? What about our children?" He was standing, pacing the small alcove. "She argued that change in the system of arrests and torture could only come by social action. If she was one of those who had to suffer, then so be it. No individuals, not even the children we might have, were more important than the cause.

"The arguments went on and on. They were fundamental. Even on the morning of our wedding we argued and fought. Two hours before the ceremony was to begin, she called it off."

He stopped pacing, stopped talking. The dim, oppressive stuffiness and the excess of emotion had caused small beads of sweat to form on his forehead. Without speaking, Sofya pressed her handkerchief into his hand.

As if brought back from some trance by the touch of her hand, he wiped his forehead, then continued. "Masha remained in the country, while I returned to Petersburg. I was in the city in '66 when Karakozov took a shot at the Tsar. But I was not among those rounded up in the mass arrests that followed. I have no idea why I wasn't. Perhaps some bureaucratic blundering, God knows there's more than enough of that. But my name did appear on a list, received by Herzen, of those arrested.

"Because of that, many came to the conclusion that I would have been arrested had I not been a police informer. For a time even Herzen suspected me. The loss of his trust was a great blow. There were rumors again that Masha had refused to marry me because she knew I had weakened and agreed to become an informer. This is of course nonsense. Masha and I are still dear friends. Her family treats me as a son. She would never be friends with an informer."

He again sat next to Sofya on the bench and took her hand in his. "But perhaps you have already heard these accusations against me?"

Sofya, biting her lip to hold back tears, could only shake her head.

"Well, if you haven't, you will, sooner or later. I thought it best for you to hear the truth of the matter from me."

Sofya was weeping now, overwhelmed by so many strong emotions in so short a time. She was sorry for her doubts and hasty accusations. Sorry for Vladimir. Sorry for Masha.

She knew with certainty now that she and Vladimir thought alike.

They hated repression of the individual spirit by authority, whether governmental or parental. And both desperately feared imprisonment, whether in a Tsarist jail or on a family estate. Escape was the correct solution, the only answer. The fictitious marriage would be Vladimir's escape as much as her own.

"It seems we will have to share your handkerchief." He gently wiped her tears. Again she thought how large his hands were; like Father's, and yet so very different.

Gently touching one of the tears on her cheek with his finger, he whispered, "Are you still angry with me? You see, my loss of Masha gives me another reason to commit my life to a cause. I must convince myself that I didn't lose her because of lack of conviction, only because of different convictions."

"Do you love her?" Sofya spoke impulsively, hearing herself echoing her father's words to her.

Vladimir looked into her eyes. "No. Not anymore."

As they stepped outside the church, Sofya took a deep breath of the chilly, fresh air. The reddish light from the setting sun gave a magical cast to the marble facing. "I hate winter. The sun goes down so early," she grumbled.

"But the fantastic glow it leaves on the marble and snow is our compensation." Vladimir's mood was surprisingly light. Leaving her at the church entrance, he went to hail a cab.

Sofya looked after him warmly. A sudden burst of wind blew dry snow in her face. She reached up and pulled the lace veil she had worn in church more closely around her. She smiled to herself. She had the inkling of a plan, but details would need to be worked out.

Having hired a cab, Vladimir returned. As he helped her into the vehicle she said, "Vladimir, promise me you'll be in your apartment next Friday around dinner time."

Vladimir, not understanding, promised.

Vasily's business meeting on the day Vladimir asked him for Sofya's hand had been a huge success. The meeting, with Aleksander Ivanovich Briullov, Elizaveta's uncle and a distinguished diplomat in the service of the Tsar, had established that from now on vodka from Palibino would be accepted for export to foreign lands. This would mean a considerable profit for the estate. Vasily was very pleased, and a week later Uncle Briullov and others were invited to dinner, to celebrate.

Vasily and his wife spent the afternoon doing some last-minute shopping. He decided to present his honored guests, Uncle Briullov and his wife, with gifts. Elizaveta's taste and judgment were essential to the selection of a silver cigarette case and jeweled earrings. They arrived home with barely enough time for Elizaveta to dress and oversee final preparations. He had planned the close timing deliberately to keep Liza from fussing about the house unnecessarily and interfering with the servants, who knew what needed to be done.

Vasily quickly donned his full dress uniform. Around his neck he placed the elegant satin ribbon from which hung the prized Order of St. Ann, awarded for valor in the Balkan campaign against the Turks. After fastening a ceremonial sword about his waist, Vasily reviewed his tall, lean reflection in the mirror. Yes, he still cut a handsome figure.

He entered the small dressing area where Liza was finishing her preparations. He silently admired his Liza in her gown. She was nervous as always before an evening of entertaining. She asked him to help her with the clasp of her necklace. As he struggled with the tiny latch, she told him that the girls both had new silk gowns, Anyuta's of light aqua, Sofya's a rich teal. Fedya was wearing his school's dress uniform. Like his father, he would present a military appearance. With no interest in her talk of clothes, Vasily kissed her neck, asked her to stop bobbing up and down, assured her the children were beautiful and an honor to them, and finished fastening the clasp.

Despite Vasily's pleading for her to relax, Elizaveta, with a few minutes to spare, began to annoy the kitchen and serving staff. She didn't settle down until the first guests started to arrive.

Pre-dinner champagne was served. At the appointed hour, a manservant approached Vasily Vasilievich and asked permission to announce that dinner was ready.

Only now did Vasily notice Sofya's absence.

Discreetly the General called his older daughter to him. "Where is your sister?" he asked quietly.

"I saw her some time ago. She was in her room fixing her hair."

"Tell her she's to come without delay. That's an order," he said sternly.

Anyuta went off, but returned almost immediately with a serious expression on her face, carrying a note addressed to Father.

"I found this on her dressing table," she whispered, handing over the envelope.

Father opened the note, read it, and put it calmly into his pocket. After a murmured word to Mother, he announced that dinner would be a little late. He would return shortly. Until then more wine and appetizers would be served. He hoped the guests would not be too much inconvenienced. As they were all old friends, they didn't mind at all, and continued their friendly gossiping.

MINUTES BEFORE MOTHER and Father had arrived home, Sofya had left the house. Alone and on foot, she hurried down the fast darkening street. She pulled her hood far over her face and walked with her head down, avoiding eye contact with passing men. She'd never before been out alone in the city after dark. She feared she might encounter unpleasantness, or be mistaken for a woman of the street.

The lamplighters were just starting to light the gas street lamps as she hurried by. The neighborhood changed from wealthy to modest to humble in only a few blocks. Her heart was beating quickly from exertion and excitement.

In about an hour she reached the shabby apartment house that was her goal. She ran up the dark stairway and knocked vigorously on the door of a third floor apartment.

Vladimir opened the door. She stood silently before him. He looked at her blankly without recognition, as if she were a stranger or a supernatural vision.

"Vladimir, it's me, Sofya. Thank God, you are at home," Sofya gasped out, trying to catch her breath.

"I promised you I would be." Vladimir was still looking at her strangely. But his stunned expression had vanished. The corners of his mouth were turned upward and his eyes were shining mischievously. "I certainly wasn't expecting you! I thought you might be sending me a note." Vladimir was dressed casually, shoeless feet in undarned socks. One large toe had escaped. His straight reddish hair, usually pushed straight back from his high forehead, now threatened to merge with his eyebrows. Behind him a lamp burned on a desk covered with papers. Books were everywhere in the small apartment.

"I wasn't sure I'd be able to come. Please close the door." Pushing past him, Sofya threw her cloak on a nearby chair, scooped books off the divan, sat down and took her shoes off, rumpled her hair a little.

"Sofya, you look beautiful!" He struggled for control of his voice, then silently stared at her. He pushed his unruly hair back into its rightful place. "Sofya! What's going on?"

"Will you close the door? Thank you. Father will be here any minute. I left him a note saying you and I couldn't wait any longer. That we had to be together. Nothing could keep us apart I told him I had fled to your apartment."

"*What?*"

"You'll see. Now he'll have to agree to our marriage. He'll find me in your apartment. I've been compromised."

"Sofya! Your reputation!" Vladimir spoke angrily, "And have you thought that your Father might just insist on a duel, or come here with a gun!"

"Don't be silly. I can predict his reactions very accurately. He's stubborn, cold, and very strict. He'll demonstrate incredible rage, shout and denounce us, but he won't insist on a duel or shoot you and he won't publicly embarrass me."

"You little fool—you've never seen a man shot, have you?" She waited silently, watching as he balanced between anger and amusement. "Your father does appear to be a remarkably sensible man. I suppose you might be right about his reactions." He smiled at her. "Well, if this is to be our plan, we must do our best to put it into effect convincingly. Don't sit there on the divan. Come here. To me."

Sofya looked at him questioningly. His eyes were gleaming in a way she hadn't seen before. When he beckoned silently with both hands, she got up slowly.

"Vladimir? Vladimir Onufrievich, this is just pretend. We don't have to do anything, just being here together is enough."

But somehow she had moved close enough for him to take her hand and draw her to him. "I know, we are only pretending." His voice was a whisper. "But let's not take any chances. I'm just rehearsing my part."

And now his arms had gone around her waist. "When we hear him on the stairs, we'll be in each other's arms. Like this." His strong arms drew her even closer. She had just a moment to put her arms protectively in front of her, her hands pushing against his chest.

He was staring into her eyes. She felt his breath on her face. A faint aroma of peppered vodka preceded his words. The words were no more than a whisper. "The pupils of your eyes are growing larger. And the iris is slowly changing from green to brown. How charming."

She felt mesmerized. She couldn't speak. This wasn't her plan!

"And when we hear your father opening the door, I'll kiss you, like this," he said. His head bent down and his lips found hers. As if it were the most natural thing in the world. Her eyes were still wide open. She felt his warm, moist lips press against hers for a long time. Her arms had fallen to her side as if by their own will. She could feel his heart beating, or thought she could. When he'd finished, she gasped. Somehow she managed to take one small step back. Her mind raced. This wasn't supposed to happen. What was wrong with Vladimir?

He took her chin in his hand and raised her face to his. Once again his voice was brisk. "You'll have to be a little more cooperative than that if we're to put on a convincing show. Don't be frightened, my little sparrow. This is just a performance."

She was speechless. What had that kiss meant? She wasn't sure. Before she had time to think, the sound of heavy boots came on the stairs. Vladimir drew her to him. She was in his arms again. It was necessary, she told herself, if they wanted to convince Father. Her arms went around Vladimir, clinging to him, as he pressed her closer to him. When Vladimir released her lips and body this time, she was trembling. She didn't want to be released. She wasn't ready. Why had he let her go? Reluctantly, her arms released him.

"Volodya—" She whispered his name endearingly, half questioning why he wasn't kissing her. She thought she heard him tenderly whisper, "My Sonechka."

Who was shouting?

Somehow, during the kiss, the door of the apartment had been opened and Father had arrived. Red-faced and trembling, he was bellowing his wrath at Vladimir. Shouting in words that Sofya had never heard before and whose meaning she did not know, beyond the fact that they must be deadly insults. Men challenged one another to duels over words like these. But Vladimir issued no challenge. He was only standing back, pale, his arms folded, now and then trying to get in a calming word.

Then Father moved toward Sofya, raging at her. She must get her things and come home with him immediately. Vladimir, playing his role to the hilt, placed himself between Father and Sofya. Now Sofya feared Father was going to strike him. Vladimir took Sofya's hand and firmly and quietly insisted that she would not leave the apartment until she was ready. And she would not be ready until and unless Father agreed to their engagement.

Father ranted, giving the impression of an angry bear.

Vladimir stood his ground calmly.

"Well, then," said Father, in a suddenly exhausted voice, and stopped. Abruptly Sofya realized that they had won.

It seemed a long time that the General stood there looking silently at the two of them, his face displaying mixed emotions. When he spoke again, it was once more to give orders, though now calmly and rationally.

"Kovalevsky, have you clothes suitable for attendance at a formal dinner? Good, then put them on. Quickly. Sofya, straighten yourself as decently as possible. I have guests waiting at home. The two of you, be down in the carriage in five minutes. No longer, do you hear?" He left the room, leaving the door open. They could hear his boots retreating heavily down the stairs, more slowly than they had come up.

Sofya and Vladimir looked at each other anxiously, then fell into an embrace. Vladimir picked her up and twirled around with her in his arms. They both burst out laughing. "We've done it. We've done it!" Impulsively Sofya kissed Vladimir on the neck as he let her down. He held her a trifle longer than necessary. Then Vladimir hurried into the next room to change.

NOT A WORD was said during the carriage ride home. Father had collected himself. To all appearances he was firmly in command again.

Calmly the three of them entered the dining room together, with Sofya clinging lightly to Vladimir's arm. Calling for the attention of the assembled family and guests, Father asked everyone to drink a toast of champagne with him. He wished to announce the engagement of his younger daughter, Sofya Vasilievna Korvin-Krukovskaya, to the lawyer and publisher, Vladimir Onufrievich Kovalevsky.

CHAPTER FOUR

Spring 1868 ❧ *The Engagement*

Congratulations were offered to the happy couple, amid a great deal of surprise. Mother hugged and kissed Sofya, then Vladimir. For a time Sofya, being kissed, hugged, and admired, felt that she was the most loved person in the world. Vladimir stayed at her side, happily accepting congratulations.

As the party sat down to dinner, Anyuta's quick, reprimanding look from across the table was not what Sofya had expected. What could it mean? For the moment, there was no way of asking. Sofya nodded and smiled, responding appropriately to the small talk of General Obruchev, who was seated on her right.

Vladimir, at Sofya's left, was consuming large amounts of food and wine, and completely charming not only Mother, on his other side, but all the guests with his knowledgeable, witty conversation. The big, reddish-haired man with the piercing eyes was clearly attractive to the ladies, and respected by the men.

By the end of the evening, only Father and Anyuta still maintained traces of cold formality in their attitude toward Vladimir.

Father had not mentioned a date for the wedding.

LATE THAT EVENING, when all the guests had gone and Mother and Father had retired, Anyuta softly knocked on Sofya's bedroom door, then entered without waiting for a response.

Sofya was in her chemise, brushing her hair in front of the dresser mirror. The image in the mirror wore a look of satisfaction and contentment that Anyuta rarely saw in her sister. Speaking to that image, Anyuta half joked, "Think you're rather clever and beautiful, don't you?"

The response from the eyes in the mirror was definitely affirmative. Anyuta sat down on the edge of Sofya's bed. "I suppose you've earned the right to gloat. That was quite an evening. Your plan worked, thank God."

Turning from the glass, Sofya gazed at Anyuta with the innocent expression of a child. "So, that's what that look meant at dinner. You think I'm gloating."

"I can see that you really enjoyed being the center of attention. A little queen holding court. Generally you're clumsy and awkward among Mother and Father's friends." Anyuta stopped short. She would have to watch her tongue. She mustn't reveal how painful it had been watching everyone make such a fuss over little Sofya.

Anyuta went on: "I saw you clinging to our liberator's arm as you entered. Ah, how quickly some of us forget our vows of devotion to our ideals!" Her voice was mocking, and she raised the back of her hand to her forehead in an exaggerated gesture.

Sofya's childlike expression had altered. Indignation sounded. "Don't be ridiculous! That was only part of my playacting."

"Impressive acting! I really hope you're not going to be one of those disgusting couples who marry on principle and then fall soggily in love. I can't stand those hypocritical, wishy-washy, name-only liberated women. Or their opportunistic, deceitful men." Anyuta was leaning back, supporting herself on her elbows. She continued watching Sofya in the mirror.

Sofya bent down, pretending to look for something. In the glass, Anyuta saw her blush.

"You'll never catch me giving up my freedom for romance," Anyuta went on. "And I've had my chances." The embarrassing moments had started at dinner, within minutes of the surprise announcement. Anyuta had heard whispered remarks to the effect that although Anyuta was clearly the more beautiful sister, she was much too willful and spoiled. No man would have such a bride.

As long as Sofya's marriage remained fictitious, Anyuta's pride could take these blows. But if it should become more than that? For Sofya to have freedom and happiness, while she, Anyuta, had nothing—that would be too much to bear.

Sofya feigned having found whatever she was looking for, and turned to face Anyuta.

"I will not allow myself a romantic involvement with Vladimir, or anyone else. Certainly not for the next five years, and probably never." A cold, controlled anger was in Sofya's voice. "I'm offended that you, my closest friend and dear sister, would doubt my resolve. You cannot possibly understand the amount of time, effort, discipline, and energy that goes into mastering a science. And when the student must struggle against all the obstacles put in her way just because she is a woman, the task is nearly impossible. There will simply be no time for romance."

Anyuta sat upright, back straight, feet pressed together firmly on the floor. From this attentive position she countered her sister's outburst with anger of her own. "Maybe I don't understand your efforts with science. But remember, I'm the one who taught you about the possibilities of freedom. Now everything, for you and for me, depends on your 'resolve' as you put it. Of course I'm concerned when I believe I see cracks starting in that concrete resolve."

Anyuta returned Sofya's silent stare.

"I'm sorry, Anya. Forgive me. I'm tired." With a slow movement of her hand, Sofya pushed a rebellious curl back behind her ear. Then she rubbed her temple slowly. Her eyes squinted slightly, her face now a picture of weariness. "It just seems so clear to me that if a romantic attachment had been any part of this plan, Vladimir would have chosen you. Don't you see, by the very act of not choosing you, he has declared that he doesn't want to be tempted into a romantic relationship? He wants to become a scientist. He will need the same single-mindedness and devotion to his field that I will. But he and I need each other as friends, at least for the present. I'd never desert you, Anya, never." Sofya reached out to take her sister's hand. "You mustn't ever doubt my loyalty."

Anyuta continued to keep her eyes from Sofya by turning her head toward the bedroom door.

"Please, Anya, don't worry. Our plans will never be sidetracked by any romantic weakness of mine."

Slowly, Anyuta turned her face toward Sofya. By concentrating on not blinking, Anyuta had managed to start a small flow of tears.

Sofya moved next to her on the bed. Placing her arm gently around Anyuta's shoulder, Sofya added, "Anya, what we should be focusing on is getting Father to agree to a date for the wedding."

Anyuta brushed away the unemotional tears, and turned toward her sister. "You'll need Mother as an ally. I can help you with that. Mother always listens to me."

"I want the marriage to be an accomplished fact by this fall." Sofya stood up and paced the floor.

"An engagement of less than six months?" Anyuta doubted the possibility. "But I like the idea."

"I want to start my studies. Even with a September wedding, there won't be enough time to plan for a fall semester in a European university. I'll try to start attending lectures here in Petersburg as soon as we're married. You will come live with us. At that point you and I and Vladimir can decide which European university we should try to attend. Right now Heidelberg seems to me like the best choice; I'd love to have a chance to work with Helmholtz. He's published remarkable papers in physiology, physics, and mathematics, all my favorites."

"Oh! Sofya, please! Please, please. No talk of sciences." Anyuta laughed with relief. All the little tagalong was interested in was pursuing her science. The shadow had proved to be resourceful, daring, and practical in prying open a window to freedom. Anyuta had no intention of letting that window slam shut. Certainly Vladimir, who had already humiliated her by insisting on Sofya as his partner, would try to control Sofya, turning her against her sister and friends. Poor little Sofya was innocent of the ways of men. Anyuta would not let Vladimir's maneuvering go unchallenged.

"Anyuta, once you and I are settled, we'll work on getting Zhanna and Julia freed. We'll never abandon anyone struggling for freedom."

Anyuta sighed. Sofya's priorities were still in place.

❧

FATHER'S BUSINESS DEALINGS in Petersburg prospered. With the lucrative vodka contract secured, operations at the estate demanded his personal attention. The family would return to Palibino, certainly for the summer and perhaps longer. The trip from Petersburg was grueling, a long day's journey by train to the city of Vitebsk, a day's rest there, then another long day in a spine-jolting carriage.

The estate was located in the westernmost part of Russia, 420 versts south of Petersburg, close enough to the Polish border to be subjected to Russian martial law whenever Poland rebelled against her Russian rulers.

Father left Petersburg for Palibino in late May. Sofya and Anyuta planned to depart in early June. Mother and brother Fedya would come along in late June when Fedya's school term ended. Vladimir, as Sofya's fiancé, was asked to accompany Mother and Fedya, and to spend the summer weeks at Palibino.

Still no date had been set for the wedding. Before leaving for Palibino, Sofya instructed Vladimir: "Strengthen our position with Mother. She's an invaluable ally in all negotiations with Father."

"I'll charm her all the way to Palibino." Vladimir lifted his arm as if taking an oath.

"Good. Mother loves charming, intelligent young men. Don't smile, I'm serious. The good will of all my relatives must be won and kept, at least until after the wedding. Remember to be especially charming to Father's female relatives. They always question Father's decisions regarding Anyuta and me. Father's sister, Aunt Anna, is a real bear."

Vladimir laughed. "I'll be charming. With bearish relatives it may not be easy, but I'll try."

ONCE A YEAR BY NECESSITY, Vladimir took the identical route from Petersburg to the city of Vitebsk. From there he headed north to his own small estate near the city of Nevel. Vladimir disliked the loneliness of the journey. Even more, he disliked the dull days spent at the shabby, deserted main house. And he hated the depressing job of going over the books for the poorly managed farm operation. Vladimir would have sold the estate long ago, but his brother would never agree.

This journey proved delightfully different. Vladimir listened attentively to Elizaveta Fedorovna's bubbly descriptions of her house with its crystal chandelier salon, large ballroom with a stage for family theatricals or musical entertainments, formidable library collection, and numerous guest rooms. From what Vladimir had heard of Palibino from

Sofya, Elizaveta Fedorovna was presenting Palibino in its most elegant light. But to be fair to the lady, she had admitted that Palibino had been built with the labor of their own servants using materials from their estate. In some places, the workmanship was short of Petersburg standards.

Young Fedya chattered on with descriptions of fishing trips at the numerous lakes on the property, hunting trips into the forests, and mushroom gathering expeditions with children from the estate's villages. He extracted a promise from Vladimir to accompany him on a fox hunt. The general refused to let the young man hunt without supervision and the general was always busy.

Vladimir's distinct impression was that Palibino spanned quite a large and diverse area of forest, meadow, and fields. He guessed the general must control something over ten thousand acres. As both Fedya and Elizaveta Fedorovna had mentioned the general's family resided on adjoining estates, the total area controlled by the Korvin-Krukovsky clan certainly made them one of the most influential families in the district.

THE SUN WAS LOW in the west when the carriage passed the postmaster's station nine versts east of Palibino. From the post station, the road ran through rolling hill country patched with clumps of poplar, oak and maple. Then an expanse of unusable land, marred with giant boulders standing like sentries, captured Vladimir's attention. He would have to examine those rocks more closely; they were probably glacial deposits and might even contain a few plant or animal remains.

And now the carriage abruptly turned onto a rough, narrow drive. Elizaveta Fedorovna and Fedya awoke.

"We're home. Thank the Lord for a safe journey," Elizaveta Fedorovna sighed.

The bumpy ride continued through a birch-lined alley. By Vladimir's rough calculation, the ride from road to house was about a verst. The carriage stopped before a sprawling house of undetermined architectural style. Vladimir's untrained eye guessed that the main house, a large, two-story structure of rock and timber, had been built before the three-story, tower-shaped building that seemed to be glued onto the main building by a wooden structure about the size of one large, long room. A balcony along the entire front vainly tried to unite the structures. The area immediately beyond the porch was filled with beautiful blooming rose bushes of various varieties, white and lavender lilac bushes, and a few jasmine. The general impression was one of warmth and comfort.

An old dog, roused from slumber on a porch step, barked furiously announcing their arrival. Three servants, among them a young boy, rushed from the main door of the house to assist the travelers. Now on the porch, there emerged the general, his unmistakably military bearing softened by a broad smile, his arm around a lovely, vivacious Sofya. On seeing Vladimir, Sofya broke from her father, rushed down the porch stairs, and took his hands into her own, her eyes shining mischievously. As they exchanged the customary kiss of greeting, she whispered that the family must see how glad they were to meet. He obliged by holding her close to him longer than custom required.

ONCE ESTABLISHED AT PALIBINO, Vladimir and Sofya set a routine. They woke at six and met to take tea together in the summer family room, the spacious airy room that connected the main house to the tower annex. Large windows overlooked the fruit orchard and kitchen garden at the back of the house. After a frugal breakfast, they separated to bathe and prepare for the day. They met again at eight in a second-floor room of the main house, which long ago had served as the children's school room. Sofya spent the mornings tutoring Vladimir in mathematics and physics. She'd given him an accelerated course on the essentials of trigonometry and analytic geometry, and touched on the basic concepts of physics. He'd studied both subjects before, but hadn't worked on them in many years. In the afternoon, they studied separately, Vladimir preferring the upstairs library, Sofya retreating to the third level of the tower, which she and Anyuta had long ago claimed as their own private space.

After the evening meal, the family gathered on the balcony for tea and the inevitable short discussion of the day's events, after which the general retired to his estate office on the ground floor of the tower. Anyuta and Fedya busied themselves with reading or cards. Elizaveta Fedorovna played the piano. Vladimir and Sofya wandered off alone. It was a natural thing for an engaged couple to walk in the coolness of the evening. They would stroll around the house toward the garden, leaving behind the pleasant sounds of the hissing samovar and Elizaveta Fedorovna's piano.

A stand of rustling poplars marked the end of the garden, but not of the couple's wandering. Into the cool and darkening woods Vladimir and Sofya would venture, happily discussing and arguing points of politics, science, or literature. They exchanged questions about people and ideas, and tried to define such concepts as freedom and equality. Always these discussions remained impersonal. About themselves, about their personal happiness, and about love, they never spoke.

Before returning from the wood, they would stop, standing on the dark path. In silence they listened to the nightingales. At these moments, Vladimir willed that Sofya should feel what was in his heart, things he hardly dared name to himself, growing sympathies, unspoken, secret, and forbidden.

On returning to the house, they would engage Anyuta in conversation. Fedya had been sent off to bed. On several occasions Elizaveta Fedorovna joined their discussions and pleasantly impressed Vladimir with her sharp observations of people's character. He found her gentle way quite refreshing after Anyuta's often abrupt and cutting comments about family or acquaintances. Some evenings, Sofya and Vladimir finished with a work session of translating English manuscripts for Vladimir's publishing business.

ON THE MORNING of his last full day at Palibino, Vladimir dressed quickly, wanting to spend every possible minute with Sofya. Pulling on his calf-high boots, he stuffed the legs of his trousers into their tops, riding style. Without putting on a shirt, he walked to the open window of his room, which looked down on the family garden of trees, bushes, and vines heavy with unripened fruit.

"I'll be back when the fruit is ripe," he told himself, wondering if his return would feel like a homecoming.

Last night, he and his three allies, Sofya, Anyuta and Elizaveta Fedorovna, had waged a final attack against the reluctant general. Their respective weapons were reason, pleading, cajoling, and tears. Under this four-pronged assault the citadel had fallen. The general agreed to let Sofya set a date for the wedding. If arrangements could be made in time, the general would give his blessing to her choice of September eleventh.

This decision required Vladimir's immediate return to Petersburg to attend to business affairs. On his way, he intended to stop at his own estate to pick up some documents and make arrangements there. His old nanny was still living on the estate—she'd be delighted at the news of his wedding.

Vladimir turned from the window. He chose a loose-fitting, open-collared shirt from the wardrobe, thinking that he was going to miss wearing the comfortable country garb. A few strokes of the brush through his hair and he was ready. Closing the door of his room, he walked down the hallway in search of Sofya.

HE KNOCKED ON THE DOOR of the upstairs library, then walked in. Sofya was seated at the table, sorting through a stack of books and papers.

She looked up brightly. "I'm trying to decide which books you ought to take with you. How are you on trigonometry?"

"Try me."

"All right. Now, in a right triangle, the side 'a' divided by the sine of angle 'A' is equal to the side 'b' divided by . . ."

"What?" He had somehow been distracted by the way dark hair curled over a pink ear.

"Finish quoting me the law of sines," Sofya demanded.

She saw him wrinkle his forehead, then scratch his head. "The sum of the squares of the other two sides . . . no. The difference of the squares of the two angles divided by the product . . ." He broke off with a sigh. "I can't think today."

"I see you had better take this trigonometry book. And you're to study the laws of sines, cosines, and tangents, again."

Suddenly she was struck by how serious he looked, almost unhappy.

She added, "You'll learn. After all, you're a lawyer."

Still his face was grim.

"Vladimir, that was intended to make you smile."

"Sorry. I'm just thinking how much I'm going to miss this room. I'll even miss you trying to teach me the law for finding the tangent of half an angle." He forced a smile.

"When we're back together, in September, I'll teach my lawyer the fundamental law of the calculus."

"Such tantalizing promises. I suppose you want to make sure that I return." Vladimir was smiling now. "The probability of my coming back to you is one hundred percent."

Feeling relieved, she returned his smile. "Come over here and decide which of these books you're taking. I plan on assigning you some problems."

Vladimir approached the table, looked over the volumes his betrothed was thrusting at him, and selected several.

The corners of his mouth just barely turned up, he said, "And I intend to assign you some homework while we're separated. There's a paper of Darwin's in this English journal of natural history which I'd like you to translate into Russian." He dug into the papers that had been stacked on the table many days ago, when the two of them had first taken over the library as their study.

Sofya could handle English, but it wasn't easy. She groaned audibly.

Finding the journal that he wanted, Vladimir quickly glanced through it, then set it in front of her, open at the page he wanted. "Be sure you think of me as you're working on this," he said, and covered her hand on the desk with his.

A long moment passed before Sofya, with the sudden sensation of an electric shock, pulled her hand violently away. She sat back in her chair staring at Vladimir, trying to understand and control her own flaring anger.

With a faint sigh he let himself down into the chair across from her. He folded his arms. "It would seem, as your friend, you would let me touch your hand." He was looking at her with serious sadness in his eyes. "I didn't mean to anger you," he added softly.

She could feel herself blushing, her anger gone.

Vladimir retreated into a silence, gazing at the window as if he wished he were outside.

Sofya wanted to explain, but how could she? Their conversations were always friendly, even intimate. When they worked together or socialized together their minds were one. She'd never felt such oneness of spirit with anyone, except perhaps her sister. Yet now, as if involuntarily, she had responded to simple physical contact with anger and withdrawal. Disturbed by her own strong response to his kisses on the night of their engagement, she feared her reaction to his tender touch, especially when they were alone. Especially today, when she knew her will was weakened by the dread of his departure.

There was a knock on the study door. "Come in," Sofya called out, glad of anything to break the silence.

Natasha, Sofya's personal maid, entered. "Sofya Vasilievna, I'm sorry to disturb you but I thought you'd like to know. A village woman with a child is waiting outside your clinic office."

"Thank you, Natasha. We'll come at once. Is Leon about?" Leon was Natasha's ten-year-old son, a quiet, strong child who often accompanied Sofya on her clinic visits.

"Yes, he's downstairs."

"Have him hitch a cart, and bring a lunch basket for us. After we visit the clinic, *Gospodin* Vladimir Onufrievich Kovalevsky and I will have lunch in the woods."

Natasha left on her errands.

"You called me 'Mister' and used my full name. I don't remember you being that formal with Natasha. From whom are you trying to distance me?" Without waiting for an answer, Vladimir was up from the chair and moving toward the door. Sofya said nothing. She didn't want him to go away angry. But she wouldn't call him back.

Before leaving the room, Vladimir turned. "The clinic and then lunch in the woods." His voice was bright. His annoyance had evidently evaporated somewhere between the chair and the door.

Sofya arose. "Yes, of course."

"Then let's get moving." He held the door open, waiting for her.

Sofya gathered up the books intended for Vladimir and approached him, to find herself holding the books close to her chest, almost as a barrier.

She continued, "There's a favorite spot of mine, a lake."

"The one just beyond the kitchen garden?"

"No, of course not that one," she sighed. "That's artificial, built by serfs before the emancipation, a depressing reminder of captivity. The lake we'll visit is west of the farm buildings, through the woods. It's big, its shore is deliciously primitive."

Out in the hallway, Vladimir said, "We'll make this a biological field trip. Never want to waste a minute." He was reaching out, obviously expecting her to give him the books. But his hands stopped just before they would have touched her arms. For a moment their eyes met. He took a small step back from her. His hands stayed dramatically frozen in midair. "May I?"

Infuriated with his teasing, for a moment she considered throwing the books at him. But he looked so comical standing as a frozen statue that she decided instead to do her own teasing. "Take them, if you are strong enough," she challenged.

Immediately, his posture changed. He came very close, putting both arms around her, so her arms and the books together were pressed against his shirt. His eyes stayed fixed on hers. His right hand moved, beginning to gently pry her left hand loose from the books. His hand gently brushed against her breast. She didn't move or let her eyes stray from his, but she involuntarily drew breath. Now he had taken hold of her right wrist. She could no longer resist effectively. She pushed the books into his chest with rather more force than she had intended, moving him back a step. He released her wrist.

"Now who's teasing?" He juggled the books precariously for a moment, then lost control of his prize and they went thudding to the floor. They were both laughing as he picked the volumes up. "I'll put these in my room. Meet me downstairs."

MINUTES LATER, Sofya and Vladimir were headed across the west lawn toward Sofya's makeshift clinic. A couple of years ago she'd appropriated an abandoned farm building and stocked her new office with simple medicines, herbs and tonics. Her diagnoses relied heavily on a book of home cures. As limited and crude as she knew her treatments and advice to be, hers was the only medical help the villagers had. The poor people were grateful for whatever the young lady could do for them.

As the couple approached the clinic, Sofya sighed. "You'll see at first hand why I'm determined to study medicine. The needs of the people are so great. Have you spent any time with the peasants at your estate?"

"No. Only the house servants. I know I should have, but . . ."

"That's too bad. I didn't really understand the urgency of the need for change until I started working with these wretched human beings. We must help them, Vladimir. Through education. Through medicine. Through science. The world must change."

"Indeed it must."

Sofya unlocked the door of the clinic, at the same time speaking softly to the ill-looking older woman who sat on a nearby bench holding a moaning child. Both looked ill, but the woman insisted Sofya help the child first.

The child's eyes were swollen nearly shut, with yellow pus oozing from beneath discolored lids. "My poor little one," the grandmother moaned as she rocked the child back and forth. "He'll be blind. A beggar."

"Don't worry, *babushka*. He'll be fine in a few days." Sofya patted the woman on the shoulder, then went to the crude workbench that served as laboratory table. Here Sofya consulted her home cure book, discovering a recipe of herbs and oils to be applied to ailing eyes. She could only hope that it would be effective.

In a few minutes she had washed her hands and created the mixture from supplies on hand. Returning to the old woman, Sofya gave directions softly. "Watch how I put this on his eyes. You must do this once when he gets up in the morning and again when he goes to bed." The woman watched carefully. "And this is very important, you must wash your hands before and after you give the boy the medicine. The power of the medicine will vanish if you forget the washing." The woman nodded her head, indicating that she understood.

Washing her own hands again, emptying basin into slop jar, she said to Vladimir, "Eye problems are very common among the peasant children. I'd like to make the study of the eye a specialty."

"If I remember correctly, you even liked the optics section of physics best."

Sofya nodded, then turned again to her patient. "*Babushka*, would you let my friend hold the child, while I speak with you?" The woman hesitated. "He is a good man! He's going to be my husband."

Smiling, the woman surrendered the child to Vladimir, who awkwardly carried the crying burden to another part of the room.

Sofya spoke briefly to the woman. Her case was not at all unusual. Intestinal distress. Sofya, getting down another bottle from a shelf, explained to Vladimir that in hard times the peasants would supplement their already meager, poor diets with wild grains, mixing the wheat grain with the wild grass grains and baking a sort of bread from the mixture. The wild grains made the regular grain go farther but the resulting loaves were barely edible and frequently caused digestive disorders.

As the woman was leaving, Sofya said to Vladimir, "I'll have a basket of fruit, vegetables, and pure breads sent to that family. At least that will provide temporary relief."

Sofya washed her hands again before leaving the clinic, and insisted that Vladimir, having held the child, do likewise.

"Why the insistence on hand washing?" Vladimir teased, "Aren't you being overly cautious?"

"No, I don't think so," Sofya responded sharply. "When I was in Petersburg, Bokova loaned me her copy of the journal *Archives of Forensic Medicine and Public Health*. Knowing my interest in mathematics and medicine, she sent the issue with statistics on disease and mortality rates."

"That article advocated hand washing?" Vladimir was incredulous.

"No! I read the other articles as well. One article celebrated the discovery of Semmelweiss, twenty years ago in Austria, that childbed fever is contagious. When he had doctors wash their hands between patient examinations, he cut the incidence of the disease drastically."

"Sofya, this isn't childbed fever."

"Of course not. Stop teasing me and listen. There's more evidence. The next article reported on Lister's work in England. Three years ago he started using phenol as a cleaning agent in surgical procedures. He reduced the surgical death rate from forty-five percent to fifteen percent. Those numbers are decisive enough to make me change my habits."

"I have heard that our government has proposed a "filth theory," relating the spread of cholera and other epidemics to poor living conditions and general squalor. Not that they've done a thing to alleviate those conditions." Vladimir moaned. "If there's one thing the bureaucratic beast is good at, it's collecting data."

"Well," Sofya continued. "My point is the data indicates a connection between cleanliness and the prevention of contagion. Just be glad I'm not making you wash three times a day with phenol."

"You really are frightened by the thought of contracting a disease."

"Dreadfully frightened."

"You do this work despite your fears," he said softly.

Sofya was silent.

Dipping more fresh water from a barrel, he remarked, "That was quite a nice job of doctoring, Doctor Korvin-Krukovskaya. Or may I say Doctor Kovalevskaya? You're very gentle. I'd not mind having you as my personal physician."

Sofya blushed faintly.

OUTSIDE, LEON WAS waiting for them. An old mare, no longer good for field work, was harnessed to a small cart.

"Ready for a bumpy ride?" Sofya asked, climbing into the back of the cart.

Vladimir hopped in beside her. "More than ready, thank you."

Leon urged the old horse past the farm buildings toward a small road lined with linden trees. The road led past the pine log huts of the house and grounds servants. A poorly dressed little girl of four or five waved a greeting. Sofya and Vladimir waved back. With the huts not far behind, Leon veered west onto a rutted path. An ancient forest of spruce and pine closed around them.

Sofya sat in one corner of the cart, bouncing lightly with its motion, one hand braced against the back and one along the side. "When I was about nine, my governess and tutor would take me for daily walks along this path."

"We must be more than a verst from the house. Quite a walk for a child." Vladimir looked over his shoulder as if to estimate the distance, but the house was already hidden behind trees.

"From the house to the point where we entered the woods is about a verst." Sofya offered the statistic. "Miss Smith was an advocate of Spartan ways."

Vladimir chuckled. "Your active imagination probably has turned your Miss Smith into a monster worthy of a fairy tale." Choosing a piece of straw from the bottom of the cart he let it hang from his lips. His eyes were on her.

"Judge a monster by its methods," Sofya said.

"Tell me more." Vladimir braced one foot against the board in front of him. The cart was moving no faster than a man could walk.

Sofya released her grip on the back of the cart and reached down to find her own clean piece of straw. She turned it between her fingers as she spoke. "Father absolutely forbade corporal punishment for us children."

"An admirable concession."

"Miss Smith did not approve of Father's lenient ways, but she didn't dare to defy him. She devised punishments which I dreaded much more than any physical pain. When Miss Smith perceived some flaw in my behavior, she had me write my sin on a piece of paper, then she pinned the sign to the back of my dress. Little labels saying, 'Sofya is very lazy,' or 'Sofya is disrespectful,' or 'Sofya is careless in her work.' I had to wear the sign all day in front of the whole family."

"Your father should have put a stop to that. There are better ways of teaching than humiliation."

"Father didn't interfere, but Anyuta protested loudly and with great energy against these methods. She was the only one who understood what torture Miss Smith's punishments were for me. But gradually I became hardened, so that I believe now I am almost immune to public humiliation. The turning point came right here, at this spot in the forest." Sofya pointed ahead with the straw. "Notice how the road comes to a rise? One early spring afternoon, Miss Smith and I were tramping up this hill, through snow up to our ankles. A cold wind was in our faces. I was walking a few paces ahead, because I wanted to be alone. Right here, at the top of this hill, I stopped." Sofya tugged on Leon's shoulder. "Stop! Right here."

As the cart halted, Sofya continued, "In the path directly ahead of me, so close I could have hit them with a snowball, was an immense brown bear and her two scampering cubs. The bear's attention was on her cubs. The cubs ran toward me a short distance and then back to their mother, playfully bumping into each other and her. I was watching with fascination, even as I started to back away.

"Miss Smith didn't see the bears until she had almost bumped into me. Then she let out a terrible scream—that got Mother Bear's attention, all right—grabbed my hand and dragged me behind her as she ran back toward the house. Miss Smith's speed was so great that by the time we reached the clearing I could have sworn I was trailing behind her like a ribbon in the air."

"And did Mother Bear make any effort to pursue you?"

"I don't know. I was being dragged about so violently I couldn't see."

Vladimir chuckled. In a moment Sofya had jumped from the stopped cart and grabbed up a fallen branch. Thrusting it into the soft ground, she declaimed: "On this spot Russian courage overshadowed British domination. May this 'tree' remain a testament to the courage of a Russian woman!"

Leon, his mouth open, was staring at her. Vladimir applauded solemnly, then extended a hand to her. Gripping his large hand, Sofya pulled herself back into the cart. A little breathless, she ordered, "Go on, Leon." The jerk of the cart starting threw her back into her seat. Laughing, she continued, "Father was furious when he heard we'd gone into the forest without an armed protector."

Vladimir was laughing too. "English forests are somewhat different from ours."

"I'm sure they must be. And Miss Smith never went near this road again. From then on she and I took our walks on a special path Father had cleared behind the house. The path leads between the fruit orchard and the kitchen garden, then around the artificial lake. The meadows and fields beyond the little lake offered far less chance of danger than the forest."

"And I'd bet my last kopeck that *you* came back here to the forest. Without a protector. Not letting bears, or anything else, scare you away."

"You're right. I love the forest."

Her companion seemed to be reminiscing. "I was carrying a rifle—almost as big as I was—the first time I met a bear." He laughed. "I was terrified. I froze, unable to move from the onrushing beast. My older brother shot the creature between the eyes."

Sofya felt curious about the nature of the man who held her future.

"Don't worry. I'm much more courageous now. I hunt bear and most other game, when I get the chance." In words barely audible and with a face suddenly turned grim, he added, "I've been in Death's service."

He must be talking about the war, Sofya thought. In silence, contemplating each other, they bumped along, having by now come a considerable distance. Where the forest joined a meadow, the ruts disappeared completely. Here Leon stopped the cart, and Vladimir and Sofya jumped out and began to climb a grassy hill. Leon remained behind, unhitching the horse and then securing the animal to a nearby tree, using a rope long enough to allow it access to a great deal of thick grass.

Vladimir, carrying the picnic basket, yelled back to Leon to bring the pail of milk. Sofya, now playfully running ahead, was already descending the side of the hill away from the road.

"There it is!" she said proudly, as her companion caught up. Before them stretched a glittering lake, so wide that trees on the far side appeared as hardly more than moss. Far to the right, the red and yellow sails of a few small fishing boats marked the smooth surface.

"The boats are your father's?" Vladimir asked.

"The ones with the red sails are. The yellow-sailed ones belong to Uncle Peter's son Nicholas." Turning from the lake, she added, "At this time of year, the fishing is better on the far shore. The boats won't disturb us."

Sofya chose a grassy spot near the water's edge for Vladimir to spread the picnic blanket. In moments blanket and picnic basket had been arranged, and Vladimir was sprawled out carelessly. He rested his head on one hand, apparently mesmerized by the beauty of the lake.

Sofya knelt on the edge of the cloth, tucking her knees and feet under her skirt. "Peasant legend tells of beautiful water nymphs, with thick blond tresses and sea-blue eyes, living in this lake."

Vladimir smiled. His comment was barely audible. "I much prefer human, full-breasted maidens to water nymphs."

Sofya felt herself blush. Quickly she turned her face from Vladimir.

"I didn't mean to be rude." His voice was slow, controlled. "The comparison is a paraphrase of a statement by Herzen. I thought you might know the reference. The point of the statement is that reality is to be chosen over fantasy. I want nothing to do with legends, or religion, or mysticism. Or idealism. Or anything else built on illusion."

Sofya had been caught off guard, but she was not ignorant of Herzen's writings. "I would have preferred Herzen's symbolism of 'the other shore' to express commitment to the material."

"Speaking of material things . . ." Vladimir's gaze turned meaningfully toward the basket.

"A good idea!" Sofya began taking things out, arranging them in a kind of display. Lunch consisted of bread and cheese, berries with cream, milk, and a small bottle of claret. Some raspberry jam was included.

The berries and dessert nuts had been gathered in nearby woods. Everything had come from the estate.

Leon finally arrived, lugging the pail of milk, then turned away after removing the pail's cover and depositing his burden on the cloth. Sofya called to him, "Leon, come and eat your lunch near us."

The boy obeyed, but reluctantly, not looking at the couple. He sprawled on the grass a short distance away. From his shirt he pulled out an apple, a small loaf of black bread, and a few curled pages barely recognizable as a paper book of the inexpensive kind obtainable from traveling peddlers.

"Really, Leon, you needn't be shy with Vladimir," Sofya assured him gently. Turning to Vladimir, she added, "I'm sure his mother instructed him to be especially considerate of our privacy."

Vladimir, mouth full of berries, grunted something encouraging.

Sofya turned to the youngster again. "Leon, after we've eaten, I'd like you to show Vladimir how well you read, and how well you've mastered sums."

The boy looked up brightly but said nothing. The prospect obviously pleased him.

As they ate, Sofya spoke with enthusiasm and pride about the teaching methods she had used with Leon, striving for a balance between reading and arithmetic. So far Leon had been her only pupil. Coming to the end of her meal and of her exposition, she sighed with satisfaction.

For a quarter of an hour or so, the two adults spoke with their young driver about reading, arithmetic, and science. The boy, his shyness gone, responded with calm, unhurried answers, asked insightful questions, and sometimes brought up related facts he had come upon in the books Sofya had loaned him.

As the educational discussion came to an end, Sofya moved the basket to the grass. She and Vladimir stood up, picked up the cloth by the corners, and shook out the crumbs. Together they folded the cloth and placed it in the basket. For a moment, all three stood looking out over the blue lake. A few high white clouds were congregating on the far horizon.

"Let's not go back just yet," Sofya said dreamily. "I love this place."

"We were supposed to make this a scientific field trip, or so I suggested," Vladimir reminded her.

"Yes." Sofya regained her vigor. "I want to liven up the clinic. I thought I might add some nature exhibits, create something like a miniature museum."

"I'd like to watch animals, or even bugs in boxes," Leon offered, now feeling free to speak.

"Do a nature study. Start a notebook, a kind of log, of some creatures' behavior in captivity," Vladimir suggested.

"I could try to catch a fish," Leon volunteered. "We could put the fish in a big tub and the children could watch it swim."

"Wonderful!" Sofya exclaimed.

Leon took the empty milk pail and started off along the edge of the lake.

"Vladimir, you and I will go into the forest, and look for a small creature or bug. Or several."

Vladimir picked up the picnic basket. "Good for gathering specimens."

They started toward the nearby woods, the shade of the tall trees engulfing them before they entered. Once among the old pines, fragrant dimness surrounded them. Insects buzzed, but none obliged by presenting themselves to be captured.

"I'll tell you a legend, if you promise not to laugh," Sofya offered.

Making himself look solemn, Vladimir promised.

"This wood harbors a werewolf."

"No!"

"Oh, yes. No one has seen him, but on moonlit nights peasant women guard their small children carefully. The women say they hear the creature's howl. A much more fearsome sound than that of any ordinary wolf."

Her companion's solemnity became real. "And they still really believe in such things, I suppose."

"I'm sure some of them do. When I was very young, I went with the peasant children on mushroom hunts. While we were riding home in the wagon, the driver would entertain us with stories."

Her companion shook his head. "What a monumental job it will be to bring science to people who can still, in 1868, think in such terms."

"Yes. Monumental," Sofya agreed. At the same time she was on the verge of admitting that as a child she'd thrilled to the make-believe— but she said nothing about that.

They walked for a while without speaking, enjoying the voices of the birds.

"Vladimir, did you hear similar legends when you were young?"

"No. I didn't grow up as you did, near your family, near nature, near the peasants and their werewolves. My parents loved city life. When I was very young, I had a Russian nanny who lived in the city with us. I think she was the daughter of a priest. I don't remember her ever telling my brother and me anything but Bible stories. When I was nine, my parents enrolled me in a boarding school in Petersburg. The family only returned to the country for a few weeks each summer. Father hated the country. He was not at all suited to managing an estate.

"After Mother died—that was when I was twelve—Father never took us to the country. In fact, we rarely saw him. He had financial problems. Emotional problems. Vodka problems. He died a few years after Mother. No family members came forward to help my brother or me. Trustees managed, or rather mismanaged, our meager inheritance. With frugal living, my brother and I were barely able to complete our education and keep the estate. I was translating books for pay when I was fifteen. A sense of reality came early to us."

Sofya was quiet for a long time. How different his life had been from her own. His life had been hard, but he had never known the tyranny of a domineering family. He had always been free to choose his own path.

Vladimir broke the silence. "I've written my brother, Aleksander, about our engagement. He's very pleased. I've described you to him in some detail."

"When shall I meet him?"

"I don't know. Aleksander's working at a marine laboratory near Naples. He writes that he's also found a very special woman. I suspect he's living with her. Without benefit of clergy, as the saying goes." There was an awkward pause as they both considered their own arrangement. "In any event, he won't be able to return to Russia this fall. There's some research he needs to finish in Italy. Aleksander's the serious one in the family. He's only interested in two things, tiny sea creatures and the history of social change. He observes both as a true scientist—but he could no more participate in social change than he could live in the sea."

Sofya laughed. Obviously Vladimir was very close to his brother.

"I've been bragging to Aleksander about you. He writes that I must send him a photo. Do you think you could find one? Or maybe two? I'd certainly like to take one with me when I leave."

"Yes, there's one somewhere in one of Mother's albums. It was taken about a year ago; in fact there may be two or three of that pose. Mother wanted photos of all her children to give as Christmas presents. I'm afraid none of the remaining pictures offer a very good likeness. I appear quite young and childish."

Suddenly Sofya paused in her walk. She had just realized one implication of Vladimir's situation. His parents were dead and his brother, his only close relative, would be in Italy at the time of the wedding. He'd be alone for the ceremony. "Then you'll have no one close to you, family or friends, present at our wedding?"

"Afraid not." The lack did not seem to bother him.

Well, and why should it? "That could be a benefit. Fewer people to deceive. This large family of mine is a bother."

"After we're married, your family will be my family."

The thought of future years of deception struck at Sofya. Would her own family ever know the truth? Vladimir was a friend, not a real husband. Not—"You needn't think of my people as your family."

"Of course they will be," Vladimir insisted. "It will be expected of me. And you won't want them to think we're quarreling, will you?"

"You'll be my brother," Sofya said firmly, grasping with relief at inspiration.

"Yes. Of course, whenever we are alone, your brother," Vladimir said equably.

They walked on, Vladimir swinging the basket, which still held only the picnic cloth. Sofya, somewhat relieved, started daydreaming aloud about their future, as she saw or thought she saw it. "We'll live just like Vera and Dmitri in *What Is To Be Done?*" Then, catching herself, she added hastily: "I mean, how they lived in the first half of the book." Now she could feel her cheeks flaming. For a moment she could not look at the man striding beside her. How could she have forgotten that in the second half of the book its fictitiously married couple begins to share a bed? Vera falls in love with another man. Dmitri again sacrifices himself for Vera by disappearing after staging a suicide.

"I understand what you mean," said her companion, with an undertone of dry amusement.

Feeling her blushes fading, she continued, "We'll start going to classes at the university in St. Petersburg as soon as we're married. Do you suppose they'll let me attend classes? You know I've never been allowed to enter a classroom."

"Inexcusable! But we know a good many people on the faculty. One of them is sure to let you sit in on a lecture. Don't worry."

There was a quiet pause. They had stopped walking, and Vladimir was staring at her with a little smile.

"Then we'll go to Heidelberg," Sofya continued. "I want to meet Helmholtz."

"Returning to the subject of science, it seems we've forgotten to look for creatures. But here is one presenting itself. It must have fallen from the tree." Vladimir lifted a beautiful red caterpillar from Sofya's shoulder.

The caterpillar went into the picnic basket, now become a collector's box. The afternoon was darkening prematurely, clouds indicating the possibility of a storm. They headed back toward the lake.

Leon was waiting for them, his pant legs rolled up above his knees and his bare feet muddy. He was sitting cross-legged and peeking into the milk pail. As Sofya and Vladimir approached he stood up and waved.

"I've caught a pike! I've caught a pike! He just fits in the pail!"

Sofya and Vladimir quickened their pace. They stared into the pail.

"Oh, Leon! He's a fine specimen," Sofya exclaimed. "He didn't bite you, did he?" The boy smiled and shook his head no. "We only have this little red caterpillar. You've done much better than we."

Vladimir was leaning over the pail examining the fish closely. "Yes, a fine specimen. Tell me, how did you catch him without a fishing pole or a net?"

"I very quietly went into the lake up to my knees. Then I stood there for some time, until I spotted a fish. I grabbed for him with my hands. It's strange, though. He didn't seem to be where I saw him. That first fish got away. I started playing with grabbing things in the water. I waited again for a fish, this time keeping my hands below the surface. That way I could judge much better where the fish really was, and when another one swam by I grabbed. I caught this pike."

"You are a bright fellow to think of such a fine way to catch fish!" Vladimir said with real admiration. "And you have discovered a good practical example of the refraction of light." He turned to Sofya. "Just what you were teaching me in physics last week."

"Yes, in the chapter on optics in Professor Tyrtov's book." Sofya recalled.

"But the poor fish seems unhappy in the little pail," Leon commented.

"We'll try to fix him a better home back at the clinic. Leon, those clouds are starting to look ominous. Take the basket and the pail with our pike back to the cart. Be careful the caterpillar doesn't get loose. Hitch the horse and wait for us there. We'll be coming along soon."

Vladimir settled down, as if absentmindedly, in the flattened grass where the picnic cloth had lain.

Sofya again sat across from him. Her mood was changing; perhaps the coming change in weather was affecting her. "Anyuta will be leaving too, in a week or so. She'll spend a month with some relatives near Petersburg, and then come back just before the wedding. Even Mother will be going into the city to get some things for the wedding. I'll be alone." On an impulse she lay back, gazing up into a patch of sky still free of clouds. Perhaps a storm was not quite imminent after all.

She could hear Vladimir stretching out nearby. Sofya reached out. Her hand lay touching Vladimir's large bony fingers. He didn't clasp her hand. Good, that would have made her pull away. At the moment she just wanted to feel his closeness.

Sofya continued to stare into the sky. All thoughts stopped. Only feelings remained alive. She felt a presence. An ominous presence, approaching as the sunlight once more faded. She couldn't break away. The presence was coming closer. It was all around her. She heard her heart pounding in her ears. Her forehead was wet with cold sweat, but at the same time she felt feverish. She was frozen. She couldn't move. All her muscles were tightening.

How long the experience lasted she could not have said, but at last she managed to break the spell and scream. She sat upright, pulling her knees up, hiding her head in her arms folded over her knees, doing all she could to make a tight little package of her body.

Vladimir had jumped to his feet with her scream. Now he was crouching over her, anxiously demanding to know if she was ill. What was the matter? Sofya couldn't answer him at first. She couldn't uncoil from her protective position just yet.

Putting his arms around her as best he could in the awkward position, Vladimir held her, so that she began slowly to relax. Neither said a word for several minutes.

Gradually Sofya regained her self-control. Vladimir's solid and kindly presence overpowered the other thing, the dark presence that could sometimes issue from an empty patch of sky. Vladimir. Volodya. She'd concentrate on his being here. On his holding her. On the sound of his heart beating.

At last she could lift her head. "I'm sorry," she began softly, staring timidly into his eyes. "I hope I didn't frighten you."

"You certainly did frighten me!" Now he sounded almost angry. "What's wrong? Are you ill? Do you need a doctor?"

"No. I'm not ill. It's something that happens when I'm overwrought. When I'm in a turmoil, I sometimes feel this—presence. It's a dark feeling of imminent evil, like an animal or a vile spirit waiting for me, coming toward me. It comes sometimes when I'm alone in a darkening room, when I stare into emptiness, or even when I see an abandoned building. It comes in nightmares as a deformed creature, a three-legged man usually. Does that sound too crazy? It's been with me since I was a child. You didn't realize that you were marrying a nervous wreck, did you?"

Gently he released her from his embrace, then squatted at arm's length, looking worried. But his words were an effort at reassurance. "You're hardly a nervous wreck. Everyone has something they're afraid of. Even me. Sometimes it's just a feeling of pointless fear, anxiety. Everyone gets that too."

"Whatever it is, it's passed now." Then Sofya noticed his hand. "You're bleeding! I did that! I grabbed you so tightly, and my nails . . ." She looked down at her own hand, where Vladimir's blood was visible on her fingertips and under her nails. "I'm so sorry!" In a fury of tender remorse she seized the wounded hand.

"I'm all right. There is no pain now." He allowed his hand to rest in hers.

Time passed.

Eventually Vladimir asked, "Are you ready to leave? We really should be getting back."

"Yes."

He stood up slowly, still holding Sofya's hand, pulling her gently to her feet. "I see that Leon has harnessed the horse. He's waiting in the wagon."

Both depressed, they hardly spoke on the trip home, where they arrived just before the storm broke.

BACK IN HIS ROOM, watching the rain, Vladimir dreaded tomorrow's departure. He didn't want to leave Sofya. After this afternoon's outburst he wanted more than ever to be with her, to reassure her that there was nothing to fear. But his business in Petersburg could not be abandoned. He wasn't done with publishing yet; far from it.

Meanwhile Sofya, retiring to her own room, had thrown herself on the bed. Vladimir had been reassuringly calm during her spell. But still she wondered if, inwardly, he had been driven away from her by the event. With sorrow, she remembered how Anyuta had been repelled on hearing of Dostoevsky's epileptic seizures.

Dostoevsky's demon had a name, given by doctors and science. Whatever pursued her was nameless.

CHAPTER FIVE

Fall 1868 ❧ *Wedding Preparations*

Sofya sat in her study, determined to maintain her strict routine. The days following Vladimir's departure were long and lonely. A chemistry book lay on the far right of the table, where she had pushed it in disgust on finding herself unable to keep her mind on the properties of carbon compounds. Directly in front of her waited a page of half-finished problems, having to do with the calculation of rates of flow in liquids. She had begun each problem with interest, but abandoned each before completion, when her mind could no longer be forced to stay in a world where time and matter were measured with precision. Absentmindedly, she had filled the borders of the math paper with floral patterns, shading the alternating leaves. She looked at her desk. An array of pencils, each as worn as the one she was holding, was spread out before her.

She sighed and looked around for her small knife, telling herself that she really must set her mind to work. Whittling away at the point of today's chosen implement, she thought, *If Vladimir were here he would be teasing me about pushing too hard on a poor splinter of wood, just as I do on my studies. He'd take out his little silver-cased penknife and trim all of these for me, meanwhile babbling cheerfully about something or other he had just read.*

Halfway through the little pile of pencils, Sofya gave up and pushed back her chair. Study was impossible. She walked to the open window and let her mind go darting down the long carriage path that started at the front entrance of the house. Fifteen minutes' walk away, the path joined the main road leading to Vitebsk. Through Vitebsk ran the iron road, rails stretching all the way to Petersburg.

What was Vladimir doing in that great city on this hot afternoon? She pictured him moving briskly from store to store, checking on the sales of his books. Or perhaps debating prices with some representative of the bookbinders. Or explaining to one of his translators why they could not be paid for another month. She shook her head. How hard it was to maintain the image of Vladimir the businessman! To her, Vladimir the businessman was a fiction. The only Vladimir she knew was a student, a scholar like herself.

He might be sipping tea at a café with one of the men from Bokova's circle, gently turning the conversation to the delicate question of how worthy women might obtain freedom. Faithful to his promise to assist Anya and the others in any way possible, Vladimir set himself the task of searching for liberators.

Perhaps today, right this moment, he was choosing their apartment. She knew that was high on his list of chores in the city. He might select rooms as simple and Spartan as his bachelor quarters. But really the details hardly mattered. Her own apartment! Freedom! The thought was dizzying.

Sofya's reverie was interrupted by a knock on the door. She turned her back to the window, putting herself between the intruder and her daydreams.

The door opened a crack. "May I come in?" Not waiting for an answer, Anyuta swung open the door.

"Anya." Sofya rested against the window sill, striving to give her sister the impression that she was relaxed. "I wasn't making much headway with my studies."

"Not developing any romantic ideas about your betrothed, I hope?" Anyuta settled in what had once been Vladimir's chair. Looking disdainfully at the titles of the books on the table, she picked up a sheaf of Sofya's papers and began to fan herself with them. "I'll never understand how you can enjoy these books," she murmured, mostly to herself.

Sofya long ago had learned to ignore many of her sister's comments. Others demanded a reply. "No romantic ideas," Sofya confirmed, moving back to her original study chair. "But I do miss having someone to study with."

"Freedom can be lonely. I wish I could be more of a companion to you academically, but just look at this." Anya tossed her makeshift fan back onto the table, and stabbed with one finger at a stack of books. "Not a single volume here on society or politics, not even a novel."

"Politics and novels I study in the evenings, after I've finished my lessons in science."

"Yes, your science." Anyuta sighed. Then, looking up brightly, "An hour ago, while you were closeted with your science, I intercepted the servant bringing Father the mail. And a good thing I did. There was a letter to me from Dostoevsky."

"Father still censors your letters from Dostoevsky?"

"What do you think?"

Sofya shook her head. "We live like prisoners in our parents' house." Her loneliness was hardening into gloom.

Anyuta pulled two or three pieces of blue paper from her pocket, and pushed them over the table to Sofya. "This is Dostoevsky's letter." Sofya picked up the pages and began to read, more or less keeping up with Anyuta's summary. "Fedor and his new wife are in Zurich. Married a little over a year, and the poor woman already has not only a sick and demanding husband, but a crying and demanding baby. To think that her fate could have been mine!" She shook her blond head, marveling. "Thank God I had enough sense to avoid that kind of slavery!"

Sofya looked up from the pages, trying to picture the man who had once been her hero. In her imagination he appeared as a dear, clumsy, somewhat sickly, graying intellectual, awkwardly holding a crying infant. Certainly he would no longer stir her to jealousy.

"He seems to think his situation is most wonderful," Anyuta went on. "He hardly mentions anything but his darling daughter."

Sofya began to read the blue pages over, this time carefully. When she had finished, she placed them on the table.

Anyuta retrieved them. "Well, I've shown you my letter from a one-time suitor. It's only fair that you let me read Vladimir's messages. I suppose he's forgotten he was to be on the lookout for a liberator for me. You told me that a code word had been arranged."

" 'Preserves.' The code word is 'preserves,' " Sofya remarked indifferently, her mind on the aching lack of any letters at all from Vladimir.

" 'Preserves'?" Anyuta laughed. "The two of you are totally mad. How did you ever come up with a word like that?"

"Mother gave Vladimir some of our Palibino jams to bring back with him to Petersburg. He made such a fuss about liking them. We thought even if Father intercepted our letters . . ."

"And did Vladimir get a message to you?" Anyuta prodded. "Let me see!"

Sofya's response was just above a whisper. "There have been no letters of any kind from Vladimir."

"None?" Her sister's eyes widened. "But he's been gone for weeks. We've had five, perhaps six, mail deliveries, and you've received nothing?" There was disbelief and concern in her voice. "Come, you're hiding a love letter from me!"

"There have been no love letters! No letters at all!" Sofya snapped angrily.

Anyuta threw up her hands. "That does it. He's walked out on us. Disappeared. Probably taken a boat to America." Her voice had the melodramatic tone she used in true exasperation.

"Don't be ridiculous!" Sofya scolded. "Perhaps he's ill. Do you suppose you could get a note to Bokova? Ask her to look in on him?"

"He's not ill," Anyuta insisted calmly.

Sofya knew that Anyuta, staring at her, could probably read the agony in her eyes. Unfortunately, there were times when being close, the way she and Anyuta were with each other, made even the smallest, self-preserving deceptions impossible.

In a softer tone, Anyuta continued, "If he were seriously ill, someone would have telegraphed. We'd have word within a day. All his Petersburg friends know you're engaged." Anyuta's voice hardened again. "To give him the benefit of circumstances, I'd say he didn't write because he regards your arrangement as a kind of business appointment. There was no progress in finding a liberator for me, so he wrote nothing."

"You're probably right." Sofya struggled to control her wavering voice.

Anyuta sounded angry. "Vladimir has been unreliable from the very beginning. And I'm concerned about your ability to handle the strain of this deception. You've been noticeably irritable ever since he left. With no letters, and your mood, Mother must suspect something's wrong. And Father's still looking for any opportunity to turn your charge for freedom into a retreat."

"There will be no retreat," Sofya assured her sister. "I'll handle my part, nervously or otherwise."

"Good." Anyuta arose and headed for the door. "You look exhausted. Try to get some rest before dinner. I'll be up in the tower getting a few books together for my trip."

"I'm going to miss you, Anyuta."

"When I'm in Petersburg, I'll make a point of seeing Vladimir and talking him into writing some kind of letter, for appearances' sake. You can count on regular letters from me. I promise!"

Anyuta was gone. The silence of the room closed around Sofya.

She covered her face with her hands. Perhaps her silly fit of terror had given him second thoughts about the arrangement, and about their friendship.

She put down her hands, folded them tightly together. Scolding herself, she said aloud, "I'm upset. I'm feeling sorry for myself. I must stop it! In a few weeks Vladimir and Anyuta will both be back with me. We'll open a path to our freedom. We will!"

SOFYA SAT ON THE TOP STOOP of the front porch and stared listlessly out over the green yard. She wiped small beads of perspiration from her forehead. The afternoon was unbearably hot and humid. She had left her study half an hour ago, hoping to catch any possible wandering breeze. For the last two weeks, she had studied every day from early morning until late in the evening. She was exhausted, but it seemed her labors were useless. Definitions, learned long ago, had suddenly evaporated from her consciousness. Sparks of intuition, so necessary to effective problem solving, could not be kindled. A kind of veil had come over her mind. When she read, there were only words, no meaning.

She stretched her arms out in front of her and moved her head slowly from side to side, hoping the act of physically relaxing her back and neck would bring about a mental relaxation.

Her ailment was easy to diagnose: loneliness. She had no one to talk to, no one to share even her simplest of sympathies. She hated being alone. Palibino was an isolation cell. Mother had left with Anyuta for Petersburg, insisting on personally inviting her elderly and influential relatives to the wedding. Even young Fedya, who could have provided some diversion with his talk of fishing, was away at a friend's.

Father remained at Palibino, growing each day more morose and stubbornly silent. When he looked at her, his eyes were cold. All her words were frozen before they left her mouth. Occasionally, at lunch or dinner, he would break his silence with short caustic remarks which demanded her equally caustic replies. She wondered if she'd have the strength to maintain her great deception if he should approach her warmly, now, when she was so starved for company.

Sofya sighed and let her head rest on her knees, her arms limp at her sides. She watched listlessly as the mangy old dog, Baka, head hanging and tail drooping, made his way slowly across the yard from the sheds. Silently he settled at her feet. She patted his head and looked into his sad dark brown eyes. Baka had been at Palibino for as long as Sofya could remember.

"Well, old dog, at least Anyuta's letters are arriving regularly, as she promised. She tells us she's having no success in locating her own 'good man.' Evidently 'preserves' are genuinely scarce this season."

The dog twitched and scratched his ear with his left hind leg.

"No," Sofya answered what she thought his twitch might mean, "I've had no news from Vladimir. Not a single letter."

The dog rested his head on his forepaws.

"Yes," Sofya responded. "That makes me sad too."

"Sofya Vasilievna." Sofya looked around. Someone had heard her talking to a dog! She could feel a warm flush come to her face. The gentle voice was Leon's. "Your father asks that you come to his study immediately."

Sofya stood up suddenly. The dog stood more slowly, then wandered back toward the sheds without looking back at her. He had left without a proper goodbye.

"Oh, drat!" She brushed her hands together and then smoothed her dress. She headed toward the study, calling over her shoulder, "Oh, Leon, be sure the dog has fresh water, this heat is wearing him down."

From the doorway of the study, she saw Father sitting in a deep leather chair, his arms folded across his chest. On the footrest, next to the chair, was a large mail pouch. Father gestured her to the vacant chair beside his.

"The mail just arrived minutes ago. Late as usual." Father's eyes did not meet hers as he spoke. His voice held an energy signifying that something of importance had occurred.

"Yes. I know. Late Thursday afternoons, Palibino makes contact with the world." Sofya sat on the edge of the offered chair, her back rigidly straight, chin up. If there were letters for her, Father would give them to her in his own good time. She forced herself fully back into the chair. She mustn't show any agitation. Why give him the satisfaction of knowing how tortured she was?

"Besides my inevitable business correspondence, there are letters for each of us from your mother, and others from your sister—and a bundle of letters that had the postman behaving quite apologetically to me." Father's face showed no emotion. The tone of his voice was cynical. "Though why the postman should apologize I don't understand. How can one apologize for being stupid? Officials of the government always apologize profusely for any incompetence. They seem to think fawning and apologizing cover all mismanagement."

Sofya could not help readjusting her position in the chair. Would Father never get to the point? He was tormenting her.

"The story the little man gave me goes like this. There have been mysterious letters arriving at the post office every day for weeks. Sometimes two would arrive on the same day. No one could read the strange squiggles on the envelopes, so the letters were put aside. The stack of mystery mail grew with each delivery from Petersburg. Moments before the postman set out on today's deliveries, another letter arrived, bearing the same squiggles. The local postman laughed as the mystery letter appeared.

" 'Why do you keep leaving us these mystery letters?' he asked the postman from Petersburg. 'Because they're for your district, you lout.' Our local man asked, 'How do you know this?' The Petersburg man responded, 'Look, that word is Palibino. Palibino is in your district.' And, if you look closely you can make out the word Palibino." Father stood, then reached into the mail pouch he had left on the footrest. "And, I believe, I can just barely make out your name." He straightened, the packet was in his hands.

Sofya could no longer restrain herself. She sprang from the chair, reaching to take the packet, still bound in the postman's string, from Father's hands. Then for a moment she hesitated. Would Father surrender the packet, uncensored?

His large hand pushed the packet toward her. "Here, take them. I haven't read them, and I'm not going to. They're obviously from your fiancé."

Sofya took them. A flood of happiness came over her. Impulsively she hugged her father. His body remained stiff and unresponsive. She quickly pulled away. Looking into his steel gray eyes, she was astonished to see they glistened with an unnatural moisture.

"Go. Go. Read your precious letters." Father had turned his back to her. "You needn't join me for dinner this evening. I'll have something sent to your room."

"Papa, thank you," she managed as she hurried from the room.

SPRAWLED ON HER BED, she restrained her impatience until she had sorted the envelopes by date. Then she skimmed quickly through all the letters. Each began, "My dearest darling Sonechka" and ended, "I can hardly wait until I see you again. I kiss your tiny hands. Your Volodya."

In fact the dates made little difference. One piece of news was always the same. Vladimir had found no prospective liberator for Anyuta.

Vladimir had dutifully visited all the relatives as requested, and felt that he had made a good impression on them.

Sofya recalled the long list of relatives' names she had given him. First on the list was old Aunt Briullova. Sofya laughed at the image of an uncomfortable Vladimir sipping tea from a fine porcelain cup, as old Auntie related the latest in court gossip and politely but firmly probed Vladimir's social connections, asking if he knew Count so-and-so or Princess whatever. Sofya knew she was Auntie Sasha's favorite niece. Vladimir would be inspected and prodded with as much attention as one of the specimens under Sofya's microscope. The humor of the imagined situation was short-lived, as Sofya sobered to the thought that her whole future might depend on Vladimir's smooth handling of the relatives.

She continued to read. He'd found an apartment near the university, on the second floor of the house of Buturlin on Sergievaskaya Line. Not exactly the best part of town, but the five rooms were light and airy. Maria Bokova was helping him decorate it, saving a bright room especially for Sofya's study. He hoped Sofya would like it.

Of course she'd like it! Just reading about it, she could hardly contain her joy. Her very own apartment!

Vladimir missed the company of his bride-to-be. He expressed that sentiment with many flowery endearments. Sofya understood that these were meant for parental eyes if they should read the letter.

He wasn't getting much studying done. He was sure she'd made much more progress than he in every field of learning. His arithmetical exercise consisted of counting the days until he returned to her in Palibino, and he had to admit that he might not have undertaken even such a trivial exercise were it not for the sentimental value it also possessed.

Sofya read the letters again, puzzling over an occasional illegible word. Then she read them all for a third time. She hugged the packet to her breast as she danced around the room. Was such happiness possible?

Needing an outlet for her happiness, Sofya quickly began to write Vladimir. She began by chiding him to practice his penmanship. The much-delayed letters had caused her great distress. Especially he should practice by writing letters to her.

THE HAPPY GLOW she had felt with Vladimir's first letter soon faded. The days of separation dragged on. Father's brooding silence returned and wore roughly on her nerves.

A string of steamy, hot days had settled on Palibino. The rare breezes brought no relief, only clouds of gnats and mosquitoes rising from the marshlands to the west. Beyond the garden, near the pond, marsh hens cackled loudly all through the days. The nights were oppressively humid, allowing only fitful sleep. The sound of crickets never ended until morning light. Day and night, Sofya tried to work. Only the Darwin translation made progress. Her own studies were at a standstill.

At least Vladimir's letters were being delivered with some regularity now that the post office had learned to decipher his writing.

Sofya forced herself to end another day of work. Ritualistically, she took off all her clothing, put on her white cotton nightshirt, opened the window, and extinguished the small bedside oil lamp. From the far corner of her chamber the glow of a small hanging oil lamp encased in dark red glass softly illuminated her icon, her window onto heaven. The dark image of a slender woman veiled in blue, the depiction of Holy Wisdom, held a small book in one hand and the white dove of the Holy Spirit in the palm of the other. The medieval woman stared into the room with large, uncaring dark eyes, as the icon's ornate silver frame sparkled as if on fire. Sofya tore her gaze from the familiar, always haunting image. All the features of her room had distorted into eerie, almost unrecognizable shapes.

She should have lain down, closed her aching eyes, and slept. Instead, barefoot and exhausted, she paced the cool, uncovered wood floor, avoiding a certain board that she knew had a tendency to squeak. Trying to empty her mind of all thought, she concentrated on her own dark shadow that first preceded, then followed her. She tried to count the number of cricket chirps per second. She stared out the window at lightning so distant that no thunder followed, and no relieving rain. She pictured Vladimir's face. She longed for his next letter.

She scolded herself for spending far too much time thinking of Vladimir. In her loneliness, she was seizing upon his offer of friendship with far too much possessiveness. She must take herself in hand. She must stop including him in her daydreams, her plans for the future. She had no reason to believe or desire that after the marriage, Vladimir would spend any of his time with her. In all likelihood, after a respectable interval, he would simply disappear. That was the customary behavior for a liberator.

Of course, there had been exceptions.

Sofya stopped pacing. Purposefully she walked to the night table and struck a match. Relighting the oil lamp, she carried it to the small writing table. Tomorrow there would be a mail pick-up and delivery.

From the table's small center drawer, she chose a sheet of notepaper edged in wildflowers. Carefully, she penned the date in the upper right corner. She hesitated only a moment, then continued:

My dearest Volodya,

The greeting flowed naturally from her pen. She told herself that the use of such endearments was a part of the formula of their letters, nothing more.

I study diligently. I have made some progress on the Darwin articles you asked me to translate. I may have them completed by your return. I am also continuing my own studies in chemistry and especially in mathematics.

No reason to bother him with the fact that her studies were not going as well as she had hoped.

I am called to the clinic several times a week. The summer has been particularly hard on the peasants although so far only one has died. I take extra precautions so that I will not catch any illness.

Perhaps he will worry a little about me. But the thought of his worrying about her was dangerously pleasing. *I must stop this foolish sentimentality!*

The clinic has experienced a great misfortune. The pike we brought back from our last picnic has died. The poor thing contracted repulsive, white worms. His death was horrible to watch. Leon is very despondent and begs not to be ordered to replace the creature. Our little caterpillar is also gone, vanished. He nibbled his way out of the comfortable cardboard home we prepared for him. These losses are a bad omen. I am now totally alone.

Vladimir will laugh at my superstitions.

Anyuta writes that she has met no one interesting in Petersburg; she had hoped to see you and perhaps she will before you return here. She looks forward with hope to the future, as I do. I dream of the happiness in store for us.

Your Sofya

Wait, I'll sign it with his last name.
Carefully she penned in her name-to-be: K-O-V-A-L-E-V-S-K-A-Y-A.
Yes, it did sound very nice, Sofya Kovalevskaya.

AFTER WEEKS IN PETERSBURG, subjected to the scrutiny of Sofya's aunts and uncles, Vladimir had returned to Palibino confident in his ability to deal with the politics of a large family. But nothing in the past weeks, nothing in his past life, had prepared him for his role in the prenuptial gathering now convening.

Fully clothed except for his boots, Vladimir lay on the bed in his room at Palibino. He'd just endured another luncheon filled with relatives he barely knew. The delightful Palibino of early June had been transformed into a theater where the audience stayed for days and both watched and participated in bit parts of the drama. He, of course, had a leading role. He was a good actor, but he despised the job.

A cool breeze moved the curtains on the open window and brushed his face gently. He stared at the ceiling, where a housefly, sluggish with the September chill, was oblivious to the large brown spider moving on an interception course.

Adjusting his hands behind under his head, Vladimir absently watched the ceiling drama. His thoughts wandered. He'd accomplished quite a bit this last month in Petersburg. He'd been able to extract enough money from his publishing business to pay a few months' rent on the new apartment, furnish the place, and provide funds for himself and Sofya. They could live fairly comfortably. The cash should last at least until the time when money from her dowry was released.

And he'd completed Sofya's assigned mission of visiting relatives. He sincerely liked her relatives. And he thought they liked him. The men were not overly concerned with acquisition of wealth, although money was not ignored. The women, like their men, were quick-witted and unusually well informed in matters scientific, artistic, and political. Of course, he'd had to watch his tongue whenever politics was mentioned. On the whole, he'd found the family was liberal and humanitarian in their views, but strictly within the boundaries set by the establishment. There were no rebels or reformers among the older generation. One thing was very clear: they were all very sincerely interested in Sofya's welfare, financially and emotionally.

Vladimir swung his legs over the side of the bed and, so as not to disturb the drama on the ceiling, slowly raised himself. He took a few steps to the wash stand, picked up the small hand towel, and with a dispassionate motion flicked the spider to the floor, then crushed the scurrying insect with a boot.

He was up now. He might as well go in search of his bride. A certain matter needed attention. He put on his boots, adjusted his shirt and pants, then took his light jacket from the chair back.

Well, he told himself as he headed down the stairs, he could honestly assert that he'd demonstrated his concern for Sofya. He'd cut his stay in Petersburg short, even though he should have spent more time on his publishing business. Her letters had sounded so forlorn, so lonely, he'd felt she honestly missed him and wanted him with her.

Her last letter to him in Petersburg had contained a frantic note that he couldn't ignore. Sofya had written that her mother had returned from Petersburg leaving Anyuta behind with relatives. The full force of her mother's attention had focused on Sofya, continually nagging her about arrangements, clothes, and the entertainment for the relatives who had already started to arrive for the wedding.

Vladimir had rushed here to assist and support Sofya. Of course, his hands were tied when it came to making any real progress at relieving the pressure. After all, he couldn't openly side with Sofya in the disputes; the risk of losing his only parental ally was too great. He could only try in vain to soothe both women.

He'd made it past the living area without being interrupted by guests.

He headed for the porch. Sofya liked the porch and they'd made a special corner of it their own. She was nowhere in sight. A few days ago, he could have counted on Sofya seeking a meeting with him. But that was before Anyuta had arrived.

True, Anyuta could manage Elizaveta Fedorovna like no one else, and Sofya was given relief from her agony, but at a price. Vladimir had fallen out of the equation. Anyuta now occupied all of Sofya's attention. When he'd tried to join the sisters, Anyuta treated him with such scorn, rudeness, and condescension that he'd retreated. He'd thought of confronting Anyuta, but that conflict would surely have upset Sofya, perhaps enough to ruin their plans. No, he'd have to endure Anyuta's barbs unchallenged awhile longer. His real pain came not from Anyuta's tongue, but from Sofya's rejection.

"Vladimir Onufrievich."

Vladimir startled, turned swiftly. The voice was that of Sofya's Aunt Anna, a tall, slender woman with silver-white hair. Presenting her extended hand for the expected kiss, he noted the unladylike hardness of her palms. Her eyes were steel gray, bright, clear and alive with youthfulness and mischief despite their sixty years.

"You're out here all alone?" she demanded.

"As you see," Vladimir answered, and nodded his head in the manner of a slight bow.

"I would have thought you'd be with your intended on such a lovely afternoon. Perhaps strolling hand in hand through the fragrant orchard, or sitting on that porch bench around the corner. But then, if you'll pardon an old lady's bluntness, I haven't noticed you and Sofya together like that. Or together in any other way for that matter." She paused. "Except of course at dinner, when the whole gigantic clan seems to amass. I certainly hope you and Sofya are not having a disagreement."

"Absolutely not," Vladimir responded as firmly as he could. "Sofya has many arrangements to make. Her time, especially during the day, is not hers to do with as she might please." Vladimir must not show this woman how correct her observations had been. He managed to put a joking tone into his voice. "And since not even your watchful eye has discovered us, I can alleviate Sofya's fear that our private meetings were observed."

"Yes, yes, of course. Sofya would worry about things like that." The woman's eyes twinkled. "And dear Elizaveta's fussing would stress a saint. My poor brother walks around with a face so glum one would think this was a funeral. Times before a wedding are so stressful for everyone. But I suppose it must be so. Such an important step."

"I don't believe it must be so. Custom has contrived to make it so," Vladimir answered.

"Point well taken, young man. But the custom has a purpose. The strains test the resolve of the participants. Any weakness should be discovered before the vows are taken. Surely, you agree."

"I agree." Vladimir looked closely into the woman's eyes. "Up to the last minute, either party must be free to decide whether marriage is their true desire." Had Aunt Anna opened this line of discussion because she knew of his earlier engagement to Masha Mikhaelis? Or was it simply by accident that she had happened to hit a very sensitive spot? Vladimir composed himself. Hardening his voice he added, "One must not, like Pushkin's Eugene Onegin, come between a couple, just for sport. You must agree, that is an unforgivable sin."

Aunt Anna smiled. "I agree. Certainly, not for sport. But if one can save a loved one from a lifetime of unpleasantness, there is a duty to do so."

"One must be very sure before meddling with the happiness of others," Vladimir responded. "If you'll excuse me, there is a matter I must attend to."

"We will continue our discussion later. I trust you have not forgotten that I am hosting an intimate dinner at my estate this evening." The woman turned and left Vladimir on the porch, staring after her majestic retreat and regretting his sharp words. He had completely forgotten the dinner arrangements.

VLADIMIR SOUGHT REFUGE in the library, thinking there was a slight chance Sofya might be among her beloved books. She wasn't.

Unable to concentrate, he stared blankly out the window. Sofya, Leon at her side, was walking across the lawn in the direction of the clinic.

He knew there was no possibility of Sofya being joined at the clinic by Anyuta. Charity had no part in Anyuta's philosophy of action.

A minute later, looking in at the clinic's open door, he found the little building crowded with ailing peasants and their bawling children. As Leon tried to organize the patients into an orderly line, Sofya was washing her hands, preparing for her examinations. Vladimir hesitated, then decided it would be best if he waited outside until her work was finished.

For a time Vladimir sat on a nearby bench, beneath which lay the mangy old dog Vladimir recognized as Baka. Old Baka's legs twitched as if he were running after an elusive dream cat. Occasionally a low growl punctuated his chase. Vladimir reached down and with his touch restored calm to the sleeping dog.

Presently, growing impatient, Vladimir began to pace slowly in front of the clinic's door. Why did she want to risk her own health, with the wedding only a few days off?

Coughing, exhausted-looking peasants emerged from the building in twos and threes. Others arrived. More than an hour passed before the crowd of patients shrank substantially. Presently Leon emerged, saw Vladimir and started talking excitedly. Sofya had allowed him to dole out medicines, as he could now read the labels on all the bottles and jars! He could even read the little book of cures that was kept in the clinic. Well, he could almost read that book.

Vladimir smiled at him and tousled his hair. "You washed your hands thoroughly?"

Leon nodded. "Of course, Sofya Vasilievna insists."

Vladimir turned toward the doorway, where at last Sofya appeared, looking tired and flushed. She didn't see him at first as she wiped sweat from her forehead, and locked the door behind her. Putting the key carefully into her pocket, she called for Leon.

"He's with me," Vladimir answered.

Her face brightened at his voice, and she came toward them. "Leon, you may return to the house." After bowing slightly to both Vladimir and Sofya, the boy turned away.

"Thank you." Vladimir lowered his head slightly. "I want a minute alone with you. These days, it seems a minute is all I'm likely to get."

"You know how busy I've been." She paused, for a moment seeming to examine him as if he were a patient.

His annoyance found words. "You find time to be with Anyuta."

Sofya stiffened. "Surely you don't begrudge me time with my sister." Assuming she was preparing a defense, he hastened on. "What's bothering me is that I'm running out of excuses when your relatives come up to me wondering aloud why I'm spending so little time with you."

For several moments his eyes locked with hers in anger.

"Let's find a place where we can talk." She had broken the eye contact first. Sofya led him to the orchard behind the house, where they sat on the grass beneath a large apple tree. Baka had followed them. Silently, the animal curled himself into a circle near Sofya.

"Well, here we are, spending time together," she said curtly without looking at him. Absentmindedly, she began to stroke the dog.

Vladimir remained silent until at last she looked up at him. Then he said: "I don't wish to keep you from whatever you had planned for these few minutes. But as the groom, supposedly the second most important player in this elaborate theatrical performance we're staging, I'd like to have a little more of your time. And a little more respect as well."

"Respect!" Her dark eyes flared at him. "May I ask in what way I have ever treated you disrespectfully?"

"My dear woman, you and I know the purpose of the marriage, but the guests don't. Nor do your parents. I am willing and happy to put your needs and desires ahead of my own, but I do not wish to become a public laughingstock." He paused for breath and to let his comment sink in.

The dog, startled by the raised voices, headed off toward the shed.

Sofya received Vladimir's outburst with a stare of astonishment. "I had no idea that your public image meant so much to you."

Her fiancé continued. "I'm beginning to feel very awkward thinking up reasons why you're never with me. The only time we're seen together is at these noisy, crowded dinners."

Sofya's shoulders were slumped forward. Only now did he notice how exceedingly tired she looked. But she still had energy to snap at him. "I don't care what the relatives think. They're important to Mother and Father, not to me. It's childish of you to have your pride hurt by such inconsequential people."

"First, as you have frequently told me, these inconsequential people could still cause us considerable trouble. We're not yet married, and you need their good will at least until we are. Secondly, I'm shocked that you can speak of your own family in such an unfeeling way. I find their prying an annoyance and embarrassment, but still I envy you having the concern of so many people, who obviously care for you, love you."

"We do still need their good will." Her voice sounded dreamy and far away as she added, more to herself than to him, "But I don't believe that any of them sincerely cares about me."

Vladimir's anger was softened by her confession.

Sofya stared off into space for a while. Then as if moved by a memory, she brightened as she said, "Do you remember meeting my Uncle Fedor? He's the young-looking, dashing one, always wears the latest English fashions. Very bright, very pleasing features. I had my first real crush on him. I was very jealous of him. I actually bit the arm of my little girlfriend who dared to climb on his lap."

"Your unfortunate friend!" Vladimir laughed.

"I was punished, of course. But my friend never climbed on Uncle Fedor's lap again. At least, not while I was around."

Vladimir could easily imagine the angry little Sofya. "So, you find Uncle Fedor attractive."

Sofya looked up sharply, and realized that Vladimir was smiling at her. She forced a tired smile of her own. "Yes, as a matter of fact, I still do. He's one of the male types that attracts me. There are others."

Nothing had been settled, but to Vladimir it seemed that the quarrel, such as it had been, was over, for the time being at least. He smiled at her. "Let's get you back to the house. You look like you could use some rest before dinner."

As they headed across the lawn toward the house, Sofya held his arm. Her head was down and he needed to lean toward her to catch her words. "I'm really dreading tonight. I can't endure Aunt Anna. I'll have trouble even being civil to her. Anyuta tells me Aunt Anna is strengthening all the doubts Father already had: Poor little Sofya is too young, she doesn't know her own mind, she should wait until Anyuta marries. And you, the potential mate, are an unknown quantity, certainly not financially secure. According to Anyuta, Father would have canceled the wedding right then, had Mother not calmed him. Thank God, Mother's firmly on our side."

"Well, the she-bear hasn't stopped the wedding plans. And we won't give her more ammunition to use against us. We'll be sure she sees us together often. The ideal happy couple." He slipped his arm around her waist, bringing her body close to his.

In the front hall, at the foot of the stairway, he stepped in front of Sofya, holding her hands in his for a moment before parting. He saw her face flush; glancing up the stairs, he saw Anyuta coming down. The older sister nodded, but said nothing to the couple as she brushed past them. Vladimir thought he heard a soft clicking of her tongue.

Sofya pulled her hands free.

Vladimir spoke in a whisper. "I can't wait until we leave Palibino."

"A few more days," Sofya whispered back. Her response sounded defeated, tired, as if she hardly believed her own words.

"We'll last a few more days. Try not to worry. Everything will turn out as we planned. Only don't shut me out, we need to work together."

She was looking into his eyes pleadingly. Then, apparently without premeditation, she pressed herself to his chest. A moment later she had disappeared up the stairs, not looking back.

"ANDRÉ WILL NOT be joining us this evening. My son has a distinct preference for the company of the young men gathered at your place, Vasily." Aunt Anna greeted her arriving guests.

"The boys are enjoying themselves," Father responded in a glum tone. "Soon enough the worries of the world will weigh on them."

Ignoring her brother's grim remark, Aunt Anna turned to Vladimir, took his arm and led the party into a family dining room. The room held a small round table and five straight-backed chairs. Along the walls, gas lights flickered. A single servant stood ready to serve.

With a motion of her hand, Aunt Anna indicated the seating arrangement. Vladimir tried to acquire a position next to Sofya, but Aunt Anna insisted this would not do. She must sit between the couple. Elizaveta Fedorovna was placed to Vladimir's right.

When they were all settled, and Anna had ordered the meal to begin, she turned to Vladimir. "Was your ride to my house pleasant?"

"Yes, quite," Vladimir answered untruthfully as he adjusted his chair. Vladimir recalled the general's stern face and Elizaveta Fedorovna's unending talk of wedding arrangements.

"We discussed the selection of music for the wedding ball," Elizaveta Fedorovna added, adjusting her napkin on her lap. "I'm just not sure the musicians are capable of playing the tunes I've selected." She added nervously, "Sofya has been no help to me on this."

"She deferred to your trained and expert taste in matters musical," Vladimir responded. Elizaveta Fedorovna smiled approvingly at him.

"Mother, you are the musician of the family. And Vladimir and I will be leaving for Vitebsk, right after the wedding dinner. We won't be able to supervise the playing." Sofya wisely added her compliment to Vladimir's as she tasted the cream that floated atop the hot beet soup.

"Anxious to be off on your honeymoon?" Aunt Anna teased. "My dear, you pleasantly surprise me." She laughed boisterously then, with no pretense at ladylike reserve. "You have more spunk and love of life than I gave you credit for."

"Then my dear aunt, you have been misjudging me." Sofya's response pleased Vladimir. He smiled at her encouragingly.

"Aunt Anna, you've heard the story of Sofya facing down a she-bear," Vladimir observed. "Certainly as a grown woman, she would face a she-bear, or a husband, with equal courage, daring, and even enjoyment."

"I recall several she-bear stories. Not all with Sofya as the heroine." Aunt Anna smiled, enjoying this exchange. "I also recall more than one time little Sofya bested her elders. Isn't that right, Vasily?"

The general disregarded his sister's question. "Anna, I know this is your home, but I am your elder brother, and I ask you to please, for the sake of family peace, control your tongue. All of us have nerves strained to breaking."

"Yes, Vasily," Aunt Anna answered in mock humility, then turning to Elizaveta Fedorovna. "Liza, however do you put up with such an overbearing man?"

Elizaveta Fedorovna blushed.

"Some of us find the trait quite attractive," Vladimir interrupted. "I'm sure Elizaveta Fedorovna and I are in agreement that a little bearishness in a partner is not a drawback."

"So, young man, the bearishness of the Krukovskys doesn't frighten you?"

"Not in the least. I find the trait charming as it manifests itself in the women, and quite admirable in the men."

"Vladimir, you are a gem!" Aunt Anna roared with laughter. "How did our Sofya ever find you? If I were thirty years younger, I'd have grabbed you up for myself."

Then, turning to Sofya, "Your eagerness to get away with your husband bodes well, my dear. I won't be surprised if by next summer you're happily in a family way."

Vladimir watched as Sofya turned a deep shade of red, then paled. He prayed Sofya would keep her mouth shut until she was under control.

"Anna!" the general scolded. "You're going too far! Sofya is not yet married. And when she is, I hope she remembers she is a lady, and does not imitate the wild talk of her aunt!"

"Vasily, your protection of womanhood is positively stifling," Aunt Anna snapped. "You've been acting like a wounded bear ever since you returned to Palibino with the news of the wedding. I thought you might have some real cause for concern. But I see your worries are unfounded. You're just reluctant to give up your favorite." She turned to Sofya, "You know dear, your Mother wasted no time starting her family. The same will be expected of you and Vladimir."

"Really, Aunt Anna! That topic is strictly our concern." Vladimir had to divert Aunt Anna. Sofya's flaring eyes indicated that an explosion was imminent, one that would offend even Aunt Anna.

"Vladimir, I apologize for my sister-in-law's prying rudeness." Elizaveta Fedorovna tried to soothe him.

"Oh, Liza, don't be apologizing for me," Aunt Anna scolded. "Vladimir's not offended."

The interruption gave Sofya the moment she needed to regain control, before Aunt Anna returned to her. "You know, Sofya, you've made quite a wise choice of a husband. Oh, I'll admit at first I was doubtful." She turned to Vladimir. "But now, I am convinced you have the character trait essential to success and happiness, a strong backbone. You stand up to my prickling admirably and manage a few well-aimed strokes in return. My, I haven't had such fun since my own dear husband, bless his soul, passed on. We fought like cats and dogs. What a pleasure!"

Vladimir's eyes sought Sofya's. Aunt Anna was theirs!

The remainder of the dinner was a joy for Vladimir. He could see the lines of nervousness and anxiety slipping from Sofya's face, replaced by a radiant, relaxed happiness. Nothing, however improper, that Aunt Anna referred to could upset either of them now.

SOFYA, ELIZAVETA FEDOROVNA and Aunt Anna were all happily arguing about the food to be served at the wedding.

The general, swaying just slightly on his feet and gripping a bottle of vodka in one fist, caught Vladimir's eye, and with a slight motion of his head indicated it was time for the two of them to withdraw somewhere.

In the library the atmosphere was quite different. The general lit a cigar as Vladimir drew a pipe from his pocket. A smoky fog separated the men. Still holding the bottle, the older man stood thoughtfully before the fireplace, that was, as always during summer, filled with cut flowers.

Vladimir placed his already lifeless pipe on the mantel. There had been no conversation, since the simple exchange in which Vladimir declared his preference for a pipe over a cigar.

At last the general spoke, pronouncing each word carefully. "I like you, Vladimir. But I still believe in my heart that this wedding should be delayed. For financial reasons, if no other. But you and Sofya have completely defeated me, and her efforts were painfully deceitful. Defeat is always bitter, but I respect you, so the situation can be borne."

"Sir, I regret you view our marriage as a battle you have lost. I promise you, your daughter's happiness was, is, and always will be my prime motivation."

The general walked, a bit unsteadily, to the table where an array of liquors waited. Throwing his cigar away among the lilacs in the fireplace, the general picked out two clean glasses and began to pour. The bottle in his hand was quickly emptied and he threw it aside. Now it was necessary to open another.

With three fingers of Palibino vodka in each glass, he handed one to Vladimir. "Your chivalry is admirable, my son. The sentiments of a young man in love are refreshing"—here he paused for a faint belch—"reminders of an earlier time, for this old and somewhat cynical warrior."

CHAPTER SIX

Sunday, 15 September, 1868 ❧ *Palibino*

The morning of her wedding, Sofya woke to the happy voices of female servants, raised in a traditional wedding song outside her bedroom door. The song instructed Sofya to rejoice in her new role as wife, aware that from today forward her loyalties would be to her husband. Last night the same women had sung Sofya a kind of lullaby, whose lyrics mournfully expressed the sadness of her last night as a maiden in the house of her parents. The lyrics claimed she would lose her freedom and become the slave of her husband.

Sofya blushed as the words of the next verse took up the subject of her wifely duties. She wished these country customs and formalities could be done away with. Sitting up in bed, she drew her knees to her chest and wrapped her arms around them. There was beauty in the voices. Sofya could make out the delicate soprano of Natasha, her dear maid. The second soprano belonged to the family seamstress, who had worked so hard sewing Sofya's wedding dress and trousseau, and many years ago had sewn her playclothes. The strong alto tones could only belong to the cook, that giant of a woman who from time to time smuggled the children cookies and other confections, and who every Easter almost smothered them with her massive, all-encompassing hug and kiss of peace.

The song ended. Sofya put her bare feet onto the cold floor and walked to the door. She knew why the servants sang so happily. After the family celebrations, Father would by tradition declare in his daughter's honor a time of rest and holiday for all the servants.

Sofya was escaping, but these other prisoners of Palibino would be left behind. She put on her robe and went into the hall to accept good wishes from each singer.

Before Sofya returned to her room, Great Aunt Aleksandrina Fedorovna Briullova came pattering down the hall. Her long, generous dressing gown swished rhythmically across the wooden floor. "I have been assigned to you for the preparations," the old woman said in a tone indicating she intended to assume command. "Everyone else will be busy with their own grooming. At my age, it matters little if I spend a moment or hours in preparing myself. So my dear, I will help you."

"Auntie, you know I chose you to help me because no one else has your powers." Sofya liked her old aunt. And Aunt Bruillova favored Sofya. The woman was an aristocrat, at home in the highest court circles. From the stories Sofya had heard, she had captivated court society with her wit, impeccable taste in fashion, and personal beauty.

"For a bride, young and full of life like yourself, I need only be sure outward trappings don't distract from your natural radiance and beauty," the old woman said. "Let's go to work, my darling."

AUNTIE SASHA STARTED by ordering a large full-length mirror be brought into Sofya's room. While the maids tended to that order, Auntie asked Sofya to lay out all her wedding garments, from her underclothing to her dress, shoes and veil. The old woman carefully inspected each item while Sofya went off to bathe. Auntie Sasha insisted the seamstress redo a tuck and tighten some of the closing hooks. Only when each item had met her approval did the old woman turn her attentions to Sofya, who had reentered the bedroom.

"Put on the undergarments, then sit down at your dressing table, my dear." Sofya smilingly obliged.

Auntie held Sofya's chin in her hand. "We'll start with a little base powder, then heighten the blush of your lips with a little rouge and put just a touch of paint on your eye lashes. Your eyes are quite large and beautiful. Ah, what I could have accomplished with eyes like that." The woman spoke wistfully.

Sofya laughed, "Really, Auntie. I don't want any powder. And I'll only stand for the slightest amount of lip rouge."

"Yes, dear." Auntie took one look at Sofya's meager array of paints and sighed, then issued a command to Natasha. "Get my facial case."

"Auntie." Sofya spoke more sternly. "I insist on doing this simply."

In a moment the woman had expertly applied a few deft strokes of paint that even Sofya admitted enhanced her natural look.

Auntie took only a moment to admire her facial artistry, then proceeded to run her fingers through Sofya's hair. "The curls are lovely, and all natural, you lucky woman." Auntie grabbed a brush and started vigorously working the instrument through Sofya's hair.

"Auntie, I can do this," Sofya insisted.

"Yes, yes," Auntie said nervously and handed the brush to Sofya. She sat on the edge of Sofya's bed, "Be sure to get at least one hundred strokes. Then, after you've put on your gown, I'll help you arrange those few errant strands that always seem to climb out from behind your ears."

Natasha helped Sofya into her gown. Sofya remembered how she had been coaxed into trying on the dress innumerable times over the last few weeks. There had been fittings and style adjustments and the constant struggle with Mother wanting to modify the dress. Sofya had stayed firmly with her idea of simplicity. And now, Sofya was pleased. The fine white silk that Mother had purchased in Petersburg had been transformed into the gown, delicate lace appliqués of wildflowers had been added. A narrow band of stitching where the gently flared skirt attached to the bodice accentuated her waist, the long sleeves puffed slightly at the shoulder, and a collar modestly covered her neck. Sofya looked into the mirror again. Natasha began fastening the long line of satin-covered buttons that ran up the back.

Auntie, still sitting on the edge of the bed, commented, "The simple lines flatter your petite figure. An excellent choice. Excellent." Auntie hesitated. "Dear, why are you squirming so?"

"The lace at the shoulders and neck is driving me mad!" Sofya burst out, more nervously than she'd expected. "I mentioned this at every fitting, and the seams still are itching me."

"Don't fuss. We'll fix it. We certainly can't have you wiggling around like that." Auntie instructed Natasha to unbutton the gown. Then Auntie expertly directed the seamstress in tacking a scrap of satin to each of the offending seams. The job was carried out quickly and expertly. "No one will notice our little adjustment and you'll be infinitely more comfortable. I can't tell you how many times I've made the same adjustment to my own clothing. Women would be far more brilliant at formal gatherings if they weren't preoccupied with their uncomfortable clothing. Sofya, comfortable clothing is the secret behind every witty and charming woman."

Sofya laughed, her nervousness dissipated for the moment.

Auntie picked up the veil. "What an excellent piece of workmanship!" The long piece of lace would reach far down Sofya's back. The edges had been hand rolled by the family seamstress who took great pride in being allowed to work on the wedding veil. Sofya had humored the dear old servant by allowing her to embroider the traditional symbols on the delicate lace. A crucifix with three cross bars, the bottom bar slanting, was the dominant design, placed conspicuously in the center, while along the edges were silken trees and delicate birds and flowers, signs that had been sewn on brides' clothing from the time of the ancient Slavs.

"I'm pleased with it," Sofya admitted. She held the wreath of myrtle and orange blossoms that would hold the veil in place. "I'd like to put the veil on now."

"I agree." Auntie held the veil in place as Sofya placed the wreath.

Aunt Briullova was fussing with one last rebellious curl that refused to stay behind her ear. "You are beautiful, my dear." Aunt Briullova stood back admiring her niece. "Now, we add a pendant with a single emerald."

"No! No jewelry," Sofya insisted.

"Perhaps you're right. Your eyes are shining like gems and your skin has just a flush of red." Auntie gave her a gentle hug. "Here is your *chrinka*." Sofya took the beautiful silk handkerchief edged with tiny pearls. Her aunt's eyes were glistening with tears. "You are ready to be presented to your family and fiancé. Be happy, my dear."

Sofya kissed her gently, then looked in the mirror one last time before leaving to greet the relatives. A beautiful bride gazed back at her. Something in the ritual of donning the dress, the veil, and the handkerchief had effected a transformation. She could almost believe she was beautiful.

DOWNSTAIRS, THE FESTIVELY decorated salon vibrated with nervous laughter and the happy talk of family and friends. Small groups had formed, one around the piano, another near the fireplace, some at tables in the corners of the room. Vases of roses and lilacs were plentiful, their fragrance mingling with the sweet smells of pipe tobacco and women's perfume. Though the morning was bright, the crystal chandelier was lit and sparkling.

Some guests had wandered from the salon through the vestibule, peeking into the ballroom. That room was filled with tables, adorned with gold-embroidered linen, silver serving cutlery, crystal glasses and more flowers. On the stage, a small group of musicians was tuning their instruments.

A loud clapping from a single pair of strong hands focused everyone's attention. Great Aunt Briullova, now clad in an elegant, high-necked green dress, announced in a strong voice that the bride was ready. The guests hurried to the foot of the stairway.

As Sofya descended, a muted chorus of admiration rose to meet her. Vladimir, looking flushed and uncomfortable in his formal suit, came up the last few stairs without speaking to take her hand in his white glove and lead her to the vestibule.

Father and Mother awaited the couple there. As tradition demanded, Sofya and Vladimir knelt before her parents. As the guests looked on silently from a respectful distance, Father gave the couple his blessing. He admonished them to love each other always and—with special solemnity, Sofya thought—adjured her to obey her husband. Vladimir gave her hand a lightly reassuring squeeze when those words were spoken.

Rising, the couple stood next to Father and Mother. After some confusion and playful remarks from the guests, Sofya maneuvered Vladimir to her right, where tradition demanded he stand. The guests then filed past bestowing their blessings. A small piece of black bread with salt was given to each guest by Sofya's cousins André and Nicholas, who were serving as Vladimir's groomsmen. This ritual complete, the party went outdoors, where in bright autumn sunshine a sleigh fitted with wheels awaited the bride and her attending ladies, Anyuta and Zhanna.

The sleigh was decorated with red ribbons and bells hung from the horses' harness. Sofya, Anyuta and Zhanna settled themselves on the satin-covered seats. Red pillows were provided to soften their ride.

Vladimir and his groomsmen mounted magnificent gray stallions, their saddles and reins decorated with ribbons and bells. The groom's party would ride beside the sleigh to the church. Sofya thought she saw Vladimir wink at her when he was settled atop his restive mount.

By tradition, the bride's parents should not attend the church service, but Mother and Father were entering a carriage that would follow behind the sleigh. Sofya had been surprised to hear that Father was the one who had insisted on defying country tradition in this instance. Why he'd want to attend a wedding he clearly wished wasn't taking place, Sofya did not understand.

Behind Mother and Father's carriage the guests followed in an assortment of vehicles.

The procession drove through the beautiful countryside, already beginning to show its autumn finery. As they passed through a village the peasant women came out hoping for a look at the bride. They insisted on serenading Sofya with earthy songs that made Sofya blush. Oh, how she wished the wedding could have been in Petersburg, where ceremony could have been kept to the very minimum. She could just barely hear the snippy remarks degrading country traditions that Anyuta was sharing with Zhanna. When Sofya dared to look at Vladimir, he was smiling approvingly at the women. To her surprise, he seemed to be enjoying all this ceremony.

Sofya was grateful the church was only a few versts from Palibino. She kept telling herself that she was getting closer and closer to freedom. Soon the sleigh stopped in front of the small, square wooden building with its domed roof. The double doors were open and the old priest, adorned in his heavy robes and elaborate headgear, stood welcoming them. Vladimir and his men dismounted and helped the ladies from the sleigh. Sofya took Vladimir's arm as they walked up to greet the priest. The priest ceremoniously led them into the brightly lighted church, where Sofya and Vladimir kissed the icon in the entry. For a moment the three were alone in the open space of the church. The brightly polished wooden floor shone with strange patterns from the many burning candles. All the walls were painted with icons of saints, whose wide eyes seemed to be staring at Sofya. For a moment Sofya felt dizzy. She swayed, but the rush of guests into the church soon broke the spell.

When all the guests had entered and were standing around the couple, the priest began the first part of the service, the Office of Betrothal. With the priest's guidance, she and Vladimir proclaimed to the guests that they were entering the marriage freely. Vladimir slipped a simple gold band onto the third finger of her right hand, then she slipped an identical ring onto his finger.

The guests moved about and exchanged comments, making way for Sofya and Vladimir, who were led by the priest to the front of the church. There, before the brilliant, three-paneled iconostasis, the screen of icons separating the main altar from the people, stood a small pedestal on which had been placed the icon from Sofya's bedroom. Her old icon awaited her like a friend.

The *a cappella* song of a lone cantor signaled the priest to begin the second part of the service, the Office of Crowning. While Sofya and Vladimir stood before the priest, Vladimir's groomsmen stood behind them holding heavy silver crowns above the heads of the bride and groom. The priest, speaking to the congregation, recalled the symbolism of the crowns. Sofya and Vladimir were rulers of a new line. The crowns were also to remind them of the crown of thorns and sufferings of Our Lord in which they would inevitably partake.

Sofya was surprised; she had asked the old priest to delete his traditional speech on symbolism, just as she had asked that there not be a full choir, and that many of the lengthier prayers and supplications to the Virgin Mother be omitted. The priest had agreed to her requests, but clearly had reverted to the traditional ceremony. Sofya could only submit.

In the final ritual, the couple shared a drink from the same golden cup. Then the priest blessed the assembly with a large cross. The rites were over. She was married. She was free. Obeying a sudden impulse, Sofya quickly stepped onto the little pink satin rug laid especially for the exiting wedding couple. Vladimir followed her.

BACK AT THE HOUSE, the ballroom tables were now filled with wonderful foods. Veal and lamb were served along with a wide assortment of biscuits and sweet cakes. The cheeses, berries, nuts, vegetables, and preserves of Palibino were abundant. An elaborate wedding cake topped with almonds occupied a special table. Before dinner, numerous champagne toasts were made by one after another of the guests.

During dinner Sofya was teased for stepping on the pink rug before Vladimir. By tradition, the partner who first stepped on the pink rug was fated to be the dominant one. Aunt Briullova voiced the opinion of most of the relatives when she exclaimed, "How can our young, shy Sofya be dominant? This time the tradition will prove itself false!"

The bride was not saved from teasing during dinner. Young Fedya and cousin Nicholas had concocted a plot. First one then the other called out, "Gorko! Gorko!" By tradition, Sofya and Vladimir had each time to put down their forks and kiss, to sweeten the meal that had been called "Bitter!"

Sofya observed that Father was gentle and gracious, but clearly he was sad. He had not smiled at her, not with his eyes and heart. Amidst the abundance of good wishes and happy feelings Sofya felt a sharp longing for the missing gesture.

The dinner went on for about two hours, with Sofya growing increasingly anxious to leave. Finally the guests adjourned to the salon for afterdinner drinks, and Sofya hurried upstairs to change her clothes. Anyuta came along to assist her. Once again, in secretive hushed tones, her older sister reminded her of their idealistic plan.

This behavior Sofya found unnecessary and irritating, but even with her growing annoyance, she felt a deep regret at leaving her sister.

Downstairs again, to one more round of thank yous and goodbyes. Sofya and Vladimir climbed into a carriage. André, the groomsman, joined them. As soon as the doors to the carriage were closed, André assured Sofya that he had no intention of accompanying them to Vitebsk, as tradition demanded. Winking at Vladimir, he informed Sofya that she would be alone with her husband just as soon as the carriage reached the post station. André would get a horse and spend the night at his hunting cabin, before returning tomorrow to tell the family all was well.

"You two can kiss or hug or whatever," André joked, "don't mind me."

"Thank you, my friend," Vladimir said as he put his arm around Sofya and pulled her closer to him. "But we'll soon be rid of you."

Amid laughing and joking between Vladimir and André their carriage turned from Palibino's private drive onto the public road, and then past the post station, where André departed. Vladimir's arm was still firmly around Sofya. "*Gospozha* Kovalevskaya, are you happy?"

"Oh, Volodya, I'm very happy! It's as if I'd been freed from prison." She looked at his smiling face, then pushed herself a few inches away from him before continuing, in as controlled and serious tone as she could manage in her state of overflowing happiness, "Thank you! I will always be most grateful to you. Thank you, thank you."

"None of that, now." His voice was playfully scolding. "We have a mutually beneficial arrangement, founded on firmer stuff."

"Of course. Mutual benefits and freedom." Sofya flushed with embarrassment at allowing herself to be carried away.

"Except, of course, your interests and benefits will come first."

"As agreed," she replied. Had there been a touch of sarcasm in his reply? No, she didn't want to think so.

They rode along, watching the birch trees go by, occasionally conversing on unimportant matters. After several hours of the bumpy road Sofya suddenly announced, "I've been composing a poem in my head. You must remind me to write it down as soon as we get to the inn."

"A poem on the wonders of being a married woman?" he teased.

"No!" she laughed. "It's going to be about my feelings on leaving Palibino. A rather dark poem, I'm afraid. A prisoner's release. And my sorrow at leaving Anyuta behind."

"I'm sorry." Her husband sounded rather glum.

"What's the matter?"

"Well, today is our day of achieving freedom. The start of our new lives. I'm putting all dark thoughts away, at least for today. I wished you would too." He looked at her. "I was sure you were happy. You were incredibly beautiful, radiant, with a sparkle brighter than any jewels. I'd hoped some of that beauty was caused by a new and lasting happiness."

"Oh, Vladimir! I am happier than I've ever been; it's just that when I think of Anyuta I feel somewhat uneasy. Perhaps even a little guilty. I want us all to be happy."

"Then it's too bad I'm not a Mohammedan." Now there was something wry and bitter in his voice. "I could have married you both. Would that have made you completely happy?"

Sofya laughed. "Yes, I suppose."

They didn't speak again for a long while. Sofya closed her eyes and tried to keep her mind blank, looking neither forward nor back in time.

Vladimir, apparently assuming she was trying to nap, suggested she rest her head on his lap. The seat was certainly wide enough. She might even be able to get some sleep. He'd cover her with one of the blankets available in the carriage.

Sofya agreed. She rested her head on his legs, curling her legs on the seat, making herself as comfortable as possible. In time, she slept.

AT THE INN AT VITEBSK their rooms were waiting; one sleeping room with a small parlor attached, a door between. On a table in the parlor a lamp was lighted against the gathering dusk. A light snack of apples, cheese, and claret had been set out for the married couple.

Vladimir raised the bottle of wine and quoted from Pushkin, " 'Plans made between claret and champagne.' "

Sofya laughed. "No doubt, in a modest way, we are revolutionaries in the tradition of the Decembrists."

Vladimir poured red liquid into two glasses, then offered a toast. "To the fulfillment of each of us!" Both drank deeply.

At Vladimir's urging, Sofya gave the next toast. "To Liberty, Equality, Fraternity!"

"Most especially Fraternity." Vladimir smiled at his bride, perhaps gently mocking her choice of a toast. He lifted the glass to his lips.

After refreshing themselves, they dined at the small café attached to the inn. Feeling the need for a walk after the long confining ride, they strolled the better streets of Vitebsk by gaslight, looking into the windows of the closed shops. They wandered past the rail station, and watched as a large passenger train departed for Moscow, accompanied by great smoke and noise.

When they returned to the inn, Sofya was unready for sleep, and settled in with a candle at the tiny writing desk. She intended to set down on paper the verse she'd been composing in the carriage. She'd include the verse in her first letter to Anyuta. As she wrote, Vladimir settled in a chair at the other end of the small room, near the fireplace. He began to read.

But before long he stood up yawning. "Sofya, we really must get some rest. We'll be traveling all day and night tomorrow. And our first day in Petersburg will be busy, settling into the apartment. I've arranged with Maria Bokova for us to have dinner at her house the evening of our return—I hope you don't mind."

"No, of course not. And I'm almost done, but I'll stop now and finish this at our apartment. As soon as the ink is dry I'll put these papers into my traveling bag."

"I'm sorry about there being only one bedroom," Vladimir repeated an earlier apology. "The innkeeper misunderstood my directions."

"It's not important. We could sleep by turns." Sofya felt faintly embarrassed by the discussion. "You're tired, you sleep first. I'll read awhile, then I'll wake you."

"No, I have another solution," Vladimir said firmly.

She watched silently as he pulled two large stuffed leather chairs together. He looked critically at the construction, poked it in several places, made some small change in the relative positions of the chairs, then announced that this would be his bed.

She was doubtful. "Can you sleep like that?"

"Old campaigners can sleep anywhere."

Almost timidly Sofya touched him on the shoulder. "There are two covers on the bed, I'll bring you one." She was gone, and back in a moment, her arms filled with a thick down quilt.

He took the item from her and fussed with the arrangement, then again stood back, his gaze fixed on her. For a moment she thought something stirred in his eyes, something almost frightening. "Have you any suggestions for making the arrangement more comfortable?"

She bit the inside of her lip, and shook her head in the negative.

All he said was, "Then good night, my dearest friend." He came to her, held her shoulders and kissed her on the forehead.

Slowly, feeling an unexpected reluctance, Sofya retired to the sleeping room. She looked over her shoulder one more time at the strange construction, then closed the door. Her hand went to the key, but she refused to turn the lock; that would have been insulting.

Mechanically she undressed, then put on a beautiful lace-trimmed nightgown, part of her trousseau. Brushing her hair vigorously, she thought, what a shame, the gown would not be seen by anyone but herself.

Everything was going as planned, she told herself. She was behaving quite properly with Vladimir and he with her. She was on her way to freedom, to becoming a doctor, a scholar. Climbing into bed, she pulled the covers closely around her, only her face exposed to the room's air, chilling with night. She had accomplished the first step in her life goal. She felt pleased with herself.

She slept fitfully. On the first night of her liberated marriage, she dreamed repeatedly of the face of her father. His sad expression lingered over her, changing grotesquely to an abstract shape that started menacingly toward her. She welcomed Vladimir's knock on her door, announcing it was time to start their day.

CHAPTER SEVEN

Fall 1868 ❧ *Petersburg*

When they stepped onto the platform in the Moscow Station of Petersburg, Vladimir held Sofya by the elbow, his eyes scanning the crowd. Leaning toward her and speaking loudly to be heard above the noise, he said, "Sechenov was to meet us, but I don't see him. I'll inquire at the porter's desk. If Sechenov's left no word, I'll see to the luggage and arrange for our transportation."

Sofya had drawn back instinctively from her companion's raised voice in her ear. But she too found it necessary to speak loudly. "Take me across the street to the travelers' inn. I want to comb my hair and wash off some of this soot." She indicated her soiled gloves and the gray streak that had appeared across the front of her dress.

Vladimir nodded, and escorted Sofya to the door of the inn. They would meet later in the tea room.

She watched as the persistent crowds and confusion engulfed Vladimir as he crossed the street and reentered the station. Thinking she would have plenty of time before he returned, she climbed the stairs to the first floor, where she planned to purchase soap, water, and the use of a room in which to refresh herself and brush her clothes.

She approached the desk confidently, removing her gloves and clearing her throat. The attendant looked up, but past her, toward the stairway. Sofya understood. He was waiting to see if the young girl was accompanied by a maid or chaperone.

Sofya firmly requested a room where she might wash. The man smiled condescendingly, as if to a lost child. Once more he turned his gaze back to the stairway.

"Sir, I am alone. I am traveling without a maid or companion." Sofya put authority into her voice, as if he were a doctor speaking to a sick peasant. She placed her hand on the desk, conspicuously displaying her wedding band. "I am *Gospozha* Kovalevskaya. A room, please." From her purse she produced a rainbow-colored bill. "Shall I pay you now?"

"Ah, *Gospozha*! My apologies," the fellow stammered, his face above his whiskers turning red. "I must, of course, ask for your documents."

Sofya handed the man a small booklet that contained a description of her and noted her place of residence.

The clerk examined the entries.

Sofya kept her face expressionless. "The room, please."

He took a key from a rack behind him, then placed her papers in the niche vacated by the key. "I'm sure you will find everything you need. If you desire further assistance, there is a bell; one of our girls will come."

"Thank you," she answered formally, accepting the key. Walking with dignity toward the indicated room, Sofya allowed herself to smile as soon as she was out of sight of the desk. Her step briefly acquired a schoolgirl bounce. She had put her new power as a married woman, a *gospozha*, to a successful test!

The room was neat and clean, containing everything she needed. As she washed her hands she twisted the gold band around her finger. There was power in that symbol, and she knew how to use that power.

IN LESS THAN AN HOUR Sofya was back in the tea room of the travelers' inn, much refreshed and again in possession of her papers. She felt wonderfully alive, her old life washed off along with the dirt and soot of the journey.

Directing the waiter to seat her at a small table by the window, she ordered fancy Bohemian-style pastries and tea. Some time passed before two vehicles stopped in front of the inn. The first was a *droshky*, small and sporty, drawn by a sleek chestnut mare, the second a *telega*, a flat wagon piled with trunks. The latter was pulled by a large, muscular gelding who kept his head down, as if he understood his inferior position.

Vladimir, hopping out of the *droshky*, motioned to both drivers to wait. Sofya quickly paid her bill, wrapped the remaining pastry in her handkerchief, and joined Vladimir in front of the inn. He helped her into the sporty vehicle, then settled himself close beside her.

"Sechenov left a note of apology, and suggests we meet him at the Bokovs' this evening."

"Sounds fine to me." In the confined space she was unable to avoid poking the man beside her with her elbow as she unwrapped the pastry and offered it to him.

"A plum *kolach*, my favorite!" His arm jostled her as he reached for the sweet. "I would die for a good, strong cup of tea to wash this down."

Under the control of the artful driver, the vehicle wove swiftly around the larger and more awkward wagons and carriages in traffic, crossing the first bridge over the winding Neva. On reaching the wide lanes of Nevski Prospekt, their small, maneuverable vehicle sped far ahead of the baggage cart.

Sofya could hardly contain her excitement. "I never noticed how busy these shops are!" she exclaimed. Then a few moments later, as she leaned toward Vladimir, "How extravagant are all the houses between Liteinaya and the Annichkoff Palace! Each is a mansion!" Once past the Annichkoff Palace the pavement changed from rough cobblestone to wooden planking, muting the noise of speeding wheels.

As they passed Rossi, the street leading to the theater district, Sofya asked, "Will we be going to the theater?"

"What? I thought you were going to devote yourself entirely to study, and now you suggest frivolity." His tone was playfully mocking.

She lowered her eyes and folded her hands in her lap, pretending to have been hurt by his remarks. He consoled her with a small hug, "Yes, of course we will go to the theater, as often as you like."

Sofya burst out laughing.

They crossed the bridge over the Ekaterininsky Canal. "Looks like they're repairing the two blocks between here and the Moika Canal. Again." She groaned in a playful, exaggerated way, "One thing is exactly as it was before."

"And what might that be?"

"Road repair."

"In all probability that will never change," Vladimir commented. "The wooden streets make for a comfortable ride, but they can't withstand our Petersburg climate. You'd think we could find some better way . . ."

Sofya was paying only half attention to his remarks. "If our wonderful ride must be slowed, so be it. I'll have more time to enjoy the views. Vladimir, look at the fine bronze statue of wild horses. Do you suppose even they had to slow down for street repairs?" She laughed. "Oh, it is wonderful here!"

"Sofya, you're behaving like a country child at her first fair. Stop sticking your head and arm over the side. You might get hurt." He pulled her close to him.

"Is this really the most beautiful street in all of Europe?" she asked, leaning her head back comfortably against his arm, letting the breeze hit her full in the face. "You've traveled abroad and seen so many places. Tell me truthfully."

"Yes," Vladimir confirmed. "Definitely, Peter's City is the most beautiful, the most mysterious city in the world. Look!" They were crossing the Moika Canal, and he pointed to the northwest. "You can see the golden towers of St. Isaac's Cathedral. That little ray of sunlight coming through the clouds is causing quite an extraordinary glow."

"I attended services there last Easter," Sofya remembered. "I prayed for my own resurrection. Apparently my prayers were heard." Then she gasped, her body tensed. The driver had narrowly missed striking a nurse carrying a small child.

"Careful, driver!" Vladimir scolded gruffly. His voice lightened as he turned to Sofya, "Traffic along this stretch is as congested and disorderly as ever. The city's most prestigious businessmen are rushing around thinking of nothing but making fortunes."

"I'll bet you're choosing to leave business for the academic world just to avoid the crowded streets," Sofya joked.

"That isn't one of my reasons, but it certainly could be."

The daring driver increased speed as they entered the region dominated by government buildings. To her left Sofya saw the massive Admiralty, great carved nymphs flanking its gateway, holding up two versions of the world's globe.

"My first assignment as a newly graduated lawyer was in this district, just beyond the Admiralty at the Senate building." Vladimir's voice sounded strained. He quickly turned his head away. Sofya followed his gaze, to the mountain of white stone that was the Winter Palace, the Tsar's most impressive residence and the largest palace in the world. "I walked past the Palace every morning. I spent my lunch hours wandering in that beautiful garden, wishing I didn't have to return to work."

"Were you here before the guards, and the closed iron gate?" Sofya asked in hushed tones.

"Before the attempt on the Tsar's life, yes. Five years before all that, in '61. The serfs had just been emancipated. We young people hoped for general reform." He groaned. "I only lasted four months at my post in the Office of Heraldry. I managed to get time off and went abroad.

I kept getting my leave extended. After a year, when I could get no more extensions, I applied for a medical discharge from public service."

"You're all right? You aren't ill, are you?" Suddenly afraid, Sofya searched his face for an answer.

"My body is as strong as . . ." he hesitated, looking around. The baggage cart was now close behind, having caught up with them at the bridge. He smiled. ". . . as strong as that horse."

"I'm very pleased to hear that, my dear companion," Sofya responded with relief. He must have faked illness to be free of his job. He certainly knew a number of physicians who would have done him this small kindness.

The *droshky* rattled across the Dvortsovy Bridge to Vasilievsky Island. Sofya and Vladimir were silent, as long as the infamous prison of the Peter and Paul Fortress, on the bank of Petrovsky Island, dominated their view. Once across the bridge they turned west, down University Embankment.

"No more gloomy thoughts of the past. Our new, happy life is ahead of us." Vladimir sounded determined that it should be so, "Look, there's the Medical-Surgical Academy. Sechenov's probably preparing for his physiology class right this very minute. And I bet that within a week, you'll be one of his students."

"A week! I hope I don't have to wait a whole week!"

As they turned onto Sergievaskaya Line, Vladimir called for their driver to stop at the Buturlin house.

Vladimir dismounted, paid both drivers and ordered the *telega* driver to bring the luggage up to the second-floor apartment. Then, turning to Sofya, he challenged, "Race you to the door."

Sofya appeared to hesitate, then dashed forward. On the first flight, despite the handicap of long skirts, she was definitely in the lead. Vladimir, with a cry of triumph, passed her on the landing below the second flight, but in the middle of the flight, his boots slipped on the stairs, and Sofya again managed to secure the lead.

At the top stood a door numbered "24." She rushed to it and tried the handle without success. A panting and laughing Vladimir was right behind her.

"You know I let you win," he gasped breathlessly. A moment later he had extracted a key from his pocket and the door was open. Sofya pushed past him, reveling in the sight of an airy, sunlit room.

"The day help won't start until tomorrow. I wasn't sure what time we'd be arriving," Vladimir called after her, his tone apologetic.

"Don't worry!" Already in the next room, she called her answer to him. "We'll manage. Vladimir, this isn't anything like the tiny student's cell I'd been vaguely envisioning. This apartment is beautiful!"

His voice called to her eagerly: "Come see the study I have prepared for my scholar."

He was standing in the hall motioning her toward a closed door. He sounded especially proud.

Opening the door, Sofya recoiled for a moment. She was facing a grinning human skeleton, hanging by the window. "Oh, Vladimir! Where did you get him?"

"He's a wedding present from Bokov. I call him Koshchey." With a deft motion Vladimir placed his hat atop the dully shining skull. In another moment one of the bony arms was extended to Sofya, much to her delight.

"Koshchey, how pleasant to make your acquaintance." Sofya accepted the long, dry fingers in her own. After a moment she inquired, "No doubt you are related to Koshchey the Deathless, famed in fairy tales?"

Vladimir came to stand beside Sofya, facing the figure. "Koshchey the Deathless and I are already old friends. I even allow him to call me Volodya. We are on very good terms."

As Vladimir removed his hat, Koshchey turned aside a little, as if he were nodding his head wisely, moving on the cord by which he was suspended. Suddenly finding the bones no longer humorous, Sofya turned abruptly, and was immediately distracted by the sight of an oversized desk, comfortably situated between two large windows whose broad sills bore an assortment of house plants. Two candles and a clock stood on the desk. "The desk will never be this neat again!" she cried, hurrying to try out her chair.

Vladimir stood on the far side of the room, leaning casually on a magnificent walnut bookcase filled with leather-bound volumes. "You've missed something. A wedding present from your devoted husband."

Sofya jumped up and rushed across the room. Eyes wide with joy, she ran her hand lovingly over the top of the wooden case, then knelt before it to examine the books, almost with reverence. The title of each was embossed in gold on leather. Stunned, she beheld in slightly smaller letters, also gold, the inscription, "Library of Sofya Vasilievna Kovalevskaya."

Vladimir explained, "There's a copy of every book I've published, along with a few others I know are your favorites."

"Vladimir, I don't know what to say!" Turning back to her treasure, she chose from it at random, and opened a volume of Darwin translated into Russian. On the flyleaf was a reproduction of Darwin's signature.

Her companion was kneeling beside her now. "I had the signature reproduced from a letter Darwin sent me, congratulating me on the publication."

Sofya nodded her admiration and carefully replaced the volume. There was a copy of Herzen's *Who Is To Blame?* Beside that, poems by Lermontov. Sofya loved his verses, some of which had been set to music. Holding up this book up so Vladimir could see the title, she began softly singing "The Cossack's Lullaby."

Vladimir put his arm around her. "You do like my present, don't you? I'm very glad."

"The books are wonderful. The most wonderful possession I've ever owned. They represent so much of you, your work, your soul."

"I gladly present my soul to you." The words were soft and quickly spoken. She wasn't sure how seriously they were meant. She looked into his eyes, and there too, for a moment, she thought she detected a very sober look.

The look faded quickly as he rose. "Let me show you the rest of the apartment." He extended his hand to assist her.

All the rooms were deliciously bright and airy, just as Vladimir had described them. One detail bothered her a little: The dining table looked somewhat small and bare.

"The silver samovar Aunt Briullova gave us will fill up most of that table," Sofya laughed. "It's somewhere in one of those trunks, piled in the corner." While Vladimir paid the porter who had just finished carrying up the last of the bags, Sofya went to the largest trunk and started to undo the straps.

Presently Vladimir came to her aid. As he struggled with the strap, he said, "I'm looking forward to inviting my friends here. My bachelor quarters weren't quite appropriate for entertaining. As you probably remember." There was a twinkle in his eye. Only once had she ever been in his apartment.

"I remember." Sofya thought she could feel her cheeks reddening. She recalled only too well the disconcerting effect of that kiss, interrupted when her father had burst in. "The unpacking can wait." She spoke with resolve, and stepped back from the trunk and from her feelings. "I'd like to see my room now."

Looking up at her with mild surprise, Vladimir freed the final straps.

He stood very erect, apparently sensing her sudden serious mood. Then he led her down a small hall.

Passing the first closed door, Vladimir pointed. "I live over there. Don't hesitate to knock. Come visit whenever you like."

Sofya shrank back a little, involuntarily. He didn't seem to notice. "Here is your room." He opened the door and motioned for her to enter.

"I'd like to be alone." Sofya entered the room without really looking about her.

"Certainly. Whatever you wish." Vladimir stepped back. "I hope the room meets with your approval. Maria Bokova and I could only guess at your preferences."

"I'm sure I'll love the room," Sofya answered mechanically. Vladimir nodded his head, then left, closing the door after him.

Alone, Sofya surveyed what were to be her private quarters. The room was very large, dominated by a grand bed decorated with a huge, flower-patterned quilt. Next to the bed was the usual night table, holding a candle. A pitcher and an enameled washbasin stood on a delicately crocheted doily. A small dressing table, a writing table and chair stood against the opposite wall. A wooden hand mirror with an etching of the snow queen on the back and a silver comb and brush all lay side by side awaiting her evening toilet. A large walnut wardrobe stood with its intricately carved doors open, awaiting her clothes. The room had a high ceiling, a well-polished floor, and a large window admitting sunlight. More luxurious plants greeted her view.

As the details impressed themselves upon her she was speechless. This was much grander than she'd imagined. Everything was very tastefully arranged. She could never do such a magnificent job of decorating. The room had that delicate feminine touch that came so easily to Anyuta.

Abruptly Sofya thought of her sister, still imprisoned at Palibino. She pushed down a wave of guilt. She would not forget her sister.

In a dark mood, she sat at her own writing table, in her own room, and began a letter to Anyuta, reminding herself to include the poem she had begun the day of the wedding.

VLADIMIR, AFTER LISTENING for a few moments to the silence beyond Sofya's door, walked to the parlor. There with a sigh he collapsed onto the large divan. Hanging his still-booted feet over one arm of the new piece of furniture, he rested his head on the other. He stared blankly up at the shiny white, freshly painted ceiling.

He was exhausted. Since the wedding he had spent two very long days struggling to conduct himself in a manner consistent with Sofya's expectations. But her moods changed with a dizzying rapidity. One minute he was sure she cared for him, perhaps was beginning to think of him as something more than a liberator, a jar of preserves. The next minute she was distant and cold.

With difficulty Vladimir worked his feet out of his boots, which fell loudly, one at a time, to the polished floor. He waited expectantly for Sofya to investigate the noise. She didn't come.

He reminded himself of the agreement they had made. He intended to honor its terms. But the situation was more uncomfortable than he'd anticipated. There was dishonesty in the relationship he and Sofya presented to the world, and, more importantly, his relationship with her was now dishonest.

The change in his feelings had come gradually upon him. Still, there had been stages. The kiss in his apartment. The picnic at the lake in Palibino. Then at the wedding ceremony—

He twisted his ring round and round on his finger. Each rotation more clearly focused the burning image of her placing the gold band, stating before everyone that she loved him. The words were meaningless to her. But to him they had been as longed for as water to a man dying of thirst. Damn! He was a complete hypocrite! He presented an untrue face to the world and an untrue face to her.

He turned on his side, facing the back of the divan, staring at the swirling paisley pattern. He wanted to walk right into her room and tell her he loved her. But if he did, she'd leave him. Walk out of his life. She'd always think of him as a cunning fox, luring her into his lair with false promises. He couldn't risk that.

He turned again, looking down the hallway to the closed door of her room. His sister's room. Now he had a sister. He had known many a man whose sensual life was a thing apart from home and marriage. Life as a correspondent among hardened soldiers had taught him that there were women enough in any city ready and willing to please a man, for casual fun, or for money if it came to that. But, at this moment, he could not imagine himself leaving the apartment, alone, going to seek out such a woman.

He must live this lie within a lie. He must play the part he had accepted. He'd made a rather tragic mistake for a partner in a fictitious marriage. He'd fallen in love. Oh, blast! Forget the brother-sister nonsense. He was married.

But the time was out of joint, as Shakespeare said. Events were out of their natural order. A catastrophic occurrence had completely turned the layers of his life upside down, putting one stratum where another should be. This would never happen with rocks. In science everything is orderly and neat. Everything has its time.

He held his hand over his eyes. He'd have to court her now. Shower her with affection and wait for her to turn to him. Finally he'd win her totally. He must.

His eyes were closing, against his will. The ceremony, the journey, the sleeping in chairs were catching up with him. He wasn't the first to find himself in this situation. Other couples had started with fictitious marriages, found they loved each other, then gone on to live happy married lives. The Bokovs . . .

SOFYA AWOKE WITH a start. Lifting her head slightly, she struggled to orient herself. She was in her new apartment, in her new bedroom, where she had been writing a letter to Anyuta. She remembered putting her head down on her arm to rest for just a moment. She must have fallen asleep.

Sitting up straight, Sofya looked at the desktop. For a moment she saw the black silhouette of a man's face in an unformed blotch of ink, drying in the middle of the unfinished page.

She would have to recopy the letter. She stood up and stretched her aching body. She needed a glass of hot tea.

Entering the living room with the intention of unpacking the samovar, she found Vladimir sound asleep on the divan. Well, he'd certainly earned a rest.

As quietly as possible she began, for the first time in her life, to do her own unpacking. She thought she knew which trunk contained the samovar. A brief struggle with straps and lock released only a snowy flood of linen. Softly closing the lid of that trunk, she glanced over her shoulder. Vladimir still slept, breathing heavily.

Sofya started to work loose the straps of her second choice, and was soon rewarded by the sight of the box holding the samovar and its accessories.

After an awkward encounter with the large box, she placed the samovar on the table. Then she set out the matching silver-trimmed glass tumblers, arranging them neatly next to the samovar. After a moment's thought she visited her bedroom, returning with the pitcher of fresh water. Again searching the bottom of the box, she found a silver container of aromatic tea leaves. A hurried examination of the apartment's several fireplaces led to the discovery of charcoal and a friction lighter. Putting all these on the table, Sofya took a step back and admired her work. She was now ready to make tea. She'd seen the business done thousands of times; it couldn't be that hard.

She pushed up her sleeves and went to work, adding a bit of water and tea leaves to the small container atop the samovar. The rest of the water went into the large urn making up the bottom. Then she filled the central tube partially with charcoal, and after several attempts, got it burning.

Expectantly she waited to see if the tea would actually start to brew. The samovar grew hot, and gurgled. Presently, to Sofya's considerable satisfaction, the delicious smell of strong tea began to fill the air.

"Well done!" came a voice from the divan.

She turned around quickly. "How long have you been awake?"

"Long enough to see some of the contest."

"You were laughing at me. You monster!"

"Let's just say I am glad the housekeeper comes tomorrow."

"But you see how well I made the tea." Sofya's pride in the achievement was undiminished.

"If you set your mind to it, I'm sure you could do most anything." Vladimir, stretching, came to stand beside her. "My wife won't do servants' work. You will be a scholar."

"Of course." She poured two glasses of tea, and held one out to him.

THE MORNING AFTER her arrival in Petersburg, Sofya woke early. Today, days before the most optimistic estimate in her original plan, she was storming the citadel of learning. She was going to attend her very first university lecture!

She jumped from bed and started sorting through a still-packed trunk. Sofya chose a very simple dark woolen dress with detachable white collar and cuffs. Her dress was completely without adornment, as lacking in feminine allure as possible, a kind of nun's habit. She brushed her hair back behind her ears and off her forehead. If all went well, the male students would not notice her, and if they did notice, they'd find her presence innocuous and not inform the administration.

Ready as she could be, Sofya went into the living room. Vladimir, in a dark suit, was sitting on the divan.

"How do I look?" she asked.

"Perfect choice. You'll blend into the background and be practically invisible."

"This was my second choice. I didn't have time to provide myself with the proper attire for this occasion."

"And what would have been the proper attire?"

"I should have liked to dress in a man's suit, as the author George Sand often did. Then the students would have taken me as a very precocious, but acceptable young man. Why, in time they might even have invited me into one of their clubs."

"What a ridiculous thought!" Vladimir showed horror in his face. "If you were caught, you'd be prosecuted in criminal court, ridiculed and debased in the papers. All sympathy for your cause and for the cause of other women seeking education would be harmed." He paused, realizing he was being teased. "I seriously doubt you would have been able to carry out this deception for long."

"Well, it might have been fun for a while." She smiled.

Vladimir sighed, "This is all happening too fast." He sat on the edge of the divan, leaning forward nervously, his hands tightly clasped.

Sofya sat next to him. Controlling her own excitement, she spoke calmly. "Now is the time for action."

"Last night you endangered yourself unnecessarily." Vladimir was still looking at his hands. "You should not have signed Maria's petition requesting full university admission for women. If the political tides change, that signature could be enough to get you arrested."

"Certainly, there's risk. But I had to sign that petition. If there's any chance of bringing change here at home, I must try."

"And if the petition fails . . ."

"We'll go abroad, as we originally planned." She leaned back trying to relax. "I was overjoyed when Sechenov offered to let me attend his lectures."

"Sechenov's gallant offer made quite an impression on you and Maria." Vladimir rested his arm on the back of the divan. "The two of you fawned over the man as if he'd presented each of you with a fortune. Bokov and I were quite forgotten, even though we are risking ourselves in helping you."

"Really, Vladimir! How absurd for you to feel slighted."

They sat silently, waiting for the remaining members of her guard of honor.

Uncle Peter was the first to arrive. After a long searching look at the young couple, he visibly relaxed. He bestowed a vigorous hug on Vladimir, then kissed Sofya gently and lovingly, in a way that reminded her of childhood days.

"My dear Sonechka." He held her hands in his. "I was upset last night when I got your message. I couldn't understand why you wanted me here so early and so soon after your wedding. And now I find you wearing this dark dress. Whatever is wrong, my darling?"

"I need your help, Uncle," Sofya began. "I'm attending a lecture at the university today."

"You're joking?" Uncle looked from her to Vladimir. "First, women don't just walk into lecture halls. Second, you've said nothing about having a permit to attend. There's no way you could have a permit. Even God could not get the administrators to approval such a request in less than a month, if at all. Third, you're on your honeymoon! You've only been married three days." Turning to Vladimir: "Tell me, Vladimir, has she gone mad? Are you both mad?"

Vladimir shook his head. "Uncle, this is not how we planned on spending the first days of our marriage. But last evening, at dinner with friends, an opportunity arose that Sofya could not let slip. Sofya was telling Professor Sechenov how badly she wanted to study medicine. And he invited her to attend his physiology lectures for medical students, which start today at nine. She must start today, or she'll be behind the others in the class."

"And the university administration?"

"We're not waiting for their approval. Later, Sofya will go to other professors and get permission to attend lectures, and then she'll get approval from the administration. She'll apply for formal admission. She'll do whatever must be done to satisfy the requirements. But she must act now. Going though official channels may delay her for years. We decided to sneak her into the lecture hall. We need your help."

"You are both mad!" Uncle looked from one to the other of them. "We might all be arrested for trespassing."

"That, I'm afraid, is a possibility," Vladimir said calmly. "This is also an opportunity to demonstrate your support for Sofya. She's told me you greatly influenced her love of science."

After a moment of indecision, Uncle sighed loudly. "Oh, I'll help you, Sonechka." He smiled. "I was regretting I had missed your wedding. Now, you have honored me." He turned to Vladimir. "What a remarkable woman you've married, sir."

"I'm well aware of that."

"Is anyone else in on your plan?" Uncle asked.

"Doctor Bokov will be leading us," Vladimir said. "He knows the design of the university."

Bokov, when he finally arrived, wasted no time in briefing the others on the day's plan. Sofya was small, and it should be possible for the three big men to surround her, shielding her from chance observation by administrators. The guard would also discourage any gathering of curious students or impolite comments.

"Sofya," Bokov advised, "you must not respond to any comments directed at you. They may be crude in the extreme. Just stare straight ahead, ignore them."

Sofya was angered. The more she thought of such unpleasant possibilities, the more outraged she became. Until now, oppression had always worn a genteel face. What if she were actually called foul names? Or spat upon?

"You honestly believe a gathering of young men hoping to be doctors could act like such animals?" Vladimir took a few uneasy paces back and forth.

"They certainly can." Bokov nodded. "And we must be prepared to ignore them."

"If anyone so much as sneers at you, he'll lose some teeth." Vladimir slammed his fist into the palm of his hand.

"If you can't control yourself," Bokov's voice rose, "you must stay behind!"

"Vladimir, for goodness sake, get a grip on yourself," Sofya pleaded. "I need you with me."

"When we get there," Uncle Peter advised Vladimir, "keep your eyes on me or on Sofya. Don't look into any of their faces."

Vladimir was well in control of himself as they left the apartment.

At the Medical Academy the four of them walked steadily to the back of the building housing the physiology lecture hall. Bokov used a key given to him by Sechenov to open the rear door. Wordlessly the quartet climbed the echoing stairs, Bokov in front, next Vladimir and Sofya side by side, then Uncle Peter.

On the landing at the top of the stairs they paused. Bokov in a whisper explained, "We must time our entry to coincide almost exactly with the start of Sechenov's lecture."

Impatiently, silently, the four stood crowded together on the dark platform, behind them the steep, dark, dirty stairway, ahead the solid door with its tiny, clouded window. They waited for several minutes, Bokov staring in silence at his watch.

"Everyone, take a deep breath," Bokov directed them softly. "Now we go," he ordered, as he briskly opened the next door and led his companions into a hallway connecting the classrooms.

In another moment, they had entered a large lecture room. Bokov indicated seats high in the rear, where the men could more or less surround Sofya.

Climbing the many stairs, Sofya made a quick calculation based on the number of rows and seats in each. Her first classroom could accommodate more than two hundred students. Having reached what seemed the dizzying height of the room's top, Sofya sank into a chair, looked straight ahead, and willed herself to become invisible.

No doubt many of the other students now filing in took notice of her. But none raised an alarm. Without turning her head she observed that a few students were even choosing seats nearby, thereby shielding her more effectively from casual observation by any administrator who might happen to peer in from the corridor.

As most of the seats in the room filled up, Sofya allowed herself to look around more freely at her classmates. All of them, of course, were male. No! Over against the wall was another woman. An older woman with a yellow ribbon in her graying hair, part of the traditional midwife uniform.

Bokov leaned toward Sofya and whispered, "Experienced midwives, older women, are sometimes allowed to observe certain classes."

Unlike Sofya, the woman was quite alone. No men sat near her. She had no honor guard.

In another moment Sechenov appeared on the stage below. He wasted no time, but began his lecture with a brief introduction to physiology, explaining that he would be examining life processes from his own special area of interest, stimulus and response reactions. His paper of '63 would form the central material of the course. A copy of the paper would be made available for student study at the library and in his laboratory. Special emphasis would be placed on the workings of the eye.

Sofya leaned forward, resting her arms on the small desk in front of her, straining to hear each word. Soon, the room around her was forgotten. She saw only Sechenov and thought only of his words.

CHAPTER EIGHT

1868–69 Petersburg ☙ Winter Holidays

In the operating theater of the Medical-Surgical Academy, gaslights fought the encroaching gloom of the late winter afternoon, concentrating their glow in the center of the large room, where ordinarily the operating table would stand. Today no blood was to be shed, and where the patient would have lain there hung a human skeleton, bits of numbered paper fastened to various parts of his anatomy. On a table next to him were displayed a variety of specimens, dried bones in open boxes and preserved organs in pans. Three students remained in the concentric rows of seats. One was on the lowest tier, hunched over the rail that served as a convenient writing area, and a second in the high top row, near the tall rear windows now opaqued by December's early darkness. Hours ago, Sofya had chosen her seat near the aisle, at an intermediate altitude.

Sofya put down her pencil. She had racked her brain over whether the trapezoid or the trapezium bone had the outside position on a hand, and where the head of talus belonged. Of course, the head of talus belonged on the foot, but where exactly? And where was the pterion area? And why was it important? Her memory just wasn't working today. Had she been reassembling poor Koshchey the Deathless he probably would have had an arm where a leg should be. She placed her examination papers on the proctor's desk, then returned to her place, picked up the case that held her supplies of pencils, paper and class notes, and left the room. Her laced winter boots made a clicking noise on the polished parquet floor as she passed closed doors along the corridor.

When she entered the cloakroom, a young man whom she recognized as one of the students from her anatomy and physics classes was fumbling through the mass of nearly identical male coats to find his own. He smiled at her. She nodded an acknowledgment. The man had spoken briefly to her on one or two occasions. She had heard his family name, Zelensky, called out in class, but had never learned his full name.

Having found his greatcoat, Zelensky struggled into the heavy garment and began fastening the buttons. He whispered, "How did you do on that examination?"

"I'm a little upset with myself. I know I missed three questions, and perhaps one or two others are incorrect."

"Ninety-five out of hundred. That's a very good showing." He smiled. "I too feel I did rather well. Now, yesterday's physics examination is another story. That was a bear of a test."

"Oh? The problems were almost identical to the ones we did on the homework."

"I see. The physics examination was a snap and the anatomy a bit of a problem." He laughed. "Well, as the saying goes: One man's meat is another man's poison." When they approached the exit he held the massive wooden door open for her. "Will I be seeing you next semester?"

"Of course, I plan on returning after the holiday." *And I won't be sneaking in the back!* she thought to herself as she stepped through the open door onto the small stone porch leading to a flight of newly shoveled stairs.

The man was all smiles as he started down the steps beside her, his student's cap still in his hand. His black hair collected tiny diamonds of snow from the air. He bowed slightly from the waist. "Sofya Vasilievna, I wish you happy holidays and a wonderful vacation."

"Thank you," she answered, smiling. "A merry Christmas and happy New Year to you."

"Zelensky! Come on!" male voices were calling from the bottom of the stairs.

"Wait a minute, you silly fools!" he yelled toward the street, where seven of his companions were now piling into an open cab designed for four. Turning his head, he added in a low tone, "Some of us wanted to be certain you knew that we are proud to have you in our classes."

"Zelensky! We're dying of thirst!" came the boisterous shouts.

Sofya held out her hand. "Thank you. You have all been very courteous to me." As he clasped her gloved hand, she added, "Your friends are waiting."

Zelensky released her hand and bounded down the snowy stairs two at a time to his waiting cab, which surely would have room for eight.

It came as no surprise to learn that she had friends among the students, but it was good to hear the words. She negotiated the remainder of the slippery stairs. She had tried to minimize contact with her fellow students, not wanting to endanger them, should friendship with her be interpreted as an offense against the administration.

Avoiding a patch of shiny black ice, Sofya pondered how surprisingly pleasant she found male companionship, especially the company of Volodya. In the mornings she woke to the sound of his grumbling and ranting to himself over some political piece in the morning paper. In the evenings while she studied, he would fall asleep, a book open on his chest, a cup of tea on the floor beside him, his long legs hanging over the arm of the divan, his rhythmic breathing keeping her company. Impetuously, in the middle of the day, he would come home to present her with candy or some silly little children's toy that had caught his imagination. And sometimes, very late at night, when she was preparing for sleep, the sweet smell of inexpensive pipe tobacco crept under her bedroom door and kept her restlessly awake.

At the bottom of the stairs, she adjusted her soft white woolen scarf to keep the blowing snow from her face. She scolded herself for the sentimental images floating through her tired brain! She needed a good sisterly scolding. And Olga would certainly provide one.

She was headed for the apartment of Olga Vasilievna Chernyshevskaya. She was grateful to Olga for providing companionship during these last months in Petersburg, a time when Anyuta's absence weighed heavily on her. And now, while the male students like Zelensky celebrated the end of the term in the bars and cafés, she and Olga would share their thoughts and feelings over a cup of tea. She had two bits of news so joyful that she could hardly wait to tell her friend. Anyuta was arriving in Petersburg next week, hopefully never again to be imprisoned at Palibino. And, this evening, Uncle Peter had arranged a meeting for her with a famous mathematician. She could picture Olga's reactions: rejoicing over Anyuta's arrival, and teasing laughter over Sofya's joy in meeting a mathematician. An afternoon with the daring, outspoken Olga would provide a light and happy change from the seriousness of examinations, just the proper beginning for her vacation.

Sofya approached one of the cabs which stood under a lighted street lamp waiting for the emerging students. The driver, dozing with a blanket over his shoulders, his bearded chin tucked close to his chest, hadn't noticed her approach. The cab was identical to the one Zelensky had boarded. The horse snorted vapor into the cold air, ready to bear his load alone. At least he would not be pulling the weight of eight young men. She liked the red ribbons and tiny bells that were tied festively on the front of the sleigh. She would fly over the snowy streets with only the sound of the bells, summer's infernal racket of wheels on stones or wood replaced with the near silent swish of the sleigh's runners. The long, dark, cold nights could be forgiven to a season that offered the delights of sleigh rides and rest from work.

She was about to nudge the driver's elbow, when she heard, "Excuse me." The masculine voice was behind her, not loud, but steady and friendly. "You are Sofya Vasilievna Kovalevskaya?"

The speaker was a tall, handsome man, wearing a somewhat worn, but nicely cut overcoat of a European style. He stood close to her smiling in a kindly way, holding a black top hat in his hands. His hair was a pleasant shade of brown with strong highlights of red.

Nodding an affirmative to his question, she scrutinized the man. He certainly was not dressed as a messenger, or anything of that sort. Could he be someone she had met at one of Vladimir's business gatherings? There was definitely something familiar about his smile.

In answer to her inquiring look, the man introduced himself. "I am Aleksander Onufrievich Kovalevsky, Vladimir's brother."

"Ah?"

Smiling, the man went on, "Vladimir asked me to meet you. He's at the museum now. We'll pick him up on our way to your apartment. Vladimir devised this plan, after my wife and I arrived. You already had left for classes."

A cold wind was blowing snow into her face. The man before her certainly looked enough like Vladimir to be his brother. He was big boned, his hands large, his blue eyes sad and intelligent. A slight difference in the quality of the facial features, the straighter, narrower nose, the slightly greater space between the eyes, the less elevated forehead, made this man compellingly handsome, a description she would not apply to Vladimir's rugged, masculine look.

"Please, believe me!" The stranger took a step closer. His voice was gentle, almost laughing. "My wife and daughter and I arrived unexpectedly, late this morning, because of a last-minute change in our travel arrangements. We are on our way to Kazan, where I have an appointment at the university. Surely Vladimir read you my letter telling about that?"

Sofya still hesitated. His facts were correct, his explanation plausible.

The man continued, "We hadn't expected to come through the city, but we detoured at the last moment. My new employer asked me to confer with some Petersburg biologists on a question concerning our researches in embryology. I'll show you my passport, if you like."

"That won't be necessary," Sofya responded, now convinced the man was Vladimir's brother. "I have another engagement. I will need to send a message canceling," she added, beginning to shiver in the cold.

"Of course," Aleksander pleasantly agreed. "Please, get into the cab, out of the wind. And write your note. I'll fetch a messenger from the school office."

Sofya did as Aleksander advised, nestling her feet into the straw on the cab's floor and accepting the lap blanket the driver offered. When a young messenger boy appeared, she gave him a note on which she had written the directions. From the way the young boy squinted at the paper, Sofya realized he could not read. She slowly repeated the written directions aloud, as she drew a few coins from her case.

"I've already paid." Aleksander motioned the boy on his errand.

Aleksander settled on the seat across from her and ordered the driver to proceed to the museum.

As soon as they were under way, Vladimir's brother leaned forward and spoke in a whisper. "I had no idea to whom you were sending a message." The good-natured smile had disappeared. "I would have been more cautious about using a university messenger had I realized your friend was Chernyshevskaya."

"Oh?"

"Yes." Aleksander's voice was stern. "The university would not look kindly on your association with the wife of an exiled author. Your friend-ship with Chernyshevskaya could be very dangerous. The authorities are suspicious of anyone with connections to her or her husband."

"I do not consult the police when choosing my friends," Sofya searched the man's eyes for the sympathy she had a right to expect from Vladimir's brother.

Aleksander returned her scrutiny. "You are far too reckless!" Then he softened his reprimand. "But, that makes you a match to my brother. I suspect your children will be quite a handful. If fortune smiles, they will favor their mother in appearance."

Sofya was startled by his mention of children. Evidently Aleksander was not aware of the nature of her arrangement. She and Vladimir would have to wear their uncomfortable masks of pretense. Silently she cursed Vladimir, even while trying to find some logic to the position he had taken. Sofya had no doubt that Vladimir loved and admired his brother, nor that the brothers were confidants on all levels. From every-thing Vladimir said about Aleksander, the man had proven by his life choices that he was one of their circle. So, why hadn't Vladimir confided the most important aspect of his life to his own brother? At times, there was simply no understanding Vladimir's behavior. She felt her cheeks growing warm with suppressed anger.

Aleksander must have noticed her coloring. "If I've offended you with my scolding or with my bold talk of children, I ask your forgiveness. My only excuse is that Vladimir has written me so much about you, that I feel we are already close friends."

"You are forgiven." She forced another wave of anger back from her voice. There was no way to explain that it would take much more than the mere mention of children to embarrass her. She was not angry with him, but with Vladimir.

The cab made the turn onto University Embankment. A cold wind blew across the frozen Neva. Aleksander adjusted his position, pulling his coat a little more closely around himself and raising the collar. "Vladimir's been bragging about you. He says you've been working very hard and successfully during your first term at university. But that you've been wavering lately as to the direction of your studies."

Sofya was still fuming. Vladimir should have clarified their relationship. She considered telling Aleksander herself, casually adding the fact to her explanation of her educational plans. No, it was Vladimir's place to tell his brother.

The Neva wind nipped at her exposed forehead. She pulled her scarf over her mouth to warm the air before she spoke. "I began my studies thinking I wanted to be a physician, like Bokova, Suslova and the other women who've returned from abroad with their medical degrees. But lately, I've been hesitant. I just don't feel an attraction to the necessary studies."

Aleksander gave up trying to hold on to his top hat in the wind and placed it on the seat beside him. Smoothing his hair, he continued, "You might consider biological research. We'd love to have someone of your quality working with us, searching out evidence for evolution."

"I'll give it some thought."

Aleksander nodded silently. "Whatever direction you choose, the fact that you are married will be a great help, not only here in Russia, but also abroad. It's incredible how many cruel gossips inhabit the halls of academia. Tatyana could tell you some unpleasant stories. Many of my colleagues scorn my relationship with Tatyana, although it is more honest and just than many of them have in their very traditional marriages."

Sofya envied and admired the man's courageous honesty, which shone so vividly against her own false position.

Seeming not to notice her discomfort, Aleksander continued, "Tatyana and I are very happy. She's the perfect woman for me. Quiet, intelligent, and ready to provide me with the kind, warm, home atmosphere I need to do my best scientific work. With the new family, I was very happy to get an offer from Kazan University. I didn't want to accept a position abroad. Somehow, even with all the problems here in Russia, Tatyana and I wanted to raise our Olga in her homeland."

The cab slowed to a stop before the Academy of Sciences. "I don't see Vladimir. We'll have to fetch him from the workroom where I left him." Aleksander helped her from the cab.

As Aleksander directed the cabby to wait for them, Sofya watched a speeding sleigh filled with laughing students. "Look!" Sofya pointed out toward the frozen Neva. "That sleigh is being pulled by reindeer! The Lapps have arrived from Finland for the holiday celebrations."

Aleksander stared at the animal skin tents set up on the vast expanse of ice. Festive sleighs pulled by the exotic animals were for hire. "I wish Tatyana and I were staying longer. She's never ridden behind a reindeer. She'd love an evening excursion with the view of all the magnificent buildings along the shore ablaze with lights."

"When are you leaving?" Sofya asked as they approached the entry of the massive brick building.

"In the morning." Aleksander turned from her and motioned to a uniformed guard. After a brief exchange, the guard led them down a narrow flight of marble stairs to the right of the main entrance. The slippery surface made Aleksander's gentle grip on her elbow welcome. A dark corridor of rooms stretched before them.

A sudden groaning of wood signaled a door opening, a voice called down the corridor, "So! Taking liberties with a pretty young girl. And you, a new father! Sasha, you surprise me." Vladimir's cheery, teasing tone filled the dark corridor. "I'll see these two don't get into trouble, Gleb. We'll be leaving shortly." Vladimir directed his words to the guard.

"Please, don't be too late tonight, sir. There's a meeting of the members this evening. This room will have to be cleaned before they arrive. Just in case one of them takes it into their head to come down here."

"We'll be gone with plenty of time to spare," Vladimir assured the nervous looking man in the blue uniform. Vladimir motioned Aleksander and Sofya forward into a large workroom, bright with gas and oil lamps.

When they had entered, Vladimir stood before Sofya. "Hello, my dear," he said as he gently pushed her scarf away from her face to quickly, roguishly kiss her on the mouth.

"And now who's taking liberties in a public place?" Aleksander's eyes were glittering with a playful smile.

Sofya felt herself blushing hotly. She stared at Vladimir in reprimand. He turned his face so only she could see and smiled innocently as if to explain that the kiss was part of the playacting.

"Sasha." Vladimir helped Sofya with her coat. "You should have insisted on a closed cab. Sofya's shoulders are covered with snow. Her cheeks are red from the cold."

"Sofya made the selection. And the choice was wonderful. The views are much better from the open vehicle."

"If it's views you're after, in my opinion, this little cellar of a room has a view unparalleled. A view into the past." He gestured toward a broad wooden table, its slanting surface divided into compartments. "Behold the remains of an ancient animal."

Aleksander and Sofya stepped closer. "Don't touch, please," Vladimir cautioned. "These specimens are not yet ready for visitors." His enthusiasm was quite evident. "I can hardly go a day without visiting this hallowed place."

Sofya looked down at the large, earth-darkened bones, sorted by their type into compartments of the table. She had seen enough of bones today. Her attention was drawn to an intense circular flame emanating from an oil lamp of a type she'd seen in a watchmaker's shop. The lamp was securely fastened to one corner of a large draftsman's desk over which it cast a light many times brighter than any ordinary lamp. She wandered to the desk and looked casually through the papers spread out on the surface.

From time to time she turned her attention to the brothers who remained at the specimen table, deep in scientific discussion. They were an impressive pair, intellectually and physically. She definitely liked Aleksander and his gentle, forthright, honest manner. And as for Vladimir and his bold ways, wild enthusiasms and incomprehensible actions that could drive her to distraction, well, she liked him, too. Perhaps too much. She quickly ran her tongue over her lips, hoping to wipe away the last feeling of his kiss.

Sofya half-listened to the men's conversation, half looked at the sketches. The sketches were very good, and the initials in the corner identified them as Vladimir's work. Vladimir was asking his brother, "You must have heard of the new exhibit up in the main hall, the skeleton of the strange creature from the past?"

"Yes, I've heard it's something like a giant reptile."

Vladimir nodded eagerly. "I was fascinated. I spent hours sketching the animal's bones. First individually, and then together, as the scientists were arranging them. The museum liked my work and has allowed me access to the geologists' field collections. I'm sketching the bones before they're extricated from the surrounding rock, and generally helping with the preparation efforts. I keep coming back to the idea that these ancient bones will play a vital part in verifying Darwin's theories. But there are so many pieces to this giant puzzle! The so-called experts are in such disagreement! The little physical evidence available from the far past is in complete disarray."

"And you want to put some of the puzzle pieces together?" Aleksander asked.

"I certainly do," Vladimir answered thoughtfully. "I'm here every moment I can get away from my publishing business."

"Why not try your hand at paleontology?" Aleksander encouraged. "I mean seriously. Really study the subject formally. Perhaps, even return to the classroom."

Vladimir smiled. "You know, brother, I've been asking myself the very same question."

Vladimir put on his tattered overcoat, then held Sofya's coat for her. As she put on the garment, he slid his arm protectively around her. "Shall we go?"

COLD, CLEAR, CALM AIR surrounded the trio as they left the Academy. Their waiting cab was swept clean of snow; blankets neatly covered the seats. Sofya settled next to Vladimir; his arm slid around her shoulders. Across the space, Vladimir began to question Aleksander on the particulars of his new position at Kazan. The cab started gently forward. The men's voices faded as Sofya searched the night sky. She sought and found the outstretched limbs of her favorite winter constellation, Orion.

She felt Vladimir grip her gently, his voice rousing her from stargazing. "We'll have a grand evening, just the family, won't we Sofya?"

Startled for a moment, she stared blankly at him.

"My dear, you'll meet your wonderful new niece. Fortunately, she favors her mother." Vladimir now turned to his brother, as if seeking verification for what he was about to say. "Tatyana let me hold the baby. Sofya, I'm a regular old uncle."

"And when the baby started to cry," the new father remarked dryly, "you were quick to give my little darling back to Tanya."

Sofya, fully aware, interrupted. "I'm terribly sorry. I won't be able to be with you this evening."

Vladimir abruptly withdrew his arm from around her. "Why?" Suddenly his voice was grimly serious.

"This evening, Uncle Peter and I are attending a lecture and discussion session at Professor Chebyshev's apartment."

"You will excuse yourself to Uncle Peter," Vladimir said sternly.

Sofya glared at Vladimir. Thinking it better not to say aloud the words that flashed through her brain, she instead turned to Aleksander. "These sessions are held only once a month. The attendees form a kind of club or association. All have a strong interest in mathematics, but none is a professional mathematician. They come to hear Chebyshev. The name is familiar to you?"

"Surely to all Russian scientists and to many scientists abroad." Aleksander sounded impressed. "One doesn't have to be a mathematician to have heard of Pafnuty Lvovich Chebyshev, and his outstanding contributions to number theory."

Sofya continued, "Uncle Peter's been attending the meetings for years. He says there has never been a woman present."

"Go next month," Vladimir insisted firmly. "Skip tonight's meeting."

"Nonsense," Aleksander responded. "Sofya must attend the lecture."

Sofya turned to Vladimir. "Uncle Peter's already told Chebyshev about me, about my interest in mathematics. And that I'll be coming this evening. Don't you see? If I choose to attend a family gathering instead, Chebyshev will think I'm not a serious student."

"Of course," Aleksander assured her, "you must go."

Vladimir leaned back in his seat. "Of course, you must go," he echoed angrily. "Your work first. Always your work comes first."

Sofya stared at people passing on the street. She tried desperately to keep her anger suppressed. Her work *did* come first. Vladimir had agreed to this arrangement.

Aleksander said softly, "Brother, don't ruin the time we have together by being angry with your Sofya. She must tend to her work, as I to mine by leaving tomorrow. And as you will need to tend to yours."

"My work?" Vladimir spoke sharply and with resentment. "Yes, my work. Unpaid translator bills, unpaid printer bills, low sales reports."

"And nothing else?" Sofya's anger weakened with the realization of the pain in Vladimir's voice. "Your new work. Your scientific work."

Aleksander leaned across the space between them and touched his brother's arm. "Vladimir, you've a marvelous start on paleontological work. You have direction now and someone to help you keep to the course."

Vladimir did not respond. He turned his face toward the street, sat rigidly, his hands clasped tightly together. During the remainder of the ride to the apartment, Sofya and Aleksander exchanged strained comments. Vladimir sat silently, unresponsively, his head turned from her.

At the apartment, Aleksander once more attempted to rouse Vladimir from his dark mood. "Brother, please, don't sulk. Sofya will dine with us. We'll get to know each other. Vladimir, we have the rest of our lives together, as a family."

Sofya dutifully admired the new baby. Tatyana spoke animatedly of her plans for their new apartment in Kazan. Sofya watched in wonder as Tatyana's light talk of trivialities gently coaxed Vladimir from his silence.

HOLDING TIGHTLY TO Uncle Peter's arm, Sofya stopped at the threshold of the large living room, converted for the evening into a lecture hall. At the far end a dining table had been pressed into service as a lectern, behind which a three-legged wooden easel supported a large tablet of blank paper and a piece of drawing charcoal, one end neatly wrapped in cloth. Most of the floor space was taken up by rows of unmatched chairs.

The front two rows were nearly filled by older men, dressed fashionably in suits cut in the European style, or in the distinctive attire of high-ranking retired military. Plenty of seats were still available in the rear, among a scattering of young men wearing university uniforms.

As Sofya came in, heads turned and the murmur of voices stopped for a moment. The sensation of everyone staring at her was becoming all too familiar. Uncle Peter gently patted her arm and announced, "Gentlemen, my niece, Sofya Vasilievna Kovalevskaya. She shares our interest in mathematics." Holding his head high, visibly beaming with pride, he escorted her into the room.

Sofya released her hold on Uncle's arm, straightened her back, and walked proudly beside him. "How different and how much more pleasant," she thought, "than sneaking anonymously into the lecture hall last fall. It seems I am making progress."

Sofya's impression was confirmed when she realized that the two vacant seats in the front row evidently had been saved for them. Only when she was seated did the voices in the room resume the murmur of casual conversation.

She sat erect, gazing straight ahead, hands folded in her lap. Uncle Peter was speaking with the older man to his left. Sofya heard her name mentioned but made no effort to join the conversation.

"Good evening, Sofya Vasilievna." The familiar voice from the right was startling. Sofya turned to look into the beaming face of Stranno-liubsky, her friend and tutor.

"Aleksander Nikolayevich! It is you!" she exclaimed with pleasure. "I didn't recognize you, this is the first time I've seen you in your naval uniform." Strannoliubsky looked quite dashing in the blue jacket and trousers of a Petersburg Naval Academy instructor.

"I knew you would be here." He lowered his voice so only she could hear. "Relax and enjoy the companionship. I'm certain that everyone here is very pleased you came and very anxious to speak to you."

Before she could respond, the room filled with polite applause. Professor Pafnuty Lvovich Chebyshev, gray-bearded and aristocratic in appearance, about fifty years of age, had appeared behind the dining table. He smiled to acknowledge the applause, then held up one hand for silence.

"Gentlemen. Tonight I perceive a welcome variation among the usual ranks of bewhiskered faces." He nodded to Sofya. "I am sure I speak for everyone in welcoming you, and hoping you will enjoy the evening."

Sofya responded with a soft "Thank you." The professor's warm smile did make her feel welcome.

"And now, let us proceed with tonight's discussion." With a showman's gesture the professor extracted from pockets of his vest a small toy gyroscope and its stand. Holding up the objects for the inspection of his audience, he acknowledged with a twinkle their murmur of interest.

Placing the stand on the table, Chebyshev carefully held the gyroscope balanced upon the stand, and gave a sharp, practiced pull upon the starting string to energize the toplike toy.

For a moment there was silence in the room, save for the buzzing whir of the small metallic spinner, blurred with speed, protected for the moment against the unbalancing pull of gravity.

Chebyshev began in a low voice. "One of the most fascinating motions in the physical world, the rotation of a rigid body about a fixed point. Special cases of this motion are observable not only in tops, but in pendulums, planets and other heavenly bodies."

The professor turned to the easel behind him. Along the paper's upper edge he quickly sketched small representations of the items he had mentioned.

When he turned back to the listeners, the top was slowing in its spin, wobbling precariously. Sofya stared with fascination; yes, a child's toy, but now she could see that it might take the eyes of genius to perceive its implications.

The top was oscillating, leaning farther and farther toward the table with each wobble, but still it did not fall. Then, with a lightning grab, Chebyshev saved the spinning object just as it was about to topple.

Silently he again turned to the easel, sketched a slightly tilted, oddly shaped figure resting on a pedestal. The point at which the object rested on the pedestal was darkened.

Sofya leaned forward, watching ideas take form. Through the darkened point the mathematician drew a system of axes: three lines, the first straight up and down along the line of the pedestal, one horizontal to the pedestal and passing through the darkened point, a third line that one could imagine as coming out of the paper into the space of the room.

Chebyshev turned back to the group. "I have drawn the fixed axes for this rotation. Another system of axes can be drawn having its origin within the tilting figure." Here he lightly sketched in the second set of axes. "When the volume, density, and acceleration forces on the top are known, equations can be formulated that will predict the position of the top at a given moment in the spin. Note that no outside forces, except gravity, are acting upon the body once the motion is begun. Unlike the problems we touched on at our last meeting."

Strannoliubsky whispered in her ear, "That was the two body problem."

Sofya, annoyed at the interruption, nodded without taking her eyes from Chebyshev.

Tearing a sheet from the paper tablet, Chebyshev was now writing out six equations, explaining as he used up his charcoal. Many of the symbols were known to Sofya from her study of calculus. She struggled now to relate them to distances and time, and then to the motion of the top.

Chebyshev was continuing. "Just a little more than a century ago, in 1765 to be exact, Leonard Euler first formulated these equations. By choosing certain initial conditions for the variables, he was able to solve these extraordinarily complex equations for that particular case." Chebyshev quickly wrote Euler's initial values next to the equations. "A second way of looking at the problem was devised by Joseph Lagrange in 1815. He described the problem with equations representing the kinetic and potential energy within the system. By taking this approach, he was able to formulate and solve equations for the motion of a top with its center of inertia not on the point of rotation."

More paper and more charcoal produced a picture of a second top. This time a point within the top was darkened.

"These two special cases cover the most important physical applications of these equations. But, there may be more solutions." The excitement in Chebyshev's voice was controlled, but undeniable. Into Sofya's mind there drifted the image of a pirate speaking about buried treasure.

Eyes gleaming, the lecturer continued, "Ten years ago, the Prussian Academy of Sciences offered a substantial prize to the mathematician who could provide a general solution to the problem of determining the position of the spinning object at any time, or who could contribute substantially to the solving of these, or similar equations. No mathematician was able to claim the prize. But many great minds have been intrigued by the problem and have uncovered, from time to time, bits and pieces of the puzzle. The elusive solution has so intrigued the mathematical community that it has come to be known as the Mathematical Mermaid."

The word Mermaid seemed to have broken a spell of absolute silence that had come over the audience. The listeners were nodding to each other and making hushed comments. Sofya, looking about her, caught an impression of reverent, cheerful appreciation, though not of understanding.

Chebyshev evidently received the same impression. "But I am speaking of things much too complex! Forgive me, my own fascination sometimes overcomes me. I have been hunting the Mermaid with great enjoyment, but, I must admit, without success." He flushed lightly. "As I mentioned, the mathematical description of the rotation of a rigid body occupied the mind of one of the greatest mathematicians who ever lived, Leonard Euler. Who, as we all probably know, made his home here in Petersburg. Tonight I will touch on some of the works of this great man, this man who adopted our city as his home."

As the lecture continued, easing down into less rarefied levels of thought, Sofya ceased to follow. The problem on the easel behind the speaker still held her attention. So the Mermaid hides in the sea of symbols, does she? We have here a mathematical version of the fairy tales' *rusalka*. The seductive creature, half-woman, half-fish, wronged in life by men, taking her revenge on men with her enchanting spirit. In the tales, the unfortunate women who in desperation over their fate had taken their own lives were not allowed into heaven, but were banished to the role of temptress mermaid.

In Sofya's head these fairy-tale images came spinning into conflict with the physical and mathematical symbols of conscious thought. Equations, motion, distance, energies, time and fairy tales twisted and twined and summed together, seeking to achieve harmony . . .

With a start, Sofya found herself back in the real world. Someone was touching her arm. Chebyshev had come around from behind his table; men were getting to their feet, forming little knots of conversation.

"Daydreaming, Sofya Vasilievna?" Strannoliubsky's voice conveyed a playful reprimand. "It appeared that Chebyshev lost you rather early in the lecture."

"Oh?"

"I shouldn't worry about it. All that talk about the equations for rotating motion was over everyone's head. You should have been paying more attention, you would have enjoyed the later part of the lecture. Chebyshev explained Euler's introduction of the notations used in today's mathematics. I hadn't realized that the use of the symbols e, pi, and i are largely Euler's doing."

Sofya nodded slowly. "I was only half listening toward the end. But it wasn't because I had given up. It's precisely the first part of the lecture that caught my imagination. Can we go over the equations at our next lesson?"

Strannoliubsky stared at her. His faint look of condescension was replaced by something else, less friendly: *Are you serious, young woman?* After a moment he said aloud, "I can't help you. Problems like these . . ." He made a gesture of inadequacy.

Sofya, getting to her feet, stood looking down at him as if she had never seen him before.

"Don't discourage the lady," Chebyshev reprimanded Strannoliubsky jovially. Then he addressed Sofya. "The Mermaid has caught your attention?"

"My imagination, at least. I'm afraid I wasn't able to follow very much of what you wrote on the board. I've an introduction to differentials and some physics. Just enough to make the work you put on the board intriguing . . ." Sofya felt the grip of frustration and impatience. The taunting *rusalka* could not be *that* far out of reach.

The mathematician was gazing at her keenly. "Imagination is the most vital ingredient in solving problems. Don't be discouraged by the rest. In time, you can acquire the skills, if the problems fascinate you strongly." He paused. "Perhaps you would like to examine the work of the masters on this problem. Don't be discouraged if you don't understand very much at first. Look at the outline of the work. I'll loan you some books. Drop in at my apartment tomorrow. We'll talk mathematics."

"Thank you," Sofya managed to say. Overwhelmed by the attention and kindness of the master. "Thank you very much."

"Good. See you then." Chebyshev smiled warmly at her, then nodded to Strannoliubsky and to Uncle Peter before moving away to speak to others.

"Well," Uncle Peter exclaimed, "You've made quite an impression. In all the times I've been to these affairs, I haven't seen Chebyshev invite anyone to a private session."

CHAPTER NINE

1869 Petersburg   ✕   Winter Holidays

In the crook of Vladimir's arm rested a bottle of fine French champagne, wrapped almost as if it were an infant. This evening, he and Sofya were going to enjoy their own private celebration. In truth, he already had made a small start on the celebration. At the store where he purchased the wine, he had sampled the excellent lemon vodka, just enough to warm him on the long walk home.

Striding along, snow crunching under his boots, Vladimir indulged in his favorite dream. After a few short years he would be a professor of geology. Sofya would busy herself teaching or assisting some research mathematician like Chebyshev. Their academic incomes would be comfortably augmented with publishing profits, the details of the business managed by a capable assistant. Someone like the intelligent bookstore manager Vasily Evdokimov would do fine. Then he and Sofya would start a family.

He stopped. He'd walked past his apartment building! Startled by the extent of his absentmindedness, he retraced his last steps. Now the doorman was looking at him strangely, evidently thinking him drunk for his distracted behavior. Vladimir gave the man a holiday greeting and patted him reassuringly on the arm.

As he hurried up the stairs, leaving in his wake small puddles of melting snow, he remembered keenly the first time he had raced up these stairs, with Sofya just ahead of him.

Hurriedly he unlocked the door and entered. Sofya called from another room, "Vladimir, you're home early! Good!"

"Be right there," he called back happily, struggling to remove hat, scarf, and coat without setting down the bottle of champagne. Leaving outer garments in disarray on the hall table, he entered the living area.

Sofya was cozily curled on the divan, a pile of books nestled around her. "I was a little lonely," she commented, without looking up from her book.

"Well, that's a good sign."

"What?"

"Nothing. Just saying that I'm glad you're ready for a little diversion." He sat in the chair across from her, the wine bottle nestled in a cushion next to him, and struggled to remove one of his overshoes. "We're going to have a celebration."

"Tonight?" She looked up, and in a smooth motion uncurled herself. The coverlet still hid her legs and feet. Around her shoulders a white knit shawl hung loosely over a brown blouse. Her cheeks were a deep rose, matching her full lips. Her dark tapering brows were drawn together in a charming look of blended interest and doubt. Her eyes danced with delight.

"Tonight," Vladimir assured her. "A small party for just the two of us, before the holiday season begins." Both overshoes off at last, Vladimir held up the champagne bottle, then collapsed back into his chair. His stockinged feet encountered a fresh puddle of melted snow, and he moved to the edge of the divan, displacing some of her novels to the floor.

"There are times when you have some wonderful ideas, Vladimir." Sofya patted his wet stockinged foot, which had somehow come up onto the divan. She drew her own covered feet up close.

Vladimir shifted position, leaned back, his arm now stretched out behind Sofya. His wet stockings were becoming more uncomfortable. He considered taking them off, but that would involve getting up, and Sofya was now resting her head gently against his arm.

"Julia's in town." Sofya turned her face toward him. He felt her breath on his cold cheeks.

"Who?" His fingers toyed with the fringe on Sofya's shawl.

"You haven't met her. She lives just outside Moscow, and only comes to Petersburg for the holidays. She's quite a brilliant woman. But her chances for an education are slim. She's . . ."

He gently placed his finger on her lips, ending what would certainly have been a long exposition of her friend's difficulties. He tightened his arm around Sofya's shoulders. "I said that today you and I should have a party. A holiday just for us." Her eyes were very close to his, and they were shining with a gleam of questioning wonder. "I've a surprise for you."

"Besides the champagne? You'll spoil me with all your presents." Laughing, Sofya sat up straight in childlike anticipation, shrugging his arm away.

"Am I really spoiling you?" Vladimir smiled. "I hadn't noticed. Perhaps I am. Hmm. I seem to remember two large bouquets of orange blossoms appearing on October 15th. Not at all easily obtained that time of year, I might add. On November 15th, a trip to the theater to see Ostrovsky's new play, followed by a rather elegant dinner. And today . . ." From his jacket pocket he pulled a small box with a bright red bow.

"French sweets! Vladimir, thank you." She paused for a moment. Looked him in the eyes. "They're very expensive." But the look of reprimand lasted for only a second. "I love them!" She had already opened the box and was hesitating over her first selection. She popped a candy into her mouth. He watched her face as she delighted in the melting chocolate. Then, as if her memory had been somehow enhanced by the sweet, she exclaimed, "Oh, Vladimir! I know! Today is December 15th!" Impulsively she threw her arms around his neck and kissed his cheek. "It's been three months since you liberated me."

"It's been three months since our wedding," he gently corrected.

"Yes, three wonderful months." She leaned back smiling. Her hands had remained around his neck. "I've never been happier." His arms had somehow come to be around her waist. He was hypnotized by her shining eyes. A tiny stain of chocolate remained at one corner of her mouth. By some magic, his lips found hers.

. . . her hands were pushing gently on his chest. Reluctantly he freed her lips. She was flushed. "Volodya." Her speaking his name in that breathless way was like a caress. He moved toward her again, but she slipped from his embrace.

She was standing. He grasped her wrist. Her shawl had fallen across the place where she had been sitting. The blanket that had covered her knees was on the floor. He gently tried to pull her back to the divan. She would not be pulled. She struggled hard enough to free herself from his grip, then stumbled to get away from the blanket which had become twisted around her feet. She moved to the chair across from him.

He watched her slow, silent, calculated motion as she placed the champagne bottle on the floor, the small open box of candy next to it. Her face was flushed and he could see and hear her labored breathing. Restraint and control, he thought. Remarkably strong for a woman of eighteen years.

Hesitantly he proceeded. "We could be much happier, Sofya." Vladimir wondered if his voice was even audible to her, for she gave no sign that she had heard. Her eyes were on her hands, folded tightly in her lap.

He went on, "There are moments, like this last one, when I'm sure you want me to be more than a friend."

Still no reaction. He searched her face for some recognition of the truth he had just stated.

At last she spoke. "We have an agreement." Her voice was soft, controlled. "You are to be my friend, my liberator, and my . . ."

"Don't say it, damn it! I'm not your brother! I'm not just a 'jar of preserves'! I'm a man!" He struggled for control of his feelings. "And there must be times you want, need, more than a friend. More than a brother."

"I admit, once or twice I may have experienced a momentary lapse. We're alone together so much of the time." Her voice was barely audible, but coldly controlled. At last she looked up at him directly. "We're fond of each other. Like anyone else, we're vulnerable to certain emotions and attractions. And we're both feeling the strain of keeping up the appearance of a marriage, when in fact . . ." She didn't complete her sentence.

"Excuse me!" He felt anger glowing in his face. "But I think you are tragically misjudging your own feelings. You are being dishonest, not only with me, but with yourself. And you're justifying it with some kind of contorted argument which passes in your mind as logic." Struggling to control an outburst of accusatory remarks, Vladimir allowed an unpremeditated question to escape his lips. A question he had been afraid to ask. "Do you want me to leave? If, as you claim, our 'lapses' are due only to our spending too much time together, then perhaps I should move, live in another apartment, another city, another country even? I could disappear from your life. You have a good start on your education and freedom. I'd give you full control of your passport and papers."

"*No!*" The answer burst from Sofya almost before he had stopped speaking. "I couldn't manage without you. Nor you without me. Good Lord, without our arrangement, you'd get yourself into some emotional muddle that would impossibly complicate your life. We're going to get an education, both of us, together. We're not going to be sidetracked by momentary impulses." She was up from the chair, skirts swishing as she nervously paced the floor.

Suddenly she sat beside him. Her hands reached for his and held them. "We've made a plan for our futures. The plan will bring us what we really want, if we persevere!"

At the moment he could feel nothing but numbness, weariness, defeat. Drawing one hand from hers, he pushed the dark curl back to its place behind her ear. "We'll go on together."

"Under the conditions agreed and as planned?" Her face turned up to him.

He couldn't answer. When she looked at him with those soft, pleading eyes so full of innocence, his anger melted. In a soft voice he reassured her, as he would a child: "Everything will be as we agreed. Just as you wish. Don't worry, my little sparrow."

Standing up, he pulled on his overshoes again and without looking back went to the entrance hall. He put on his coat and hat. He needed more than chocolate now, and something stronger than champagne to drink. His hands were shaking as he opened the door. He had made a start at confronting their situation honestly. He would not reproach himself as a total hypocrite. He would try again to renegotiate their arrangement. He knew that despite his offer, he would never have had the courage to leave her forever. He cursed his weakness, and the fact that he had allowed this child to assume control over his soul. Mixed with these feelings was an urge, absolutely irrational, to bless the goodness of a God who had granted him the light of this woman in his life.

THE DOOR OF THE apartment slammed shut.

Frozen with disbelief, Sofya sat motionless, holding tight to the back of the divan. The heavy wooden door appeared to shimmer as she stared through her tears. He had fled, not to his room or behind one of his books or papers, but further than ever before. He was a horrid, cowardly man.

She hid her face on her arm and sobbed. He might never return. She'd be alone, perhaps forever. She couldn't stop her sobbing. Her throat ached with the pain.

She had no idea how much time had passed, when she lifted her wet face from her now equally wet sleeve. All she knew was that she must blow her nose.

With a sigh, and feeling somewhat better for the emotional release, Sofya rose from the divan and started toward her room. She needed a handkerchief, and to change her blouse whose wet sleeve was sticking to her arm. Kicking aside the blanket that was on the floor, her bare foot touched a cold wetness. With a start she realized that she'd stepped into the puddle of cold slush left by Vladimir's overshoes. That inconsiderate, uncouth man, had removed his dirty, wet overshoes in her living area.

Reluctantly she admitted to herself that Vladimir was an interesting person to share an apartment with. She felt the sharpness of hurt and fear recede, then begin to grow again, taking the form of anger. There were times when Vladimir really displayed an unattractive streak of selfishness.

Suddenly her gaze fell on the champagne and box of sweets. Standing still, she touched her lips, recalling the sensation of the chocolate and the kiss.

There had been a hint of liquor in his kiss. She'd thought it quite appealing at the time, but now she understood. He'd started his celebrations without her and would finish them without her. He'd left her alone with only alcohol and candy.

She would not let him ruin the anniversary of her freedom. She would celebrate, and not alone. Madame Chernyshevskaya had given her a standing invitation to her Sunday evening soiree. Anyuta would be there, as would many friends. She would go to the gathering without Vladimir, as a free woman.

ON THE EVENING before the Day of the Magi, the Epiphany, Vladimir and Sofya were closing the annual round of social events with their own large party. He sat on the divan awaiting the arrival of the first guests.

Both he and Sofya were nearly exhausted by the frantic social life they'd led since Christmas. As newlyweds, they had been obliged to attended endless family gatherings. Then there had been the social affairs demanded by his business, the round of parties given by and for owners of bookstores, translators and printers, all of whom had to be kept on friendly terms if his new line of books was to have any chance of showing a profit. Sofya had played to perfection her role as his attentive, brilliant young wife. She quickly caught on to business details and her facility with numbers allowed her to follow some very complex financial discussions. She was becoming an effective business woman. Of course, all his business acquaintances were convinced he had made the perfect match and enjoyed a perfect marriage.

Vladimir groaned. How easily people were fooled by appearances.

He had almost fallen asleep, when the doorbell rang. Shaking himself into alertness, Vladimir opened the door. In walked Sofya's sister, accompanied by a young woman he did not recognize.

Anyuta's kiss of greeting was quick and formal. He felt her cold, smooth cheek against his. She smelled wonderfully of a floral fragrance, and her big, blue eyes sparkled with laughter. Neither woman waited for his help in removing their coats. Anyuta placed the garments on the rack in the hall.

Vladimir admired her smooth, white arms and the perfection of her blond hair, pulled back in a luxurious braid that twisted to hug the back of her head.

Turning to him, she introduced her companion, Julia Vsevolodovna Lermontova. Julia was of average height, and very slender, though he noticed she possessed a particularly well defined figure. Her face was not appealing.

Anyuta stood back, crossed her arms over her breast, and devoted herself in mockery to a critical examination of the man before her. Then, turning to Julia, she demanded boldly, "This is our Sofya's conquest. What do you think of him?"

Vladimir flushed with embarrassment. To judge by the reddening of her cheeks, Julia was experiencing a similar discomfort. Anyuta, oblivious to the awkward situation she had caused, walked past them into the living area. Exchanging apologetic looks, that quickly turned to smiles of shared recognition of Anyuta's rudeness, Vladimir and Julia followed her.

"I see none of the other guests have arrived," Anyuta announced, turning to inspect all the corners of the room. "Where is my sister? Probably still dressing. Well, she can always use help and advice with that task." Anyuta headed toward the bedroom hall. "Vladimir, be nice to Julia." Having issued her orders, she disappeared behind Sofya's door.

"That's Anya," Vladimir said smiling, trying to put at ease the young friend who seemed on the verge of turning painfully shy and embarrassed. "I'm afraid she doesn't have much confidence in my social graces."

A wide smile pleasantly transformed the young woman's face. Still she was standing timidly near the entrance of the room. Vladimir motioned her to the divan. Nodding, she seated herself gracefully. She was silent, but watching him intently, making him just the slightest bit uncomfortable.

"Fruit juice or tea?"

"Juice, thank you."

He moved to the dining table, where overflowing platters of crackers and cheese were flanked by pitchers of tea and various fruit juices. A large array of mismatched cups and glasses and several ashtrays occupied the space at the table's ends. Choosing two of the nicer glasses, he poured a purple liquid into them. He resented not pouring wine into those glasses. Some of the customs of this group were definitely becoming tiresome.

When he handed Julia the drink, she moved to one side of the divan, suggesting that he might be seated with her.

Then, in a soft, pleasant voice, she began to question him about his work. When Vladimir informed her that he had published Darwin's works in Russian, her shyness vanished. She was a great believer in Darwin's theories.

Her eyes seemed to stay locked on him. The look was not critical, but rather approving. Vladimir found himself forgetting her somewhat homely appearance, and speaking quite freely, almost bragging to her of his accomplishments. It turned out that she had read several books that he had published. She named them and commented knowledgeably on their scientific content.

Vladimir felt a twinge of resentment at the interruption of their conversation when a knock at the door signaled his need to resume his duties as party host.

In half an hour the room was filled with people. At the first opportunity, Vladimir returned to Julia, who was still sitting on the divan. Fortunately, there was a place next to her.

"Has my cousin Zhanna arrived yet?" she asked with some concern, looking around the room.

"No," Vladimir answered. "I think Sofya said that Zhanna would not be able to attend."

"Zhanna has an unbreakable appointment for this evening. But she promised to come if she could get away early." Julia turned back to him.

"We'll keep watch for her. I can see the front door from here. Meanwhile, why don't you tell me about yourself?"

"I suppose the most interesting thing about me is my love for chemistry."

He nodded approval.

The rising noise of the party induced Vladimir to move closer to Julia, to hear. She was becoming animated as she spoke, her face no longer plain but attractive. She felt strongly that chemistry, of all the sciences, had the best potential to advance the welfare of the people. Great strides in basic understanding were being made, right here in Russia; if Mendeleev's ideas were confirmed, a whole new way of classifying and ordering elements would come into use. She'd love someday to work alongside a giant like Mendeleev. But that was a dream.

"Why only a dream?" Vladimir demanded.

"My parents are very dear and have always treated me with love and kindness. But they cannot accept that I might need any education beyond what tutors can provide. They'll let me study as much as I like, in any field I choose—as long as I don't go far from home." She smiled. "So you see, my opportunities are limited."

"Nonsense! Such parental authoritarianism is unforgivable."

"Please." She spoke quietly, but firmly. "I must ask you not to speak harshly of my parents. Believe me, they mean well. I wouldn't hurt them for the world. My plan, my hope, is to find some way of convincing them, gently, that advanced study is really best for me. They do have my best interest at heart."

Vladimir, surprised and interested, considered this girl, this woman, carefully. Obviously Julia was sincerely gentle and intelligent. She did give the impression of a person who had been loved and cherished as a child; such people, he'd noticed with a certain envy, tended to be quietly self-assured.

He told her: "If anyone can convince your parents, it is Sofya. She has an uncanny ability to charm almost anyone."

Julia nodded. "She has offered to try, and I most certainly intend to take advantage of her help." In a quiet, almost apologetic tone, Julia added, "Sofya is very fortunate in having the assistance of such a kind man."

"And if there is anything I can do, please ask." What a rare modern woman this Julia was! Apparently she nursed no hatred or resentment for the older generation. "If there were anyone I knew who could help you . . ." Vladimir let his sentence fall unfinished.

"Oh, no. Nothing like that." Julia spoke quickly, her face reddening. She had picked up the implied possibility of a fictitious marriage. "Sofya's help will be quite welcome, but nothing more." Her gaze, for the first time in the conversation, wandered away from him.

Hurriedly Vladimir changed the subject. He found himself telling her the newest discoveries in paleontology, the nature of the evidence which would be required to provide firm support for Darwin. Paleontology desperately needed an organized method of dealing with the information being uncovered. Just as Mendeleev was bringing order to chemistry, someone must bring order to paleontology.

He would have enjoyed spending the entire evening telling Julia of his studies. She certainly gave him the impression of being interested. Despite his promise to watch the door, he lost track of the arrival of other guests. The increasing noise around him only made him feel more like he and Julia shared an island of their own making.

"Julia, there you are!" Zhanna's familiar voice invaded their space. "I had a most frightening time at the ball. Thank God I'm here and safe!" She had materialized before them, a vision of perfect blond beauty clothed in green silk, a rich ball gown conspicuously out of place at this informal party. The beauty possessed delicately sculptured features, large gray-green eyes, small red lips, and a flawless complexion, all framed by luxurious blond curls. Only the piercing harshness of her voice ruined the picture.

Zhanna seated herself on the other side of Julia. Seeing the two women next to each other, Vladimir was again jolted by the realization of how plain—almost ugly—Julia really was. While they had been speaking, he had all but forgotten her physical appearance. But now, next to this beauty, her plainness was painfully accentuated.

The beauty in green silk was slowly peeling white gloves from her small hands. "Oh, Julia, the Grand Duke was simply offensive tonight. I must find some way out of his clutches." Actually Zhanna did not look in the least frightened, only resolved. "I feigned illness to provide myself with an excuse for leaving the Palace ball early. Fortunately, Mother and Father decided to stay on. I was allowed to take the family carriage. So, of course, I came on here."

"You poor woman!" Julia offered comfort. It was impossible to tell whether she was entirely sincere. "You're among friends now."

"Yes." The beauty folded her gloves in her lap. "I'm sure somehow, with my friends' help, I'll get free of that man." Turning to Vladimir with a knowing look, she appealed to him rashly. "I'm serious. Actually I'm trying rather desperately to find a liberator. Just as our fortunate little Sofya has evidently done with such great success."

"Zhanna!" Julia flushed with anger. Her voice was a controlled, insistent whisper. "Watch what you say. Even here, among friends, you must guard your tongue."

"Well, of course. But what have I said?" Zhanna looked from one to the other, completely unperturbed, with a kind of surprised innocence. "Quite honestly, Vladimir, you certainly must be aware that Anya has arranged for me to meet a potential liberator here this evening."

He frowned. "I knew nothing of the sort! Who is the man?"

"How should I know? I'm here to be introduced to him." Zhanna responded lightly.

"How dare Anya make such arrangements without telling me or So-fya."

"Well, I'm sure Sofya knows." A mocking smile appeared on Zhanna's lips. "You could ask her, Vladimir. She's over there! See, with her tutor Strannoliubsky. Yes, I'd say totally absorbed by the presence of that handsome, handsome tutor. Apparently, Anya has taken over the hosting duties for both of you."

Vladimir could feel his cheeks redden. "Excuse me, Julia, but I must have a word with Anya. I'm sure Zhanna will keep you entertained, in one way or another."

He stood up quickly, scanning the room for the first time in—how long? An hour? There were Peter and Maria Bokov, and Sechenov and Anyuta with them, congregating in a corner. The look on Anyuta's face suggested that she was definitely flirting with Sechenov.

To reach them Vladimir had to maneuver around a group of five or six blocking his way. Their attention was centered on Madame Chernyshevskaya, the consort of the imprisoned champion of freedom, almost sacred to the generation who followed her husband's words.

Vladimir disliked contact with this set. He didn't know if his distaste sprang up despite, or perhaps because of, his great admiration for the persecuted writer. A smartly dressed young man stood to one side, fawning over Chernyshevskaya, waiting on her every word. Vladimir had not met this man, but knew he was only one in a line of amusing partners intent upon keeping the famous author's wife from loneliness. At Chernyshevskaya's other side, nervously smoking a cigarette, was a man whose shabby dress suggested a prepared kind of carelessness. He was taking frequent puffs, blowing the smoke into the air, and mindlessly letting the ashes drop to the floor. A look of rebelliousness and cockiness radiated from this one's stance, his exaggerated hand motions, his too-loud voice, his intense look. His whole being betrayed a condescension toward everyone and everything.

Vladimir edged past them. From this new vantage point he was able to see, beyond another barrier of bodies, the short, appealingly rounded figure of his own wife, and Strannoliubsky leaning toward her, the two of them appearing lost in some animated conversation. Vladimir felt a twinge of possessiveness and jealousy as he watched Sofya smile warmly at her friend.

Suddenly Vladimir paused, struck by what he had observed as he passed through this room. What was happening? Zhanna, the Chernyshevskys, the Bokovs, even he and Sofya. All these people, these searchers for, experimenters in, and devotees of freedom, all were becoming hopelessly entangled in one way or another, their lives restricted by their very search for liberty. All people in pain. Yet all around him they were laughing as if there could be nothing frightening in the world. As the cloud of the rebellious man's cheap and malodorous cigarette engulfed Vladimir, the room became grotesque. A sinister yellowish veil seemed to have fallen on everyone and everything within the room.

The image was so strong that for a moment Vladimir was unable to move and feared he would be sick. He held his breath, and started making his way to the front door of the apartment, fighting down a panicky urge to knock people out of his way. Once at the door, he held it open to let a draft of cold air into the stuffy apartment. He stood outside in the empty hallway until he felt he was no longer in danger of physical illness. When an old, gray head appeared frowning in the doorway of a neighboring apartment, Vladimir gave a little apologetic salute and plunged back into his smoky rooms. Before closing the door, he managed to open the transom above. At least some air would enter.

"I opened a window." Anyuta, for once approving, was beside him. "You're right. This apartment needs air."

"Anya, Zhanna told me that you've arranged a meeting for her," Vladimir began without preamble, taking her by the elbow. "Why wasn't I told about this?"

"Frankly, because you haven't been very cooperative lately." Anyuta pulled her arm away sharply. "In my opinion, you have lost sight of our ideals. I can sense this in your behavior with Sofya. Therefore, it seems to me that arranged meetings are no longer any of your business."

"This is my apartment."

Anyuta's eyes blazed. "This is *Sofya's* apartment!" She spoke with confidence and control. "It shouldn't be your place at all."

"What do you mean?"

"Isn't it obvious? You should have vanished, disappeared, immediately following the wedding. That was what any honorable, sincere liberator would have done. You're taking advantage of my sister's immaturity and insecurity. Well, this is Sofya's place, her apartment. She is the only one I will consult about what is done here. She, of course, has approved of Zhanna's meeting with her potential liberator. I invited the man. Fortunately, he's found a friend in Madame Chernyshevskaya. He certainly wants nothing to do with you, in fact he would not have come had he known you would be present. He feels tainted by remaining in the same room with you. He knows of your secret association with the authorities."

Anyuta started to turn away. Vladimir, momentarily stunned by the attack, recovered swiftly, grabbed her arm, and pulled her back.

Anyuta, just as quickly and fiercely, once more pulled her arm from his grasp. "What do you think you're doing?" she demanded in a savage whisper.

"I'm going to explain a few rather important things to you. That's what I'm doing." Taking her arm once more, this time in a grip she could not break, he pushed and pulled her toward a corner of the entrance way, out of sight of the general party. Her back against a laden rack of coats, he took hold of her shoulders.

"I have not broken my contract with your sister," he informed her in a biting voice. "Sofya wants me to stay with her. Furthermore, my personal arrangements with your sister are no longer your concern."

"My sister is always my concern," Anyuta snapped back. Her full breasts rose and fell. Her eyes showed no fear, only a disdainful anger. She struggled to pull away, but he refused to let her.

"Second, I am not an informer!" When she relaxed, he loosened his grip, then added more gently, "Anyuta, how can you believe that vicious lie?"

She freed herself. Stared intently at him. "I believe you are a man who doesn't act in accordance with his stated beliefs. I don't trust such people," she concluded firmly. Pushing past him, she rejoined the party.

Vladimir felt as if she had slapped him. He had to talk to her, to change her view of him. Automatically he followed her. She was joining the group surrounding Madame Chernyshevskaya.

As Vladimir approached, Zhanna and the liberator were standing near to each other. The disheveled potential liberator appeared to be delivering an oration. His back was to Vladimir, but Vladimir could distinctly hear his grating, overly loud words. ". . . conditions at the university are reaching a crisis. A strong leader will arise and the students will demand their rights. The only way to stop the oppression of this administration, and for that matter the oppression of the whole Tsarist system, is to make a show of force. Force is all the administration knows and respects. The students of today are ready to speak the language of the Tsar!"

At that point the man, as if alerted by some extra sense, turned to look over his shoulder. His eyes met Vladimir's. Without another word, the orator broke from the group and walked toward the opposite side of the room. Zhanna unquestioningly followed him. Vladimir and the remaining members of the group watched with surprise.

"Well, I wonder what that abrupt exit was all about? He acted as if he thought you were sneaking up on him." Madame Chernyshevskaya was addressing Vladimir. "No matter. But what a mysterious and charming man that Tkachev is!" She indicated the potential liberator. "I had no idea you were acquainted with the radical elements of the movement, Vladimir. The man's ideas are quite startling. How refreshing he is. I sense he is a man not only of ideas, but one of action."

"So, the man's name is Tkachev," Vladimir noted with exasperation. "We owe the pleasure of his company completely to Anya. I take no credit for his appearance."

"How gracious of you to give your sister-in-law all the credit." Chernyshevskaya smiled condescendingly. "How astute of you, my dear Anya, to find Tkachev. So many of our modern men are only good with words. Words, words, words. I'm tired to death of men of words." Then she laughed again and turned to her young companion, grasping his arm in a very familiar manner.

Vladimir nodded to her and to Anyuta, then left the circle. Clearly Chernyshevskaya meant she was tired of her husband, who must be a man of words above all else. Vladimir felt disgust at her open unfaithfulness to her devoted husband.

WHEN THE LAST of the guests had left, Sofya collapsed on the divan, took off her shoes and lifted her stockinged feet onto the cushions. Vladimir had extinguished the gas lights. He lingered by the tree, making sure that all its candles were entirely extinguished.

"Thank God this evening is over!" he sighed.

Sofya nodded in silent agreement. She disliked the dead smell from the newly extinguished candles. She was tired. She dreaded the darkness that closed in with each puff of smoke from an extinguished candle. Soon only the glow from the hallway lamp would keep the room from total darkness.

Wearily Vladimir sank down beside her, and lifted her feet onto his lap.

"The tension between you and Anyuta threatened to disrupt the whole party. Can't you try a little harder to be at least civil to her? For my sake, for the sake of peace."

Vladimir stared at the dark tree. "Your sister is meddling in issues she knows nothing about. She persists in taunting me with innuendos about my supposedly wicked past. I know I'll always be suspected by some. That's part of the brand the authorities put on me. But I didn't expect such treatment from your sister."

Sofya sighed. "She must be temporarily under the influence of that Tkachev fellow. I'll have a talk with her. Forgive her, Vladimir. For my sake."

"I'll excuse her on the basis of her naiveté. She doesn't understand my situation at all." He rested his head against the back of the divan, and spoke to the ceiling. "You should have consulted with me before allowing Anyuta to invite that young rebel. Men of his type are dangerous."

"I'm sorry. I told her she could invite whomever she liked. And poor Zhanna is really desperate for a liberator."

"Tkachev should never be trusted as liberator, not for any of your friends, not for Zhanna and certainly not for Anyuta. The man's passions are out of control. And I don't mean his passion for lechery."

Sofya turned, swung her legs down from the divan and placed her stockinged feet on the cold floor. She stretched her arms in an effort to relieve the tired ache in her back, then moved to sit in the arm chair across from Vladimir. He was leading this conversation in a direction that would require her attention.

Vladimir was looking at her. Perhaps he was a little hurt by her avoidance of him, or perhaps his look just meant he too was tired. In the dim light she could not be sure. He went on, "Anyuta has no sense about these matters." His voice lowered. "And she's making another grave misjudgment. She'd better stop flirting with Sechenov."

"Why?" Sofya felt a need to defend her sister. "Anyuta knows Sechenov objects to being viewed as merely a liberator. I'm sure Anyuta honestly finds him attractive. And from what I see of them together, he seems to share her feeling. I think they would make a rather striking couple."

There was silence. Then she heard Vladimir sigh, "Maria Bokova is in love with Sechenov. They've become intimate."

"You can't mean that!" Sofya stiffened with shock.

"Peter loves her. He's loved her from the first." Vladimir's voice sounded like a groan. "He's miserable. He isn't sure how serious Maria's infatuation is. He's concerned enough to feel the need to confide in a friend, me. Not that the situation isn't partially his fault."

"Peter must be imagining Maria's involvement. The three of them have been such close friends for so long. I can't . . ." Her voice dropped off. Sensing dark complications, she tried desperately to reason them away. "Sechenov has been responsive to Anyuta. You saw them tonight."

"Peter told me more. For some time now, there's been a *ménage à trois.* Our Maria Bokova is no longer happy with this arrangement, she wants only Sechenov. The gallant Doctor Peter Bokov agreed to leave. He'll start looking for another apartment after the holidays."

Sofya's tired mind tried to accept the situation. Maria must have been in torment, not wanting to hurt Peter, nor destroy his friendship with Sechenov, but needing to follow her heart. And what of Sechenov's beliefs? Was he trying to draw Anyuta into a second *ménage?*

Vladimir's voice conveyed a tired resignation. "Ask Anyuta not to get involved with this mess."

They sat in silence, Vladimir again staring at the ceiling. When he spoke once more, his voice was just above a whisper. "You know about Madame Chernyshevskaya and her new friend?"

"She's told me. They're lovers. She insists that Chernyshevsky offered her an open marriage. He's even agreed to support any children from these other unions. When they were married, he assured her she'd be free to take lovers if she wished. There was to be only freedom between them, no ties, no chains, on either partner."

Again there was long silence, ended by Vladimir's quiet reply. "I've talked to some of Chernyshevsky's friends. He's allowed to write from exile now. He knows of her affairs. He professes that he loves her, only her. His friends say he's very upset, but he'd never reproach her. He's too 'noble.' " Somehow his tone conveyed quotation marks.

Reaching across the space between them, Vladimir lightly touched her knee. "Sofya, our friends are hurting each other so desperately, mortally. Their experiments failed. You and I are headed on the same road, but we can still turn off." He stood up with a sudden nervous energy that frightened her. "Sofya, I'm tired of the lies, but I'll still go along as we agreed. But there's one thing that you must understand. While I'm your husband of whatever mode, you will not take a lover!"

"You have no right to make demands, and no need to make this one." She struggled to control a growing anger. "But I accept, on the condition that you abide by the same stipulation. You will not take a lover while I am your wife of whatever mode!"

He stood up stiffly from the divan. She watched him walk to the bedroom hallway, heard his door close. He might not have heard her.

She sat in the chair for a long time. She stared blankly, unthinkingly at the darkened tree that seemed to loom toward her.

ON RETURNING to her university classes, Sofya immediately missed the presence of her classmate, Zelensky, who had wished her well on the day of her departure. After making a few discreet inquiries of fellow students she learned that during the holidays, he had been put under house arrest at his country estate. Zelensky was an active organizer of a student financial cooperative. The cooperative had made it possible for certain borderline "politically undesirable" students to continue their educations after the government had rescinded their scholarships and subsidies. The government was responding with its usual excessive repression.

Another disturbing fact greeted her return. In Sechenov's physiology class, a new student had suddenly appeared, though it was unheard of for any student to begin this class in midyear. The man was more neatly dressed than most of her classmates, and seemed to pay more attention to his fellow students than to the professor. Her first thought was that a government spy had been assigned because of her unofficial presence in the class. But within a few days she was certain that she was not the target. Spies had appeared in almost every class.

Days passed and the silent, threatening presence persisted. She sensed the anxiety grow among her fellow students and professors. Everyone wondered who would be brought before the Ministry of Education because of a carelessly worded remark. What innocent interaction with a fellow student would be construed as a subversive meeting? They all knew that such an accusation might destroy a career. For a student, the action meant the loss of the right to complete a degree, condemnation to a bleak and dismal job in the lower rungs of society. For a professor, the action meant the loss of his position, and possibly of the right to teach anywhere in the country. Or the punishment could be years of exile in a backwater village or even Siberia.

Sofya found that because of her own irregular status, she was trusted by the daring students. Word was passed to her that a street demonstration was being organized. She was given a packet of pamphlets being secretly distributed among the students.

"Vladimir, look at these!" Sofya exclaimed, tossing a pair of pamphlets on the divan. Vladimir was seated there, reading a newspaper and smoking a pungently aromatic Russian cigarette.

Without a word, he put his paper down and took the documents in hand. "Well, I am quite familiar with this one," he said, immediately putting one aside. "The words of my old mentor, Herzen. Now, what's the other? Ah, I've heard rumors about this one, but I hadn't seen it yet. Quite inelegant and amateurish, don't you think?" Calmly he glanced over the pages containing threats of retaliatory action against the police, the Tsar, and the royal family.

"Vladimir, these pamphlets appeared at the university only this morning." Sofya, with growing apprehension, picked up the documents and sat on the divan next to him. "Tell me how you came to know about these."

Vladimir's normal, somewhat melancholy expression gave way to a sly smile. His eyes were twinkling. Just above a whisper, he said, "I know about Herzen's letter because I arranged for it to be printed. Are you proud of me? You see, I'm as willing to promote the movement as that man your sister brought to the party. In fact, this rival pamphlet, this amateur piece of trash, is the product of your sister's friend, Tkachev. And that man knows everyone with legal or illegal access to a press in this city."

"But why did you get involved?" She hoped she had controlled her voice well enough to hide the panic struggling to take possession of her.

"Why? Because Herzen needed my help to get his letter to the students. Read this carefully! Herzen understands the indignities and injustices the students are being subjected to, but he is pleading for rational behavior. The fact that foolish schoolboys, like that Tkachev, are misinterpreting or ignoring Herzen's advice cannot be blamed on me or Herzen." Vladimir picked Tkachev's pamphlet from her lap. "This document's a cry for a street demonstration, the ranting of a small child throwing a temper tantrum. The effects can only be disastrous." He crumpled the pamphlet and hurled it into the fireplace, where it quickly burned to ashes.

"Are you in danger?" She could hardly hear her own voice.

"I hardly think so. Tkachev's pamphlet will draw all the wrath."

"Then thank God," Sofya whispered. "Thank God for Tkachev's pamphlet."

"Before you offer up any more thanks, realize that Tkachev's pamphlet may also make your scholarly position much more precarious. Faced with such a challenge, the authorities will not be inclined to give way on any point. Your petition for the admission of women to the universities will remain on the desk of the university provost. He will never have the courage to pass it on to the Minister of Education, much less to the Tsar. There is no chance of formalizing your position as a degree candidate at the University. And it's just a matter of time until they get around to dismissing you completely."

"Vladimir, if you are right . . ."

"Of course, I'm right. Can't you see it?"

Sofya nodded slowly and spoke quietly. "I'll go abroad. As soon as possible. We'll go abroad."

VLADIMIR SAW ONLY one obstacle to their immediate departure: money. The debts of his publishing business had to be paid before he would be allowed to leave the country. Had book sales been as robust as he'd anticipated, his debt would be paid by now and he'd be a hundred thousand rubles richer. But the profits weren't coming in.

He had taken the company ledgers home for the fifth night in a row to try once more to find some place among the jumble of figures where he could free some money.

"How much do we owe?" Sofya asked as she pulled up a chair beside him. She was carrying a single piece of paper. A pencil rested behind her left ear.

"Twenty thousand." He closed the ledger in disgust.

"Can we count on at least ten percent of that coming in royalties by April?"

"Yes. Even with the most conservative projections we'll have that amount." He wondered what the point of her questions might be. Two thousand rubles would not be enough to get him cleared by the government for travel abroad.

"I've done some figuring and planning, while you've been moaning over the books this last week." She put down the paper she had been holding, and removed the pencil from behind her ear. "You'll be getting the first installment on my dowry, that plus the two thousand will cover the debts. I talked to Papa yesterday, before he returned to Palibino. Papa promises to get you the dowry money by April."

"I can't use your dowry to pay my business debts! Put that money in the bank, invest in property, do anything you want with the money, but do it in your name only. The whole dowry system is a despicable custom, treating women as property. Even giving your father the benefit of the doubt in thinking he may be regarding this payment as a kind of advance on your inheritance, or a wedding gift, or some other more civilized motive, he is putting a large sum of money under my control because he believes you are married to me. Sofya, we are not married in the way your father assumes! I'm already deceiving the man. By accepting the money I'd be cheating him."

"You have a finely developed sense of honor." She patted his arm gently. "It's charming and most attractive, but perhaps a wee bit too refined when applied to money matters. And you are just a wee bit late in voicing this concern."

"What do you mean?"

"My money was always part of our agreement, our special arrangement. Remember, I promised to help you. You knew that meant not only my personal efforts, but my money."

Vladimir groaned.

"If you insist, I'll take control of the dowry money. I choose to invest it in your business. That will pay the debts, and you'll be free to go abroad with me."

He let his aching head rest pillowed by his arm on the cluttered table top. Without lifting his head, he turned to her. She was sitting erect and alert. "I consider this infusion of money not as an investment, but as a loan. I'll repay the money when the sales come in."

"Think of it any way you wish, Volodya. We've got to get out of the country as soon as possible." She looked at him. "Volodya, please, pay attention and don't mope. I have no idea what it costs to live abroad, but you do. Now, help me do this figuring."

On her command, he straightened up. She was already engrossed in the numbers on her paper.

"I persuaded Papa to give me a thousand rubles a year toward my studies, the same amount he pays for Fedya's schooling."

"Oh, Sofya, really! You emotionally blackmailed your father! Have you no pride where money is concerned?"

"Vladimir, please, just concentrate on the figures now. You can bemoan the situation later." She was writing something. "How much annual income can you count on from your estate? Give me a conservative estimate. No, make that the least possible amount."

"I've never received less than five hundred rubles a year."

"We've got fifteen hundred a year to live on. Plus, whatever royalties come in after April. Can we study abroad on that sum?"

Vladimir looked at her. "Maybe. We'd have to be truly frugal, much more frugal than you've ever been in your life."

"I can live frugally." Sofya sounded enthusiastic. "After all, the average schoolteacher's salary is three hundred rubles a year."

"Yes, but they do not have the expenses we'll have. Let me have that paper a minute." Vladimir pulled the piece toward him. He forced himself to think calmly of numbers. He took up his pencil and tried to recall the prices of room rent in the student quarters in various European cities he'd visited. Plus train fares, food, some clothing, some allowance for books and fees. He scribbled numbers. "Yes." He hesitated and looked over his figures once more. "We can both live on fifteen hundred a year."

"At fifteen hundred for two, that's seven hundred fifty per person."

"I managed abroad one year on my five hundred from the estate. But I was living in conditions I would not have for you."

"Well then." She smiled coyly. "Three could certainly live on two thousand five hundred a year, that would be nicely over eight hundred each."

For a moment his mind reeled at the possibility that she would tell him she wanted to have a child. But that of course was nonsense. "What are you leading up to?"

"When I was at Papa's discussing these money matters, Anyuta was with me. Oh, Vladimir, you should have seen her manipulating Papa. I think he's just tired of arguing with her. At any rate, he agreed to give Anyuta the same thousand-ruble educational allowance. Then Anyuta and I both talked him into letting her go to Europe. Papa agreed, with only one condition: you must act as her chaperon and guardian, or some such nonsense. We assured him you would watch over both of us."

"You conniving little demon! You had this all decided before you ever showed me the figures."

Sofya considered. "No. Not really. I needed your opinion and approval on several matters, the debt, the amount of living expenses, and your willingness to be a chaperon for both Anyuta and me."

"Seems you've been successful on all counts. All right." Vladimir tried to sound well pleased. "We'll leave in mid-April, the three of us."

He pushed away from the table and the numbers. Settling wearily onto the divan, he put his arm over his eyes and tried not to think of his humiliation. He hadn't depended on anyone for financial support since he was fourteen. Now, at twenty-seven, he was being supported by his wife. And by her father, the man they were deceiving. He was being bought, like a jar of preserves!

CHAPTER TEN

Spring 1869 ⊛ *Vienna*

Days of discomfort on one train, followed by more days, more discomfort, on another. South to Moscow, west to Minsk. Change trains. Arbitrate another quarrel between Anyuta and Vladimir. West again to Warsaw.

Exhausted, her enthusiasm sapped, all Sofya could think of was that she was heading not to Heidelberg, as she had dreamed, but to Vienna, the city of music, art, and Vladimir's geological idol, Eduard Suess.

They had ten minutes to change trains. The Russian line ended here in Warsaw, and all passengers proceeding west must transfer to trains which ran on the smaller gauged tracks of Western Europe. Carrying a heavy bag in each hand, with another tucked insecurely under her arm, Sofya struggled along the wooden platform. For the first time in her life she was surrounded by a crowd in which no one spoke Russian. All the signs were in the Western alphabet. At five in the morning, her mind rebelled at interpreting the unfamiliar symbols. Struggling unsuccessfully to read the Polish words, she caught sight of a large sign. Her mind accepted the German, *Wien*. The train to Vienna. Vladimir, carrying four of their personal bags, was just ahead of her, clearing a path through the crowd, and she hoped Anyuta was still behind her. Her sister had charge of one bag, an armful of books and newspapers, and a small basket that contained their breakfast and luncheon.

As Vladimir stowed the last of the bags on the shelf above the seats of their compartment Sofya and Anyuta collapsed onto the narrow, padded bench. Sofya nearest the window, Anyuta, next to her, had already closed the door of the compartment and was resting her feet on the opposite bench. Options for a place eliminated, Vladimir sat across from Sofya. As the train jerked to a start Sofya jumped to her feet to close the window, too late to keep out the accompanying first belch of black smoke. A whispered curse of all trains escaped from her lips as she slumped back into the seat.

Turning to the side and resting his back against the closed window, Vladimir brought his own long legs up onto the bench, forcing Anyuta to adjust the position of her feet. His voice was unusually dreamy and soft. "Every time I've made this switch from our Russian rails to the Western, I'm overcome with a strong feeling." His head was tilted up and his eyes half closed.

"Exhaustion," Anyuta snapped. "The feeling is exhaustion."

"No." Vladimir straightened to a rigid sitting position, looking at Sofya. "It's as if there were some depressing spirit who plagues me, but who can only travel the rails of the Russian Empire."

Sofya stared at him. She had never heard him speak so mystically, so poetically.

"What a pathetic attempt at imagery!" Anyuta reproached him. "Vladimir, stick to science!" Removing her feet from the bench, she rummaged in the food basket and brought out an apple. After crunching into the fruit and wiping a small dab of juice from the corner of her mouth, she added, "I do agree, Vladimir—"

"Gads! You agree with something I said!" He reached out a long arm for his own red fruit.

"Stop it, you two!" Sofya flared.

"I was just going to say," Anyuta continued, pulling out her kerchief to blot at apple juice, "that I share Vladimir's feeling of increased independence. This transition in Warsaw is the mark, at last we are free."

"I feel I'm leaving some spirit behind. And parting with that spirit is somehow sad and draining." Sofya's voice unexpectedly caught on the words.

"The child's homesick!" Anyuta teased. "Listen to her! Look at the dreaminess in her eyes."

Vladimir stared into Sofya's eyes. "I believe you're right. Our Sofya is definitely homesick. Come now, Sofya, you'll love it in Vienna."

Sofya sighed. Certainly their laughter and gentle chiding was meant to bring her to her senses. Which it did. She determinedly pushed aside the sense of loss.

For a long while no one spoke. Anyuta had taken out paper and pencil, apparently making notes for a short story or article. Vladimir was hidden behind an open book. The rhythmic clatter of the train filled the compartment. Sofya closed her tired eyes as the first light of morning met the rain-soaked Polish countryside.

"SOFYA?" VLADIMIR'S HAND rested on her knee. "You've been asleep for several hours. You started murmuring as if you were having a bad dream."

"I think I was. But I can't recall anything about the dream now." Her back and neck ached terribly. "I could use some fresh air."

"How about joining me on the observation porch?" Vladimir was trying to stretch his arms, but the narrow compartment could not accommodate the span.

"Perhaps that would be pleasant." She had to shake this depressed, tired feeling. She should be feeling happy and free.

"Of course, it will be," Anyuta snapped, waking from her own nap and regaining something of her usual form. "He'll stop at the dining car and buy you hot chocolate. He's bought you a present of sweets every day of the trip! And he's taken you for a little tête-à-tête on the observation porches of all the trains we've been on. Although he does prefer moonlight to mid-morning sunlight. Don't you, Vladimir?"

Vladimir, ignoring the outburst, left the compartment.

"Sofya, it's time you put a stop to this blatant display of juvenile romantics. Good God, you're free now. You're in Europe."

"Anyuta, you must stop baiting Vladimir!" Sofya nearly screamed the words. She folded her arms across her chest and clung to her sides, trying desperately to control her anger. "I can't take much more of this. You two are going to have to find some way of getting along, or I'll go mad!" Slamming the sliding door of the compartment behind her, she headed for the observation porch.

She took the seat next to Vladimir. They were alone. Vladimir was taking long puffs from a cigarette and staring at the passing scene of rich green dotted with patches of white wild flowers. She touched his arm. He turned to her, said nothing, but taking out a silver case from his inner jacket pocket offered her a cigarette.

She declined with a silent gesture; there was no one here who needed to be impressed with her liberal ways. She looked out. The train had left the swampy terrain of Poland and entered northern Austria. Rich green rolling hills spread out on either side. The air was clear; in the distance she saw a few mountains and a clustering of cottages. The hills harbored spas renowned for their beauty and the health-giving properties of their waters—places of rejuvenation. If only some of that peace would float her way.

She drew in a deep breath, and gently broached the problem. "Vladimir, try to be patient with Anyuta. And you know, some of the things she says are true. Do this for me. I've done my compromising to make this trip successful for all of us."

"You mean, you're still pouting about going to Vienna instead of Heidelberg."

"Well, yes."

He heaved a sigh. "Sofya, we've been through this. You'd have no chance at university admission in Heidelberg. Women just aren't accepted there. In Vienna you'll have a chance. Your father agreed, Vienna was where he wanted his daughters to be. 'A civilized city,' those were his words. I'll have a chance to start my work. Anyuta will have a chance to—achieve whatever foolishness she finds appealing."

"Vladimir, you've won the argument. We're all going to Vienna and you'll work with your revered Suess."

Vladimir smiled. "Suess knows what someone with my background has to contend with. He was imprisoned for his part in the uprising of '48, then, because of his police record, denied entry to the university. Still he's made a great name for himself."

"As far as I've been able to discover, Suess's main interest is in the formation of the Alps. Your interest is in the evolution of animals, not mountains."

"The histories of both lie in the rocks." Vladimir tossed the cigarette away, and put his arm around her. "Now, if you'd just relax, we could be having a wonderful time."

WHEN THEY RETURNED to their compartment a few minutes later, Anyuta had curled up on one of the benches, her arms pillowing her head, her blond hair covering her face. Sitting next to Sofya on the opposite bench, Vladimir whispered, "She looks like a sleeping princess, an illusion broken when she awakes."

Sofya glared at him.

WHEN THE TRAIN pulled into Nordwestbahnhof, Sofya whispered a prayer of thanksgiving that the journey was over. Stepping out onto the platform, she felt freedom, like a clean breeze after train smoke, or the warmth of the sun chasing away winter. Space had expanded around her. No more confining walls and touchable ceiling of a train. The station's high, peaked dome spanned the entire width of the structure without the help of intermediate supporting pillars. A real feat of modern engineering worthy of some further study, she thought. As in all other stations, a flowing mass of people, intent on greetings or farewells, occupied the platforms. But these people were wearing lighter, less cumbersome clothing than in Petersburg. She saw no flowing woolen scarves, no fur hats.

Vladimir was at her right side, Anyuta at her left, her arm linked with Sofya's, as the three made their way through the stream. Vladimir excused himself and headed toward a kiosk selling papers from around the world. In a few moments he was back.

"I had to have a copy of *Neue Freie Presse*." His arm slid gently around Sofya's waist, guiding her to the exit. "The financial section is the most insightful in all Europe and the literary essays are first-class."

"Their political analyses are ridiculously naive," Anyuta snipped.

"We'll have a chance to test your opinion. The front page has an article headlined 'Disturbances at Petersburg University.' It appears there have been more student arrests. More disciplinary measures, including a dress and grooming code. Student meetings of any kind have been forbidden."

"I suppose you'll get around to searching the paper for apartment ads?" This was Anyuta, her voice hard and critical.

Sofya glared at her sister. Clearly, Anyuta expected Vladimir to manage most of the practical details of their lives. Of course if he were to do so, she would doubtless blame him for interference, or bestowing undue attentions on capable women.

Vladimir held open the door leading to the street. Two porters had followed carrying their baggage. Vladimir motioned to a waiting cab. The baggage was stowed as the trio climbed in.

"Hotel Seejungfer," Vladimir told the driver.

"The Seejungfer is much too expensive!" Sofya protested. The cab began its struggle to enter traffic. "We can't afford rooms there."

"If you'd planned ahead, you could have found us comfortable rooms in a respectable hotel among the more common people," Anyuta grumbled.

Vladimir scowled at her, then with a visible effort made himself relax. "We've been at each other's throats for days, Anyuta. What we need after that trip is a good dinner, perhaps the relaxation of a show, and a comfortable night's rest. Then maybe the three of us will be able to start a civilized life together." He turned to Sofya and smiled. "We can afford this little luxury. We're celebrating our arrival."

Sofya welcomed the blessed silence of her companions as the cab worked its way toward the heart of the ancient city. The streets were lined with chestnut trees; their leaves showed the first signs of budding. Ancient stone buildings stood proudly in neat rows. Flower boxes, newly painted and awaiting the first blooms of spring, hung from many windows. A tall spire in the distance loomed above the rooftops. "Vladimir, is that Stephansdom?"

Casting a glance that way, he responded in German. "It certainly is. I think you ladies could use a little orientation to your new home, and a little practice in the language. I'll give my one-schilling tour. If you don't understand something I say, hold up your hand."

"Really, Vladimir, how childish," Anyuta grumbled, in the same language. "We're both fluent. We spent summer of '66 with our German relatives in Switzerland."

"I could use the practice," Sofya admitted timidly. "Reading German comes easily, but speaking and listening are always difficult for me."

"Here goes." Vladimir cleared his throat. "The Cathedral of St. Stephen is dedicated to the first Christian martyr. The five-hundred-year-old church stands in the heart of the city. Near the church is a two-hundred-year-old column commemorating the end of the plague."

"Vladimir, if you're to do us any good you're going to have to speak more naturally. You can't pause between each word." Apparently Anyuta was paying attention.

"Behind us is the breathtakingly beautiful Schönbrunn, the summer palace of the Hapsburgs. The palace was redecorated about two hundred years ago by Empress Maria Theresa. She managed this while ruling a country, fighting a war, and bearing sixteen children. On special holidays the formal gardens are open to visitors, and across the street is one of the oldest theaters in the city. I'll take you there, Sofya."

Sofya raised her hand. "Stop! Please!" She laughed. "I caught all the numbers—five hundred, two hundred, two hundred, and sixteen!—then something about gardens. For now I'm just going to enjoy the view of this beautiful park we're passing."

"The name of the park is Volksgarten," Vladimir answered in Russian.

Sofya could barely tear her eyes away from the fairy-tale city, when the cab pulled up to the imposing entrance of the Seejungfer Hotel.

They checked into the hotel, reserving the smallest and cheapest available two-bedroom suite. In their room, Anyuta and Sofya collapsed into their beds. Staring up at the ceiling, Anyuta announced that she would not go out to dinner. Instead she'd order something light to eat, and stay in the room and write a letter to Mother and Father.

Welcoming the idea of a dinner without dissension, Sofya gave Anyuta no argument.

Vladimir's face, when he saw Sofya emerge alone from the bedroom, wore an expression which could only be interpreted as relief.

"VLADIMIR, ARE YOU sure we're dressed formally enough?" Sofya whispered, as she looked around at the elegantly dressed diners settled around the outdoor tables. They were in a small plaza adjoining the Hotel Seejungfer. "The men look as if they might be Grand Dukes, and the ladies, Balkan princesses."

"You look wonderful!" Vladimir assured her. "And I, my dear, will never look dashing. But, the management has a reputation for giving special consideration to young couples who are out for a special night. They believe such customers add to the color and atmosphere of the restaurant. Pretend you're in love, and no one will expect much from us in the way of finery."

Even as he spoke, an attentive, owlish-looking waiter approached them, and at once conducted them to a table near the street. Vladimir whispered to her, "You see? We're going to be on display, as this evening's young couple in love."

Seated, Sofya raised her menu to hide her discomfort at his teasing. Quickly she decided on her meal. Then from behind the cover of her menu, she examined her surroundings. Directly across the street was the magnificent new Opera House, its exterior obviously complete. But Vladimir told her that according to what he had read in the paper, the interior still needed much work.

Nearby, at one end of an open plaza, stood a wooden platform from which tables were being cleared away. Vladimir commented, "Later this evening the platform will be transformed into a dance floor. I'll wager you're a marvelously graceful dancer."

"The truth is that music almost frightens me."

Vladimir looked at her strangely, then smiled, "You're frightened by the little gypsy the music awakens in you. Your dark features betray your origins. Somewhere deep inside the serious, dedicated scholar lives a wild gypsy girl."

Sofya felt herself blushing deeply.

"But what sets you most apart are your piercing eyes. They quite fascinate me." After an awkward moment when he stared directly into her eyes, Vladimir returned to his study of the menu.

Suddenly in search of distraction, Sofya lost herself in watching the parade of people passing on the street. The evening was warm, and much of Vienna seemed to have come to the city center to enjoy a stroll. Uniforms, mostly those of high-ranking military officers, were much in evidence. The Viennese soldiers were the most smartly dressed in Europe, or so she had heard. She could vouch for the fact that the blue jackets, the bright red trousers tucked into high black boots, made even the plainest soldier look dashing.

Vladimir's dry voice broke in on her thoughts. "If you keep watching the soldiers, no one will believe we're a young couple in love." She felt his hand on her chin, gently turning her face back to him. "They might ask us to find another restaurant. And then you'd miss out on the most wonderful chocolate tortes in all of Europe."

Blushing and smiling, vowing to pay her escort more attention, Sofya felt the strain of the trip draining away.

The dinner was just what Sofya needed, excellent beef with noodles, accompanied by delicious hot, Capucin coffee served with a glass of chilled mineral water. And, as Vladimir had promised, a most wonderful exquisite chocolate torte.

When she finished the last bite, Vladimir, who had been silently watching her with an expression suggesting a satisfied cat, announced that she was not to become too contented. "We just have time to walk to the Theater an der Wien and catch the last show. The newspaper said a charming new operetta was being performed tonight. I can't recall the title, but the composer is Offenbach."

"After a meal such as this, I can't even think of moving," Sofya groaned. But in fact she rose quickly from the table and was ready to walk. Surprising herself, she wanted to prolong the evening.

As they strolled along the narrow streets, Sofya linked her arm with Vladimir's. "There is music everywhere in this city."

"Yes," he agreed. "I find it wonderfully refreshing. After the show I will take you to a beer garden with a famous 'signature room' where Beethoven, among other celebrities, has signed his name on the wall. They still allow visitors to sign the wall. You might add your name."

"Thank you, no. Modesty prevents," Sofya laughingly declined. "Although Beethoven would be wonderful company. When I was sixteen I mastered *Pathétique*."

"I had no idea you played the piano with such accomplishment."

"I've barely touched the instrument since I performed that piece."

The evening of her humiliation, when she had found Anyuta flirting with Dostoevsky, returned, strangely flooding her with the same childish emotions. Only three years ago, but it seemed half a lifetime. "Actually, tonight, I'm not in the mood for music. Would you mind terribly if we didn't attend that operetta?"

"Well, then." Gently he took her shoulders and turned her around. "We'll go to the Burgtheater. They're doing a version of Goethe's *Faust*."

"Much better," Sofya laughed. "I've read *Faust* in the German. Still, after my miserable attempts at understanding your descriptions this afternoon, I wonder how much I'll comprehend?"

"And I can wonder if you, like Goethe, find music a mixed muse, both soothing and provocative."

WHEN THEY RETURNED to the Hotel Seejungfer, Sofya, as tired as she was, suggested that they stop for a drink before retiring to their rooms. Vladimir gave quick approval, and led her to a small group of tables set off to one side from the hotel desk. Only a few of the tables were occupied.

As he was helping her adjust her chair, Vladimir leaned over her shoulder and murmured, "Look who we have with us, three tables to your left. Her back is to us now, but I'm sure it's Anyuta."

Sofya looked. Facing her from the distant table was a very handsome uniformed young man. When Sofya's gaze happened to meet his, he started to nod and smile in a friendly manner. Embarrassed at having been caught staring, she quickly looked away. Then, slowly, turned back, this time being careful not to look directly at the officer.

The woman at the distant table was wearing a familiar-looking street dress. The close-fitting blue poplin jacket worn over a blue flower-printed dress that draped gracefully to the floor indicated the lady was not wearing the fashionable bustle and hoop, but had allowed the material to flow naturally. Sofya did not need the extra clue of a distinctively beautiful abundance of thick, wild blond waves that hung well past the woman's shoulders. Sofya was staring at her sister. Presently Anyuta turned her head, no doubt wondering what it was behind her that her companion found so interesting. When and where had Anyuta obtained that delicate hat with a white feather and butterfly?

Vladimir, who had not yet seated himself, started toward the other table. After a brief hesitation Sofya followed.

For an awkward moment the officer, now standing, extended his hand to Vladimir and it was not immediately accepted. Vladimir's expression was one of irritation, accompanied by a faintly ironic amusement. And Anyuta, who remained seated, wore an indefinable look of satisfaction and concern.

Avoiding Sofya's gaze, Anyuta turned to her unfamiliar companion and made strained introductions, speaking in French. "Captain Leopold Wolf, this is my sister, Sofya Vasilievna. And my brother-in-law, Vladimir Onufrievich Kovalevsky."

The awkward pause prolonged itself a little longer. Then Vladimir accepted the extended hand. With a look of relief the handsome man turned to Sofya and gallantly kissed her fingers. Immediately he suggested, "Please, join us."

"We most certainly will." Vladimir drew two chairs to the table, as he continued to favor Anyuta with a look of disapproval.

"Captain Wolf came to my rescue," Anyuta offered somewhat awkwardly. "I had come downstairs to ask the desk clerk how to post my letter to Mother. My German is a little weak, and I was getting nowhere. And the clerk's French was weaker than my German." Anyuta turned her eyes to the handsome soldier who was looking admiringly at her. "Fortunately the good captain came to my rescue," she repeated. "He kindly offered to escort me to Volksgarten for an evening stroll, and when I could not help admiring this charming hat in one of the shop windows, the captain purchased it for me."

"But I was delighted to be able to be of help!" Captain Wolf's eyes twinkled mischievously.

Anyuta lifted her chin at Vladimir, as if daring him to object. A waiter appeared before the conversation could proceed, and Vladimir, instead of arguing, ordered wine.

Sofya, beset by wine and weariness, realized that her mouth was hanging open, and forced it shut. She struggled against the feeling that something fundamental in the world had changed. What in heaven's name was Anyuta up to? Anyuta, of all people!

Meanwhile, the other three at the table were making small talk, about the city, the university, literature, and, of course, the weather. Inevitably the conversation touched on the fringe of politics. To Anyuta's inquiry, the soldier admitted he had heard nothing recently of conditions in Paris. "But I fear that Louis Napoleon is hungering for conflict with the rest of Europe. All Europe, even France herself, is growing tired of that warlike family."

Even that modest dose of politics was enough to start Vladimir looking at his pocket watch. "We really must retire now," he announced, pushing back his chair. The officer also rose to his feet.

"Thank you again for rescuing my sister," Vladimir said with a light bow. "It's been a pleasure talking with you, sir."

"Thank you so much for your generosity and for a charming evening," Anyuta told the officer demurely as she arose, offering him her hand. Sofya still looked on in mute astonishment. Was this helpless, flirting maiden the liberated woman?

Gallantly Leopold Wolf drew his heels together and made a formal bow as he kissed Anyuta's hand. Evidently emboldened by her attitude, he looked into her eyes. "It is my pleasure to offer the hospitality of my city to such a lovely visitor." Sofya could hardly hear her sister's murmured reply; it sounded indecisive, but hardly chilling.

A FEW MINUTES LATER, when the three had ascended to their suite, Vladimir began his cold criticism. "Anya, how could you, an unaccompanied lady, have started talking to a soldier!" were his first words when the door of the room was closed behind them. "Really, Anya, Father entrusted you to me and on your first day abroad your behavior is frivolous, flirtatious. Accepting gifts from strange men, next thing I suppose you'll be inviting men up to the room."

Again Sofya gazed in disbelief. Her liberal-minded husband was suddenly sounding very like Father.

Anyuta's response came in icy, measured tones. "I remind you, sir, that I am a liberated woman. I will talk to whomever I please, at any time, without feeling it necessary to defend my behavior. And you, supposedly a sworn supporter of women's equality, are the last person who should be lecturing me!"

Vladimir stared at her for a moment, then stalked away to his bedroom.

Anyuta, almost immediately cheerful again, shrugged off the incident, "Sofya, this is just another example of Vladimir's uncontrolled emotionalism. I do not understand how or why you put up with such an unpleasant man." Kissing the bewildered Sofya lightly on the cheek, she added, "I'm exhausted. I think I'll retire now."

But just as Anyuta reached the bedroom door, she turned, as if reminded of something, and came back to Sofya. Silently she hugged her sister and whispered, "We're free now, you and I. Just as we planned."

Sofya silently clung to her sister, then kissed her cheek. Anyuta went off again to the bedroom.

Alone, not ready to follow her sister to sleep, Sofya noticed a piece of paper on the small writing table. She picked up and read the beautiful rounded script of her sister's letter to Mother and Father. A disturbing discovery, for it meant that Anyuta hadn't tried to post the letter. Her encounter with the officer must have begun in some way even less excusable.

Sofya, hardly knowing what she wrote, added a few words in her own hand and closed the letter.

NEXT DAY IT WAS late afternoon before Vladimir returned to the hotel, met the two women for whom he had somehow become responsible, and conducted them on a tour of a small two-bedroom apartment near the university. The weekly rent was a little more than he'd expected, but not really out of their range.

The sisters generally approved of his choice, though Anyuta could not resist one comment on how small and dark the rooms were considering what they cost.

Moving in their baggage was soon accomplished. Tomorrow Vladimir and Sofya would try to enroll in lectures, while Anyuta planned to spend the day working on a new idea for a short story.

SOFYA MADE HER way carefully over the uneven, dusty ground, treading on boards which had been laid as a temporary pedestrian passageway. A little way ahead, the lamplighter was beginning his evening round. A few steps in front of her, Anyuta and Vladimir picked their way, engaged in another round of their sporadic bickering.

"The plan is to encircle the center with a wide boulevard, to be called the Ringstrasse." Vladimir steadied Anyuta as she took the long step from one board to the next. "Adding even more beauty to the city, enhancing the cultural opportunities. New museums and theaters are planned. Existing structures, like the Opera House, are being refurbished. Traffic will flow easily around them, alleviating this annoying congestion." He nodded toward a line of carriages, some with their own lamps glowing, slowly merging onto the thoroughfare.

"Vladimir, how naive you are!" Anyuta pounced. "If you'd stop reading the editorials in the papers that are only tools of the government, and instead read the really free ones I've been bringing home, you'd know that the boulevards are broad so they can't be blocked with barricades. The parks are vast to give cavalry room to maneuver. They have nothing to do with cultural enrichment. They are to enable the authorities to crush rebellion more efficiently. Similar renovations are taking place in every major European city." Anyuta's voice rose up in scorn. "Fear is what's driving the changes. Fear of a repetition of the revolts of '48."

"In a little over a month, your Anya's become expert at cavalry movement," Vladimir observed to Sofya as he assisted her across the same wide span between the boards. "Can her new interest in matters military be attributed to the handsome Captain Wolf?"

As they proceeded along the narrow way, Vladimir was once more beside Anyuta, who continued expounding her newly acquired ideas on city planning as a tool of authoritarian government. Trailing behind the couple, Sofya listened with uneasiness. Since their arrival in the West, Anyuta's political ideas had become much more radical. Of course, Anyuta was not above taking a position simply for the sake of annoying Vladimir.

Content to be left out of the conversation, Sofya silently made her way around construction obstacles. The day had been exceptionally warm for late May. She savored the evening breezes and she yearned to reach what promised to be the refreshing atmosphere of the park. A restless, brooding, foreboding mood of discontent had taken possession of her soul since her arrival in this glittering city and it would not let go.

Vladimir half-jokingly attributed her black mood to a touch of envy. While Anyuta enjoyed the company of her officer friend, he said, Sofya allowed herself no distractions and was developing an exaggerated concern for their budget. She had responded that the real reason for her discontent was the inadequacy of Viennese mathematical society; but she doubted that Vladimir had taken her seriously. He teased that she was unique among the women in Vienna, not because of her mathematical talents, but because she had not danced the waltz. Tonight she would. After dinner, while the music mingled with the breeze, she'd remind him of her mathematical needs. He might fuss a little, but she'd console him by waltzing all night with him.

"Sofya?" Vladimir was far ahead, turning to her, calling. With a start, as if being awakened from a dream, Sofya realized that she had fallen considerably behind the others. "Sofya, the music will be starting in a few minutes. We'll have to hurry if we're to get a desirable table."

She quickened her pace and in a moment had caught up with him, and taken his arm. Anyuta was at his other side. Vladimir hustled them across the street, to the grassy expanse of the Stadtpark. Clearly, he knew exactly where he was going, heading toward a row of cafés edging the south border of the park. He had no hesitation choosing the café he wanted. And to Sofya's surprise, the waiter seemed to know Vladimir. A table was found for them immediately.

The park was quickly becoming crowded as couples and families moved closer to the orchestra shell. Some spread blankets on the grass. Children ran beneath the streetlights, dancing on the pavement's shadow patterns cast by burning gas. All Vienna seemed to be awaiting a summer evening in the changed world created by music.

The waiter quickly accepted their dinner orders. As the band started to take its position on the stage, Vladimir commented. "Tonight the music will be particularly beautiful. Johann Strauss is conducting. Various members of the Strauss family have been conducting here every summer since the park's opening in '09."

"How remarkable." Sofya loved listening to Vladimir's small talk. Everything interested him. Everything was a source of wonder. No doubt, he would entertain her with hundreds of facts on Heidelberg, when they'd settled in. He certainly could be a charming companion.

"Vienna is indeed a shallow city, easily distracted from the important events of the world," Anyuta remarked haughtily. "A city content to hide itself in music—as long as times are good for its oppressive businessmen."

Vladimir cast a sad, pleading look at Sofya, a glance intended to express his frustration with Anyuta; it happened to coincide with Sofya's own heartfelt sigh, uttered in the same cause.

Then the trio fell silent, the music of Strauss casting its spell. As they had each ordered a sausage plate dinner, a round of beer seemed appropriate. Vladimir generously paid the waiter, assuring that they would be well supplied with beer during the evening performance.

Vladimir's foot was tapping and his fingers drummed on the table as the orchestra moved into the strains of the *Blue Danube*. Sofya noticed her sister watching the waltzing couples, her admiring eye on the officers.

A truce had taken effect between Vladimir and Anyuta. Now was the time for Sofya to make her announcement.

"I've decided we must go to Heidelberg," she proclaimed in a sure, steady voice, at the next pause in the music.

Anyuta and Vladimir both stared at her in stunned surprise.

Vladimir was the first to comment. She thought his voice quavered a little. "So, you've decided."

"I've given Vienna a fair try, Vladimir. I've attended physics lectures with Lange, and sat in on a few mathematics lectures. At Heidelberg I could receive a far higher level of training in analysis. None of the Viennese professors seem interested in the developments in the calculus, or differential equations. The mathematicians here are consumed with the new geometries."

"New geometries?" Vladimir's brow creased, uncomprehending. Anyuta still looked blank.

"Yes, the systems that replace Euclid's fifth postulate, the parallel postulate, with alternate conjectures. The work is fascinating and quite important, but it's not what I want to do." She wasn't going to be distracted from her announcement. "I want to study with Professor Königsberger in Heidelberg. He'll get me started on a serious investigation of space, time, motion and infinity. Professor Lange assured me that Königsberger is on the very edge of the new work in analysis. And Lange is so impressed with my work in class this last month that he's agreed to write me a letter of introduction."

"Evidently your plans are set for Heidelberg," Vladimir observed coolly. "How soon must you leave?"

"As soon as possible." Actually she hadn't made any arrangements yet. There was something alarming in his calm.

"You remember," her husband cautioned, "Sechenov thought there was no hope for a woman at Heidelberg."

"He may have been wrong. He may have been basing his view on experiences there with Professor Bunsen, who's a known woman hater. But Bunsen's in chemistry, and I don't need him." She spoke hurriedly, hoping to be convincing. "Other professors won't be that narrow-minded. Lange also advised me to see a Professor Frederick, who's sympathetic to women students. If all goes well he'll help me deal with the administration."

Vladimir turned briskly to Anyuta. "What are your plans, dear sister?" Still he sounded cold and indifferent. "I assume that nothing holds you here—now that Captain Wolf has been called to join his regiment. Sometimes the threat of war does get in the way of military adventures."

Anyuta tossed her long blond hair. "I'll go to Heidelberg with Sofya," she answered calmly. "Whatever is best for Sofya's education is my main concern. And should be yours, Vladimir."

Vladimir nodded slowly; he seemed to be recovering from the shock. "Well, I can offer some help in your resettlement. I'll telegraph an old acquaintance of mine, Lamansky. He's in Heidelberg studying physics. He should be able to help you find an apartment."

Anyuta answered. "We've met Lamansky, once, long ago. The night we first met you."

"Good. Then you'll recognize him," Vladimir said coolly.

There was a silent pause. Sofya studied Vladimir as he stared blankly at the couples dancing.

What was he thinking? What could possibly delay his departure?

He turned toward her with a critical look. He turned the same gaze to Anyuta.

At last he spoke. "As for myself, I'm staying in Vienna." The tone was as definite as that of a military order.

"You can't mean that!" Sofya burst out.

"My dear, I mean exactly that. At last I shall be able to devote myself deeply to a field I really enjoy. I have a full schedule of geology lectures for the summer, and the fall sessions appeal to me even more. I may even be able to hear lectures by Suess. For the first time, in a very long time, I have hope for my own future, as something more than a jar of preserves." He took another long drink of beer. "And, in a manner of speaking, I've fallen in love."

Sofya felt her heart jump. She was afraid to look at him, afraid to look away. Afraid of what she herself might think or do in the next minute.

After a long pause, he added, "With geology, I mean, of course."

Sofya found her voice. "Vienna isn't the only place where you could study geology. Heidelberg must offer at least as wide a selection of courses." Suddenly she was astounded to hear herself begging. "Vladimir? Please come to Heidelberg?"

From the corner of her eye she could see Anyuta glaring at her: How could Sofya plead with him, this man who had served his purpose long weeks ago, who should have removed himself from their company then.

"No." Sofya's husband shook his head. There was pain in his eyes but he was not wavering. "You won't need me, Sofya. You'll have Anyuta, Lamansky, and others to help you. I'm staying here. I love Vienna and her people."

After a moment of silence he got to his feet, standing tall. "And now, good evening. Surely two ladies capable of going to Heidelberg alone will be able to find their way back to the apartment."

"You can't leave until we've discussed this more thoroughly." Sofya to her horror discovered that her hand had gone out and was gripping the sleeve of Vladimir's jacket.

Silently he waited until she let him go, then bowed slightly to both women, turned, and disappeared into the crowd.

CHAPTER ELEVEN

1869 ❧ *Heidelberg*

"This apartment is much brighter, pleasanter than the one in Vienna. And I love the neighborhood!" Anyuta called out as she unpacked in her bedroom at 13-A Utere Neckarstrasse, Heidelberg. "And it's cheaper!"

"I love the view!" Sofya fully opened one of the twin parlor windows that faced north. Resting her hands on the ledge, she leaned out as far as she could, taking in as much of the city's beauty as possible. From her third-floor vantage point she gazed over an almost continuous surface of tiled roofs.

Beyond the crowded buildings, the narrow winding cobbled streets, her eyes followed the windings of the Neckar River, its broad surface reflecting the wooded hills beyond. Tranquilly the river divided itself to pass through five arches of a majestic bridge. Then it meandered past the town, under a second bridge, before curving at last off to the west, through fertile fields and plains.

On the opposite shore were only a few buildings. A steep green wooded hill rose up behind them, and beyond the hill was the most remarkable translucent blue sky Sofya had ever seen.

Taking in a deep breath of wonderfully fresh air, Sofya reluctantly withdrew from the window. The oak-paneled walls of the parlor, the green divan and matching chairs, the sturdy table with four wooden chairs continued the impression of coziness. Obtaining such a nice apartment had been a stroke of luck. Lamansky knew the former renter, a student who had been called home unexpectedly. The building was only a block from the oldest section of the town. The university was within easy walking distance, as was most everything in this small town.

Lamansky had insisted the best views were to be had from the gardens of the thirteenth-century castle that dominated from its hill. Sofya would enjoy investigating that claim. But not today. Today she must unpack.

Struggling to hoist one of the heavier bags onto the bed in her room, she called to her sister, "I like Lamansky."

"I could tell." Anyuta was suddenly standing in the doorway, one hand resting on the frame. "He won't interfere with your studies, will he? Such piercing black eyes! He's got Tatar blood in his veins, no doubt. Those short brown student jackets show off their figures to good advantage. And the jaunty way Lamansky wears his student cap, I'll wager the man has every sweet little *fraulein* in Heidelberg sighing."

Sofya turned to her sister. "I'll be cautious about him." More softly she added, "I thought he showed more interest in making friends with you."

"Especially when he thought I was married." Anyuta entered the room and settled into the armchair, propping her feet on the edge of the bed. With her elbow resting on the arm of the chair Anyuta's forearm moved slowly back and forth, index finger extended as she continued in a semiserious voice, "Be careful! Lamansky appears to be the kind of man who likes to be very friendly with women who are no threat to his freedom."

"I got the same impression." Pushing baggage aside, Sofya cleared a small space for herself on the bed. "Still, he is charming. And he's studying physics. He could be quite helpful." Sofya gently pushed her sister's feet from the bed. "Don't worry, little mother, I can handle him. My only interest is in study. Tomorrow I start making arrangements with the university."

"As for me, I plan on visiting the town's newspaper offices. I will waste no time in making contact with this city's writing community."

"Don't be distracted by any officers," Sofya reminded her sister. "This is a small town. People will be making note of everything we do. There must be no hint of impropriety."

"Ah, officers!" Anyuta sighed overdramatically. "I doubt there's a man to compare with Captain Wolf among these milksop students. What a shame the captain's regiment was called up just as our friendship was blossoming."

"So that is why you didn't mind leaving Vienna. Oh, Anyuta!"

TIRED AND DISCOURAGED, Sofya trudged from the university eastward down the broad, cobbled main street. The late afternoon light reflected brightly from her landmark, the gothic Church of the Holy Spirit, with its baroque spire and roof. At the church she would turn north, toward the river and the bridge where she was to meet her sister and Lamansky.

Sofya walked as quickly as she could manage, considering her aching feet, passing blocks of brick buildings pushed tight against one another. The ground floor of each was painted red, white or green.

When she reached the church, she found merchants' stalls nestled in the narrow spaces between the gothic buttresses along the sides of the great building. The church would afford a cool place for a few moments. As she settled in a back pew, she noticed an ugly, incongruous brick wall separating the choir from the main section of the church. Trying to think of a possible reason for this disfigurement, she decided that some petty administrative whim must be to blame, as for so many of the world's troubles. She left the church feeling refreshed neither in body or in spirit.

At the foot of Alte Brücke, Lamansky and Anyuta were waiting for her.

"My day was a disaster!" Sofya moaned at them by way of greeting.

"You certainly look like you've been through some kind of catastrophe." Anyuta's critical glance prompted Sofya to push a wandering curl back behind her ear and to brush lightly at her dusty skirt.

Lamansky's black eyes examined Sofya with concern. "Dinner and a stein of one of the local brews will revive you. I've a place in mind on the other bank of the river, but it's a bit of a walk. Would you rather take the ferry across? There's a station right below the bridge entrance."

"My feet are aching, but I'd still rather walk." Sofya maneuvered herself between Anyuta and Lamansky and started the trio through the bridge gate, an entrance between two massive, rounded towers, both striped horizontally in orange and white, and connected with a stone arch.

Lamansky saw her examining the structure. "These towers once contained prison cells. The lower levels were for common criminals. The debtors, up in the archway, had a better view of the river and town."

It was all too easy to imagine prisoners' faces, shadowy forms in the arch windows. Quickly Sofya walked under the old bridge gate, ahead of her companions. With the towers behind her, she stopped short. To her left was a statue of some sturdy German burgher, no doubt the bridge's patron. Around his stone feet curved the bodies of sea nymphs, river gods. She smiled. The mermaids were here, waiting for her to capture them. And capture them she would!

"Is that a smile I see?" Lamansky put his hand under her chin. "Well, you are reviving. Good."

"Tell us what had you so depressed," Anyuta urged. "Maybe we can leave the gloom outside when we go in to dinner."

"The day started off badly." Sofya ran her hand along the edge of the thick brick parapet following the side of the bridge. "To begin with,

Professor Frederick is out of town. I went to the university and asked who was handling Frederick's affairs. A clerk suggested I see Kirchhoff and gave me his address, and I went immediately. All I could think of was that I mustn't embarrass myself before this giant of science. But of course the man didn't know me at all—no idea of who I am, or my background in science. I could see at first that he thought me some kind of madwoman to propose entering his classes."

"But you persisted," Anyuta prompted.

"Of course. I mentioned Chebyshev and the books he'd lent me. I told him Lange had praised my work in physics. I tried to speak intelligently about the different classes of functions I'd studied. Fortunately the theorem he asked me to explain was one I'm familiar with. I managed to recall and discuss several different proofs for it. I hope, by the end of the meeting, I convinced him that I am a serious, well-prepared student."

"Kirchhoff's a good fellow." Lamansky sounded encouraging. "He's helped many a student."

"I'm sure," Sofya sighed. "However, he didn't do much for me. He simply shuffled me off to the university's admission office."

"You went?" Anyuta asked.

"What choice did I have? The interview at admissions was, shall I say, difficult. Well, I suppose no worse than an afternoon with an interrogation officer from the Third Section."

"Come now," Anyuta snapped back.

Sofya ignored her sister's remark. "After two or three bureaucrats had talked to me, it was decided to hold a hearing of some kind. A committee will be established to judge my worthiness. By that time Frederick will be back. Judging by the questions I was asked today, my academic merits will not count for much. Apparently it's my character and motivations that most interest the authorities."

"It's because you're Russian," Lamansky lamented. "Being a young Russian is becoming synonymous with being a troublemaker. Everyone here has heard about all the problems at Petersburg University."

"Yes. But even more of a threat to these men is the fact that I'm a woman!" Sofya shot back. "I'd wager they never asked you about your marital standing, or what your father thought of you being in Germany, or who was responsible for you while you were here. They acted like I was nine years old."

"What did you expect from these tight-laced professors?" Anyuta snapped.

"I didn't expect an interrogation committee."

"I swear, I'll help," Lamansky vowed as they reached the north bank, where the bridge was guarded by a statue of St. Nepomuk. "I'll find out who's on the committee. Then I'll try to arrange for each member to have an individual meeting with you before the committee convenes." He took an arm of each of his companions, and led them westward along the riverwalk.

Anyuta remained determined. "And I'll stand as your chaperone. I'll be wonderful in the part of the stern, sensible older sister."

Sofya tried to visualize her sister in this role, and even serious gloom was unable to stand against the image. Laughing despite herself, she said, "You couldn't convince a child that you were stern and serious. Angry, yes, but that's not the same. And as far as these fellows are concerned, I'm chaperoning you! After all, I'm a married lady."

Anyuta's face turned pale. "How dare you—"

Lamansky quickly intervened. "You're far too beautiful, Anyuta. You'd frighten the scholars even more than Sofya. And you're far too fiery! I will stand as Sofya's second in her duel with the authorities."

Sofya was shaking her head. "Neither of you will need to do anything of the kind. I will face these people on my own. But I do thank you both for offering. Really, my spirits are restored. I am ready to do battle."

Lamansky guided them to a table at one of the riverside outdoor cafés. Soon, steins of foaming beer appeared. Sofya sipped the warm, pale amber brew and felt its calming effect. The scene before her was magical and romantic. The wide river reflected the majestic bridge, the church steeples, and, standing guard above the town, the ruins of the castle, red sandstone against the dark green of the forested hills.

Gradually the feeling grew in her that she had been right to insist on starting her career here. No matter what the obstacles, or the sacrifices, this was where she belonged. She took another sip of beer. She wondered what Vladimir was doing at this moment. She'd write him tonight.

In the background of her consciousness she heard Lamansky mention his recent trip to Paris. Eagerly Anyuta was encouraging him to tell the story. Her interest in things Parisian was becoming insatiable.

SOFYA SAT AT THE HEAVY DARK WOODEN TABLE in the parlor of her apartment. Today, at last, the committee reviewing her application was meeting.

After breakfast, she had spread her lecture notes from Vienna onto the table, halfheartedly hoping to distract herself during the long anxious hours of waiting. She would remain in the apartment until she was notified of her fate. Lamansky had cautioned that the procedure might take more than a day. Blessedly, Anyuta had announced that she would be gone for the day. Sofya would be free from her sister's ranting which most recently centered on the insufferable provincialism of Heidelberg, at least as its reality contrasted with the romantic image of Paris that Anyuta had conjured for herself.

Drawing pictures of four-leafed flowers on a paper meant for equations, Sofya tried to put aside her discouragement. For three weeks she had carried her credentials from the office of one administrator to another, suffering through a seemingly endless series of grueling interviews. She was sure her letters of reference and responses to mathematical questioning had made a strong positive impression on the Herr Professors Paul Dubois-Reymond and Leo Königsberger. Those two men were only in their thirties, and she felt they were open to working with a woman student as well prepared as she. She had not made as strong an impression on the physicist, Kirchhoff, despite the fact that she had a solid grounding in his field. She guessed the man was in his middle forties and lukewarm on admitting a woman to his classes and especially into his laboratory.

But of course her real opposition would come from the famous chemist, Herr Professor Robert Wilhelm Bunsen. He was fifty-eight, a confirmed bachelor, fanatically dedicated to his calling, and all too set in his ways.

With a struggle, Sofya forced her mind back to constructive work. Equations were again taking their rightful place on the paper.

Around midday a knock at the door announced a visitor, Lamansky, who thoughtfully had brought her a boxed lunch and news.

"The whole town's talking about you," he began, tossing his hat onto one chair, pulling up another to the table. Sofya quickly cleared away her papers. He went on, "You're a celebrity. The town's buzzing with word of the mysterious foreign lady who wants to be a scholar."

"All I want is admission to the university, something hundreds of men seek every term." She unpacked two bottles of mineral water, a large wedge of rich yellow cheese, a half roll of hard salami, and heavy black bread.

Her visitor fumbled in his pocket, brought out a small knife which he unfolded and began cutting the meat and cheese. "This is a small town. The university is its life. This morning I heard two bakers discussing the pros and cons of admitting a woman to *their* university!" He tore off a large chunk of black bread. Chewing vigorously, then wiping a crumb from the corner of his mouth, he added, "The administrative assistant appointed to gather information on you submitted his report to the committee this morning. They'll probably deliberate on it this afternoon and into tomorrow morning. I've heard the report's quite extensive. People have been streaming in and out of his office for the last few days."

Playing with the piece of cheese he'd put before her, she made a helpless gesture. "Every time I walk down the street, I see heads turning my way. Still, I can't imagine what the committee thinks they'll discover about me. I don't know a soul here, except yourself."

There was a knock on the door. "Perhaps the committee's come to a decision!" Sofya quickly wiped her hands, pushed back her chair with such force that its old legs wobbled precariously.

Opening the door, she froze in stunned surprise. "Vladimir!"

He stood shyly smiling at her. Was it possible that she'd forgotten how tall he was? In a moment she found herself pressed against his chest, his strong arms around her. Just as quickly, she felt his hands on her shoulders, and he pushed her gently away. His eyes examined her, as one would a child. "Your beautiful eyes are all bloodshot."

For some reason her knees felt weak. "Why didn't you write me you'd be coming?"

He shrugged. He turned and dragged his traveling bag into the room, then dropped it to exchange greetings with Lamansky. Slipping an arm around her waist, he looked from her to Lamansky.

At once she was aware that the casual appearance of Lamansky, his tie loosened, his brown jacket hanging over the back of a chair, his hat strewn on the armchair, must have startled Vladimir. Her hand went to the collar of her dress; in her nervous state, she had left the top two buttons comfortably open.

"We were just having lunch. Lamansky brings the two essentials of life, food and news." Sofya led the way back to the table.

"Thank you so much, Sergei Aleksandrovich, for helping Sofya get settled so comfortably." Vladimir's tone of thinly veiled sarcasm and jealousy surprised and embarrassed Sofya.

"Unfortunately, things aren't completely settled yet." Lamansky ignored Vladimir's sudden formality.

"Vladimir, I'm glad you came," she assured him a few minutes later, when the three were finishing the remnants of lunch.

"When I received your letter describing the trials the administration was putting you through, I started worrying. I can make it quite clear to this committee that you have the support of your husband." He shot a glance at Lamansky as he emphasized the last word. "I've told my professors that I'd be here until you started the term."

"Thank you." She reached out and touched his big hand. She had always liked the red hairs clothing the backs of his fingers.

Lamansky cleared his throat. "In my opinion, you've arrived just in time. A day later, and all might have been lost for Sofya. I was trying to think of a way to tell you, Sofya, but now . . ." Lamansky looked at Vladimir. "There are some very interesting developments. A wife of one of the professors, I can't find out which one, says she knows Sofya's a widow!"

"What?" Two voices exclaimed the word at the same time.

"And I hear that the committee believes her."

"But this is ridiculous!" Sofya jumped up from her seat. "I don't even know any of the professor's wives. How could one of them make up such a lie?"

Lamansky shrugged. "I can only guess. Your landlady, and I suppose others, must have noticed there's no man living here. People gossip and speculate. Now several of the committee members are convinced you're here to find a husband, probably among the professors. They've reasoned you must be one of the free-living Russian liberals they've heard about. The poor dears are worried about your threat to their virtue."

"Those small-minded bigots! Even Russian widows are to be feared?" She suddenly realized her hands were clenched before her and she was shouting.

"Do you still want to go to school here?" Vladimir's voice had risen to match hers.

"Yes!" she shouted back.

"Why, in God's name?"

"Because *these fools are the best scientists!*"

When Vladimir spoke again, after ten seconds of silence, his voice was lower. He managed to sound stern and soothing at the same time. "I must talk to the committee. Lamansky, how soon can you get them to call me as a witness?"

"Tomorrow. I know the people to contact."

THE NEXT MORNING, Vladimir stood before the committee. He was introduced to the four inquisitors, who were seated behind a long oak table: mathematics, Herr Professors Paul Dubois-Reymond and Leo Königsberger; chemistry, the most esteemed Herr Professor Robert Bunsen; physics, Herr Professor Gustav Kirchhoff. The venerable Professor Kirchhoff did not acknowledge his introduction. His cane rested on the table, upon which he leaned with one arm in a crooked position, his large hand hiding much of his face.

Vladimir knew the reputation for excellence that each of the men had earned, Kirchhoff and Bunsen being of almost legendary renown.

Calmly Vladimir addressed this quartet. "Gentlemen, there seems to be some confusion about my wife's intentions for study here, and her personal status. I stand ready to answer any questions you may have."

Bunsen, frail and sickly looking, began. "We have had witnesses who stated that Frau Kovalevsky was a widow. For all we know, you may be a sympathetic friend posing as her husband." Bunsen adjusted the pirate-like patch that covered his right eye, ruined years ago in a laboratory explosion. The left eye was fixed cold and unblinking on Vladimir. "Can you prove when and where you were married?"

Vladimir controlled his temper. "Sofya and I were married eight months ago in Russia. I have shown the clerk my passport, and my wife tells me you have examined all her credentials. I had not thought it necessary for us to bring our certificate of marriage."

"Why were you not here with her at the time of her petition for admission?" The man's voice carried bitterness and conceit. His reputation as a misogynist was almost as solid as his reputation as a chemist, and not without reason.

"With all due respect, Professor Bunsen, your question has no bearing on my wife's qualifications as a student." Vladimir paused, sighed as the panel only continued to look at him. He went on: "Because of my wife's strong desire to work at your university, she left Vienna where we were both studying. I remained behind to complete a project in geology. My wife arrived here accompanied by her older sister. You must have been informed of her situation. I fail to see what bearing this might have on her ability to comprehend your lectures on chemistry."

"Please, try not to be too defensive," DuBois-Reymond pleaded, apparently embarrassed by Bunsen's blatant expression of ill will. "I've interviewed the candidate, and will vouch for the excellence of her mathematical preparation. Still, when admitting a woman to university lectures, especially a woman as young as Frau Kovalevsky, character and background are also factors." The man wiped his brow with a very large white kerchief, before continuing in a tone and manner meant to ease the tension. "Herr Professor Königsberger, you found the young woman's mathematical background acceptable."

"More than acceptable! Her preparation for my courses is outstanding." Königsberger's answer was stronger than Vladimir had expected from a young professor who had just solidified his own position at Heidelberg. He could not be expected to take a controversial stand at his first committee hearing.

Vladimir had one more card he wanted to play. "You should be aware of my wife's maternal line, the Schuberts." Vladimir stressed the obviously German surname. "Her family boasts of many illustrious scientists. Her great-grandfather was a native of your country, educated at Göttingen. He loved mathematics and astronomy, and corresponded with the greatest German mathematician of all time, Johann Gauss. His adopted countrymen, recognizing his great talent and putting aside the fact that he was not a native, honored him with election to the prestigious St. Petersburg Academy of Sciences. His son, Sofya's grandfather, was a geographer who published many papers and books, both in Russia and abroad. Her grandfather Schubert also was elected a member of the St. Petersburg Academy of Sciences. For character references, you might consult Sofya's aunt and uncle who are living in Stuttgart. Sofya's uncle is the personal secretary to the Queen of Würtemberg. Perhaps Sofya should have supplied references from the queen, rather than from her tutors. Gentlemen, for background and character, you could hardly have a more well-positioned candidate than my wife." Vladimir was grateful he had retained some of Sofya's mother's conversations about the family background.

After a long pause, Dubois-Reymond responded in a steady tone, "You have made a strong case for your wife. Both her intellectual and national heritage will stand in her favor."

Vladimir stood silent. He had done what Sofya would never do, presented her as a German. For three generations her mother's family had been loyal Russians, constantly forced to defend against the prejudices caused by their German name. It was time some benefits came from the heritage. He calculated that Dubois-Reymond, a German, must have encountered the evil effects of nationalistic fervor because of his French name. And it seemed to Vladimir that it was Dubois-Reymond who was most sympathetic to Sofya's admission.

Addressing Vladimir in a tone almost congenial, the mathematics professor continued, "I seem to recall the name 'Kovalevsky' coming into a scientific discussion I was having with my brother. The context was biology, or rather embryology. Are you, by any chance, related to Aleksander Kovalevsky?"

"Aleksander is my brother."

DuBois-Reymond looked at his colleagues. "The members of this examining board should be aware that Professor Aleksander Kovalevsky is widely respected as a dedicated and brilliant scientist, and a proponent of Darwin's theories."

Vladimir nodded. "Both my brother and I have been in correspondence with Mr. Darwin. Before taking up scientific work, I had the honor of translating and publishing Mr. Darwin's essays."

The interrogators took a moment to whisper to each other. It seemed that Dubois-Reymond and Kirchhoff had been won over. Bunsen was the holdout.

As he watched the gesturing scientists, Vladimir tried to weigh the effect of the introduction of Darwin into the situation. He was never sure, in the case of older scientists, whether his support of Darwin would be helpful or do him harm.

"Herr Kovalevsky, are you planning on continuing your own studies here in Heidelberg?" Kirchhoff inquired.

An automatic "no" was on Vladimir's lips, but it died there before it could be spoken. His mind was racing through the implications. If he told them now that he would be returning to Vienna, Sofya would almost certainly be denied entrance to Heidelberg; the great dream of her life would be shattered. On the other hand, if he actually stayed here, he must abandon his work with the great Suess. Gone was his own dream of a scientific life surrounded by the gaiety and friendliness of Vienna. Instead, years spent in the oppressive provincialism of Heidelberg awaited.

Kirchhoff's eyes had never left Vladimir's face. Breaking the deadly silence and evidently willing to make a gesture that would arouse Vladimir as well as appease Bunsen, Kirchhoff added, "You realize, Mr. Kovalevsky, that some members of this committee would view your wife's position entirely differently, if she were studying primarily to be your assistant."

Clearly, Kirchhoff was offering a way of presenting Sofya's case so that Bunsen could feel he had not given way on the "woman" question.

Vladimir still had not replied, and now Kirchhoff was speaking again, stumbling over the words as if he were embarrassed. "Your wife is quite young and, as we have all noted, quite, ah, pleasant in appearance. Heidelberg is a very small town. The committee is concerned with reputations. Frankly, your presence would greatly strengthen your wife's position."

Bunsen quickly added in a tone that made no attempt at hiding sarcasm, "Of course, she will be judged only on her own qualifications."

Vladimir looked into the faces of the examiners. Clearly Kirchhoff, Königsberger and DuBois-Reymond were pained. Bunsen's one eye remained fixed on Vladimir with an expression that said "checkmate."

Vladimir hesitated. The question and his answer were too important to him to tolerate the slightest risk of a misunderstanding. "She will be allowed to attend class only if I attend with her?"

"Of course not." DuBois-Reymond tried to smooth things. "It's just that a positive decision would be easier, for some of the committee, if it were understood that her main purpose was to advance your career." His eyes turned down shamefully as he added, "The condition need not be formally stated."

Vladimir struggled against his urge to rebel against these bigots. To tell them to go to hell and take their damned degrees with them. But he couldn't do that. He wasn't fighting for himself, he was fighting for Sofya. "I assure you gentlemen that my wife has my complete support in her efforts to obtain an education." He would tell them what he must, now, and try to find some way around it later. He drew in his breath before he added, "I will make arrangements to continue my studies here in Heidelberg."

"Thank you, Herr Kovalevsky." DuBois-Reymond seemed much relieved. "If you would wait in the next room for a little while—?"

IN A FEW MINUTES he was summoned back. DuBois-Reymond spoke for the professors. "We are happy to accept you, Herr Kovalevsky, as a student. Your wife's situation is more complicated. She will not be allowed to work in a program culminating in the granting of a degree. However, if she can obtain individual permission from the professors involved, the university will not object to her attending lectures. If an individual professor refuses her admission, the university will not force him to accept her.

"The decision of the committee will be committed to writing and sent to Frau Kovalesky, immediately."

Vladimir turned and left the room. He had the feeling of having stepped into a trap, and at the moment he could see no way out.

☙❦☙

VLADIMIR RETURNED TO THE APARTMENT and informed the sisters of his hard-won partial victory, omitting at first any mention of the special condition that had made it possible.

Sofya sighed tiredly. "I'd hoped for more. For something that would set a precedent. Women should be able to study without relying on the goodwill of individual professors. Goodwill is a rare and delicate commodity."

"You're right, of course. But something definite has been gained, a precedent has been set. Now liberal professors won't have to worry about repercussions from the administration when they open their lectures to women. I've discovered that you're the first woman to be officially recognized by the university administration since the Italian scholar, Olympia Morata, was invited to lecture here."

"Was she invited to stay?"

"She must have been. She was buried here, beside the Jesuit church, in 1555. Believe me, Sofya, you've taken a big step. The rest will come in time."

"In time?" Sofya looked at him sourly. "In three hundred fourteen years two women have won conditional recognition, the first as a lecturer, the second as a student."

"Stop pouting and enjoy your victory," Anyuta scolded her. "You may not have won everything you wanted, but you've won a lot. Fight them again tomorrow."

"I've brought wine for the celebration, if either of you are interested." Vladimir drew a bottle from his jacket pocket and placed it on the table. As he struggled with the cork, Anyuta brought glasses.

"To your victory." Vladimir raised his glass to her. "Through diplomacy and perseverance you have managed a feat our Petersburg friends said was impossible." They all drank.

"To *our* victory." Sofya proposed the second toast. "With help from my loyal and dedicated supporters"—she nodded to Anyuta, then to him—"I have kept to my goals."

Now it was Anyuta's turn. "To freedom. May we all one day just be free to follow our own dreams."

"Amen!" Vladimir and Sofya chorused.

Glass in hand, Sofya settled into her favorite reading chair. Her sister occupied the divan. Vladimir remained standing, refilling his glass with the last of the wine. Squinting through red liquid at a candle flame, he announced, "Attached to this partial victory was a certain condition."

He sipped his wine before continuing. "The committee assumed I was staying in Heidelberg. I did not contradict them."

It took her a moment to comprehend. "You're really staying? You've given up Vienna?"

"If that was the only way to get you admitted, of course, Vladimir had to do it," Anyuta put in firmly.

Vladimir sipped again. "Your education comes first."

"Thank you," Sofya whispered.

"For once, your action pleases me, Vladimir. You'll be of some real use. You know how she hates being alone." Anyuta's face had the look of a cat ready to pounce on a ball of yarn. "With you here, I can leave for Paris."

"Anyuta!" Sofya nearly shouted. "To Paris? Alone?"

Vladimir turned to stare. "In Paris, Anyuta, every woman alone is assumed to be dishonorable. You have no idea what you're getting into. None whatsoever." These sisters were impossible.

"Anyuta, I know you've wanted this for a long time, but won't you consider finding another woman to accompany you?" Sofya pleaded.

"I promised your father I'd look after you." Vladimir's statement sounded tired, defeated and half-hearted.

"You could come with me, Vladimir," Anyuta jeered. "But then you'd have to leave Sofya alone. And I believe you've promised Sofya, Father and the university that you wouldn't do that. You seem to have over-extended your store of gallantry. Short of physical restraint, there is nothing you can do to stop me. I'm going to Paris, and I'm going alone. I'm perfectly capable of taking care of myself. I won't spend another month in this boring little German town while the world remakes itself in France."

Anyuta sipped the last of her wine before continuing, "There is a difficulty. Mother and Father will make a terrible fuss when they find out I'm not staying with you. And I suppose Father could force me to return home by restricting my passport or even by coming to get me."

Sofya had seen Anyuta's stubborn determination many times. Nothing could stand against it.

"There's no need to upset Mother and Father," Sofya reasoned aloud. "We just won't tell them about your move. You send letters to me, and I'll post them here with my letters to Mother and Father. The postmark will read Heidelberg. They'll never know we've separated."

"Very clever." Vladimir's lips were pressed tightly together, giving his face a cruel and cynical look Sofya could not remember having seen before. "I can't help but admire the persistence and ingenuity of the Krukovskaya sisters. I sincerely congratulate you both." He drained his wine and set down the glass. With a last small nod to Sofya, he withdrew to the room Sofya had vacated for him.

Sofya started after him, but immediately Anyuta was on her feet to stop her. As the door closed behind Vladimir, Anyuta began scolding, "Really, Sofya, he has no reason to be upset. In staying with you in Heidelberg he's doing no more than he agreed to do when you made your bargain. I never asked for his protection. He had no right to make any agreements with Father concerning me. His own relationship to our parents is completely false; he certainly has no grounds for outrage at my little deception."

Sofya allowed herself to be restrained. "You don't understand him at all, Anyuta."

"Oh, don't I?"

"No, you don't. Vladimir has hopes for his own life, his own career. Today he made a great personal sacrifice for me. It was a noble act, and I won't let you belittle it."

"I repeat, little sister, the man is only following the terms of the contract he made with you. I've said he has my approval for doing that." Anyuta moved aside. With a dramatic wave of her hand she motioned toward Vladimir's room. "Could it be you're succumbing to romantic ideas, forgetting the very contract your knight has defended?"

"Anyuta, you're insufferable!" Feeling her face grow warm with anger, Sofya pushed past Anyuta, and knocked gently on the closed door. "Volodya, open the door. Volodya?" Softly she spoke the endearing form of her husband's name. No answer came. Hesitantly she tried turning the knob. The door was locked. Once more she called his name. Nothing, no answer. For a moment longer, her arms hanging limply at her sides, she stared at the closed door.

Slowly she turned away. The sneering, self-satisfied face of Anyuta awaited her. Feelings Sofya had not known since childhood overtook her, a flood of humiliation and rejection.

Sofya retreated to her reading chair and hid her face behind a book of mathematics. Mercifully, Anyuta did not disturb her. Sofya's thoughts would not focus on the equations. Her mind raced. She had to blame herself that things had gone so wrong. For a moment she had let herself forget the bargain, the arrangement. She had wanted to be close to Vladimir. She had let herself be swayed by romantic emotions. Her lapse had brought only rejection and degradation.

RETURNING FROM THE LAST GEOLOGY FIELD TRIP of the semester, tired, dirty, and weathered by exposure to sun and wind, Vladimir felt pleased with himself. This trip, like the others, had proven worthwhile. Despite his earlier doubts, his professors, these small town Pharisees, were giving him a solid foundation in geology. Now that his thoughts were on the subject of unearthing remains and moving dirt, he wondered in what state of disarray he would find Sofya and the apartment. During the four months since she'd started classes she frequently had not bothered to eat, because he had not been there to arrange the meal. She had taken on a heavy load of course work. If they could both stand the strain for three more weeks the term would be over, and next term he'd try to convince her to ease up. Twenty-two hours a week in a classroom was too much for anyone. Out of necessity he supervised the occasional servants and attended to matters of housekeeping. Even the details of both their wardrobes had fallen entirely into his care. Which reminded him, he'd never seen her wearing the new dress he'd slipped into her wardrobe. In fact, she never even mentioned its appearance. Never thanked him, not that he expected thanks.

Preoccupied with his concerns for Sofya, Vladimir entered the vestibule of their apartment building. As he started up the three flights of stairs, Frau Müller, the landlady, called to him in her loud, harsh German. "Herr Kowalewsky, I have a letter for your wife."

Vladimir cringed inwardly, as usual, at the German mispronunciation of his name, the vibrant "v" stretched out into a whining "wa."

"It arrived when the young student was out." The short, fat, old owner of the apartment house dressed cheaply, and might easily have been taken for a washerwoman. She handed an envelope to Vladimir.

"Thank you." He turned immediately and trudged on up the steps. The postmark was Petersburg and the fine, legible script looked like the general's hand. Maybe a letter from her father would take Sofya's mind away from her work for a few moments.

"Herr Kowalewsky!" called the harsh voice behind him. "I remind you, your rent for this month is overdue. I can't pay my bills if I do not receive the rent due me. You must make a payment soon or I will be forced to ask you to leave."

He turned, staring down at the woman with what he hoped was an appearance of dignity. "We are good, quiet tenants. I'm sure you won't want to lose us. I'll make a payment within a few days. A little more patience, Frau Müller."

Frau Müller did not seem pleased, but a moment later her broad backside was disappearing behind a first-floor door. He felt contempt for her. In Russia, the owner of an apartment building would never harass tenants for bills. Such matters were dealt with by a building supervisor who served the owner, and as everyone understood, also served the government with the spying eyes of an informer.

Trying to imagine Frau Müller as a spy only made him dizzy. Vladimir finished his climb slowly and tiredly. Expenses were spiraling out of control. He'd closed the Vienna apartment with a loss on the lease. At least that was only a one-time expense. Anyuta had needed a large sum of cash to establish herself in Paris. Only a loan, she'd insisted, that she'd repay from her allowance checks. Maybe she would. And the expenses of his geological field trips were an ongoing drain that was taking a serious toll on resources. Of course, the trips were absolutely necessary to his work. Geology wasn't a pencil-and-paper science like mathematics.

He reached the apartment, took out his key and opened the door.

Expecting to enter a monastic atmosphere of study, he felt his jaw drop open as he took in the unexpected scene. Seated at the dining table was Sofya, smiling happily. Her beautiful, expressive eyes were shining as she studied, not lecture notes, but some article in a newspaper. What sounded like the last echo of a girlish giggle was on her lips; it had been a very long time since Vladimir had seen her in so playful a mood. Bending over her shoulder was Lamansky. His left hand, pointing to the paper, almost touched Sofya's hand. His right arm was on the back of Sofya's chair, his face was very close to hers.

She was wearing the blue flowered dress Vladimir had bought her. She looked absolutely charming. Her eyes turned toward him, but she didn't rise in greeting. "Vladimir, come see! Lamansky's found an article about me in the local paper."

Lamansky straightened, and Vladimir thought he noticed a slight reddening of his face. Had he been about to kiss Sofya?

Sofya, far from appearing guilty, or even sensitive to Lamansky's mood, was all caught up in her own publicity. "The editor is commenting on the 'foreign, woman student.' They also refer to me as their 'wonder student.' "

Lamansky added, calmly enough, "Sofya's becoming the pride of Heidelberg, Vladimir. The people are taking her to their hearts."

"Some of them are, certainly." Vladimir walked to the table and sat in the chair across from Sofya, gazing at her.

"Look, it says here that the professors are impressed with my 'quiet, shy manners.' " With a little laugh she turned the paper so Vladimir could read it properly. "They don't realize a good part of my shy manners are embarrassment at my poor German.

"I think I'll save this article and send it to Anyuta."

Ignoring the paper, Vladimir tossed the unopened letter on the table before his wife. "Here's some more news."

"I'll be going now." Lamansky had sobered rapidly. "I'll see you at Kirchhoff's lecture, Sofya."

"Yes." She arose and accompanied the visitor to the door. When he was gone, she at last took full notice of Vladimir. "You look tired."

He grunted agreement.

Dismissing his disturbed state, Sofya opened the letter. Vladimir watched an expression of dismay develop on her face. He didn't know what the bad news was, but somehow he was not surprised.

"Oh, Vladimir. Father's found out Anyuta's not with us."

"Already? How?"

"It seems she refused the attentions of some dunderheaded Russian student in Paris. The student had the gall to write Father, complaining of Anyuta's bad manners toward a fellow countryman."

She was skimming rapidly through the pages. "Then there's a long, sad paragraph about how hurt Mother is that Anyuta deceived her. And a good many paragraphs of Father's outrage. His own daughter, living unchaperoned in wicked Paris! He always knew, he says, that once she started writing fiction, she was on the road to damnation. He says here that he and Mother have disowned Anyuta. If she wants to live on her own, well then, she can try managing on her own. They'll not send her any more money.

"Vladimir, we'll have to help Anyuta. I'll send her a third of my allowance."

"And anything we can spare from my publishing income." The sarcasm in his voice went unnoticed. His thoughts turned to the business. He hadn't had any income in months. The books he published were a meaningful contribution to science in Russia, but they just weren't profitable. He might improve sales with a translation of another Darwin book.

Sofya interrupted his thoughts. "Father ends with a note to you, Vladimir."

"Go ahead, read it."

"He forgives you and understands how you were not able to control

Anyuta's wild impulsive behavior. And he understands that your silence to him on this matter was probably necessitated by your wife's demands. He concludes by saying how much comfort it is to him knowing you're with me, taking care of me!" Sofya handed over the letter. "He's siding with his son-in-law. Male camaraderie. For his daughters, only reproach. For you, understanding and forgiveness."

Vladimir glanced at the pages briefly, then laid them aside. "Can't you see how deeply you've hurt him? I suppose we all have. He doesn't even know I'm not really a son-in-law. The poor man loves his daughters."

"Father loves me?" Sofya sounded surprised.

"You're incapable of recognizing love." Vladimir whispered so softly he was sure she hadn't heard him; she was staring at the letter again. When she lifted her gaze he looked into her eyes and spoke firmly, with as much control as he could muster. "While we're speaking of relationships, let's get something cleared up. What's going on between you and Lamansky?"

The sheer bewilderment in her face eased his worry. "What's wrong with you? Sergei is a friend. Just a much needed, much appreciated friend." In a moment her bewilderment vanished, replaced by a hard, cold stare of challenge. "Now and then, he's a little too flattering and flirtatious. His playfulness means nothing to me. And if it did, I didn't think you'd care."

He jumped from his seat. He shouted in her face. "Are you deaf and blind?" The shocked look on her face made him realize his fingers were pressing hard into her shoulders.

"Take your hands off of me!" She glared at him, her hands clenched. Clearly she was struggling to control her outrage.

He let her go and dropped back into his chair. Humiliation welled up. He had completely overreacted. He'd let her goad him into a rage. An all-possessing dread followed the realization. He was ruining any chance for her love and respect.

She didn't move or speak. He thought a look of disgust was beginning to replace the anger.

"Forgive me," he muttered.

With no sign of forgiveness, she turned and left him alone. He heard the door of her room slam.

SOFYA LOOKED UP from papers scribbled with diagrams and formulas spread before her on the dining table. She had one more examination, introductory mechanics, to complete the term. In the easy chair, not far from her, Vladimir sat with his long legs crossed at the ankles. A geology text on glacial formations opened on his lap, a glass of tea, as usual, within easy reach.

How unlike the raging man who had roused her own fierce anger a few weeks ago. He had let unwarranted, unjustified jealousy threaten their relationship. She understood the force of jealousy. And she felt she was on the whole rather generous to the failing in others. Gradually, over the course of days, her anger had passed. His mood of depression and remorse had not. Forced to concentrate on her examinations, she had pushed aside a disturbing feeling of concern for him. A feeling disturbing enough to have caused her episodes of night terrors.

Perhaps sensing her eyes upon him, Vladimir looked around. "Sofya, the term will be over in a week, and—"

"Thank goodness!" Sofya interrupted. "We desperately need time away from our work."

He went on, not acknowledging her comment, as if following a rehearsed speech. "—and I've been making arrangements for the vacation period. I'm going to the British Isles, first to London, then field trips to the countryside and possibly to the Isle of Man."

"London?" She gazed at him in astonishment. "Vladimir, I promised Mother and Father we'd visit. With Anyuta estranged from them, they'll be counting all the more on seeing us."

"I agree, you should visit your parents. But I'm not going with you. For one thing, I can't imagine visiting them and not have them realize how things are between us."

"We could work something out so they wouldn't suspect." Sofya flushed. She felt herself becoming nervous and agitated. "How could I return alone? How would I explain your absence?"

"I'll stand by any story you concoct."

"I won't go back without you," she said firmly. "I can't."

Vladimir smiled at her with his look of sad understanding. An unpleasant thought must have caused his face to twist in a grimace. "And what will you do with your vacation? Stay here with Lamansky?"

So, the jealousy monster had only been asleep. *I just will not discuss Lamansky.* "I don't want to stay here *alone.* I hate being alone, you know that. If you insist on going to London, I am coming with you."

"No."

She thought she detected a brief hesitation in his refusal, a lack of resolve. She tried for her most pleasing voice. "Why go to London? From what I hear, it's a frightening place, with hordes of poverty-stricken factory workers. Crime and suffering and child labor."

"Have you been reading Dickens again?" he looked at her pityingly. "I've lived in London. The city is alive with fabulous museums, libraries, theaters, scientific and philosophical societies. I have friends I want to visit and some fossil research I want to do. I might be able to do a little publishing business."

Sofya would not be left behind. "Well, if you insist on London, then it's London. I suppose we could stop in Paris, going over. Perhaps again on our way back. We'd visit Anyuta."

He frowned. "Think, Sofya. The long train rides, the boat crossing, strange cities, hotel living. You hate those things."

"Vladimir, I want to be with you." She spoke softly.

He looked at her for a long time, examining her with the wonder he usually reserved for his fossils. She turned her eyes away.

The hint of cheerfulness she had been waiting for broke through his melancholy. "If you won't go home, I suppose you had better come with me." Rising from his chair, he spoke while pacing, his big hands hidden in his pockets. "I'll have to make some changes in my arrangements. You can't live in the cheap bachelor quarters I had reserved. I'll write my brother and ask for a small loan to cover the added expenses. I'll show you the real London. And I'll show London you." At last she saw his smile. "You're quite a beauty and a marvel, Sonechka, my little sparrow."

She warmed to the sound of the diminutive. A very long time had passed since he'd called her his little sparrow.

CHAPTER TWELVE

1869 ❧ *London*

Vladimir was pleased at having arranged accommodations in one of the more favored sections of London: Primrose Hill. The area was within walking distance of the British Museum. Theaters, a bustling business district, and cafés galore could be reached without resorting to expensive cabs. And, the north bank of the Thames offered pleasant views for an evening stroll.

The streets of Primrose were lined with elegant rowhouses, many boasting front entrances with pseudoclassic pillars. The house Vladimir had obtained was just such a rowhouse. The neighbors were doctors, lawyers and high-level civil servants. Vladimir knew from his previous stay in London that this area was also home to a few successful men with liberal political leanings, and these men were inclined to offer hospitality to like-minded foreigners.

The housekeeper had been dismissed for the evening, and Sofya was in one of the other rooms. Vladimir picked up the photo that rested on the mantel in a silver frame. The family of his old contact, Frederick Margels, looked out at him, plump wife and two daughters on the brink of womanhood.

Replacing the photo on the mantel, Vladimir wandered from room to room in search of Sofya. He marveled at just how well his friend, who had no obvious means of support, had done for himself. The ground floor offered a spacious parlor with a fireplace and a large window overlooking a lovely park. A second, less formal room lay behind large double doors.

Up a steep flight of stairs, on the first floor, were two rooms, one a very spacious study. A desk, carelessly stacked with books and papers, was turned to take advantage of the view of the park. An oversized morocco leather divan stood against one wall. The smaller room, with warm blue walls and a white-trimmed window frame, served as a sleeping chamber for the owner and his wife.

The second floor was divided into three rooms of equal size. It was somehow obvious that not only a successful man, but a successful family lived here. Two sleeping rooms for the owner's daughters, and a third chamber in transition between playroom and study. Twin desks piled high with serious looking books shared space with a sorority of dolls atop a bookcase of children's stories. These last were mostly in English, some in German. Clearly at least one of the daughters had a strong liking for plants: pots of thriving greenery were lined up along the window sill, and grouped in the corners the room. Philodendron vines sprouted from hanging containers, and struggled to close a curtain of vines over the window.

Vladimir paused at the open door for a moment, looking in. Sofya was seated in a rocking chair, staring vacantly out the window. The rhythmic creaking of the chair on the bare wood floor went on, uninterrupted by his arrival.

"You need some cheering up," he remarked. "Come out with me."

"I'm exhausted." Sofya looked up at him, her face expressionless, her body limp.

"I'm meeting a very interesting Englishman." Vladimir moved a desk chair to face Sofya's. Straddling the seat and resting his arms on the back, he spoke in a gentle, coaxing tone. "Ralston's a curator at the British Museum and a scholar of Russian folklore. He knows more peasant customs and songs than our two old nurses put together. The conversation will be wonderful, and in Russian."

She studied him briefly, then turned her gaze back to the window. "Thanks, but I won't be very good company."

Vladimir reached out and placed his hand over hers. "You're worried about Anyuta. Well, so am I. Your sister is getting involved with radicals."

"She appears to be content." Sofya didn't look at him when she spoke. "And she enjoys earning money writing articles and translating news reports for that small publishing house."

Vladimir felt himself tensing. He withdrew his hand from Sofya's. It was a struggle to speak calmly on the subject. "The stuff that publishing house puts out is very inflammatory. Here in Britain the press is relatively free, but . . . I tried to warn her."

"Of course, but she won't listen to you." Sofya said fatalistically. She got up and wandered about uncertainly. "Anyuta thinks you've lost all your convictions. And she's worried I'm losing mine. Perhaps I am. Look at this house, it's absolutely decadent."

"I grant you, far above the scale your sister has chosen for herself. But we have it only by a stroke of good luck. So accept our good fortune." Sofya's pacing was already wearing on his nerves. "Sit down!" he commanded.

Obediently she went back to the chair, sat down in it without rocking, her back straight. She looked down at the dark wood of the floor. Her hands were clutched tightly together.

"Stop fretting about Anyuta! And stop feeling guilty!"

She didn't move or answer.

His tone softened, "Oh Sofya, try to cheer up! Come out with me?" Again he reached over and took one of her hands.

"Not this afternoon."

"Well, at least come down to the parlor. I'll settle you there comfortably. It's warm for October, but I'll build a cozy little fire to keep you company while I'm gone." He stood up, still holding her hand. This time she rose gracefully from the chair.

Vladimir led her downstairs to the living area. "Settle here." He motioned her to a brown, overstuffed bear of a chair that faced the fireplace. Then, kneeling before her, he gently removed her shoes. "You need a cup of tea and a great book. When I return this evening, you'll be rested in mind and body."

The tension in Sofya's body was evidently starting to melt. "I've started Dostoevsky's new novel. You know, one of the characters reminds me of Anyuta. Please, would you get the book from my traveling bag?" Her voice hinted at an improving mood. "My slippers are in the bag as well. Just in case I feel energetic enough to move."

"The slippers I'll fetch. But no Dostoevsky, no Dickens, not even Eliot. Nothing with the least hint of politics. I've a new book for you."

Her lips turned up in a controlled smile. Early in their friendship he'd learned to keep a surprise or two in reserve for her moody times. He held up his open palm to her. "Stay put for just one minute."

He trotted up to his own room on the first floor, grabbed a plainly wrapped object from the pile of clutter on the floor and put it securely under his arm. Then up another flight of stairs to Sofya's room, where he fumbled through her traveling bag and found the soft satin slippers. For a moment he looked at them in wonder. They were tiny enough to fit a child.

When he reentered the parlor, she was sitting just as when he left her. "Curl your feet under you," he ordered. "There's an afghan on the divan. I'll get it for you." He leaned over her, tucking her in. "That's the idea."

He placed the delicately embroidered slippers next to her shoes, then took the package from under his arm and held it out to her.

With obvious delight, Sofya took the package, tore open the wrapping, and stared down at the cover. "*Alice in Wonderland?*" She read out the title in an English strained and accented. "Is this a book for children?" Sofya gave him a pleased look, half playful and half wondering.

"Just read it. You'll like the verse, especially the Mouse's Tale—very Russian in flavor." He lit the already-prepared fire, stoked the logs a little, then turned to her. "I'm told the book was written by a mathematician, Professor Charles Dodgson. Lewis Carroll is the name he uses for a little playful deception."

"Already I like the author." Sofya laughed. "A Russian sense of humor, a mathematician, and a player at harmless deceptions."

"Now for your tea." He opened the double doors leading to the smaller room. "The day servant left us a pot with a cozy and some sweets on the sideboard."

He returned with a warm cup of tea, brewed as strongly as English tea can be brewed. Sofya had swung her legs over one arm of the chair, her head rested on the other. The afghan was draped over her, covering her from neck to toe. The book was wedged between the cushion and the back of the chair.

Her small hand emerged to grasp the cup. He gently touched her lips with one finger, at which signal she obligingly opened her mouth to accept the dark chocolate rosebud.

"I'll want a report on the book at dinner." He reached around her and placed the book in her lap. "Read. No more brooding." He placed a quick kiss on the top of her head, an action she did not seem to be aware of, and went out.

SOFYA HEARD the front door close. Vladimir was quite attractive, she thought, especially when he was in a high mood. Anyuta's parting words in Paris came back: *don't succumb to romantic tyranny.* She had not surrendered to Vladimir's rugged charms. However, she saw no purpose in denying the man his due. He was handsome and attentive. Pulling the comforter closer around her, savoring the melting chocolate, she started to read. Alice was falling, down, down the rabbit hole.

Moments later, Sofya rested the book in her lap. The passage had sparked a mathematical image. The rabbit with his little pocket watch embodied time. The course of the little girl's life—or anyone else's— was a function of time. Alice was falling through a break in the graph of her life function! She was entering a Point of Discontinuity, a magical opening into another world where all natural laws were suspended. So- fya imagined the graph of the rational function $1/(x-1)$. It started some- where out in the uncharted regions of negatives clinging to the x-axis. Then dipped down, at $x=0$, changed course and headed back to the x- axis. Just as it was about to cross the x-axis, at $x=1$, a great abyss opened. There was the point, the rabbit hole, where x equaled one and the function became meaningless, a point where all established laws of calculation ceased. She was comforted in the realization that the func- tion would recover, come back into the realm of law, adventure a little farther from the favored x-axis, then turn and cling once more to the axis from which it had come, now from the opposite side.

What a wondrous opening to a novel! If she ever took up writing fiction, she would find a way to incorporate the rich images and relationships encountered in mathematical work.

With pleasant anticipation she picked up the book and read on.

A FEW BLOCKS of brisk walking in the welcome autumn sun brought Vladimir to the British Museum. He stood watching the parade of Museum visitors. Men wearing black top hats, carrying walking sticks or umbrellas, assisted fashionably dressed women down the museum's stone stairs. A young boy in a frilly collared suit with short pants was held in tow by his neatly uniformed nanny. A line of waiting cabs had anticipated the closing time rush.

Vladimir turned away from this scene of the bourgeoisie indulging itself in intellectual distractions, enjoying the bounty of their Empire. He pondered whether these folk could understand anything of what they viewed inside the museum. Were they widening their view of the world, or was this just science as circus?

Just down the street from the main entrance stood a small café. Stopping under the café's awning, Vladimir consulted his watch. Ten minutes past the appointed time. Ralston should be here.

A tapping noise caught Vladimir's attention. At a table just inside the café's clear glass window, sat a grayer, heavier version of the Bill Ralston who lived in Vladimir's memory.

Signaling to the waiter to bring another pot of tea, Ralston, conversing in excellent Russian as soon as Vladimir was inside, continued his welcome. "You look very hardy and ruddy, my boy. Your adventures must have agreed with you." A handclasp of greeting failed to interrupt the flow of remarks. "I loved your letters from Italy, Vladimir. Thanks for thinking of me under those most trying of wartime conditions. But then, not a word for over a year."

Vladimir apologized for his lapse in correspondence.

After they had emptied their first cups of tea, Ralston lowered his voice. "Tell me of Russia; how are things?" The question sounded hopeful.

"I left about the time you were starting your '68 visit. So, my news is secondhand." Vladimir's voice, too, had fallen until it was barely audible. "What I hear is not encouraging. The universities are cracking down on student organizations. The noose of literary censorship is tightening. And conditions in the factories surrounding Petersburg are utterly intolerable."

Ralston looked disappointed, but not surprised. The conversation continued in hushed whispers. Even in London, fearing spies employed by the Tsar, Vladimir kept a steady lookout as they spoke.

But soon, indicating that he had told all he knew of the current Russian political situation, Vladimir leaned back in his chair.

Ralston paused for a moment, as though sifting, sorting and storing Vladimir's comments. Drawing a silver case from his jacket pocket, he offered Vladimir a cigarette. Then, in a fatherly tone, inquired, "You've recovered from the affair with Masha Mikhaelis?"

"Fully recovered. Masha and I are friends. That reminds me, she and her mother send you their warm regards. They insist that you visit them when you're next in Russia."

"I've a research trip this fall. Any letters you'd like me to carry?"

Vladimir inhaled deeply on the weak English cigarette. "No letters. I've left the movement, Bill. No more social activism for me."

Ralston looked as if he did not entirely believe the claim. "I understand you're staying in Margel's house? I've been there. It's a lovely place, I've wondered how he could afford it."

Vladimir nodded. "I certainly couldn't. Fortunately he's letting me have it free of charge. He and his family are spending two months in Germany, on some kind of business trip, I gather."

"Yes, his business. And the meetings, they will continue while Frederick is absent?"

Vladimir reddened slightly, then forced himself to relax. "Yes, Frederick did put one condition on the arrangement. I found it disturbing, but I agreed. Twice this month, I am to host the regular political meeting at the house. Simply a gathering of friends, nothing more. In London the police are very unlikely to take an interest in such things. I will take no part in the meetings, I'll let people in at the door, and that's that." He had seen no reason to worry Sofya about this part of the housing arrangement. If she questioned the meetings, he'd try to tell her they were related to his geological work; she'd probably be off in her room reading anyway. Such accommodations were worth a little deception.

Ralston seemed politely skeptical. "Let them in at the door, and maybe make them tea?"

"Maybe make them tea. No, on second thought I don't think so. Let them do without tea."

"And your publishing? How's that going?"

"I still dabble. The business is limping along. But when the debts are finally paid, I'll close that down completely."

Ralston sighed. "Such a brilliant mind lost from the movement, just when things are starting to happen. There's real activity in Paris. And right here in London, building a theoretical foundation for the movement, Marx and Engels. Would you like to meet Marx, by the way? He is frequently in the reading room at the Museum doing research. I've a passing acquaintance with him. He lives not far from where you're staying. He might even show up at one of your meetings."

"No. They're not my meetings, and I don't care if he does. I'm serious, no more politics. I'm devoting myself to science."

"Well, you have the brains for science. But still . . ." Ralston hesitated.

Vladimir brushed aside his friend's doubts. "Which brings me to a subject I wanted to talk to you about. There are a few people I'd like you to introduce me to."

"If I can, certainly."

Vladimir extinguished his cigarette, then poured himself more tea. "I'm studying geology, with a concentration in paleontology. I'm going to try to do some work to support the theory of transformation. You've heard of it?"

"From the work of Darwin, isn't it?" Ralston looked a little quizzical. "Something about species evolving in response to environmental changes."

"There's not much evidence to test the theory. I'd like to start organizing what data we have and adding to it." Vladimir felt he was going out on a limb, proposing too grand a goal for a beginner, but he pressed on. "Of course, the theory is much too broad for one man to try to cover. I'm not sure where to concentrate my own study. Perhaps dinosaurs, mammals, or maybe fish. I'd like to talk to some experts before I decide. Could you get me an introduction to say Owen, Lyell and Huxley?"

The other nodded. "I can arrange that. Wouldn't you rather talk with the master, Darwin?"

"Darwin has already invited me to visit him at his home."

Ralston's eyes widened slightly. "Quite an honor for a student scientist, Vladimir. Quite an honor." His tone expressed admiration and perhaps a touch of envy. "But a word of warning, my ambitious friend. Don't expect to find Owen and Huxley in the same room. Owen has made enemies in the Darwin camp."

Vladimir's lips curled in a smile that became a laugh. "It's impossible to escape politics!"

"Quite impossible," Ralston affirmed rather loudly, in Russian.

"What's impossible?" The English words that startled Vladimir were spoken in a musical voice by a stylishly dressed young lady, who suddenly was standing at Ralston's side.

Vladimir straightened, instantly alert.

Ralston, clearly flustered, blurted out a reprimand in English. "Oh, Jenny! Why do you sneak up on us like that? And what are you doing here?"

The young woman had already pulled a vacant chair up to the table.

"Now, Uncle, don't be upset. Auntie told me you were here. I'm on business." The redheaded young woman kissed Ralston lightly on the cheek and then occupied the chair she had just moved.

In a moment Ralston was performing introductions. The young woman, Jenny McKay, was his niece, who worked for what he described as a very progressive women's magazine.

With a quick gesture, Jenny added, "My magazine does some political articles, but we're trying to appeal to all the concerns of today's modern woman."

Ralston was plainly under the spell of his charming niece, and Vladimir could understand why. Jenny McKay was young and full of life. Her frivolous manners couldn't hide a sharp wit and keen intellect.

Jenny's eyes burned into him. "So, you don't remember me, Vladimir."

That gave him pause. Had he ever met her, he didn't think he would have forgotten. Shining green eyes, set against a creamy skin marred only by intriguing patterns of freckles, and framed by rich auburn hair . . . there was indeed something familiar about those freckles.

"I'm very sorry, but . . ."

The young lady spoke in quite passable Russian. "I know it's been six years, and I was only sixteen last time we met, but I didn't think you'd forget."

"Yes! Yes of course!" he burst out in English. "I tutored you in languages." Once more he looked at Jenny, this time in astonishment. She had grown into a beauty. "Your Russian has improved notably. You must have found a more adept teacher."

"You were my favorite," she answered softly, her eyes teasingly dropping, then looking up quickly to catch him staring at her.

Ralston steered the conversation back to business. "Well, Jenny, what is this urgent business that made you track me down?"

"I'm doing a feature article on Waterhouse Hawkins's models of prehistoric animals, on the grounds of the Crystal Palace. I need an expert consultant to explain the creatures to me, so I can write a meaningful article that the average Englishwoman can understand. With your Museum connections, Uncle, you can find someone to help me."

"What luck! Vladimir is a student of paleontology. Perhaps he would be your guide." Ralston nodded to his companion. "If you talk him into the project."

Jenny was intrigued. "Vladimir—paleontology? What about the social movements? What about women's rights?"

"As I was just telling your uncle, they'll have to get on without me. I'm concentrating all my efforts on science."

"Be my guide. Please, I need both your brain and your brawn. I want to make photos of the models. A big, strong fellow like you will be ideal for carrying plateboxes, cameras, and all the rest of the equipment. Agreed?" Jenny coaxed.

"Well, I've never tried my hand at that technology. How could I refuse an opportunity to advance my knowledge?"

Jenny's green eyes sparkled. "I shall be at the Museum the next few days."

Vladimir thought about it. "May I meet you, here, at noon tomorrow?" he offered. "I might possibly be of some assistance."

Jenny smiled. "Agreed." Turning to Ralston she continued, "You see, Uncle, how painless my interruption was. And everything is all settled. How fortuitous! Now you may go back to your conversation and I must go back to work."

With a little wave to Ralston and Vladimir, she left.

"The girl is something of a pest," Ralston said, a little sheepishly. "I'm sorry for the interruption. She draws on my contacts quite frequently. And I must add, it gives her magazine a scientific and technical depth not common in women's papers."

"She's absolutely charming." Vladimir was still watching her departure. Turning to Ralston, he added, "I can hardly blame her for making use of such a valuable resource as yourself. As an old newspaper man, I can tell you, I'd behave exactly the same."

Ralston was looking at his pocket watch. "Vladimir, I'm sorry, but I must return to the Museum." He reached to touch Vladimir's hand. "Please, come to dinner on Wednesday. My wife will be so pleased to see you again."

"Yes, I'll try to come." As Ralston stood up, Vladimir reached to detain him. "Oh wait! I'd almost forgotten." He felt his face growing red.

"Yes, what is it?"

"I'm traveling with . . ." Vladimir hesitated. The idea flashed across his mind that he would introduce Sofya as his sister. He'd be free of the lie. She'd be free from the awkward social situations that tended to arise from their deception. But somehow he couldn't say the words. Compromising with himself, he substituted, ". . . with a student mathematician."

"Of course, your friend is also welcome." Ralston smiled, "You know that. I'll even arrange for Professor Arthur Cayley to join us. That should make the invitation irresistible to any serious student of mathematics."

"But . . ." Vladimir stumbled, suddenly wanting to confess that the mathematician was his wife.

Ralston was already waving his farewell. "I must go. It really is wonderful, having you here in town again. Goodbye now." He walked away from the table.

The opportunity for confession had passed. Vladimir lit another cigarette, a strong Russian one. When the first deep breath of smoke had filled his lungs, had been exhaled and transformed into a surrounding cloud, any guilt or regret over his hesitation to reveal himself as a married man had been blown away. He again felt euphorically contented. The pleasant possibilities of his stay in this foreign land took form in delicious daydreams.

THE AFTERNOON OF REST and reading hadn't cured Sofya's depression. Nor had she been able to put aside her concerns for Anyuta.

At dinner, Vladimir had been annoyingly and uncharacteristically gay and frivolous in his conversation. He jabbered on about the invigorating effect the people of London had on him. Then, with great satisfaction at his own wit, jokingly expounded on a theory of his that there was something in the air of London, something carried in on the fog, perhaps, that made the island inhabitants more aware of and engaged in life. Someone must collect and analyze data on whether a Darwinian change had occurred among the people of Britain which precipitated their evolution into pleasant, cultured companions for the rest of humanity.

This was the first time Sofya had heard him jokingly refer to anything having to do with Darwin. She had frowned at him across the table. Either he was slightly inebriated, or childishly overreacting on returning to a place he loved and where, years ago, he had been happy. Whatever was going on in his brain, he was taking no notice of her mood.

Now, back in their borrowed home, just before it was time to retire, he was pestering her with talk of the *Alice* book.

Unable to control her annoyance, Sofya snapped at him. "I will not discuss that disturbing book."

"Disturbing?"

"Definitely! Points of Discontinuity. Shrinking and stretching transformations. The confusion experienced by Alice regarding her own identity." Simmering angrily, Sofya settled herself into the armchair in which she had spent most of the afternoon.

"We've come to a strange land, Sofya. Not too unlike Alice's. I'd suggest that you heed the Caterpillar's advice." Vladimir proceeded to remove his coat, tie and shoes. In one smooth motion he sprawled himself across the armchair opposite her. His head rested on one of arms of the chair, his long legs dangled over the other.

"The Caterpillar's advice was for Alice to keep her temper. What do you mean? My temper is perfectly under control, thank you." It struck her how foolish he looked, with his big toe protruding from a hole in his stocking. He must purchase the garments with holes. In a year's time she had never seen him with an intact pair.

"I realize you're not in the proper mood for seeing things my way, but I want this settled today, our first day in London. And I want you not to be angry when you answer." Vladimir spoke without looking at her. "I think it would be a good idea for us to do a little playacting."

"What kind of playacting?"

He jerked into an alert position, both feet on the floor, body leaning toward her. "I want to introduce you to my London acquaintances as my sister."

"Why?"

Vladimir spread his big hands nervously. "It might make things easier." He hesitated. "In certain social situations that I—we—might encounter, here in London."

"That's absurd!" Suddenly she was on her feet. She felt warm blood rushing to her face, her temples. "How? How could you suggest such a thing."

"It's closer to the real truth, than . . ."

"No, absolutely not! I will be introduced as your wife. You saw the problems in Heidelberg. What if someone we meet here reports back to the university that I'm your sister? All our work at convincing them that I'm a reputable woman would be lost."

"Remember the Caterpillar's advice." Vladimir's flippant attitude was enraging. "As my wife, you'll find some awkward times ahead," he added calmly.

"We'll manage," she announced firmly, then turned her back to him. Tears of anger were blurring her vision. They had endured awkward times together since they had begun their relationship. She had no idea why he felt these situations would prove any more troublesome in England than anywhere else.

"Very well. You will be known as my wife." Vladimir's hands were firmly gripping her shoulders. His breath touched her ear. "In this strange land, people may not behave as you expect."

She didn't turn around. She heard him bound up the stairs to his room, then the door closed loudly. Certainly, he was not behaving as expected.

When she finally went to her own bed, sleep was fitful, her dreams peopled by grotesque figures from *Alice*.

SOFYA SAT at a large oak table in the reading room of the Royal Academy of Science, mathematical journals spread out before her. She hadn't planned on spending her vacation reading mathematics, but when this opportunity came, she couldn't help herself. Through Vladimir's friend Ralston, she had gained access to this excellent mathematical collection. Ralston had even introduced her to some of the leading mathematicians in England, including the prolific and acclaimed Arthur Cayley of Cambridge; the charmingly shy author of *Alice*, Charles Dodgson of Oxford; and the inventor Charles Babbage.

Cayley made the biggest impression. After one of Ralston's dinners, Cayley had taken her aside and discussed his work in some detail, talking at length on developments in function theory. An older man, almost fifty, he looked thin and frail, but when she spoke with him she found he was strong in mind and body. She found him rather attractive, despite his age. The man's interests were vast. He loved mountaineering and tramping. He painted in watercolors, he admired art and architecture. He had spent fourteen years as a lawyer, and was no stranger to the world outside of mathematics. And he supported the idea of women acquiring mathematical education. He was tutoring his young niece whom he thought quite promising. The man liked to read, and suggested Sofya vary her diet of Dickens with some Jane Austen, his second favorite author after Sir Walter Scott.

Instead of following Cayley's suggestion on Austen's writing, Sofya was now pursuing Cayley's work. He had published on a wide range of mathematical topics in both analysis and geometry. Journals containing his articles lay open before her. His early work on Invariants held the greatest interest for her. Struggling to keep her attention on the line of reasoning behind a long string of calculations and substitutions, she felt a gentle tap on her shoulder.

She turned. A darkly handsome man, tall and slim, spoke just above a whisper. "Excuse me, the clerk told me that you were using journals containing the earlier works of Cayley. Would you mind if I shared them? I've a point I absolutely must clear up for a paper I'm preparing." There was a faint flavor of Ireland in his speech.

When she nodded her consent, the man settled across the table from her and began his work. From time to time over the next hour she looked up from her own reading and studied the somehow intriguing figure jotting notes and drawing elaborate diagrams in a small black notebook. His forehead domed out in a white curve, barely covered by long strands of straight black hair. His deeply sunken eyes were a shade of blue so dark that at first she had judged them to be black. His complexion was pale, suggesting a man who spent many hours indoors in study and contemplation. The man was a little older than most graduate students. Perhaps he, like Vladimir, had been involved in some worldly endeavor, become completely disillusioned and sought refuge in science.

The man suddenly looked up just as Sofya, intrigued, was about to conclude her construction of his imaginary past. He'd caught her staring.

He addressed her boldly but calmly, completely without awkwardness. "Would you like a cup of tea? I'm having trouble concentrating. Perhaps, if you'd be kind enough to let me talk about my work and show you my diagrams, I'd clear up some little difficulties. I find talking frequently helps my thinking." His voice was pleasant and persuasive.

As they strolled to a nearby café, her companion simply introduced himself as James More. He was interested in mathematics and legal systems. At one point he had considered a career in law. He had been active in political reform movements, but disillusioned, he turned to mathematics. Shyly he confessed that something seemed to be drawing him away from mathematics and back to contemplations of truth and justice and morality. He hoped his current investigations into mathematics would prove compellingly interesting enough to keep him in the sciences.

Sofya warmed to his openness. She gave him her name, and admitted she too had wavered for a while in her choice of careers. Now, she was firmly committed to mathematics. And like any thinking Russian, she was to some extent concerned with politics.

With a cool disregard for convention worthy of any revolutionary, he suggested that they begin immediately upon a first-name basis. Loving the challenge of defying a social norm, Sofya readily agreed.

A few minutes later, as she sipped tea and examined the neatly drawn diagrams, James tried to explain his investigations in celestial mechanics. He was particularly interested in asteroid orbits of great eccentricity. She couldn't follow his reasoning, but he seemed to be deriving great benefit from her questions. It was late in the afternoon when Sofya reluctantly withdrew. They would meet again tomorrow for further discussions.

Walking back to the house, Sofya pulled her white woolen scarf over her head. An autumn wind had sprung up, and she was shivering. Hurrying her steps as she passed the shops and dwellings of the less respectable areas along the way, her thoughts returned frequently to her intriguing new acquaintance. He was suave and witty, with a controlled excitement in his nature that added to his attractiveness. His dark eyes had held her almost hypnotically. The mathematical discussion had strayed to modern technology and from there to the Crystal Palace Exhibition. James enthusiastically proclaimed his willingness to act as her personal guide to the exhibit. She had promised to consider his offer.

As she opened the door of her borrowed house, she realized with a start that she had never mentioned to her new friend that she was in London with her husband. Suddenly it struck her as strange that he had asked nothing about her personal situation, nor she anything about his. Since she had not mentioned Vladimir to her friend, James, there was no need to mention James to Vladimir.

WHEN VLADIMIR ANNOUNCED that he would be absent all day Friday on a geological field trip, Sofya asked to come along. Coolly he insisted that the trip would be far too strenuous for her. She was genuinely disappointed, until he added sarcastically that surely she could entertain herself for one day.

Then her anger returned. Indeed she could entertain herself, she thought. She'd ask James to try to arrange a trip to the Crystal Palace.

FRIDAY DAWNED SUNNY and unseasonably warm. She carried her coat and scarf in anticipation of a possible sharp change in weather. James was waiting for her, as they had agreed, on the walk in front of the Royal Academy of Sciences.

His expression softened when he saw her. "You're a little late. I was beginning to wonder if you'd changed your mind." His extremely tall, spare figure impressed her as quite dashing in a black frock coat and top hat. One gloved hand held a fashionable cane, the other was extended to her.

"I'm ready, walking shoes and all." Sofya rested her hand on his arm.

"Good. We'll start with a little stroll to the train station. The train will take us as far as Sydenham, where we'll rent a fast little vehicle that we English call a fly. It's a two-seater and makes very good time when the roads are clear. You're not frightened by speed, are you?"

"Not in the least. Russians love speed. If you're an enthusiast, there is absolutely nothing to match a ride in a troika."

"I wish that I may someday have that opportunity. With you as my guide, of course." James's deep-set eyes sparkled. "Fast horses and beautiful women are my obsessions. And to have the two together is sublime."

"And what of mathematics?" Sofya teased. "In the days I've known you, you've show a definite obsession with the subject."

"Yes. A subject of intrinsic beauty." He looked distant. "And it offers opportunities of success."

"Do you mean success in science? Or invention? Or—?"

"I mean, Sofya, in establishing one's superiority. Surely you must be familiar with the delectable exhilaration that comes from winning an intellectual game. Forcing one who is almost, but not quite, your mental equal to admit inferiority."

"I have felt that, sometimes," Sofya impulsively responded. "And I feel I will be able to do so more frequently, when I finish my training. I know something of the thrill that comes from possessing a talent, an insight, more acute than others. Of course that shouldn't be the most important thing."

"And what should be more important?" James inquired.

On the train, and in the fly, James elaborated on his views of life and challenges. Sofya sensed a suppressed aggression in her companion, that had been absent in their London meetings.

She was about to counter his arguments against the existence of true personal happiness, when reaching the top of a small hill a glimpse of the Crystal Palace rose before her. She gasped. The enormous glass building shimmered in the sunlight like a palace from a fairy tale. The vast, tall spiderweb of steel and iron, clad entirely in glass, covered as much ground as a small farm.

James's eyes followed her gaze. "Ah, the castle is in sight. I will now transform myself into a tour guide." He began to expound on facts she already knew. But she didn't interrupt. She liked hearing them again as she stared in amazement. The Palace had been erected first in 1851, in Hyde Park, as part of the first World's Fair for International Industry. Later the building had been disassembled and rebuilt on its present site. The whole effect was of light and openness. The design had been copied many times, for railway centers and shopping areas across Europe.

James suddenly abandoned the tone and manner of a tour guide. "I think, my dear, that you and the Palace are well met."

"Whatever do you mean by that?" For the first time since sighting the building, she gave her companion her full attention.

His eyes twinkled darkly. "Certain concepts, descriptions like 'innovative, beautifully original, and causing quite a stir' apply equally to yourself and the Palace."

Sofya allowed the corners of her mouth to turn up in what would appear to be a smile, but her eyes were scrutinizing the man's face trying to discern his sincerity. His voice was too practiced and controlled for his compliments to be taken seriously.

On stepping into the building Sofya froze. The high, sunlit spaces of glass and steel geometry threatened her obscurely, as if strange visions might come out of them. She fought back a spell of dizziness and disorientation. Focusing her gaze on James, she regained her stability. "It's a whole city street—more than that, a marketplace. More than that— but I don't know exactly what."

Offering her his arm, James led her into the bustling throng.

Exhibits exemplifying the latest advances in science and industry lined the sides of the main walkway. Each exhibit was surrounded by interested groups of humanity. Crowds moved slowly up and down three tiers of walkways. "The exhibits seem to go on forever." Sofya had to speak loudly to be heard above the steady murmur of the crowd.

Her escort nodded a polite agreement, while weaving them skillfully toward the main science section. "I've chosen a few special exhibits I'd like to show you. If something else interests you, just let me know."

"I'm overwhelmed." She clung tightly to his hand. "Lead on."

James guided her from the latest electromagnetic dynamo designed by Siemen, to a cross-section of the underwater telegraph cable designed by Kelvin in 1866. Then it was on to the latest steam engine, and the latest weaving devices. Even a model of Babbage's unfinished calculating machine was on display.

"You know the story of Babbage and his charming female assistant?" James asked.

"I heard the story directly from the elderly Mr. Babbage." Sofya caught sight of James's head oscillating slightly from side to side, a habit she had noticed once or twice before, and which now seemed vaguely threatening. It was as if he were appraising her vulnerability, like a cobra looking at its victim. Her stare must have made an impression on him, for the apparently unconscious motion stopped.

"There's a charming invention." James indicated a display on the far side of the aisle. "This is the alarm bed. The frame, you see, is connected to a large spring controlled by clockwork. When the set time arrives, the bed will be jolted to a vertical position and the sleeper tossed to the floor. In another variation, the sleeper is tossed into a cold bath."

"Oh, how my English governess would have loved to have this device!" Sofya joked. "Even now, I sometimes have terrible fits of laziness, and love to stay in bed." The sly smile with which James received this news made Sofya regret the remark.

"How charming!" James jostled against her.

"It certainly is crowded in here," she complained. It was not the first time he had pressed his body against her, and as before, he unnecessarily maintained the pressure, his hands finding their way to her waist.

"Then I suggest we go outside." James unhurriedly released the contact. "There's a lovely garden which may offer a respite from the crowds. Perhaps, now would be a good time for lunch."

Sofya quickly agreed. As they made their way to the exit, James again assumed the air of a charming and knowledgeable guide. "The garden is an extension of the exhibitions. Placed among the trees and shrubs are life-size concrete models of prehistoric animals, created by a Mr. Waterhouse Hawkins, under the direction of the geologist Richard Owen. We'll see dinosaurs, iguanasaurs, ichthyosaurs, plesiosaurs. Ancient amphibians, crocodiles, and various mammals who came after the dinosaurs. Our repast will be in another time, another world, far removed from nineteenth-century Britain."

"How exciting! I'm most interested in seeing the models." When James maneuvered his arm around her waist under the pretense of guiding her through the throng, Sofya decided it was time for clarification. "My husband is a geologist," she announced in a firm voice.

"How interesting." His voice indicated no surprise at the existence of a husband. And his arm stayed tightly around her waist. He was leading her to a deserted spot.

Not wanting to go any farther from the crowd, she settled determinedly on a bench. "This is a fine place." The position offered a good view of two concrete iguanasaurs. The creatures, posed on the fringe of a nearby clump of trees, appeared ready to fight each other.

James placed the hamper of food he had purchased on the bench. He began to settle next to her, but paused in vexation. "Ah, we must have something to drink as well. Would you prefer fruit punch, or something more warming?"

"Whatever you like."

Sofya felt a sudden relief at his departure. The murmur of human voices was remote, no louder than the sound of birds. She leaned back on the bench, closed her eyes, and imagined herself falling back to the time of the igaunosaur. In that far distant past, the quiet was interrupted by the fighting lizards' loud bellows, the damp air would reek with the giant beasts' scent, the ground shook as they stamped their massive feet. So, this was where her husband worked. She envied Vladimir his world, one that could be made graphic, whose beauty could be displayed and shared with the uninitiated.

Sofya opened her eyes, the sound of laughter drawing her back to reality. Some fifty yards away, a lively, well-dressed couple was approaching the iguanasaurs from the far side. She caught only a fleeting glimpse of a large man loaded down with camera equipment and boxes of what were probably photographic plates. The woman, a slender, tall, fair-skinned redhead, carried only a writing pad and a wicker picnic basket.

The way the woman carried herself, so sure of her beauty and attractiveness, the way she subtly and expertly flirted with her escort, all reminded Sofya of Anyuta when they had been at home at Palibino, and suitors came to call. Sofya fondly watched as the young woman gave orders—in a gentle, teasing way—to the man, who had moved out of sight behind an ivy bush. The woman was too far away for Sofya to hear her voice, but the gestures were easy to interpret. The man should set the camera here, the plates there. No, the camera wasn't level yet, he must adjust the legs.

From the increasing drama of the woman's gestures, Sofya imagined the man was pleading exhaustion from his labors. He must be sitting on the grass, for as the woman approached the spot she gave a little cry and abruptly sank from sight, as if in playful struggle he had pulled her down next to him. Her laughter bubbled from an invisible source.

Sofya smiled wistfully. The couple were obviously enjoying themselves thoroughly and scandalously. The scene stirred another memory of Palibino, of the picnic she and Vladimir had shared an eternity ago.

"Hello there. You seem to be lost in some kind of reverie." James startled her with his return. His eyes followed Sofya's gaze.

"I think . . ." He walked a little to one side, gaining a clear view of the couple. "Yes, I'm quite sure. I recognize that man." A joyless little smile flickered across James's face.

Suddenly Sofya wished that she was somewhere else. "Really, James!" Her tone was one of reprimand. "They want their privacy."

"I'm sure they do. Nevertheless, I'm going over there to join them."

To Sofya's astonishment her companion, having scooped up the food hamper under one arm and carrying the small tray of drinks in the other hand, walked toward the couple. Uncertain of what else to do, Sofya followed.

As she passed the concrete monsters, Sofya felt her eyes widen. Her stomach jumped to her throat. When she finally remembered to breathe, the air entered her lungs in short gasps. The young man who had turned at the sound of their approach was Vladimir!

Groping with one hand, Sofya established her balance against the concrete flank of a great lizard. Beyond that point she couldn't make her body move. Vladimir had sprung up from his reclining position on the grass and was coming toward her. On edge of this picture, James stood innocently at a little distance, smiling, watching.

"Sofya," her husband whispered as he approached her, his back to the others. "Sofya?"

"What?" Her voice was dazed.

"I can see what you're thinking." He was speaking in quick, low-toned Russian. He had taken hold of both her arms. His eyes were opened wide and shining. "We'll talk later. Compose yourself." Then she could see a new idea dawning on him, and he interrupted himself for a moment: "Why are you alone with this man?" He dropped his grip on her. Next moment he was once again trying to soothe her. "Please, join us in a civilized manner."

"Of course I'll join you." Sofya could feel her shock evolving into hurt, anger, and wild jealousy. But for the moment her voice was well controlled.

Vladimir's face was almost as red as his hair as he introduced Sofya to Jenny. She and Vladimir learned that James and Jenny were acquainted. Neither James nor Jenny showed discomfort at the awkward situation.

"You're as charming as Vladimir described you, Sofya." Jenny's smile simulated friendliness. "Vladimir, you didn't mention how young she is. Sixteen? Certainly not more than seventeen."

Sofya couldn't bring herself to reply. Instead she turned to Vladimir and said in hushed Russian, "I won't put up with this artificial sweetness. It would require a degree of civility that is beyond me at the moment."

"Sofya, I speak Russian rather well," Jenny's voice said, in that language. "Your husband was my teacher."

Sofya rounded on her. "You realize how awkward my situation is?"

"Why? You are here with your friend James, and I'm here with Vladimir. There's nothing awkward about this, unless you make it so."

James had been listening and watching attentively, but his face showed no trace of understanding. When he spoke it was in English. "Sofya, I'm sure they'd love to have us join them for lunch."

"How do you know my husband?" Sofya demanded of him.

"Evidently your husband travels in much wider circles than you realize," he murmured coolly. His head had resumed a slight reptilian oscillation.

Presently the four were picnicking together. Sofya amazed herself by managing to eat a little of the sandwich passed to her. No English woman was going to drive her away from her own husband. Nor was any going to display greater self-control.

Sofya listened numbly as Vladimir described the project he and Jenny were working on for her newspaper. James in turn related how he and Sofya had enjoyed the science exhibits. He was hoping Sofya would accompany him to some of the entertainment events.

"Yes," Sofya heard herself saying. "I'll accompany you to the other events. I'd love to."

"Vladimir, it's time for us to return to work. And James and Sofya want to return to the exhibit," Jenny announced, as she rose gracefully. Looking down at the trio still seated on the grass, she added, "I'm hosting a party at my father's this evening. I hope you all will attend." She looked at Vladimir. "You haven't given up that kind of social work have you, Vladimir? The party starts at nine. There'll be dancing, good food and fine company."

Both Vladimir and James were on their feet before Sofya. Each extended a hand to help her. As she started to reach for Vladimir, she heard Jenny's sharp voice, "Vladimir, you must promise me at least one waltz."

"And I must have the promise of a waltz from Sofya." James didn't wait for her to extend a hand to him. He stepped between her and Vladimir and took both her hands firmly in his.

With brief, awkward farewells, Sofya and James proceeded to the Palace. James's arm was again around her waist. This time she welcomed the support and the restraint. Sofya wanted desperately to run back to Vladimir, to cry, to shout her outrage. But she would not allow herself to do that, not in front of his English friends.

CHAPTER THIRTEEN

1869 ❦ *London*

The strains of a Viennese waltz filled the brightly lit ballroom. Handsome men in smartly tailored suits were escorting elegantly dressed women in flowing gowns. Vladimir stood alone at one side of the room as smiling couples twirled past. He scrutinized each dancing pair, but the couple he searched for had not appeared.

From the opposite side of the room, Jenny, dazzlingly beautiful in her green gown, was making her way to him, with another attractive young woman in tow. Jenny must have introduced him to every young woman in the room, and he found them all indescribably boring. With the exception of Jenny, each of his dancing partners had moved stiffly, without life. Leading them through the turns put him in mind of pulling a raft down the Volga. He shuddered to think what fools they'd make of themselves if they ever attempted a mazurka, not that they ever would. Russian girls, now, were born to dance. A Russian girl with gypsy blood, like Sofya, that would be supreme delight. She'd float gently in his arms, her tiny feet barely touching the floor.

"Vladimir?" Jenny's voice recalled his wandering thoughts. "I've been praising your dancing skills to my friend, Mabel. She thinks I must be exaggerating. Won't you prove me an honest woman?"

Smiling sweetly up at him was another beautiful woman, this one tall, with light eyes, white complexion, a vacant face that promised only empty chatter.

Vladimir bowed slightly. Mabel's gown was more than a trifle daring, exposing her white shoulders, long smooth neck, the contours of her full breasts.

As he took the woman's hand and led her to the dance floor, he wondered what Sofya was wearing at the moment. She'd best not show up here in a dress like this woman's or he'd take her right home, and have something to say to her on the way. He twirled his partner with the sparkling blue eyes. Sofya hadn't packed a ball gown, that might be the only reason she wasn't here. But James, as he liked to be called, would have connections. It was easy to see that he had money and lots of it. And a reputation with women. Any one of his lady friends could see to it that Sofya was outfitted for the ball. Vladimir could see the scene in his imagination. The experienced woman and James would exchange leers as they prepared his Sofya, dressing her provocatively, daringly, Sofya innocently going along with their plans.

But Mabel was playing her own scene. "Oh, how exotic it must be, to be Russian! You must tell me about your mysterious country." This woman was going on very much like all the rest. He must try to pay attention to his partner, to listen to her silly babbling.

His arm slipped more tightly around the girl's waist. As he twirled her around he found no attraction in her beautiful bare shoulders, or her breathless pink lips, or her heaving bosom. He kept scanning the room, anticipating another awkward meeting with Sofya and James.

At midnight, Jenny was again at his side. "I hope you're enjoying yourself, Vladimir."

"Your party is charming. The musicians are very skillful, the food delicious, and the drink superb." He took her hand and kissed it.

"And the company?" Jenny's eyes were sparkling mischievously. "Too bad your wife and her friend were unable to attend. They must have found other entertainment."

"London is full of opportunities." Vladimir forced a smile to his lips. "However, by missing your party, they can only have chosen a lesser joy." He offered his arm to Jenny. "I could use a little break from dancing. I'd love to see something of the rest of the house. Would you take a moment from your guests and give me a brief tour?"

"I'd be delighted." Jenny accepted his arm. She pushed gently against him as she led the way into a darkened hallway.

Vladimir's thoughts turned gloomy with the lighting. He had already angrily concluded that Sofya and James had found better entertainment. Sofya, the little flirt, was sneaking around on the arm of a London academic with a well-earned reputation as a Don Juan. Or worse, she and

James were alone. She might have gone to his apartment, or she might have invited him to their home. Sofya had insisted on making their marital status known. Well, then, she had better behave like a wife. She must act with some propriety. He would speak sternly to her. If tonight she could behave with such wanton disregard of their agreement, then so could he. He would drive her from his mind. He would drink and dance and flirt outrageously. He pulled Jenny even closer to him.

Suddenly she seized his hand and guided it to her breast. "My room's not far away," she breathed into his ear.

"Lead on," he murmured, and was guided into deeper darkness.

FEELING TIRED AND GUILTY, Vladimir left Jenny McKay's at three in the morning. The dancing would probably go on till dawn. As hard as he had tried, he had not been able to drive Sofya from his thoughts. On returning with his hostess to the party, he had offended Jenny first with a bold remark made in his more-than-half-drunken state, and again when Jenny had seen him going into the garden with her friend, Mabel. And *that* willing girl had not appreciated his whispering the name "Sofya," even though he'd tried to convince her that in Russian the word *sofya* meant darling. He had made an unholy mess of the evening. And perhaps of his life as well.

He arrived home to find the house in total darkness. Quietly he entered, and managed to get a candle lighted. Half expecting to find Sofya snuggled in the arms of that man, he began to search the ground-floor rooms. He didn't want to know, and yet he had no choice. His search was futile. One hand on the wall, and one holding the candle, Vladimir made his way upstairs. The door to his room was open. A quick look showed it vacant, as was the adjoining study.

With dread, Vladimir climbed the next flight of stairs. Two doors at the head of the stair were open. The third, the door to Sofya's sleeping room was closed. She was home.

He should turn and go back down to his room and collapse on his bed. But his head was swirling, and he didn't want to negotiate the stairs again until it stopped. He'd rest a while in the rocking chair in the study.

Putting his candle down on the desk, he noticed the *Alice* book lying there, opened to an illustration of strange creatures on a seashore. Unable to focus clearly, and too tired to keep trying, he blew out the candle flame. Fumbling in the dark, he sat on the edge of the chair and tried to remove his boots. This produced extraordinary bumping and banging noises, but he made little progress. Very well, the boots would remain on. The truth was he'd had too little to eat and too much to drink. He'd spent himself, mind and body, on beautiful women. Or on women who looked beautiful until you got to know them. Jenny in particular.

But that wasn't the real problem. After months as a scholarly monk, he deserved a little romantic company without the guilt of betraying some impossible promise. Letting his head fall back against the high top of the chair, he rocked in it slowly. In the morning, he'd have a serious talk with Sofya. Living under the terms of their original agreement was simply impossible. Apparently, Sofya felt the same. She had flirted with Lamansky, and now she was carrying on with More.

Vladimir changed his position, hanging his legs over the arm of the chair. The chair creaked loudly, as he tried to adjust a pillow behind his back. Well, perhaps he had overreacted to Sofya's friendship with Lamansky, but James More was another matter. Very dangerous, brilliant, and completely without scruples. Vladimir recalled meeting him at the political gathering he had been unable to stay clear of, here in this very house.

Sofya definitely needed some brotherly advice where men were concerned. He yawned uncontrollably, he was falling asleep. He'd nap a little in this chair. He was too tired to get up.

A low groaning sound drifted into his fading consciousness. At first he thought it was part of some dream. But no, it was definitely real. Vladimir listened, his eyes still closed. Could it be a small animal outside the window? Impossible, he was in London. He listened again, eyes open now. The sound came from the next room.

He got up, maintaining good balance with an act of will, and walked on his still booted feet to Sofya's door. Suddenly he was completely awake. Did he dare to enter her room? What if she were in bed with More, moaning in passion? No, she wouldn't, she couldn't. He knocked. He waited. No one answered. Another moan.

Quietly turning the knob, he discovered that at least the door was unlocked, and entered. The window blinds were partly open, and for a moment he feared that his worst suspicions were confirmed. In the dim English moonlight he could see that the bed covers were in wild disarray. But Sofya was alone, tossing around on the bed in her nightgown.

Vladimir silently approached. Sofya's eyes were closed. She was sweating profusely. She must be ill, some kind of fever. Her breath was coming in short gasps. Maybe More had hurt her, drugged her, then left her here alone . . .

Sitting on the edge of the bed, he seized her shoulders and gently shook her, at the same time calling her name. He had to get her out of this delirium.

"Sofya. Sofya? I'm here. It's Vladimir."

Her eyes flew open, huge with fear. She uttered one more cry, almost inhuman, then sat up with a spasmodic movement, staring into the empty room. Vladimir still gripped her by the shoulders. In a few moments he felt the tension in her body relax just a little.

She looked at him, with recognition now, and her body began to quiver. She pressed herself to his chest. "Hold me," she murmured.

His arms went around her, and he pressed her hard against him. "I'm here now," he whispered. "I'm here now."

He held her tightly in this position. When her breathing returned to normal, she gently pushed herself away.

His heart was beating madly. No mere dream, he thought, could have such an effect upon a grown woman. What had happened to her, one of her fits? But they were so rare. He took her small hand in his, and looked into her face. "Tell me, did he hurt you?"

She looked at him blankly.

"Are you ill?" he asked gently.

"No, nothing like that. Just terribly frightened." Another sob raked her body, tears were on her face. He wiped them with the back of his hand, and saw that his own hand was shaking.

Sofya struggled to speak. "I was upset, confused, lonely. The evening with James ended badly. I had to struggle to keep his hands off me the whole way back from the Palace. I'm never going to see him again."

"Did he hurt you?"

"No. No. I controlled him." She dismissed his concern. "When I got back, you weren't here. I didn't want to think about you and—with that woman. Trying to calm myself, I came upstairs and forced myself to read. I picked up that book you gave me our first day in London. At midnight, I gave up reading, and waiting for you. I went to bed. I had this terrible dream."

"Talk. Talk about it." After getting up to fumble for matches on the table, Vladimir lit a candle near the bed. Only rarely and by accident had he ever seen Sofya in her nightclothes. Not realizing the effect she was having on him, she took his hand and drew him back to sit on the edge of the bed.

She readjusted her position on the bed, a movement all the more provocative because it was not intended to be so. "I dreamt about a dance. Like the one in *Alice*. At first it was pleasant. You were there, and Anyuta, and a great many others. We were on the beach, trying to dance, and among us were strange creatures, a kind of giant turtle, and an ugly lobster with a man's face. The music was terrible, discordant, and the people, even you, were chanting loudly, 'Will you, won't you, will you, won't you.'

"When the chanting reached a fever pitch the lobster grabbed one of the dancers and threw her into the sea. I was afraid the lobster would grab me next, but he seized you instead. I tried to pull you back, but I couldn't. He threw you far into the sea. I could see you struggling. You were drowning. The turtle kept yelling, 'He's near the other shore, he's near the other shore.' I screamed. I wanted frantically to attack the turtle, but I couldn't move. I made out the faces of Jenny and James, they were laughing. And there were other people I didn't know, they all just sat on the beach laughing, even Anyuta. The turtle's face was turning very red as he yelled 'would not, could not, would not, could not.' "

Abruptly Sofya fell silent. She again pressed herself against his chest. "You see how childish I am," she murmured, and tilted up her face, inviting a kiss.

"I see," said Vladimir, and accepted. He pressed his lips hard against hers and enjoyed their quivering movement. His arms wrapped tightly around her. He felt her arm slide around his neck. His own hands were now exploring her back. He kissed her neck. He heard her catch her breath as she turned again to him.

If he hadn't drunk too much, if she weren't so frightened, he could have her now. She was responding to his touch. But he wouldn't let himself take her under these conditions. He wanted all of her, her body, her mind, and her will. He wanted her freely and resolutely to accept him as her husband. He would not take her when she was so completely vulnerable, the result of the day's emotional tortures. His longing and devotion should not end so, in drunkenness and terror.

He pushed her away gently. She tried to pull him back. He looked into her eyes and said, "I love you."

Sofya turned her head so he could no longer see her face.

"I've loved you since I first met you. I wanted to protect you then, and I still do. And I want more than that . . . but I'm confused. We're both confused."

"Don't leave me alone," she begged. Her bright eyes reflected a profound inner fear.

Standing again, in a swirl of dizziness, he pulled a chair up beside the bed. "I'll stay till you fall asleep. Then I'll be in the bedroom next to yours. I'll leave both our doors open." Collapsing onto the chair, he leaned forward, hiding his face with his hands, repeating over and over, "It wouldn't be good like this. It wouldn't be. I'm drunk."

Eventually the sound of her weeping ceased. Timidly he allowed himself to look at the bed. She was asleep. Only her dark wavy hair showed above the gently rising and falling bed covers.

SOFYA AWAKENED EARLY. As she opened her eyes, she turned to where Vladimir had been sitting. Disappointed at finding herself alone, she slowly rose, chose a simple dress, and while reviewing the previous night's events, prepared without enthusiasm for the morning. Brushing her hair at the vanity table, she stared critically into the silvered glass. Her face around the eyes was swollen from the hour of terror and weeping. For several minutes, she applied a cold wet towel. Returning to the glass, she doubted the treatment had been a success. But she couldn't wait any longer to begin her search for Vladimir. Quickly glancing into the neighboring bedroom, she saw the rumpled covers, but no Vladimir. Nor was he in the study.

As she started slowly down the stairs her mind for the hundredth time tried to evaluate the events of last evening. Her hand slid slowly over the smooth oak banister. The episode of a night terror was embarrassing, but completely out of her control. From time to time, not often, she experienced vivid, disturbing dreams and unnamable dreads. She had reacted this way since she was a child. Of course, she scolded herself, she could avoid situations that precipitated them. The last twenty-four hours would have been a trial for anyone's nerves. Her test of wills with James More, the man turned octopus, had been only the half of it. Less than half. What had been worse was seeing Vladimir with that woman. And then, to come home and try to relax by looking at the fantastic creatures in that book. No wonder she had lost control.

As she passed the opened door of Vladimir's sleeping room, she noticed the neatly made bed. He had not slept in this room, though the smell of his tobacco lingered in it. With a thrill, she suddenly remembered his kiss. A kiss so compelling all reason had been driven from her mind. A kiss that promised passage to another world.

With a rush of embarrassment, she recalled that Vladimir had been the one to bring them back to reason. Gently pushing her away, he had held her from him and dispassionately declared his love. She understood and appreciated that he acted nobly and honorably from a higher love than most men were capable of. But a naggingly playful part of her, moving in tune with the music on the beach, felt disappointed that he had not, just this once, forgotten about high ideals and noble thoughts.

At the bottom of the stairs, any remaining playful feelings were brought under control. Reason must reign. With luck, Vladimir wouldn't mention anything about yesterday, or last night. Perhaps, everything between them could proceed comfortably as before. She would suggest that the past twenty-four hours be forgotten.

She smoothed her hair and pulled a loose string from the cuff of her sleeve, then looked into the living room. Vladimir, still dressed as he had been last night, even to his boots, was asleep on the divan. Moving quietly to the sideboard, the smell of fresh-brewed leaves told her she was not the first to think of tea. Pouring herself a cup of the steaming beverage and drinking deeply, she stood and watched her husband sleep. He was quite a wonderful man. More wonderful now, in comparison with other men she'd met. He definitely possessed a rugged attractiveness, but it was his great intelligence and ideals that really set him apart.

Vladimir awoke, suddenly and quietly. She had been caught staring. Somehow misinterpreting her look, he offered a vague apology. "Forgive my appearance. As you see, I never undressed last night." The tips of his ears were turning red. His eyes seemed to be avoiding her. He yawned dramatically. "I came down here when it was light. You were sleeping peacefully and I badly needed a cup of tea. Quite an unsettling night."

"I wish we could forget what happened." Thinking he must have drunk far too much, she turned from him and settled herself into the great bearlike chair.

"Impossible!" His blue eyes glistened.

"The nightmares are worse since we've been in England," she said softly. Placing her tea cup on the floor, she reached over and touched him gently on the arm. "Sorry I am such a child."

Vladimir stretched, rubbed his head where sleep had left his hair in mad disorder, and swung his booted feet to the floor. "Whatever you are, you are not a child," he said emphatically. He got to his feet, wincing a little, and stood looking down at her. He reached for her, holding her hand tightly in his strong grasp. "I wanted very much to provide a much different kind of comfort."

She pulled her hand from his inflaming grasp.

Slowly, purposefully Vladimir closed the room's large double doors, creating a well-defined space of their own, free from any chance interruption by the day servant. He turned and faced her. His eyes stared determinedly.

Sofya felt cold perspiration on her forehead. Perhaps Vladimir wanted to marry Jenny. Something kept trying to be heard over the rational part of her mind. The turmoil was unbearable. She sank back into the chair.

He was still speaking in a low voice. "Something must be done. I can't go on hurting you, as I did yesterday, when you saw me with Jenny. And I can't go on being hurt by you. Ever since we made our arrangement, I've hoped for . . . for a change in your attitude toward me. Then seeing you with More . . . seeing that you had wanted, had chosen, another kind of relationship, but not with me . . . I was completely unsettled. It was unbearable."

There was a long silence. She was afraid to speak. Afraid of pushing him away from her forever. And still fearful of letting him come too close.

Vladimir broke the silence with the half-hearted, self-critical remark she most feared and had heard before. "I should have walked out of your life as soon as we were married, as Anyuta has continually advised."

Sofya, stealing a frightened glance at her husband's face, saw pain.

"Do you want to leave me now?" she whispered.

"No!" The answer was quick and sharp. Kneeling beside her chair, he took her hands in his. "I love you." He kissed the palms of her hands. She let her head drop to his, his hair just touching her cheek. She pulled back before he looked up at her.

His voice was a warm breeze. "What would be the difference if we lived together, really lived together? Who would be hurt? We could both continue to pursue our studies." He smiled gently. "Dear Sofya, don't you understand?" His finger gently traced the outline of her lips, transporting her back to last night's kiss. "Your husband is proposing to you."

Something like an electrical storm seemed raging in her mind, lightning bolts of reason and logic striking relentlessly into the ocean of her feelings. She turned her face from his.

"Sofya." He gently turned her head back toward him. "Sofya, last night, I felt you . . ." His voice was soft, hesitant. She wanted to turn away, but her eyes had locked onto his and would not let go. "Sofya?" His voice pleaded for her to respond. What could she say?

He was suddenly on his feet. Pacing the floor in front of her. "Sofya, I will not let this rest. You must tell me, now." He stopped in front of her. His hands shaking as he clasped and unclasped them nervously. "Do you . . . Will you ever . . ." He resumed pacing, then stopped resolutely in front of her. "I am not asking you to give up your freedom to study. You know I would never do that." His fingers touched her chin, and led her face gently back to his. His eyes locked on hers, they softened, he gently touched the corners of her swollen eyes. As if suddenly seeing into her soul, he touched gently at her fears. "Of course, there will be no children."

"Vladimir, my darling, you are making a statement that no man, living with his wife, can make with certainty." Her head was bent and she spoke so softly, she wasn't sure he had heard her. "Should I become pregnant, any chance I might have at a scientific career would be over. And the financial burden of a child would also end your pursuit of a scientific career. Try to understand the implications, Vladimir. Think!"

His face showed a glimmer of understanding. Then his voice softened, "Sofya, we will not always be students. I must know, now, what you think of me. I can't go on being near you and believing I'm nothing to you but a jar of preserves. I can't go on like that, Sofya. I can't. I love you and I want you as my wife. My true wife."

"Oh Volodya, I want to be your wife! Really, I do." In the fleeting instant after the words were spoke, she realized her heart had taken control. The ocean was unchanged by lightning. She felt as if she were floating.

She slipped her hands into Vladimir's. In a moment she was in his arms.

SOFYA REFUSED to open her eyes. She was warm, rested and deliciously comfortable. She had no idea how much time had passed since Vladimir had taken her into his arms. She recalled the first breathtaking kiss and then another. Somehow, intertwined, they had found their way to the divan. He held her tightly in his arms and whispered wonderful things. Her hands had rested on the back of his neck, she remembered the feel of the muscles holding his head, the soft downy hair near the center of his neck. Then her arms had slid along his solid arms. She remembered how clearly and strongly his heart beat as she pressed herself to his chest, ignoring the pressure of his shirt buttons against her cheek. She remembered his hands gently stroking.

She blushed. She had pushed down the shoulders of her dress. His large, warm hands had reached for her bare shoulders, caressing them, then gently he had held her from him. His hot breath whispered, "Enough, for now." He kissed her on the forehead, and touched the end of her nose gently with his finger. For a moment he sat next to her, not touching her. Then he had gone upstairs.

She must have fallen asleep waiting for his return. She opened her eyes slowly. A blanket was draped over her and her shoes were lying next to the divan. The doors to the room were open.

Vladimir was sitting in the large chair. He looked refreshed and smartly dressed.

"I was waiting for you to awaken." He looked up from a paper, the size of a train schedule. He had never looked so completely handsome. She felt herself blushing as she stared at him.

Putting down the schedule and moving to the end of the divan, he lifted her stockinged feet into his lap. As he gently squeezed her arches, she let her head fall back onto the arm of the divan, and sighed.

"Sofya, you do remember that we are promised to each other now."

"Hmhmm." She closed her eyes again as he gently petted her feet.

"Our wedding night will follow immediately upon the conclusion of our respective formal educations." Vladimir's voice was steady, though she thought with perhaps just a touch of humor. Entirely appropriate.

"I promise, Vladimir. I promise." She squirmed slightly as his hands moved up to her ankles.

"I'd like a token of our agreement. Something small, but a token. Something I can use to remind you, just in case you forget." Now his voice definitely carried a note of jest. "We can't very well exchange rings. We've done that."

She put her hands behind her head. "Did you have something in mind?"

"Yes." His hands were stroking her calves firmly. "The Jews in my village have a rather quaint custom that might serve us."

"Well, we've already had a Christian ceremony. What might the Jewish custom be?"

"When they wish to seal a contract, the seller offers the buyer his sandal as a sign of good will, and as a renunciation of his claim. If the buyer rejects the sandal, the deal is broken."

"I assume you mean me as the seller. A bit patriarchal for my taste." Sofya turned up her nose meaningfully. She was far too physically content to be angry. And clearly the matter was too serious to be approached without a little humor between them. "I seem to recall a story of that sort in the Book of Ruth." Sofya also recalled but didn't mention that, as a child, her tutors had always praised her easy mastery of religion. As with mathematics, the teachings of religion, the doctrines of theology, had come naturally to her. She prided herself on excelling in areas that drew heavily on imagination like mathematics, fiction, and religion.

"Yes, the Book of Ruth." Vladimir coaxed, "I would like to have you give me those small, silk slippers of yours as a sign of our betrothal."

"They're yours," she said at once. "Though I'll have to go about barefoot in my bedroom."

"Only until we share the bedroom." He laughed and squeezed her feet again.

"And what will you give to me?" She reached down and picked up one of his enormous boots which lay abandoned next to the divan. With a thud she let the weight fall to the wooden floor. "I don't believe I want to wear one of these next to my heart."

"Well, then." He reached into his pocket. "Will you take this?" He was holding out a beautiful, engraved silver timepiece, one that she had never seen before. "I purchased it many years ago, when I was coming home from Italy by way of Switzerland."

"It's magnificent!" Wondering, she handled the piece carefully.

"For a long time, I've hoped to give this to you. I wanted to find the right occasion. You see, I bought it after I came very close to losing my life in a skirmish. For me it symbolized my future—a time I almost didn't have. Now, my future lies with you."

"Oh, Vladimir. I'll keep it always. Always!" Sofya sat and kissed him tenderly on the cheek. "We will be happy."

A moment later, she bounced to her feet and poured two fresh cups of tea. She handed her husband a cup and sat next to him. For a long while they were silent. She fingered her new watch admiringly.

He didn't look at her as he spoke. "I've an invitation from the Darwins. They live in Kent, a pretty countryside area not far from London. I'm to visit there late this afternoon. If you'd accompany me, after the visit we might spend a few days alone in the country."

"Of course I'll come."

CHAPTER FOURTEEN

1869 ❧ *Darwin's Home*

The noises of the train made serious conversation all but impossible, so Sofya silently watched the English countryside roll by. Vladimir sat beside her, his shoulder pressed gently against hers. They were fortunate in having the compartment to themselves, although their privacy was limited by the glass in the door and the knowledge that at any stop the bench across from them might be occupied by another passenger.

From time to time Vladimir's hand would pass familiarly over hers, or she would feel the pressure of his leg against her skirts, his actions bringing back delicious memories of the morning. With pleasant anticipation, she wondered if he was signaling a reminder to her. But when she glanced at him, his face was expressionless. He appeared to be deeply engrossed in rereading his copy of Darwin's *Origins*.

At Bromley Station, one stop past Sydenham, site of the Crystal Palace, they disembarked. A rented carriage was available for the short ride to Down. After making sure their light baggage was adequately secured, Vladimir joined her in the carriage. Cheerily announcing that they would be the only passengers, he slipped his arm around her shoulder. She let her head rest against him as the vehicle jounced along the poorly leveled country road.

For the first time in several hours she felt she could speak to him. "I hope my joining you isn't a mistake. Perhaps I should wait for you in Down. After all, the Darwins aren't expecting two guests. My presence may be an imposition."

"Nonsense. Mrs. Darwin is a gracious lady, quite accustomed to entertaining her husband's guests, expected and otherwise. She'd never forgive me if I left you alone in town." He leaned over and kissed her lightly. "My worry is that you've only agreed to come with me so you can meet Darwin."

"Well . . ." Sofya playfully drew out her response.

For no reason she could comprehend his mood changed. "I've got you here with me." He solemnly intoned, "If it took trickery and bribes, then so be it." He withdrew his arm from around her shoulders.

"Vladimir! I was joking!" She tugged at his arm. "I came because I want to be with you. Today, tomorrow, and all the tomorrows after that."

He smiled weakly, took her hand from his arm and kissed it gently. Then he turned his sad eyes away.

They rode in silence, Sofya frequently glancing at him, as he pretended a preoccupation with the countryside. She doubted she would ever understand this man.

IN DOWN, the driver stopped at the town's one small inn. As Vladimir helped her from the carriage, Sofya squeezed his hand affectionately. He looked at her with some surprise, then the corners of his mouth turned up slightly. She hoped this meant his mood was lightening. The driver handed down their bags.

A piece of luggage in each hand, Vladimir nodded in the direction of the small inn whose signboard read *George and the Dragon*. The letters were scripted above a carving of a man and beast, done in would-be medieval style.

Entering a dim room, Sofya approached an oaken serving bar. A slender, balding, old man stood behind the bar polishing it with a towel. In answer to Vladimir's question, he assured them that a room could be obtained for the night.

Vladimir firmly asserted that two rooms would be preferable.

A heavyset woman emerged from a small door behind the innkeeper. "Oh, brother and sister, vacationing together. How nice! My brother and I traveled the continent together. That was before I married this one. Now, where do I travel? Up and back to the kitchen, that's where. See the world now, deary, before you're tied to one of these." She poked the innkeeper in a less-than-gentle manner.

Sofya quickly corrected the bold woman. "We're not brother and sister. We're married." She looked at Vladimir. A broad smile now dominated his features. Holding up her handkerchief as if to cough, she softly spoke in Russian, "Remember! No rumors must fly back to Heidelberg." Grinning, Vladimir nodded his head in agreement.

The woman stared disapprovingly at Sofya, before turning to leave through the door by which she had entered. From beyond the door, a barely audible mumbling drifted back. "Separate rooms and married. There's no telling with foreigners." With the words came a wave of odors escaping; the room was certainly the kitchen.

Vladimir handed the innkeeper payment reserving two rooms.

Clearly pleased with the amount, the man apologized for his wife's outspoken manner. Then he leaned over and whispered to Vladimir, just loud enough for Sofya to hear, "To tell the truth, sir, you have the right idea with your Missus. Gives you some peace, you might say."

Sofya felt her face growing warm. Her own sense of modesty could not be disturbed by such a vulgar man or his wife. But Vladimir's honor as a husband was being attacked by these provincial innkeepers, and that infuriated her.

Forestalling more domestic advice, Vladimir informed the innkeeper that the rooms need not be ready until early evening. If for any reason the innkeeper needed to contact them, they would be at the Darwin residence.

Leaving their baggage with the innkeeper, Sofya and Vladimir turned and started to leave. Before going out the door, Sofya clutched Vladimir's arm tightly, then stood on tip-toe to kiss him scandalously on the cheek. She made sure her whisper was loud enough for the innkeeper to overhear. "Thank you darling, thank you! You really must let me have some sleep. I promise you, it will only be for this one night!"

Vladimir could not resist turning back to the man, and giving a knowing wink.

Outside, the couple burst into laughter.

"You behaved like a very naughty lady!" Vladimir mockingly scolded.

"No more than warranted," she smilingly responded. When they had walked a few paces, Vladimir turned around and pointed at the sign. "I would bet that our innkeeper is named George."

"And we know who the dragon is," Sofya commented.

The early afternoon sun was warm on their shoulders as they silently climbed the slight rise in the road, between thick, towering hedges. After a quarter of an hour's brisk walk, the shrubs were beginning to thin, allowing glimpses of distant countryside.

"There it is!" Vladimir increased his pace.

At first she could barely see the house. Gradually it came into view, very large and white, and set back only a little distance on the right side of the road. A background of rolling hills and a strip of forest formed the perfect setting. Sofya stopped and stared. "It's like home. It could be Palibino!"

"Come on." Vladimir reached for her hand and led her up the dusty drive. In a few minutes, they were entering a broad gateway in a low flint wall.

Not until they reached the door, did Sofya slide her hand away. She reached for the door knocker, anticipating his move.

DARWIN AND HIS WIFE, Emma, must have been in nearby rooms, for they were at the front door to greet their visitors almost as soon as the servant who opened it.

Darwin was as tall as Vladimir, and as well proportioned, with the look of a man who had once been robust but was now somewhat debilitated by age and illness. The top of his head was totally bald; a bushy white beard covered the lower half of his face. Full, scraggly eyebrows accentuated his long narrow nose. His large eyes sparkled. Obviously he was delighted at their arrival.

So this is the great scientist, Sofya thought. The man whose ideas are changing the world. Without the beard and the sparkling eyes, the man might pass for the innkeeper's brother. The image she was forming was not just of Charles Darwin, but Darwin and a woman. The two made one picture.

Sofya guessed Emma Darwin was about sixty, the same age as Charles. Unlike Charles, Emma was still robust. She'd kept a fine figure, now highlighted by her simple but flattering dress. She wore her graying hair combed over her ears, parted in the middle. Her face appeared more kindly than beautiful.

"Welcome." Charles Darwin shook Vladimir's hand warmly. "How good to see you again after so long a time!"

Presently the four of them were in a spacious sitting room. A maid brought in an English teapot with elaborate accessories and began the ritual of serving tea. While the men discussed publications, Emma Darwin engaged Sofya in small talk. Emma was glad to see Vladimir again. How nice that he had married! Was Sofya enjoying England? Was this her first visit? The questions came with barely a pause between.

Sofya felt herself flush and asked Emma to speak more slowly. The rush of English words were hard to understand.

Graciously and naturally, Emma obliged.

When Emma had poured each of them a cup of steaming tea, Charles again directed himself to Vladimir and to business. "How are my books doing in Russia? Am I as much scorned for *Origins* there as I am here?"

Vladimir shook his head. "The books sold well. There was much controversy about your ideas at first, but even in Russia the scientists are beginning to realize the importance of your work. Your appointment to the Imperial Academy of Sciences in St. Petersburg was a major victory."

"Yes, the Russians are noticing me. Well, Englishmen are noticing you. I regret to say, my dear Kovalevsky, that I have recently seen an article denouncing you as what is termed a 'nihilist.' "

Startled by the reference to nihilists and somewhat fearful for Vladimir, Sofya put down her cup of tea and focused her attention on the men's conversation. Being publicly labeled could have severe consequences. European institutions, particularly the universities, wanted nothing to do with students known to have nihilist leanings.

"I have been called worse than 'nihilist' at home. In print and in conversation, I have questioned established ways and institutions. I like to swim against the current," Vladimir answered lightly.

"So do I," Darwin chuckled. Replacing his cup and saucer on the table, pushing himself up out of his chair, Darwin bowed slightly to Emma and Sofya. "Ladies, you will please excuse us," he announced somewhat abruptly. With a nod and a slight wave of his hand, Darwin indicated that Vladimir was also to rise.

"Emma dear." Darwin sounded apologetic. "I'm going to steal Vladimir away for just a little while." Turning to Sofya, "You do not mind, Mrs. Kovalevsky."

Sofya, of course, had no objections. Vladimir was beaming delightedly. His smile exactly that of a little boy, on being invited to an amusement park.

Taking Vladimir by the arm, Darwin guided him from the room, conversing all the while. "Come into my study, young man, I'd like to talk to you in detail. Your brother Aleksander is doing fine work. If, as I suspect, his findings support my transmutation theory, perhaps I'll include them in the next revision of Origins."

"Aleksander would be honored indeed, sir. That reminds me, my brother asked if you'd autograph a book for him. I brought along a copy of your Variations of Plants and Animals Under Domestication."

"Certainly." Darwin looked at Vladimir keenly. "I hear you're studying science, geology?"

"I have begun an effort in that direction, yes sir."

"That's my field. Or it was originally. I'll want to know what you're planning as a specialty."

Sofya could hear their voices receding down the hall, until a door closed somewhere to cut them off.

Emma turned to her with a resigned smile. "They'll be in the study for hours, if I know my husband. Charles is very much engrossed in his new project, and it's been a while since we've had a scientific visitor. It will do Charles a world of good."

From certain hints dropped by Vladimir and others, Sofya understood that Darwin was, or at least for a long time had considered himself to be, chronically ill.

"Shall we take a walk in the garden, my dear? Or have another cup of tea first?" Emma touched Sofya gently on the hand.

"I'd love to see the garden."

Sofya liked the older woman, deciding, as they talked, that Emma Darwin was sincere in her concern for people. Emma's lively nature combined with an apparent inner peace that Sofya envied.

A few minutes were sufficient to dispose of the usual flower garden near the house. Emma then suggested they take a turn around what she called the sandwalk. Curious, Sofya agreed. The older woman linked her arm in Sofya's in the carefree manner of a sister or friend of her own age. As they progressed, Emma related the story of the sandwalk. It was Charles's creation, a great looping path about a third of a mile in extent, running out from the house among the fields and woods and back again. He walked the path daily, seeking exercise and quiet thought at the same time. Emma laughed as she told how Charles, methodical-minded in everything, would establish a small pile or row of stones before he started, one stone for each round he planned on walking, then kick one stone aside as he finished the round. Would Sofya like to do something like that?

"Let's put out three stones," Sofya suggested as she placed the markers. "My father had a walk cleared in the woods behind our country home. When I was little, my governess and I took an hour's walk daily. In winter the path was kept clear of snow so we could continue our walks. Only extreme cold kept us inside."

As Emma seemed eager to hear more, Sofya found herself telling the older woman about the country house in Palibino, about the family and the governesses. Before their first trip around the sandwalk had been completed, Emma requested they call each other by their Christian name. Pleased and honored, Sofya agreed.

Their talk led on to other subjects, and Sofya did her best to convey the excitement and satisfaction she found in her work in mathematics.

"My son George is also interested in mathematics." Emma's voice filled with pride. "George is twenty-four now. He's doing advanced work at Cambridge."

"The mathematics department of Cambridge is respected around the world," Sofya offered. "I'm looking forward to the day when I am prepared for advanced work at such a prestigious university. For now, my courses at Heidelberg University are challenge enough."

"You're allowed to take courses at the university?" Emma looked at her in amazement.

"I am, yes. It's rather a long story."

The older woman was shaking her head. "English universities are simply not admitting women students. They probably never will. We did the best we could for our two daughters. They were as well educated at home as we could manage. Still, when the boys went off to university, the girls were envious. Especially our Henrietta, she's the older one, twenty-six now. She's quite gifted in science and literature. Our Etty frequently helps Charles edit his papers before he sends them to a publisher, and she always goes over the publisher's proofs with him. Charles frequently praises Etty for her insightful suggestions."

"How very unfortunate your Etty was never able to pursue formal training."

"Most unfortunate," Emma sighed.

They walked in sad silence. Sofya wondered if somehow she had depressed Emma. In an effort to enliven her, Sofya asked, "Do you have other children, besides George and Etty?"

"Oh my, yes!" The older woman glowingly described her brood of five boys and two girls. She'd lost three other children to illness, but such tragedies were well-nigh universal, and she had come to accept them.

"Someday, you and Vladimir will find great happiness in your children," Emma spoke with assurance.

"I don't want children!" The words came bursting forth of themselves. Then Sofya bit her lip. She desperately hoped she had not offended her new friend. Yet the need to express her own inner feelings to this caring woman had become overwhelming.

In the face of a shocked but patient silence, Sofya did her best to explain. "I want desperately to attain the highest level of mathematical education. I can be as good as any man. I know I can do this. I'd be the first woman with a doctorate in mathematics. The very first! Then, other women would have an easier time. Women like your Etty wouldn't have to waste their talents . . ." Sofya stopped, "Oh, Emma, I didn't mean it like that."

"I know what you mean, my dear." Emma smiled. "You're young and clever and full of dreams for the world. But while you're making the world a better place, try to remember to make your own world happy.

I know, there are many ways to be useful and happy. Together, you and your husband will find a way that's right."

For the first time, Sofya felt she had received a blessing on her true relationship with Vladimir. Along with the blessing came a flash of revelation. She and Vladimir must find a way that was right for them. Not the path of her parents. Not the path set by the expectations of their well-meaning friends. A new path all their own.

With a feeling of inner peace, Sofya refocused her attention. Emma was reminiscing. "Charles and I were thirty before we married and started our family." She patted Sofya on the arm. "And to tell you the truth, I don't think Charles could have accomplished nearly as much in science without me. My nursing him when he was ill, supporting him when some of his trusted friends deserted him, standing by him when the public criticism came. There are many topics on which we still don't see eye-to-eye. But we respect each other, we love each other. And now that the children are grown, I have more time to 'help the world' as you might say. I work with the animal humane society, and I help my son William with his work among the poor. I've found many ways to be happy. But the greatest happiness has been sharing life with Charles."

The last pebble was kicked aside by Emma. Slowly the women turned toward the house. Both were silent. Sofya's thoughts had turned to the future. She tried visualizing herself alone, then herself with Vladimir.

On her way across the lawn to the house, Sofya paused, distracted by a large stone in the shape of a torus with flattened sides, a thick disk an arm's length in diameter, with a central hole. This lay in the grass with what appeared to be the tips of steel rods projecting up slightly through the hole. With a feeling of horror, she thought it must be some kind of unusual gravestone!

"I see you're interested in Charles's wormstone." Emma's eyes were twinkling.

Sofya blinked. "I beg your pardon? Wormstone?"

Emma Darwin waved away any need for caution. "One of my husband's experiments. The idea was to determine at what rate a heavy stone, undermined by the natural burrowing of worms in the soil beneath it, would sink into the earth."

"Ah!" Sofya almost laughed with relief. This object was not a gravestone. "You speak in the past tense of some experiment?"

"Charles first did this experiment years ago with one of our sons. He's decided to re-do the work. Nostalgia for the children perhaps." Emma lowered her voice. "Charles has been taking such careful measurements—I haven't thought it wise to tell him yet—but yesterday I observed a small boy, the gardener's son, standing on the stone and most energetically jumping up and down. Ah—children!"

As the ladies reentered the house, Charles Darwin and Vladimir were just returning to the sitting room from the study.

"Enjoyable walk, ladies?" Darwin inquired as he went to Emma's side, touching her arm affectionately.

"Yes, very. Now, if matters are running smoothly in the kitchen, dinner will be ready in a few minutes." Emma looked to her guests. "You will be able to stay?"

Sofya turned to Vladimir. His eyes pleaded that she agree. She nodded her acceptance.

"Thank you," Vladimir answered for them. "We'd love to stay. I recall that you set a most delightful table, Mrs. Darwin. I'm glad my wife will have the pleasure of experiencing your hospitality."

"The pleasure will be ours, my boy." Charles patted Vladimir on the back. "Emma and I love the company of young people."

Dinner was a leisurely affair. When it was over, lamps were lighted and the men retired to the front porch with their cigars. Emma and Sofya went to the living room to sit by the small, cozy fire. From a cloth bag beside her chair, Emma took out crochet work. Sofya stared at Emma's swiftly moving fingers. "I crocheted when I was a child."

Emma responded, "Would you like to start working on a piece?"

"Very much." Pulling her chair next to Emma's, Sofya took the offered crochet hook and some thread. She fumbled with the thread for a moment, then Emma leaned over and helped. A few brief reminders were all Sofya's fingers needed to bring back familiar movements.

After a time the men rejoined them. "The evening is as warm as summer," said Charles, moving to the back of his wife's chair. "You ladies should come out and see the stars."

"Sofya!" Vladimir had come to a halt, staring down at her. "I had no idea you knew how to do that sort of thing."

"This is crocheting, Vladimir. I also am rather accomplished at embroidery."

"I never suspected . . ."

"Seems your wife has talents you are unaware of, my boy," Charles chided. "Women are full of surprises. Now my Emma . . ."

"Your Emma has just realized how late it is," Emma said. "Our guests may be tired." She addressed Vladimir. "You and Sofya will spend the night with us, I hope. Charles and I insist upon your company." And indeed her husband looked upset at the suggestion that the visitors might leave tonight.

Sofya heard her husband saying, "We'd love to spend the night. Thank you for your generous offer."

"But our bags are at the inn in Down," Sofya began, in feeble protest. "We made a reservation."

"That's no problem. We'll send our man, Parslow, down to fetch your bags and arrange things with the innkeeper." Emma began to give the necessary orders to a servant, stressing that a reimbursement for Mr. Kovalevsky ought to be strongly suggested to the innkeeper.

With no great surprise, but only a sense that fate was conspiring, Sofya accepted the new arrangement.

Their host brightened. "Kovalevsky, my friend, we still have much to talk about. I'd like to dig out some scientific papers you might be interested in. Then we could discuss some other thoughts on your work with fossils. I've more suggestions on possible lines of study for you. Things I'd like to do myself, but never will. I'm no longer up to the field work."

A FEW HOURS LATER, on indicating politely that she was ready to retire, Sofya was shown to one of the many bedrooms up on the first floor. As she ascended the stairs she could hear Emma yawning, urging Charles to retire. He mustn't tire himself on his first good day in weeks.

The spacious room Sofya entered contained a large wooden wardrobe, a straight-backed chair, and two bed stands, one on each side of an oversized bed. Pushing back the blue satin spread, Sofya uncovered four luxurious feather pillows and a serviceable brown woolen blanket. An additional woolen blanket lay folded at the foot of the bed. If the evening remained as warm as it now was, she would have no need for an extra blanket. Even the glowing coals in the small fireplace opposite the bed seemed to be radiating too much heat.

Sofya pushed aside the light drapes and opened the window full. She took in a deep breath of the night air. Turning, she noticed that two traveling bags had been placed next to the wardrobe, hers and Vladimir's. Of course, Emma would assume they would share a room. There were plush throw carpets on the floor and the extra blanket and pillows. Quickly she arranged a comfortable sleeping place for Vladimir on the floor.

With a sigh of release, Sofya wiggled out of her travel-worn dress, hung the garment in the tall wardrobe, and placed her shoes beneath it. Tonight, she decided, she would sleep in her more modest chemise rather than change to the nightgown packed in the bottom of her bag. She stood before the small round mirror which hung over the wash stand. Slowly she brushed her hair, taking pleasure in the soothing touch of the soft bristles.

Lying in bed at last, the satin cover pulled up over her breasts, her bare arms held a book she'd found on the bedside table. Adjusting the position of the candle, she tried to concentrate on the words.

After she'd read only a few pages, she heard a soft knock, then Vladimir entered. It seemed strange, yet somehow reassuring, that he scarcely looked at her, as if he had seen her in bed a thousand times before.

His expression was joyful, and in a quiet voice he began to recount the minor triumphs of the day. Darwin had suggested that Vladimir study Cuvier's fossil collection in Paris. Much work was going to be needed to explain the evolution of the horse. And Darwin had made some suggestions as to the best universities for Vladimir's continuing study and preparation for a teaching or research position.

Her husband went on talking, glancing at her frequently with merry eyes, and all the time it was plain to her—it must be plain to him as well—that all his talk, however pleasant, was, at this moment, unimportant.

Quietly but excitedly Vladimir continued to converse with her as he walked around the room, brushing close to the large bed. Certainly, he must have seen the sleeping arrangements she had made for him near the open window. Now he'd taken his boots off, and his jacket. Sofya put her book back on the nightstand. Self-consciously she pulled the satin cover to her chin. She had placed the book precariously and it was now threatening to fall. She reached out to push the object to a secure place. The cover slipped from her shoulders, exposed except for the thin straps of her chemise. Her eyes met Vladimir's.

"Surely you're not cold. The night is a little brisk but wonderfully freeing, don't you think?" She felt herself blush, but Vladimir didn't seem to notice. He continued with his talk. Darwin was working on a new book. One of the chapters was on birds. Vladimir had offered observations, gathered on his hunting and shooting trips in Russia, as supporting evidence for some of Darwin's ideas. Darwin had seemed pleased and would acknowledge the contribution in a footnote. Also, the great man had promised Vladimir the Russian publishing rights.

Perhaps this would be the book to earn the Kovalevskys the added income that they needed.

Vladimir, barelegged now, wearing only his shirt, was standing at the open window with his back to her. The muscles in his calves were well defined. A reddish coarse hair seemed to cover them from his ankles to his knees. She had never seen his legs. Embarrassed, she wondered if Vladimir had noticed her staring.

He appeared to be absorbed by whatever it was he saw outside the window. Softly he called her to come and look. She obeyed. She could see that a brightly gibbous moon had arisen, and as she moved toward the window Vladimir put out a hand hardened by the handling of many rocks, and pinched out the candle. "Let your eyes get used to the darkness," he advised softly. "Then you will see more clearly."

Standing beside her husband, she could see how the moon silvered the treetops clothing the rolling hills. Except for the air, so strangely warm, it might have been a Russian forest spread before her. Vladimir, standing behind her now, pointed silently. Quite near at hand, a fox was crossing an open, moonlit field.

Sharply Sofya drew in her breath, but somehow she knew she could not, must not, speak. Vladimir's arms were around her breasts. His head was bent beside hers, his lips just brushed her throat. Her hands touched his arms, then clung to them. She bent her head to gently kiss those strong arms that held her. Her first kisses released a hungry series, and she did not know and did not care where and when and how they were ever going to stop. Clinging to his arms, but now gasping for breath, she pressed herself tightly against him.

IT WAS HOURS LATER when a low, steady noise awakened her. The room was dark. She was naked. Vladimir, her husband, as naked as she, lay beside her on the bed, his back to her, his red hair rumpled. He was snoring. Sofya rose, grabbing up her husband's shirt, which lay rumpled at the foot of the bed, and slipped the garment on over her head. She went to the open window. Settling on the rug before the window, clutching to her chest the pillow she had once laid aside for Vladimir, she forced herself to think. My God, she might be pregnant! In an impulsive moment she might have ruined her future and Vladimir's.

Turning her head, she gazed at the calm, rugged face of the man who lay there snoring lightly, innocently. She must not let him feel guilty for what had happened. She had been as willing as he to forget their carefully worked out compromise, to forget ideals and goals. For one night, in this enchanted room, in this wondrous home of dreams, on this mysterious foreign island, she had lived and loved. Tomorrow she'd return to her well-planned life. Please God, she prayed, I mustn't be pregnant.

Feeling a sudden chill, she quietly closed the window. Returning to the rug, she wrapped the blanket over her shoulders. She stared mindlessly at the dark, mirror like glass that reflected a frightened little girl. Drawing her legs under the shirt, she clutched her knees to her chest. She started to sob. Tears came freely and silently.

CHAPTER FIFTEEN

1869 ❦ *Paris*

Heavy waves struck the side of the vessel; the Channel was in an extraordinarily ugly mood today. Vladimir stood alone, gripping the wooden rail that rimmed the passengers' deck, his eyes searching for the approaching shore of France. Cold, damp air wet his face as the ship entered the thick fog that clung to the continental coastline. A chill shiver passed through his body. For just a moment a nearby patch of fog had assumed the shape of a giant hand, like the paw of an angry djinn reaching out for him. Turning up his coat collar, he sternly scolded himself for such mystic imaginings. At any rate, a djinn was nothing to compare with the very material problems confronting him.

He shuddered again, this time with self-loathing. His physical need for Sofya haunted him like an addiction. And she, she had distanced herself from him with a stony coldness that he feared carried contempt.

For two unnerving weeks Sofya had been agonizing over the uncertainty of her condition. Had she gotten pregnant or not? And he had had no choice but to share her suffering. Then, only an hour ago, just as they were boarding the ship, Sofya had informed him she planned to see a doctor friend of Anyuta's as soon as they arrived in Paris. Frightened beyond words, he had steered her into an isolated corner below decks. Grabbing her by the shoulders, perhaps a bit too forcefully, he had demanded that she not endanger her life. Sofya had stared at him in seeming disbelief. Then, gathering all her forces, she had calmly stated that she took orders from no one. Pulling away, she demanded he leave her alone. He had not seen her since.

He was to blame for her dangerous position. He could well imagine that, if she saw the abortionist and survived, in her pain, she would hate him and never want to see him again. As for him, there could be no meaning to a life without her. Gripping the rail, he stared into the dark, rolling waves beneath the fog.

A moment later, a small, warm hand slipped over his. He looked up. The breeze was pushing Sofya's dark curls from her face. She said: "I won't need to see a doctor in Paris." Her voice was barely audible.

Heaving a sigh of relief, he slipped his arm around her shoulder and drew her to him. She clung to him, pressing her face against his chest. He felt the short little jumps of her shoulders, moved by her sobs. Lifting her chin with one finger, he looked into her eyes, as green and dark as the waves. "We'll be all right, Sofya. We're back on course."

"Vladimir." Her voice was tentative. "Vladimir, I want you, but . . ." she hesitated. "I mustn't let myself . . ." She gripped him tightly, so tightly that he felt pain. "Please, try to understand."

ON ARRIVING IN PARIS, Vladimir and Sofya went straight to Anyuta's small apartment. Over a simple dinner of bread and cheese, followed by tea and wine, Sofya related the highlights of their trip, omitting the most memorable part of the stay at Down. When Anyuta interrupted her sister's enthusiastic description of the mathematical community in London, to query her on her impressions of the political climate, Sofya pleaded ignorance and Vladimir was more or less forced to take over the narrative.

After what seemed to Sofya an interminably long discussion, an argument between Vladimir and Anyuta threatened to erupt. Anyuta questioned Vladimir's wisdom, and beyond that his sanity, in declining a meeting with Karl Marx. With an exaggerated yawn, Sofya consulted her new watch and announced that it was well past midnight. She was retiring.

For once Anyuta was ready to abandon an argument. "I do have to go to work tomorrow." She pushed back her chair, stood up and stretched. "How long will you be staying?"

Vladimir spoke reluctantly. "I'm afraid we're going to need your hospitality for a few days. Certainly not more than a week. I was expecting a royalty check I ordered sent to this address. At the moment our resources consist almost entirely of our tickets back to Heidelberg."

That got his wife's attention, as he had feared it would. "Why didn't you say we were low on funds?" Sofya looked at him with tired exasperation. "We could have left England immediately after our visit to Down, and saved weeks of travel expenses."

"I needed to visit the chalk sites for my work." Not able to face her gaze, he lowered his eyes. "And I didn't want to burden you with money worries."

"That was foolish!" Sofya scolded.

"I suppose it was, but I was certain the check would be here. I'll borrow the money. I know quite a few Russians here in Paris."

"From your political days?" Anyuta looked at him with what could only be called disdain.

"As a matter of fact, yes, Anyuta." Vladimir poured the last of the wine into his glass. "Sofya, don't worry, we'll be back in Heidelberg in plenty of time for the start of the new semester."

Too exhausted to debate further, Sofya retired to the bedroom. With one curt motion Anyuta relegated Vladimir to the divan where a pillow and blanket were stacked on one side. Then she followed her sister.

SOFYA SILENTLY WENT through her bedtime rituals. She was exhausted, emotionally and physically. Putting on a simple cotton nightgown she looked into the mirror. There was Anyuta's shy, little, clinging Sonechka. With a loud sigh, she climbed into the large bed and pulled the covers up to her chin.

When Anyuta joined her, she began whispering further questions about the trip. Yawning at intervals, Sofya obliged with impressions of the people and places she had visited, promising more details in the morning.

"Sofya, what really happened?" Anyuta was leaning on one elbow. Sofya touched her sister's single long blond braid. Anyuta was again a beautiful goddess, the all-wise advice giver, the guide to life, just as she had been in their childhood. The goddess was looking sternly down at her. "I can read you like a book, Sonechka. Something has changed you."

"Oh, Anyuta." Sofya felt her voice crack. "At Down, Vladimir and I shared . . ." Her face was warming. She turned from her sister's intense gaze.

"Oh . . ." Anyuta reached over and put out the bedside candle. She remained quiet for a long time. When she spoke her voice had a hard quality of practicality. "I saw from our bedtime preparations that you escaped this time." Anyuta's head now rested on the pillow next to Sofya. The darkness of room was broken only by a small night candle that burned in a red glass container in one corner of the room. Its flickering arrows of light reminded Sofya of the icon lamp in the bedroom they had shared as young children many years ago in Palibino.

"I don't suppose Vladimir took any precautions." Anyuta's voice was just audible. "And even if he had, that's no assurance you'd be safe. Vladimir's such an impractical fool."

"Don't say that!" Sofya instinctively wanted to protect Vladimir. "I was as much to blame as he."

"God, Sofya, how could *you* have behaved so stupidly?"

"Oh, Anyuta!" Sofya drew in breath to keep herself from bursting into tears. "For a time, all thought and reason were driven from me. Anyuta, I'm not at all sure I won't be drawn to him like that again. I don't know what I'm going to do." A sob escaped.

"I knew you wouldn't be able to handle this 'arrangement.' " Anyuta's whisper conveyed a certain, motherly conviction of her own wisdom. "Here's what you need to do. First, you're going back to your work. Don't risk your future. You told me you have the backing of the leading mathematicians in Heidelberg. They'd all have a good laugh and then forget you, if you took a year off to have a baby. You'd never be given another chance. Second, you're going to arrange your living conditions so that you don't succumb to temptation." Anyuta was relentless in her certainty. "Surround yourself with women of like ideals. Spending weeks alone with Vladimir, away from your work, was very foolish. Of course, you turned to him for affection and comfort. And he gave you the only kind of comforting a man knows how to give."

"I love him, Anyuta." Sofya's voice was a whisper, hardly recognizable even to herself. "I want to be with him, again and again, forever."

"I've heard that's what awakened passion is like," Anyuta sighed. "You're not the first to confide in me, you know. For goodness sake, get a grip on yourself. Remember your ideals, *our* ideals. Do you want to be a whimpering nobody? That's your fate if you give in now. You'll be an empty, used-up woman, just like mother."

Sofya stared at the ceiling, with its dancing shadows from the lamp that was not an icon.

After a pause, Anyuta yawned, then gently hugged her sister. "You're vulnerable now. In another week or so, your logical, sensible spirit will return. Don't disregard my advice. You must find yourself a group, like the one we had back in Petersburg." After placing a light kiss on Sofya's forehead, Anyuta turned and moved as if trying to find a comfortable position.

"Julia will be joining me in Heidelberg," Sofya whispered. "Her parents have agreed to let her study abroad."

"That's good, dear. Julia's a very sensible woman." Anyuta's words trailed off into a yawn.

Sofya listened to her sister's quiet breathing. Perhaps Anyuta was right. From the parlor, the sound of Vladimir's steady snoring mocked her resolve evoking memories of Down.

VLADIMIR PACED THE ROOM awaiting Sofya's return. She had spent the day at the publishing concern where Anyuta worked. Vladimir feared that place, feared that Sofya, again under Anyuta's spell, would be sucked into the mire of radical politics. He had spent the last few days fruitlessly tracking money. His requests had all been curtly denied. Men with whom he had shared very trying and dangerous times, to whom he had given money when he had it, were refusing him any help at all.

The sisters arrived, each carrying a part of the evening meal. The food was spread out on the bare wood of a small table. As long as he was here, he'd have to eat food paid for by Anyuta and endure the constant irritation of her negative comments. More upsetting was Sofya's aloofness. The sooner he and Sofya were out of Anyuta's apartment, the better.

"I don't understand why they all gave me such a cold reception," Vladimir heard himself confessing, after his mood had been mellowed by half a bottle of wine and the remnants of a loaf of bread. As the sisters cleared the table, he refilled his glass and withdrew to the divan.

"All Vladimir's friends can't be struggling for funds, can they?" Sofya looked to Anyuta for an answer.

"None of them is struggling for money." Anyuta took a clean napkin, and wiped the crumbs from the table. "That's not the reason for their tight fists."

"You know more about my friends than I?" Vladimir snapped.

"In this case, yes," Anyuta retorted. "One of your friends," she put a vicious emphasis upon the word, "is seeing the typesetter I work with down at the paper. Of course, the girl didn't know I was your sister-in-law."

"Well?"

Anyuta, hands on hips, faced her brother-in-law directly. "She told me that everyone in the Parisian Russian community believes you're working as a government agent. None of them will lend you a sou."

He started to his feet, then sank back on the chair, his jaw sagging.

"I don't believe it!" But even as he protested, he knew he did. The old rumors were back again, and there would never be an end to them. "Both of you know that I never worked as an agent!"

"I know," said Sofya.

Vladimir stood up again. "Sofya, I'm leaving this damned town tomorrow. I'm going back to Heidelberg. I'll give you your ticket before I go, you can join me when I've got a place."

"I'm coming with you."

Her sister shook her head. "It would be wiser if you waited until Vladimir makes suitable arrangements."

"We have at least one true friend in Heidelberg. Vladimir, write to Lamansky. He'll help us." Sofya went to pack.

That evening, Vladimir wrote, not to Lamansky, but to his brother, pleading desperately for money.

CHAPTER SIXTEEN

1869 ❧ Heidelberg

Sofya and Vladimir arrived at their Heidelberg apartment at midday. With dread, Vladimir knocked on the landlady's door, wondering how he'd ever manage to convince her to let them stay until the money from his brother arrived.

To the couple's surprise, the old woman greeted them calmly and pleasantly, inviting them into her simply furnished, immaculately clean living room. A cat on the window sill awoke, sprang to the floor, and with tail raised circled slowly around her legs.

Ignoring the animal, the lady cordially invited the couple to sit and have tea. They must tell her all about their vacation in England. Vladimir and Sofya exchanged confused looks. The landlady was behaving much too civilly.

"Thank you for your kind invitation, Frau Müller. However, at the present we are concerned about a certain family matter. Has there been any mail for us?" Vladimir hoped against hope that his royalty check might have been sent to this address.

With a kick of her leg she sent the cat scurrying. She walked slowly to a desk in a corner of the room. Taking a stack of envelopes from the desk, she handed it to Vladimir. Quickly he shuffled through them.

Nothing from Evdokimov, the man in charge of his book business. He handed the useless pile of paper to Sofya.

"If you don't mind, Frau Müller, we're quite tired. We'd like to go to our apartment." Vladimir waited for her to pounce, demanding the money owed.

But the landlady only blinked. "I was so hoping to hear all about the Royal Palace in London. You did see the Palace?"

"I'll stop in tomorrow, Frau Müller, and tell you all about Buckingham Palace. And the British Museum, the Crystal Palace, the shops, the theaters, and the countryside," Sofya assured her.

"Oh, I'd love that my dear girl!" The lady beamed. "I'll invite my friend Frau Blüker. She'll be so envious! None of her tenants are noted university scholars and world travelers!"

"And I will be in to settle our business matter very soon," Vladimir added as they were leaving.

The landlady made a peculiar sound. "Herr Kovalevsky, if you are referring to the rent, it has already been paid. A few days ago a young lady arrived who said she was your friend. She paid the back rent, and for this month as well. I hope I did not do wrong by letting her into your apartment. She seems a very pleasant, respectable fraulein."

"Julia!" Sofya whispered to Vladimir.

"You did as we wished," Vladimir reassured the landlady. "We were expecting Fraulein Lermontov. Thank you. We are anxious to be reunited with her."

THEY RACED up the stairs and burst into the apartment. In a moment the women were in each other's arms, hugging and laughing. Vladimir stood patiently by while they completed their reunion. Then he extended his hand to Julia. With some embarrassment, he thanked her for seeing to the rent. Right now, he wasn't able to reimburse her, but in a day or so . . .

"We will not speak of finances on the day of your arrival." Julia's words were spoken firmly. Then, as if to soften what she must have perceived as harsh words, she smiled warmly at him. "I'm so very grateful to you for allowing me to join you and your wife. I don't believe Mother and Father would have let me come abroad to study, if Sofya hadn't offered your protection, Vladimir. I'll try not be in your way."

"Oh, Julia!" Sofya moved to her friend's side. "Of course you won't be in our way."

"I'll put our traveling bags away and we'll set out for some tea and conversation." Vladimir headed toward the sleeping rooms.

"Oh, just a moment. I've made a change." Julia's voice wavered. "I ordered a spare bed for the larger sleeping room. I've put my things there."

Vladimir studied her intelligent face. Julia would have had no difficulty discerning which was Sofya's room. And, she must have seen his geology books, spare smoking pipes and shaving cups in the back sleeping room. She'd drawn conclusions based on circumstantial evidence and information, now outdated.

"If this arrangement isn't convenient . . ." Julia's face was reddening. Her uncertainty was evident.

An awkward silence filled the room. Vladimir looked hopefully at his wife.

"Really, it would be no trouble for me to move to the smaller room." Julia looked from Sofya to Vladimir. She was giving them every chance to gracefully acknowledge that there had been a change in their relationship.

"Don't be foolish." Sofya's eyes rested on Julia. "Of course, you made the proper arrangement."

With stoic resignation, Vladimir moved his bags into the small room.

RIGOROUS EXERCISE became a fixed part of Vladimir's daily routine. For a while, he had considered taking up fencing. Rumor had it that a flat in the apartment building next to his was used by Heidelberg students for just such practice. For some days, Vladimir had watched the students who entered the building, then decided that the benefits of the exercise were not worth the cost of keeping company with these juveniles. He'd retain his regimen of vigorous walking and stair climbing.

Sofya scolded him for taking precious time from his studies for athletics. He countered with the need to stay fit for field trips. Of course, what he hadn't mentioned to her was the calming effect his efforts had on his need for her. Although, an even more potent calming effect had entered his life—Julia.

Even-tempered, serious, studious, and very plain, Julia was ever present at the apartment. She never criticized his show of affectionate attentions to Sofya but in Julia's presence, there was no danger his attentions would be anything but proper. Julia had worked magic on Sofya, as well. During the weeks since her arrival, his wife had grown content. As before, she studied like a fiend, but now she at least found time to laugh. She gratefully acknowledged his management of the mundane details of life, and, most wondrously of all, she received his most proper attentions and reciprocated them in a charming manner, every now and then spontaneously kissing him on the cheek. If real marriage must be postponed, then having Julia as a chaperone was the best arrangement Vladimir could imagine.

On this particular Sunday, a fine day in autumn, the trio were strolling at a good pace down Haupstrasse, past the faithful parishioners hurrying to services at the Church of the Holy Spirit. Vladimir guided them on toward the cluster of shops known as Corn Market.

"Somehow, in all the weeks I've been here, I've never had time to visit the castle," Julia commented, staring up at the brown-red structure, its outline vague with ruin, that dominated the hilltop overlooking the city. She leaned a little forward, talking across Vladimir. "Sofya, you must have visited it last semester?"

"No. I never found the time."

Taking each woman by the arm and striding along between them, looking straight ahead, Vladimir murmured, "Such a shame. The castle's a romantic old place."

"Let's go today," Sofya pleaded. "It's been ages since Julia and I had an outing."

Vladimir looked at Julia, whose smile said she was ready. He shook his head. "Ah, if only you two were not weak and fragile women, robbed of your vigor by hours of intellectual strain, we could hike the Short Hill straight to the Charles Gate. I've made the tramp several times, but then I'm a vigorous geologist, hardened by numerous field trips. Ah," he looked from Sofya to Julia, "I see your spirits are daunted. You bookish ladies are in no condition for such rigors." Still holding each woman's arm, he started to turn them back toward the town.

"Really!" Sofya poked Vladimir lightly with her elbow, releasing herself from his grasp. "Julia, can we allow this man's remarks to go unchallenged?"

"Definitely not!" Julia pulled away from Vladimir.

The women lifted their skirts a few inches and broke into a run. They were racing and laughing with all the abandon of children. Only when the town was well at their backs did the three slow to a fast walk.

"Ladies, ladies!" Vladimir scolded when he had caught up with them. "Such disregard for propriety! Your skirts are quite dusty. Sofya, I believe you are glowing! Should a proper young man be returning to town on this path, and encounter you, however would you explain your disheveled state?" His finger gently brushed Sofya's moist forehead, then feathered against her upper lip.

Gasping for breath, she seized his arm and laughed, "If I chose to explain, I'd tell him I'm a gypsy, not bound by his rules."

"And you, Julia, what would you say?"

"Why, that I was under the spell of a gypsy, of course."

Vladimir proceeded to climb, motioning his companions to start moving.

"Slow down, please," Julia pleaded between gulps for air.

"And tell us about the castle," Sofya gasped out the words. "I know you're going to set an impossibly fast pace. Talking might just slow you down a little."

"Clever." Vladimir laughed. "And here I thought you just admired my erudition." He paused for breath, but kept up the pace of his walking. "The worthy townspeople started building the castle in 1300 and kept at it more or less for the next four hundred years. The Renaissance wing was added about 1559." He held the branches of a bush back from the path. When Julia had passed the obstacle, he offered his free hand to Sofya and smiled. "I'll let you ladies set the walking pace."

"Thank you kindly, sir." Sofya touched his hand gently. Their eyes met and he knew she was pleased with him.

Now the two women were in the lead. Following Sofya, Vladimir found his gaze helplessly fixed on the swaying motion of her hips.

"Please continue with our lesson," she called back to him.

"Oh, yes." Vladimir forced his attention to the narration. "Various rulers added to the site. The seventeenth-century ruler, Frederick V, was very romantic. He married an Englishwoman whom he adored, and had one of the gateways built overnight just to surprise his wife on her birthday."

"Certainly, you can vouch for the attractiveness of English ladies," Sofya reproached softly.

"Yes. Well." Vladimir felt his face warm and hurriedly continued. "A little over a hundred years ago, the French stormed the castle and reduced most of it to rubble. A few years later, lightning added to the damage. What is left is what we will see today."

"Only a ruin," Julia observed sadly.

"A very romantic ruin," Sofya added.

Vladimir stepped up beside her on the path and slipped his arm around her waist. "I can do old Frederick one better. For my Russian lady and her friend, I will rebuild the whole magnificent castle. And I'll do it in much less than a night."

"In our imaginations!" Julia called back to him.

"What finer setting." Sofya rewarded him with a most charming smile.

They had reached the top of the hill and a junction of paths. Vladimir explained that one footpath branched past the Castle wall to a garden overlooking the town. The other path led to the Charles Gate and into what had been the castle.

"Let's storm the castle." Sofya chose the path.

Passing through the Gate, Vladimir led them into the central courtyard. On three sides stood the scarred walls of what once had been tall, magnificently crafted stone buildings. A look over the fourth side, where the wall had been reduced to a low fence, offered a breathtaking view of Heidelberg.

When they had admired the view for some time, Vladimir steered them back to the courtyard. They were not alone. Other townspeople and visitors were wandering the grounds, some carrying picnic baskets. There was even a young boy selling juices and small pies.

After purchasing some refreshment, they found a spot to sit on a low ledge near the Well Tower at one end of the courtyard. As they ate and drank, Vladimir announced he would begin reconstructing the castle for his ladies. He pointed to one building after another. "That's what's left of the Ruprecht Building, the oldest part. There the ruler had his living quarters, offices, and halls for entertaining. The large structure near it was the Women's Building. The ladies of Court and their servants occupied the upper two floors, the lower floor served as a banquet hall."

"No doubt the ladies were kept under guard. For their own good, of course," Sofya sighed.

"No doubt," Vladimir continued. "On the opposite side of the courtyard, safely distant from the ladies, are the buildings most frequented by the knights. You can just make out the remains of a giant fireplace where oxen were roasted whole. The little structures on the far side are the remains of the bakery and butchery. The larger building is called Ottheinrich. It contained a tower where the town's medicines were prepared. A furnace and all kinds of utensils used by the early sorcerers, or should I call them chemists, is still intact. But you have to climb over some piles of rubble to reach it."

"I've got to see that," Julia asserted. "After all, I am a chemist."

"Perhaps, something of a sorceress too," Sofya teased.

"There are other attractions." Vladimir pointed. "Directly across from us is the Friedrich Building. It had the dubious distinction of housing an oaken wine vat holding fifty-five thousand gallons. Castle residents were not noted for their sobriety. One of those heaps of rubble was the Bell Tower. Where will we go first, ladies?"

"Climb or no climb, I'm headed for the Ottheinrich Building and the chemist shop." Julia turned to her friends. "Are you two coming?"

"No. I want to stay in the courtyard a while longer and try to take in the whole scene." Sofya looked at Vladimir. "You're headed for the wine vat room?"

"No. Too sad, looking at that broken vessel." Vladimir smiled at her. "I'll stay out here with you awhile."

"I'm glad." Sofya lowered her voice. "Actually, seeing the ruins of these buildings has been a little unnerving for me. What looked so romantic from afar, up close is haunting. I dislike the sight of destruction, even when it happened centuries ago."

"I think I understand." Vladimir leaned against a granite wall near the well and stared across the ruin toward the quiet town below. Without effort his mind re-created the scenes of violence that must have occurred on this now tranquil hillside. He smiled. Somehow Sofya's strong imagination was building the castle for him, and not the other way around.

"Vladimir?" Her voice brought him back abruptly. "There's another reason I'm glad you stayed with me." He turned to see her fingering sheets of brownish paper. She must have had them in her pocket, for they were far from crisp and stiff, as ladies' stationery tended to be. "Zhanna needs help."

"Zhanna?" Vladimir's attention was still focused more on the tattered appearance of the pages than on Sofya's words. "Oh, yes, one of your sister's good friends. The third member of your liberation group, when you were all looking for 'good men.' Or was it jars of preserves?"

"Yes, that's Zhanna." Sofya's voice hardened. "She's a close friend of mine, too, and Julia's cousin."

"Well, what's the trouble?"

"She writes that conditions in Petersburg are unbearable. Worse than what we've been reading in the papers." Sofya's tone expressed resignation.

Vladimir nodded wearily. Neither of them expected anything but the worst in the way of political news. "Does Zhanna give details of the university situation? Or the city's problems with factory workers? How about the fate of the liberal press?"

"I'm afraid she's too centered on her own immediate difficulty." Sofya lowered her voice as she continued, "The Grand Duke is making her life hell. Almost daily he contrives to meet her in the park when she's out walking, then he proceeds to make the most improper proposals. They're becoming more demands than suggestions. Worst of all, Zhanna's parents are encouraging him. Poor Zhanna's afraid she'll be forced to become his mistress."

"If the situation becomes serious, her parents will send her on a trip abroad, just as your father did when Dostoevsky became too attentive to Anyuta. At least that's the story Anyuta tells."

"Vladimir, Dostoevsky was a destitute ex-prisoner. But the Grand Duke is the Grand Duke! For God's sake, if her parents showed defiance, they could all end up in Siberia."

"There I think you exaggerate." Vladimir kicked at the dirt. "The penalty for parental defiance would be banishment from Petersburg and Moscow. The family would be forced to live at their country estate, no one would come to see them, no one would do business with them. They'd be ruined. But they wouldn't be in Siberia."

"Vladimir! Zhanna's desperate. She says she'll end her life if she doesn't get away soon."

He sighed. "Let me see that letter."

Reading it, he had to agree that the tone was desperate. Zhanna even talked of drowning herself. Vladimir could not be certain if the threats were feminine hysterics or serious depression. But he had known enough desperate young people to understand that a threat of suicide, even a hysterical one, was not to be taken lightly.

"Vladimir, something must be done. We can't abandon her."

He was reading the letter again, looking for but not finding signs that such concerns were unreasonable.

"Vladimir?" Sofya called softly. He looked up startled. "What can we do for her?"

Automatically he glanced around. No one else was near. "There may be a way to get her out of the country." His voice had fallen to a whisper. "But of course it's dangerous."

"She has no alternatives."

"Failure would mean death or prison. Not just for her, but for the people who helped her."

"She's in a prison now, and she's ready to die by her own hand."

Vladimir began pacing thoughtfully around the courtyard area, circling the Well Tower several times.

When he came around the last time, Julia had returned from her own excursion, and was saying, "You look terribly pale, Sofya. Are you all right?"

"I didn't realize how much the sight of this old ruin with all its destruction and disfigurement would upset me." Sofya shuddered.

"She showed me Zhanna's letter. You've seen it?"

Julia nodded. Her gray eyes filled with despair.

"I'm working on a plan." Vladimir stood close to Sofya. He felt her lean against him.

"This place is too public to even think the thoughts you must be having now," Julia whispered. "Let's go home."

THE WALK BACK to town was conducted in thoughtful silence. When the door to their apartment was closed and locked and all three were sitting at the table, Vladimir began to disclose his plan. "Sofya, you'll write Zhanna immediately. I think I can get her out of Russia. Get the paper and pen. Everything must be very discreet. If our letter is intercepted by the police, no one must be implicated."

When Sofya had gathered the writing materials, Vladimir pulled his chair close to hers. He sketched the plan, watching as Sofya constructed a first draft. "Zhanna is to go to my business contact, Evdokimov. She must tell him that she is my friend. She will have to give him two hundred rubles in cash, and say that I insist a ticket be purchased for her on the railroad to Zurich."

"Zhanna's allowance gives her access to that much cash," Julia noted.

"But she has no passport or papers," Sofya objected. "She can't travel by rail without papers."

Vladimir was shaking his head. "Her whole speech is a code. She won't be traveling by rail. And she won't be going to Zurich. Evdokimov will take her to a small town outside of Petersburg where he will leave her with a peasant family. He'll instruct the peasants that she's to be delivered to the bookseller. She'll be passed from village to village through a system of sympathetic, and easily bribed, peasants. Eventually, she'll arrive here in Heidelberg."

Julia interrupted softly, "Something like the American underground railroad for slaves, before their civil war."

"Yes." Vladimir looked admiringly at Julia. The longer he was with this woman the more she impressed him with her knowledge, intelligence, and common sense. "The actual crossing will be through a swamp on the Polish border. It's guarded, but not very heavily. With any luck

Zhanna will slip through." Vladimir spoke very softly, "I've taken this route in reverse several times. The last time was a few years ago, when I wanted to get some forbidden books into the country. It's not too demanding physically, but it is dangerous." Vladimir turned first to Sofya then to Julia before asking, "Does Zhanna have the nerves for this kind of adventure?"

Sofya answered, "Zhanna's desperate enough to try anything."

Julia countered, "Zhanna's eccentric enough to try anything. And despite her delicate appearance and sometimes flighty conversation, she is not a woman of delicate nerves."

Again Vladimir looked admiringly at her. Julia was a good judge of character, sympathetic without being romantic. Quiet, patient, plain Julia was proving herself a very wise and useful woman.

A carefully worded letter was mailed.

CHAPTER SEVENTEEN

1870 ⚬❧⚬ Heidelberg

At the table filled with books and papers, Vladimir's chair was pulled close to Julia's. One of the articles he had been assigned to read in a geology journal described the effect of thermal changes on gases confined in pockets within the earth's surface, and the ideas taxed his knowledge of chemistry. With Julia's help, the salient points made by the author were becoming clear.

Across from Vladimir sat Lamansky, his chair pulled close to Sofya's, papers with equations, rough sketches, and short charts of data strewn on the table in front of them. "That makes no sense at all to me," Lamansky was saying as he leaned even closer to Sofya. "I can't see how you knew that the tension on that string would cause it to snap." He pointed to a long row of numbers and letters that Sofya had just finished writing. "Why did you use that formula?"

"Did you study problems five and seven? The ones Helmholtz did in class. I think you forgot to take into consideration the force acting perpendicular . . ."

"Don't bother to finish explaining." Lamansky pushed his chair back. "I really don't care anymore. I understand just enough to get a decent grade in the mechanics course this semester."

"That's a pretty bad attitude, Sergei," Sofya scolded gently.

"I don't want to be the best physicist in the world, just good enough to get myself a teaching position. I'll get a recommendation for graduate work next year. And I'll slide by. I may even give up physics and go into finance with my brother. A position in a Moscow bank is certainly more lucrative than a professorship."

Julia and Vladimir had stopped their whispered work. They were staring at Sergei.

"I know." He smiled at each of them in turn. "You three are all alike, you want to be the best of the best in your respective fields. Well, more power to you. I just don't care about that. I don't have your kind of talent."

"It's been a difficult term for you," Julia offered. "You'll have easier times."

Vladimir looked at Sofya. "This term has been my best. There's been peace in this apartment."

"And you, Sofya." Lamansky turned to her. "Has this been an ideal term for you too?"

"Actually, it very nearly has. Professor DuBois-Reymond assures me that in less than a year I'll be ready for graduate level work. And I've found a field for specialization." Her excitement was growing. "This fall DuBois gave us an introduction to elliptical functions. They're fascinating! The physical problems described by elliptical functions . . ."

"Whoa, Sofya, whoa . . . ," Vladimir's voice pleaded.

"The question was, 'Have you been happy?' " Julia reminded her.

"Dangerously happy," Sofya confessed.

"Well, let's celebrate all this contentment and happiness. I just happen to have a bottle of wine in my bookbag." With the ease of a magician Lamansky produced the refreshment, then awkwardly struggled with the cork.

Julia set out four glasses. Lamansky poured a small amount of wine into each and offered a toast. "To the three musketeers of Russia, may they bring light and justice to the world."

"A bit overdramatic, my friend." Vladimir emptied his glass, and held it out to receive more wine. "My toast is to Julia, a true friend and peacemaker."

"Thank you." Julia nodded to Vladimir. "Now, my toast to my new friends."

She filled the glasses. "To you, Lamansky, for your constant good nature. To you, Sofya, a dear friend and the most talented woman I have ever met. And to you, Vladimir, the most intelligent and gallant of men." Julia's eyes rested on him warmly.

Lamansky was measuring out the last of the wine. "And I must have my turn. To Sofya . . ." He stopped at the sound of a loud knocking at the door.

AFTER A MOMENT'S HESITATION, Vladimir went to the door. "Who's there?" he called in a stern voice.

"Please, let me in." The words were in Russian, the voice was a woman's, high-pitched and hysterical.

Pushing ahead of Vladimir, Sofya quickly opened the door. The eyes of the wretched waif who stood outside were wide with fear, her grimy cheeks tracked by tears. Long blond hair, coming loose from what had been a twisted braid, hung to her shoulders in dirty disarray. Her torn scarf had once been fine yellow wool, but now resembled a cleaning rag. The young woman's coat was stained in several places, and her shoes were caked with mud. Exhausted and weeping, she swayed precariously, clutching a small parcel in her arms.

"Zhanna! It's Zhanna!" Julia cried, recognizing her cousin.

Vladimir managed to get an arm around Zhanna, just before she fell. At his touch she cried out weakly, her eyes widened in fear. As soon as she was inside, Lamansky shut the door.

"For goodness sake, help her to the chair," Sofya commanded.

Moments later the newcomer was seated, her scarf and coat having been removed. For the space of a few breaths Zhanna sat motionless, staring into space; then she burst into hysterical crying.

"You're safe now." Sofya was sitting on the floor next to Zhanna's chair, holding the girl's hand. "You're safe." Julia at Zhanna's other side was trying to comfort her also.

Sofya gave orders. "Vladimir, get a cup of hot tea and some bread. Lamansky, I think you'd better leave. Our visitor will have a story to tell, and it may include something you really don't want to know about."

"Oh." Lamansky was still staring dumbly at Zhanna. "I suppose she's here illegally."

"Sergei Aleksandrovich, get out of here!" Sofya shouted. "Go! Forget what you're seeing!"

Lamansky came to his senses. "I'll go. But you can trust me, Sofya. I'd do anything for you . . ."

"Leave!" Sofya shouted.

The door closed behind Lamansky. Vladimir brought a cup of steaming tea from the samovar which stood ever ready in one corner of the living room. "Here, drink this."

Zhanna reached for the cup, but her hands were shaking so that Sofya had to help her. A moment later, the newcomer was attacking a piece of bread with great enthusiasm. As soon as the edge was off her hunger, she seemed to realize that everyone was staring at her. Brushing away crumbs, Zhanna sat up straight, the first signs of her strong pride and natural elegance returning. "I've been without food for more than a day," she explained. Then she looked down at her dress. "I want to get out of these filthy rags and wash. I feel all crawly."

"Come with me." Julia helped her to her feet.

A quarter of an hour later, Zhanna reappeared in the living area, wearing a loose shift of Julia's. She still looked exhausted, but she was clean, and her hair was combed. Sitting at the table, Zhanna with ladylike etiquette consumed the remainder of the loaf of bread along with half a jar of preserves, and two cups of tea. Then, moving like a zombie, she returned to the big chair in the living room, where she sank down to rest.

"Would you like to lie down?" asked Vladimir. He and Julia had been busy transforming the living room divan into a bed.

"I can't!" Suddenly Zhanna began to cry hysterically. "I can't rest! It was all so horrible. I must tell someone what happened."

"Zhanna, you can tell us all about it in the morning." Vladimir's voice had a stern fatherly tone.

"Oh, Vladimir!" Sofya scolded. "If Zhanna feels she needs to talk, we will listen. Get the blanket from my bed for her knees." Sofya turned to the sobbing Zhanna. "You'll have a proper audience for your adventure."

Zhanna reached to touch Sofya's hand in thanks. When the blanket had been tucked in around her legs, and her audience had settled themselves to hear, Zhanna began:

"Two weeks ago, I received Sofya's letter." She smiled weakly, thankfully at Sofya. "Immediately I made contact with Evdokimov. Then days passed in which I heard nothing. I would have gone mad if I had not had the hope of escape before me. Finally word came. Vasily Jakovlevich Evdokimov had made all the arrangements. Under the pretext of staying overnight with a friend, I left my home carrying my light traveling bag, and all the cash I had saved. Mama kissed me goodbye, as she always does when I leave the house."

Here Zhanna interrupted herself to weep again. "Poor mama, she must be out of her mind with worry."

Julia was calmly reassuring. "I'll send a telegram tomorrow. She'll know you're safe."

"Tell mama I'm with you, Julia. Mama likes you. She trusts you."

Vladimir cleared his throat and asked a question, as Zhanna began to sink into a whimpering state. "Did you meet Evdokimov again?"

"He was waiting for me at the bookstore." Zhanna continued. "He drove me outside Petersburg, and left me at a peasant house near the sea. Then I was passed from one rural family to another, traveling across the countryside in crude peasant wagons, each day a little farther west. I was always cold, always hungry. Everyone had to be bribed. Finally I arrived at a small town near the Polish border. I didn't even know the town's name. A boy led me on foot deep into a swampy area. He pointed to a house, barely visible on the other side of the swamp, and said that was Poland, and I must walk across alone."

"He lied," Vladimir said angrily. "He is supposed to go across with you. That's what he's paid for."

"How was I to know that?" Zhanna snapped, showing some signs of energy for the first time. "I started the long walk with my little package under my arm. When I had almost reached the house, a foot patrol came along. The two guards spotted me and started shooting."

"Oh, Zhanna darling, how terrifying!" Sofya cried out.

"I ran madly, and somehow I made it. The border guards gave up the pursuit. The people in the house wasted no time in getting me farther into Poland and onto a freight train. The engineer of the train was bribed. I rode into Heidelberg hidden in the crew's quarters. From the train station I walked here. I'm totally out of funds. I have no papers. If the Heidelberg police find me, they'll send me back to Russia." Zhanna again burst into sobs. "The Russian police will put me in prison."

"We'll take care of you," Sofya assured her. "We won't let the police find you. And we won't let them send you back."

"You must rest." Julia urged Zhanna gently to the makeshift bed.

Vladimir had extinguished the lights in the living room, and the trio were going back toward the sleeping rooms, when Zhanna called after them in a pleading voice. "Julia, you'll wire mama first thing in the morning? Even if I'm still asleep?"

"As soon as the office opens, I'll send the wire," Julia reassured her.

"Julia," Zhanna continued. "Wire Anyuta too. Tell her I've arrived safely. I wrote her I was trying to escape." Sofya, with her hand on

Vladimir's arm, could feel him stiffen and hear him mutter angrily. "I wonder who else the little fool has told."

Sofya hissed at him to be quiet.

"I'll wire Anyuta," Julia confirmed. "Now go to sleep. I'm going to my room to rest. Sofya and Vladimir need to rest too."

"I'm sure she was discreet," Sofya whispered, trying to placate Vladimir before they separated for the night. "She probably used a code," she added hopefully, though she doubted that Zhanna would have that much sense. The only reply was another angry mutter.

WITHIN A FEW DAYS, Anyuta arrived with two large traveling bags, and announced that she had come to celebrate Zhanna's freedom.

At dinner that evening Anyuta confessed that she had had an ugly disagreement with a fellow worker and quit her job. At any rate, the job simply consumed too much of her energy. She needed more time for her writing. She had no immediate plan for returning to Paris.

The little apartment now had five occupants. Vladimir was sleeping on the divan, his things stored in his traveling bag. Anyuta had another bed squeezed into the back bedroom she now shared with Zhanna. Julia and Sofya occupied the remaining bedroom.

The evening study sessions, so congenial before the arrival of Zhanna and Anyuta, were transformed into times of pure agony. Each evening, five chairs crowded around the small table. Books and papers spread in confusion everywhere. The three real scholars tried to study as Anyuta impatiently and noisily drilled Zhanna on Latin verb declinations and vocabulary. Zhanna wanted to study law, but needed a stronger command of Latin.

Vladimir decided that tonight he would offer to take over as Zhanna's tutor. He could assure enough quiet so that at least Julia and Sofya could get their studying done. Anyuta should be happy to have time for writing her precious short story.

Before taking his seat at the table, Vladimir went to the divan and began unfastening the laces of his shoes. He was rubbing his stockinged foot when Zhanna burst with outrage.

"Just what do you think you're doing, Vladimir?" Zhanna's voice was high and loud. Her eyes were wide.

"I'm taking off my shoes. I got a blister on last weekend's geological tramp." He continued to take off his sock.

"Stop that!" Anyuta yelled at him. "You can't do that in front of us."

"We have a right to a certain decorum here," Zhanna added. "You will not take your shoes off while there are ladies present."

Sofya looked toward Julia. Julia shrugged her shoulders in bewilderment.

"Whose apartment is this, Zhanna?" Vladimir demanded. "Mine. Isn't that correct? Mine and Sofya's . . . and Julia's. I will take my shoes off when I please."

Anyuta looked at Vladimir critically. "We're living under very crowded conditions. We women have a right to civilized behavior. After all, we're not able to relax while you're around either. And I might add that your pipe smoking in the living room must end. As long as you are here, I suppose you must sleep in the common area. But otherwise you will use that area in accordance with the wishes of the majority."

"Anyuta!" Sofya pushed back her chair and stood beside Vladimir—just in time, she thought, to prevent a disastrous outburst from him. "This is Vladimir's home."

"Well, it shouldn't be!" Anyuta burst out. "Little sister, if you had the courage of your ideals, Vladimir would have been long gone. You have your friends around you now. You don't need his emotional support. If you can call his presence a support. Frankly, from what I've seen and what you've told me, he's an emotional drain and a danger to your freedom."

"Anyuta!" Sofya looked at her sister with shock.

"Vladimir is rather overly attentive to you, Sofya." Zhanna looked at Sofya with sympathy. "I know how men are. He wants something from you. Probably to seduce you. That's what all men want. You need to keep your guard up."

"Don't be ridiculous, Zhanna!" Julia slammed down a book on the table, and everyone looked at her in amazement. "Vladimir has never made an improper gesture to Sofya in all the time I've been with them. You are wrong to judge every man by your own unfortunate experiences!"

Vladimir had been staring angrily from one woman to the other, his face growing a deeper and deeper red. Now, with energetic movements, he began to put on his shoes.

"Ladies—and by that term I mean you, Sofya, and you, Julia—I am leaving now. Before I forget I am a gentleman." The shoes were on and he stood up. "I will not spend another night here." Focusing his attention on Sofya, he asked simply: "Are you coming with me?"

"I . . . ." The room was suddenly silent. They were all looking at her. Simply walking out would mark her as a failure, in the eyes of Zhanna and her sister, while staying would win their approval. But that wasn't the reason why she couldn't move.

She looked at Vladimir. His eyes were so pleading, so persuasive, that she felt herself slipping under his spell. She must have taken a step forward, for she felt the gentle pressure of Anyuta's hand on her arm. She pulled away from her sister, but that touch broke the spell Vladimir's eyes were casting.

"I'm staying here," she barely whispered. Her eyes were down, not daring to look at him.

"Well, good for you, Sofya. You do have some sense." Anyuta looked smug. "Goodbye, Vladimir."

She received no reply. There was no delay required for packing, as Vladimir's belongings were already in his traveling bag. As the door of the apartment closed behind her departing husband, Sofya headed for her room and slammed her door. She threw herself on the bed and cried. She was still crying several hours later when Julia entered the room to retire.

"I wish we could have prevented his leaving." Julia's soft words as she prepared for sleep were no comfort. "Anyuta has a very sharp tongue and Zhanna only encourages her." Julia kept talking, although Sofya's only answers were sobs. "And, of course, there really is no way Vladimir could be comfortable in a small apartment like this, with four women."

"I can't throw my own sister out!" Sofya sobbed. "And I can't send Zhanna out on the street, into the hands of the police."

"I'll find my own place," Julia said, suddenly contrite. "I should be the one to leave. Your husband should be here, in this room, with you."

"Oh, Julia, he and I can't share a room, not now. We'd lose our future. We both know that." She turned her head on her pillow so she could see her friend. "I don't even dare to share an apartment with him, unless there's someone with us." She paused to dab at her tears with a handkerchief. "The weeks before all this were wonderfully happy."

"I was happier than I'd ever been," Julia confessed softly.

"How I wish our trio had stayed together!" Sofya sat up in bed. "Julia, don't you leave me, please. If I lose both you and Vladimir, I think I'll just wither to nothing."

"I won't leave you." Julia put out the candle and settled into her bed. "I wonder where Vladimir will spend the night. I'm going to miss him."

"Oh, so will I, Julia!" Sofya sobbed again. "So will I." And she didn't want to think about where he might be going to spend the night.

❦

ON THE FOLLOWING AFTERNOON, Vladimir and Sofya sat at a table in a small bakery near the university. A cup of chocolate steamed in front of Sofya. Putting down his own cup of strong Turkish tea, Vladimir started simply. "I stayed at a hotel last night."

"You look very tired."

"I didn't get much sleep. I kept wondering why my wife hadn't come with me."

"Vladimir, Anyuta and Zhanna helped me find freedom. And they helped me find you. I know they're very hard to get along with. But I will not just abandon my sister, or any woman who needs my help to obtain an education. That doesn't mean that I don't need you." Sofya put her hand over his. "I didn't sleep much either."

He pulled his hand away from her. "I'm moving into Lamansky's place today."

"Oh? I wouldn't have thought you'd pick him as a roommate."

"The price is right. He's letting me stay free. It's degrading, not paying my way at his place. But with you supporting Anyuta and Zhanna, there's no way I could afford a place of my own."

"Vladimir," Sofya heard herself pleading impulsively. "Come back to our apartment. We'll work this out."

He looked at her steadily. "How soon are your sister and Zhanna leaving?"

She couldn't respond.

"I didn't think they were." With a sigh he continued, "I must have some peace and freedom for study. Frankly, I don't see how you stand that overcrowded, vicious atmosphere."

"Won't you please come back?" Her eyes were smarting with tears.

"If the others leave. Not Julia, of course, but Anyuta and Zhanna. I don't like being the resident eunuch in this harem you've created."

"What a cruel thing to say!"

"Meanwhile, if you want to see me, I spend my afternoons at the library and I dine at the little place across the river."

SOFYA DID VISIT him in the library, every day for the next week. When she arrived on the seventh day, she began abruptly: "Certain developments at the apartment have me totally bewildered. I must speak with you." She did not remove her coat or scarf, nor did she sit.

"And I must speak with you." Vladimir was already on his feet, putting on his coat. "I have an assurance that Lamansky won't be home until late. He's out drinking with friends. A frequent occupation of his."

On the street, Vladimir stared straight ahead intently, as if to avoid her questioning eyes. The pace he'd set was so swift she had trouble keeping at his side. More than once she found herself trailing far enough behind that passersby would not have guessed that they were together.

When they arrived at Lamansky's apartment, Sofya sat in the larger of the room's two giant leather armchairs. She was exhausted. Vladimir's back was to her, as he prepared their tea. She could hear the agitation in her own voice, as she spoke hurriedly and softly.

"Zhanna received word from her parents." Sofya tried to control her voice. "All is forgiven. They are ready to help her in any way they can, she need only write and tell them her needs. Her mother and sister will send her clothing and funds. Her father will arrange to have her papers put in order. He's giving her legal permission for her travel and study in Europe. They're planning to come to see her as soon as possible."

"Love, parental love! An illogical, incomprehensible phenomenon." Vladimir's faint smile appeared indulgent and false as he handed Sofya a steaming cup. He settled his own drink on the small wooden table he used for study, and positioned the other armchair so that by turning only slightly he was able to rest an elbow on the table and still see Sofya's face.

Sofya inhaled the warm vapors and pungent aroma that rose from her cup. "I don't understand Zhanna's parents, any more than I understand her." Sofya sighed, before taking a long drink of the hot liquid. "You know, had she stayed with them, they would have refused her all these things. But because she ran away, they are ready to fulfill her slightest whims."

"Don't waste your time and energy trying to find reason in the emotions and motivations of Zhanna's family."

She looked at him. "What do you mean?"

He countered her question with another. "Will Zhanna be moving out of your apartment?"

"No." Sofya stared at him coldly. "She's still quite shaken by her experience, perhaps that's why she's so disagreeable. She says she's not ready to venture on her own. She plans on staying on with me at least another term."

"You'd better get her out of there."

"You know I can't turn her out." Sofya hesitated. "The atmosphere at the apartment is worse than when you were with us. Zhanna and Julia are fighting."

"How could anyone fight with Julia?" Vladimir's words were exasperated. Then he pulled a letter from his vest pocket. "I say get her out, because she is dangerous. I've just had news from a friend in Russia. Evdokimov is in jail. The shop in Petersburg where the stock of books for my publishing business is housed was shut down."

"What happened?" She reached for the letter, and skimmed the text as she listened.

"Apparently, your brilliant friend, who wants to be lawyer, wrote Evdokimov a thank-you note for his help in her escape." Vladimir sighed loudly.

Sofya looked up and her mouth fell open. "I can't believe it."

"That's not all. She asked Evdokimov if he planned to attend a workers' meeting to be held in Berlin. How she came to know about that meeting, I can't imagine. Evdokimov was already under suspicion for collaboration with radical elements. For years his mail has been carefully watched. Zhanna's letter gave the authorities their first solid piece of evidence."

"And now he is in prison!" Sofya could only whisper.

"Do you or any of your harebrained friends have any idea of what that means? I doubt it." Vladimir's anger was directed at her. He jumped from his chair and paced in front of her. "This isn't a reprimand from loving parents. This is the Russian government."

"I'm sorry. I never wanted to make trouble for you or your friends."

He searched her face. "Oh, I'm responsible too." He sat down again. "I'll have to try to free my friend. But I don't know where I can find the kind of money I'll need, to pay fines and bribes. My book business is lost, the entire stock will be confiscated. I won't even be able to recover the cost of the books."

"How much will you need?"

"To help Evdokimov? Probably three thousand rubles."

Sofya lifted her chin. "Borrow the money from my father."

"I can't. I won't get your father involved in this."

"Tell Father we were foolish and ran out of money. Make some excuse that involves me and Anyuta. He doesn't have to know the real situation."

"Parental love, again. So, you do believe in parental love," Vladimir said under his breath. "You're right, though. The general is the only possible source for that kind of an advance. I'll leave for Russia tomorrow. There's no telling when I'll return."

Sofya sank back into her chair. "I'll miss you," she said tiredly, leaning her head back and closing her eyes.

"I sincerely doubt that." The tone of his voice gave her shivers. But she was too tired to fight.

TWO WEEKS LATER, when Vladimir returned from Russia, Sofya and Lamansky were waiting for him at the train station. After a strained dinner where Vladimir related the general happenings and gossip in Petersburg, Lamansky excused himself. He had plans for the evening, but his companions were free to use the apartment if they had private matters to discuss.

"I told Lamansky you were in Russia on business for Zhanna," Sofya confessed. "He won't be back until late. He knows I don't want him involved with this."

"Did you see him often, while I was gone?"

"As a matter of fact I did. He offered his apartment as a quiet retreat." She watched for Vladimir's response.

"And did you accept?" His eyes blazed with anger, as she had hoped they would.

"Of course not. Such behavior would inflame my husband's jealousy."

AT THE APARTMENT Vladimir went to his room. Placing his worn brown leather bag on the bed, he began to unpack. In a moment Sofya was standing in the doorway. He indicated that she might take the chair next to his work desk, but her stern look discouraged him.

Carelessly he dumped the entire contents of his bag onto the bed. Rummaging through the dirty socks and shirts, he found a jar of preserves and a bottle of vodka, both with Palibino labels. Sofya's mother had given him the jam, her father the vodka. "Here are some choice 'preserves.' " He pronounced the word in a manner he knew would provoke memories. "This jar is from your mother."

Sofya took the gift. "Vladimir, you don't have to unpack now! Come back into the main room and tell me what happened in Petersburg."

He pushed aside the dirty clothing, placed the vodka on his desk, motioned for Sofya to precede him, then slammed the bedroom door behind him.

He sat on the divan, with Sofya across from him in one of the two leather armchairs. She sat rigidly alert, her eyes sparkling with anticipation.

He began, "When I arrived in Russia, I went straight to your parents' home. After your mother fussed over me and saw that I was well fed, your father and I retired to his study for brandy. I confided the truth of the whole Zhanna affair. Your father was not surprised. As a friend of Zhanna's father, he had heard something of the situation. And I might add, he has great insight into the personalities involved. By the next afternoon Father had arranged a meeting with the grand duke, where he explained Zhanna's departure in a way most flattering to the duke's virility."

"Go on. Tell me how," Sofya insisted. She was turning the jar of preserves nervously in her hands, picking at the label and struggling to remove the wax seal. He handed her his pocket knife.

"Your father has unsuspected literary talents. In a very convincing tone he relates that Zhanna, having vowed to herself that she would become a scholar, was forced to run away from what would otherwise have been an irresistible temptation: that of falling hopelessly under the duke's romantic spell. After reaching Heidelberg, by some means never clearly spelled out, Zhanna joined the general's younger daughter and his son-in-law in pursuing academic interests. Naturally I confirmed this."

Sofya nodded thoughtfully. "Zhanna truly is very intent on becoming a scholar, she must have at least hinted at this when the duke was pursuing her." Her voice quavered slightly, "And the duke was satisfied?"

"Yes. Fortunately, as your father already knew, the grand duke is now quite taken with another Petersburg beauty. He only needed a little salve to soothe his vanity. The general even maneuvered the duke into quite a jovial mood, by telling a few humorous stories. I will not embarrass you by repeating them."

"And you went along?" She looked at him critically, her dark brows coming together over her piercing eyes.

"Don't wrinkle your nose at me. Yes. I told a few camp stories. So, after much back-slapping, winking, and a few nudges in the ribs, your father, the duke, and myself found ourselves in agreement on the subject of 'beautiful women and how they try men's understanding.' By that time the duke was feeling quite pleased with himself. Your father passed around some imported cigars. As we were lighting up, I seized the opportunity to ask His Nobility if he might arrange a pardon for my friend, Evdokimov. The duke was receptive to the idea; nothing was too good for your father, his brave and honored general, and a pardon seemed a fitting tribute to the memories provided by the delightful, beautiful Zhanna. The duke offered us a round of cognac. We drank to Evdokimov's weakness when subjected to the pleas of a beautiful woman, and to his imminent release. Then we drank again, to all beautiful women."

Vladimir got up, went to the sideboard where a samovar was steaming, and poured himself a cup of tea.

"The disgusting depravity of aristocrats!" Sofya slammed the now open jar of preserves down on the table next to her chair with such force that the lamp shook precariously. "Of course, my father would understand precisely 'noble' thinking, and how to play on the royal weakness. A woman's desperate escape is easily interpreted as a source of amusement, somehow flattering to the man who forced her into it!"

"You really don't understand the risk your father took. Or how cleverly he handled this situation." Vladimir considered lecturing his young wife on her harsh judgment of her father, but he decided he would be wasting his words. He stared into his tea. "Ah, that cognac!"

"You might have offered me some tea!" She held out his closed pocketknife to him.

"Sorry." He took the implement, then as he turned to prepare her tea he continued, "More to the point, Evdokimov is out of jail, thank God. And even my book business has been salvaged. I managed to retrieve the confiscated stock, though that cost me some money in bribes."

"Where did you get the money for that?" Sofya sipped cautiously at the steaming cup he handed her.

Unable to meet her eyes, Vladimir stared at the spoon as she stirred the cup. "Another loan." His voice dropped. "From your father, where else?"

"Don't look so forlorn. We'll pay him back." Her voice was cold, it would seem, easily cold enough to freeze the tea she was so intently spooning.

"Naturally your father asked about your health. And he would like you to come home for a visit, soon."

"Was that his condition for the loan?"

"No. There were no conditions, no interest, no time limits on repayment. Your parents only request that you come home. They nearly begged me to return with you for the Christmas vacation."

"And you promised them our vacation time."

"Not exactly. I explained that I had to make up the university work I'd missed, and that required a field trip over the holidays. As disappointed as they obviously were, I believe they understood. I tried to assure them that their daughters were fine. Your mother was especially concerned about Anyuta. They've had no communication with her. Sofya, you must visit them without me. Assure them that you and Anyuta are all right."

"I'll write them a letter. But I'm not going back home without you."

"Sofya, there are times I feel I hardly know you." Disgusted with her reaction, Vladimir walked to his sleeping room, where he picked up the bottle of Palibino vodka, expertly popped out the cork, and poured a generous amount into his tea. Taking a long swallow and feeling somewhat fortified, he returned to the living room.

Sofya was adding to her tea a large spoon of raspberry jam from the jar Mother had sent. She looked at him. "There's been a change in the make-up of my little women's community since you went to Russia."

"Chernyshevsky strikes again! I must re-read *What Is To Be Done*, to see what's coming next." Vladimir gulped tea and smacked his lips. "Don't tell me, let me see if I can guess. You now have fifteen women with you. All scholars, all terribly oppressed by their parents. You're going to start a sewing cooperative! At least I won't need to arrange rescues, only needle and thread," he added as he sank back into his armchair.

"Very funny! Do you want to hear the real news or not?" She took a long sip from her sweetened cup.

"Well?"

"Anyuta's returned to Paris." Sofya's voice was low, her eyes downcast.

Vladimir's sarcasm vanished, leaving him sober and serious. "When?"

"About a week ago. She received a letter postmarked from Paris. Her face glowed when I handed it to her. She evidently recognized the script. She tore open the envelope and read in silence. When she looked up she had a smile on her face like that of a child with some wicked, secret plan. But she said nothing."

"Did you question her?" Vladimir placed his empty cup on the sideboard. Returning to the divan, he sat leaning forward, almost touching Sofya.

"Of course. That kind of behavior is very unlike my sister. But I learned nothing." Sofya sighed and placed her cup on the table next to her. Her small hands clasped the arms of the chair. "Anyuta immediately began to get ready to go back to Paris. When she talked about it at all, she made a point of emphasizing that she was returning to a life of solitary dedication to her ideals."

"Strange behavior." Vladimir scratched his head. "Sounds almost as if the note might have been from a gentleman."

"Don't be ridiculous! Anyuta never, ever swoons over an admirer. She probably received a job offer, or sold a story or article. Whether the letter contained money I couldn't tell, but she asked for some cash, and I gave it to her. From the food fund."

"She gave you no details?"

"None," Sofya confessed, "I am a little worried about her. But in all honesty, her departure has eased some of the strain at the apartment. And the physical crowding was relieved a little."

"Exactly how crowded is it now?"

"My cousin, Natalia Armfeldt, joined us. Before Anyuta left, there were five of us in that apartment. Now we're back to four."

"Madness!"

"It shouldn't matter to you, you've already left me." Sofya paused to sip her tea and calm herself. "Natalia came to study mathematics. The problem is, she isn't very good at mathematics. Quite inadequately prepared, and even more inadequately motivated. Apparently her real forte is politics."

"Another political. She should fit in quite smoothly." He settled on the divan and reached down to remove his shoes. He lifted an eyebrow mockingly to ask permission.

Sofya ignored the gesture. "Natalia joined with Zhanna to harass Julia and me. So the mood in the apartment is not good. Really, I'm glad you're not there. Zhanna and Natalia argue, viciously and constantly. Julia's retreated into silence."

"Poor sweet Julia, she's got no defenses against those vipers." Vladimir wiggled his freed toes, noticing for the first time that his sock had a rather large hole through which his toe protruded.

"Yes." Sofya looked at him. Whether she noticed his toe or not he couldn't tell. "Well, I'm worried Julia may leave me and get her own place. I don't think I could stand being deserted by both of you."

Vladimir looked at her for a long time. "I won't argue about who is deserting whom, we've been through all that. But do you realize that you are carrying your dream of helping your fellow countrywomen to a ridiculous extreme? Must you take every dream to the extreme?" The room was silent. "For your own sanity's sake, Sofya, I strongly suggest you change your living arrangements. You and Julia are going to have to find a place where you can have enough peace to study."

"I can't plan a move now, Vladimir." Sofya rubbed her forehead. "I'm swamped with work. When I've got through this term, I'll be able to think about improving my living arrangements. I can think about it over the Christmas break, when we're back at Palibino."

"I told you, I'm not going back to Russia. I'll need the time to do field work and try to write some papers."

"Let me stay with you over the break? I could help you." She was pleading. "I must get away from the apartment. I can't go home and face Mother and Father without you, and without Anyuta."

"What of your fear of living alone with me? That's what this whole crazy term has been about, hasn't it? You're afraid of me." He rested his head on one end of the divan, raising his feet onto the other. One arm dangled over the edge and brushed against her skirts.

"No." Then she hesitated. "Yes. Perhaps that entered into my decisions, a little."

"As long as we're being honest, I am almost as frightened as you. I don't want to risk your getting pregnant any more than you do." He stared at the ceiling as he spoke. "I know I was glad to have Julia with us. Now you're suggesting we take a chance on being alone together."

"It won't be the same. You'll be occupied with your studies, gone most days and some nights on field trips. When we're together I'll be all business, help you prepare your papers, clean your collections, draw sketches, anything to help you." She leaned over and touched his hand. "After our night in Darwin's house I'm much more aware of my own weakness. I promise I'll behave more cautiously."

"Are you sure this is the risk you want to take?" He pulled his hand from hers. Even her innocent touch must not be allowed.

"There will be no risk. We can handle this, Vladimir." She continued in a softer tone, "If we don't spend some sane time together, we'll drift so far apart that when we've finished our studies you won't want to be with me."

"The chance of that is small. No, nonexistent."

"And I want to be with you." She spoke softly. He saw her face color as he turned his head at her response.

CHAPTER EIGHTEEN

1870–1871   ❧   *Jübingen-Marseille-Paris*

The morning of the first day of Christmas holiday a horde of students crowded the Heidelberg train station. Encumbered with traveling bags, Vladimir and Sofya navigated their way through the throng. Three trains were puffing steam, getting ready to depart. The first would rush northeast for Berlin, the second southwest to Tübingen, the last due west to Paris. As they pushed through the crowd waiting to board the Berlin Express, Vladimir explained again why they were getting aboard the second.

"The fields around Tübingen are littered with fossil bones," Vladimir was saying as he stumbled along behind her in the train's corridor.

"So you've been telling me," Sofya commented gloomily. She preferred either Paris or Berlin.

"I'll see the remains of some of the earliest, most primitive dinosaurs. The bones lie exposed in the nearby rocks just waiting for someone to sketch them. All of southern Germany is dotted with outcropping of Keuper beds."

"What kind of beds?" She tried to hear his enthusiastic comments. Bodies bumped and pushed against her as she struggled through the narrow corridor. She tried to check the number on their boarding ticket against compartment numbers.

Vladimir leaned his head over her shoulder to read the number. Taking a step backward, he pushed on a door she had just passed. Shoving the bags into the tiny compartment and tugging Sofya in after them, he closed the door. The noise and confusion from the corridor was muffled.

Climbing over the bags, Sofya claimed the seat nearest the window.

"I was saying," Vladimir continued as he tossed one of the bags onto a rack above the seat, "the area around Tübingen contains Keuper beds, rocks from the earliest of the Triassic System."

"Trias. That's Greek meaning Three."

"Right!" Vladimir sat next to her and let out a sigh of relief. "About forty years ago, a geologist named von Alberti grouped three kinds of sedimentary rocks into what he called the Triassic System. We're interested in the Keuper rocks, they're reddish brown or gray in color and they contain lots of bones. Keuper rocks are the youngest of the three kinds of rocks. We saw some examples of Keuper rocks when we were in England. The ones near Tübingen are said to be much richer in fossil remains. I'll be poking around in the limestone, clay and shale in ponds, streams and fields. I've arranged for field trips with professors from the geology department of the city's university."

"I'll read all the geology books you assign me. I'll even tramp beside you through field and stream, if you ask." Sofya groaned. "But, I don't want to go near a university. I'm on vacation."

"For me this is not a vacation, I've plenty of work to do. And I'm counting on your help." Already he was pulling out a large book on fossils. "Just don't expect me to entertain you on this trip."

"I'll find my own entertainment, thank you. I have half a dozen Flaubert novels I'll consume. When I'm not helping you, that is. And I have a distant cousin on my mother's side living in Tübingen. Gretchen writes that the countryside is perfect for walks. The Black Forest is worth some investigating."

AFTER TEN DAYS in Tübingin, Sofya pleaded with Vladimir that they move somewhere, anywhere away from the rain that kept her confined indoors. Cousin Gretchen had proved an extremely boring companion, interested only in talking of her latest conquest, a handsome Prussian soldier.

To Sofya's surprise, Vladimir agreed, suggesting a move to the south of France. The weather might be more pleasant. And he could do some collecting from the chalk and limestone fields along the Mediterranean coast. He could work that data nicely into his paper.

AFTER NUMEROUS STOPS in the towns along the coast, they made their way to Marseille, where Vladimir finally declared he had sufficient data to complete his paper.

Sofya walked slowly, her hands clasped behind her back. She and Vladimir had been silent since they left the noisy Promenade de la Corniche whose shops and wooden walkways paralleled the coast. The late afternoon breeze was cool and Vladimir, without a word, had removed his jacket and put it over her shoulders. She slipped her arms into the sleeves and held the sides of the too large garment crossed over her breasts.

Vladimir walked purposefully toward a large outcropping of rock. The busy harbor was before them, the Promenade now far behind, out of sight and inaudible. Vladimir led her up onto a rock that jutted over the water's edge, then sat down with his boots hanging over. Silently, Sofya took a place near him, keeping her feet away from the occasional splash of spray. For a long while they sat wordlessly looking out over the harbor. Ships were bringing in cargoes of petroleum to France, others heading out to sea, carrying, she imagined, wines and perfumes to the West Indies and North Africa.

"Sofya," Vladimir spoke without looking at her. It was as if he were talking to the sea, or to one of the ships that looked so small with distance. "I won't be returning to Heidelberg."

"Why not? You've completed a brilliant paper on reptilian fossils.

You'll be ready to continue your classes, as if you'd never missed those weeks last fall."

Vladimir's voice was still remote. "I've been reconsidering the options for my advanced training. I've heard the University at Jena has a very liberal policy. They don't care about political or professional opinions. Questions are restricted to the field of study. Degrees are granted solely on the basis of a candidate's demonstrated knowledge."

"What a wonderful idea!" Sofya said sarcastically. "Do you think other institutions might copy their ways?"

Not responding to her try for a lighter mood, Vladimir continued gravely, "My reputation as a political is bound to prejudice a conservative university against me. And I'm certain the thrust of my scientific work will be a search for data supporting Darwin's theory of evolution. That approach is going to disturb many of the older professors."

"Your work will be construed as mixing science and politics." Sofya sighed.

"Very likely," Vladimir agreed. "And that's why I must choose my places of study carefully. The advice I keep getting is that the courses in Munich are better than in Heidelberg or in Jena. Munich would give me a solid, respected background. And Munich is close enough to Jena for me to establish some professional connections. Sometimes, at Jena, degrees are granted in absentia, the quality of the aspirant's dissertation being the only consideration. When I have a dissertation ready, I'll submit it to Jena."

"You've decided to study at Munich and get your degree from Jena?"

"Yes. I realize the plan's somewhat bizarre, but in my case, I believe that it will be successful."

"Why not finish one more term at Heidelberg?"

He looked out to sea. "You know I've been unhappy at Heidelberg."

"I just have one more term!" Sofya couldn't believe he was telling her this. "Stay with me just one more term."

"Stay in a separate apartment? I might see you for a few minutes each day, and during most of those minutes you would be studying. And at the end of the term, what then?"

Sofya spoke softly, "The best place for advanced work in mathematics is Berlin. I'll be going to Berlin." She paused. "Surely, you could do your course work in Berlin and submit your dissertation to Jena."

"Munich is the best place for my work." His words were cold and definite.

Sofya pulled her knees up to her chest, and rested her head on them.

Her arms hung limply at her sides. "Munich is so far from Heidelberg. And even farther from Berlin."

"You won't be alone, you have your friends." His voice was bitter, and he was still looking out to sea, not at her. "Doubtless there are many women you could help."

"I know last semester's arrangements were difficult for you." She must convince him not to move away from her. "But the situation will change. There's only going to be Julia and me. We could be together, the three of us, as when we first returned from London. Oh, Vladimir! Please say you'll stay with me in Heidelberg."

"What about Zhanna?"

"Her family has connections. She's been admitted to the university at Leipzig."

"And Natalia?"

"She's returning to Russia. She wants to go into the country to teach."

"I've heard you and Julia talking about 'rescuing' cousin Olga. Of course, Olga would need a place to stay. Sofya, this dream you have of being a helping hand to other young women is very noble. Follow your noble dreams. But it's time I pursued my own dream."

There was a long silence.

"It's not a noble dream for me, Vladimir, it's a very practical matter. For some women, there is nothing more important in life than an education, and there's no way to get an education without help. You gave me that help. If I can give it to others, I must," Sofya said softly.

"I'm trying to understand." Vladimir put his hand under her chin and lifted her face toward him. He looked strangely blurry through her tears. "I'll come to see you as often as possible. We'll spend every vacation together. I promise." He gently wiped her tears with the back of his hand. She thought she saw him put that hand to his lips before asking, "Would you come to Munich?"

"I couldn't," she whispered, then once more hid her face in her arms.

SHE AND VLADIMIR parted ways in Marseille. He headed for Munich, she for Paris to spend her last vacation days with her sister.

Over the rattle of the wheels, Sofya could almost hear Anyuta's reassurances. "Little sister, your concerns for living without Vladimir are ridiculous. After all, I have been managing quite nicely on my own. If I can manage, surely you, with your great scientific brain, can manage. I've always said, Vladimir should have moved away right from the start."

❦

ANYUTA RETAINED the same Paris apartment she had when Sofya and Vladimir last visited on their way back from England. In the shadows of winter's early darkness, the building appeared even older than Sofya had remembered, and the neighborhood much less friendly.

At apartment numbered 3A, no one answered Sofya's knock. Anyuta must be at one of her workers' meetings. Sofya left her bag at the door and retraced her steps down the dark stairs. A few minutes later she was back, having seen the landlady and obtained a key.

Inside the apartment, two large, well worn chairs stood before a cold fireplace. On a small table between the chairs, covered with a checked cloth, she discovered cheese, bread and a half bottle of wine, evidently remnants of Anyuta's dinner. Sofya settled herself into the larger of the chairs, and from time to time nibbled at the food. To her surprise, she soon drained the half bottle, and was licking her fingers for the last of the cheese. She curled up on the cushion of the chair and rested her eyes. Travel was so tiring. Even before she was fully asleep her mind was weaving a kind of dream, involving Vladimir and some laughing woman.

SOFYA HEARD the animated voices. A man and a woman were speaking French. She strained to listen. Somewhere between waking and sleeping, Sofya marveled that she must be dreaming in French.

She was not dreaming. The woman's voice was Anyuta's, and the man's was some stranger. The stranger was expressing his approval of Anyuta's behavior at the evening's meeting, evidently just concluded. Anyuta was a beautiful, articulate woman. She'd made a strong impression on the attending publicists. He was sure, soon she'd be offered a job working with them.

Anyuta's reply complimented her companion's forcefulness and logic. Soon he'd be leading a section of the organization.

Sofya rose from the chair. She was staring at a scene of such inexplicable nature that words were held captive somewhere between her mind and throat. Anyuta pressed against a tall, good-looking young man, obviously a Frenchman. Her arms clasped his neck, his hands held her waist. He was kissing Anyuta's lips, her neck, her ear. Sofya gasped. Anyuta turned slightly at the sound.

"Who's there?" Anyuta asked in French. Her face changed. "Sofya! I thought you were coming in tomorrow." Gently Anyuta freed herself. Coming closer, she whispered in Russian, "Sofya, please, get a grip on yourself. He's a very special friend. Speak French."

Finally Sofya managed some automatic greeting.

Anyuta's voice wavered slightly, "Sofya, this is Victor Jaclard. He works in the movement. He was a professor of mathematics, before he discovered his talent for more important work."

Sofya could do little more than stare.

Victor was laughing, in what Sofya imagined was supposed to be a charming manner. "You, of course, are the little sister. Anyuta's told me about you."

An awkward silence followed. Sofya gave her sister an icy stare. What was going on?

Soon the three were settled at the dining table. As expected, Anyuta greeted the news of Vladimir's move with enthusiasm and approval.

When the light snack had been concluded, Jaclard announced he must get some rest, and arose politely to exchange a formal good night with Sofya. Anyuta had risen also, and seemed to be showing her visitor to the door. At last, Sofya would be able to talk candidly with her sister.

Jaclard kissed Anyuta good night, boldly, as if no one else were in the room. Then, instead of putting on his coat as Sofya had expected, he approached the door of the bedroom. Entering, he closed the door behind him.

Only Russian would serve for this conversation. "He's living here!" Sofya marveled in a shocked whisper.

Anyuta's face turned a deep red. In a breathless voice, just above a whisper, she said, "Please try to understand. I love him. We've been together since I returned from your place last month."

Sofya continued to stare at her sister in utter disbelief.

"Don't look so hurt!" Anyuta pleaded in a subdued voice. Sofya realized that she was being very considerate of her lover, not wanting to disturb his slumber. "Victor's strong, intelligent, a leader of men. Together we'll accomplish great things." Then, dropping her voice to a whisper, she confessed, "I want to be with him more than anything."

Sofya's astonishment was turning to anger. She couldn't comprehend what she was hearing. This wasn't Anyuta, this was not her sister, but some changeling. Her sister scorned and made fun of women who succumbed to the power of a man.

Waves of emotion, hurt, betrayal, anger, overwhelmed Sofya, salty tears ran down her face. A great, numb silence seemed to overlay the world.

Mercifully, Anyuta stopped her endless explanation of Victor's wondrous nature. "Sofya, how cruel of me to go on like this. You must be very, very tired from your trip. Make yourself comfortable on the divan. We'll talk again tomorrow." Kissing Sofya on the cheek, Anyuta retired to the bedroom.

Sofya turned and stared at the divan in the corner of the parlor. She remembered it well. It was the very one on which Vladimir spent the night, during their last visit with Anyuta.

CHAPTER NINETEEN

1870 ⚜ *Berlin*

A rush of wind set a pile of leaves sweeping into the air, magically twisting them into a twirling cone. As Sofya watched, a gray horse with its head drooping wearily pushed into the vortex, scattering the leaves. The horse stopped, and turned his head quizzically to Sofya. The animal's soft brown eyes were pools of disappointment and sadness, cutting at her heart.

"*Droschke*, Fraulein?" the voice of the cab driver called.

"*Nein, danke.*" Despite the threatening storm, she would walk to her destination. The cabby's call had startled her. She looked around her. She must have been sitting on this iron bench under this protective oak for over an hour, thoughts and fears racing around in her head like dry leaves.

She was alone in Berlin, a city of a million people. Vladimir had come in from Jena for a weekend, helped her find an apartment, and then, despite her pleadings, had left her alone.

She checked the time. She had a few minutes before she needed to start on her mission. Absentmindedly she fingered the lovely timepiece Vladimir had given her, on a day that now seemed as remote as the Triassic Period. With a rush of annoyance at Vladimir she thought he should be here, with her, not flitting from city to city, museum to museum, rocky site to rocky site. There was no understanding him! Last term he had insisted on Munich, this term Jena. He should be here in Berlin with her.

A burst of thunder reminded Sofya of her own mission. She stood, smoothed her coat, brushed a leaf from the hem of her simple dark dress, and began to walk, into a crisp fall wind. With one hand she held her unaccustomed hat on tightly, with the other she gripped the folder tucked under her arm. She looked for the numbers on the neat row-houses that lined the block. Each was individualized in some way, here a flower box in a window, there a crocheted curtain, or a distinctive door knocker. All she knew of the residence she searched for was the number, 40 Potsdamerstrasse, the home of Weierstrass.

Hesitating in front of Number 40, a house very much like all the others, she gripped the decorative iron railing of the stone stairway. Her future depended on the outcome of this visit. Everyone agreed that Karl Weierstrass was a mathematical genius. More importantly for her, he had a reputation for training outstanding explorers on the frontiers of research. The endorsement of Professor Weierstrass was a ticket to the highest realms of the world of mathematics.

Well, she had prepared as thoroughly as possible for this moment. There was nothing more to do but try.

She climbed the stairs, lifted the knocker and, fully aware of making a fateful decision, let it fall.

A woman answered the door. She was tall, thin and large boned, towering over Sofya ominously. Her graying hair was pulled severely back from her face and parted by a straight line. Sofya guessed her to be in her late forties.

"May I help you?" When she spoke, any threat suggested by her height and rugged build evaporated. Her voice was pleasing, her eyes gentle.

"Is Professor Weierstrass at home? I wish to speak with him concerning my attendance at his lectures." Sofya blurted out the words too quickly. She heard the heavy accents of her own speech.

The woman looked somewhat surprised, but she unceremoniously stepped aside and held the door wide open. "My brother is not at home. However, please, come in. The weather is turning nasty and you don't appear to have a cab waiting."

As soon as the door closed, they heard a dash of rain against it. "My goodness, it seems the storm held back just until you found shelter." The woman indicated the room to the left of the entry hall. "You may wait here until the weather improves."

"I'd very much like to wait until the Professor arrives." Sofya spoke in a low slow voice. She hadn't moved from the hallway.

"There's no telling when Karl will be here. He's probably in a pub surrounded by a half a dozen students discussing some mathematical theorem or other, and has completely forgotten the time." A loud clap of thunder shook the house. The woman's eyes quickly assessed Sofya. "You haven't even brought an umbrella."

Another woman of about the same age as the first and with the same rugged facial features and majestic bearing appeared in the small hallway. "Oh, Clara, we have a visitor. How nice." Her voice was pleasant also.

"Yes. This young woman is looking for Karl. Something to do with his mathematics." Clara was occupying herself with the contents of a container near the door, that appeared to hold nothing but walking sticks. "Elise, where's Karl's big, black umbrella? The one with the duck carved into the handle."

"Really! Concerning mathematics!" Elise smiled broadly at Sofya, and ignored her sister's inquiries. She reached her hand out to Sofya, "I'm Elise, Karl's younger sister."

"I'm Sofya Kovalevskaya. I hope to study with your brother." She removed her gloves, then grasped the warm extended hand.

"Our brother's a whirlwind of activity lately. You know he's been elected Dean of the Philosophical Faculty." The woman beamed with pride. "All his new duties are keeping him very busy. And, of course, he loves spending hours and hours with his students. I just hope he doesn't overwork himself. A few years ago he came right to the brink of a breakdown. And he, a man with a rugged athletic constitution!"

"Elise, how you do go on." Clara scolded. "Now, help me find that umbrella."

Elise had barely moved from a vulnerable position in front of the large oaken door, when it suddenly flew open, and a powerful body entered. Sofya stared at the man. Bushy eyebrows were knitted together over his large nose, as if he were in deep thought or worry. His balding head was bare against the cold and wet, his face clean shaven. His tall, robust, bulky appearance was strangely to her liking. He was probably in his middle fifties. Leaves and wind had entered with him, and his coat was dripping water onto the polished floor. Brushing rain from his face with a huge paw of a hand, he turned slightly to toss his scarf onto the bench, his shining blue eyes brushing Sofya's as he did so.

"Oh, Karl," Clara rushed to take his coat. "You'll catch your death of pneumonia. This is Fraulein Kova . . . Kova . . ."

"Frau Sofya Kovalevskaya. Some Germans say Kovalevsky—it doesn't matter. I've come to study mathematics." Sofya spoke firmly, but discovered that it needed an effort of will for her to keep looking steadily from under her hatbrim at the man, this man, who was the master wizard of her world.

As soon as she mentioned mathematics, it seemed that Weierstrass had already seen quite enough of her. "Elise, show the lady into the living room." He shook his head and body, like a wet lion spraying droplets in all directions. He cast one more fleeting glance in Sofya's direction. "Excuse me, I'll be with you in a few moments."

Clara followed her brother through the hall and up a flight of stairs.

Elise murmured something and disappeared into the rear of the house. Returning almost immediately, she led Sofya into a tastefully decorated parlor and motioned her to a chair. "You'll have time for tea and a little pastry. Clara will insist Karl change from his wet clothing before he meets with you." She looked at Sofya. "My goodness, I forgot to ask for your coat and hat."

"You're most kind. But I prefer to keep them. I'm a little chilled right now. I suppose it's nervousness. I don't think I'll be able to eat a bite, but hot tea sounds wonderfully fortifying."

"You're nervous? About meeting with Karl?" Elise looked sincerely surprised, as she placed a cup of steaming liquid before Sofya.

Sofya nodded and smiled weakly.

"My goodness, you mustn't be nervous with Karl. He wasn't always a stuffy old professor." Elise passed the cream and sugar. "He never even finished his own university studies. Father was furious, and accused him of spending more time in the beer gardens than in the lecture halls." Elise giggled, a girlish sound, then sipped from her cup.

Sofya murmured something.

Her hostess shook her head. "Not that Father wasn't right to be upset. Karl was involved in more than one frivolous student duel. He might have been injured." A gleam of humor came into her eyes. "But Karl is too sturdy, too agile, too capable of total concentration. None of his opponents could touch him with a sword. To this day my brother regrets never receiving that so-fashionable male badge of honor, a facial scar."

Sofya blinked, unable to reconcile this image of Weierstrass with the one she'd received from his mathematical admirers. Could there be another brother? She asked tentatively, "Professor Weierstrass never studied for a doctorate?" Perhaps this non-mathematical woman did not have the facts quite straight.

Elise shook her head with decisive pride. "No he did not, not in the way everyone else does, at a university under the guidance of professors."

"How amazing." Sofya sipped her tea.

The mathematician's sister stopped to sip her tea. Her cup rattled noisily on the saucer as she replaced the fine china on the table. She dabbed at her lips with a delicately embroidered napkin. She clearly was enjoying the chance to elaborate on one of her favorite topics. "Karl was awarded a doctorate based on the quality of an independent research paper. Professor Kummer liked Karl's work, invited him to Berlin, and offered him a teaching position at the university. All that excitement, and Karl was already thirty-eight years old.

"That's when Clara and I came to keep house for our brother. He was nearing a breakdown. I'm certain overindulgence in mathematics was the cause."

She makes it sound like strong drink, thought Sofya to herself. Well, perhaps it is, for some.

Elise was going on. "I have no understanding of why a subject so coldly logical has such a debilitating effect, but the work consumes him. Left on his own, he forgets to sleep, to eat, to rest." She looked up again at Sofya, and after a moment of silence added softly, "He needs looking after."

KARL WEIERSTRASS WALKED UP the stairs to the large, comfortable chamber that combined the functions of his bedroom and second study. He was quietly pleased to hear Clara's footsteps behind him. His doting sisters were at times a bit annoying, but they provided him with a comfortable, quiet home, the perfect environment for a mathematician, with no family worries to distract him.

All those years locked away teaching secondary school. No such homey comforts then, when he was young. He had occupied his days with teaching, his evenings reveling with his friends, and late at night he lost himself in the cool beauty of the writings of Abel and other mathematicians. Alone he had mastered the masters.

Then one day fate tapped him on the shoulder. The state required that each school yearly submit a paper demonstrating that its teachers were actively involved with their subjects. An annoying business, but the authorities required it. Could Weierstrass handle it this year? The other instructors were overburdened with important work.

Of course, he could write a paper. And he had. His paper rocked not only the foundations of the staid mathematical community, but those of the very calculus itself. He described a function that was everywhere continuous, but had no derivative! First local people, and then eminent professors, had fallen all over themselves trying to refute his finding, but none could do so. He'd triggered an earthquake from which the dust had yet to settle. And now he was rebuilding the foundations that he'd shaken.

Feeling rather pleased with himself, warmed by the glow of memory, he started into his room.

"Don't close that door!" Clara's voice behind him sounded a warning. "I'm coming in. I know you, Karl, you'll see some paper with scratchings on it, sit down at your desk and completely forget that nice young woman waiting for you, completely forget to get out of those wet clothes, and catch your death of cold."

Weierstrass turned. "Clara, really! You treat me like a child. This is going too far. Wait for me downstairs." His glow of contentment had evaporated.

"Karl, please." Her tone softened. "I want to know about the war. I've read the papers from front to back, but I know the pubs are where the real news is exchanged."

"So, General Pedtke has turned your head," Karl teased. "A woman of your age, Clara, really!"

Clara blushed furiously. "Please, Karl, if I asked in front of Elise she'd tease me mercilessly, even more than you. And the general's letters are so vague. I can't tell if he's in danger." Having come past him into his room, she busied herself straightening his papers.

Weierstrass stepped behind a screen and began to remove wet clothes. "I doubt I've heard anything that you haven't read in the papers. France is beaten. Napoleon's been captured—after all, not nearly as tough as his uncle was. The Empire has fallen. The borders between our countries are closed tight. Paris is surrounded. Bismarck is drumming up a lot of support for uniting the German-speaking areas, while the French can't find an ally. Our troops are having an easy time of it." He thought, then raised his voice slightly. "Oh, I did hear one interesting item. Paris is totally cut off, as I said. But every few days they launch a large hot air balloon. A craft big enough to carry men and some supplies. Imagine, these devices fly right over our lines carrying men, a few refugees, mail and whatever else will fit in one of those hanging baskets. It's amazing!"

Emerging from behind the screen in dry clothing, Weierstrass began to search a drawer for the woolen vest Elise had made for him. It would please his sisters to see him wearing it. "I'll be glad when the war's over. So many empty seats at the lecture hall. The young men all off. I'm down to twenty students. Before the war there were fifty capable young men following my course of lectures. Where is that vest?"

"Karl, the woman downstairs hopes to study with you." Clara found the neat gray waistcoat, for which he had been looking in the wrong place, and handed it to him, straightening the contents of the drawer before closing it. "If your student load has been reduced, perhaps you should consider taking her on. At least we women would get some good from this horrid war."

"Good grief! There may be a shortage of students but I'm not sure I'm ready to take on a bored Russian aristocrat. And from what I read in the papers about the Russian women students, I don't think I'll involve myself with them. Their government claims they're revolutionaries who study only for purposes I cannot mention in front of a lady, my dear sister. Damn, if I see that woman now, I'll have to wear a jacket and tie."

"I read the papers too, Karl," Clara piped up. "They accuse the Russian women of studying medicine so that they can perform abortions, and of studying government and law so that they can go home and preach revolution. God knows what evil purposes they attribute to a woman wanting to study mathematics. Probably they'd think she wants to build bombs. What nonsense! Just because a girl wants to get some schooling she's subjected to slander."

"I'm not ready to waste my time on a wealthy woman who doesn't know what to do with herself, and has illusions of studying something for which she couldn't possibly be prepared."

"Karl, stop grumbling, you haven't met her yet. At least give her a chance. And never mind about the jacket, the vest will do just fine. She's come unexpectedly and you've just been caught in a storm." Clara looked at her brother, and straightened the collar of his shirt. "I think you look rather dashing."

WEIERSTRASS UNCONSCIOUSLY TUGGED at the front of his vest as he arranged papers on his desk in his downstairs study. He was interrupted by a gentle knock at the door.

"Are you ready to meet with Frau Kovalevskaya?" Elise's voice had its usual note of urgency. "The woman's been waiting some time."

Weierstrass nodded, barely raising his head from his papers. The meeting could not be put off any longer.

When he looked up he found a small figure occupying the large leather chair across from him. The woman had unbuttoned but not removed her coat, a rather worn and inelegant garment for an aristocrat. A simple dark woolen dress with clean but frayed collar and cuffs showed itself as she shifted her position in the chair. Her only visible jewelry was a small gold watch, hanging from a delicate chain around her neck. Her hat of black silk was her one concession to fashion. Although Weierstrass was aware that the floppy brimmed style of hat was all the fashion this season, he disliked it. For one thing, it shaded this woman's face in such a way that he couldn't see her eyes or very much of her face at all. Out in the entrance hall it had been so dark that he hadn't had a good look at her there either. The cape and tassels on her coat made it impossible to tell if she was fat or thin or in between. Weierstrass stroked his face. Not that he really needed to see her to know what she was like. He'd been right, this was a waste of time. Before him sat a dowdy dreamer who undoubtedly had as little sense for the order of science as for the order of fashion. A twang of pity prompted him to kindness. The poor woman was probably a widow trying to find something to do with her life.

Well, it was necessary to get the business over with. He cleared his throat. "So, you are interested in studying mathematics?"

"Yes sir." Her voice was small and pleasant.

"I don't mean to be abrupt, but the University has a policy against admitting women. I'm sure there is no hope of your enrolling."

"I'm not ready to concede that point, professor."

The answer was immediate and firm. There might be more strength of character in her than he'd guessed.

She continued, "I want very much to attend your lectures."

"*My* lectures."

"Yes sir. To do that, I will need administrative permission. Of course, first I need to know that you'll admit me."

Weierstrass let out a slow breath. "What formal training do you have in mathematics?"

"I studied in Heidelberg for over a year. My mathematical adviser there, Professor Leo Königsberger, recommended I continue my studies with you."

That was a jolt. "Königsberger! He was one of my best pupils, and one of my earliest. So he's sent you to me. Well, do you have a letter from him?"

"Yes, here it is. And another letter as well." Eagerly the woman opened the folder she had been clutching. She fumbled with some papers then leaned over and placed two pages on his desk. The professor still was not able to get a good look at her, except to see that her hands were small and well shaped. A simple gold band encircled the right third finger.

The letters looked genuine enough. Now Weierstrass didn't know what to think. Certainly it was necessary to be polite at least. "Königsberger and Paul Dubois-Reymond both recommend you. Well. Dubois-Reymond's brother, Emil, is here in Berlin on the staff, I'll see if I can get more information."

Her small voice pursued him. "I also studied with Professor Helmholtz when I was in Heidelberg. He's here in Berlin now. I'm sure he'll vouch for me. And there is a professor here, Doctor Virchow, in pathology. He is acquainted with my family."

He wrote the names down carefully. "Your recommendations are outstanding, but before considering you for any of my classes, I'll need to make my own evaluation. Would you do some problems for me? Perhaps my courses would not be appropriate."

"I'm willing to try, sir." Although her hands were tightly clasped, the woman's voice was steady. She showed courage and confidence in her abilities. Whether her confidence was based in fact he'd soon find out.

After rummaging briefly in his desk, Weierstrass found what he was looking for, a paper of seven problems, the first assignment for all his prospective graduate students. The sheet contained some elementary problems, and some others, very difficult, meant to challenge the more talented students. Applicants were routinely given a week or more to work out the problems. It was not uncommon for even the better students to leave a problem or two uncompleted. Part of the process of teaching, Karl felt, was to demonstrate to the students that the methods and tools he would impart in his courses would give them power over otherwise intractable problems. He doubted that his visitor was going to get very far with them, but they'd give her some idea of exactly what it meant to study with Weierstrass.

Handing the paper across the desk he said, "Call again when you have these completed. Then we'll decide how you should continue your studies."

"Thank you." She glanced over the paper, put it into her folder, rose gracefully, and with her face turned away walked to the door.

"Well, that's the last I'll see of her." the professor thought to himself as he too arose. Moments later, looking out through his curtained window, he noticed two things: first, that the rain had stopped. Second, that a figure unaccountably resembling that of the woman he had just interviewed was skipping down the street, swinging a man's large umbrella in a very charmingly girlish manner.

As SOON AS SHE ARRIVED at her apartment, Sofya cleared the writing table in her bedroom of everything but the mantle lamp. She placed the folder containing Weierstrass's problems precisely in the upper right corner of the table as she faced it. She tore the wrapping from the clean white sheets of paper she had purchased on her way home and placed them beside the folder. Opening the old oaken wardrobe that stood opposite the bed, she extracted her traveling bag of work materials and began to rummage through it, bringing out her mathematics notebooks, a few precious textbooks and a well worn book of tables which contained integrals, trigonometric values, known physical constants, and other minutiae of data representing endless hours of meticulous calculations by generations of mathematicians. These references she arranged on the bed within reach of her desk chair. From the bottom of the bag came three graphite pencils, already whittled to half their original size, and again in need of repointing. A stack of scrap paper whose reverse sides could be used for trial calculations was placed on the left side of the work surface. Removing her collar, opening the top buttons of her dress, and rolling up her sleeves, she arranged the light to her satisfaction and was ready to begin. She sat up straight-backed and reached for Weierstrass's folder.

Quickly she glanced over the seven problems: five were purely theoretical, the last two applications. A few of the problems seemed at first reading encouragingly simple. She reminded herself to be very careful not to make any slips with the many intricate, but routine computations that would certainly be required.

Undecided on where to begin, she reread the list with care. *Determine which, if any, of the following three infinite series converges. Find the sum of any converging series.* That was simple. All the series could be reduced to geometric series. And she recalled the conditions under which those series converged and the formula for calculating their sum. The first problem could be dealt with without even referring to her textbooks.

The next two were more of a challenge: *Using Maclaurin's series for the sine function, differentiate to obtain his series for the cosine function. Find the Taylor series for the sine of x at a.* She was comfortable with Maclaurin and Taylor, mathematical giants from the last century whose works had become classic.

The next problem came from a giant of her own century, Cauchy.

Cauchy popularized a ratio test for convergence of a series. Using this tool, decide if the following series converge. There should be no difficulty with that.

But problem five would be very tough. *In 1720 Nikolaus Bernoulli conjectured that for a two-variable function, the order in which successive partial differentiations are made on the variables does not affect the final result. Reproduce and annotate Euler's 1755 proof of Bernoulli's conjecture.* Sofya leafed through her notes and the books she'd placed on the bed. Unfortunately, she didn't have a copy of that proof and she suspected the mathematical library at the university was closed to all but students and faculty. She'd just have to rework the logic herself.

The problems certainly confirmed the rumors she'd heard that Weierstrass demanded his students acquire a command of the old masters.

The remaining two problems dealt with matters of practical physics, one with heat transfer, the other with the description of a vibrating violin string. She'd have to be careful that all the initial conditions were incorporated into her function, choose the appropriate constant of expansion from her book of tables, and be sure that the function she finally derived was convergent. Sofya let out a small sigh of relief; there was nothing here beyond her ability. She reminded herself sternly to be meticulously careful at each step of her calculations.

SITTING IN HIS STUDY, Karl Weierstrass absentmindedly fingered the note from the mysterious Russian woman. It said that she had completed the assigned problems and would like to present them to him.

Only two days had passed since their meeting. Yesterday afternoon at the pub, he'd quite by chance met Virchow, and mentioned the woman.

"I believe I've heard some talk of her," Virchow scratched his chin. "She made something of an impression on Chebyshev when she attended one of his lectures."

"Really! I've read several of Chebyshev's papers. He's quite an outstanding mathematician, although his ideas on the nature of the calculus are not to my liking." Weierstrass sipped his beer.

Virchow nodded agreement, then continued, "I am acquainted slightly with the woman's maternal aunts. They are deeply involved with the intellectual community surrounding Petersburg University. Their father, Fedor Fedorovich Schubert, was a geologist whose work on the shape of the earth is well respected."

Weierstrass slapped the table. "Why, I know Schubert's work. I quoted him in the opening paragraph of a paper I published nine years ago. So, that's this woman's grandfather!" Karl looked at Virchow. "Schubert was a German."

"The family moved to Russia generations ago," Virchow explained.

Of course, as Virchow had cautioned him, heritage was no guarantee of either ability or respectability. Many prominent Russian families were split along ideological lines these days. Many of the younger generation and not a few of the not so young had taken hold of unorthodox views of politics and flaunted the rules of "civilized" society.

Weierstrass had already determined that he would set his own criteria for accepting the woman. No matter what her family background or current political leanings, she'd have to prove herself mathematically. Evidently he hadn't frightened her away with his problems. The woman would be here in a minute and he'd have the task of going over her work and, in all probability, telling her face-to-face that she wasn't qualified.

The professor heard the doorbell ring. Clara answered, as the maid traditionally had Sunday off. Taking Sofya's coat, and placing the returned umbrella back in the container near the door, Clara showed the visitor into the study.

Weierstrass rose in greeting. Wasting no time, he inquired, "Frau Kovalevskaya, may I see your efforts?" Taking the folder from her gloved hand, he motioned her to the seat across the desk from him.

The woman was again wearing that black floppy silk hat. At intervals Weierstrass looked up from the pages of calculation to that shadowed face. The first problems were done quite competently. She had a firm grasp of trigonometric and infinite series.

Among the problems he had set was a difficult proof fraught with logical pitfalls. This was where he really gauged the extent of a good student's talent. One who was competent, but not truly gifted, might laboriously work through a proof, coming to the conclusion by brute force, as it were. A more ambitious and talented student might have read widely enough in the field to be able to generate a proof in a style similar to existing proofs by outstanding mathematicians. That meant that the student had understood an elegant approach and had been able to apply it, the indication of an ability that a professor hoped to discover in his top graduate students.

Weierstrass frowned. As he looked at Sofya's work he found neither of these methods. Here, instead, was something new and unexpected. He rested his head in his hands. Was this correct? Minutes passed as he bent over the papers, forgetful of the world around him, even of the presence of his visitor in her chair across the desk.

At last he sat up straight, giving an unconscious sigh. No doubt about it. Here was an original, short, insightful proof, clearly presented. A proof he would only have expected from the most gifted, mature mathematician.

Weierstrass stared at the floppy hat in disbelief. Perhaps the woman had come across some paper in a recent journal he'd missed. Perhaps she had a gifted friend helping her. He had to know.

Not wanting to cast doubt on the woman's honesty, when the truth could be found much more courteously, he gently confronted her. "Frau, the approach you've taken on the last proof, the one in which I suggested Euler's method, is quite novel. Would you mind explaining your reasoning to me step by step?"

The woman's gestures became a little flustered. It was as Weierstrass had thought, she wasn't going to be able to explain the work. Removing her gloves, she placed them on the desk in front of her, then she walked around to his side of the desk. As she leaned over the papers her hat brushed his arm.

"Oh excuse me!" she said, removing her hat. A curl of dark hair fell toward the papers as she leaned over again, one small, pale finger pointing to the steps she had taken in the problem. "I've shown that a special function may be constructed such that when the mean value theorem is applied twice the result follows. I'm sorry, I couldn't recall Euler's proof, so I devised my own." She spoke rapidly in her heavily accented tones, while staring at the paper. At the moment, Weierstrass was hardly aware of her appearance, while he followed her concise and flawless reasoning. She had seen a new approach to this old problem of Euler's. Quite extraordinary. Quite extraordinary, indeed!

On finishing her explanation, she was a little breathless. Her eyes looked up, not thirty centimeters from his. Now it was suddenly the professor's turn to be breathless. The large, captivating, intelligent green eyes were staring into his. Her skin and hair were dark, faintly suggesting a gypsy origin, rather than German or Russian. She was very youthful with nicely proportioned features. Her figure was full, her stature charmingly petite.

He kept staring. He felt his face grow warm, then his hands grow clammy.

"Professor, was my approach incorrect?" His visitor's eyes were sparkling, her lips half smiling. She noticed his discomfort. They shared a quick unspoken moment of understanding, before she went on. "The procedure I've followed seems perfectly clear to me. Did I forget something? Perhaps that last substitution was invalid. Where is the difficulty?"

Weierstrass recovered himself. "There is no error. Your proof is valid and decidedly innovative. You have the gift, that rare unteachable talent for seeing old problems in a new way." He paused, then added slowly, "I'll see that your case is brought before the University Senate."

"Will you accept me into your classes?"

"Most definitely. With hard work and guidance, you'll be a first-rate mathematician. Now to convince the University Senate that you're to be admitted."

The meeting ended. Closing the door after the departing woman, Weierstrass slapped his large hands together in delight. He felt his Teutonic blood warming, as his imagination produced from somewhere an image of himself as a knight, carrying this lady's colors into battle.

A moment later he was laughing out loud. Laughing at himself. He was behaving like an old fool, all because of a pair of eyes that betrayed an uncommon brilliance of mind.

SOFYA ENTERED HER APARTMENT. A woman's coat was hanging on the cloak rack. And a suitcase leaned against the wall.

"Hello," Sofya recognized Julia's voice calling from the back of the apartment. In a moment Julia stood before her. "For the second time, I've had to ask a landlady for admittance to your apartment. You were supposed to meet me at the train station this afternoon. It would seem you aren't very thrilled to have me as your roommate."

"Oh, Julia!" Sofya fell into her friend's waiting arms.

"My God, you look pale. What have you been doing?"

"Work. I haven't stopped day or night for over a week. But I'm pleased with the results. Weierstrass has agreed to have me as a student."

"I should have known you'd throw yourself right into your work." She gestured at the room around her. "This apartment is a mess. There are books and papers everywhere, clothes on the floor, and the only sign of food I saw were a few very stale rolls. You don't even have a samovar set up."

"Don't scold like a mother. I really had to work every minute. But Weierstrass is pleased." Sofya held on to her friend's hand as they sat next to each other on the divan. "Why didn't you let me know you were coming?"

"I did. I wrote and asked you to meet me at the train. But, judging from the stack of unopened letters I now see you haven't opened your mail for some time."

"I suppose it's been well over a week. I just didn't have a spare minute."

"I'll get things back in order," Julia soothed. "This must be one of the gloomiest apartments in all Berlin. There's so little light in here."

"You'll stay, though?" Sofya asked tentatively.

"Most of my things are already in the second bedroom." Julia stood up and started toward the table where a small, cold samovar stood. "I've written to several of the chemistry professors here in Berlin. They're going to let me audit classes. That way I won't have to go through the process of petitioning for official admission, probably a futile exercise in any case. After I've proved myself and gotten to know the staff, I'll choose an advisor and begin work on a dissertation. I've been told that Göttingen University will grant doctorates on the basis of research and an oral examination. With a doctorate, I can go back home and teach at the higher levels, or possibly work in one of the laboratories."

"But, if there isn't a particular professor you wanted to study with here in Berlin, why didn't you just try to make contacts directly at Göttingen?"

"I don't make friends quickly, Sofya. And I don't like being totally isolated. I can work here as well as at any other university." She lowered her voice a little. "Vladimir asked me if I could make arrangements to be with you."

"I see, he refuses to stay with me, but he doesn't trust me to be on my own. So he sends a keeper for me." Sofya stood up and paced angrily.

"Don't fault Vladimir. And I'm not here as your keeper, I'm here as a friend and fellow student. I won't stay if you don't want me."

"Oh, Julia, of course I want you to stay." Sofya let herself fall back onto the divan. "I'm just so tired. My nerves are stretched tighter than a violin string."

"I've unpacked my samovar and I'll get us some tea in a minute. If you're not totally exhausted, I'd advise you to read your mail. I noticed there's more than one letter from Vladimir and one from your sister, I didn't recognize the others."

Sofya leaned down and untied her shoes. Putting her feet up and covering them with a well worn throw, she ruffled through the stack, arranging the letters by postmark date. The top letter, the oldest, was from her sister. As she read, she called the news in abbreviated chunks to Julia.

"Anyuta's spent the last weeks of August in Switzerland. She says Victor's been implicated in a workers' riot outside Paris. The situation became violent, with people killed on both sides. The police are blaming Auguste Blanqui's group, and have made a number of arrests. Victor decided to flee to Geneva, and Anyuta went with him."

Sofya swung her feet down. She sat erect on the edge of the divan, gripping the pages tightly in her hand, reading as quickly as she could. Julia had abandoned her unpacking and was standing over her.

"Once Anyuta got to Geneva, she wrote mother and father and begged their permission to marry Victor. They've refused. They refused to send her baptismal certificate, or any of the other proper consent papers. They've refused to release her dowry."

Julia spoke softly, "I can understand their position. They've never met the man. Surely they've heard from other Russians who've been in Paris, that this Jaclard has been living with their daughter in what they consider a highly dishonorable relationship. And the man is now a fugitive from the law."

"I can imagine what it must have cost my sister, to put aside her own beliefs and beg a concession from our parents." Sofya held the letter tightly as she looked up into Julia's innocent face. "Silly paternalistic legalities about marriage are standing in the way of Anyuta helping the man she loves. If Victor were to be arrested, Anyuta, not being his legal wife, would have no visiting privileges and no right to seek help for him. If they both were arrested, they would have no chance of seeing each other or even of being informed of each other's fates. It sounds paradoxical, but while they're engaged in illegal activities, it's all the more important that they be legally married."

"Anyuta must love this man very much." Julia, looking rather confused, sat in the chair across from Sofya.

"She does." Sofya sighed. "Why, I don't understand, but clearly she does." She returned to the letters. "Listen to this. Anyuta goes on to say that in September, when the Empire fell and the New Republic was established, she and Victor immediately returned to France. Oh, Anyuta! You fool!" Sofya was nearly shouting. "You should have stayed in Geneva!"

Regaining some composure, Sofya said, "My God, Julia, has the empire really fallen? I haven't seen a paper in weeks."

"Yes. The Empress has fled to England, a new republic has been formed in France. Victor Hugo is back in Paris, filling the press with his fiery speeches. The new government is still opposing the Prussians, but how long they'll be able to hold out is questionable. You haven't heard any of this? No, I don't suppose you have."

Sofya was reading on again, leafing through pages. "Anyuta spends paragraph after paragraph talking about a new organization, something called the Internationale. She and Victor must have joined, though, of course, she doesn't say so plainly. Victor has some kind of political position in the new French government. She goes on about how he was overwhelmingly elected as a representative from his home district in Lyons. Then more paragraphs, all glowing praise of her hero. The only interesting point being that Victor is an acquaintance of Marx's son-in-law."

"Nothing about how they're managing? I've read that the Prussian army has Paris under siege. I've seen mixed reports on the conditions in the city." Julia's attention had returned to the bubbling samovar.

"Yes, here, near the end. They are without funds. Victor's office pays him almost nothing. They're both giving private lessons in the evenings, she in Russian language and literature, he in mathematics. Apparently some of the citizens are still living more or less normal lives. She insists that she and Victor are doing better than many others. Their food supplies are holding. Listen to this, she hasn't needed to resort to rats' meat, which is being sold now by many grocers. She's tried some of the new canned carrots and says they're quite edible . . . the rest of her letter is assurance that she's under no real hardship. Her only fear is that Victor is flirting with arrest. He makes no concessions in his criticisms of the government."

Julia brought two cups of tea to the divan, "You must persuade Anyuta to join us here." She handed one cup to Sofya.

"She'll never leave Jaclard. Who, in my opinion, is a moody, impractical dreamer with more daring and bluster than common sense. I really don't know what Anyuta sees in the man. Except he does present a very dashing figure, and he's a radical, that's always attracted Anyuta. And he has many contacts in the liberal press. When I was in Paris, she showed me one of his articles. He writes acceptably well, with force and spirit, but he's certainly no Dostoevsky."

Sofya hesitated for a moment, contemplating the swirls in the hot dark liquid. "I don't know what to do. I can feel Anyuta's about to be caught in a whirlwind. Do you think I should try to go to her?"

"Definitely not," Julia snapped sternly. "There's nothing you could do for her there."

Logic was on the side of Julia's advice. After some minutes of silence, Sofya responded with a tired sigh, "You're right. The most helpful thing I can do is try to convince Mother and Father to allow the wedding. From here, I can keep sending Anyuta at least a little cash from my allowance." Sofya put her sister's letter to one side, and took up another, addressed in a different hand. "I wish I could talk this over with Vladimir." Sofya unfolded the scrolled, nearly illegible paper. "Vladimir writes that he won't be able to visit here for several weeks. Perhaps not until the Christmas vacation."

"Write him, Sofya. He should be told about Anyuta."

KARL WEIERSTRASS WAS ON a crusade now. The young woman must be admitted to the university. With the memory of his own youthful difficulties ever before him, he felt a special calling to encourage and develop young talents. And this was indeed a special case.

Systematically, Weierstrass gathered around him some of the leading scientists of the prestigious Berlin faculty. Helmholtz, the physicist, had known Kovalevskaya as a student in Heidelberg and was ready to champion her here in Berlin. Emil Dubois-Reymond, the physiologist, had gotten a glowing letter about the woman's abilities from his brother Paul who had been one of her mathematics professors in Heidelberg. Emil would stand proxy for his brother and support her claim before the senate. Rudolf Virchow, professor of pathology, was ready to defend her character as well as her reputation for brilliance. Weierstrass would testify that he had assessed her mathematical abilities and would readily have her in his classes.

Only Professor Kummer, the brilliant mathematician and member of the University Senate, Weierstrass's friend and first supporter, held strongly against them. Kummer would not admit a woman to the university, nor would he allow a woman to audit any mathematical lectures. The mathematics department was Kummer's realm of absolute power.

Disgusted with his old friend and benefactor's inflexibility, his blind adherence to tradition, Weierstrass reluctantly reported the decision to Sofya.

"There's no appeal from this decision?" Sofya sat erect on the edge of the divan. Clara, her eyes blazing with indignation, sat on one side of her, and Elise, sad and retreating, on the other. On Clara's invitation, Sofya had spent the afternoon waiting for the senate's decision with the sisters, who now reacted to the bad news with sympathy and outrage.

"I'm afraid, none." Weierstrass stared down at his big hands. "Perhaps, if Kummer hadn't come out against you, there might have been a chance to audit in mathematics. But the other members of the senate won't offend him on his own ground." Weierstrass was pacing before the small fireplace. "You know, the scandal of this situation is that other university departments will have women auditors this term. Kummer can refuse them admission as full students, but he can't stop the departments from admitting women as auditors. I've heard the chemistry department's supporting one of your countrywomen."

"Yes, her name is Julia Lermontova. She's a friend of mine." Sofya said softly.

The professor's eyes softened when he looked at her. "I can't tell you how sorry I am, or the shame I feel for my colleague. Please, accept my deepest apologies."

Sofya swallowed the lump of disappointment that had arisen in her throat. "Sir, if there is no recourse to the university administration, if I am not allowed even to audit mathematical lectures, would it be possible for me to take private lessons from you? In Russia, when I was beginning my studies, only private lessons were available to me. I found I was able to make acceptable progress with this arrangement."

The professor was staring at her, and she thought she saw the beginnings of acceptance. She rushed to fortify her position. "Of course, I realize this would be a great imposition on your time. I would offer my services in lightening any administrative duties. As a small compensation, I would of course pay you the equivalent of the university's fees."

"Why didn't I think of tutoring!" Weierstrass sat back in his chair. "But you are to devote your energies entirely to study. And there will be no paying! I insist. This is a point of honor for me. It will perhaps help cover my university's and my department's incredible and disgraceful pig-headedness."

"How wonderful!" Elise leaned over and gently touched Sofya's hand. "You'll be visiting us regularly. I'm so pleased."

Sofya felt a warm glow. She would have the undivided attentions of the most brilliant mathematician in Europe.

"Lessons once a week?" Clara looked from Sofya to her brother. "If Sofya came on Sunday afternoon, she could have a lesson with you and then join us for dinner. Elise and I would love the company. You could bring your friend, the chemistry student you mentioned."

"And Herr Kovalevsky would also be welcomed," Elise added tentatively.

"There will be no Herr Kovalevsky," Sofya felt her face grow warm. She couldn't explain about Vladimir. These sweet Catholic matrons would never understand a husband who was never present. Embarrassed she cast her eyes down.

"Oh, I'm so sorry," Clara said softly. From Sofya's tone, she had understood her to mean that her husband was dead. Sofya could not find the courage to correct her. Clara rushed on to cover the awkward moment. "Karl, Elise and I would love the company of the women students. Please, say yes."

"You seem to have it all worked out, Clara. But there is one thing." Weierstrass looked at Sofya. "I think lessons twice a week would be more effective. You've only had one year of formal training past the calculus. Your work is brilliant, yes, but you will need to do some catching up to match the background of my other students. I want you to start reading about the geometries: Riemann's work and Lobachevsky's. Then there's Crelle's Journal, the last few issues . . ."

"Karl, please . . ." Elise interrupted.

"Oh, yes, we can go into the details later." Still excited, he continued, "I intend for you to follow the exact same lectures I'm presenting to the other advanced students. I'll give you my notes before I present the work to the class. We'll meet once during the week and again on Sunday. Would that suit you?"

"I love the arrangement," Sofya affirmed.

"Well, that's settled," Clara stood up. "Let's all have some dinner. Tell us, Frau Kovalevskaya, what are your favorite foods?"

Sofya made her way to the dining room, with Clara's arm linked in hers, following Elise and Karl. Defeat had turned to an extraordinary victory.

CHAPTER TWENTY

Spring 1871 ❧ Berlin

Sofya hunched over her papers, the sleeves of her dressing gown rolled above her elbows. She put down her pencil with a feeling of accomplishment. The stubborn integral involving the square root of a 7th degree polynomial had finally been conquered.

Wearily she straightened, pushing herself away from the table.

For the last six months she had been struggling with problems like last night's. Each challenging problem progressively more complex, all in one way or another involving elliptic functions, whose seemingly harmless little exponents stretched docile circles just enough to grossly complicate calculations and shatter seemingly simple relationships.

For today's meeting with Karl she would bring her handwritten copies of the professor's last few lectures, along with his published papers of 1849 and 1854, copied from Crelle's Journal. She studied these works for so long and with such concentration that she felt if she closed her eyes, she could draw up an accurate picture of each page, complete with the K's, J's, Σ's and $\pi/2$'s, all in their proper places.

Pleased with herself, she rubbed her eyes and stretched. Her efforts of the last months were not in vain. She could honestly say that she was adept, if not a master, at manipulating the three kinds of elliptic functions Legendre had classified in his 1820 book, *Exercises du Calcul.* A copy of that book had been a gift from Weierstrass. She treasured it as much as she imagined other women might treasure a book of French poems from an admirer.

My God, she thought, sitting on the bed, the fleeting thought was painfully accurate. She was happy only with Weierstrass and mathematics! What was happening to her? She was deceiving her parents. She loved, but no longer trusted, her sister. And her every meeting with Vladimir started hopefully, then ended in bitter accusations and recriminations about money.

And, of course, about that other matter. Like money, that other matter seemed always present with Vladimir.

With Karl at least money was never a concern. At her last session with Karl, the professor's clear blue eyes had taken on a new look, almost dreamy. He had held her hand when he confided, that she, of all his students, best understood the workings of his mind. She had felt herself blushing furiously. He dropped her hand, coughed nervously, and told her that her potential as a mathematician was limited only by her devotion to study. Then the professor had asked her to think of him, not only as a mentor, but as a friend.

That was the moment when she ought to have told him that she was not a widow, that she had a living husband, even if that relationship was in name only. But she hadn't said a word.

Smiling, she ruefully shook her head. She was calling the world's greatest mathematician by his given name! But then, he'd asked her to do so. She remembered his words clearly.

"When we are with mathematics, you must call me Herr Professor Weierstrass, or my muse may become jealous of you. When mathematics is put aside, you must call me Karl." . . . yes, after today's lesson they all would enter the dining room for light, intellectual conversation and the most sumptuous meal of Sofya's week. Karl would compliment her on her pretty dress and perhaps dessert would be Elise's delicious chocolate cake.

JULIA SETTLED HERSELF comfortably into the large leather-bound chair in the small parlor that along with the two bedrooms made up the tiny Berlin apartment she shared with Sofya. In a few hours, she and Sofya would visit the Weierstrass household as they did every Sunday. Perhaps, if Sofya finished her work early, and the nice weather held, they might even be able to spend some time walking in the park. Julia's mind wandered back to the wonderful afternoon walks in Heidelberg with Vladimir.

Dear, kind, awkward Vladimir! His last visit had been weeks ago. She remembered his arrival, his joking and saying he'd come to celebrate the vernal equinox. They must all rejoice, for spring had arrived. He'd brought them presents, a fine Swiss muslin dress with a heart-shaped neck for Sofya and a light gray cashmere mantelet for her.

The day of Vladimir's departure, Sofya received a letter from her sister. Anyuta and Victor had married in a civil ceremony performed by an official of the new government of Paris. Even with so much to celebrate, Vladimir's visit, like all the others since coming to Berlin, ended badly.

Her friends' bickering began over when they would visit Anyuta and ended with a skirmish over available funds, and Vladimir's extravagance in purchasing Sofya a new dress.

Julia waited until the screaming stopped and a silent standoff had been reached. Then she suggested they all go to a coffee house to try to smooth matters out before Vladimir was forced to catch his train back to Jena. While Sofya and Vladimir silently glared at each other over coffee, she had tried to open a civil conversation by discussing her current experiment with petroleum-based substances.

At the next table, a pair of wealthy Frenchmen, clearly recent refugees from the war, were loudly complaining. Their French, definitely not Parisian, betrayed their origins in the Alsace.

"First the German invaders trample over my estate," a fat man in a black top hat groaned. "Then Napoleon drags his army through the area, only to surrender. We were left with a toppled government, and an army in the hands of the idiot Trochu."

The fat man's companion was thin and bony, sporting a gold watch and white silk gloves. "You survived that without too great a blow to your pocketbook," he observed mournfully. "Whereas I—"

"A man must know whom to support, and when," the fat one interrupted. "Our fledgling Republic under old man Thiers may offer some real opportunities for an enterprising businessman."

"If the conservative Thiers can keep control," the thin man snickered. "Just five days ago, your man Thiers marched the government and the soldiers out of Paris and off to Versailles, leaving our beloved city in the hands of a rabble of armed hoodlums and ruffians."

Vladimir, his temper already worn thin by argument, was unable to restrain himself. Leaning toward the other table, he suggested, "Gentlemen, the ruffians you refer to have organized a responsible and responsive government. They are the only ones now defending your beloved Paris, standing up to the German invaders. Gentlemen, France was betrayed by your Republic. An unjust and humiliating peace agreement will turn the Alsace over to the control of Germany and extract high reparations. Your Republic will require grave sacrifices both in taxes and reduced public programs for the poor. But I see, as you are here in Berlin, that you are not concerned with these matters as long as the flow of profits is maintained. Of course, wise businessmen, such as yourselves, will know how to avoid taxes. And reduced benefits to the poor mean a larger, more desperate band of workers who must labor for whatever meager wages you deem to pay and endure whatever miserable conditions you impose."

"I beg your pardon," the fat man said angrily. "But what business is this of yours? Your speech betrays you as a Russian."

Rising to his feet, Vladimir continued, "Even a Russian can see that the only French people of honor are the rebels of Paris. The fighters of the Commune are not a rabble, sir, but an inspiration to the world. They are testifying with their lives, that government belongs in the hands of the people!"

Sofya was tugging at Vladimir's sleeve. The manager of the restaurant, who had been hovering in the background, signaled, and two waiters positioned themselves, one on either side of Vladimir. Among them, the two waiters and the two women maneuvered him out of the restaurant.

Once back at the apartment, Sofya mercilessly attacked Vladimir's judgment and common sense. When Julia added her voice to Sofya's, Vladimir looked repentant. Yes, thought Julia, remembering the scene now, Sofya should have sensed his remorse was sincere, but she hadn't. Soyfa's anger always burned too fiercely and too long.

Julia wondered sadly if her two dear friends would ever again behave gently to each other, as they had those first weeks in Heidelberg. She looked down at the notes she was preparing for tomorrow's session in the laboratory. She tried to concentrate, but without success. Her pencil, as if of its own volition, drew a small outline image of a castle, in the margin of a chart plotting reaction times and solution temperatures.

A loud and somehow awkward sounding banging at the door interrupted Julia's less than fruitful efforts at study. With a sigh she rose from her chair. The landlord's child must be bouncing a ball against their door, again. The front door led directly onto the street. The boy could not resist tossing his ball at the junction of the door and stoop and trying to catch it. She would have to speak firmly to him, and not for the first time. The child knew she did not have the heart to complain to his father. And in all likelihood, after listening to her lecture, he would try to convince her to play catch with him. Well, not today, she told herself. Putting on what she thought to be her best schoolteacher look, Julia opened the door.

Before her stood, not the little boy from upstairs, but Vladimir, his arms filled with newspapers. He must have been knocking on the door with his elbow, she thought. His eyes wide with a dreadful excitement, he rushed past her into the parlor, dropping his load of papers onto the divan and throwing off his coat.

"Where did you come from?" Julia gasped. It was as if she had conjured him all the way from Jena with her thoughts.

He ignored the question. "Get Sofya."

His tone compelled. Julia rushed to Sofya's bedroom, knocked once, then flung open the oaken door. "Vladimir's here. He wants to see you immediately."

"Here? What's happened?" Sofya almost dropped the button hook. Something must be dreadfully wrong. Wild thoughts rushed through her mind. The police were after him.

When the two women entered the parlor, Vladimir's large frame was sprawled on the parlor floor, a newspaper spread out before him. On the divan were piled at least a dozen more, their headlines in a jumble of languages, German, French, Polish, English, Russian. Vladimir's head was bent down in such a way that his rumpled red hair hid his expression.

"Sofya, you're here. Good." He pushed aside his hair and stared up at her. She glimpsed his face. Something was wrong, very wrong.

"For God's sake, Vladimir, of course I'm here. The question is, why are you here?"

"Paris is under heavy bombardment. The army of the French Republic has begun to reclaim the city!" he said excitedly, barely glancing back at her. "They are meeting resistance in the streets."

"Anyuta," Sofya said, almost in a whisper.

"Yes, I know." Leaning on one elbow, he thrust one of the papers at her. "Here! Read these!"

The two women began to devour the papers, trading them back and forth. In a few minutes, they had grasped the outline of the situation. The new French government under Thiers, backed by what was left of the regular French army, had begun to crush the rebellious rabble in the capital. The reports in the German papers were the most disturbing. The victorious German forces stood on the banks of the Seine and watched in pleased amusement as Frenchman attacked Frenchman.

"This will be the worst kind of war," Vladimir was muttering. "Not just uniformed men on a field of battle. A vengeful slaughter, men, women and children. I saw how the Tsar crushed the Polish rebellion in '65. A government can have no mercy for rebels. And these poor Parisian devils have no way out. They are squeezed in a vise between the army of the Republic and that of Prussia."

Julia coolly corrected him. "Bismarck's army is no longer merely Prussian. He's united the Germans into a Second Reich. King Wilhelm is now Kaiser Wilhelm, who thinks he's caesar. A conquering emperor with Krupp cannon."

Vladimir was nodding. "An apt description, Julia. The Parisians haven't got a chance. Now it won't even be the Germans who slaughter them, but their own French brothers. Disgusting." He pushed aside the papers and sat clutching his knees.

"Is there no hope?" Sofya looked from one of her companions to the other. "In Anyuta's last letter she seemed certain that the Paris rebellion will spark others, all across France. All across Europe."

"You don't see any here, do you?" Vladimir sighed. "The poor fools in their Commune must imagine this as 1848, all over again. In my mind, the only question is, how long can they hold out?"

Julia was shaking her head stubbornly. "I say there's a chance, even if it's only a thin, crazy, idealistic possibility, that the fires of a world revolution have been ignited. People just might rise up and seize power away from the big governments. Cities across France might send fighters to help Paris. Then suppose the fervor spread to England."

"No, Julia, that's a dream. The Parisians will be crushed." Vladimir pushed back his hair. "It's just a matter of time."

Sofya's fear and anger had been growing while she listened. Now she almost screamed, "Stop this, you two! The point is, Anyuta is in Paris. I've got to convince her to leave before the final blow is delivered."

"And how will you do that?" her husband demanded.

"I'm going there, of course."

"Don't be ridiculous!" Vladimir's voice was tremulous with excitement. "Remember last January? You and I wasted most of our vacation trying to get into France. The Prussians stopped us at the border. They're certainly not going to welcome us now." He stared at her, his hand waving the Berlin newspaper. "Neither the Germans nor the French are going to let a couple of crazy Russians just wander in for a little family reunion."

"Anyuta must be reached," Sofya murmured, as if to herself. She rose from her chair and walked quickly, aimlessly around the room. Then she confronted Vladimir. "I'll tell the Germans we need entry for scientific reasons. I must make contact with mathematicians who are delivering papers on differential equations. Weierstrass mentioned it to me, the French Academy of Sciences really is holding a session on the equations this month."

"In Paris? At a time like this?" Julia gasped in disbelief. "A scientific conference on theoretical mathematics?"

Sofya nodded.

"The Parisians certainly are interesting," Vladimir observed. "So, my dear wife, you would forsake your studies? I thought nothing and no one meant more than studying your precious mathematics with your idol Weierstrass."

"My work is as important to me as yours is to you," she shot back at him. "And my friendship with Weierstrass has a tenderness and oneness of spirit, a purity, that you are not capable of imagining!"

Vladimir flushed red. He got to his feet.

Sofya glared at him. "I tell you I am going to Paris. I will not abandon my sister."

"I can't believe what I'm hearing." Vladimir cut at her. "Only two weeks ago you were berating me for being too political when I voiced my views in a café. Now you're running off to become a rebel!"

"Sofya's concerned for her sister," Julia interjected.

"I knew your sister was trouble from the first time I saw her. 'Another one of those revolutionary types,' I said to myself. 'Stay away. You've had enough of that.' And now here I am again."

"Stop criticizing Anyuta!" Sofya leaned back on her heels. Her voice softened, took on a pleading tone. "You don't have to go, Vladimir. Just get me through the lines. You have contacts, friends, I know you have. Just help me get to Paris."

"No." Vladimir's eyes hardened as he spoke. "You have no idea what you're getting us into, the hardship, the danger, the madness, the violence."

Sofya did not turn away, but matched his hard stare with her own. "I'm leaving for Paris. Tonight."

Then she looked over her shoulder at the other woman. "Julia, please, talk to Herr Professor Weierstrass. Tell him there's been a family emergency. A close relative is dangerously ill and needs me to look after her. Whatever story you think best, but don't let him know where I am. Tell him I'll come back as soon as I can. And, keep the dear Weierstrass sisters company."

Julia nodded, then turned her gaze to Vladimir.

He closed his eyes for a long moment, then opened them again. Suddenly his voice was very weary. "Damn, Julia! Don't look at me like that. You know I can't let Sofya go alone."

CHAPTER TWENTY-ONE

April 5, 1871 ❧ *Saint Denis*

"Well, we've made it to Saint Denis." Vladimir sighed as he pushed Sofya's traveling bag to the floor, then sank down on one end of the narrow cot in her tiny hotel room. It was an almost windowless and lightless chamber ordinarily used by the maids as a changing room, but the only space available in a hotel overcrowded with refugees.

"I was right," Vladimir continued in a self-congratulatory manner, opening the top buttons of his shirt. "The best entry into France was from the north, by way of Belgium. Every German guard on the route believed we were headed for London. Clear, comfortable passage all the way to the coast and Calais. No special papers needed, just our passports and a good story."

"Hardly comfortable. It took three grueling days!" Sofya looked around and tried to push back the feeling that she was in a cell. There was no furniture, or room for any, other than the cot and a small dressing stand on which she had thrown hat, gloves and cape. There were no pictures on the dingy gray walls, no books or magazines or other signs of intelligent life. The one small gas fixture on the wall gave more smoke and heat than light. Tired and depressed, she collapsed onto the other end of the cot, letting her back rest against the wall. "We had to waste almost a whole day at Versailles. I grant you, getting from Berlin to Calais was easy. But from Calais to here, was exhausting, frustrating and expensive." She withdrew a small leather purse from her dress pocket, extracted a slim roll of bills, and tossed it onto the bed between herself and Vladimir. "This is what's left of our funds. We can't afford many more bribes. That farmer charged outrageously for the last bone-jostling ride from Versailles."

"That was money well spent, my dear. Money to seal lips." He struggled to a standing position and pushed back the flimsy, faded cotton curtain from the small, dirty window. "We're within sight of our goal. Only two kilometers northeast of the city limit. We'll be in Paris tomorrow."

"You said that yesterday in Versailles." She squirmed, trying to find a more comfortable support for her spine on the cold wall, then pulled the slim pillow from the head of the cot and pushed it behind her. "A whole day wasted tramping from office to office."

"We gained information, my dear. Information." He looked at the wad of bills still lying on the bed. She watched silently as he leaned over, separated what seemed approximately half of them, and stuffed that much into his pocket. "We learned that from here the press are allowed to enter and leave the city with relative ease. We may at least be able to get a message to your sister."

"I could have sent her a message from Berlin! Having come this far, I intend to see Anyuta." Sofya sighed. "Do you think the Prussians will be any more sympathetic to our story than the French were at Versailles? Let's see: you are a keen scientist who absolutely must visit the bone collection at the University, and I'm your loving wife, and 'whither thou goest . . .' "

Vladimir was shaking his head. "That didn't work in Versailles, it won't work here." He sat on the cot again, pulled off one boot, and let it drop with a thud.

As if in echo came the bang of a piece of field artillery. Sofya instinctively turned to the window. She saw no flare of light. Yesterday, as they were approaching Saint Denis in the farmer's wagon, Vladimir had explained to her some of the fine points by which the sounds of the various types of armament could be distinguished. She found herself surprisingly fascinated by his technical description of the giant destructive machines, and almost disappointed when he said he didn't think they'd hear the monstrous fifty-ton Krupp gun the Prussians had rolled up on its specially constructed railway car; that gun had been silenced with the armistice. All the shelling they'd heard since their arrival had been of Frenchmen trying to kill Frenchmen, not to mention women and children, in an effort to break the will of the Commune, and reclaim Paris. Many of the shells were of the incendiary variety and when she'd looked through the window earlier this evening she'd seen the light of unextinguished fires that dotted the opposite bank of the Seine.

"Sofya." Her husband's voice was insistent and broke through her tired, wandering thoughts. "I have a plan, based on intelligence I've gathered."

"When have you had any chance to gather intelligence?"

"May I remind you that while you are luxuriating in these lavish private quarters, I am across the hall sharing sleeping accommodations with an English adventurer and two American reporters. I'm privy to quite a bit of gossip."

"And . . ."

"The Versailles troops have control of the Courbevoie province just west of the city, and they control Fort de Mont-Valérien. From that position of strength, they've been hammering away at the city. The Parisian troops from Montmartre and Belleville have been engaged. The Neuilly Bridge into Paris has been destroyed. Two of the Communards' best military leaders, Flourens and Duval, have been killed."

Sofya sighed "Our friends face war with inadequate leaders and inferior weapons." A copy of the morning's paper lay folded on the dressing stand. She tossed it toward him. "See the headline. The Versailles troops have this horrible new weapon, the *mitrailleuse*—a man turns a crank and bullets come pouring out of it like rain. At Neuilly they cut down a group of young convent girls just as they were leaving church. At least public opinion may turn against Versailles."

"I'm afraid it's the Parisians who are losing public favor, my dear.

Arresting the Archbishop of Paris is not going to gain them support from outsiders."

Sofya blinked. "Why did they arrest him?"

"No visible reason, except the Central Committee leaders are unabashedly anti-clerical. And they probably have some idea of trading him for Blanqui. What's important to us is that now even more reporters will be trying to get into Paris."

"And how does that help?" She brushed back a curl of hair that escaped from behind her ear.

"The American journalist sharing my room is going in tomorrow. I've told him of my experience covering the Italian civil war, and he has volunteered to take my name to the American consulate in Paris and get me a journalist's pass into the city. I'd work as the American's assistant."

"No, I won't let you do that! I won't be left behind." Sofya poked angrily at his bootless foot. "I don't want any government, any consulate, breathing down our necks and checking into our movements. We'd lead them right to Anyuta, and who knows what her political position is by this time."

Vladimir, who had looked ready to argue, subsided. "You have a point," he conceded. Both boots on again, he rose abruptly, to bump his head on the slanting ceiling. "We need another plan," he mused, rubbing the injured spot. "I'm going to spend the rest of the afternoon visiting whatever bars and cafés I can walk to from here. I'll do better at gathering information if you're not with me."

"I suppose you're right," Sofya reluctantly admitted. "I'll stay in the hotel lobby, read whatever papers I can get my hands on, and try to strike up conversations with the incoming guests. Perhaps I can learn something useful."

"I don't know if you've noticed, but most of the women hanging around the hotel lobby are not wives and mothers."

"Why do you always think me so naive? Of course I've noticed." Sofya went to the door. "I can talk with whores. No doubt they have plenty of information from sources on both sides of this war."

"We'll meet for dinner. Hopefully, one of us will learn enough to let us formulate a plan." His hand was on the door handle. "I see you're wearing the watch I gave you. Meet me in the lobby at seven."

DEPRESSED AND DISCOURAGED, Sofya greeted Vladimir at the appointed hour. "I wasn't able to find out anything helpful. I spoke with innumerable women of vast worldly experience. All of whom treated me like a little sister. They were only too willing to complain of their lost comforts, but that was all. Nothing about their escapades with officers and government officials. Not a crumb of serious information."

Vladimir chuckled. "You just look too young and innocent."

"I do not!" she protested, without thinking.

"Have it your way then, maybe you look too wicked." He touched her elbow. "I'm starving. Let's get something to eat."

The café Vladimir chose boasted tables with a view of the Seine. He ordered dinners with delicate French names, which Sofya identified as boiled potatoes, roast beef, and boiled greens.

Sofya silently observed the bright coloration of the birds of prey occupying tables. In recent days, under Vladimir's tutelage, she'd become as skilled as any ornithologist in spotting and identifying them. There sat a blond mustached dandy of the Black Prussian hussars. His tasseled boots reached high on his calves, his crimson tunic was trimmed with white piping. His cap, left conspicuously on the edge of the table, sported the emblem of death, the skull and crossed thigh-bones. The yellow and blue tunics of the dreaded Uhlans, Prussian lancers, vastly outnumbered the dull greens of the infantry and smattering of the pale blue tunics of the Bavarian Corps. The dragoons were well represented, the various units identified not only by their plumage but by the regimental numbers on their shoulder straps, the number 7's in blue and salmon, the number 1's of the guards in blue and white, and the number 2's in black and blue tunics.

The fashionably dressed Frenchwomen who accompanied the officers were no less brightly bedecked birds. Their song identified them as Parisians. All were jeweled and liberally rouged. One nodded and smiled at Sofya. The woman was wearing a particularly bright crimson gown with long white feathers across the bosom, a black feather drooped from the crown of her head which was piled high with red curls. After a moment without recognition, Sofya acknowledged the greeting. Earlier in the day, in the hotel lobby, Sofya had received from this woman some unnecessary advice, which the donor now apparently felt was being followed. Making a small gesture, the woman clapped her hands together in a sign of approval as her eyes indicated Vladimir.

Sofya felt a surge of revulsion, that she hoped her face did not betray.

"You look lovely," Vladimir commented gallantly as he reached across the table to gently touch her hand. Apparently he was misattributing her discomfort to her simple dress.

Keeping her hand in his, she nodded toward the café patrons nearest her. The woman in the crimson gown was giggling coquettishly and remarking in French on the magnificence of the fires and stunning explosions across the river, joking and laughing as if viewing entertaining fireworks.

"I don't like it here," Sofya whispered.

"Ignore them. Would you like to change seats, so your back is to the window?"

She shook her head. "No, I'd rather see."

Vladimir enclosed her hand in both of his. "You must eat well and heartily."

Amidst a background of gunfire and exploding cannon shells, leaning toward her and stroking her hand like an attentive admirer, Vladimir softly disclosed his plan.

"We're going to our destination tonight." He had pulled his chair nearer to hers and was leaning very close. She felt his warm breath on her cheek. "We'll leave very late," he whispered. "By a route . . ."

Sofya touched her fingers gently to Vladimir's lips. The waiter was approaching. With a fiendish smile, Vladimir took her hand in his and brushed his lips against her palm. She felt a warm flush rising to her cheeks in response to his lips' caress.

Vladimir mouthed the words 'nicely done my dear,' as the waiter cleared his throat discreetly, then placed the dishes before them.

When the waiter left, Vladimir, seeming unaware of her discomfort, moved his chair to a position across from her. He picked up his fork and leaned over the steaming dishes. "When we've finished here, we'll return to the hotel and lie down till midnight." He smiled sardonically at her reaction. "You, of course, in your room and I in mine."

Annoyed at her momentary loss of composure, Sofya quickly started to bombard Vladimir with questions. She wanted details. Vladimir shook his head and put his finger to her lips, indicated there was to be no further talk on the subject.

AN HOUR LATER, sitting on the cot in Sofya's tiny room, Vladimir divulged his plan in a whisper. "We might as well forget about any official entry papers; my becoming a reporter was our last chance along that line. So we will simply walk east out of Saint Denis until we come to the Seine, then follow the bank of the river southwest for a little over a kilometer. I'm going out in a little while to see if I can make some arrangement for our crossing. The Prussians on this side of the river are pretty relaxed right now."

Sofya thought aloud, "We'll abandon our luggage here. Anyuta will supply whatever we need in the way of clothing."

"I might be able to sell some of these things," he said as he rummaged through one of the traveling bags. "A task I'll undertake while you're resting."

He went to the door of her room. "Change into what you're going to wear for our adventure, and give me everything else. I don't need to remind you to dress practically."

While Vladimir waited in the hall, she quickly took off her dinner gown and slippers. She set her simple dark woolen dress and the boots that had served over the last three days as a traveling outfit onto the dressing table. The garments were badly in need of cleaning, but would serve well enough. She also set aside her hooded cape and gloves, they might be needed if the night turned cold. She then gathered her remaining things, pushed them into the traveling bag and closed the clasps. Keeping herself behind the door, she handed the bag out with a caution. "Don't waste too much time on running errands. You need rest, too."

"In war, my dear, one must never underestimate the need for money or information. Pawnbrokers are an excellent source for both." He grinned at her. "Don't worry, I've done this sort of thing before."

SOFYA LAY DOWN to rest. She pulled the worn quilted coverlet up to her chin, then slipped her arms back under the covers and rested them straight at her sides. Unable to sleep, she stared wide-eyed at the ceiling. She felt no fear, only an extraordinarily keen sense of being alive.

Just before midnight, as Sofya lay listening to the intermittent sounds of distant rifle fire, she heard a knock at her door. She wrapped the coverlet around her.

Vladimir stood there, looking calm, almost matter-of-fact. "Dress quickly."

"Yes," she answered with equal calm.

"DID YOU GET any rest?" Sofya asked as they walked along the hotel corridor. Her cape was open over her wool dress.

"About two hours." His voice dropped to a whisper. "I found a pawn-broker, and managed to come away with a little cash, and some information. By the way, that loud burst of fighting we heard was centered at Neuilly Bridge."

"But that's the way we're headed!" Sofya warned. "Did you notice, the moon is full?"

"We can't avoid Neuilly, or the moon either. The more direct approach would take us across an open plain. Certain exposure and infinite vulnerability." Vladimir's voice held a new undercurrent of excitement.

"So we go by way of Neuilly." Sofya confirmed. "How are we going to cross the river?"

"The pawnbroker told me of a man who rents boats. His establishment is closed, officially. But someone will be there tonight. No more talking now."

She nodded in agreement.

On the street, Vladimir put his arm around her shoulder and drew her close. He whispered in her ear, "If anyone questions us, we're just a romantic couple looking for a place to be alone."

She slipped her arm around his waist.

They walked out of town, over the railroad tracks, and into the lightly wooded grove through which she could see the river. Vladimir took her hand and quickened their pace to a near run. From here on, if they were discovered, explanations would be hard to come by.

In what she estimated was ten minutes, they had reached the bank. Vladimir stopped. "We'll rest here."

They sat, almost comfortably, on a large tree root. The healthy old tree hid them behind its gigantic trunk, while its branches leaned over the river's edge as if searching for the water. Vladimir whispered, "The river is low. Damn. We'll be more exposed crossing the bank."

His eyes were never still. His head turning first to the right then left, then staring intently straight ahead. "What are you looking for?" she whispered back.

"A boathouse." Vladimir reached for her hand. He must feel how her palms were sweating. She stood up and indicated that she wanted to proceed.

Picking their way along the bank, they stepped carefully over twigs and shore debris. Something that sounded like a rat squeaked loudly at them, then ran back toward the water. Apparently the rat was the only sentry taking his duties at all seriously. Farther along the bank, the crackle of their step was answered with heavy snorting and the sound of lightly stamping hooves. Vladimir stood motionless. They had disturbed some Prussian horses, almost invisible behind a dark screen of trees. Sofya turned in the direction of the sound. Her eyes locked with the glowing brown eyes of a giant mare. The mare was the first in a row of horses fastened with ropes to a long row of pickets, their harnesses piled on the grass behind them. No guards or sentries were roused. It seemed to Sofya that the horse was wishing her luck. She nudged Vladimir to continue. They heard one last muffled snort, then nothing from animals.

A little farther, and Vladimir stopped again. He pointed ahead of them. Sofya squinted, but could not quite make out what Vladimir was trying to show her.

Putting his lips to her ear, he whispered, "That must be the boathouse the pawnbroker promised. You wait here. If you hear a commotion, head back to Saint Denis."

Sofya grabbed his sleeve. "I'm coming with you." She tried to speak as forcefully as she could, without making a sound that would be audible ten feet away.

"No," he said firmly. "I'll return in a minute." Drawing her close, he held her tightly for a moment. Then he was gone.

Sofya could be quieter, she supposed, if she were sitting down. The musical sounds of the night insects, interrupted by her presence and Vladimir's, soon resumed. The shadows swallowed him up immediately, without a trace.

A minute passed, and then another. Alone and motionless, she was aware of every sound, every change of the night breeze, even the movements of the stars.

As she stared into the dimness ahead, there came a faint squeak from the direction of the water's edge, like a hinge in need of oil. Her attention focused in the direction of the sound, she vaguely began to discern a solid bulk that she supposed must be the boathouse. Then she heard a murmuring, as of whispered voices briefly raised, and a short succession of faint thumping noises, as of someone bumping into things in the dark.

Then, once more, silence.

It seemed a thousand minutes, an eternity, before she heard the branches of the willow, almost beside her, being pulled back. Her hand slipped around a rounded river rock. She would fight if necessary. A dim colorless form whispered in a barely recognizable voice, "Let's go. We've got a boat."

Letting the rock fall from her hand, Sofya jumped up. Vladimir's eyes caught the moonlight. They were alive with a strange fire she had never seen before. Sofya could smell his sweat, hear his heavy breathing. His clothes were ruffled and dirtied. A spot of darker wetness was just visible on one sleeve of his jacket.

"I'm not hurt," he whispered, aware of her unspoken concern. He moved his arm freely with no sign of pain in his face or voice. "If I ever meet that double-crossing pawnbroker again . . ."

"Vladimir," she gasped, "you . . ."

"The boatman was in the shed, as promised. Waiting. He wanted more money, too much money. Then he gave up bargaining and drew his pistol. But he was a little drunk and careless with it."

Vladimir had already taken her by the hand and was leading her quickly to the boathouse, whose door, she saw as she approached, stood open.

"Where is he now?" she demanded anxiously.

"Where he'll be quiet." Vladimir pushed open another door, a broad one leading out right into the water. Faint light from fires across the river outlined a rowboat waiting on a kind of launching ramp. "Help me shove this into the water."

She pulled her eyes from a long, bloody knife that lay not two feet from her. She hesitated, kicked the weapon into the river, then jumped into the boat as it began sliding briskly down the ramp. Vladimir followed, almost soundlessly, a moment later.

He had made sure that they had a pair of oars. Sofya watched, grateful for his skill as a soldier and as a boatman. He gently dipped the oars into the water and strongly pulled them back. The craft glided downstream. Vladimir's eyes intently searched first one shore then the other, as if with every stroke of the oars he was deciding whether it was time to cross to the opposite side. Several minutes before his eyes met hers, his command came in a harsh whisper. "Sofya! Get down off the seat and onto the bottom of the boat. Tuck yourself into as small a space as possible."

Sofya considered a protest, but swayed by the fire in his eyes, decided to defer to Vladimir's superior knowledge in this situation. She felt foolish and uncomfortable huddling on the soggy bottom of the boat. Now he was rowing hard, almost careless of the noise. And she couldn't see what was happening. She lifted her head, stiffened her back, and held onto the sides of the boat. Vladimir frowned at her, but gave no further commands.

He kept the boat near the shoreline. The shadow of the trees gave them a little cover from the bright moonlight. Ahead of them appeared the branching where the Seine flows around an island. Vladimir steered toward the smaller eastern branch. He whispered, "We've got to get to ashore before we reach Neuilly bridge, the guards there will be exhausted and edgy from days of battle. I'm going to make a break for it. Stay down."

The area on either side of what was once Neuilly bridge came into view. Fires glowed against the night sky. Half-demolished buildings covered with gray soot appeared as from another world. Sofya stared in disbelief at the massive destruction eerily illuminated in the moonlight.

She saw a small orange flash on the far shore, and simultaneously heard a popping sound nearby. Cold water splashed against her face and soaked her sleeve. Before she had brushed the wet hair back from her face, another spray erupted just beyond the bow. More shots and raucous shouts followed. Then silence.

"Drunken idiots!" Vladimir cursed in Russian. He rowed furiously toward the shore. Quickly they hopped out. She helped Vladimir push the empty boat back into the moonlit river. A few more shots fell near the drifting boat. Vladimir grabbed her hand. They ran toward the protection of the inland growth.

Dried brush crunched under her feet and struck at her skirt. When they reached the shelter of a few taller trees, Vladimir hesitated. He cast a worried look back at her. She brushed back the hair that was sticking to her sweating forehead, gulped in a few deep breaths, then grinned at him, completely exhilarated.

Still holding her hand, he turned his back on her, pulling her forward. She heard him mutter to himself, "Definitely a general's daughter!"

At this moment, she relished that half-heard comment more than any compliment her husband might have given her. And for the first time in many years, she felt proud to be her father's daughter.

CHAPTER TWENTY-TWO

April 1871 ⚛ *The Paris Commune*

Quickening their pace, keeping under cover of trees as much as possible, they made their way toward the distant hills and windmills of the Montmartre district. Near their destination the streets became narrow and steep. At the sight of the first barricade, Vladimir pulled Sofya close against the wall of the nearest building. She gazed in moonlight at an unimpressive pile of paving stones, an overturned carriage, discarded furniture and mattresses, topped by a wheeled device that she took for a piece of field artillery, until Vladimir whispered that it was a *mitrailleuse*. Sleepy looking soldiers, rifles tucked under their arms, were passing a bottle from hand to hand.

Vladimir murmured, "Best if we don't trust to their judgment. We'll find a way that's not blocked."

"When we reach the railway that rings the city, we could follow the tracks," she whispered back.

"Yes, I remember, two spurs cross the ring and enter Montmartre. There'll be some guards."

"Let's try." She stepped away from the wall and hurried forward.

THE MOON HAD SET, and the sky was its darkest, the morning star glowing against a black background. Tired, scratched by thorns, covered with dust and dirt, Sofya and Vladimir arrived at the foot of the Montmartre butte. On the high ground she could make out the shadowy forms of cannon. The street along the base of the mount was nearly deserted. Vladimir took her hand and hurriedly led her around the corner of the nearest building. She caught a glimpse of a young man carrying a rifle on his shoulder and walking their way.

"Militia," Vladimir whispered, as he hurried her along. In the next block, Sofya pushed against him to avoid colliding with a tattered peasant hunched over and carrying a bundle. The bundle bumped Sofya's arm, the stiff fingers of a corpse brushed her hand. She shuddered and pressed closer to Vladimir.

The next street climbed. They had covered several more blocks before he pulled her to a halt. "Look, that must be a meeting house of some sort," Vladimir pointed to a two-story structure on the opposite side of the street. A large red flag hung over the entrance, at the top of an uncovered stair.

"It's open." Sofya whispered. In the doorway the figure of a woman appeared, sturdy but bent, and clad simply. A cleaning or washerwoman, Sofya supposed.

"Let's go in," Sofya suggested.

Vladimir shook his head. "The sign says 'Working Women's Club.' You'll have a better chance at getting information without a man present. And the stains on my jacket might need some explaining."

Sofya nodded in agreement.

When the washerwoman was well out of sight, Sofya quickly crossed the street and climbed the stairs. Pausing at the open doorway, she gazed inside. Flickering gaslight illuminated a large room where a plain woman in her late thirties stood refilling an oil lamp. A large, sleek cat emerged from under a table strewn with papers and began rubbing against the woman's feet. As if by some unseen prompting, the woman looked up and met Sofya's stare. Her face was long, the bones pronounced, her dark eyes glowed like a prophet's. She was dressed neatly and simply, the red sash around her waist obviously part of a makeshift sort of uniform. Her harsh stare melted into a vague smile just before she turned, placed the lamp on the table and picked up the cat.

Sofya drew a deep breath and walked in.

Still holding the cat, the woman extended one hand in a friendly manner. Her eyes, large and set far apart, were definitely her most attractive feature. Her nose, prominent and poorly shaped, would have made her truly ugly were it not for the high forehead. Her long, light brown hair was pulled severely away from her face, not a wisp escaping to that noble forehead. Everything about the woman gave the impression of being larger and stronger than average.

After a moment Sofya realized why the harsh features seemed so benign. They reminded her strongly of someone she liked, but at the moment she could not think who.

"I'm Louise Michel." The woman's voice was deep and sure, with the flawless enunciation and tone of an aristocrat.

Her grip was firm, the hand surprisingly rough. Immediately on Sofya's contact with Louise, the cat had wiggled from the woman's grasp and dashed under the table.

"Please excuse Mimi's manners," Louise laughed. "This is the second siege of Paris she's endured. She lost many friends to the stewpot during the first, and she's somehow correctly concluded that their loss came from trust too quickly given."

Sofya released Louise's hand. "I'd say Mimi chose well in her friendship with you."

"She is a beauty," Louise turned her piercing gaze from the animal back to Sofya. "And how may I help you?" She motioned Sofya to a bench along the side of the room, where they sat side by side.

Before Sofya could respond, Louise continued, "Has one of our Parisian men been too forward with you? If you wish to avoid his company the Vigilance Committee can offer you shelter."

"I . . ." Sofya hesitated briefly. "I don't need protection."

"Your hair is rumpled and there's dirt on the hem of your dress, I thought perhaps . . ." Louise Michel smiled, looking sympathetically at Sofya. "Would you like something to eat or drink? Refreshments are available."

"No, I'm fine." Nervously Sofya brushed at her dress. "Actually I'm looking for my sister, Anna Jaclard. She sent me a note posted from Montmartre, but I don't know her address."

Louise Michel's gaze turned cool and calculating. She drew a small notebook from under her sash, turned pages, read something, then stuffed the little book away again. In a neutral voice she began to ask questions: the names of Anna's favorite aunts, the name of the village nearest Anna's childhood home, and finally the date of Anna's name day.

Sofya provided each answer without hesitation.

The corners of Louise's mouth turned up slightly, "Like my Mimi, I've learned to use caution with strangers. Anna is a dear friend. In some quarters, particularly outside of Paris, the Commune has enemies who intend to destroy our leaders."

Moving to a desk at one side of the room, Louise took out paper and a pencil. "The cottage your sister and Commander Jaclard occupy is on the Rue de Rosiers. Because of Commander Jaclard's vital services to the Commune, his home is guarded at all times. You'll need this note."

After giving directions to the cottage, Louise added, "Your sister was at my side that first day of the insurrection when we women faced down the National troops and stopped the confiscation of our two hundred cannon."

Sofya stared at the woman and tried to imagine Anyuta, at this woman's side, fighting for possession of cannon. Regaining some measure of composure, Sofya thanked Louise.

"Before I leave, may I ask you a question about your family?"

"That seems only fair. I've asked some prying questions."

"Are you related to Miss Mary Ann Evans, a British writer who uses the pen name of George Eliot? I met Miss Evans last year and have kept in contact with her." Sofya hesitated. "I ask because your features are so strikingly like hers I guessed you might be sisters, or perhaps cousins."

"My God! Two women cursed with these features!" Louise laughed. "No, I am not related to Miss Evans, although I have read and admired her books." Her eyes were twinkling as she continued, "It's fortunate that relationships are not told by appearance, for I was struck by the fact that you look absolutely nothing at all like Anna Jaclard."

"And that is my misfortune," Sofya smiled.

Out of the lighted entrance and down the stair, Sofya crossed the street and turned a corner. Vladimir appeared at her side. "You were successful?" he inquired anxiously. In answer she hurriedly guided their steps toward the Rue des Rosiers.

TWO DAYS LATER, Anyuta briskly led her sister along the narrow walk of Rue des Rosiers. Anyuta pointed to the building where the National generals had been held under arrest, that first day. With pride she mentioned that Victor had served as a judge in the military court that had quickly been set up to try the soldiers accompanying the generals.

"The generals were shot," Sofya noted grimly.

"Yes, that was unavoidable." Anyuta increased their pace.

After hours spent trying to convince her sister to leave Paris, Sofya weakened and reluctantly agreed to accompany Anyuta to an evening meeting of the Women's Vigilance Committee.

"You'll see, Sofya. When Thiers pulled the national government out of Paris, he didn't realize what a chance he was giving the real people. The Vigilance Committee is working wonders in improving the lives of working women. We're setting up humane conditions in the factories. We're seeing that women have a chance at education. That they get a fair break from their landlords, even from pawnbrokers. We won't let this opportunity to establish a just society slip through our fingers."

Sofya sighed, and wondered to herself if this was the proper moment to raise the point that the just society of the Commune refused to let women vote. Anyuta was chattering, as she had been since they left the cottage, her voice blending with the raucous sounds of jays flitting from tree to tree.

"Listen to reason, Anya." Crossing the railroad tracks, Sofya lifted the skirt of the plain blue dress Anyuta had provided her. At Anyuta's insistence, a red sash had been tied around the waist. "The French army is going to crush Paris, it's just a matter of time. Thiers has strengthened his forces with seasoned soldiers released from Prussian prison camps." Sofya tripped on a cobblestone, then regained her balance. "Didn't you listen to anything Vladimir was saying?"

"Vladimir's a pessimist. A man with no backbone."

"Anna!" Sofya protested.

Anyuta went on, "Last night at my place, you saw Victor and the other officers of the National Guard. These men drove Thiers from the city and they won't let him back until our demands are granted. Paris will be independent. Paris will have a voice. This time, Paris will not accept humiliation and surrender. She will fight to the death!"

"Is death what you want?" Sofya had not been impressed by Victor and the others; in comparison with her father and Vladimir, they had seemed to be strutting little boys playing soldier.

"I was speaking rhetorically. The fighting will end soon."

"The fighting's just begun, Anyuta." Sofya controlled her anger. "I wish you'd come away with me, before things get so bad that you can't get out. This experiment hasn't got the chance of a canary in a Siberian winter."

"Nonsense. I don't need rescuing. Now is not the time for cool scientific analysis, now is a time for action. We're making history, Sofya. And we need every worker we can get. We need you." Anyuta took hold of Sofya's elbow and started down a flight of stone stairs. Sofya's right hand slid along the low iron fence that bisected the stairway from top to bottom.

Anyuta continued her sermon "When you see how enthusiastically the citizens of Paris embrace our changes, you'll want to be a part of it all. Just as you were a part of my circle in Petersburg."

"Anyuta . . ." Sofya felt her throat tighten. Anger would win her nothing.

"It will be wonderful having you by my side, just like old times."

Anyuta abruptly turned a corner. Before them stood the Women's Club where Sofya had asked directions not two evenings earlier.

"We're joining some of our local members here," Anyuta explained. "Then we'll march over to the main meeting as a group."

As many as fifty women were milling about in the street, under the shadow of the huge red flag, enjoying the cool evening air. Some carried small children in their arms. The women's simple dress and lined, tired faces made it easy for Sofya to classify them as from the working class. Some were clearly from that group of unfortunates who had been driven to the lowest rank of society. Fascinated, a little uneasy, Sofya leaned closer to Anyuta.

Tugging Sofya with her, Anyuta walked among the women, nodding to one or another of them, introducing Sofya to teachers, milliners, seamstresses, makers of artificial flowers.

The introductions held tantalizing indications of life stories worth hearing. Stories not unlike the ones told by Dostoevsky.

In a couple of minutes Anyuta had maneuvered to the top of the stairs, stopping every few steps to greet a woman by name, patting a child on the head, offering words of thanks to one and another of the women for coming. In quiet amazement Sofya realized that here among the working women of Paris, Anyuta was acknowledged as an important leader.

Anyuta slipped her arm around Sofya's shoulder and drew her close. "Every one of these women is helped by the new government. We've given them better jobs and more money." Anyuta's eyes were shining, her voice sincere. "We've given them hope. Do you see why I must stay in Paris?" With a warm breath that Sofya felt as well as heard, Anyuta whispered, "And you must stay with me."

Not waiting for a response, Anyuta released her, indicated with a gesture that Sofya should stay where she was, turned and disappeared within the entrance of the Club.

Sofya waited outside the door. Crossing her arms over her breast, focusing her gaze on the boards of the porch, she tried to rethink her position. She had left her studies and come to Paris determined to argue her sister into leaving, but what were arguments, what was logic, against this kind of an emotional appeal? She caught bits of the conversations around her, but the women were speaking too quickly to be understood. The smiles on the women's faces and the enthusiastic way they waved their hands gave the impression that they were celebrating. With a start, Sofya noticed every woman present wore some kind of red adornment. Those who were better dressed wore a red artificial flower, the poorer a rough scarf of red.

Sofya shuddered, and pulled her arms more tightly around herself. She was being absorbed into this restless red mass. She wanted to run down the stairs, back to the cottage where Vladimir waited for her, back to her studies with Weierstrass.

Just as Sofya was on the verge of bolting, Anyuta reappeared, her face flush with excitement. Sofya hesitated as her eyes met Anyuta's. Before Sofya could speak, Anyuta linked arms with her and led her to the bottom of the stairs.

A loud roar erupted from the crowd. Louise Michel had appeared in the doorway. Louise's arms were outstretched, reaching just above her head in a triumphant gesture. Each of her hands gripped one side of the doorframe. She was wearing the uniform of a National Guardsman, complete with holstered pistol and trousers. A red sash, not unlike Sofya's, was tied about her waist.

Another loud cheer rose from the Montmartre women gathered at the stairs.

Louise spoke, her voice forceful, audible to the entire street. "Citizens! Sisters! You see me in the uniform of our men. I will fight along-side our men on the battlefield. I ask every woman who is fit and capable to join me. Today, I will be enlisting volunteers for a women's battalion of the Guard."

A cheer went up.

Louise held her hands up for quiet. "Some of you are serving the cause as sewers of uniforms, as workers in our munitions factories, as hospital workers, as teachers and caretakers of our children. Some of you have already been on the battlefield at the side of our men, bringing food and drink, serving as ambulance nurses. Some have even fired rifles alongside their loved ones. All these things are done when a city is in peril. Now, we women claim the right to have our own battalion, to be officially recognized as fighters along with our men!"

Another roar rose from the women.

"Tonight, before and after our meeting, I will record the names and addresses of those of you who are willing to fight for our dear city in this special way. I ask you, please, if you can, sign up with us. Encourage your friends to sign. We women will share equally with our men both the fighting and the fruits of the victory."

Wild applause.

Louise, tall and stiff as any soldier, walked down the stairs. Anyuta took her place right behind the woman soldier. Sofya followed in dazed amazement.

Louise turned once more to the women following her. "We, mothers, sisters, wives, will be a visible reminder to the soldiers on the battlefield that the ideals of the revolution of 1789 must not die." Arms were raised above her head, face turned skyward, she cried out with an emotion that poured over the crowd, "Liberty, Equality, and Fraternity!"

The revolutionary cry was echoed, louder than ever, by the crowd.

Sofya's voice joined with the others. Her arm, like those of all the women around her, raised in defiance and salute. She was walking in a march step at the side of Anyuta and directly behind Louise Michel.

They marched down the center of the Rue des Trois Frères, all of them singing the *Marseillaise*.

In haphazard array and party-like merriment, children ran before the group, singing and cavorting at the head of the parade. Sofya sang so loudly she felt her throat ache. Still, she could hardly make out her own voice among the others. Anyuta, singing right next to her, was indistin-guishable.

The group turned onto the Rue Yvonne Le Tac. In sight, not far ahead of them was a church. Women, much like the ones with whom Sofya was marching, filed into the building.

One woman carrying a large red flag stood at the entrance and waited for Louise Michel to mount the stairs. As they entered the vestibule of the church, Louise was shown to a table. The flag bearer stood at attention beside Louise, who was soon seated and taking names of volunteers.

Anyuta motioned Sofya to one side of the main entrance, where women were streaming in.

"Louise is wonderful, isn't she?" Anyuta's eyes blazed. "And wait till you hear my friend André Leo. She's speaking tonight."

Sofya stared at her sister. "Anyuta, what are we all doing at a church?"

"It's a great place for meetings, plenty of seats. During the day the religious rituals still go on, for those who think they need them. The black crows nest during the day, but at night, we brush out superstition with truth." She patted the solid stone beside her. "This is government property now."

Sofya nodded, only half hearing her sister's response.

Anyuta waved and called to a woman at the bottom of the stairs. The woman, small, fortyish, neatly dressed, noticed Anyuta and was waving back.

"That's Leo," Anyuta spoke to Sofya. "André Leo. Her real name is Leodile Champseix, everyone calls her Leo."

When the pretty woman joined them, Anyuta made a brief introduction.

André Leo grasped Sofya's hand in both of her soft hands. "I'm delighted to meet you, Sofya. Anyuta's told me about you. I admire the courage and intelligence of a woman who can push open the gates of science. After this meeting, we must get together and talk."

"I'd like that," Sofya said. "I've read your novels with enjoyment."

"Well, then, now that you're in Paris, you'll certainly want to join us," Leo went on in an easy manner, "We'll just have to recruit you to help us on the paper, won't we Anna? *La Sociale* can always use another intelligent helper, especially during these trying days."

"It's time we were going in, Leo," Anyuta said, then turned to Sofya. "I'm giving a brief financial report, and saying a few words on educational programs. I'll be sitting with the speakers. Relax and enjoy the meeting."

"We'll talk later." André Leo smiled warmly. Her eyes were calm and intelligent. Her manner gentle. Sofya liked her.

Anyuta and Leo hurried toward the front of the church.

❧

STAYING TOWARD THE BACK, Sofya noticed that the wall above the nearest pew bore a carved plaque, rather like an icon, depicting Veronica offering a cloth to wipe the bloody face of Christ, who had fallen under the weight of his great cross. The pew was empty. Well, why not? she thought. She would sit beneath the symbol of compassion, loyalty and service.

Awkwardly stepping over the kneeler, Sofya pushed herself all the way in, against the wall. Her eyes searched the room. The arched ceiling, even the tiled floor, seemed to be covered with art. The rows of benches gave a disciplined order to the gathering. Here there would be no tightly packed, standing mass of humanity, as in the churches at home.

Off to one side Sofya could just see the shimmering light from tall cylindrical glasses holding burning candles. An old grandmother, alone, her head covered with a lace veil, bent over, a strand of wooden beads swaying in her hands, knelt before a statue of the Woman in Blue. The grandmother swayed and moved her lips and hands, completely unaware, or perhaps deliberately unresponsive, to the activity around her. Sofya turned her eyes; even looking at her felt somehow intrusive.

Along the sides of the church, stiffly standing guard, Sofya identified a plaster statue of Jeanne d'Arc, the warrior, another of Francis of Assisi, the man of peace. Her eye wandered along the wall noting the small plaque-like sculptures, like the one above the pew where she was sitting. The walls were lined with them, she counted ten or twelve, each plaque depicting a scene from the last torment of the Great Reformer.

The light in the church was quickly fading. Some women working at preparing the chamber for the meeting were smoking cigarettes, joking and laughing loudly as they went from lamp to lamp along the sides of the chamber, lighting the flames with their cigarettes. Large lanterns that might have been borrowed from a theater had been placed at the foot of the altar and around the pulpit from which elevated position Sofya expected the speakers would address the group.

The stained glass windows, at their best when backlighted by the sun, now gave off an eerie reflected light, looking more like Russian icons than Papist portraits.

A large crucifix dominated the center of the wall above the altar. In the semi-darkness, Sofya could make out the figure of a woman who had climbed on the altar, and was now reaching up toward the cross and its carved wooden figure, draping a red loincloth around the waist.

Meanwhile, a few of the women in pews near the front hooted their amusement and offered applause.

The pew in front of Sofya was now full, and the one behind her nearly so. She saw no men among the congregation, only working class women, neatly and simply dressed, like the women she had met in front of Montmartre Vigilance Committee hall. Some wore bonnets trimmed with cheap white lace. Some with a clear gesture of defiance removed their bonnets on entering. Every woman present had some sort of red decoration on her dress.

A young woman whose face bore the lines of illness, or extreme tiredness, slid into the pew next to Sofya, and smiled at her.

"Hello," Sofya offered in greeting, hoping the woman could be persuaded to talk. Like others she had met this evening, this one seemed exotic and fascinating.

"Hello," the woman responded. She pulled out a well-used handkerchief and coughed into it. "Just come from the factory." She squinted at Sofya, as if trying to decide who she was. "You wouldn't have a cigarette, would you? Or maybe a little something to drink that might ease the cough?"

"No, I'm sorry, I didn't bring anything with me," Sofya said.

"When you been working eleven hours straight, you sure could use a lift. Not that I'm complaining. Eleven hours ain't nothing compared to what I had to do before these nice Communey people took over. I work down the street, sewing uniforms. What do you do?"

"I'm a student," Sofya answered.

Again the woman squinted at her, her expression quickly hardening into dislike. "No place here for aristocrats. Maybe you come here to see how the animals live?"

"I'm a friend of the speaker's. My name is Sofya." Sofya responded in as friendly a tone as she could manage.

Once more the other's expression altered. Every thought on her part seemed to require a major effort. "Well, maybe you're all right. You're a for'ner, sounds like. Some good for'ners helping us in the army and such. My name is Lily." She extended a rough hand, nails black at the ends. "I can read, you know. Really, I can. I read that Leo's column every day. She's taken a man's name. Can you beat that? She's got a man's brain too. But she's sure got a woman's heart." Lily would have said more, but a baby in the pew behind them cried out noisily.

Lily turned around angrily. "When the speaker comes, you better keep the damn brat quiet."

An older woman, next to the young girl holding the baby, looked up from her knitting. "You just mind your mouth in here. We've got a meeting, sure. But this is still our church."

A loud chord from an organ reverberated through the church. Instinctively Sofya turned in the direction of the sound. Above, in a choir loft, she could see the tall, unmistakable figure of Louise Michel seated at the organ.

A woman Sofya didn't recognize was standing in the pulpit. When the chord faded, she loudly proclaimed that the meeting was now to be in order. The meeting would begin with women rising and singing the *Marseillaise*. From the organ came a few preliminary chords, then voices filled the church. After several choruses, the music stopped, and the women sat down.

The chairwoman announced that the first speaker would address the problem of "The Role of the Church in the Commune."

The prepared statement was delivered with strength and passion, outweighing certain shortcomings of reason and logic, Sofya decided. During the discussion period that followed various views were expressed.

Lily rose and was recognized by the chair. "I don't want no black bird bitches in our city. Ruined us sewing girls, selling their stuff so cheap, but they won't do it no more. If they stay, make them buy their food and pay rent, just like us."

"Oh, shut up!" came a call from the pew behind. "The nuns are pretty good to me and my kids. And the priest, he came and gave us some food just last week for Easter. They ain't hurting no one."

Voices called out from other ends of the room. The speaker recognized one, then another. Some favored Lily's harsh approach, some sided with the old woman.

Listening to these poor women torn by a sense of duty to an organization and their own need to make a living, Sofya thanked God that she had never doubted her conviction that no authority, no organization, civil or religious, would ever have control of her mind or will.

The discussion was brought to a swift end when the leader announced that it was time to introduce the main speaker. The respected journalist, André Leo, would speak on "The Role of Women in the Commune."

Loud applause came from the audience. Leo had barely quieted the crowd and straightened her papers, preparing to begin, when a loud bang vibrated through the assembly. Turning, Sofya saw that the heavy doors at the back of the church had been flung open.

All eyes were now fixed on the young woman who had just entered.

Strikingly attractive, dressed in a black velvet riding suit. In her belt were thrust two large revolvers. A fashionable black felt hat sported a large red feather. Around her shoulders and draped from right to left across her breasts was a red silk scarf with broad gold trim. The woman's carefully arranged chestnut hair, bright grey-blue eyes, fashionably pale complexion, smooth features and especially her elegant mannerisms and carriage were not those of the working class Parisian.

Confidently she came striding down the central aisle, the red feather bounced jauntily with each step. The room was silent, everyone mesmerized.

"Lizzie Dmietrieff," Lily murmured, leaning toward Sofya. "One of those for'ners. Russian, I think. Come all the way from there to help us!"

Sofya nodded acknowledgment, while her eyes remained fixed on the new presence. Dmietrieff reached the pulpit, where Leo was exchanging words with her.

Now Dmietrieff nudged Leo aside, and when she authoritatively motioned the others nearby to resume their seats, to Sofya's surprise, they obeyed. Dmietrieff stood at the pulpit, hands gripping the edge. "I have an announcement." Her voice was amazingly strong for a small person. "It is a story of rape and murder."

A gasp went up. In the silence that followed, everyone in the church could hear the shocking details. A young Commune nurse, really no more than a girl, had been carrying water to a wounded man on the field of battle just outside the city walls. Suddenly, she had been ambushed from behind. Brutishly attacked, not by one man, but by five. Attacked and dishonored by five troopers in the service of Versailles!

"Is this an enemy that can be reasoned with?" Dmietrieff asked rhetorically. A vibrating yell of "No!" rose from a thousand throats.

"We women must defend ourselves!" Dmietrieff yelled as she raised her arm, pistol drawn. "We will give no quarter to these beasts from hell!"

"Avenge the girl!" Lily shouted. Then, with an air of inspiration, "Kill a prisoner!"

"Kill five prisoners!" Another voice called. "One of us is worth five of them, at least!"

Leo managed to force her way back to the pulpit. Shoving Dmietrieff aside she shouted, "No! Remember who we are, and what we want! Think! Just yesterday, we burned the guillotine in the public square, vowing to end all capital punishment. We must not fall into the Terror!"

"We will have our righteous revenge!" Another voice shouted.

"Silence the voices of opposition!"

Sofya was on her feet. The crowd around her turned suddenly ugly, vicious, uncontrolled. Emotions, pent up and furious, were spilling out.

"Everyone who is not for us, is against us!"

Dmietrieff had again shoved Leo aside. "There is no room among us for those who side with the devil! Listen, women. We will have our revenge. Tonight, we will march on the offices of the enemy sympathizers."

"Yes! Yes!" came the call from uncountable voices.

"And tomorrow . . ." Dmietrieff called out. But she had to stop. The uproar drowned out her words. She tried again.

"Tomorrow, we will attack the slackers among us. We will force the leaders to pass a law. All who are not actively for the Commune are against it . . . all men who are not actively serving the Commune must be arrested and shot!"

Suddenly Sofya's blood turned cold. She stood still, gasping. It was impossible to doubt that this woman meant exactly what she had said. Might she truly have the power to get such a draconian law enacted? A law straight from the days of the Terror? She certainly had the power to lead a crowd to action.

Not a woman was in her seat. They flowed into the aisles, climbing onto the altar. Some were lifting Dmietrieff to their shoulders.

A few steady voices, especially that of Leo, tried to regain control of the assembly, but none of them could be heard over the growing excitement. The chairwoman called for an adjournment of the meeting, but no one was paying her any attention.

Sofya pushed and shoved her way to her sister and together they reached the side of André Leo, who was still feverishly trying to refute the calls to violence that sounded from every side. Shouting to make herself heard, Anyuta urged Leo to leave off her futile attempts at reason, and to retreat.

It took the sisters several minutes to nudge and urge a still debating Leo to the door. While Anyuta stood guard, somehow Sofya managed to get a cab. The three of them, at Leo's insistence, headed for the office of *La Sociale*.

WHEN THEY ENTERED the paper's office, a man, no more than thirty, tall, with wavy black hair, jumped up from behind his desk and came to meet them.

"Leo, whatever has happened?"

"Oh, Ben, things went terribly wrong at the meeting. I'm afraid there might be a mob on its way here to destroy our paper," Leo cried out in an emotional, near hysterical tone. She tried to explain the details of what had happened in the church.

Leo pulled from Sofya's gentle grip and nearly fell into the arms of the man. Sofya and Anyuta stood awkwardly by, as the man, Benoit Malon, held a sobbing Leo in his arms.

Recovering under Benoit's gentle touch, Leo gently pushed away. Smoothing her hair, she began to pace nervously around the room, talking as quickly as she paced. Tomorrow, if the presses were still intact, she would bring reason back into the movement. She would remind women of their important role in the new society, a role equal to that of men. When women gave themselves time to think, they would react more with logic and less with raw emotion.

Meanwhile, Anyuta was quietly raging. "Dmietrieff wants total and sole control of the women of the Commune. All other organizations, all other ways of thought, are to be wiped out. And she has some powerful friends in England ready to help her with pen and pocketbook."

"And how do you know so much about the little vixen?" Benoit stared at Anyuta.

"I met her in Geneva, briefly, when Victor and I sought refuge there at the start of the war. Her real name is Elizabeth Tomanovskaya. She has family in Petersburg, we know some of the same people. In Geneva she was elected to represent the Russian section of the International Working Men's Association at a meeting with Karl Marx. She's become a close friend of the Marx family."

"Marx, the German professor who publishes all those pamphlets?" Benoit asked.

"The very one."

Leo lowered her voice, "In justice, I admit, Dmietrieff, or Tomanovskaya, or whatever her name is, has done some good things. She's set up cooperative sewing factories where women obtain work directly from the government. Without middlemen, wages are higher. She's recruited women of the street and offered them a chance to make an honest living. I've praised her work in my writing. But now I see what she's really up to." Leo's face grew red as she continued furiously. "Anna's got it right. Completely and totally right! Dmietrieff is after sole control of the women. And she wants blood. I can't believe it. She's only twenty years old! She'll destroy the whole movement!"

"Anna, Leo's very upset now." Benoit turned to Anyuta, his eyes more pleading than his tone, "Leave us, please. Go home." He turned to Sofya. "Mademoiselle, if you have any influence with Madame Jaclard, please, take her home immediately. I will close the office quickly, then accompany Madame Leo to a safe place. If a crowd does come to the office, it will be better if no one's here."

FROM ALL THE ATTEMPTS at persuasion, from all the discussions and debates, from all the emotion charged rhetoric of the day, one phrase had burned itself into Sofya's mind.

"All men who are not actively serving the Commune must be arrested and shot!"

After everyone had retired, Sofya lay awake on her bed staring at the ceiling. Vladimir was sleeping in a small alcove off the kitchen. She had to find an opportunity to talk to him alone, and quickly. Putting on her robe, she tiptoed barefoot out of her room, past the door of Anna and Victor's room, and on into the kitchen. There she stopped suddenly, seeing the glow from Vladimir's pipe, smelling the tobacco.

"You're dressed!" she whispered as she stood before him. His large dark shape was only a shadowy outline, sitting on the edge of the cot. Soon she made out that he was wearing the army issue clothing Victor had given him on arrival and which he'd refused to wear till now.

"Yes, I was about to wake you." Vladimir's voice was as low as hers. "I don't plan to join the Guards and be shot in battle, or to refuse to join and be shot for that. So I'm leaving Montmartre. I'll have a better chance at crossing the barricades in this outfit." He brushed at the leg of his uniform with disgust.

Sofya, relieved, sat beside him on the cot. "But you're not leaving Paris?"

She felt the weight of his hand gently resting on her arm. "Not unless you come with me."

She shook her head.

"I didn't think you would." He withdrew his touch.

"I can't." She hid her face in her hands for a moment, then stared out into the blackened room. "There's still a chance I'll be able to help Anyuta."

"Be careful," he whispered. "The people here are turning vicious, Sofya, very vicious."

"You don't need to tell me that. But there may still be hope for a rational end to this situation. I know Anyuta will follow Leo."

"But Victor won't. He likes this business of war too much. He loves issuing orders, and prancing around in his gold-braided uniform, a sword clanking at his side. On top of that he drinks too much. Your sister's fascination with him defies reason."

Vladimir stood up. From the foot of the bed, he took a small cloth packet wrapped in the shirt she recognized as the one he'd worn when they arrived in the Commune. Tucking the packet under his arm, he started toward the door.

"Where will you go?" Sofya demanded anxiously.

"Not every area of the city is as demented as this one. It's dawned on me that here I actually have a chance to do something that may someday be of some slight benefit to humanity." Taking in Sofya's bewilderment, he added a succinct explanation. "I can study. Cuvier's collection of fossilized mammals, the one Darwin recommended to me, is right here in Paris. I'll make some drawings and take some notes. I might just get a publication out of this. After all, we vowed to spend our lives in pursuit of science, didn't we?"

Dazedly she nodded.

"If you need my help, or if by some miracle you convince your sister to leave, a message sent care of Professor Albert Gaudry at the Natural History Institute in the Jardin des Plantes will reach me. If you actually manage to get away for a few hours, come at noon, any day, to the statue of Buffon in the park near the Institute."

"I'll meet you there as often as I can."

"Good. I don't need to tell you that no one else should know my whereabouts."

"I'll be careful."

"Keep your eyes open and your head clear." He lifted her chin, kissed her lightly. Then he was gone.

CHAPTER TWENTY-THREE

May 1871 ⊶ *The Paris Commune*

Sofya sat at the kitchen table alone, staring blankly into a cup half full of cold tea. She wondered what Vladimir was doing this very moment. Perhaps he was already at the Institute involved in some academic work.

Vladimir had been gone two weeks. She should have attempted a rendezvous, but hadn't. She'd let herself be swept up in Anyuta's hectic life of meetings, speeches, and official gatherings, had accompanied her sister on visits to factories for everything from ammunition to ladies' parasols. But today she was going to locate her husband.

Thoughts of Vladimir were jarred away by a hand on her shoulder. "Up early aren't you, Sofya?" The light, joking tone in Anyuta's voice was grating. Her sister was invariably cheerful these days.

"Earlier than your husband," Sofya snapped, in no mood for Anyuta's domestic flutterings. Anyuta, dressed in a very feminine nightgown, had begun busily preparing Victor's breakfast tray. "Anyuta, I can't believe the things you do for that man."

Anyuta ignored her comment and chattered on as she lighted the flame beneath a pot of water. "Victor says the Central Committee has been doing some reorganizing. I expect I'll be asked to take on new duties. Of course, I'll accept whatever positions I'm offered."

"That's nice," Sofya responded, turning the pages of the newspaper absentmindedly. She wondered at the fact that despite months of war and deprivation, the Parisians, seeing themselves as the most civilized people in the world, had not been without their numerous daily papers.

Anyuta placed a large serving of Brie along with a slice of cured meat on Victor's plate. "You'll be more enthusiastic once we're at the meeting."

Anyuta took fragrant tea leaves from a canister and placed them in a ceramic pot. This was English tea making, Sofya thought, not Russian. Anyuta should have at least set up a samovar.

"I won't be at the meeting. I have other plans for the day." Sofya watched for Anyuta's response.

"And how, may I ask, will you spend your day?" Someone had dropped off four fresh eggs, a gift, the visitor had said. Somehow, good food kept appearing on the leaders' tables, despite the chronic shortages; Sofya had noted the fact, had filed it with other matters that she was not prepared to think about. Now Anyuta was fingering the eggs, clearly debating with herself whether to prepare them for Victor's breakfast. Finally deciding against using them, she stared directly at Sofya, awaiting an answer.

Sofya turned from her sister's demanding gaze. "I'm going to Parc Monceau." She pointed to an article in the newspaper. "Some enterprising fellows have set up telescopes, and for a few francs they'll let you get a good look at the fighting at Neuilly and Passy."

"I wouldn't have thought that you'd be entertained by cannon blasting." Anyuta broke a large piece of bread from a loaf on the table. She smeared some thick cream, also a gift, onto the uncrusted surface.

"I want to see what kind of optical instruments the amateurs are using, then cross over to the left bank and visit the observatory." Sofya more than half expected a scolding, and some comment on the irrelevance of science to the all-important changes now being wrought in society. But it seemed that Anyuta really wasn't paying her that much attention.

Instead, she said, her voice soft with reminiscence, "You know, when Victor and I first returned to Paris, we spent a wonderful fall evening at Parc Monceau. It's beautiful. The telescopes were there then, and we saw Venus and the face of the Moon. We lay on a blanket, staring up at the stars, holding hands." She sighed.

"Anna?" came an impatient voice from another room. "Where's my breakfast?"

"Coming!" Anyuta hurriedly poured the now boiling water over the tea leaves. "Sofya, if you insist on going to the left bank, I need to warn you. Stay away from the area around La Salpêtrière asylum. The National Guard's planning a raid. All the male employees are to be recruited, forcibly if necessary."

"And stay clear of the Palais Royal," Victor's voice came booming. In a moment he was standing behind Anyuta, his hair rumpled, and lacking shirt, shoes or socks. He had pulled on only a pair of trousers on springing out of bed. Sofya glanced at him and away, feeling more disgusted than embarrassed by his rude display.

Victor was not interested in her reaction. He had slipped his arms around Anyuta's waist and was kissing her neck. "We're going to pick up any slackers in that area too." Releasing Anyuta's waist, he snatched up a piece of bread. Mouth full, he continued, "Good thing for Vladimir he ran when he did. We caught several cowards making their way out over the ramparts, lowered on ropes. Some we arrested in the train stations were dressed as women." He laughed, an ugly sound. "I don't suppose Vladimir tried that. He would be the ugliest damn cow imaginable."

Sofya pushed her chair back and retreated toward her room.

"I'll write you a special transport pass and leave it on the table," Victor called after her. "You'll be able to cross the barricades freely and be safe from harassment if you do encounter our troops."

෨✤෨

FOLLOWING THE PLAN she'd outlined for Anyuta, Sofya made her way to Parc Monceau. It proved impossible to really see much of the battle through the telescopes, but the little Sofya did see was sobering. After a few minutes she took a cab to the observatory where she impatiently hurried through the section of the building open to the public. En route she made mental notes of what was on display, just in case Anyuta questioned her at dinner.

Now at last she felt free to look for Vladimir. Remembering that the La Salpêtrière asylum lay just to the southeast of the Jardin des Plantes, Sofya entered the park from the northwest. This put her far from where Anyuta had warned her about National Guard troops. She would have to walk the diagonal length of the park to reach the statue of Buffon, but the safest route lay away from the main streets.

After eight months of war, the cages of the zoological garden were all empty, the elephants, lions, zebras, and giraffes having long since gone to feed the human population of Paris. Next came the botanical garden, where she noted that the plants had fared far better than the animals. An extensive bed of herbs displayed basil and chamomile, along with innumerable mints and other medicinals she couldn't identify. Rows of flower beds offered their finest spring display.

When she reached the statue of Buffon, the time was well past noon. Vladimir might have already come and gone. She looked hopefully about on the chance of spotting him, then settled on a bench. After a few minutes, too nervous to wait any longer, she crossed the Allée Buffon and hurried to the imposing building on the southwest corner. Inquiring inside, she eventually reached the secretary of the paleontology department, who directed her to the offices of Professor Albert Gaudry.

Turning the handle of a massive oak door, she found it unlocked. Before her lay a broad, long room, lighted by a row of windows and lined with wooden tables. Under each table was a chest containing many drawers and pigeonholes, while the tabletops were strewn with trays holding miscellaneous bones. The nearest trays held what appeared to Sofya to be dried yellowed teeth, hundreds of teeth, most of them too large to possibly be human.

In a glass case on the table to her right crouched the skeleton of what appeared to be a large rat, or perhaps a small dog. The table to her left contained jawbones of various sizes, worn teeth still in place. Immediately in front of her on a long table were laid out the bones of what might have been a complete animal, but all in disorder, like a giant puzzle awaiting someone's attention. The room seemed ominously quiet.

She called out, "Is anyone here?"

From the far end of the room, a reddish head and large body rose from behind the tables.

"Sofya, you've come!" Vladimir's deep voice echoed through the cavernous space. He advanced toward her, dressed now in shabby civilian clothes, still holding a large bone in each hand, like some hungry savage.

"Thank God you're safe!" Sofya made her way around the tables to him, and slid between the bones, still held awkwardly in his outstretched arms.

She laughed, "Can't be parted from your work for a minute."

"These?" He juggled the white shapes thoughtfully. "I was just cleaning them up. Here's a rib from a horse, just obtained from a restaurant down the street. And this is a pig's foot from the neighborhood butcher. It may have been the last live pig in Paris. They came with traces of meat still on them, by the way. It was delicious. How are you faring over there? Getting enough to eat?"

"More than enough. The Jaclards are very well liked by the butchers, bakers and restaurant owners. Gifts, as Victor calls them, of one delicacy or another appear daily, as if by magic."

"I should have realized that the family of a National Guard Commander never lacks."

"Actually, I'd rather we not discuss Victor."

"Fine with me," Vladimir smiled.

"And now that you've cleaned these bones—?"

"They'll be useful for some rough comparisons. I've become fascinated with herbivorous mammals, both odd- and even-toed ungulates."

"The horse being odd with one digit, the pig even with two." Sofya laughed, "You're impossible!" She took the bones from him, put them on a table, then gave him a big hug, which he warmly reciprocated.

Some moments later, his arms still tightly around her, he asked, "Are you ready to leave? Will Anyuta go?" The questions came quickly.

"No." She pushed him firmly away. "Neither of us are leaving."

"All right." To her surprise, he actually seemed relieved. "Now would not be a good time for me to leave Paris, either. Of course, if you needed my help . . ."

"Nothing like that. I just wanted to know that you had found some place of safety. That you were all right."

"I'm absolutely fine. I appreciate your concern." He smiled warmly.

"I've accomplished quite a lot here." His eyes shone with enthusiasm. "I'm onto something, Sofya. Something important. Let me show you."

Willingly she let him lead her to a corner of the room that contained a case with a pony-sized skeleton.

"This is *Hipparion*. From the Miocene age, that makes it about seventy million years old. Ten years ago, Gaudry pieced it together. Then by showing similarities in bone structure, he proved that this is an ancestor of our modern day horse."

Sofya examined the bones carefully. "A horse? I don't understand, a horse has a single toe. This creature has three digits."

"Actually some of the really old specimens had five digits. Gaudry took note of the change in number." Vladimir chuckled. "He meticulously examined the bones, especially the teeth and leg bones, and from their shape, size and position derived theories of how the animal's body functioned. To make a long story short, he was able to conclude that this creature is from the same family as our modern day horse. Every reputable expert in the field has accepted his arguments."

"Then it offers support for Darwin's theory?"

"Exactly!"

"Ah!" Sofya stared at the bones. Here was true science, the realization of a theory in the real world. It reminded her of the way the abstractions of an equation could be seen in the actual motions of planets.

"Now look over here." Impatiently Vladimir was dragging her on, to a case where another full skeleton was displayed. "*Palaeotherium*, the animal Cuvier uncovered in the gypsum fields at Montmartre well over forty years ago. He showed it's from the horse family as well."

By now alerted to the importance of toes, Sofya examined the skeleton carefully. "This one is only the size of a dog, and it has four digits on each of its front feet, and three on each of the back."

"So it does. This specimen is several tens of millions of years older than Gaudry's. But they're both from the horse family, and they're both from the same era, the Cenozoic."

"If the scientists agree." Sofya nodded.

"Now, come over to this table." He led her to the table where she had already noticed the confused bones of some uncompleted puzzle. "These bones were collected by one of Professor Gaudry's students, a young Parisian, I think his name was Lartet."

"This is a front foot? It has three digits, like the Gaudry model."

"Very good, my dear!" Vladimir held up a large tooth, a molar she thought. "Take this, and compare it to the teeth in the two skeletons I just showed you."

A minute or two later she looked up. "This tooth looks more like the Cuvier model than the Gaudry."

"Precisely!" Vladimir was grinning from ear to ear. "I think I can build a solid case, showing that the specimen on the table here, is an intermediate form between Cuvier's and Gaudry's."

Sofya stared at him as what he was saying sunk in. "You'd have found one of the links supporting Darwin's theory of the continuous evolving of a species!"

For once Vladimir seemed too happy to say anything at all. He nodded his head affirmatively.

Sofya gasped. "Can you do it? Do you think you really could prove this form is an intermediary?"

"I can!" Vladimir clapped his hands together. She'd never seen him this delighted. "I won't do a sloppy job like so many others who spend pages and pages on the teeth and never look at the animal's bones, or the surroundings in which they are found. I'll document every nob on every bone, every cusp on every tooth, then I'll relate the function of the bones to the facts that are known about the grasses and vegetation existing at the time this creature lived, and to the geological facts known about the conditions of the earth at that time and place. I'll present so much data in such a clear logical manner that no one will be able to contest my conclusions. I'll show not just that the animal has evolved, but the context in which evolution took place. I'll show that natural selection was at work."

"That's wonderful. Wonderful!" She was almost too excited to think.

"One minor point, there's not quite a complete skeleton here, but that shouldn't matter." He rattled on, "I'll have to gather a lot more data, from Puy in central France, Aymard might help me. Then I think I'll take these specimens with me, back to the British Museum and compare them with the skeletons from Hampton and Hampstead. With luck I'll get Owen and Hawkins interested. God, there's going to be a lot of work involved in this."

Sofya frowned. "Vladimir, doesn't this skeleton belong to another scientist? What about that young Parisian student of Gaudry's you mentioned? He's not going to let you steal his claim to scientific greatness."

"He's certainly not going to object." Vladimir's face turned suddenly serious. "He was killed at Neuilly, in the first battle, fighting for the Commune."

"I am so sorry," Sofya whispered.

"Gaudry was devastated by the senseless loss of his friend, and of a brilliant young scientist. He gave me the bones. He said it will take a young man's energy and drive to develop the ramifications of the theory they suggest. I'll fight the dead man's battle, the one he should have devoted himself to. Pick your battles, Sofya. That's the lesson here." He paused. "Won't you consider coming back to science? You realize you're endangering yourself, just as that young man did."

She hesitated.

He saw her indecision and pressed on. "Professor Gaudry's arranged for my use of several rooms in the old Cuvier home. We could be quite comfortable there. I'd continue my work at the Institute and you could take up your mathematics. I hear Paris has more than its share of powerful mathematicians. Of course, you would keep in touch with Anyuta. If she needed us, we'd be here."

"I'll return to mathematics later," she said softly.

Slowly Vladimir's shoulders slumped. "So, you've been converted to the cause. What do its glorious leaders have you doing? Certainly not solving equations."

"I haven't done much of anything so far. I've just been tagging along with Anyuta. But if Anyuta and her friend André Leo have their way, there will be a great relief of human suffering, great advances of opportunity for women, for everyone."

He stared piercingly at her. "I've also heard that the Commune is recruiting scientists for weapon development. They've approached several of the more radical professors here at the institute. Your humanitarian friends want to develop poison gases, and to investigate ways of spreading disease among the enemy troops. Simple incendiary devices are being perfected, that can be used effectively by the untrained."

"That can't be true!" Sofya flared. "I've heard nothing of this perversion of science. I wouldn't use my knowledge of science for such ends. How could you think such a thing of me?"

"Yes, that's what Nobel is saying about his development of dynamite." Vladimir sighed. "I just wanted you to be prepared. As the Communards are pressured and pushed, they will react like all other trapped animals. They'll fight any way they can."

"No they won't, Vladimir. I know they won't."

"I see we don't agree." He turned his back to her.

She didn't have to stand for his moralizing. She stalked to the door, opened it, then turned back and shouted, "Can we discuss this again?"

"I'll be watching for you." But he didn't look at her. He was staring at his damned skeleton of a horse!

"STILL UP, Sofya? Good." Anyuta tiredly hung her cotton shawl on a peg near the kitchen door, and pulled one of the wooden chairs back from the table where Sofya was eating the last of her dinner.

Anyuta slumped into the chair. "Did you enjoy your trip to the park and observatory?" She pulled over another chair and put her feet up. "That was probably your last chance for a day of leisure. According to the reports I heard today, things are going badly. Everyone is going to have to work double duty from here on out. We'll have to find a job for you, little sister."

Sofya searched Anyuta's face, discovering an extraordinary look of content. The time was right. If she acted gently, persuasively, she could take the initiative out of Anyuta's hands. She could assure she would not be forced into weapon development.

Rising to put her dishes into the sink, Sofya began, "Seeing the battle through a telescope, seeing the faces of the injured men, moved me deeply, Anyuta. I want to work for the Commune. I want to serve as a nurse."

"That's wonderful! You're really with us. What a perfectly wonderful day this has been." Then Anyuta hesitated. "As a nurse?"

"Of course. I've had a year of medical school."

"But you have years of training in chemistry and physics, along with all your mathematics. Victor's spoken about some interesting science related projects that are in the planning stages. Perhaps . . ."

"Anyuta, I want to do something real and immediate. I want to be among the working women, among the soldiers."

Anyuta looked at her questioningly. "Are you sure?"

"I'm absolutely certain."

"I can arrange it," Anyuta said confidently, obviously coming to a decision. "I've been assigned some heavy responsibilities." She had taken off her shoes and was now rubbing her tired feet. "Along with my women's educational duties, the Montmartre Vigilance Committee has put me in charge of the operation of ambulance nurses and military hospitals in our district. Casualties are increasing at an alarming rate. You'd be kept very busy at a hospital."

"I understand."

"But really, you'd be under-utilized as a nurse. I'd like you to take charge of the hospital, arrange for training a new nursing staff, assume administrative duties. The Committee plans to dismiss the nuns who are running the hospitals as quickly as possible. Someone must see they're replaced with dedicated women of the Commune."

Sofya stared at her sister in disbelief "Anyuta, you mustn't do that. You can't run hospitals without trained staff!"

"We'll get dedicated volunteers. You'll train them."

"Anyuta, I'm sure all these hardworking mothers, daughters, and sisters of the National Guardsmen mean well, and want to help. But they know nothing about medicine! You can't train a nurse in a week!"

"You won't have a week, you'll have to train them on site, Sofya." Anyuta turned. "Oh, while you're up, bring us both a cup of tea, would you? Is there any of that stew left? I'm starving."

As Sofya prepared the tea and ladled out stew onto a clean dish, Anyuta went on. "I'll assign you to the aid station at l'Elyée-Montmartre. You did a great job at running the clinic for our peasants in Palibino."

"Anyuta, that was a makeshift country arrangement, one idealistic young girl trying anything to relieve suffering. That doesn't qualify me to take charge of training nurses, or running a hospital in the most civilized and advanced city in all Europe. There are many people in this city who know medicine, skilled doctors and teachers. You must find someone better qualified than I am."

"There may have been many, but it seems most have fled. Don't be dramatic. You'd be wonderful at the job."

"It would be tantamount to murder." Sofya set the cups of tea on the table, then placed the steaming dish before her sister. "I will work as a member of the nursing staff. I will not attempt to train nurses or administer a hospital."

At last Anyuta lowered her eyes. "Oh well, if you're going to be stubborn about this, I'll see you're assigned as a nurse. The supervisor at one of the temporary facilities on the left bank has been demanding trained help."

CHAPTER TWENTY-FOUR

May 11, 1871 ❧ The Commune

The cab slowed as it turned off the quay onto the Boulevard de Invalides. The sounds of sporadic bombardment were clearer here and the occasional flash of a bursting shell brightened the morning sky. Since the beginning of the Commune this section of the city had served as the first line of support for the troops stationed just outside the city wall. To the southwest, the forts Issy and Vanves had long been under heavy attack. To the west, the district of Passy was being heavily shelled. Just north of there, Neuilly had been under attack since the first days of the conflict.

All vehicles in this area were subject to military inspection. After being stopped for the second time in less than a block, Sofya decided it would be less troublesome to walk the remaining distance.

Obtaining directions from a young Guardsman, she headed east on foot soon reaching the grounds of a three-story building that once served as a modest hotel. A white flag with the red cross flew above the doorway. A tent stood on the lawn outside, with a makeshift sign stuck in the ground identifying it as belonging to Marie Paulette, head nurse. There was no way to knock effectively on the canvas flap or wall, so Sofya lifted the flap and called "Excuse me?"

"Come in," a bright, feminine voice answered.

Sofya entered a dim, warm space. "I'm Sofya Kovalevskaya, reporting for nursing duty."

A young woman in nurse's garb, sitting at a small table strewn with papers and set between two field cots, turned her head slightly to examine her visitor. "Ah yes. I received your application yesterday. There is a very simple, lightweight garment for you on that cot, another will be supplied tomorrow. I strongly advise you to wear it while on duty, as it is easily washed. Change, and I'll give you a tour of the hospital." She pointed to one side. "Put your street clothes in the trunk at the foot of the cot. I see you've brought a bag. Better put that in the trunk as well. Lock the trunk when you're not here." She pushed away from the desk, stood up and looked Sofya over critically. "You're about my height, though a bit more substantial in front. The garments are cut generously.

They should do just fine. By the way, I'm Marie Paulette, head nurse and the only trained nurse at this station. I'll be sharing this tent with you as living quarters. All the available space inside the building is occupied by wounded. The doctor occupies the tent next to ours."

Sofya guessed Marie Paulette's age to be about twenty-eight. Her unfashionable black hair, even shorter than Sofya's, stuck out at odd angles from her oval face. She was fine boned and very slim. Her sparkling eyes of deep turquoise seemed to reveal a mischievous nature, in contrast with lips that smiled with an innocent warmth. She wore sturdy shoes, a small white cap, and a simple gray dress with an arm band bearing a red cross on a patch of white. Over the dress, she wore a crisp, clean white apron with large pockets.

Sofya picked up an identical gray dress from the indicated cot, and held it against her body. It would fit.

The nurse went on, "I've devised a curtain between our cots, to give us each some privacy." She pulled an old drapery along a line connected to tent poles. "You might as well get used to this," her voice came from behind the divider. "We're terribly understaffed. You might go days without being able to go home."

"I won't mind." Sofya began to unbutton her dress with steady fingers. There was more truth in that statement than her casual answer implied. These last days, as the war efforts became more intense, she'd felt very uncomfortable at Anyuta's.

"I love nursing," Marie Paulette chattered cheerfully from behind the heavy drape. "I was at Sedan, last year when the Prussians attacked. Overnight, my patients changed from the old and sick to the very young." Her voice turned very solemn. "After the truce, I decided to visit Paris and study the latest techniques for nursing wounded men."

"I've read that the American ambulance here in Paris has quite a reputation for excellence," Sofya called.

"They do. When I learned the Communards were barring nuns from nursing duty, I knew there would be a terrible shortage of trained help. I volunteered and was assigned here. What about you? We're going to be sharing a tent, I'd like to know more about you than what's on the paperwork. That's more concerned with politics than qualifications."

Sofya hesitated briefly. "Like yourself, I happened to be visiting the capital and saw the need. When this is over, I'm going back to Germany to complete my studies in mathematics." Finishing the quick change, she proudly adjusted the white arm band with the red cross.

"Math, is it? You must have brains. Something most of the other women assisting here are lacking. They mean well, but can barely read. Any experience in nursing?"

"Book learning, a year of medical school before I decided on mathematics as my field of study. I have an excellent command of anatomy. I've read a lot of home remedy books, herbal books, that kind of thing. I established and ran a clinic in one of the unused sheds on our parents' rather large farm and dairy." She avoided the word "estate," as liable to rouse suspicions in this world. "Where I grew up, one doctor served hundreds of square miles and few people could afford to go to them."

"You ran a clinic?" The words were filled with weary hope. "Finally, the Commune sends me someone who can help! To start you'll assist me with dressing wounds, and the doctor with setting fractures. If that goes well, the doctor will probably want you in the surgery when I can't be there. Also I'm putting you in charge of stocking the drugs and medical supplies. I'll give you a basic list."

"I'll do my best." Sofya pulled back the drape.

Marie Paulette assessed Sofya's appearance. "You look quite professional in that uniform. A little too pretty perhaps, but I've found that if you conduct yourself professionally, the men will respect you." She colored faintly, as if at some personal memory. "Turn around, let me see the full effect." Sofya obliged. "You're going to need an apron. I forgot to set one out for you. Here, take this." She reached into the trunk at the foot of her cot.

During the few seconds when the trunk was open, Sofya caught a glimpse of a black book, a crucifix, and a string of wooden beads. Marie Paulette quickly closed the lid again and handed Sofya an apron.

Sofya pulled the loop of the garment over her head, and tied the strings behind her back. Meanwhile she studied the woman who would be her supervisor. She was pretty, peppy and happy. Not at all what Sofya had expected from a nun.

"Let's get started." Marie Paulette had moved to the entrance of the tent.

ON ENTERING the converted hotel, the fresh outside air, the song of birds, the warm sunlight were abruptly left behind, replaced by the stench of human waste, the smell of chloroform, and a background of low groans, now and then punctuated with screams of agony and whimpers of despair. Behind the elegantly carved reception desk sat a young girl, crocheting a piece of what appeared to be lace.

"Good afternoon, Francine," Marie Paulette placed a hand on the desk. "Any new admissions?"

"Yes. Two. And one death. I've sent in the report."

As they walked past the desk, Marie Paulette explained, "The Commune receives daily lists of the dead. Family pensions are given on the basis of these lists. The girl's job is rather slow right now. But just after a battle, when the newly wounded are arriving, her work, like ours, becomes nearly impossible. What with relatives begging to see the list of wounded and new arrivals coming in faster than she can handle. She's the only aide who can read and write."

Now they were ascending stairs. "The owner of the hotel abandoned it when Thiers's army left the city. The Commune took it over about two weeks ago when crowding at the other facilities reached crisis."

At the head of the stairs stretched a long hallway, lined on either side with tables holding supplies of medicine and bandages. The doors to what had been hotel rooms were open.

Sofya looked into a room of modest size. A small table, probably once draped with delicate French lace, was now hidden under oilcloth. The room designed to accommodate one or at the most two beds, now held eight, so close that a nursing aide, a hefty young woman, carrying drinks of water, could barely maneuver between the rows. Each bed contained a wounded man, some of them no more than boys. The thick hotel carpets were dark with blood and muck. Heavy drapes were drawn over the rooms, one small window closing out light and air.

Marie Paulette must have seen the look of shock on Sofya's face. "We put as many wounded as possible into a room, that makes it a little easier to serve them all."

Marie Paulette made her way across the crowded room to the window, where she pulled back the drapes and raised the sash, letting in a flow of light and air. The girl passing out water looked apprehensive, and Marie Paulette winked at her.

Then she returned to Sofya. "Our doctor served for years with the National Guard, and is rather set in his ways. Dark rooms for the sick, and still, quiet air, no matter how it smells. I have no authority to change the rules. However, from time to time, someone might leave a window open. As soon as the doctor sees it, he swears like the old soldier he is, and closes it again. But for a while the men have some relief."

Marie Paulette gently nudged Sofya on. "Patients with less severe injuries are put into rooms like this one." She pointed to her right. The room had no beds; simple mattresses covered the floor.

In the dark, cavelike room, Sofya saw one soldier, wracked by desperate coughing, his face inches from the bandaged head of the man next to him. Several of the men had the flushed red faces of fever.

"Have your patients been vaccinated for smallpox?" Sofya asked. She tried to put out of her mind the chances of an epidemic in this fertile ground.

"Unfortunately, the French army falls way behind the Prussian in this endeavor. And of course, many of these men were not in the regular army at all. We should separate the men with fevers from the ones with wounds, and until the last few days we tried to do that. Now we're putting men wherever there's space."

Sofya had to repress an urge to make some excuse and run. She had stood up to gunfire, she had seen ugly wounds now and then in her clinic at home, and faced contagious disease. But this . . . scolding herself for faintheartedness and gathering her nerve, she stared at Marie Paulette, who showed no fear at all.

The tour had brought them to the end of the hallway, where a beautifully carved buffet, once no doubt loaded with fine china and rich food, now bore an array of surgical devices for cutting and probing human flesh.

"There's an instrument table at the end of each hall." Marie Paulette pointed to the steel probes with some pride. "The doctor keeps a wide assortment of blades, scissors, probes and a few saws. One of your duties will be to see that the instruments are boiled after each use."

She pulled back a white enameled cover from one of a series of bowls, like chamber pots, but this one held red tissue and blood. Clearly visible was part of a man's hand, including two fingers with black hair growing on their backs, one still wearing a cheap ring. "You will also see that these containers are emptied regularly and cleaned. The women who serve as aides consider this job revolting, and you will have to be sure they do their duty regularly."

They moved on a few steps, but Sofya still stared at the bowl at the far end of the table. A background roar, generated in her own mind and body, was rising in her ears, but over it she could still hear Marie Paulette explaining that the chloroform was kept in a compartment under the table along with other drugs and ointments. The bandages were in the boxes to the right as were the lint pads. The lid had been put back on the bowl, but she had no trouble still seeing the two fingers, and the ring.

Sofya felt the room sway. Somewhere in the middle distance she could hear a man vomiting, then the voice of one of the nurses' aides, complaining about the mess. Presently the fresh, sour odor came to compete in her nostrils with older smells.

Marie Paulette gently turned her from the buffet, where no one any longer found good things to eat. "Want to sit down? Shall I help you to the outside?"

"No, I'm all right."

She handed Sofya a glass of cool water. "Still want to work here?" Her voice was gentle, but businesslike. "I'm sure with your training there are other jobs you could do for the Commune."

The reminder of what those other jobs might be was enough to strengthen Sofya. She fought back her dizziness. "I'm staying."

DURING THE SEVEN DAYS since Sofya had begun nursing, the forts of Issy and Vanves had both fallen. Injured were rushed to the city's already crowded ambulances for treatment.

Five large field tents now stood on the grass outside, surrounding those in which doctor and nurses were sometimes able to grab a little sleep. Wounded men were brought straight from the fighting to the tents. Those who survived long enough were transferred to the main building. Sofya, like Marie Paulette and the doctor, slept when they could no longer stand on their feet.

Looking over the dining room turned ward, tired and disheartened, Sofya struggled to balance a heavy tray filled with newly boiled steel instruments and clean basins. With care not to stumble, she stepped to the bedside of a soldier brought in during the night.

"It's about time you got here." The bent old doctor snarled at her. He looked up momentarily from the dressing he was changing. "Get that tray over here."

Sofya moved closer. Dropping the soiled bandage onto the floor, the doctor dipped a clean cloth in a bowl of warm water on the tray Sofya held, washed the wound, and applied a lint compress.

"Why the hell isn't there an antiseptic on this tray?" He looked up at her. "You're that jackass Jaclard's sister-in-law. At least you could use your family influence to procure our share of antiseptics. That would have made you good for something."

"Doctor Bouroche." Holding tightly to the tray helped Sofya controlled her urge to slap the man. She kept her voice steady, devoid of emotion, "if there were supplies to be had, we would have gotten them. I assure you, I filed our report."

The patient cried out as the doctor probed the wound, then began to apply a new dressing.

Sofya winced inwardly. Lint tended to stick to the sores. In the last week, she had witnessed even minor wounds go gangrenous after this treatment. A serious wound, like this man's, very likely meant death from blood poisoning.

The doctor wiped his hands on his already blood-stained apron. "Come along," he ordered.

Once in the hallway, Sofya deposited the tray on a large table filled with supplies. As she turned, she nearly bumped the doctor who stood with his arms folded over his chest. His lips set, his eyes blazing angrily.

Her fighting impulses responded to his anger, she could no longer hold her tongue. "Doctor, that wound could have been treated with warm compresses. I saw it done that way at the American ambulance. The patient would be spared a very painful and dangerous change of dressing."

Bouroche pushed his glasses back up onto the bridge of his nose, and glared at Sofya through them. "One visit to that new American ambulance and you've set yourself up as an expert in medicine. I run this ambulance, just as I ran field hospitals through the last war, and the one before that. This isn't the first time I've had to tell you to keep your suggestions to yourself. Brother-in-law or no brother-in-law, I won't stand for your insolence; I have some influence too."

Sofya flushed with anger. Not for the first time, she regretted not accepting Anyuta's offer to manage the hospital. She certainly could do better than this man.

The doctor entered the next room. Sofya didn't follow him. With a sharp command she ordered one aide to fetch the dirty dressings from the floor, another she directed to the doctor. The man didn't want an assistant, he wanted a servant. She had sent him one.

She washed her hands in a bowl of warm water placed outside the room. She felt intolerably hot, tired and exhausted. She must slip away from the sickrooms, just for a minute. She heard the cries of the boy from whom the doctor was now removing a dressing applied yesterday. She poured herself a glass of tea from the pitcher that stood next to the wash basin, and headed for the front door.

Outdoors, sitting on the front steps of the building in the sunlight, she held the cool glass to her forehead. She must learn to adopt Marie Paulette's methods of quiet defiance, avoiding useless confrontation. But somehow, it was impossible to keep quiet in the face of deadly idiocy.

She had no energy left for self-control, not when she was this exhausted.

The rattle of wheels on brick made her look up. A small cab approached. More wounded coming, no doubt; they arrived in every imaginable kind of vehicle. Putting down her glass, she raised her tired body from the steps and dragged herself toward the slowing cab.

When the door opened, she could only stand watching in dull surprise as Anyuta and Louise Michel stepped boldly out. Anyuta looked happy, vibrant and beautiful. Louise, eager and energetic, was wearing her sash and pistols.

"Sofya, I've brought Louise to see the aid station. I'm so proud of our work." Anyuta gave her sister a hug, then frowned at her in concern. "You seem very warm. Not ill, are you?"

"Just tired. Anyuta, I must talk to you. There are some changes that must be made here at the ambulance."

Anyuta didn't seem to hear her. She spoke hurriedly as the ladies headed into the makeshift hospital. "We've been working very hard on the new educational committee. I got your note, but I simply couldn't get away to see you any sooner. It's been one meeting after another—what's wrong?"

Sofya had stopped, and for a moment stood staring at her sister in disbelief. "I had forgotten," she said, "about all the meetings you must attend."

"Yes," said Anyuta vaguely, a half smile on her face, no comprehension in her eyes.

"I had forgotten, you see, because I now live in a different world. The only meetings I have are with the men who are dying here. They keep getting blown up and cut to pieces, and when they arrive here, diseases spread among them."

Anyuta had only been half listening, and now she was already droning on. "Louise always has such a good effect on the morale of the wounded." Anyuta turned to Louise as she said this. "Many have seen her on the battlefield of Neuilly and at the defense of the fort at Issy. Fighting right alongside the men."

Louise seemed to relish hearing the description. She stood dressed in a National Guard uniform, the handles of two revolvers protruding from the red sash around her waist. Her face, never pretty, had taken on a sinister hardness, making it easy to believe that this woman had enjoyed her time on the battlefield, and was ready to go back. Sofya gazed in half-feverish horror, thinking the war had done this to Louise, driven her mad.

Pushing back an overpowering feeling of tiredness, Sofya offered, "I can show you the station. Then we'll discuss the changes that must be made."

"Lead on!" said Anyuta brightly.

Sofya brought her two visitors first to a room on the ground floor where victims of stomach wounds were kept. Awful sounds of moans and groans filled the room. The three women stood just outside the doorway. "In my opinion," said Sofya in a low voice, "every one of these men will die. We're desperately short of quinine, opium and oakum for the dressings. Our requests have gone unanswered." Sofya stared at her sister bleakly.

Anyuta nodded with seeming sympathy. Then she said, "I brought Louise here to encourage the men. We don't have that much time. Take us among the men who are expected to return to battle."

"All right." Sofya stared at her sister. "I just thought you might want to know what was happening."

"Of course, dear. I can see you're doing a marvelous job."

"Marvelous!" Louise echoed. Her eyes were glittering, probing ahead as she walked.

Sofya led the visitors to a ward filled with leg and arm wound victims. "The men here have a fair chance of survival," she told the women tiredly before they entered. "At least the ones who don't require amputations. All our amputees have died of gangrene. The doctor keeps doing them, though they seem rather a waste of time."

At that moment one of the men recognized Sofya and called to her.

Sofya went to his side, and tried to put some cheerfulness into her voice. "Jacques? How are you today?"

The patient took hold of Sofya's hand. She returned the pressure of the sweating palm. The boy was the same one who had first directed her to the ambulance. Since his injury from an exploding shell, he had become her special friend. He wanted to become an engineering student. Someday, he had told her, he would make a great invention using electricity, a really efficient motor. Perhaps, someday, his invention would be on exhibit at the Crystal Palace right alongside all the wonderful inventions she'd told him about. Talking about inventions and science was the only anesthetic she could offer him.

"Sofya, Doctor Bouroche says he'll have to operate on my leg. Will you be with me then?" His eyes looked into hers.

She held his hand. "I will," she whispered. "Now meet some important members of the Commune. This is my sister, Anna Jaclard, she's responsible for establishing new military hospitals—it seems we'll need them. And I'm sure you recognize Louise Michel."

"I'm honored." the boy managed to say as he tilted his head to the two women. He was still holding onto Sofya's hand.

"You must rest and heal, so you can serve the Commune again," Louise said, briefly looking at the boy's face, then moved on to the next bed. In a hearty voice she began to tell the occupant how much his heroism was appreciated.

When Anyuta and Louise were out of earshot, Sofya leaned toward Jacques and whispered, "I'll be here tomorrow."

"Promise?"

"Promise." Sofya patted his hand and gently loosened his grip. "I must move on now." She could feel the boy's eyes follow her as she rejoined Anyuta and Louise.

Louise, in her element now, was making her way among the beds, speaking briefly to each patient.

Sofya firmly pulled her sister to one side. "Anyuta, the situation here is desperate. Just being able to keep the windows open would help. And the morphia."

"I'll see what I can do."

"And we must have trained nurses."

"What would you have us do? Hire the black crows back again?"

"What difference if they are nuns, or were? Such women are not a political threat! The policy of mass arrests is terribly wrong, Anyuta."

"Keep your voice down!' Anyuta moved to put her body between Sofya and Louise, who was still campaigning in the middle distance. "Give me the names of the trustworthy ones. Women who will put aside their nuns' garb and take up the work without religious trappings. I'll see they're released."

How am I supposed to know which nuns are politically trustworthy? Sofya hadn't raised the subject with Marie Paulette, but probably she could help. Sofya lowered her voice again. "I'll send you a list of names."

"Good." Anyuta took Sofya's arm, and the tour resumed.

When it was over, Sofya shook Louise's hand and thanked her for the visit. She implored Anyuta to use her influence to have changes made at the ambulance. Then, before saying goodbye, Sofya, feeling an overpowering need for comfort, drew herself into the arms of her sister.

"You're doing a wonderful job, Sofya," Anyuta repeated, patting So-fya's back gently. She swept a few strands of hair back from her forehead, then whispered, "I'll try to have your ideas implemented. But please, don't talk politics to anyone!"

"Believe me, Anyuta. The last thing any of us talks about in here is politics."

SOMEWHAT ENCOURAGED, Sofya returned to Jacques.

"You're much prettier than your sister." Jacques's blue eyes were staring up at her.

Sofya smiled. She knew she looked exhausted, her hair a mess, her eyes bloodshot. "I'll be with you tomorrow," she promised again.

"And we'll talk about electricity?"

"Perhaps. Perhaps about the planets and stars. When I was a student, I read some interesting theories on Saturn. There are very intriguing speculations on the shape of the rings. We'll talk about it," Sofya added smiling at him. "We'll talk about someplace far away."

"I'll be here waiting for you." Jacques winked flirtatiously.

FOR THE FIRST TIME in many days, Sofya left the hospital and its grounds. She had some money in her pocket, saved from lunches and dinners she never had time to eat. She walked hurriedly through the streets strewn with debris of fallen trees and broken glass from the recent shelling. She stopped in a nearly deserted bookstore and coaxed the proprietor into finding her a volume on astronomy. Slipping the small book into one of the large pockets of her uniform's apron, she hurried back toward the hospital.

It was just after five in the evening, she could spend a few minutes with Jacques before her next nursing shift. She turned the corner onto the street leading to the hospital.

Without warning, a deafening blast seemed to split open the clear sky above her head, from horizon to horizon. *Another shell*, she thought, in the first dazed half second following. Then: *No, a thousand shells.*

But with shells, one usually heard them coming. This might have been the end of the world, shaking the earth beneath her feet. A fraction of a second later, an unimaginable fist of wind lifted her from the ground, flattened her against the wall of the nearest building. When the wind abruptly let go, she felt herself falling. She caught at a gutter with her free hand and pressed herself against the rough bricks of the wall. Her free arm was in front of her face, glass from a thousand windows was flying in all directions, falling in a tinkling rain. A wave of intense heat made her exposed skin tingle.

Not a thunderbolt, not a shell. This was something far beyond the common events of war. If not the end of the world, then what? She waited for the next hit. It didn't come.

In a moment her ears, recovering from the blast, were filled with screams as women, their clothes in flames, ran from the remnants of the munitions factory two blocks behind her. Sofya had once visited the place with Anyuta, had seen shells, cartridges, and bombs being assembled by women recruited by the Commune.

Somehow standing on her feet again, Sofya looked around in horror. Now she could hear a rattle of rifle fire. An infantry attack? No, she realized, it must be exploding cartridges. Flames leapt from gaping openings in a building that had stood next to the factory. The heat coming from that direction was almost unbearable, two blocks away. She tried, but couldn't force herself to move. There was not a scratch on her own body, but her eyes had fixed on a bloodied, disembodied leg that lay on the pavement just before her, the leather shoe and cotton stocking neatly in place. Another body was dangling limply from the porch banister above her, blown there by the force of the blast.

A young woman walking in a daze bumped against Sofya, the woman's face red as if burned by the sun. Her arms were stretched out unnaturally away from her body, her hair was smoking, her eyes saw nothing.

Sofya gasped for breath. Her heart was pounding furiously. Finally able to move again, she started down the street toward the center of fire and devastation. Smaller blasts continued to fill the air. Before she had progressed more than a few meters, a National Guardsman grabbed her by the arm. His eyes were glaring madly.

"The munitions factory! It's sabotage!" The man held tightly to her arm. He was staring at her red cross arm band. "Thank God, you're a nurse. Help us!" He dragged her to a cart that must have been just around the corner from the blast. Mercifully, the driver had come to the scene.

The soldier was now half carrying, half dragging a woman toward the cart. Her face and arms dripped blood, large pieces of glass stuck out from the bleeding wounds. The woman was crying and pointing back frantically to the building. Sofya followed her gesture. Against a building lay the body of a child, the girl's hand clutching a container from which white milk had splattered to mix with the blood from her injured head. Sofya ran to the child, lifted the small, limp body and carried her to the cart. Beside the little girl the soldier was placing another victim, a shivering mass of burned flesh.

"There's an ambulance only a few blocks ahead!" she shouted to the soldier who now sat holding the reins. "Get us there. Fast!"

THE NEXT HOURS were a living hell. Not until well after midnight had she been relieved from tending the dying women. She'd fallen onto her cot exhausted.

A few hours later she emerged from dreamless oblivion. Her first coherent thought was that her friend Jacques must now be facing his own horror. By some miracle, the book she had bought for him was still in the pocket of her apron.

She must see Jacques. Together, before his leg was cut away, they would explore the universe. For a time, they would escape this planet's pain and madness. She hurried through the dark yard toward the ambulance and his room.

At Jacques's bedside, Marie Paulette was spreading clean sheets. She let the sheet fall floating in a jumble onto the empty bed. "When we finished with the factory women, I couldn't rest. I came in here." Her voice was just above a whisper. "Jacques's fever was climbing. He was delirious much of the time. I stayed with him."

Sofya stared at the empty bed, barely hearing the nun's words. Her own voice said, "We were going to talk about astronomy."

"Yes, he mentioned that. He spoke of you and of his mother." Marie Paulette stared into the empty space. "Like so many of the others, when he realized he was dying, he asked for a priest. And of course there's no . . . I tried to comfort him." She brushed away tears. "There's so little I can do."

Then Marie Paulette slid an arm around Sofya's shoulder. "He has gone to be at peace with the good God. At least he didn't have to endure the operation."

Sofya pulled away. She wanted none of this rationalizing, no claims that death was a blessing. Unsteady on her feet, she tightened her grip on the book she had brought for Jacques, as if the bound paper might offer support. She continued to stare in disbelief at the bed occupied only by a fluffed sheet.

She felt Marie Paulette's cool hand to her forehead. "You're burning up!" She heard Marie Paulette say gently, firmly, "Sofya, my friend, you're not well. You must rest. Go home. Go home."

Sofya was not conscious of saying anything in reply. Angry, fighting back tears, clutching her book, she made her way through the hall to the hospital entrance. Home? Where was home? More casualties were arriving, this batch more routine, not women factory workers but men and boys from the front again. She pushed herself against a wall to make way. She stared out at them, looking for Jacques, who might be coming in with this batch. But she couldn't see him. Some were hobbling on crutches, some leaning on comrades for support.

One man seemed to be staring at her in the oddest way. Then she saw that it was because the side of his face and part of his neck had been carried away by a fragment of shell. The eye on the injured half of his face hung limply from its socket. Sofya gasped and ran for the open door. Just as she reached the grass, she leaned over and was sick.

When she could straighten up, she was still clutching the book in front of her like a shield. She staggered to the walkway, keeping the hospital behind her, keeping it out of sight. She wouldn't turn around, she wouldn't stop. She must keep going. She headed toward the cool river.

Blindly she stumbled along, the wide flowing water visible to her left. Hadn't someone told her to go home? Yes, she must get home. The faces of people she passed seemed to glow green and yellow in the flickering light of the street lamps. They all grinned at her maliciously. One, unmistakably female, stepped from a bar, a bottle in her hand. The bottle's label bore mathematical symbols instead of words. The woman leaned into Sofya's face, "You'll never catch me now." Then she threw back her head and laughed wickedly.

Sofya stared, the woman's legs, bound close together in an immodestly tight golden skirt, had a strange appearance because they were really not legs at all, but unmistakably a fish's tail. The creature, the mermaid, tottered on her tail, but before she fell, a big, rough man came up behind her and seized her in a supporting arm. Turning his familiar, large-boned face to Sofya, he said in German, "Where have you been? I've been expecting you." One of his eyes fell from its socket but he pushed it back. Then he too laughed, then beckoned her to follow.

The couple disappeared back into the bar, Weierstrass carrying the mathematical mermaid. Sofya's pulse was pounding at her eardrums. Home. She must keep going. She must get home.

SHE STAGGERED nearly to the edge of the water. She hurried on, afraid to look at the shops and bars, she kept her head turned to the ever flowing river. Human bodies floated past, like small boats. She tried to count them, but she couldn't remember the French word for ten. How strange! Overhead the sky was bright with midday light, but this time at least it did not split in two from horizon to horizon. She waved goodbye to the moon.

She must have been walking for hours. She had to rest, just for a moment. She'd sit down on that bench. She stared across a garden of flowering herbs and plants. To one side, she heard the bubbling of a fountain. Not far to her right, she saw a large building, a museum or library perhaps. She would stay here.

With vague satisfaction she discovered that she was still holding a book, the one she intended to give to Jacques, close to her breast. Her thoughts started and stopped, existing only in fragments, like dismembered bodies, no longer containing any real life. Carriages with wounded were going by, mixed with the normal, healthy, walking movements of the unwounded, the men and women on whom the war seemed to have little or no effect. They were still exchanging small talk. She must be watching a play.

For Sofya there was no time. Hours may have passed. Her tongue, too large for her mouth, repeatedly slid over her cracked lips, her throat ached with each swallow, she listened to the bubbling water that was just out of reach.

Someone was touching her arm, someone talking to her. Someone was sitting next to her. She turned her head.

"Vladimir?" she whispered, half questioningly.

"Sofya, thank God I saw you! I might have missed you altogether. I was walking . . . what's happened?"

"I want to go home, Vladimir." Her voice was a plaintive Russian whisper. "But I don't know where home is." The words seemed to come out as if someone else were speaking them.

"Vladimir." She reached for his hand. "I saw Weierstrass."

"You saw Weierstrass?"

"Yes. Just now. I must go back to Berlin. Please, Vladimir, help me."

He held her hand gently, stroking her fingers. "You're burning up with fever, Sofya. I'll keep you safe, my love, my dear. I'll help you do whatever you want."

CHAPTER TWENTY-FIVE

1871 ✧ *Berlin-Paris*

In Berlin, no bombs burst, no squads searched door-to-door for slackers. If there were no rats to be seen, it was because of cleanliness, not because they had been eaten.

Vladimir was sure he would not have long to wait until the capital of France regained stability. During their first week in Berlin, only sketchy reports of the continued fighting, the decline of the Commune's resistance, appeared in the German papers. Toward the end of May the dispatches grew longer and more frightening. The Republican forces had entered Paris, still meeting some determined but disorganized resistance. With utter defeat staring them in the face, the Communards had topped their previous record of stupidity by shooting all their hostages. Gradually regaining control of the whole city, the Republicans were intent on matching and surpassing the violence of the Communards. Blood was flowing.

VLADIMIR NERVOUSLY FINGERED the Berlin paper spread before him.

Julia, who had been watching in silence for some time, at last burst out. "You can't keep this news from her, Vladimir. You must tell her today that Victor and Anyuta are on the list of prisoners. She doesn't read the daily reports only because she's afraid of what she'll see. She trusts you to tell her if anything like this should happen."

"I don't know if she trusts me or not." Vladimir looked sad. "She's scarcely looked at me these past four weeks."

"She finds a refuge in mathematics."

"And with Weierstrass."

"He is reassuring, that's all. You wanted her to recover, didn't you? Of course you did."

"Of course. Just as quickly as possible," Vladimir protested.

"You wanted to be the agent of that recovery."

"I suppose I did," Vladimir admitted. He couldn't lie to Julia.

"Don't be offended by her actions, Vladimir. She can't help it. Mathematical ideas are like quicksand for her." Julia's soft voice drifted to him.

"Yes, I know what effect they have on her. How well I know." Vladimir crumpled the paper and threw it to the floor. Standing up, he stretched, rubbed his face with both hands, and made a decisive announcement. "I'm going back to Paris, Julia. I should never have left. I should have just put Sofya on a train and sent her back here to her beloved Weierstrass."

Julia's eyes twinkled and her voice was sweet. "But then, sir, you wouldn't be in possession of the Russian proofs for an edition of Darwin's *The Descent of Man*. They were waiting for you here when you got back."

"Well, the printer had no address for me but general delivery in Berlin." Vladimir's voice took on some enthusiasm. "With luck, I'll have the book ready for publication by fall. I can certainly use the money it'll make. I mean to take the pages back to Paris with me for one final review."

"A good idea. And, when you tell Sofya about her sister, I'm sure that she'll be going with you too."

WHEN VLADIMIR SHOWED SOFYA the list of Versailles prisoners, she sobbed hysterically. He took her in his arms and tried to comfort her, meanwhile explaining the plan he had begun to formulate. "To do Anyuta any good, we must try to make contacts in very high places, military contacts. But I don't have those kinds of friends. I may not be able to reach the right person in time."

Sofya looked up, wiped her eyes, and said solemnly, "My father knows military men."

"Would he help?" Vladimir gripped Sofya's shoulders and held her a little away from him. "He's disowned Anyuta. And he's nearly disowned you for your part in her deceptions. And I'm not much in favor either, I haven't repaid last year's loan. I wouldn't blame him if he's washed his hands of the lot of us."

"Vladimir!" Sofya's voice expressed exasperation. "Anyuta's life is in grave danger! Of course, Father will help."

Vladimir nodded. "All right. Send your father a telegraph immediately. The idea is to explain, but only in some cryptic way, that Anyuta needs his help in Paris. He probably suspects she's in trouble, he may even have seen the same Berlin newspaper, so you won't need to say much. Tell him to meet us as soon as possible at the hotel in Saint Denis, the one we stayed in before entering Paris."

Sofya immediately started composing the telegram.

"And start packing," Vladimir added. "I'll get our train tickets."

ON THE TENTH of June, almost exactly one month after the day of their departure from Paris, Sofya and Vladimir arrived again in Saint Denis. For a few moments it was possible to believe that they had been on some hopelessly misdirected train, arrived at an impossible destination. On the platform they stepped into a festive, vacationlike atmosphere, moving among well-dressed crowds as foreign as themselves, and in a mood grotesquely out of place.

Sofya drew back against a wall. "What is this? I don't understand."

Speechlessly, Vladimir pointed at flyers and posters on the station wall. Each promised, for a modest fee, an escorted tour of the scenes of war. See the ruins of the Hôtel de Ville by moonlight!

LODGING WAS DIFFICULT to find amid the bustle of tourism, but in the end proved not impossible. The next morning, Sofya and Vladimir's train trip into Paris was filled with confusion. Great numbers of people were struggling in and out of the devastated city, making all travel extremely slow and difficult. Many who had fled during the Commune were returning. Others, mostly Commune sympathizers, were trying to leave, fearful of arrest if they remained. Sofya and Vladimir disembarked at St. Lazare Station.

Somehow Vladimir was able to get a cab. The enterprising driver, like many others, had decorated his vehicle to accommodate the new rush of tourists. A pair of opera glasses securely fastened to the side of the vehicle by a long leather strap rested on the seat beside her. A hurriedly published flyer the cabbie had handed Sofya, "Through the Ruins," lay on the floor. Now, in Montmartre, the territory where the Communards had found most of their support, the streets were only half familiar. The scenes of destruction forced themselves upon their minds. Here was a stream of water from a broken main. Evidently it had flowed unchecked for days, and had begun to carve itself a riverbed among the cobblestones; an elderly woman, intent on filling a cooking pot, bent over a miniature waterfall. Recent rains had turned all unpaved soil to mud. Many buildings lay in ruins, and those still standing were streaked by rain and sooty smoke from their demolished neighbors. Sofya caught a glimpse of an unexploded shell, now the centerpiece of some game among a group of ragged children. Debris was everywhere. Leafless tree trunks, broken and half burned, lined unshaded avenues.

There was a twisted piece of grillwork, torn from the porch of some fancy house, lying like some giant pretzel in the street. Deserted barricades still blocked some streets. Flies were everywhere. Blotches of fresh paint marked some walls, evidently where revolutionary slogans had been eliminated.

"Vladimir."

"Yes, I see," he said in Russian. "Damn them." Atop the last half barricade, two dead bodies were still visible. The corpses had been lightly sprinkled with lime, the victors' concession to humanity. Over a burned archway, a large plaque still proclaimed to all, in mockery: Liberté, Fraternité, Égalité.

A crisp volley of small arms fire sounded from one of the side streets. "What was that?" Vladimir asked the driver, in French.

"What it sounds like, sir." The driver turned back briefly, and shrugged philosophically. "People are suspected of setting fires, or of who knows what. They are taken out into the street and shot. And there their bodies lie."

An omnibus pulled by a team of six horses, tourist faces gawking from every window, rumbled by in the other direction.

Sofya suddenly put a handkerchief to her mouth. She had caught a sudden whiff of unbearable stench, and she feared she would vomit. Suddenly the nightmare of the hospital was back with her, full force. Vladimir was at her side, holding her hand, murmuring words meant to be reassuring. She told herself forcefully that she was not going to see the mermaid again, no, not here and now. She was going to find Anyuta and help her, and then get out. There was another lime-sprinkled heap of decomposing corpses, looking like a vision of madness but all too real.

AS THEY APPROACHED the Rue de Rosiers, the street where they could hope to find Anyuta's cottage still standing, Vladimir stopped the cab and paid the driver, who made no offer to wait.

Vladimir held tightly to Sofya's arm as they advanced on foot, across a pavement littered with bricks and broken glass. A ragged, staring, mumbling, man came stumbling out of nowhere to bump into her, then cringed away when Vladimir raised a threatening arm.

Save for a few broken windows, the house where Anyuta and Victor had spent their last days of freedom was still intact, the first reassuring sight they had seen. The front door stood open, and there was no one about. More glass crunched underfoot.

Vladimir entered without bothering to knock, and Sofya followed on his heels. A whirlwind seemed to have gone through the rooms, capsizing furniture, scattering and breaking everything. But at least there were no bodies and no blood.

"I hoped," Sofya admitted weakly, "that we would find her here. Even if her name was on the list. Lists can be wrong."

Vladimir tried to sound hearty and reassuring. "Naturally, if she is free, this would be the very last place she'd stay, knowing that they might be coming after her."

"Anyuta. Oh Anyuta!"

"I was hoping we might find some clue here, that she might leave some indication of where she was going. I had to look. Now we can get organized, and down to the serious business of finding her."

Finding an unbroken bottle of ink, he dabbed a message on the wall, in Russian. "So if she or Victor do come back, they'll know we're in Paris and where to find us."

"You at least are still thinking. I don't know if I can."

"You can. You will, you must."

VLADIMIR DIRECTED THE CAB to a café on the Avenue des Champs-Elysées. The signs of the horror of war had already been swept away by the energetic businessmen on the west side of the city. Cafés, shops and entertainments awaited those with time and money for the frivolous.

Vladimir ordered two cups of tea. "If you're feeling well enough, I suggest the two of us split up temporarily. With our papers to prove we're tourists recently from Berlin, I think we'll be safe enough from the Republicans. I will go back to the Jardin des Plantes, the museum, and see if the people I know there can tell me anything useful, or put me in touch with someone who can. The scientists were more or less neutral during the upheaval. Some of them may have contacts in the Republican government."

"I'll go to the hospital where I worked." Sofya lowered her voice. "My supervisor, Marie Paulette, is the only person I know in Paris who isn't now classified as a criminal. She meets people from all levels of society. She may be willing to help me." Sofya drank the steaming beverage, hot enough to cause her pain and the beginning of a small blister. "I owe the woman an explanation and an apology for my sudden departure."

"We'll meet back at the hotel." Vladimir took a small roll of bills from his pocket and handed them to her. "You may need extra money for bribes. Just be discreet."

"I sincerely doubt that Marie Paulette will be impressed by money."

"Probably not by the small amount that we can offer—all right, I'm sorry, I'm sure she's a good, holy woman." Secretly he was pleased to observe that Sofya had not lost her ability to assume good in others.

TENTS FILLED WITH INJURED BOYS no longer checkered the lawn. Only the patches of dead grass showed where they had been. Even the tents of Marie Paulette and Doctor Bouroche were gone. The red cross flag waving before the front door identified the hospital. The windows were open now, a sign of new administration, the light curtains billowing with the summer breeze.

Sofya walked hesitantly to the front desk. "Is Marie Paulette here?"

A pretty young woman in the black habit of a Sister of Charity looked up. "Sister is in her office. May I tell her who's calling?"

"Tell her . . . tell her it's the woman with whom she shared a tent last month."

The receptionist looked at Sofya quizzically.

"Sofya!" Marie Paulette's voice called before the young nun had emerged from behind the desk. "I'm so glad to see you! Come into my office."

Sofya turned to behold a familiar face above a long black gown, below a huge, white-trimmed wimple, just like the one worn by the receptionist.

The nun turned back to the woman at the desk. "Sister, please have the novice bring tea for us, and a few of those cakes we had left from luncheon."

Marie overrode Sofya's protest that she was not hungry, and embraced her warmly. "It's nothing, food is plentiful again. I'm so glad to see you looking well. I've been so worried, the last time I saw you, you were quite ill."

"Yes, I'm sorry to have left you so abruptly."

"The important thing is that you are well now. And I'm so glad to see you." Marie Paulette closed the door of her small office behind them. Motioning Sofya to a chair, the nun returned to her seat behind a simple oak desk. The curtain of a single window fluttered in the breeze. "Of course the changes since you left have been enormous. Now, I'm in charge of dismantling this hospital. The building will be returned to the owner as soon as we're able to relocate all the wounded."

"Marie," Sofya started hesitantly, "I'm here to ask a favor."

"But of course. What can I do?"

"I don't know where else to turn. My sister and her husband have been arrested." She broke off abruptly at the sound of the door opening.

A white-robed novice entered the room, to set down a tray of tea and cakes on one corner of the desk. Just behind her came the burly figure of an officer of the Republican military police.

Taking brief notice of Sofya, the foreign tourist, he absently bowed to her, then gave Sister Marie an informal salute. "Sister, we have checked the roster of your remaining patients' names. No one else there that we want, as far as I can tell."

"Thank you, colonel." The voice of the nun behind the desk was neutral.

"Naturally I don't suppose all these young men were really hurt in accidents, though they may have told you so. We'll be back, if new evidence comes to light. This time we mean to make a thorough job of rooting out the murderous scum—right, Sister?"

The last words were directed, with a kind of ferocious jocularity, to the novice.

"Oh, yes sir—yes sir!" She stuttered her reply, and Sofya, with a sudden sense that the mermaid had once more appeared before her, looked intently for the first time at the figure in white. A moment later the officer was gone.

"Anyuta!" and the sisters were in each others' arms.

When Sofya finally recalled that she and Anyuta were not alone, she looked around for Marie Paulette. The nun, a wide smile on her face, was still sitting at her desk. "Pull up another chair, and sit, please, sit." She laughed merrily. "That is, if you can let go of each other for a moment."

Sofya sat in amazed silence as Anyuta explained how several days ago she had come to the hospital, tattered, exhausted, frightened, fresh from prison and in need of food and first aid. It was the only possible place of refuge she could think of. She had been arrested after fighting on the barricades, among a band of women led by Louise Michel.

Holding Anyuta's hand tightly, Sofya murmured her joy that her sister was not in prison, her apologies for having left so suddenly.

Anyuta did not seem to hear. Retelling the Commune's last hours had thrown her into a kind of trance. "Do you know where Victor is? My Victor." She kept looking from Sofya to Marie Paulette, and back again. "Has there been word? Sofya, Marie, tell me, where is my Victor?"

"Yes, Anna, yes. We'll find him." Marie Paulette reached across the desk to hold Anyuta's hands. "Now you must calm yourself. We'll take care of you."

Raising her head, the nurse whispered to Sofya, "She's fine most of the time. I've seen this before, in survivors of battle, of abuse and torture. A kind of hysteria triggered by one word or thought. Anyuta is able to recover quickly."

"Victor, Victor must be helped." Anyuta whimpered, then covered her face and burst into tears. But in a few moments she was quiet again, her eyes staring blankly.

Sofya was decisive. "Marie Paulette, I can't thank you enough for what you've done. But now I want to take Anyuta back to my hotel. I'm certain I can get her to safety from there."

The Sister thought about it and nodded. "I think that's wise. I don't know how long we could keep her safe here. If she should have an episode, like the one you just witnessed, while one of the policemen happened to be present, well, that would be very difficult behavior to explain in a novice. Or if my superiors in the Order should discover her . . ." She let the sentence die away.

"I can't thank you enough . . ." Sofya began again.

"Nor I you," Marie interrupted. "I remember your efforts to help us, myself and my sisters, when the Commune ruled. It seemed only the Christian thing to do, to try to return the favor."

"God bless you," Sofya heard herself blurting out. That must have come from some deep well of her childhood.

"Thank you. Now to practical problems," Marie went on briskly. "You may of course be stopped between here and your hotel, and I doubt you have two sets of legal papers. Besides, a single novice traveling anywhere, even with another woman in street clothing, would draw too much attention." She sighed and came to a decision. "I'll get a novice habit for you, too, Sofya."

Sofya's eyes met those of Marie Paulette. In a moment the two women were laughing outrageously.

"May we meet again in saner times, Sofya!" Marie Paulette hugged her warmly, and left her with her sister.

IN THE PRIVACY of their hotel room, Anyuta again insisted on speaking of the last hours of the resistance. She had fought at the barricades, seen her friends wounded and killed beside her. She had held a rifle in her hands, and shot men down with it. She had watched a massive street execution by the Republicans, women and children lined against a wall along with captured soldiers, all of them shot.

Later, after she had seen Victor taken away from the fallen barricade, she had tried to follow behind the prisoners. A soldier had spotted her, and arrested her. Despite the evidence of gunpowder on her fingers, she had admitted nothing. After hours, or perhaps it was days, she could not be sure, she was released; simply turned back out on the street.

Sofya listened with horror. Evidently the reports reaching the outside world had not been exaggerated. The Parisian papers were boasting as many as ten thousand people executed by firing squads during the first week of Republican reoccupation. Nearly thirty-four thousand people arrested, and some twenty-five thousand still being held.

Exhausted, Anyuta rose from the bed, insisting she must go back into the city, in search of Victor.

Sofya pulled her sister back. But she could only quiet her by swearing a solemn oath that she and Vladimir would take up the search.

When at last she was convinced that Anyuta had fallen into a deep sleep, Sofya left her sister's bedside. Without fully closing the bedroom door, she made her way to the living area and the comfort of the cushioned chair.

Vladimir sat across from her, rubbing his forehead. "Sofya, Anyuta must be gotten out of France as quickly as possible. They'll realize her release was a blunder and start searching for her."

"I understand." Sofya sighed, pushing a curl of hair from her sweating forehead. "I've convinced Anyuta that she has no hope of finding Victor herself, and that you and I will not leave Paris until Victor is free."

"We'd need a lot of luck to fulfill that promise," Vladimir shrugged. "A more realistic goal is to find out where Victor is being held and what the Republicans plan on doing with him. I suspect that if we don't get him out, he'll either be shot or sent to prison in New Caledonia. I heard that's where Louise Michel is bound for."

Sofya shuddered slightly. "We're definitely not mentioning anything like that to Anyuta."

"No. But where to send her now? That's the question."

Sofya thought aloud. "Russia is out of the question. They're fanatical about keeping out anyone from Paris who might possibly have been in the insurrection. She'd be stopped at the border, and sent back here to a firing squad."

"What about Germany?" Vladimir mused.

"All indications are that Communards will have no friendly welcome in Germany." Sofya sighed. "Thank God, Julia was able to convince Weierstrass that I've gone off to tend a sick relative. If the truth were ever known in Germany, my academic career would vanish, even if I escaped arrest."

"You should have thought of that a month ago." When Sofya ignored that, Vladimir added, "What about Zurich or London? I heard André Leo and her friend Benoit Melon are safe in Switzerland. Of course, the British are the most obliging about people who seek sanctuary. And I have friends there who would shelter Anyuta."

"Probably London is our best choice." Sofya tried to make her tired brain think. "But I'm sure Anyuta would prefer to stay with her own friends. Karl Marx is there, of course."

"Yes, writing his endless pamphlets. I suppose he's in a huff because the Communards refused to take his orders from afar."

"Actually Anyuta, in one of her calmer moments, told me Marx is helping settle refugees. Among others, Elizabeth Dmietrieff. Anyuta might be willing to go there."

"She'd better be. All right. It's London, on your passport, with your identity as a student. I'll get the ticket." Vladimir started toward the door.

JUNE WAS DRAWING to an end. Sofya lay on the divan, her tired feet resting on the cushioned arm. She had spent another morning waiting in government offices and checking for information with Marie Paulette. Victor seemed to have disappeared from the face of the earth. She stared at the ceiling above her, counting the cracks. She wondered if it was worth the effort to go to lunch.

A knock on the door interrupted useless thoughts. A hotel pageboy reported that there were people in the lobby who wanted to talk to her. Hurriedly Sofya straightened her dress and hair. Perhaps one of Vladimir's contacts had found out something about Victor. With anticipation tempered by past disappointments, she followed the boy downstairs.

"Mama! Papa!" Sofya exclaimed as she caught sight of her mother and father, standing beside a small mound of luggage. Tearfully she hugged them both.

Sofya led her parents to her rooms. Not until the luggage had been brought up, and the three were alone in the apartment, did Sofya tell them that Anyuta was safely in London. Victor in all likelihood was in the Savory prison.

Father, greatly relieved, praised Sofya for her quick thinking, and promised to arrange for the replacement of her passport.

The remaining problem of Victor dampened the joy of celebration.

Unless Victor's freedom could be somehow achieved, there was no reason to think that Anyuta would remain in safety.

Father and Mother were sitting next to each other on the divan, as Sofya prepared three glasses of sherry. The room was quiet, when Vladimir walked in. Father sprang to his feet and started thanking Vladimir, praising him for keeping Sofya safe and for helping Anyuta. Impulsively, Father hugged him. No less demonstratively, mother was at Vladimir's side. How glad she was that Vladimir was her son-in-law!

Vladimir taken by surprise, quickly recovered himself. At the parents' insistence, Vladimir again related what had been done for Anyuta.

The younger couple tried to comfort the elders by explaining how much Anyuta and Victor loved each other, and reminded them that Victor and Anyuta had been truly married, under the laws of the Commune. That those laws were not recognized by Russia or by France was a mere legality. Victor must be considered one of the family.

The room was silent. Mother wiped her eyes with a small lacy handkerchief. Father stared at his clasped hands. Then, breaking the solemn mood, Mother gently reminded Father that they had not yet acquired a room.

Sofya watched in startled silence as Vladimir offered Father and Mother his room. There was no hope of their getting their own suite in this overcrowded hotel.

Father began explaining that their delay had been caused by a necessity of obtaining certain papers before leaving Petersburg. Father had come with letters of introduction from important Russian diplomats requesting he be granted the privileges of an *agent extraordineire* of the Tsar.

As Vladimir moved his things from the bedroom he had been occupying into Sofya's room, he commended Father on his foresight. Father accepted Vladimir's compliment graciously, and began moving his things into the room Vladimir was vacating. With weightier matters on his mind, the general seemed oblivious to the fact that his daughter and son-in-law had been occupying separate bedrooms.

But Mother stared in bewilderment, first at Vladimir who was carrying his clothing to Sofya's room, then at Sofya who felt her face growing warmer under Mother's glare.

FATHER ASSIGNED MOTHER the task of striking up acquaintances among the other guests. Someone among the refugees might drop a useful piece of information. This was a chore she relished and performed superbly.

Vladimir brought Father up to date on the local political situation. Sofya had another message from Sister Marie: Several reports suggested Victor was still at the Savory prison, and that he was alive.

"I'm going to the very top," Father announced abruptly. "I'll get a hearing with old Thiers himself."

"Is that possible?" Vladimir stared at him with a mixture of disbelief and admiration.

"We'll see. Actually, I've met the man, and we're both old war horses."

"You've met him?" Sofya was dumbfounded.

"Several times, on state occasions, here in France and back in Russia. It's a matter of whether he remembers me at all, and what impression he retains. I'll just have to try."

FATHER RETURNED FROM HIS VISIT with Thiers, and waved aside the first eager questions. "Wait. Let me tell the story once, and tell it to all three of you."

The four family members assembled in the sitting room. Father sank down wearily in a chair, still in the uniform he had put on for the occasion, his neck conspicuously adorned by the ribbon supporting his precious Order of St. Ann medal.

"Well. Things aren't too different here from at home. I discreetly mentioned Victor's name and my 'personal regard' for him. The old war horse nodded and commented that a pardon for such an active leader of the Commune would be out of the question. I agreed instantly, and we went on to other topics. When he pushed a box of cigars toward me, I reached out to take one and at the same time dropped an envelope, a nice thick one, on his desk. When he pulled the cigars back to his side, the envelope went with it."

"But he gave you no promise?" Mother was anxious.

"Officially nothing. That's not how these things are managed. We went on talking of old times, and the difficult present. He went to the sideboard to pour us each a brandy, and had a chance to peek into my little gift. After that he called in an aide and asked him a few questions, and when the man was gone again Thiers let me know that tomorrow some prisoners from Savory were to be transferred to a different prison. He said he was somewhat concerned, because the route they were taking led down a certain busy street, right past an exhibition hall, which he took care to name. Escapes, he said, were possible and even likely under such conditions. 'But what can one do?' he concluded. 'The army has so many responsibilities.' "

"Will he keep his part of the bargain?" Vladimir wanted to know.

Father looked at him sourly. "People soon stop paying bribes to one who gets a reputation for cheating."

MINGLING WITH THE LARGE VERSAILLES CROWD, assembled for what was evidently the opening day of some kind of artistic exhibition, Sofya tried not to stare down the street. The doors of the exhibit hall were opening now, the crowd starting to push its way in. Sofya had all she could do to resist the flow of people pushing forward. Deftly she maneuvered to keep her position on the edge of the throng nearest the street.

In a moment, she heard loud military voices, shouting orders to civilians to stand back. Sofya kept her position. More than one hundred tired, dirty, unshaven men, stumbling in a loose formation four or five abreast, were filing past. Their sunken eyes were staring at the ground. Soldiers scattered around the periphery of the mass herded it forward at a steady pace. A few of the exhibition goers cursed at the interruption, but no one wanted to be reminded of the war.

Her eye fell on a tattered, bearded figure, slumped at the very end of the procession. Victor. Somehow Anyuta's husband seemed to have become invisible to the nearest soldier, the last guard supposed to be bringing up the rear. That guard had actually stepped ahead of Victor now, cursing the other prisoners to keep them moving steadily forward, all eyes to the front.

Before Victor could well begin to wonder what was happening, Sofya was at his side, walking along with him. With bold familiarity she took his arm, slowed his steps, guided him across the pavement on a different course. No guards looked back. A couple of passersby were staring, but what incentive did they have to become involved?

The mass of prisoners was already far ahead, now almost out of sight along the busy street.

In a low voice Sofya began to murmur words of encouragement to the man beside her, who still had said nothing, had scarcely looked at her. After a few agonizing attempts at getting his attention, he grunted back a sound of recognition.

A small store, a tobacconist, stood near the exhibit entrance. Sofya pulled Victor toward it, and quickly the two of them were inside.

The owner, his cooperation already purchased, looked up nervously but said nothing. The couple walked straight through, beyond a curtain to the back room, where Vladimir was waiting, to grab the dazed Victor and start unbuttoning his shirt. "We must get you into different clothes." Turning to Sofya, he demanded, "Did anyone take notice?"

"A couple stared." Sofya was shaking now with nerves. "I don't think they're going to raise any alarm."

"That's good. Versailles crowds have a reputation for anything but generosity to Communard prisoners."

"Perhaps even they have had their fill of brutality." Sofya looked at the ruins of what had once been the dashing Victor.

Too stunned and exhausted to utter a word, Victor mechanically changed into the civilian clothing Vladimir had brought. Food and drink were ready as well, and when he was dressed he fell upon them hungrily.

"We are going to the railroad station," said Vladimir. "Here's a ticket to Geneva. And here's my passport. You'll have to be a Russian, a more or less respectable Russian, and only for a few days. Language won't be a problem, all upper class Russians speak French fluently; some prefer it to Russian." He pushed the papers toward Victor. "Go ahead, I'll have a new one soon. It's all arranged."

Victor hesitated, then reached out to take the papers. "Thank you," he said. He seemed to taste the words, as if they were unfamiliar. "Anna?" he asked at last.

"Safe in London," Sofya told him. "Here is her address. Send her a wire when you reach Switzerland."

Victor stuffed one more paper into the inner pocket of his new jacket. "Where will you be?" he asked her.

"Back in Berlin," she promised fervently. "Studying, as hard as I can, as soon as I can manage it. There is a doctoral degree that I must have."

"Thank you," Victor said again, still practicing.

THE TRAIN TO GENEVA had pulled out, and another one was loading. Some of its passengers would land eventually in Berlin, others in Warsaw, and still others in the strange, remote lands even farther east.

Sofya, having seen her parents aboard, and with one hand on the car herself, turned to Vladimir. "*Spaseeba*," she said. "*Spaseeba za fsyo.*"

"*Pazhalsta*, little sparrow. You are always welcome to everything."

Forcing a cheerful tone, she began, "I know you want to stay in Paris for a time."

"Yes. For a time." Vladimir hesitated, then repeated the explanation he had given her before. "There's a lot of work yet to be done with the

Cuvier collection. I'll be gathering material for my dissertation."

"I know, we've decided on our plan. It's just that right now, parting seems so painful."

Vladimir covered her hand with his. "My darling, the sooner we each finish our doctoral work, the sooner we can start our life together, really together."

"When will I see you, Vladimir?"

"I'm not certain. The work here in Paris may take some time. Just as soon as I'm finished, I'll rush back to Jena in search of an advisor for my dissertation. When that detail is settled, perhaps we can arrange a meeting."

"That could be months."

"Sofya, you won't be alone. Julia will be with you. You'll be with people you really love—Julia, Weierstrass and your mermaid."

"And you?"

"I'll come to you. Just as soon as I can."

"Vladimir!"

"Rest for a while. Get well. And then work like the devil."

"Won't you even ask me to stay with you?"

"You can't stay in Paris." He let his eyes roam around the station, the chattering tourists. "All this," he added, vaguely. Then, "I'm very tired. I suppose you can believe that, I'm very tired? It would be too much for me to go on with the deception. Really too much. Surely you see that? I must have some time to think, to work. You may not have noticed, but I have trouble doing that when you're around." His voice softened. "I know you don't mean to be disruptive, but it seems there's always a crisis of one sort or another."

She nodded, slowly. Tears were forming in her eyes.

"Take care, my little revolutionary." He touched her cheek gently.

Suddenly, surprising her, he pulled her close and kissed her fiercely. A moment later he had torn himself away, and vanished in the crowd. The way her tears were flowing, it was hopeless to even try to look for him.

CHAPTER TWENTY-SIX

December 1872 ⚜ *Berlin*

Crash!

The big clock slid down the wall.

Sofya watched with shock as fragments of glass along with metal wheels and springs spilled to the floor and rolled to her feet. The heavy book she'd just thrown at the wall bounced from the impact, flapping its covers and pages like a wounded bird, to go skidding across the private desk of her mentor, Professor Karl Weierstrass. A well of blue ink toppled, and so did one of black, sending twin floods to defile fine wood and precious papers. Sliding on, the book fell at last with a thud on the fine carpet of the professor's study.

"Sofya!" Karl's bright blue eyes, unencumbered by glasses, were wider than she had ever seen them. The big, burly mathematician stared at his prize student in horror and disbelief. He had started up from his chair, but was frozen in mid-movement, his athletic body bent as if he were about to cringe behind his desk. As if he feared she had been trying to hit him with the book.

Well, maybe she had been, maybe he deserved it. Right between the eyes!

She straightened, small fists clenched, refocusing her anger. "Karl, you can't mean my research paper has to be thrown away!" Sofya could hear her own voice going up and up, out of control, as she stood before her mentor's desk. At the moment, there seemed to be nothing else worth throwing within her reach.

"I'm afraid there's nothing else to do." The big man's voice was hollow and apologetic. "Hermann Schwarz's paper contains the same results."

"Damn it, Karl! There must be some way to save my work!" Her mentor was the world's leading mathematical analyst, yet she, Sofya Kovalevskaya, a stubborn twenty-two-year-old, strong-willed Russian female with only four years of substantial mathematical training, somehow found the audacity to challenge his word.

Now Karl lowered himself into his chair, absently pushing it back to a safe distance from his dripping desk. There he sat slowly folding and unfolding his hands, his eyes down, never meeting hers. He cast one side glance at the broken clock, and shook his head. The job of cleaning up could wait.

At last he said, "We'll start again on another problem."

She couldn't put aside her rage, not yet. "It is wrong, wrong, wrong, and it is damnably unfair! After a year of intense preparation, to get to a point where I can do research. Then another half year on that minimal surface problem. Now I'm supposed to throw away all my work and start over! Karl, I wanted that paper to serve as my dissertation. I want a doctorate!"

"Sofya, your work was certainly of dissertation quality." Now Karl's voice grew agitated. "We've been through all this before. There's no guarantee that you'll ever be granted a degree, no matter how outstanding your work. But the degree only has importance if you're intent on joining a university faculty, something no woman ever has managed. So, you must concentrate on establishing your reputation as an independent researcher. There I am sure you will do first-rate work, and the bigots cannot stop you."

Sofya felt her rage abating. Karl truly wanted to protect her, to help her find her way. In a voice that no longer screamed she asked, "Is there no hope of saving the research I've done?"

"Your work on that paper taught you how to do mathematical research. Your time was not wasted, but any hopes for its publication I'm afraid are gone." Weierstrass shrugged big shoulders. "Schwarz's paper is already in the hands of the reviewers. It will be published within a month." He picked up from his desk a paper dripping blue ink, looked at it uncertainly for a moment, then dropped it in the wastebasket. Now at last he looked at her. "He has written an excellent paper, Sofya."

"Of course he has!" Her anger flared again. "For God's sake, Karl, he was one of your star students! He attended your lectures and undoubtedly took excellent notes! He's had over ten years to digest ideas I first encountered just last year. Of course, you point out topics for further study, for research, to all your students." Now, it was she who couldn't allow their eyes to meet. "What an ironic twist of fate that Schwarz set out to tackle the problem, just as I did." She turned her back. She could feel a huge sob developing somewhere, deep in her chest, and struggled not to let it escape. She had invested so much time, sacrificed so much of her life, worked so incredibly hard to produce this paper. From sheer frustration she began to cry.

Karl's chair creaked, and in a moment his arm was around her shoulders. "Such coincidences happen in science, Sofya. You mustn't take it so hard."

"But I could have beaten him." She turned and buried her face in Karl's strong, comforting chest.

His arms enfolded her, and he stroked her hair soothingly. "It's my fault," he murmured. "My fault. I shouldn't have made you write and rewrite, polish every phrase, follow every possible implication of every minor statement. If I'd let you publish a month ago, you'd have the honors now."

Slowly she pulled back from him. She brushed at the spots of tears she'd left on his shirt. "Yes, and if I hadn't spent four months away from Berlin last year, the paper would have been completed months ago. I'm the one who really caused the delay."

Karl had pulled out a silk handkerchief, with which he dabbed tentatively at her cheeks. "Your duty was to your sister in her illness. You yourself were ill. Thank God it wasn't serious."

Sofya sighed. She grabbed the handkerchief and used it, for the tears had started again. She could never tell Karl the truth about those lost months. Nor that her illness had been a mental and physical exhaustion brought on by living through the horrors of war. And she shuddered at the price her participation in the Commune, if known, might cost. To the French government, Communards were criminals. Across Europe they were being hunted down and extradited to France to be shot, imprisoned or exiled to the tropical hellhole of New Caledonia.

"I'm sorry about the clock," she said in a small voice, "and the spilled ink."

"Never mind that." Karl reached for her hands, gripping them firmly, one in each of his, as if to form a solid connection by which his strength might flow to her. "We'll start again with another problem."

WEIERSTRASS, HATLESS and coat open despite the cold December fog and breezes, walked briskly along the wooded paths of Tiergarten. His university lecture had gone exceedingly well, one of the better students asking a question that had started thoughts rumbling through his brain like a steam engine.

He wished Sofya had been present, so that he could discuss the student's comments with her. How stupid of the authorities to deny her entry to his classes! Now he'd have to wait until their Sunday meeting to hear her views on the thoughts racing through his brain.

He took a deep breath. He needed open air, the feel of nature to determine the most profitable direction for these new thoughts. Only when he'd tired his brain with the dancing equations, and his body with walking, would he head for his favorite beer hall, a fashionable meeting place frequented by the university's professors and more affluent graduate students.

"MORE STOUT, Herr Professor Weierstrass?" A meticulous waiter, white towel across his left arm, inquired. The beer garden boasted polished oak tables, a spotless floor, wood paneled walls, and good food. A chalkboard listing the names of frequent customers covered most of one wall. Weierstrass's name stood at the top, and unlike many others was followed by no count of unpaid beers.

"Not yet, Ludwig. Oh, tabulate these last three on the board for me." Karl looked at his stein, still half full. The drink had freed his mind of equations, but replaced them with visions of his favorite student, along with the beginning of a deep melancholy. After her disappointing experience with the Schwarz paper, Sofya had come to their meetings with an air of moodiness and withdrawal. She looked pale, almost to the point of illness. She worked with her usual intense effort, but she was brooding and unhappy and nothing he said or did relieved her agony.

Karl glanced around at the room in which he'd spent so many happy hours, often in the company of his favorite students, all except the most favorite. Today neither the room's delicious aroma of kraut, nor the merry clinking of glasses and silver, nor the excellent service, could lift Karl's spirits.

As the slender, bent server retreated, Karl took a deep drink of red stout. He leaned an elbow on the highly polished oak table. Actually, why the woman was so fanatical about getting a degree she'd never be allowed to use, was beyond him. No doubt about it, she was a natural research mathematician. She didn't have to keep butting her head against the wall of university administrations. He didn't think that financial considerations were that important in her case. He'd met Sofya's parents last summer, and her father, a Russian general, obviously well-to-do, was clearly supportive of his daughter's efforts. Anyway, she was a married woman. Although her husband, somehow involved in scientific publishing, was never around. The husband must be helping her financially. Sofya, with her degree or without it, ought to be able to look forward to a leisurely life of producing elegant mathematical papers.

He sighed. What really bothered him was the effect this woman had on his emotions. When he saw her so hurt and discouraged, he wanted to take her in his arms and . . . and what? What an old fool he was. He was old enough to be her father! Still, the attraction between them was undeniable. He was sure that from time to time she flirted with him. And where *was* her husband, come to think of it? What kind of man would leave such a lovely young woman alone? Probably some drunken Russian beast, or immoral aristocrat, who cared nothing for her.

"Why so glum, Weierstrass?" The scraping of chair legs on the floor accompanied the inquiry. Karl looked up to see the short frame and scholarly looking face of a fellow faculty member, Rudolf Virchow. The great biologist and public health advocate had never lost his gentle physician's manner.

"Oh, hello, Rudy," Karl grumbled. "I've got graduate student difficulties."

Virchow sat across from him and waved to the waiter. He nodded with immediate understanding. "Graduate students! What a pain they are." He sipped deeply from the foaming stein that had appeared almost instantly.

Karl said nothing. The good doctor was just trying to draw him out. The man never stopped trying to heal people.

Virchow prattled on. "I'm here to meet a former doctoral student of mine. A formality, pure formality. The man upsets me. I can't understand how such a brilliant student could be so completely enraptured with Darwin's ideas. If there's one thing I try to teach it's a respect for facts. This evolution, it's just a theory, there's no solid evidence. Or very little . . . do you know Ernst Haeckel?"

"I'm afraid not."

"Once my star pupil, now a professor at Jena, and doing very well— Haeckel is ready to come to blows with anyone who challenges his beloved belief. You'd think I was attacking the man's religion."

Karl nodded. He had only a layman's knowledge of the controversy raging in biology. Mathematics and physics had vicious squabbles enough for any man. He and Kronecker had been at each other's throats for years over points in the calculus.

Virchow sipped his beer. "Haeckel's here in town for the Academy of Sciences meeting. Says he has some new evidence for his theory that will bring me to my senses." Virchow adjusted his circular lensed glasses, then took them off and wiped them with a large kerchief. "By the way, congratulations on your presentation at the Academy's session. I've heard it was very well received."

Weierstrass muttered something. "Just another example of my procrastination. You know I made the discovery of that deviant equation years ago. I just never got around to doing a formal paper."

"So, you enjoy the study of deviants. Well, so do I. In fact, it's my work with deviant animal specimens that makes me so doubtful of Darwin's mutation theory." He scratched his neatly trimmed beard.

Karl smiled weakly. Even this mild talk of science was helping to raise his spirits.

"Here comes Haeckel," said Virchow suddenly, and rose to wave to a tall, strong looking man of about forty. The newcomer's light, fine hair was already receding, adding to the high forehead that rose above intent eyes. His nose protruded, large and straight, over a massive blond mustache and a full dark, curly, unkempt beard.

Proper introductions were exchanged.

"Professor Weierstrass. I've heard so much about you." The words sounded almost derisive. Haeckel's eyes were alight with merriment, and a smile that to Karl resembled a smirk slid across the man's face. "I hope my good colleague, Herr Professor Virchow, is going to let me share some of your company. In fact, there is a question, a problem, that you could shed some light on for me."

Weierstrass looked at Haeckel, then at Virchow who was frowning. Virchow's eyes pleaded from behind his little round spectacles. "We shouldn't impose on Herr Professor Weierstrass."

Haeckel had already pulled out a chair and motioned for a stein. "Nonsense. The professor has a reputation for hospitality." Again, to Weierstrass, the tone carried a suggestion of mockery.

"The mathematical master won't mind a little shop talk." Ernst Haeckel prattled on. "One of my graduate students has completed a remarkable work, filling in a major gap in my genealogical tree of the horse. The paper was read before the London Academy by Huxley himself. I'm sending you a copy, Virchow." He turned to Weierstrass. "Our brilliant, public-spirited comrade will be won over to Darwin's camp someday."

"You know, Ernst, I'm going to need a lot more evidence . . ."

"Well, my pupil, whose name by the way is—" Haeckel paused momentarily before pronouncing the name. He was looking directly at Weierstrass. "—Kovalevsky, has come up with enough solid evidence to satisfy even an old skeptic like yourself."

Weierstrass sat up straighter in his chair. "What did you say the name of your student was?"

"Kovalevsky. Vladimir Kovalevsky." Haeckel pronounced each syllable distinctly. "A Russian, quite a brilliant man. Came to science a bit late in life, after working as a publisher of science and popular science. He introduced Darwin's works in Russia. Good man."

Haeckel's voice took on a mocking tone. "Like myself, the man is an avowed atheist. So he has none of the prejudices on the nature of creation which a believer like yourself, Professor Weierstrass, will need to confront. Nor is he tortured by the uncertainties of an agnostic like the good doctor Virchow." Then turning to Weierstrass, eyes gleaming maliciously. "Kovalevsky will make a first-rate scientist as soon as he frees himself from the witch of a wife he's tied to. Poor fellow, everyone knows his wife's exchanging favors for, of all things, mathematical influence! Quite a joke on my poor student." The man's ugly face contorted in what passed for a smile. "Don't you agree, Professor Weierstrass?"

Karl felt the nails of his hands digging deeply into flesh, a pulse thudding in his head. He leaned forward, his face warmed, his eyes stretched open, short forceful breaths escaped his nostrils. "Sir," Karl pushed himself up with such force his chair clattered to the floor. All eyes in the café fixed on them as quiet fell.

"Sir," Weierstrass reached across the table and grabbed Haeckel by the front of his jacket, effortlessly lifting the large man half out of his chair. "You will withdraw your slander of Frau Kovalevskaya, or you will meet me on the field of honor."

Haeckel's eyes were wide, his hands pulling at Karl's, but the iron grip wouldn't loosen.

"Gentlemen!" Virchow grabbed at Weierstrass's arm. "There will be no talk of a duel. Haeckel, withdraw your remarks."

But at the moment Haeckel could not say anything. Karl's bear paw of a hand had closed around his throat, and he was turning red.

Waiters rushed to Virchow's assistance. With each man tugging on one of his arms, Karl's fingers were at last torn loose.

Coughing and gasping, Haeckel sank back into his chair. Weierstrass, with waiters ready to grab his arms again, stared at him from across the table.

Haeckel looked defiantly into Karl's eyes. "I have only spoken openly what every scholar in Germany has heard privately." Haeckel coughed. "Virchow, you can't deny you've heard of 'Weierstrass's weakness.' "

"He's right, Karl," Virchow admitted softly. "I have heard the rumor."

"False and vicious!" Weierstrass snarled.

Haeckel rubbed his neck. "On your sterling reputation as a speaker and seeker of truth, Herr Professor, I will withdraw my remarks concerning the lady in question and decline your challenge."

"Well done," Virchow patted Haeckel on the shoulder. "No sense anyone dying over rumors."

Karl slammed the table with his hand. "If I ever hear you speak of the lady in such a manner I will personally see that you carry my saber mark across your forehead, like a mark of Cain." He grabbed Haeckel's beard. "This, sir, will offer you no hiding from my mark."

Karl heard the tittering of the crowd behind him, as he stormed to the door. Then a loud cheer. A contingent of graduate mathematical students stood with raised steins in salute. Apparently Sofya had supporters.

THE WINTER WINDS of Berlin blew bits of snow against the window of Sofya's room. Soon she would be able to see nothing of the outside world.

Sofya sat at her desk, too tired to get up and close the curtains which had been open since early morning. She braced her elbows on the cluttered surface, her head resting in the spread fingers of both hands. She was meeting with Karl this afternoon. He had suggested they continue with their well-established biweekly schedule. He'd keep presenting advanced methods, continue to broaden her mathematical background, and discuss recent developments published in the journals. Soon some question would catch her fancy, and she could start on a new research topic.

As she saw the situation, the difficulty wouldn't be finding a new topic that fascinated her. The field of mathematical physics was alive with problems just waiting for attention. One in particular, that of describing a kind of spinning motion, had captured her imagination almost from the time she started her studies. But ensnaring the mathematical mermaid was still far beyond her capabilities. Karl would select problems she could handle with some hope of success. He had guided many students to their doctorates and to prestigious positions on faculties all over Europe. She would trust his judgment.

She stared blankly at the confused heaps of papers littering her desk. The nearest ones were in her handwriting. They were filled with Greek and Arabic symbols with only a rare number here and there, a sprinkling of parentheses, a plus sign, a minus sign; a mysterious magic code, on long, dog-eared sheets of paper. She was privy to this powerful code. She could escape to that magical world and now, after years of preparation, she had set out to explore its uncharted regions.

"The journeys of a fearless explorer," she said aloud with a sigh. "Only my last expedition was a failure, another flag was placed ahead of mine." She crumpled a page in disgust.

Bunching a stack of personal letters together, she pushed them into a drawer, leaving only her mathematical papers on the desk surface.

Last night had been one of those confused, intense nights where her mind had jumped from topic to topic. She willed the mathematical problems to dominate her attention, but family matters managed now and again to edge themselves to the front of her consciousness. She had pulled out the letters, one by one. Letters from her sister Anyuta, her mother and father, and a precious few from her husband Vladimir. She'd read and reread them, tossed them aside, and returned to her mathematics.

She glanced at the small gold watch pinned to her dress. She had some time until her meeting. She fingered the pretty timepiece. Vladimir had given her the watch, in what seemed another era in London, as a pledge of their future life. Well, so much for pledges. She hadn't seen him in over a year and his most recent and hurtful letter was months old.

Annoyed at herself and at him, she stood up quickly, and in doing so, pushed the chair back with a scraping sound. It fell to the floor. She didn't bother to pick it up, but went to the snowy window.

In the last year and a half her life had been in this room, here in Berlin. Nothing else. Only letters reminded her that once she had lived a life of action.

One memory, more unreal, more dreamlike than all the rest, was the memory of Vladimir. She had seen him only a handful of times since they'd said goodbye at a Paris train station. Disagreements derived from impatience, mistrust and weakening hope ended each strained meeting in bitterness followed by anger and hurt and months of cold silence.

It was from Vladimir's brother, Aleksander, that she had heard her husband had completed his doctorate in paleontology at Jena. Vladimir had not asked her to share his victory. From Aleksander she learned that Vladimir's work was being read before the London Academy of Sciences by the great Huxley. And from her own sister, Anyuta, she heard Vladimir was living in England and could think of nothing merrier than settling down there. Settling down! With whom? She hadn't been consulted.

She turned from the window angrily. "Vladimir! What are you doing to me?"

Only the snow answered, tapping gently at the glass.

Unable to remain still in her agitation, she turned from the window, circled around her desk, then paced the length of her bed. Again facing the snowy window, she stopped, her mind momentarily mesmerized by the luminous crystal white beauty. The respite from feeling was short. Anger flooded back into her consciousness.

For the hundredth time she recalled the cruel words in Vladimir's last letter. The words had burned into her mind the first time she read them:

Now you can manage without me. You are an independent, intelligent person. Our temperaments are quite different, as you know. My work demands travel, I've become a regular gypsy. You prefer stability. I need solitude. You need to be surrounded by devoted friends. I long for the closeness of a family. You are happy with your friends. Linking our destinies for the rest of our lives must be reconsidered. I'm certain you will do very well on your own. This 'arrangement' of ours is becoming a hindrance to your emotional freedom. The closeness you feel for your professor with whom you spend so much of your time would surely develop into something more satisfying if you were free. At a word from you, I can make life easier for both of us. What instructions do you have for me?

The mention of Karl infuriated Sofya. Vladimir, concerned about malicious gossip! He of all people should understand that a man and a woman could have a deep relationship of mutual respect and sympathy, without romance!

And his closing request for instructions. She felt the blood rush to her face. The anger rising again. "What instructions? If Vladimir wants a change in our relationship he'll have to initiate it. I have all the freedom I need to study, to finish my work with Weierstrass. What I don't have is time for changing the legalities of our arrangement. Certainly, I have no time for a family commitment. I'm not going to make the next move! For goodness sake, Vladimir, stop shouting at me!"

There was a pounding. The voice calling her name wasn't Vladimir's. She was sweating. She must have been pacing around the room. She'd caught herself pacing a lot lately. The habit had resurfaced along with her night terrors. She was not unfamiliar with her willful mind's mode of rebellion against unhappiness and overwork. She slammed shut the half-open desk drawer. The call came again. The call was real.

"Sofya. Answer me. Sofya!"

She opened the door. She stared blankly at the homely face of her housemate, Julia Lermontova. "What's the matter?"

"I heard you running in your room again, Sofya. And I could hear you mumbling. Shouting, rather. Are you all right?"

"Yes," Sofya said softly. "Yes. I'm fine."

Julia's eyes were full of concern. Taking Sofya by the elbow, she half led, half pushed her to the living area. Tiredly Sofya let herself fall into a stuffed chair.

"Sofya, I'm worried about you. I know you've had a horrid blow with your work not getting published. But you'll find a new topic soon."

"What can you know of how I feel?" Sofya snapped. "Your chemistry professors have let you attend their lectures, work in their laboratories. They're helping you with research suitable for a dissertation. And they've promised to help you get your doctorate."

"Sofya, it's because they know I'm unmarried." No anger crept into Julia's tone, only a kind of resignation. "The professors know I'm going to have to make my way in the world without a husband. If the degree won't get me an academic position, they know it will get me a respectable position in a research laboratory. They feel sorry for a spinster."

Julia's eyes were fixed on Sofya's hands. Sofya glanced down. She was surprised to see she was holding Vladimir's last letter. She jumped to her feet and pushed the paper into her pocket.

Running her hand through her hair, reminiscent of Vladimir's habitual gesture, she stared at Julia, then started to laugh hysterically. "They're helping you! *Because* you're unmarried!" She raised her fists and shook them at the ceiling. "This is truly maddening! I had to marry before I was allowed to do anything at all!"

"Sofya. You must get hold of yourself." Julia gently pushed her toward the divan. "Calm down!"

Sofya sat stiffly. Then willed herself to breathe more slowly. Julia was sitting beside her, eyebrows drawn together in a look of concern that made her face even less attractive than usual.

"Sofya, you've been working too intensely." Julia rested a hand on Sofya's shoulder. "You're making yourself ill, pacing around, mumbling, even shouting to yourself at all hours. When you do sleep, you cry out with nightmares."

"Sorry to have disturbed you," Sofya said sharply, her self-control now fully restored.

"You know I'm not complaining." Julia withdrew her hand from Sofya's shoulder. Seemingly to avoid Sofya's eyes, she looked to the opposite end of the divan and started to toy with an unfinished baby blanket Sofya was knitting. Winding the loose ends around the red, white and blue balls of yarn, Julia said, "I'm worried about your health. You're not eating. You look pale and thin. You can't keep pushing yourself like this."

Sofya scooped her knitting bag from the floor and handed it to Julia, who put the unfinished blanket in it. Sofya stood up and offered a hand to Julia. "In a few months Anyuta's baby will be born. We'll visit her in Zurich. That will give us a much needed break from our routine. Now, we both need to get over to Weierstrass's for our Sunday meeting."

Julia rose and smoothed the folds of her dress. "I'm ready for another Sunday well spent. You enjoying your mathematical session with Karl, while I have a good talk with Clara and Elise."

Sofya began collecting her things. "Followed by a wonderful dinner all together, and a quiet evening of chatter and knitting by the fire. I promise I'll eat two of everything the dear sisters offer us."

CLARA AND ELISE FUSSED as they always did, each in their own endearing way, when Sofya and Julia arrived for the Sunday meeting.

"My dears." Elise fluttered around her guests. "You've heard of our brother's confrontation in the café?"

Sofya looked at Julia, whose face showed as much perplexity as Sofya felt. "We've heard nothing." Sofya answered.

"Karl challenged a young man to a duel!" Elise's excited words spilled out.

"Really, Elise," the calm Clara interrupted. "I'm sure Karl wouldn't want Sofya worrying about that."

"Clara." Sofya stood back shocked. "I know Karl is a very physical person, but he is not rash. Whatever prompted him to put himself into such danger?"

Elise giggled nervously. "He was defending a woman's honor." Her eyes shone with glee. "I think it's very romantic."

"Fortunately," Clara sensibly explained, "Professor Virchow defused the situation. Virchow has sense."

Elise interrupted, "Virchow doesn't like duels. He declined Chancellor Bismarck's public challenge just a few years back." She hesitated. "But that wasn't a romantic encounter, only a political disagreement."

Half hearing Elise's nervous chatter, Sofya gasped, "Karl could have been killed!"

"Oh, no, Sofya," Elise assured her. "Karl has excellent reflexes. He dueled with sabers in his student days, and never got a scratch. I'm sure he'd be just as quick with pistols. No one could ever touch our Karl."

"It was a foolish thing for him to do," Clara's stern voice entered. "But understandable, under the circumstances. I'm proud of him. Sometimes a man must risk his life for honor." Clara still wore a black armband in honor of her friend General Pedtke, killed more than two years ago in the Franco-Prussian war.

"Clara, am I the woman who . . . you said Karl was protecting a woman's honor." Sofya tried to keep her voice calm. It was foolish to even ask the question. Who else could it be?

"And his own." Clara's eyes lowered.

Julia spoke quietly. "Men fear you, Sofya, as *Rusalka*."

Sofya looked at Julia without at first comprehending. Then she nodded her agreement.

"*Rusalka?*" Elise looked puzzled.

"*Die Wassernixe*, a mermaid," Clara explained. "A temptress. A goddess who leads men to destruction."

"In our Russian folk tales, she is also the goddess of life and renewal," Julia added.

"A quality of healing frequently overlooked. And one which I will now try to emulate." Sofya turned her back on the women and pushed her way into Karl's study, closing the door firmly behind her. Karl, surprised, looked up from behind his desk.

"Clara tells me you've been challenging someone to a duel. And somehow, over me."

He pushed back from his chair and walked toward her. The look on his face was strange, unsettling, haunted and at the same time self-satisfied. "So, now you know, I care for you. It was not a very personal way of letting you find out."

"Karl, this is no time for teasing. You could have been killed!"

"The man slandered you. Slandered both of us, really. I couldn't just sit there. And why do you think I am teasing?"

"No, I know you're not. But no public humiliation, no scandal, no slander is worth a life. Not yours, not anyone's!" She backed up half a step, struggling with several emotions. "Death for honor. Male nonsense. Nonsense!"

"I would do the same again."

"No, you shouldn't, you mustn't." Sofya paced the room. "Slander and scandal follow me like demons. If you can't deal with that in a safe way, I will have to stop seeing you. I will find another mentor. I will not have you risk your life for me."

Karl drew a deep breath and let it out. "Very well. I promise, I will never challenge anyone to a duel again. But in exchange, you must give me an explanation of exactly what your position is, with regard to your husband."

"That's fair enough. Vladimir and I . . ." She paused, sighing. How to begin to explain? "There's a lot more to me than you've seen. A part of my being which you've no inkling exists and which I doubt you could ever understand."

"I don't believe that, Sofya. I know you, perhaps even better than you know yourself."

Sofya spoke softly, still unable to look at him. "I should have made my position clear from the start."

"Why? Your marital state has nothing to do with your mathematical ability. Nor should it preclude your maintaining male friendships."

"Your views are far more advanced than most of your countrymen."

"You're right." He continued, "I've had several well-meaning friends tell me, 'man to man,' about your living husband. I also know you haven't seen him in over a year." The words came more huskily. "Recently, I have come face to face with the realization that my feelings for you are not at all as well defined as I had assumed. In fact, they most certainly exceed the bounds of traditional friendship. On this basis, I am pressing you for an explanation of your private status."

"It's an unusual situation." Opening her eyes, Sofya spoke in a whisper. "Only a Russian would understand."

"Is he a drunkard? Does he beat you?" Karl's gaze bore at her from across the room. "No doubt he is a womanizer. Whatever the situation, I deserve to hear the story from you."

"Yes, of course you do." She drew herself into a rigid position, hands folded and head high. "My husband is not a drunkard, and he treats me with the greatest respect. Whether he is involved with another woman, I cannot say. I've heard gossip." She fought back tears.

Karl had crossed the room and was sitting next to her. He reached for her hand.

She went on, "Vladimir and I have what we moderns at home call a fictitious marriage. An arrangement, an agreement that we entered into with the sole purpose of enabling me to leave Russia and continue my education. It was the only way."

Now at last Karl was shocked. He dropped her hand. His eyes never left her face. When he spoke, his voice had a cutting tone to it. "I've heard of these 'arrangements.' I never thought you capable of such a calculated mockery of marriage and family."

She sniffled. "I told you, there is a depth of my being that you cannot even imagine."

"I'm trying," he spoke gently. "Sofya, you wanted to study so badly that you agreed to sacrifice your personal life. And this Vladimir, your husband, he agreed as well?" Karl spoke in disbelief. Half whispered to himself, "What kind of a man can this be?"

"My husband also wanted to study." For some illogical reason she wanted Karl to like Vladimir, or at least to respect him. "With the help of my allowance from Father, my husband had the financial freedom to study. He now has his doctorate in paleontology, from the university in Jena."

"And where is he now?"

"I think in England. Probably consulting with some of the best minds in his field."

"You don't even know for sure where he is!" Karl's struggle to control himself was visible. "So, this man took advantage of your situation to help himself to a chance at an education."

"I could help him, and he could help me. He always put my welfare first. Always!" Sofya spoke firmly. "He is a brilliant and devoted scientist."

"That's a rather cold description of a husband."

"He is physically brave and daring. As you are. He's morally strong. As you are. He believes that each individual has the right to choose what his or her life will be. As you do. He believes in a woman's right to education. As you do." She paused to draw breath. "And like you, he is a very noble man."

"Perhaps. That tells me very little about your feelings."

Sofya struggled. "Oh, Karl!" She tried to examine her heart more closely than she had allowed herself to do even in the solitude of her room. She was afraid of what she might see. After a time, she answered, "All I know for certain is that Vladimir is dear to me. He has been a dear, dear friend, a brother, a champion and . . ."

"I suppose those were the terms of your arrangement," Karl interrupted. "But did you never think of him as a lover? Or he of you?"

Sofya blushed deeply.

"I apologize. I had no right to ask that," Karl whispered. "Of course, when I first realized your husband was still alive, what I imagined was quite different. I saw you as the victim of a parentally arranged marriage to a cruel man, a Russian drunk, a womanizer, or a compulsive gambler. I saw myself as your rescuing knight. What a fool I've been!"

"Karl . . ."

"No, let me finish. I see now that this is not a marriage, it never was. You and your so-called husband have both achieved your goals, acquired an education. So now there is nothing to stop you from freeing yourselves. Surely the Orthodox Church would see this was never really a marriage and grant you an annulment."

She was shaking her head. "How little you know Russia! No. There can be no public declaration of our arrangement. We have committed sacrilege. If the whole truth were known at home, my husband and I would be considered criminals. In my country, sacrilege is an imprisonable crime."

Karl was thinking. "Then you must get a divorce. That will be a painful, time-consuming ordeal, but you must."

Sofya whispered, "That's what Vladimir has been hinting in his letters. He hasn't actually come out and asked me for a divorce. Not yet."

"And you don't want a divorce?"

"No," she snapped. "Yes, I suppose . . ." She faltered. "Oh, Karl, I don't know what I want. That's why I've been so miserable. When Vladimir and I are together we argue and fight, but when we're apart I feel helpless and deserted."

"Sofya, you must settle this. I will help you. I want to meet your husband. When will you see him?"

"I've written, asking him to come here to Berlin, at Christmas." Her letter had been posted care of Aleksander, who quite probably would know where his brother was.

"And may I meet him then?"

As she stood up, she nodded agreement. She could hardly see through her tears. Karl took her in his arms. She felt surrounded by his huge mass. "I'll always be here for you. You'll always be my dearest, most cherished—" He paused, unable to utter the word 'friend.'

"WEIERSTRASS ASKED about my relationship with Vladimir," Sofya calmly confided to Julia as she moved toward one of the chairs placed before their modest fireplace.

"And you told him about your arrangement?" Julia's eyes widened with just a touch of alarm.

"Karl has earned the right to the truth."

Julia settled into the twin chair, positioned within touching distance. The more comfortable divan, Sofya's favorite place, was strewn with books and papers, too cluttered for either of them to sit.

"I explained as well as I could." Sofya pulled off her shoes and lifted her feet toward the fire. "I feel incredibly relieved. Oh Julia, I'm so tired of deceptions."

They had just finished the midmonth financial accounts and were enjoying hot tea with spoonfuls of cherry jam. A small, cheery fire burned steadily, its light just reaching the narrow table set along the wall. The shiny silver samovar reflected the light and added its own faint but steady glow from the hot charcoal under its bright belly. Next to the silver vessel stood a large jar of jam tied with a festive red ribbon and a humidor filled with black tea leaves, both Christmas presents from Sofya's mother and father. Her parents had also sent extra money, as had Julia's. Going over the accounts and paying the financial bills had been almost pleasant this month.

"I'm feeling rather homesick," Julia confessed, staring into the glowing fire. She placed her glass on the hearth rug. Then, wrapping a knitted throw around her shoulders, she slid from the chair to the rug. She drew her knees up to her chest, and clutched them with her arms. "I hate not being home for the holidays."

Sofya touched her friend gently on the shoulder. "You can't leave your work at the laboratory. You've said so, many times."

Julia's eyes stayed on the flames.

Sofya tried to soothe her. "Julia, this work could result in a research paper that will get you your doctorate. You can't leave your experiments untended."

"I'm glad you're staying with me." Julia leaned back and rested against Sofya's legs. "I couldn't stand being alone."

Sofya mouthed words of comfort. "I wouldn't leave you alone." Here she was pretending again. The real reason she'd remained in Berlin, the reason only she knew, was that she couldn't face her parents nagging her about her relationship with Vladimir. Months ago, he had flatly refused to visit her parents until they had settled their "arrangement."

Julia sipped her tea, then asked, "Will Vladimir be coming? I haven't seen a letter from him in months. I always recognize his scrawling hand on the envelope."

"I invited him." Sofya curled her stockinged feet up under her. "Karl made a point of asking me to bring Vladimir to meet him. I'm afraid Karl may try to counsel us. That will be very awkward."

"Karl and Vladimir both love you." Julia stood up. "Each in his own way, of course." In one smooth gesture, she stood up, leaned over, picked up her glass, and placed it on the mantel. She held her hands palm up toward the fire. "You're a very fortunate woman, Sofya."

Julia sounded almost cheery as she turned to face Sofya, all probing of emotional wounds evidently done for the time being. "We really should have new dresses made, as a Christmas treat. Our wardrobes have grown quite shabby."

"I suppose I'll have to find time for the dressmaker." Sofya picked at a thread that hung from the cuff of her sleeve. She recalled wistfully that when she was first married, Vladimir had tended to all the time-consuming details of living, while she devoted herself to study. He'd brought her silly presents for no reason at all, just to see her laugh, and serious presents full of meaning and caring.

The fire sputtered and crackled.

Sofya tilted her head back and looked deeply into the face of Julia, standing behind her chair. "Did I drive Vladimir away?"

"You didn't mean to, Sofya, but—" Julia would tell the truth. Julia always told the truth "—you made such demands on him, running him from city to city. Then Paris, into the war zone to help your sister. The death, the destruction, the politics. He'd thought he'd left all that behind when we made the arrangement with you."

Sofya was becoming agitated. "Vladimir got exactly what he wanted." She caught her breath, surprised at the bitterness with which she had spoken. She felt the blood rise to her cheeks as she quickly added, "He got his education, his precious degree."

"You believe that is really all he wants from life?"

A knock on the door saved Sofya from having to answer. She sat unmoving in the chair, while Julia opened the door. A delivery boy in a blue uniform held out a package. "For Frau Kovalevsky,"

Julia took the package from him, offering a few coins in exchange. The smiling lad thanked her, bowed politely, and wished her the happiest of holidays. She closed the door on the sound of whistled carols and skipping steps.

"It's from Zurich. Anyuta." Julia was reading the label as she handed the package to Sofya.

Sofya opened the note attached to the package and silently read her sister's message:

Vladimir is in England. He asked me to forward this package to you. He has again expressed his desire for a more 'traditional' family life. He's very anxious to know what action you want him to take regarding your 'legal' arrangements. Sofya, dearest, please send me your decision soon. For both your sakes.

Love.
Anyuta.

ps I'm feeling well, although I unmistakably look in a very motherly way, and hate being confined almost totally to the apartment. Victor sends regards.

Sofya tossed the note onto the table, among the household accounts. Of all the cowardly actions! Apparently, Vladimir was refusing to meet with her, here in Berlin or anywhere. He should have at least sent a note in his own hand declining her invitation. Still, he had sent her a present.

She tore open the package. *No! How could he!* The top of a small feminine slipper showed itself. Her slippers, the ones she had presented so ceremoniously to Vladimir in England, a few months after their marriage. The slippers had been a pledge, a silly, romantic wonderful pledge that someday she would be his real wife.

He must have put a note in with them. But no, she could find no note. The meaning was clear. He was, symbolically, divorcing her! He must be involved with that English woman again. That's why he hasn't come back. Sofya fingered the watch he had given her in London, his part of the pledge. No matter what happened, she would never part with his watch. His pledge of his future with her.

Julia stood looking anxiously at Sofya.

Sofya's eyes met Julia's, but she said nothing. Holding the package close to her, her eyes filled with tears. She rose from the chair and stumbled her way into her room. Ceremoniously she placed the package under her bed. Feeling very tired, she stayed a moment, kneeling beside the bed, her hand on the quilted coverlet. Wanting to crawl beneath it, she rested her cheek on the smooth surface and closed her eyes, pretending she was back in London.

But she wasn't. With effort, she forced herself to rise, wiped her tears, and told herself that there were times Vladimir behaved very cruelly. She returned to Julia.

"A Christmas present from Vladimir," Sofya announced as she reentered the room. "Something personal." She hurriedly put on the shoes she had left before the fire. She couldn't face Julia's questions now, she had to walk and think. Going to the rack that stood near the door, she chose her overcoat and a wool scarf.

Her hand resting on the door latch, she didn't turn to Julia when she announced, "Vladimir is not coming for Christmas. I have no idea when, or if, I will ever see him again."

When the door closed behind Sofya, Julia sighed loudly and turned to go back to her room. Her eyes fell on the table with Anyuta's note. She picked it up, then hesitated, suddenly feeling she was about to betray a trust. But her hesitation was only brief.

CHAPTER TWENTY-SEVEN

1873 ৵৹ *Zurich*

Anyuta awoke to the sound of a baby crying. Her baby, though that still seemed a miracle. Urey's next cry refocused her attention. Oh, for a maid! Anyuta sighed. She hadn't enjoyed the luxury of having servants since leaving her parents' home in Russia. Rising, she pushed back a strand of hair that had fallen before her eyes and made her way to the tiny bedroom that served as a nursery.

Victor had been right in choosing Zurich for their refuge. The city teemed with Russians and Poles seeking escape from tsarist tyranny. And the proper, bourgeoisie citizens had a tradition of tolerance dating back at least three hundred years to the religious rebel, Zwingli.

From the one small window, soft spring sunlight illuminated the baby basket. An old, serviceable wooden rocker obtained from a pawn shop occupied the space between the window and the basket; a simple cot had been pushed against the remaining wall.

Anyuta leaned over her son. Her hands skillfully unwrapped him. As she fitted a clean linen to his body, tucking in corners, he seemed to stare up thankfully at her. She loved those brown eyes, his curly brown hair, and long lanky body.

Picking up the dry baby, Anyuta gasped as pain shot through her back. She held the baby close to her breast with one hand, stabilizing herself by gripping the edge of the basket. Slowly, carefully she made her way to the wooden rocker, its seat and back now covered by a thick quilted pad that Mother had brought with her from their Russian country home in Palibino.

She undid the fastening of her blouse and prepared to nurse. The baby hungrily locked onto her offered nipple. Anyuta sighed and rested her head on the back of the rocker. She felt herself dozing off.

The sound of an outer door opening jarred her back to wakefulness. She called out in French, softly for fear of disturbing the baby. "Victor? I'm in the baby's room."

"Yes, Anna, I'll be with you in a moment." Her husband's voice came back. He entered, heavy boots thumping carelessly across the uncarpeted floor. He was tall and slender, dashing and romantic, despite his somewhat worn appearance. There were signs of fraying on his shirt cuffs and his trousers were taking on an unfashionable shine. His well-tailored brown woolen vest, a gift from Mother, flattered his trim build. His jacket, Anyuta knew, would be neatly hung on the rack in the hall. He was one of the few men of their group who valued a neat appearance.

Victor gave her a quick kiss on the top of her head, then whispered at the bundle she held close. "How's Daddy's little Frenchman?" He squeezed the blankets covering the baby's feet. The baby gave a startled cry, then continued nursing.

Victor sat on the edge of the cot. From his pocket he took a short-barreled pistol, which he inspected briefly and balanced in his hand.

"What are you doing? Put that away!" Anyuta gasped. Her body tensed, and Urey responded by letting out a squeal.

He slipped the weapon back into his pocket. "Smirnov's coming in a few moments. I'm giving him the gun." His voice was quietly eager, but at the same time uneasy.

"Smirnov! No!" She glared at Victor. "You are not giving that man a gun."

"I must." Her husband brushed a piece of lint from his trouser leg. "A bad situation is brewing, Anna. The Bakuninists claim we stole some political documents from their office. They're threatening to come after us with clubs."

"Some of our group *did* steal documents, against my advice," Anyuta said with disgust. "And now, if you put a gun in the hands of that fool

Smirnov, the conflict will expand from theft to murder. I won't have it, Victor!"

"I have my orders from Karl Marx, orders to support the Lavrovists. They must have control of the Russian group."

"Yes, I suppose they must. But—"

"You suppose? You suppose? You owe Marx your undying loyalty, after all that his family did for you in London."

"Yes, Victor." Anyuta sighed. After the collapse of the Commune she had been smuggled to safety in London where Marx's family provided her with lodging until Father could arrange for her return to Europe.

Victor stood up, hands behind his back, adopting a pose that she had seen him use when commanding his irregular troops in Paris. She had seen the same pose in certain portraits of Napoleon. "We've been instructed by Marx's own son-in-law to destroy Bakunin's influence in the Internationale."

"Murdering some insignificant supporter won't accomplish that. What it *will* do is bring down on us all kinds of hell, first from the Swiss government and then from the Russian government. I really wish you would put that gun away somewhere. And whatever happens, don't give it to Smirnov."

"I won't take orders from you, Anna," Victor snapped. "There are times when you seem to think you're an expert on strategy and tactics."

Anyuta glared at him. "Try not to wake the baby!" She knew that at the moment it would be worse than useless to argue any more.

With a confident manner worthy of Napoleon, Victor went to raise the window, then stood in front of the opening drawing deep breaths. The chill spring air rushed in, flushing out some of the room's foul odors, but leaving Anyuta shivering. She reached over to the cot to pick up Mother's shawl, and with one hand awkwardly draped it around herself and the baby.

Presently Victor turned back to her, wearing a smug look that meant his irritation had passed. "I'm preparing an editorial for the next edition of *Forward!* I believe the piece will please you. Of course, you'll do the Russian translation."

Anyuta nodded. "Your words, darling, are very effective weapons." *Much better than that foolish gun.* But she would not raise that subject again, until little Urey was fast asleep and out of range of the heated argument that would certainly ensue.

Thoughtfully Victor turned back to the window, closing it almost entirely as he looked out into the street. "I don't see Smirnov. Something must have detained him," he remarked. "Is there tea ready? Smirnov will need refreshment. The man never remembers to eat or drink when he's working."

"I think Mama set up the samovar in the living room before she and Papa left for the train station."

Victor's expression turned quizzical.

"You haven't forgotten, have you?" Anyuta reminded him. "Sofya and her friend Julia are arriving today from Berlin." The baby wrapped his little hand around her finger, without stopping his vigorous sucking.

Victor blinked. "Today? Well, don't expect me to entertain visitors. I have to finish work on the paper. Some of the articles need editing."

"You're editing for the *Forward!?* I should think not, you barely know ten words of Russian."

"Of course, I'm not actually doing the editing." Victor's voice was condescending. "I'll oversee the layout and then supervise typesetters. The contact who will smuggle the papers into Russia will be here any day now. This edition must be finished by the time he arrives."

"You will make time for Urey's christening. Mother's made arrangements for the service to be held tomorrow."

"Yes, well, I suppose. But one feels so hypocritical about that."

"We've been over this." Anyuta kept her voice calm. "Urey must have a baptismal certificate, just as you and I must have passports issued in my family name. These are political necessities."

"I find all this deception very distasteful. I am Victor Jaclard, not Victor Korvin."

"There was no other way for Father to get us papers. For the sake of sanctuary you will assume the identity of a distant member from the Korvin branch of the family, whom I married while abroad. We've been over all this, darling." Anyuta's words soothed. "At any rate, Urey's baptism is very important to Mama and Papa."

"And I do owe my freedom to your family's efforts," Victor admitted grudgingly. Then, looking out the window again, he brightened. "Aha, Smirnov at last." In another moment he had turned away and left the room.

Anyuta stared after him. She fought back the tears. As if sensing her feelings, the baby awoke and began crying. Lifting Urey awkwardly to her shoulder, she patted him gently on the back and started to pace painfully up and back.

The nursery door stood half open. Anyuta looked down the short hall and into the living room. Already Smirnov and Victor were sitting on the divan, their heads close together, talking in excited tones.

She'd met Smirnov at the organization's office, and hadn't liked him. He was a short, sturdy man of thirty or so. She thought him good looking in a rugged, unpolished sort of way. His speech and mannerisms clearly those of a self-schooled, intelligent factory worker. But for all his professed liberal notions, he never appeared at ease with a woman's participation in political discussions. He was quick to anger and all too often acted without thought of the consequences.

Hands shaking, Smirnov lit a cheap, ill-smelling cigarette and inhaled with agitation. His eyes roamed the room like a nervous cat's, and when Urey gave a little cry, Smirnov's gaze quickly discovered Anyuta looking through the doorway. He nodded his head in recognition, then quickly turned away, as if embarrassed by the sight of her and the baby.

Victor looked up briefly noting the exchange.

The talk between the men went on. The words "library" and "documents" drifted to Anyuta's ears. Then she saw what she had been watching for: Victor reached into his pocket and passed the small pistol to Smirnov, who hurriedly stuffed the weapon inside his own jacket.

Baby Urey gave a healthy belch, depositing a small, sweet-smelling stain on her shoulder. His little body relaxed in her arms. She placed him back in his basket. Pushing her hand hard against the aching spot in her back, she straightened. Sucking in breath to stop from crying out with the pain, she closed the nursery door separating herself and her child from Victor's folly. Then she lowered herself into the rocker. Resting her head against the high back, she closed her eyes and gently rocked. The rhythmic creaking smoothed her way to welcome oblivion.

A TAP on the nursery door roused Anyuta and startled the child back to crying wakefulness. Dazed, Anyuta looked from the door to her crying baby for a moment not knowing to which call she must respond.

The decision was taken from her. In less than a moment Father was stepping into the room, and kissing her lightly on the cheek. "Hello, hello! I've brought your little sister." Despite his seventy-three years, Father's military bearing had not deserted him. He stood tall, straight and lean. His eyes gleamed with energy, intelligence and the strength of a true general.

Mother, a full twenty years his junior, brushed past him in a hurried effort to get to the crying baby. In her youth Liza had been a Petersburg beauty sought after for her charm, wit and musical accomplishments. Her hair, once as blond as Anyuta's, showed more gray than gold. Her bright eyes sparkled mischievously. Her figure was now more plump than voluptuous, and the haughtiness Anyuta remembered from her childhood had rounded into a dignified pride. Gently, Mother lifted Urey into her arms.

Anyuta struggled to stand. She turned to follow Father's merry eyes and saw Sofya standing pale and hesitant in the hallway outside the nursery door. There was hardly room for her in the nursery. Anyuta's eyes met her sister's.

Anyuta held out her arms and moved toward the sister she had not seen since the destruction in Paris, almost two years ago. Warmly exchanging the kiss of greeting, she hugged Sofya tightly in a strong embrace. She heard Father clear his throat. Pulling back just a little from her sister, unwilling to totally release her, Anyuta examined Sofya.

With surprise Anyuta raised her hands to her face. "Sofya! You've let your hair grow long."

"So you have," Father observed, without much interest. Years ago, he had almost thrown a tantrum at Sofya's defiant bobbing of her hair in Revolutionary fashion. But now he hadn't even noticed that she had reverted to the conventional style.

"Doesn't your sister's hair look lovely, Anyuta?" Mother murmured between coos at little Urey.

"I can't wait to take a comb to those thick waves." Anyuta laughed. "Just as I did when you were a child."

"I remember you took quite a wicked delight at pulling at the tangles." Self-consciously Sofya pushed a chestnut curl back behind her ear and patted the small braid that barely stayed secured to the nape of her neck.

"So I did," Anyuta agreed good-naturedly.

"Sofya, you haven't held your new nephew." Mother turned and proudly presented the now cheerful and contented baby for Sofya's inspection. Anyuta watched with humor as her sister timidly offered the required admiring remarks and awkwardly bounced the bewildered baby. But no infant would hold Sofya's interest for very long and the child was soon back in Mother's care.

"Enough!" Father put his arms around both his daughters and nodded to his wife. His voice was a little loud and exceedingly joyful. "My daughters, we are forgetting our manners. Victor and his guest are in the living room. We should join them."

There was a quiet, but unmistakably firm tone to Mother's voice.

"Vasily, as long as Urey behaves himself, I see no reason he, or I, should be banished to the nursery."

"Of course, my dear," Father agreed softly.

VICTOR AND SMIRNOV rose from the divan.

Father bowed slightly to Victor. "My apologies. We rushed through the room a moment ago barely nodding our greetings to you and your guest. Our rudeness can only be explained by our great desire to reunite our daughters."

"I've explained the situation to my friend." Victor placed his hand on Smirnov's elbow. "No apology is necessary, sir."

In a short, curt manner Victor presented Smirnov as a dutiful Russian nephew on an extended visit with an aging aunt. Smirnov had generously offered his services to the newspaper being prepared by a small group of Russians in Zurich. The same newspaper he and Anyuta assisted.

Anyuta noted with something like despair that Smirnov's hand kept returning to his jacket pocket. The gun must still be resting there.

The ladies were offered seats on the divan. Father assisted Mother as she cuddled the contented baby. The gentlemen settled on chairs. The ensuing awkward silence was broken by Smirnov. "Sofya Vasilievna, I have long admired your husband's efforts as publisher, particularly his line of highly readable scientific works. Will there be more?"

"I'm afraid I can't say," Sofya answered, "My husband's publishing business has become little more than a hobby for him."

"How unfortunate." Smirnov's prying eyes never left her. "Will your husband be joining you? I would like to meet him."

"His current scientific work demands his attentions and presence elsewhere. So I'm afraid you will not have the pleasure of meeting him anytime soon."

Father looked at her with surprise. "Too bad. I've been looking forward to Vladimir's company." Turning back to Victor he said, "I hear an old acquaintance of mine, Peter Lavrovich Lavrov, is involved with the publication you and your friend here are working on."

"Yes, sir," Victor responded. "He is our chief editor."

"Hasn't Mother told you?" Anyuta inquired. "Peter Lavrovich has agreed to stand as Urey's godfather."

"Well, then I'll be sure to see our old neighbor. A good political discussion with someone of my generation is just what I've been hoping for."

"My dear," Mother interrupted, "I hope you're planning on including me in your meeting."

Father's jaw opened, but no sound came forth, his eyes wide with disbelief.

Then, turning toward Victor and Smirnov, "Well, gentlemen, will you be my guests? I suggest we adjourn to the café down the street, for cigars, brandy and conversation. We'll leave the womenfolk to the care of the child and to catch up on their gossip."

Just as they had when they were girls at home, Anyuta and Sofya silently shared their exasperation at Father's depiction of the "womenfolk."

Victor awkwardly declined Father's invitation, explaining that he and Smirnov must leave for a work session at the paper's office.

"And you, sir," Mother announced to Father, "are taking little Urey and me out for a walk. It's a lovely, sunny spring day. We'll stroll along the quay. The gardens are greening and the lime trees are just starting to bud. I've planned a lovely route zigzagging over the river bridges all the way to the lake, where I am told there is a breathtaking view of the Alps."

"The air will do us good," Father agreed as he stood and offered Mother a hand in rising from the divan. As if by order, the others all rose.

Anyuta impulsively hugged her father. She kissed him on the cheek and whispered in his ear. "Father, Mother would like you to explain the town's new constitution to her."

Father looked at Anyuta with surprise, then he frowned at his wife. "Elizaveta, are you really interested in politics and the town's government?"

"Yes, Vasily, I am. All the young women are interested in politics and I don't want to be left out of their discussions." Mother started toward the nursery. "Get our coats, dear. I will get Urey ready."

"I really must get your mother back to Russia." Father winked at his daughters. "Zurich and you girls with your modern notions are having quite a disturbing effect on my Liza."

In a few minutes the proud grandparents had left with their grandson settled into the handsome new pram Mother had purchased on arriving.

"In 1869," Father was saying as they left, "the canton of Zurich adopted an amazingly democratic constitution. A model, really." His voice faded as Anyuta closed the apartment door.

⚬╬⚬

GRATEFUL FOR TIME alone with her sister, Sofya returned to the cozy nursery and settled into the wooden rocking chair. Anyuta soon entered the room and sat across from her on the small cot.

"Julia will be joining us here for dinner," Sofya informed her sister. "She's resting at the hotel."

"I haven't seen her since before you were married." Anyuta lay back on the cot, pulling the pillow under her head. "Why, that's almost five years!"

"She hasn't changed. She's as shy and full of common sense as ever."

"She isn't interested in anyone romantically?"

"Julia?" Sofya remarked incredulously. "She thinks only of her studies."

"What a shame." Anyuta pushed a loose strand of blond hair back behind her ear, then let her arm rest on her forehead. "Julia has such a strong domestic nature. She could be both a scholar and a mother. With the right kind of husband, of course."

Sofya rocked slowly as she stared at her sister. If Anyuta was headed for a discussion in which domestic nature and marriage would be delicately and pryingly discussed, Sofya planned to divert her. "How are you and Victor getting on?"

"We argue about politics and about other things." Anyuta closed her eyes. "Our endless poverty is weighing on both of us. Our little Urey was somewhat unexpected. And, as devoted as Victor is to the child, he feels trapped by our marriage, by the responsibility."

Anyuta lowered her arm and began to fidget with the front of her blouse, where a wet spot had appeared over her left nipple.

"Oh Anyuta, whatever happened to the rebellious girl who wanted only freedom and her own career? Where's the girl, the young woman, I idolized when I was growing up."

"Don't despair of me just because I've had a child. I mean to continue my writing, my work for social change." Anyuta smiled faintly. "I do take credit for teaching you something about freedom and ambition."

"So you should." Sofya's voice softened. She looked away from her sister's penetrating eyes. "I think I've lost my way, Anyuta. I've been so indecisive, so depressed since Paris."

"It's your relationship with Vladimir that's troubling you, isn't it." Anyuta lifted herself partly on one elbow.

Sofya nodded, avoiding her sister's eyes.

"Sofya," Anyuta reached out one hand and gently rested it on Sofya's knee, "Vladimir's written me that he's returning to Russia. He's going back to take the magesterium examination. With that formality out of the way, he plans to apply for a university teaching position, probably in Odessa. He'll be near his brother."

Sofya stopped rocking. She felt her body tense. For the moment she could find no words.

"Apparently, he's very determined to start a new life somewhere—England, the Continent, Russia." Anyuta's voice dropped. "Has he written you about his plans?"

"Vladimir confides far more in you than in me." Sofya felt her temper rise. "What a change! From the time Vladimir offered to be my liberator, the two of you could barely stand to be in the same room. Then after my marriage, when the three of us went abroad, you were constantly ridiculing him, calling him an ineffectual dreamer."

Anyuta shifted on the cot, as if trying to get comfortable. "I misjudged him, Sofya." Her words were utterly sincere; her sad gaze met Sofya's eyes. "When Victor and I were so desperate, in Paris, Vladimir helped even though Victor and I had treated him badly."

Sofya's temper cooled. "The war changed many things, for all of us. It would be impossible to live through that kind of hell and not be changed."

Solemnly Anyuta nodded agreement. "When Vladimir visited Zurich, a few months after Victor and I were reunited here, I invited him to settle with us. From the way he talked, I felt he wanted to be near family. But he refused my invitation. He said he feared being swept up in the political turmoil brewing among the Russian exiles."

"Vladimir wants no part of politics." Sofya rubbed her forehead. A vague headache was beginning. "Still, if he goes back to Russia, I don't see how he can avoid being dragged into it again. He simply believes too strongly in justice and freedom." Sofya fought back despair. "God only knows what that man is really searching for."

"He's searching for a human life." Anyuta's candid words struck cruelly. "He is very lonely. It isn't hard to see what he wants: a career, a home, a wife and family. Sofya, Vladimir is an intelligent, attractive man, only thirty years old. You won't be a real wife to him, and you won't free him."

"We have an agreement," Sofya choked.

"Yes, I know all about your agreement. I was there, if you remember." Anyuta continued, "Sofya, he got you out of Russia, and he helped you get started on your education. More than a start. That's what your agreement called for, and that's what he gave you. Now it's time for you to let go."

"You mean get a divorce?" She struggled to control her voice. "I'm much too involved in my own work to spare the time and emotional energy for lengthy legal action." She hoped she sounded firm. "I've told him as much in letters. If he must have the divorce now, he'll have to initiate proceedings."

"To do that, he would have to claim you were unfaithful. Then, wherever you tried to live and work, you would suffer terribly from the label of adulteress. You'd never be allowed to teach. Your chance at any academic career would be destroyed. Whereas, if you are the one to initiate proceedings, Vladimir will stage some incident between himself and some woman. It won't hurt a man's career any to be thought guilty of an affair."

"What need is there for staging? From what I've heard, he probably has a list of women who would support my claim. Russian, French, German or English corespondents." Sofya hardened her voice. "I could claim he deserted me, but he hasn't been away five years, so that won't satisfy the requirements. Or I could claim he's been impotent for the last three years, but I think there would be too many witnesses to dispute that statement."

"Stop that!" Anyuta's voice was firm, but not loud. She swung her legs down from the cot and sat up straight, hands clasped together. "You and he are torturing yourselves with rumors. Certainly you know that he's heard rumors about you and your professor."

There was a long silence.

Anyuta slowly stood up. A twinge of pain momentarily distorting her beautiful features. She touched Sofya on the shoulder. "I haven't asked Vladimir's permission, but I'm going to have you read the letters he's written me." Without waiting for a reply, she turned and left the room.

Sofya sat alone, rocking monotonously, for several minutes. Then she rose, pulled the large linen kerchief from her pocket, wiped her tearing eyes and blew her nose. She went to the open window and looked down. She ran her fingers through the moist black dirt of the flowerless window box.

In a few moments, Anyuta joined her at the window. Sofya still played mindlessly with the soil. Anyuta slipped a packet into Sofya's pocket. "Read these letters. You must find some way to end the torture you are inflicting on each other."

Sofya nodded. She didn't turn as her sister left the room and closed the door.

Sofya brushed the dirt from her hands and sat in the rocking chair. The envelopes bore Vladimir's unmistakable, nearly illegible handwriting. The stack of letters rested in her lap. She hesitated. Afraid to open them, she fingered their edges, then studied each postmark and arranged the envelopes in chronological order. With a deep sigh, she forced herself to open the first. She began her reading.

When she had finished the last letter, her hands were trembling. She struggled to control her emotions, to try to make sense of the progression of feelings Vladimir had exposed.

In the early letters, his concern was that she had been unfaithful. That there must be truth in the gossip about her and her professor. He was jealous. In a controlled way, he really was jealous.

More recently he wrote of his struggle not to have an affair with his English friend. Honor would not allow him to involve his friend in a relationship that would quite likely result in a child but could never lead to marriage. So, his sense of honor, not his concern for his wife was all that stopped him, if it had stopped him, from this affair. Sofya thought she knew the lady, undoubtedly the attractive red-haired woman who had so blatantly made advances to Vladimir when they were last in London.

The last letter from the pack cut more deeply than all the others. Vladimir had written to Anyuta knowing she was near the time of her delivery. After expressing his great happiness for Anyuta and Victor, and certainty of how pleased they must be, he confessed that he doubted that she, Sofya, could ever be a good mother. He had never seen the slightest inclination of maternal feelings in her behavior. Although he deeply wanted to be a family man, he doubted that he would be a good father. In addition to his personal shortcomings, his field trips would make family life difficult.

Sofya wanted to tear that letter apart. How could Vladimir have thought her so cold and unfeeling? He'd seen her caring for the sick, the wounded. He knew how much she needed friends and family. Of course she didn't want a child, certainly not now. She had her studies to finish.

She folded the last letter back into its envelope. Fighting back emotions, she forced herself to analyze the situation in light of the new information.

The evidence was unquestionable, her logical mind could no longer ignore it. The uncertain state of their relationship was destroying both her and Vladimir. Her dread of being alone would have to be faced. Her determination to finish her studies was unshakable. His determination to have a family—equally unshakable. The situation had to be resolved.

Sofya picked up the envelopes and carried them into the living area. She found Anyuta sitting in an oversized, tastelessly upholstered chair, her feet resting on a matching hassock, an open book in her lap. She lifted her head from the back of the chair as Sofya entered. For the moment, the sisters still had the apartment to themselves.

"I've decided to write to Vladimir," Sofya announced quietly. "I'll ask him to meet with me, so we can arrange for my starting divorce proceedings."

"Good," Anyuta responded tiredly. "That will be for the best. Sofya, it's not in your nature to suddenly become a devoted wife, even less so a doting mother."

"I have no idea why he and you seem to think I'm not suited to be a wife or mother. I find this whole issue to be an incredibly unwarranted and insensitive attack. What he really means is he believes I'm selfishly engrossed totally with my own affairs."

"Sofya, certainly you don't believe either Vladimir or I would misjudge you so cruelly."

Sofya's thoughts raced back to the painful time when she and Vladimir had thought she might be carrying his child. Of course she hadn't wanted a child then. She was just beginning her studies. That didn't mean she never wanted a child. How could Vladimir have thought that? She swallowed hard before speaking. "Of course, Vladimir, in his charming," she pronounced the word with irony and followed it with a long pause, "self-deprecating, illogical manner, claims he'd be a terrible husband and father. Still he insists he must have a family."

"Vladimir's letters are filled with emotion, not reason. Don't expect them to have the cold logic of a mathematical proof," Anyuta softly added.

"He harps on the smothering effects of my overpowering will." Her voice cracked. His accusations couldn't be true. She was the one who had been overpowered by her need for him. This last year without his affection and attention, with only constant bickering followed by long periods of silence, she had been the one to suffer. Struggling against a desire to melt into tears, she managed to strike out. "He follows his attack with that self-pitying, whining tone of his. He is unworthy of being a husband, particularly my husband. And the confession that he feels guilty for marrying me when he really loved me. And the mad man's remedy for this guilty, pitifully proclaimed love? To dissolve our marriage! He drives me mad, Anyuta. Absolutely, mad."

"You really love him." Genuine surprise and pity filled each word. Looking down at her hand and turning the gold band, Anyuta barely whispered, "I know the pain of loving someone who has weaknesses you can't understand. Weaknesses you think will drive you mad. Sofya, now may be the best time to put an end to pain. Your pain and his."

Sofya threw herself down on the divan, and lay silent, her eyes closed. She felt Anyuta's hand calmly stroking her forehead.

Sofya murmured, "I just don't have the energy to fight any longer. I'll do whatever he wants."

CHAPTER TWENTY-EIGHT

1873 ❧ *Zurich*

Sofya held baby Urey in her arms as she paced before the nursery window. Surely, if she could learn mathematics she could learn to hold a baby. Confirming her hypothesis, Urey smiled charmingly up at her. She thought of the small brain growing behind the smile, and wondered if it would later interest itself in politics—or, perhaps, in mathematics.

Julia was settled in the old wooden rocker, the rhythmic creaking soothing the child. "He's certainly the perfect gentleman now," she commented. "Not at all the abysmal manners he showed us this morning during the baptismal service."

"One can hardly blame him." Sofya patted the bundle tenderly. "Strange chanting, the strong smell of incense, and then three dips in the font. What we put our children through in the name of religion!"

"I notice it didn't take Victor long to remove the gold cross from the baby, even if it was a gift from the revered Lavrov. As if he thought there might be some contamination."

"I'm sure the gift was a sign of Lavrov's respect for Father, rather than for any sincere religious feelings."

"Agreed." Julia got up from the chair and peeked into the bundle. "The child is handsome, isn't he? May I hold him?"

Gratefully, Sofya passed the baby over.

Anyuta appeared in the doorway, looking tired. But her voice was pleased. "The caterer has brought the cheese, bread and pastries, I've prepared the samovar, and Victor's opening the bottles of wine. The guests can arrive.

"Sorry, Julia, but I must nurse Urey once more before they come."

Julia passed the bundle to Anyuta.

"The guests are from the Russian community here in Zurich, aren't they?" Julia asked.

"Yes. Mostly politicals, some academics." Tiredly Anyuta leaned her head back against the rocker. "I'm hoping you and Julia will like the academics enough to consider staying here in Zurich."

"No matter how well I like them, I have to return to Berlin," Julia announced in a tone that gave no hint of uncertainty. "I've still got a lot of work to do in the laboratory, maybe another year or so, but I'd have to start my experiments over from the beginning if I moved now."

"And you, Sofya?" Anyuta nodded to her. "There's a professor at the Polytechnikum, Hermann Schwarz, who studied with Weierstrass. If my informant is correct, Schwarz has an excellent mathematical reputation."

"I know of Professor Schwarz," Sofya responded quietly. "He's the mathematician who beat me to publication."

Anyuta continued, undaunted and undistracted. "I've given your stay here quite a bit of thought, Sofya. Studying with Schwarz would give you a fresh outlook on your work. After all, you've been with Weierstrass for three years now."

"You may have a point." A change certainly would dispel some of the rumors surrounding her relationship with Weierstrass. Perhaps even save him from engaging in dangerous acts of gallantry in defense of her honor.

"Doctorates are easier for women to obtain in Switzerland, at least I've heard that's true in medicine, and the Swiss universities are very highly respected." Anyuta looked at her sister. "Please, give the idea of staying here in Zurich some serious consideration. I would love to have you near me."

A knock at the door announced the arrival of the first guest. The sound of male voices reached them as Victor greeted two of his friends.

SOON THE SMALL APARTMENT was filled with cigarette smoke and friendly conversation. As the party broke into small groups, Victor made his way toward the gathering that had quickly formed around Lavrov.

"Victor, what a charming party!" the elder statesman congratulated him as he approached. "But Goldsmith and I were just noting that Smirnov isn't here."

"Smirnov told me he was visiting you this afternoon," the bespectacled Goldsmith added. "I assumed he'd be here when we arrived."

Victor dug a cheap watch out of his pocket. "When I visited him at the office he was doing some editing. That was about three this afternoon, after the christening. He's probably so absorbed in the work that he's forgotten the time. He said you were coming by for him, Goldsmith."

"My God, how embarrassing!" Goldsmith's face colored. "I received a note from him just before I left to meet my wife at the university. I assumed the note had to do with some editorial matter. I haven't opened it."

He reached into his pocket and pulled out an envelope. Tearing it open, he read it aloud. " 'Let's share a taxi to Victor's. I'll be waiting for you. Smirnov.' "

"You'd better go back for him now," Lavrov suggested.

"I'll leave immediately," Goldsmith agreed. "Victor, tell Katerina where I've gone. She's immersed in some discussion with Anyuta and your sister-in-law."

"So she is." Victor looked across the room at the three women. "You'll be gone and back before she even misses you. My Anyuta's arguments tend to be long and forceful, and her sister is even more of an orator."

Goldsmith hurried out. Lavrov and Victor were soon deep in a discussion of the articles Smirnov was now editing, to be published in the first edition of the new paper.

SOFYA, ANYUTA AND KATERINA GOLDSMITH nibbled at small slices of rye bread. Their discussion had turned naturally from politics to current literature. Anyuta deftly turned the conversation to Dostoevsky's newest work, *The Damned*. Cleverly she defended her ex-suitor's artistic abilities, while Katerina argued against his reactionary political ideas. He was a religious fanatic, an ultraconservative and a threat to progress. Sofya felt a flush of embarrassment. She had not read the work and wanting neither to defend nor disparage her friend, she politely broke from the little group.

She had just reached the samovar when a faint cry from the baby made her turn toward the nursery. Through the half-open door she could see Julia pacing with Urey on her shoulder. Thinking to bring her a little refreshment, Sofya put some sweets on a small dish. She was just reaching for a glass when one of the guests approached her.

The woman introduced herself as Elizaveta Fedorovna Litvinova, a fellow mathematics student. With a swift glance, meant to appear casual, Sofya tried to take Litvinova's measure. Was this a possible rival for the honor of first woman doctorate? Or, more likely, a beginning student, to be helped on her way?

Elizaveta Fedorovna extinguished her cigarette and reached for a glass. "I'm quite an admirer of yours."

"Really!" Sofya acknowledged the compliment without taking her eyes from the glass of hot tea she was pouring.

"Oh, yes. Like you, my preparatory studies were in Petersburg with Strannoliubsky. You were very much his star pupil. He tirelessly sings your praises."

"He may have exaggerated my abilities. He likes to tell a good story." Sofya studied the young woman, a blond beauty with pale skin and beautiful blue eyes that sparkled with intelligence. The same type of beauty as Anyuta, but not at all in Anyuta's class for grace and manner. "I haven't heard from Strannoliubsky for many months. How is he?"

"He married recently. His wife is very much a modern woman. She often helps in arranging his schedule of classes and even does some tutoring. Clearly, theirs is a union of love." Litvinova paused for just a moment, as if to draw breath. Then more softly added, "unlike many others from his circle of friends." Her gaze met Sofya's directly.

Nothing more needed to be said; Litvinova knew, or strongly suspected, that Sofya's marriage had been an "arrangement."

But now Litvinova was hesitating, "I received a letter from our teacher only yesterday. He related news of your husband." The word "husband" was pronounced with a sharp emphasis.

"And . . . ?" Sofya prodded encouragingly. Perhaps she would learn some real news of Vladimir.

Litvinova continued in hushed, conspiratorial tones, so that Sofya could barely hear her through the babble of party noise. "Strannoliubsky told of your husband's unfortunate encounter with the magesterium examining board at Odessa."

Sofya's eyes widened for just a moment. She turned to the samovar, mainly to hide her face, which judging from the warm flush and quickening of her breath, must be showing shock. She had no desire to reveal how ignorant she was of Vladimir's affairs. She poured a second glass of tea, silently commanding herself to composure. While her face was still turned she spoke in a controlled voice. "Rumors in Petersburg about that incident in Odessa? I would be amused to hear what everyone is saying."

Litvinova innocently obliged. "Well, as I heard the story, Vladimir approached the examining board without reviewing his university course work, even though Strannoliubsky and others had advised him to study."

Sofya interrupted. "Vladimir studies constantly. His work and recent publications are proof enough of his competence."

"I'm sure that's so," Litvinova responded, then continued. "Perhaps more surprising, shortly before the examination, Vladimir challenged the qualifications of one of the examiners, publicly, in a professional journal."

Sofya struggled to hide her reaction. How could Vladimir be so unwise?

"According to Strannoliubsky, the examiner confronted Vladimir with the accusations." Litvinova paused, her eyes searching Sofya's face. "Did your husband actually write letters discrediting the examiner?"

Sofya hesitated only briefly. "And why wouldn't he? If the man's research is faulty, I'm sure Vladimir felt it was his duty to point that out, no matter what the consequence to himself."

"Well. Be that as it may, the examiner felt he had been insulted."

What a snippy thing she is, thought Sofya. She's enjoying carrying tales. And perhaps she's even enjoying weakening my emotional state. Is this the way she chooses to compete?

Litvinova continued, "It seems to me an unwise thing for an applicant to do, just before his examination."

"Vladimir always does what he thinks is just, not what is politically correct." Silently Sofya blamed herself. She should have been there to advise him. He could be so impractical, bold and foolish!

Litvinova stopped to taste a sweet, in the process moving so she now stood between the nursery doorway and Sofya. "And that's not all. Strannoliubsky says that at the examination, Vladimir again challenged the credentials of the examiner. The examiner responded by questioning Vladimir on the most obscure areas. When he couldn't give suitable answers to the first two questions, the board dismissed him." Litvinova paused, her eyes seeming very innocent. "Tell me Sofya, is this one of Strannoliubsky's exaggerations?"

Sofya responded quickly. "Would it matter if I denied the gossip? It would still be passed from person to person. Better if I let this rumor run its course."

"That is wise." Litvinova flushed red as she spoke. Her tones were much softened.

Sofya noted the change. Apparently Litvinova realized too late, that she might have seriously offended a potential ally. Sofya forgave her. The woman must have assumed that like most women in fictitious marriages, Sofya had no regard, and perhaps even a little contempt, for her partner.

Still flustered, Litvinova tried to recover the situation. "But when information is so limited . . ."

"I'm sure Vladimir will be offered a suitable position elsewhere. His research papers have been very well received both in Germany and in England." Trying to think of something else to add, Sofya realized that Peter Lavrov was standing at her side, pouring himself a glass of tea. He must have overheard the last part of the conversation.

With both women now staring at him, Lavrov commented quietly, "Unfortunately, there may be some who reason that Vladimir acted this way to impress certain political groups with his defiance of Russian authority. And others may interpret his actions to mean he is putting up a show, and he is really working with the Russian authorities."

"Oh, not that again! What a horrid accusation! And what nonsense!" Sofya retorted angrily.

"Yes, total nonsense." Lavrov placed his hand lightly on her shoulder in a fatherly manner. "I relate it to you, not to hurt you, but to protect you. You need to know what is being said about your husband. Unfortunately, a number of government agents have been recently uncovered in our ranks, and we are all suspicious of each other. Which, I am sure, is one effect the government is trying to produce."

Sofya stared at him in silence.

"You must admit, Sofya," Lavrov's voice was now soothing, "Vladimir's attacking prominent scholars is no way for him to win a position at any university. Least of all in Russia, where administrators seek excuses to disqualify those trained abroad."

Sofya swallowed, successfully dispelling the tightening in her throat. She sighed. "You have a point, sir."

There was a pause. Lavrov glanced at his watch and then expectantly at the door. In the brief space of time, Sofya was able to recover her composure.

"Enough talk of the depressing situations at home." Lavrov turned to Litvinova. "I hear you are a student of mathematics."

"Professor Schwarz has taken me under his guidance." Litvinova beamed. She turned to Sofya with a look that seemed to ask forgiveness. "Would you like to attend one of his lectures with me?"

"I'd be delighted. We'll make arrangements," Sofya answered politely. Actually she wanted very much to see Schwarz teach. His techniques and amiability would factor strongly in her decision on staying in Zurich. And she also wanted to discover just how far advanced Litvinova was in her studies.

"You'll be impressed," Litvinova continued. "Of course, he's not Weierstrass. I envy you working with the grandmaster. I'd do almost anything to have Weierstrass as my doctoral advisor. Perhaps when I've finished my undergraduate work you'd put in a word for me."

"Perhaps." Again Sofya's heart leapt. So, that was this rival's plan! Litvinova wanted to study with Karl. And she was after a doctorate. Sofya felt a sudden rush of jealousy, all the sharper because she knew it was irrational.

Sofya nodded to Litvinova and Lavrov, and then motioned to the bedroom. "Excuse me. My friend has been waiting patiently for me to take my turn walking the baby."

When Sofya entered the bedroom, her eyes met those of Julia, who clearly had overheard the remarks concerning Vladimir. She clutched the baby close to her, comforting him. At the same time she whispered to Sofya, "You must help Vladimir. You must."

Interruption came in the form of Anyuta, announcing that she needed to nurse the baby again. Sofya and Julia were to rejoin the party.

In less than a party mood, they obeyed, securely closing the bedroom door behind them.

As THEY RETURNED to the group, Sofya noticed a young man clearly making his way through the crowd toward them. He had straight black hair and bushy black brows over sharp green eyes. He was rather tall with slumping shoulders and his large head extended forward like the prow of a ship.

Sofya touched Julia's arm to halt her motion into the crowd.

When he was before them effectively blocking their passage, he stood awkwardly, his eyes downcast. Running a nervous hand through his hair, he explained that he was a student in the chemistry department of the Polytechnikum. His eyes lifted to Julia and her soft smile encouraged him. He continued. He hoped to start graduate work in the fall, with luck in Berlin. He would very much like to hear the ladies' impressions of the chemistry faculty there.

Julia's gentle response seemed to set him at ease. And she and the student were soon engaged in a conversation.

Sofya, having nothing to contribute to the assessment of chemical laboratories, turned away, wondering if Julia had even noticed how attractive the shy fellow was, with his piercing green eyes.

Looking over the crowded, noisy room, Sofya's gaze settled on Victor, who was smugly occupying the place of honor on the divan, immediately to the right of Lavrov. Litvinova and several other students were sitting on the floor in front of the old master, raptly listening. Crossing her legs at the ankle, she gracefully lowered herself to a sitting position between Litvinova and a stocky, dark-haired male. The man extended his hand in assistance, and now offered a cigarette. She accepted silently. Adjusting her skirt, she pulled her knees up under her chin, her arms wrapped around them.

Lavrov was expounding his political philosophy, with which Sofya felt quite comfortable. The ideas of Herzen and other early thinkers were brought out and reaffirmed. His voice boomed, "Individuals must prepare themselves and others through education and propaganda for the time when the old authorities will be no more."

The mention of fading authority prompted one of the young women to mention the Paris Commune. Litvinova leaned over to Sofya and whispered, "That's Vera Perovskaya, one of the Frichi group."

"What's that?" Sofya whispered back.

"Women students here in Zurich who lodge at Frau Frichi's. They've displayed a budding interest in social issues. Vera's the brightest and most energetic of them."

Sofya took a closer look at the woman. She was about twenty years old, strikingly beautiful with a strong forehead, a delicate nose, a mass of luxuriously wavy, honey-colored hair, and sparkling gray eyes that were a little small, but very lively.

Soon a brisk debate was under way, concerning the effects of the Paris Commune on the movement to social reform. As always in these discussions, no consensus was reached.

When the comments turned to the possibility of further violence, Sofya struggled against the urge to scream out her objections. She mustn't let the surging memories of the bloodbath block a reasoned response. There would be no convincing these students with shouts.

But at last she could hold back no longer. "Violence accomplishes nothing." Her voice was louder and firmer than she'd expected. "I was in Paris, tending the wounded. And I, for one, have seen enough of senseless suffering and wasteful loss."

Victor immediately pounced in contradiction. "My dear sister, when one is actually in the front lines, one takes a different view. What of the greater violence that is being enacted against the working classes every day? Although peaceful change is an admirable dream, human nature being what it is, that is most of us not having the patience of saints, find that violence is a tool that can and should be used."

Sofya glared at Victor, as a babble of small arguing groups arose around her. How could Victor support violence? Yes, he'd been on the barricades—or at least he claimed he had been. Certainly he'd seen the horrors committed by both sides in war. She knew her sister Anyuta had fought to the end, risking her life and her sanity.

Anyuta had joined the group. She sat on the divan, leaning tiredly against her husband, whose arm had gone around her shoulders. Evidently Urey had been peacefully settled for the evening.

Straightening her back and pushing a little away from her husband, Anyuta voiced her view. "Victor, I'm sure Sofya didn't mean to imply that the Commune accomplished nothing. It will always be a beacon of hope to those wishing justice. And Victor, you agree that wanton violence serves no end. However, in circumstances of self-preservation, even saints may be violent."

Sofya noted that Anyuta, tired though she was, was taking on the uncharacteristic role of mediator. This post-Paris Anyuta was not the sister Sofya had grown up with. Anyuta's jaw was set when she fixed her steely blue gaze on Sofya. Any disagreement between her guests, much less between her sister and husband, was not to turn ugly.

Anyuta continued to speak now addressing one, now another, of the guests. Sofya contributed what she could, taking her cue from Anyuta and also playing the mediator.

Just as a more friendly atmosphere was established, the door to the apartment flew open. Sofya looked up, half expecting a landlord come to complain of smoke and noise. But the figure bursting in was that of Goldsmith, out of breath, flushed, looking half crazed with excitement.

"Smirnov's been attacked," the man in the doorway choked out. "He's barely alive!"

Gradually silence fell. The guests stared in disbelief. Goldsmith had to repeat and amplify his announcement. "Smirnov's been beaten! Our office ransacked!"

Now Lavrov and others crowded around him anxious for more information, which Goldsmith did his best to supply. "Smirnov says it was some of Bakunin's supporters. He recognized Sokolov among his attackers. The beasts came for the documents. Smirnov was alone. They became violent."

Anyuta's thoughts immediately leaped back in memory, to the gun. But surely Goldsmith would have mentioned the fact if Smirnov had fired at his attackers.

Now a dozen voices rose up in indignation. Sokolov, the attacker, was a big brute of a man, Smirnov a sharp-tongued but frail fellow.

"I found Smirnov on the floor." Goldsmith was gradually getting his breath back. "Bloodied, bruised and bewildered. He kept murmuring something about his jacket hanging on a hook. He wouldn't lie still until I'd brought him the garment which he clutched to his chest. Then I ran next door for help. One of the medical students living there, a Russian girl, agreed to care for him. She's taking him to your place, Lavrov. I rushed home and got my revolver. Then I came here."

Some of the guests spoke of calling the police. But the idea was quickly overruled; involving the authorities would cause trouble for the whole colony and draw attention to their political activities.

CHAPTER TWENTY-NINE

1873 ❦ *Zurich*

Sofya sat on the edge of the cot in the baby's room, where late morning sunlight fell through thin yellow curtains. Anyuta's copy of Dostoevsky's novel, *The Damned*, lay next to her, open, face down, the last chapter unread.

Sofya and the baby were alone in Anyuta's small apartment. The three days since the abrupt ending to Anyuta's party had been filled with turmoil and deception. Since that night, Sofya had not seen Victor. She assumed he was away at political meetings. Anyuta had made lame excuses for him to Mama and Papa, who had announced last night that they were returning to Russia.

Sofya assumed her shrewd father had learned of Smirnov's beating. Father was no fool when it came to political struggles. He would guess a retaliatory response from Lavrov's followers was being planned and that Victor and Anyuta were involved. The ensuing violence of attack and counterattack between the groups would soon draw the attention of the Swiss government and eventually the attention of the Tsar. Father must have come to the conclusion that he could best help his politically troublesome daughter from his base of contacts at home.

Sounds of movement in the quiet apartment brought Sofya back from her musing. Presently Anyuta opened the bedroom door and looked in to ask softly, "Did Urey give you much trouble?"

"None at all. He's been sleeping contentedly for the last half hour." Sofya stood up and stretched. "Did you get much done at the paper?"

"Everything is in such a commotion. No one's really working. I was able to sit down most of the time, thank goodness." Anyuta lowered herself onto the cot.

"I wish you wouldn't overextend yourself, Anyuta," Sofya scolded gently. "The birth was hard on you. And you're just starting to get some of your strength back."

"I'm much better, really." Anyuta's tired voice did little to assure Sofya. "Did Julia come to help you?"

"Julia's gone, on the early morning train to Berlin. She insists she must resume her studies."

"I suspected that Julia was equally concerned with removing herself from the temptation of the handsome, young chemistry student she met at the party."

"Poor Julia!" Sofya gently adjusted the blanket more tightly around the sleeping Urey. "She runs so frantically from any chance of romance. If she only realized how helpful some of these men could be to her career, and how easily they could be kept at a comfortable distance. I suppose it's lucky for me Julia is shy of men. It makes her a wonderfully reliable companion. Except of course, when she runs away from them and leaves me behind."

Little Urey let out a soft cry. Sofya began to gently rub his tummy, but the cry became louder.

Anyuta struggled to her feet and picked up the baby. "What about your plans, Sofya?" With little Urey leaning against her shoulder, Anyuta began walking back and forth in the bouncing step often favored by mothers with small children. The bouncing made her words come in oddly punctuated phrases. "Classes have started . . . and . . . you aren't . . . returning? . . . Have . . . you decided . . . to stay in Zurich?"

"For a while longer," Sofya answered as she watched her sister's rhythmic bobbing. Days ago she had stopped being distracted by the bouncing motions of her sister with the baby. Some of their most sisterly conversations had been interspersed with Anyuta bouncing and cooing to little Urey.

Sofya continued. "Weierstrass writes that he wants to get out of Berlin. A case of cholera has been reported in the papers. So it's no use my going there, he and his sisters will be at their retreat on Rugen Island for the next few months."

"I'd . . . hoped you'd . . . decided to study . . . in Zurich."

"Weierstrass knows my mathematical strengths and weaknesses. Staying with him will speed up my research work." Sofya picked at a loose string in the bed's cover. "For a while I thought I had the luxury of changing mentors. But now I realize that if mine is to be the first mathematical doctorate awarded to a woman, I better not lose any time. Others have seen the goal."

"Your . . . competitive spirit . . . has been roused. Pity your opponents." Anyuta treated the matter as if it were a joke. She placed the now sleeping Urey back in his bed and motioned to Sofya that they should leave the room.

Keeping the door to the bedroom open just enough so they would be able to hear the baby's cry, the sisters went into the living area.

Anyuta settled herself on the divan. Sofya pushed the foot rest toward Anyuta. Then, going to the samovar, she poured two cups of hot tea.

As she handed Anyuta the steaming brew, Anyuta spoke, "So, I have just a few months with you. You aren't planning on staying at the hotel, are you? It's far too expensive."

"Litvinova's recommended a boardinghouse near the university. I'll meet other students, have an opportunity to talk mathematics." Sofya sat next to her sister.

"Why don't you move in with us?" Anyuta placed her cup on the near table. She stared into Sofya's eyes. She looked away and hesitated. "And if you take your own place . . ."

"Yes?" Sofya gently touched Anyuta's arm.

"Well, I'm worried about you going about the student section alone. If you stayed with us, I could see to it that you always had a companion when you went out. Since the night when that idiot Smirnov was beaten, three more of our friends have been threatened with violence."

"Threats," Sofya said firmly. She did not want to accept that two groups of Russian reformers struggling against an oppressive Tsarist government and in principle against all world tyrants would actually wage war against each other over a few pieces of paper. She didn't want to believe intelligent people could act so irrationally. She reasserted firmly, "Just threats."

"Sofya, Smirnov was armed on the night when the attackers broke into the office. But he'd left the weapon in the pocket of his jacket, and the jacket hanging in the entry." Anyuta's eyes were fixed on Sofya. "They are not all as inept as Smirnov. Some are experienced fighters, veterans of the Commune. The Bakuninists know you're associated with us; they might attack you. The streets are filled with bands of sympathizers for one side or the other. Victor and his friends have taken to carrying guns."

"Oh, please, Anyuta!" Sofya rose and walked to the window. Looking out she saw one old woman walking with a tote bag filled with groceries. Sofya turned back to her sister. "The streets of Zurich aren't really filled with anyone but peace-loving Swiss. Save your mothering for Urey."

Anyuta was silent. Her face was turned to Sofya, the beautiful features drawn with exhaustion and worry.

Sofya sighed. She went to the divan, stooped next to her sister. Taking Anyuta's hands in her own, she gently said, "I'll be fine."

The corners of Anyuta's mouth turned up just a bit, her eyes flickered with a spark of her old contentiousness. "I suppose you don't decline to stay here on the hypothesis that you would have to help care for the baby?"

"Not at all! Not at all." Sofya laughed and straightened. "I'll visit as often as you like. And, I'll help with little Urey."

SOFYA AND LITVINOVA walked down Oberstrasse toward the lecture hall at the Polytechnikum. The area was the center of the colony of three hundred or so Russian émigrés in Zurich.

"I met Schwarz several weeks ago," Sofya explained as they hurried past pawn shops, bakeries, and resale bookstores. "A chance encounter at the library. Then I invited him and his wife to dinner at my sister's."

"I meant to introduce you to him." Litvinova apologized. "I find him an attractive and charming man. His wife tends to put on airs. I suppose that comes from being the daughter of one of the world's leading mathematicians. You knew she is Kummer's daughter?"

"No!" Sofya sighed. "Well, that explains her attitude. She probably heard horrifying rumors about me from her father. Kummer is head of the mathematics department in Berlin. It was his objection that blocked my admission."

"Well, Schwarz is of a completely different mind. He welcomes women students. Especially, when they show promise." Litvinova added, "Did you have a chance to talk mathematics?"

"Not much." Sofya silently recalled the awful night. The dinner had been dismal, talk constantly interrupted by the baby crying. Anyuta and Victor were having one of their disagreements and the air had been thick with tension.

"I did discover," Sofya continued, "that Schwarz and I share some areas of interest."

"I can guess what those are, differential equations of course, probably those involving trigonometric functions. Schwarz is always emphasizing their importance, even to his beginning students."

"Yes, and some topics on converging infinite series and complex numbers." Sofya went on. "A few days later, I met Schwarz again, in his office. I was able to go into some detail with him on my fascination with describing the motion of toy tops, gyroscopes, planets, that sort of twirling movement." She moved her forefinger in a small circle for illustration.

"The elusive problem of the Mathematical Mermaid," Litvinova nodded. "He's mentioned that in some of his lectures. It seems you and Schwarz are off to a good start. You didn't need me to invite you to this lecture."

"Don't be silly! I'll be much more relaxed in the lecture hall having another woman with me." Sofya linked arms with Litvinova. But shortly they separated again, detouring on the walkway to avoid a vendor's cart whose owner was violently disputing the price of a piece of fruit with a young student. Sofya turned back to stare at the handsome student who bore all the marks of her countrymen. He was tall and sturdily built, his loose-fitting red shirt hanging carelessly over his trousers, his black boots well dirtied. His reddish hair was worn longer than fashionable among the Swiss and the start of a bushy beard was apparent.

"You know it's even a pleasure to hear street arguments, when they're in Russian," Sofya commented when she and Litvinova were again side by side. "You can't imagine how I've missed that."

"I understand completely." Litvinova relinked arms with Sofya. "For all my experience with German and French, I feel I'm only totally myself when I'm speaking Russian."

"Precisely. It's like taking off a mask." Sofya confirmed her friend's feelings. "Yesterday evening, the young men were singing peasant songs in the cafeteria. I retired to my room humming. I haven't done that in years."

"You've been away from familiar things for too long," Litvinova scolded mockingly.

Sofya's thoughts jumped to Vladimir and her hand instinctively touched the letter hidden in the pocket in the folds of her dress. In the two months since she'd written him requesting a meeting regarding their divorce, there had been a number of exchanges, some angry, some not. Still they had not managed to arrange a meeting, because it seemed impossible to agree on an exact time and place. And so the flurry of short letters had continued.

The letter now in her pocket was Vladimir's latest, in which he kept repeating how sorry he was that he had hurt her feelings. He had been cruel. He welcomed her concern for him. However, he could not meet her in Berlin as she had requested. Would she come to Jena, to talk with him there?

Just this morning, she'd quickly dashed off yet another note, saying that a meeting in Jena was impossible. The meeting must be in Berlin. Although she was now in Zurich, there was no sense his coming here as she expected Weierstrass to summon her back at any moment. She'd wire him the minute she arrived in Berlin. She decided to included a joking reminder to Vladimir that her relationship with Karl was most poetic and platonic. So, he need not fear she was insisting on Berlin as meeting place for any but practical reasons.

"Watch out!" Litvinova clutched Sofya's elbow just as she was about to step out in front of a moving carriage. "You certainly were lost in your thoughts. Mathematical ruminating, I suppose. I often do that."

Shocked a little by her own absentmindedness and a little frightened, Sofya murmured her thanks. "Actually, it wasn't mathematics that distracted me." She hesitated, then hedged the truth. "Thoughts of home, friends."

"Be careful," she cautioned. "You might have been seriously injured."

They had come now in full view of the Polytechnikum. Sofya slowed her steps to look at it. Here was one of the most renowned centers of engineering and science in Europe, indeed in the world. Of the hundreds of students enrolled only thirty-four were Russians and of the Russians only three were women. The other three hundred or so Russian students in Zurich were attending the university.

"If you're impressed with the exterior, just wait until you see the inside," Litvinova promised. A minute later, Sofya caught her breath. The oak-paneled halls and tiled floor inspired a mood of majesty. Heavy doors opened onto large rooms filled with dark benches and writing tables. Long, narrow windows of frosted glass provided illumination.

Now they were entering a lecture hall. Sofya had forgotten how overwhelming the atmosphere could be.

"Let's sit in Kamchatka," Litvinova whispered. Sofya smiled her agreement as they took seats in the very last row: Kamchatka, the Russian province farthest removed from the capital.

Sofya's escort leaned forward to whisper in her ear. "There will be over fifty engineering students attending today's lecture. I'm certain you're familiar with the techniques for handling second order differentials."

"I'll be concentrating on his teaching techniques," Sofya whispered back. She sat still with her hands folded on the desk in front of her. The last time she had been in a classroom had been in Petersburg, just after her marriage. Flanked by Vladimir and her dearest uncle, Sofya had been smuggled into the hall. She remembered how frightened and determined she had been. And how protective and supportive Vladimir had been.

A nudge and another whisper from Litvinova brought Sofya back to the Zurich classroom. "Are you daydreaming again?"

Sofya straightened. She must not let her mind wander so. Her object in coming here was to study and analyze the various methods and techniques of presenting the precise, refined ideas of mathematics.

The last of the students were finding their places. Not surprisingly, there were no other women among them. Those who sat near the two ladies acknowledged their presence respectfully, with nods and murmurs.

A few stopped to say a word to Litvinova whom they recognized. Sofya overheard one of the Russian men excitedly ask, "Elizaveta, have you seen the article in this morning's paper? The Tsar's taken notice of his subjects in Zurich."

Litvinova shook her head. Neither she nor Sofya had read the newspaper. Before the student could tell them more about the article, Schwarz entered. The class rose and awaited a nod from the professor before resuming their seats. The room fell silent.

The professor stepped onto the raised platform. He settled his papers on the lectern, then checked the supply of chalk.

The students waited expectantly, pencils in hand, ready to start taking notes.

The Professor scanned the room, saw Sofya and Litvinova in the last row and nodded in recognition, then began his lecture.

"Gentlemen and ladies. As engineering students you have all encountered potential functions in your study of gravitation. Today, I will present the first theorem of George Green from his masterly paper *An Essay on the Application of Mathematical Analysis to the Theories of Electricity and Magnetism*, which I am informed, will be used in your fall class on electricity."

A massive groan rose from the hall.

With a smile of mock sympathy, he turned to the board, and began writing a very involved equation filled with triple integrals and second order derivatives.

The class copied furiously.

He paused and turned back to the class. "Take heart, class, I will not present the full proof, which doubtless few of you are equipped mathematically to appreciate. Instead, I will present a few examples of its application to electrical and magnetic problems."

He turned back to the board, then hesitated, and faced the group. "First, may I mention that in 1828, the very year Green published his classic paper with his proof of the above theorem, a Russian mathematician, Michel Ostrogradsky, presented a proof of the theorem to the St. Petersburg Academy of Sciences." His eyes were riveted in Sofya's direction. "These things happen in mathematics, when two strong, well-trained minds tackle the same problem. The duplication is quite innocent of devious intention."

Sofya understood. Schwarz was offering her his sympathy, not an apology. He had not willfully snatched her work.

The lecture proceeded, Schwarz stopping now and again to ask pointed questions of his class, which helped the students follow his calculations.

Sofya's mind drifted. So, Ostrogradsky had also tackled this problem. She would search out the reference. After all, she told herself, the last time she had looked at any of Ostrogradsky work she had been a child of six delighting in the swiggles, circles and lines of the makeshift wallpaper of her nursery.

Now her mind, only half engaged, easily kept up with the substance of the lecture. The delightful swiggles were no longer strangers, but old friends.

When Schwarz had finished his mathematical presentation, the class awaited his formal dismissal. But he had one more thing to tell them.

"You have been privileged and honored to attend this lecture with one of the most promising mathematical students of our day. In the back row is the Frau Sofya Kovalevsky. She is currently studying with the great Karl Weierstrass. Her notes on his lectures and procedures have made available to the mathematical community some of the thoughts of today's greatest mathematician. I have had the pleasure of reading her notes and speaking with her. She is the finest example of the Russian woman student. Please, Frau Kovalevsky, stand and greet our students."

Sofya blushed as she stood. The eyes of the entire class were upon her. The students broke into a spontaneous applause.

As the students filed out, many stopping to shake hands with Sofya, Schwarz approached the women. He asked if they had seen the morning papers. Sofya and Litvinova again exchanged worried glances.

"Please, come to my office," Schwarz invited them. "You must see this article."

On his desk lay the *Government Herald* of June 7, 1873, folded open to a page with the headline "Russian government addresses women students of Zurich." Sofya and Litvinova bent over the article, reading the German text as fast as they could.

Sofya skimmed key phrases.—center of propaganda—revolutionary organizations—socialist theories—equality of the sexes—free love—local inhabitants scandalized . . .

Litvinova, reading at a faster pace, gasped and pointed out these words:

Under the guise of medical training, the women concentrate their study on the branch of obstetrics with the particular intent of practicing that procedure which in all countries is punishable as a criminal offense.

"What slanderous lies!" Sofya's anger was so intense that she could barely choke out the words. "Russians are dying for a lack of doctors. Half the women won't let a male doctor near them because of 'modesty.' And the authorities worry about abortion!"

"I agree with your assessment completely, Frau Kovalevsky," Schwarz assured her.

"Wait until you read this!" Litvinova was again leaning over the paper, her finger tracing along the top of the next column of type.

All Russian women studying in Zurich, whether at the University or at the Polytechnikum, are to discontinue their study as quickly as possible. Degrees earned after Jan 1, 1874, will not be recognized in Russia. Furthermore, any woman attending lectures at these institutions after the given date will not be allowed a government position, nor will she be allowed to take the magesterium examination certifying her for positions at institutes of higher learning in Russia.

Hastily Sofya ran through the implications in her mind. This edict irresponsibly slandered and ruined the personal reputations of the women studying in Zurich. It threatened to ruin their careers in Russia. Most of the 104 women students, motivated by a desire to help their suffering countrymen, were studying to be physicians. However, as every Russian knew, doctors were certified by the state and for that matter, virtually all intellectual jobs depended on government approval.

Sofya looked at Litvinova, who was standing silent with her face pale, her eyes wide. Sofya understood.

Schwarz folded up the paper and handed it to Sofya. "Is there anything we professors can do to convince your government to rescind this order?" he asked. "Anything at all?" His tone indicated sincere willingness to help.

"I couldn't say." Sofya stumbled over the words.

"Thank you for the offer," Litvinova murmured. She was already heading for the door.

"We must meet with our friends," Sofya finally managed to get out. "Please, excuse us." The force of the edict reminded the the women of their Russian-ness, of their citizenship in a nation with an autocratic government, of their need to be cautious in expressing any opinions regarding their government or its edicts in the presence of any but the most trusted friends and relatives.

"I assure you, the citizens of Zurich do not hold the opinions expressed in this edict." Schwarz's words followed them. He was leaning against the door frame, calling after them as they walked down the long hall. "The Swiss government will make every effort to rectify any erroneous impressions your Tsar may have about your work here!"

Sofya and Litvinova hurried their steps. They needed a safe place to talk, to think. Sofya felt infinitely relieved that she was a private student of Weierstrass, putting her out of the scope of the ukase, beyond the notice of her government.

❧

THREE DAYS LATER, Sofya moved from one end of the living room to the other with a bouncing step, trying to imitate her sister's walk. She held Urey tightly pressed against her left shoulder. His little legs struggled against her breast as if he meant to climb it. With her right hand she patted his bare back as he fussed and cried uncomfortably. She had removed his blanket in an effort to cool him from the day's heat.

For the last hour, nothing Sofya tried would settle the child. She had cleanly swaddled him, laid him across her knees and patted him, cuddled and even sung to him. Somewhere along the line her exasperation had turned from the child to Anyuta. As she jiggled Urey now she whispered some rather sharp remarks to him concerning his mother.

"In the unlikely event that I someday have a child," Sofya informed her nephew forcefully, "I swear, by all that's holy, the child will always have a nanny. If I have to earn the necessary funds by translating English articles, operating a typing machine, or teaching runny-nosed little boys their sums, I swear, I'll do it."

Urey, pursuing his own agenda, took no notice of her declaration but went on crying.

Sofya recalled her own nanny, a strong peasant woman who encircled her with loving arms. If only she were here now to comfort Urey! What wonderful fairy tales nanny had told, complete with demon witches, idiot princes, and magical beasts. No one could tell stories like a Russian nanny.

Urey's head rested heavily against his aunt's neck. For the moment the child was quiet, but she dared not stop her pacing.

Sofya let her mind travel back, to the sweet smell of her nursery, the outrageous joy of jumping on nanny's giant feather bed. Mother was a stern disciplinarian, concerned about educating her to be a lady. Nanny was love and play, and not at all averse to Sofya's tomboy manners. A child, every child, needed a nanny. Perhaps every mother needed one even more.

A knock at the door came sharply enough to rouse her from her daydream, and Urey from uneasy sleep. "Oh, please, let it be your mother knocking because she's forgotten her key again!"

Holding the wiggling, crying baby against her breast with one arm, Sofya struggled with the other hand to turn the latch. Exasperated, she called out, "Just a minute, I'm having trouble with the lock." There was no answer. Finally, after she pushed against the wooden panel with her hip, the metal turned, the door opened.

Sofya stood back, one hand supporting the baby. The figure taking up most of the opening was lean and red-haired, with a close-cropped beard to match. The corners of his mouth, just visible, were turning up in the beginning of a foolish smile. The eyes were unmistakable.

"Oh, Vladimir, that beard!" Sofya said, laughing after the instant of recognition.

CHAPTER THIRTY

1873 ✦ *Zurich*

Striding into the room, Vladimir seized her in a hug of greeting, pressing the fussing baby between them.

As he released her, their eyes met, and they both laughed awkwardly.

"Your hair!" Vladimir ran his fingers through the strands that were now long enough to reach below her shoulders. "You've let it grow. The style is very flattering."

It was hard to savor her compliment, with Urey's crying again pitched at a disturbing level. Sofya paced and jiggled as she tried to carry on a conversation.

"I expected you to be in Berlin by now." He picked up his bag from the hall and brought it into the apartment, then closed the door.

"I thought I would be by this time, but Weierstrass is still worried about cholera. I'm staying at one of the boardinghouses."

Sofya walked to the open window where the day's first breeze fluttered the lacy curtain. The summer heat, the strain of caring for Urey, and Vladimir's unexpected arrival had completely unsettled her. Now Urey's hand had managed to clamp onto a stray curl of her hair. As she tried to free herself from his grip, she felt a drop of perspiration making its way down the side of her face.

Vladimir's eyes were on her. She felt herself flush under his gaze. Trying to compose herself, she searched for some intelligent line of conversation. "You've heard the Tsar's ukase?"

Vladimir's expression became serious. "Yes. Actually that's why I came. I know something about European universities, and I may be able to help the women find positions elsewhere. I have contacts in Bern, Geneva, and Paris. Even one in Philadelphia."

"They're accepting women at all those universities?" Sofya spoke incredulously.

"They certainly are. If the women are qualified and have the language skills."

Urey's crying had dissolved into gurgling. Vladimir walked up behind Sofya and put a finger gently under Urey's chin. "Another reason I came here is to meet my new nephew."

Sofya propped the baby in the curve of her left elbow. Urey was still for the moment, his eyes all wide and dark. "Urey Jaclard Korvin, may I present your uncle, Vladimir Onufrievich Kovalevsky?" She turned to Vladimir. "Now you've been formally introduced, you must get to know each other better." She motioned Vladimir that he was to take the burden.

Uneasily he put out his long arms, and Sofya settled Urey into them. "Be sure to support his head," she warned.

"You, young man, may call me Uncle Vova." Vladimir's eyes didn't leave the baby. Urey stopped fussing and offered his uncle a most charming smile.

Sofya sighed and sank onto the divan. "It's been a long morning." She wiped back a moist curl from her forehead. Marveling at the man and infant, both obviously content, she added, "How did you ever manage to quiet that child?"

"He does seem to like me. I may have a knack for this kind of work."

Someone was at the door, and it opened suddenly. Anyuta burst into the apartment, Victor close behind her. "Sofya, I'm so sorry we're late. We've been . . ."

She stopped. It took a moment before she recognized the man holding her baby. Then she cried out, "You've come! I'm so pleased!" A moment later she had scooped the child into her arms, kissing Vladimir lightly on each cheek as she did so. "Excuse us, I must tend Urey now," she added. Moments later the bedroom door had closed behind them.

Vladimir and Victor exchanged restrained greetings. Then Vladimir settled onto the divan beside Sofya. One arm came behind her and rested along the back of divan, his long legs stretched out before him. "Well, Victor, how are things going for you? Personally, I mean, I don't want to hear about politics."

Victor pulled a chair close to the divan. His words came quickly. "Hasn't Sofya told you?" He looked at Sofya with some displeasure. "Anyuta and I are returning to Russia just as soon as our papers can be put in order."

Sofya added, "Father has telegraphed, advising Anyuta and her family to return home."

Victor looked over his shoulder reflexively, and lowered his voice. "Reading between the lines of the telegram, the general seems to be saying it will be easier to explain our stay in Europe as being connected with the Zurich University affair. There's a good chance our activities in Paris can be hidden from the Russian government." Standing up from his chair, Victor unconsciously struck a pose. "If it were not for Anyuta and the child, you understand, I would immediately return to France and join the underground. But . . ."

"I understand," Vladimir interrupted softly. "A return to France is out of the question."

Sofya said, "I told Anyuta that I think it would be better for them to stay in Zurich." She avoided her brother-in-law's glare. "At least here, there is no fear of extradition to France. The Swiss have given asylum to all refugees from the uprising. In Russia, as we all know, it is different."

Vladimir added sadly, "I've heard that Anyuta's name is on the list of insurrectionists France has classified as probable incendiaries and common thieves." Vladimir leaned forward, his hand brushing against her back as he drew his arm to his side. He tapped his fingers nervously against each other for a moment. "You, Victor, being listed by the French as a political might someday be safe even in Russia, but Anyuta . . ." He turned to Sofya. "I agree. The family is safer here in Zurich."

Victor shifted his stance. "You two are wrong! Absolutely wrong. Anyuta will be perfectly safe. Her father can see to that." Victor glared at them in turn, then began to pace. "Surely you understand, Vladimir. The problem is money. The general has offered financial aid once we're in Russia. We'll stay at the apartment building run by the girls' aunt, as guests. The aunt and her maids can help Anyuta with the baby. I'll try to establish myself as a private tutor. Perhaps do a little writing as well. Anyuta and I have been talking about translating some French children's stories into Russian. They might be quite popular."

"I still have some connections in Russian publishing. I may be able to help." Vladimir nodded slowly, then shook his head. "I for one am rather ashamed at the way our wives' father always seems to be bailing us out of political and financial difficulties."

Sofya moved uncomfortably. She broke the awkward silence by addressing Victor. "When will you be leaving?"

"A few days. A week at most."

Anyuta reappeared just as Victor was speaking. "For as long as we're here, you're welcome to stay with us, Vladimir."

"Thank you, no. I may be in town for some time. I'll find a place of my own." Vladimir smiled warmly at her.

"You could take a room at the boardinghouse where I'm staying," Sofya offered.

Vladimir turned so only she could see the brief mocking smile. "I'll give that some consideration."

"Your effort to help the Russian women here in Zurich is admirable, Vladimir." Anyuta stood behind him and placed her hands on his shoulders tenderly. "But many of them are abandoning their efforts at an education. They're returning home in despair."

"Not despair, my dear," Victor contradicted, "just a redirection of their effort and rather formidable will. I expect most of those women will now devote their full attention to social reform. I know some of them well." Victor laughed wickedly. "What an opportunity! The government has no idea what it's unleashing. What asses they are! I say, thank God for this insane edict. Thank God, and Father, we'll be in Russia to take part in this." Victor threw back his head and laughed again.

THAT EVENING, Vladimir and Sofya walked to the boardinghouse where she was staying.

Sofya motioned to a building across the street. "That's the place."

She took his arm before stepping off the walkway. He pulled her back gently. "Just a moment please. I want to be sure I've really heard what you've been telling me about the accommodations. If single accommodations are available, and I do not have to share space, I'd have one small room with a bed, a desk and a wardrobe. No room to walk around. A very small window that, as you've assured me, will probably not open. The un-openable window most likely will overlook a filthy, cluttered yard. You're uncertain if the men have access to a water closet. Women board on the second floor, men the third. No visiting in each other's rooms. One small common room for receiving callers. Still, noisy chatter can be heard through the wall until at least midnight, every night. But if you ignore the occasional roach and protect against bedbugs, the rooms are not too uncomfortable."

"That's a fair, if blunt, summary of my comments," Sofya responded.

Vladimir spoke in a firm voice. "I'm sorry, but this will not do." He nudged her gently along the sidewalk. "Sofya, I'm not a student anymore. I'm looking for a respected position on a faculty. I need a place where I can entertain professors as well as students. And I must have a quiet place where I can read and study."

"You're becoming quite soft and bourgeois," Sofya teased. "Next you'll be donning a black top hat."

He laughed and patted her hand which was resting on his arm. "Nothing of the sort."

The hard calluses she could feel on his hands convinced her he spoke in truth.

"It's not the hardship," he continued. "I endure plenty of that while digging for old bones. In fact, I rather enjoy the rough life. But not the rough life of an overcrowded boardinghouse."

He had been guiding their walk toward a nearby hotel. "What do you know of this place?" he asked her.

"Guest speakers for the university are lodged here. I've dined here with Professor Schwarz and his wife. The atmosphere is quite cozy and comfortable, the food plentiful and good." She looked at him with a teasing twinkle in her eye. "Nicely bourgeois."

"Let's take a look."

"What sort of rooms will you require, sir?" the clerk asked Vladimir, then turned and smiled pleasantly at Sofya.

"My wife and I would like a suite with a moderately sized living room, two bedrooms, and a bath. We prefer at least one window overlooking the street."

The man consulted a ledger at his side. "There is a suite available on the second floor. Would you like to see it?"

"Yes," Vladimir affirmed.

The rooms were bright, and simply furnished. Vladimir quickly walked through the suite, opening doors and drawers, checking table tops for cleanliness.

"Thank you. We'll take them," he announced shortly. "You may remain, my dear. I'll go downstairs and sign us in." Sofya settled on the divan, while her husband went out with the clerk, talking about rental rates and deposits.

In a couple of minutes Vladimir was back. He had ordered his bag to be fetched. Tea and a light snack would be sent up to the room. Smiling, he threw himself down in a large armchair across from her.

"There are advantages to being bourgeois," she admitted.

They talked about everything and nothing. Of course, Vladimir inquired about Julia, and in turn entertained Sofya with new stories of their mutual acquaintances and scientific friends in France and England.

Alone together, behind locked doors, Vladimir had an attentive listener for his vivid description of the restoration of Paris after the war and uprising. The city would soon be its joyful self. He bragged shamelessly of the enormous success his edition of Darwin's *The Descent of Man* was enjoying in Russia. For once, he was not without funds. And he described the warm welcome he'd been given by Huxley, who had introduced his paper before the Royal Academy. London was easily his favorite city, with the exception of Petersburg and Moscow, of course.

"Speaking of Russia, of home," Sofya interrupted hesitantly. Her eyes as well as her voice dropped as she spoke. "I heard of your unfortunate encounter in Odessa at the magesterium exam."

"Yes." Vladimir's hand was clenched and he was striking the arm of the chair in a rhythmic fashion. "It seems it will be some time before I am allowed a teaching position at home."

"I wish you had told me you were planning on taking the examination." Sofya rubbed the soft velvet fabric of the divan with the back of her hand. "I could have come and helped you evaluate and compensate for the personalities of your examiners. Your examination would have gone more favorably, had you taken their idiosyncrasies into consideration." She couldn't raise her eyes to him. "I remember how much you helped me in Heidelberg."

"My dear Sofya." Vladimir's voice was sad, not in the least accusing. "You would not have left your studies to join me. I believe you were in the midst of preparing a research paper to be submitted as your doctoral thesis."

Then she told him of her bitter disappointment. She could not submit her research for a doctorate. Schwarz had published the results before her. She would need at least another year of work to develop a new topic.

Vladimir's outrage, as great as her own, came with the freshness of surprise. He had known nothing of her disappointment, the tragedy too recent to have been in Anyuta's letters and her own notes had said nothing of this. Then his words of encouragement and confidence somehow soothed.

After some time, Vladimir rose to stretch his legs. As he walked from room to room again examining the quarters, Sofya slipped off her shoes, and curled her feet under her.

She closed her eyes and rested her head against the high-backed divan. How relaxing the last few hours had been, she thought. How strange that although she and Vladimir had been apart, angry and hurt for so long, after they had shared their disappointments and ignored any reference to their future, they had reestablished the relaxed, affectionate feelings she remembered from their first years of friendship.

WHEN SHE OPENED HER EYES, Vladimir was standing before her, staring down at her as if studying one of his paleontological specimens. Their eyes met.

"Sorry," he said with embarrassment. "I couldn't help admiring you, while you slept."

"I wasn't asleep." She pushed a wayward strand of hair behind her ear.

"Oh?" Vladimir smiled. "While you were not asleep, I smoked my last bit of tobacco. I'll go to that little shop we passed this afternoon and be right back. Then I'll take you to supper in the hotel restaurant."

Her legs felt stiff when she moved them out from under her; she must have been curled up on the divan longer than she thought. "I can't possible eat another bite. But if it is really late enough for supper, I'd better be on my way."

"You don't have to leave. I could send one of the hotel maids to retrieve your things from the boardinghouse." His voice softened. "Stay here with me."

Sofya looked up from tying her shoe.

Vladimir clumsily pushed his unlit pipe back into a pocket. "You'll be a lot more comfortable. And you'll get more studying done. Here there are no students fighting and yelling down the hall."

"Are you sure that's what you want?" She spoke hesitantly. "You understand I can't . . ." This was so difficult. "I won't . . ." She sighed.

"I understand. Yes, I'm sure I want you to stay." His eyes shone. "On our usual terms, of course."

"Thank you," she whispered. Then, to fill what threatened to become an awkward silence, she hurriedly added, "You needn't send for a maid. While you're getting your tobacco, I'll gather my things. I don't have much. And I'll show the hotel clerk my passport. I wouldn't want to raise any eyebrows."

Both shoes now tied, and feeling more composed, she stood up to face him. "I must say I admire your confidence."

"Oh? My confidence about what?"

"In asking for a suite with two bedrooms. That was a little presumptuous, don't you think?"

"Quite the contrary. I wanted the larger bedroom for my things. I'm traveling with a trunk of specimens, bones. I'll do some work. I'm something of a vagabond now. Never knowing how long I'll stay in a place or where I'll go next. Always searching for a home . . . an academic home that is. If I'd ordered a suite with only one bedroom, the room would have been much too small. You, my dear, will have to make do with the smaller quarters and I shall have to retire among the bones."

"The smaller quarters it is." She smiled. When their eyes met, she hesitated, then added solemnly, "With this arrangement, we will certainly have the opportunity to discuss serious matters relating to our futures. You haven't mentioned the last letter I sent you."

Vladimir looked away. "Some things I suppose I am afraid to talk about."

Impulsively Sofya reached out to lightly touch his hands. "Vladimir, I can leave for Russia with Anyuta. I'll initiate the request for our divorce. You'll be free."

He looked into her eyes. Pushing aside her hands, he took a step back from her. "That will be a very disturbing process, for you and for your family. They'll all be dragged into this. I suppose I should be the one to talk to your father, to explain as best I can."

"No! I will manage my parents." Sofya felt a rush of anger. "I assume I'm to file on grounds of infidelity." She could hardly say the word. "I suppose, when the time comes, you'll give me some names."

His face flushed deeply, but he said nothing. She wanted him to deny this. To say it was all a formality.

He stepped behind her. Of course, he would want to conceal his embarrassment. His voice was unsteady. "When I wrote asking you to— to do this thing"—he stumbled over the words—"I had no idea you would still not be finished with your degree." His hands gently brushed at her hair and came to rest on her shoulders. She felt her body go rigid, not knowing if his touch was meant as a caress.

She felt his breath pass her ear. He whispered, "Don't return to Russia now."

"Vladimir, you want . . ." He didn't let her finish. His grip on her shoulders was firm. She didn't try to turn to him. If he looked into her eyes, he'd see the desperate pain the words were causing her.

"I promised I'd help you with your education. I mean to keep that promise," Vladimir stated firmly.

"That promise was made years ago." Infinitely saddened by his loveless answer, Sofya could barely hear her own voice. "I release you."

"I decline your release. I mean to fulfill my part of our bargain." He lowered his voice. "We made another promise to each other. After London. After Darwin's house."

"You're free of that obligation, too." She pulled from his grip and turned to face him. If he had just said that he loved her—but he had not. Their future life together, which had once seemed almost within reach, was fading into unreality. Now she was ready to strike with a defiant claim of not wanting or needing his help, ready to tell him exactly what she thought of his devotion to "honor." But his eyes gleamed with tears, his face contorted with pain. How could she tell him how ridiculous and meaningless his sense of honor was to her? She wanted freely given loyalty, friendship, companionship. She wanted devoted love. Still, if gratitude and honor were all that was keeping him with her, well, she could settle for that. Anything to delay the awful time when she would lose him completely.

FOR MORE THAN A WEEK, Vladimir stationed himself at the student library. The displaced women, desperate for information on universities that would accept them, anxiously sought his advice and help. Sofya offered her assistance, encouraging the women, helping with packing, shipping books, and making travel arrangements as the women hurriedly organized their academic credentials and sought out their professors for letters of recommendation.

Exhausted, Sofya and Vladimir vowed to spend Sunday in peace at their apartment.

The dinner dishes had been removed by the hotel waiter, whom Sofya generously rewarded with money for his tea. A day with good food, the wonderful company of Vladimir, and relaxation, punctuated with a glorious walk along the riverbank with Vladimir expounding as he always did on wonders of science and glories of literature, had put her in a mellow and generous mood. The prospect of a whole evening of reading a new novel which Vladimir had chosen for her from a dusty little bookshop was almost too self-indulgent.

She sighed so loudly as she settled into the overstuffed chair with her book resting on her lap, that Vladimir turned briefly and smiled. She treasured the book as much for the emotional pleasure of a gift from Vladimir as for whatever intellectual pleasure it might give. She opened the cover, the book's author was French, a man named Jules Verne, the title *Vingt Mille Lieues sous Les Mers*. She opened it to the place she had marked.

"I read somewhere that Verne consults a friend, a mathematician, for verification of all his scientific data. Wish I could remember the mathematician's name," Vladimir offered, as always ready with bits of fascinating trivial detail.

"I might have recognized the name."

Vladimir grunted an "oh" and returned to his papers. Shoes off, he had stretched his long legs to rest on one arm of the divan, while his head lay on the other. His chest was buried in a cascade of newspapers, French, German, and English mingled with Russian pages. A cup half full of tea rested on the floor within his easy reach.

She opened the book, and examined the frontispiece engraving, a disturbing illustration that perpendicularly sliced sky, sea, and undersea. A large whalelike creature, half-in half-out of the water, dominated the page. In the lower corner two small humans in strange attire, their heads engulfed in a large bubble, stared up at the animal and at the sea's surface. In the distance, on the surface, a ship at full sail made for the edge of the paper.

Sofya tore her eyes from the fascinating but disturbing picture. "Vladimir, I'm so glad we spent today together. No visits with students, no professors, and best of all no politics. Just us, alone in a world of wonder. Like these two figures below the sea."

Vladimir grunted agreement. But he did not sound terribly interested.

Men. With a smile she turned up the lamp light and began to read. No wonder Vladimir liked this book. On the first page there was a mention of the French paleontologist and naturalist, Cuvier, whose collection of bones Vladimir had studied in Paris, while the world around him flamed and died in war. Sofya pushed aside thoughts of those dark days and read on.

She had just reached the part where Professor Aronnax had been asked to sign on the frigate *Abraham Lincoln* when a knock at the door interrupted her reading.

"I'll get it." Vladimir grunted again, this time more emphatically, as he swung his feet to the floor and stuck them into his boots. He ran his hands quickly through his hair and pushed the pile of papers under the divan.

Sofya carefully positioned the silk place marker, closed the book, and placed it next to the lamp on the table. Then she stood to greet the unexpected guest.

At the entrance of the apartment the attractive, neatly attired Elizaveta Fedorovna Litvinova was speaking animatedly with Vladimir.

With a catlike grin Litvinova took in the domestic scene.

"Sorry to disturb you." Litvinova moved toward Sofya, hand out-stretched in greeting. "I felt I needed to consult with you on an important question."

"Would you like me to leave you ladies alone?" Vladimir looked from one to the other. "I can just as easily read the newspapers in my room."

"Yes, thank you," Litvinova nodded to him. "I must discuss with Sofya matters regarding," she paused, "Weierstrass and my chances in Berlin."

Vladimir's face darkened, but Sofya doubted that Litvinova would notice the change in his manner. Or that she would interpret it for the jealous reflex that Weierstrass's name always brought to Vladimir.

"Well, Liza, may I get you some tea?" With difficulty Sofya pushed aside her annoyance at a ruined evening. She would try to sound friendly toward this woman whose presence had rekindled some very unpleasant feelings between her and Vladimir.

Litvinova settled onto the divan, and began calmly.

"Like every other Russian woman in town, I've been trying to decide how to deal with the Tsar's ukase. I've heard that you and Vladimir have been most helpful. I realize that you, in particular, may be able to help me." The woman hesitated, coyly looking down at folded hands before again locking her gaze on Sofya. "If Weierstrass would sponsor me, I could leave Zurich for Berlin."

"I doubt that even I could assure you of Weierstrass's help." Sofya spoke calmly and confidently, although a pang of fear knotted her stomach. Was this woman going to replace her as Weierstrass's protégé? "Of course, Herr Professor Weierstrass is anxious to help talented women. And, I would gladly support your request." Sofya hoped the slight blush she felt creep across her cheeks as she lied about her willingness to approach Weierstrass was not too obvious. She knew she would never support another woman's efforts at gaining mathematical intimacy with her Karl. She wouldn't even mention the woman's name to him. "But, Weierstrass only takes advanced students. I'm afraid, Liza, that although you show great promise and determination, you just haven't achieved the level of proficiency Weierstrass demands. In another year or two, perhaps."

"Yes," Litvinova sighed. "I was afraid Professor Weierstrass wouldn't consider taking on an undergraduate student. But, you understand, I had to be sure. You see, Professor Schwarz has offered continued support of my work. Or, if I prefer, he'll recommend me to the faculty at Bern."

"He's certainly an admirable mentor. You're very fortunate he's taken an interest in you."

"Yes, but if I stay, I'm defying the ukase. There may be no place for me when I return home." Litvinova's voice softened, "I want to return home someday, Sofya. You understand that, don't you?"

The woman became so upset by this confession, that Sofya moved to the divan and gently touched her arm to comfort her. "Is there no other mathematician in Europe that you would like to work with?"

"No. Only Weierstrass or Schwarz." Litvinova nervously picked Vladimir's red hairs from the arm of the divan. "Really, Sofya, you know that they are the very best in our field. Why would I settle for less. Certainly, you won't."

"No. I won't. Although Schwarz also has offered to sponsor my work, I've decided to return to Weierstrass. It's not the ukase, mind you, I just think I can get my doctorate sooner, if I stay with Weierstrass."

"And he is the very best of the best," Litvinova said. "I had to be sure there was no chance for me now with Weierstrass before I risked my whole future by staying in Zurich."

"Liza, for you, Zurich is the best mathematical option, if not the best politically."

"Well, that's settled." Litvinova stood and again extended a hand to Sofya. "I'll let you and Vladimir continue your quiet, domestic evening." Her voice sounded just a bit catty.

Certainly, Sofya thought, Litvinova was not so naive as to be unaware of the effect of Sofya's private life on her race to a doctorate. All Litvinova saw was a tender, attentive, supportive husband and a grateful wife. Sofya apparently was again in control of her emotional life. Good, that was the impression she needed to give any potential rivals.

Sofya met Litvinova's hard eyes. Sofya had no intention of becoming a complacent hare to Litvinova's plodding tortoise.

ON MONDAY AFTERNOON when Sofya arrived at the library, she found Vladimir alone, seated at one of the large tables. He appeared to be reading a letter, and took no notice of her entrance. As she approached, she saw his brows come together in a look of deep concern. Now she was close enough to smell the faint odor of expensive perfume as he turned the pink pages. When she was directly across the table from him, she could see that the letter was written in English. "Something wrong?" Sofya asked in way of greeting.

"No," Vladimir answered shortly, apparently startled by her presence.

He collected the pages from the table, carefully folded them and put them into his jacket pocket. "How was your morning?" His voice was now emotionless. "I hope your goodbyes with Anyuta weren't too draining."

"No more than you would expect," Sofya said coolly. "I see you have a foreign letter." She let her voice linger on the word "foreign." "I also have received a letter. Weierstrass is back in Berlin. He wants me to return as soon as possible. He's come across a problem he thinks will interest me, a problem that just might be worthy of a dissertation. I'm returning in two days. I've bought my train ticket."

"You might have spoken to me before purchasing your ticket," he said with a note of hurt. He didn't wait for a response from her. Holding the fragrant pink letters in his hand, he continued, "I've been asked to return to England, to continue my studies." He paused. "With a friend."

Sofya felt her face grow warm. With an unsteady jerking motion she moved to one of the heavy, nearby chairs and sat down across the table from Vladimir. Unable to bring herself to look him in the face, she thumbed the pages of a book that lay to her right. The silence grew heavy. Her eyes still down, she asked in a soft voice, "You'll go?"

"I haven't bought my ticket," he said in a flat, almost accusatory voice. Vladimir got up from his chair. He moved to the entrance of the library and closed the door. "The singing coming from the cafeteria is a little loud. You recognized the tune?"

"It's a folk song. I recall hearing it sung by the peasants of our district,"

"Correct. We heard it the last time we were together at Palibino. Remember?"

She did remember. It had been their wedding day.

"So you'll be in London while I'm in Berlin. We'll go on as we have, until I've finished my degree." Sofya fought back tears.

"That wasn't what I had in mind." Vladimir paced. "As we decided, being free of our 'ties' to each other is not possible, at this time. And being apart, without being free, didn't work very well for either of us."

She looked up. "I can't, I won't 'normalize' our marriage. Not now. Not while I'm still completing my degree. You know that."

"You've repeated it many times," he said in a whisper. After a painful pause he continued, "What I have in mind is my taking a tiny bachelor apartment in Berlin. I could store my collection there, and establish a place conducive to writing scientific papers. Of course, I would travel frequently, to London, Paris, Petersburg, other centers of science. And

I'd have my field work. Still, I'd be stationed in Berlin. You would remain with Julia. We'd see each other regularly. I could be of support to you while you finish your work. And you would advise me on my search for a position. I'm not tactful or skilled at this aspect of developing a career in science."

"And when I've gotten my degree?"

"We'll reevaluate our situation." Vladimir nervously ran his hand through his hair.

Sofya looked at him. Did this make sense? Probably not, but still they could help each other. The pain of losing him would be postponed, for a year, maybe more.

CHAPTER THIRTY-ONE

1874 ◆ Berlin
A Doctorate for Sofya

In Berlin, spring was fickle. One day the sun shone brightly on the mud-darkened piles of snow; the next, she never appeared.

The gray evening sky threatened snow. Vladimir pulled at the collar of his overcoat, securing it more closely around his neck, then tucked his chin down into the warmth. His ears were cold. Sofya would scold him for not having brought a hat.

The weather could not dampen Vladimir's joyful anticipation. It was Friday. For the first time in many weeks he would be with Sofya. Tonight dinner, tomorrow a picnic in the country, and Sunday morning before her mathematical session they'd visit the zoological gardens. He'd impress her with his knowledge of biology and the evolution of the different animals. He still had fun impressing Sofya.

Over the months, he found himself planning more and more time in his small Berlin apartment. Sofya had actually suggested that she stay at his place on weekends. She explained that her relationship with Julia had become just a trifle strained as each worked at a fever pitch on their dissertations. A break from their routine would leave Julia some much needed privacy. A certain green-eyed chemistry student whom Julia had met in Zurich had taken to appearing at their door on Saturdays. The incomprehensible chatter between him and Julia was really quite distracting.

Vladimir's weekend nights in Berlin were relegated to the divan. But still, Sofya was near. Her presence had worked its old magic. He was again under her power.

He pushed the slippery package he carried under the arm of his overcoat back securely in place. He had arrived at her building. He hurried down the stairs to the basement apartment, knocked on the door.

"Come in, Vladimir." Julia opened the door wide for his entrance. "My, you look happy."

He smiled broadly. "Where's Sofya?" he asked anxiously as he strode into the living area.

"Patience, man, patience." She laughed and put a warm hand to his cheek. "You're cold. Your ears are almost as red as your hair."

"It's starting to snow. Very lightly." He put his package on the table and hung his coat on the simple coat tree.

Julia had already poured him a cup of tea.

"Thanks." Still standing, he sipped his tea. "I hope Sofya's ready? I have dinner reservations at a little place near Alexanderplatz. It's recommended by a very prominent Russian acquaintance here in Berlin on business."

"So fancy?" Julia commented.

"Well, yes. Just this once." Vladimir sounded almost apologetic. "I received some money from my brother, a gift of sorts. And I want to celebrate. The monograph I've been preparing for months is finally ready."

"Vladimir, that's wonderful! I'm so happy for you."

"My victories are all due to Sofya. She keeps me focused on the task." Vladimir beamed with pleasure. "I've planned a weekend devoted to pampering my lady."

"You, sir, are an incurable romantic."

Good-naturedly nodding agreement, he put his cup down and strode to the closed door of Sofya's room. He knocked lightly. "Are you almost ready?" A moment passed without an answer. "Perhaps you'd like me to help choose your gown?"

Silence. Vladimir shot Julia a questioning look.

Julia made a helpless gesture. "She was sequestered in that room when I left this morning. When I came back from the lab about an hour ago, I knocked on the door and called to her. I was worried she might not be well. Her response was just to growl at me to go away."

Grimly Vladimir knocked again, this time more firmly, then gently opened the door. The room was dismally dark and stuffy. "Sofya?" he whispered softly, not wanting to startle her from what must be deep concentration. There was no reply from the figure at the desk, back to the door. He entered, gently closing the door behind him.

The gas had not been lighted, and only the yellow glow of a large candle illuminated stacks of crumpled papers. He drew closer. She was leaning over, her head resting on one hand, her other hand scribbling unrecognizable symbols, now and then crossing out lines. Starting over. More scribbles. She appeared to be in some kind of a trance. Afraid to interrupt her concentrated state, he softly retreated toward her bed, where he sat and waited several minutes, in silence, thinking. What a strange woman! The almost inhuman intensity of her concentration both attracted and repelled him. He envied that world of symbols that could so completely possess her soul.

When he saw her stir slightly in the chair, he called her name. Sofya started, her body twitching. Her head turned until her eyes met his, but it was a second or two before he saw recognition in them.

"Sorry I startled you," he told her warily.

"Why are you here? Go away!" Her voice was husky, strained. She turned to her work, then looked back at him again and spoke in softer tones. "Later. Please, later."

"Sofya. We're having dinner together tonight. We planned this last weekend." He could hear the pleading in his voice and he detested it.

"I can't stop now. I'm onto something." Her eyes were shining as she talked on, obviously more to herself than to him. "I've had a feeling from the start that there was an exception to the cases I had claimed I could solve by substituting the differential equations with analytical ones. But till now, all my counterexamples were too complicated, too obscure. Now I've hit upon a beautifully simple, counterexample of a class of equations that can't be solved by this method. I think I can show that the heat equation is the simplest of these. Oh Vladimir, it's wonderfully beautiful! If I can do this, even Weierstrass will be amazed. I knew it was an exception, I just felt it." She turned back to her work.

"I suppose you realize I don't know what you're talking about." His feelings of tenderness were turning to anger. "Obviously, you're not coming out this evening."

Sofya's lips parted, as if she might be about to speak, but no sound came. Her eyes were on the papers.

Vladimir's voice rose. "Can you understand that I wanted to be with you? Or is there some equation I have to write before I can get you to accept that truth?"

Somehow he had got through. Sofya put down her pencil and turned to him, a look of anger growing on her face. "You're acting like a spoiled child. To miss one dinner upsets you so? You know I have to finish this paper. I can't control when an idea's going to strike me. If I stop now it will take hours to get back to this point. Perhaps I never could get back." Her eyes were puffy from strain, her face lined with exhaustion.

Vladimir could only stare at her. "I will not bother you further." He left the room, slamming the door behind him.

Trying desperately to control his anger, he entered the living area to find Julia sitting, obviously pretending to read. She had overheard too many of their outbursts for him to be embarrassed by her hearing this one.

After taking a few deep breaths, he said, "There's no sense our going hungry. Can you be ready for dinner in fifteen minutes, Julia?"

Julia stared at him. "I don't think I should accept."

"I need to talk. I don't want to be alone. I'm afraid I'll act too rashly and destroy what I'm so close to possessing." His voice was halting. "Please, Julia, as my friend and Sofya's, please be with me tonight."

As THEY WERE SHOWN to their table, Julia was surprised to hear snatches of Russian conversation, coming from nearby tables. To judge by the fine dress of the customers, in this expensive decor, it seemed her fellow diners were Russian aristocrats, indulging themselves in the high culture of the new capital of a united Germany. Or perhaps they were businessmen. The filthy factories springing up on the outskirts of Berlin apparently were drawing not only unprecedented numbers of peasants to the city, but also moneyed men, seeking to further enrich themselves through the new industries. In the more than three years she had lived in this city, she had never experienced this side of the new Berlin. She felt more than a little uncomfortable.

Fortunately, Vladimir had reserved a small room, separated from the main area of diners by a curtain. She would not be reminded that she was a part of the group beyond the curtain.

The meal was excellent, though her mind was elsewhere. When the dessert of fruit, nuts, cheese and a delicate champagne appeared, Julia bravely decided to open the topic of real concern. "Sofya's been working long hours these last few weeks—I mean long hours even for her. So be patient with her, her nerves are raw. She can't stand the thought of being beaten out again, as she was by Schwarz."

"Simultaneous breakthroughs happen in all the sciences. Sofya recovered magnificently. She's not a one-problem person. Since she returned to Berlin, she's finished two papers. Either of which, she tells me, could be used as a dissertation. There's the paper on Saturn's rings and the one on . . ."

"Abelian functions," Julia finished for him.

"Whatever they are," he snapped. He cracked a walnut in his rough hands and dug the nutmeat from its shell before continuing. "Why doesn't she leave it at that? Is she intentionally delaying the finish of her studies?"

"I understand your position. Really I do." Julia sipped at her drink. "She must have told you that Weierstrass thinks she's on to something very important with this latest paper on partial differential equations. If it proves as fruitful as he expects, not only would she be assured of a degree, but her place in mathematical history would be secured. Vladimir, you can't ask her to give up a fair chance at that kind of accomplishment."

"She doesn't hear me, when I ask her things," Vladimir commented without enthusiasm, reaching for another nut.

"Come, now. You want her success as much as she does." Julia sighed. "At least, that was what you told her six years ago."

"But must she always drive herself so? No matter what the cost to her personal life, to our life?" Vladimir lowered his voice. "Julia, she even treats you poorly when she's in one of her moods."

Julia's silence was agreement. Without looking at Vladimir she commented, "I think it's precisely the intensity of her personality which makes her so attractive to you."

Vladimir smiled. "Perhaps you're right."

He refilled his glass, drank the contents, then refilled it again. A long silence passed before he said, "You're completing a dissertation too. Still you make time for dinner, a walk, a talk with a friend."

"Only for a very special friend. I'll have you know, sir, I work very hard."

"I know, I know." Vladimir smiled. "Forgive me, I didn't mean you were not working."

"Actually, my work is going very well." Julia blushed. Then, covering her discomfort, she continued, "My sponsor is about to submit my petition for a doctorate to Göttingen University. By fall, with luck, I may have my degree."

"I'm very happy for you." Vladimir nodded slowly. "I assume you're planning on returning home to Russia."

"Yes, of course. I've missed my family, Moscow, our estate. All those familiar people and places."

"Sofya says she wants to go home too. When she has her doctorate in hand." Vladimir ran his hand through his hair nervously. "She says she's tired of being a gypsy."

"And you . . ."

"Me? My career?" Vladimir drew a breath. "I haven't said anything to Sofya, but I've been considering an offer from Professor Suess in Vienna. It would mean delivering a series of lectures on paleontology for beginning students, starting this fall. And I'd be paid! My new monograph will be published by then, and I'm preparing a little pamphlet explaining the unfortunate situation surrounding my failed magesterium examination. I expect other offers.

"And, when I abandon myself to daydreams where money and other obligations have no hold, I dream of going to America. Cope and Marsh are making some magnificent finds in the American West."

"Escaping to America? Just like Chernyshevsky's hero?" Julia mocked him. "You are such a dreamer." She looked searchingly into his sparkling blue eyes, "And no longing for home? For Russia? I'd miss you, Vladimir. Sofya would miss you. She needs you."

"All Sofya wants or needs is her work." The words were emotionless, flat.

"You're very wrong," Julia said softly. "She needs you, desperately. I'm amazed two brilliant scientists can't assimilate the simple fact that they need and love each other." Julia's gaze turned down to her napkin. "Take my word as a chemist. The structure of Sofya's nature is such that she must combine herself strongly with another. And she has decided that other is you. And the structure of your nature is such that you, unfortunate man, must combine with her." Julia smiled. "Although my analogy is weak, the chemical bond between you and Sofya is not. I've observed it, quite unscientifically, for the last six years."

"Thank you, for spending this evening with me." Vladimir reached across the table and touched her hand.

She felt her face grow warm. Vladimir was a hopelessly lovable fellow.

WHEN THEY REACHED the apartment, Julia invited Vladimir to come in, just for a moment.

"Just for a moment." He gently accepted her offer. "I'll keep the cab waiting." He returned to the cabbie and handed the man a few bills.

Julia had her latchkey in hand when the door suddenly flew open.

"Well, here you are at last," Sofya greeted them breathlessly. She was wearing a very flattering gown and her hair was arranged neatly. She seemed barely able to stand still. Her face was aglow, her eyes wide, showing no sign of fatigue or strain.

Staring in disbelief, Julia edged past her into the living room.

As Vladimir entered, Sofya threw herself at him and kissed him ardently.

"I'm done! My God, I'm done!" The words came out in something like a scream. A moment later she had released him, and started pacing around the room. "And the work is wonderful, beautiful! After you left my room, Vladimir, I looked at the work again and everything fit into place. I don't think it took me more than an hour to finish. I was writing so fast my hand cramped. And it's absolutely magnificent!"

Vladimir and Julia stared at her, then looked at each other, half afraid that they were dealing with a madwoman.

But Sofya's speech was rational as she paced the room and talked. "I'll show the papers to Karl on Sunday. Oh, he'll pick and poke at the details, but I just know, I feel that my work is unshakably correct, beautiful. And I'm starving. Absolutely starving. I've eaten half the box of chocolates you left, Vladimir. And I've had endless cups of tea, waiting for you. I may have worn a spot in the rug from dancing around in circles. Oh, how I wish you'd been here." She went to Vladimir and once more threw her arms around him, tugged at him, humming and urging him to dance with her. "I'm free now! Free! This paper is as good as my degree. The rest is formality."

"If you think you can sit in one place long enough, I'll take you for a real meal and perhaps a little something to calm you down."

"Oh yes, now, right now," Sofya insisted. "Then, you'll take your wife home. I want to go home, to our home. I don't want to return to that room that cave and cage. Not tonight. Maybe not ever."

He looked at her for a long moment, in silence. His lips moved, but he seemed unable to find words. At last all he said was: "The cab is waiting. And my apartment will have to do as home tonight."

Sofya ran to the door.

"Here's your coat." Julia hugged Sofya's shoulders as she placed the garment around her friend. "Celebrate, my dear friends." Putting her lips close to Sofya's ear, she whispered, "I won't expect you back tonight."

๑๖

JUNE HAD ARRIVED before Karl had submitted her smoothly polished dissertation, along with her two earlier papers, to Göttingen. A flurry of notes had been exchanged between Karl and Professor Lazarus Fuchs, her supporter in Göttingen. Karl insisted she be excused from the customary oral examination. She felt she could stand before an arena of hungry lions and defend herself, if that would hasten a favorable decision, but Karl's understanding of academic tactic was far better than hers, so she had agreed.

And now she waited, and waited, for the judgment of the Göttingen mathematicians. Once again in the apartment she had shared with Julia, Sofya sat staring aimlessly into a cold fireplace, useless in August. Once she had commented, half in jest, that she found the gaping emptiness of a fireplace in summer vaguely frightening, like watching moving clouds or shadows in the night. On hearing this, Vladimir had insisted on filling the opening with plants, but in this dim, poorly ventilated room, the plants had withered. Now, an arrangement of bright paper flowers filled the void, with a brave imitation of cheerful life.

Sofya picked up a chemistry book and thumbed mindlessly through the pages. Vladimir, almost as frustrated as she by the waiting, had gone to Vienna for a few days to take care of some details and say farewell to his beloved Professor Seuss.

Sofya hated waiting alone. A book wasn't going to fill the emptiness, not now. She let it fall back to the table, then checked the time on the small watch she had pinned to her dress. Julia, completely absorbed in preparing for her oral examination, had left early for the university library, but perhaps she would be back for lunch.

Leaning back in her chair, Sofya dreamed of her new life. She and Vladimir would be professors in Petersburg or Moscow. They might accept a position at some respected university outside one of Russia's two capitals. Or even teach at one of the higher gymnasiums, until something better became available. They would settle into domestic bliss, like Vladimir's brother. At night they'd study and do research. She could visualize their small house, the home Vladimir had always wanted, crammed with lots of books and perhaps even a few noisy red-haired children—watched by a nanny of course. Sofya smiled to herself. This daydream was not unlike the one she'd had years ago when she thought she was in love with Dostoevsky. To be with a loved one, performing some great service, perhaps even in some far-off land had been her girlish dream. Now Russia had become the far-off land.

A knock at the door roused her. She hoped it was not Julia's troublesome green-eyed admirer.

"Karl!" Sofya stood motionless, staring at the large man who occupied the whole doorframe.

He blushed and stammered. "I believe my unseemly arrival at a time when your husband is out of town will be excused—I have received a telegram."

"For goodness sake, Karl, don't be ridiculous . . . a telegram?" Mechanically Sofya stepped aside to let him in. Suddenly her heart was hammering, at a possibility she was afraid to let herself believe. "Not illness in the family—?"

"No, no, nothing like that. It comes from Lazarus Fuchs." He drew the envelope, already opened, from his jacket pocket. Karl's eyes were riveted on her, and the strange joy in them seemed to confirm the unbelievable.

"Oh, let me see!" She snatched the envelope, fumbled with fingers that seemed half paralyzed, read hastily. "Fuchs says the committee was . . . very impressed with my work . . . and the degree is to be awarded . . . the doctorate . . . oh, Karl, this is wonderful!" Impulsively she seized him around the neck and kissed him on both cheeks.

Carefully he freed himself. "I'm sure you also noticed those three little words in Latin? The degree is granted *summa cum laude*. Of course, I expected nothing less from my star pupil. Didn't I tell you, Frau Doctor Kovalevskaya, what a marvelous, insightful piece of work you did?"

"Would you say that again, please?" She was clinging to his arm, laughing almost uncontrollably.

"Frau Doctor Sofya, you appear nearly hysterical." He slipped his arm around her shoulder. "But you have earned the right to some hysteria. Yes, earned the right. May I escort you on a vigorous walk? Perhaps over to my house where Clara and Elise are nearly as hysterical as you."

TONIGHT WAS SOFYA'S LAST in Berlin.

A week had passed since Sofya first heard of her victory. The telegram was in her pocket. It had not been more than an arm's length from her since she had torn it from Karl's grasp.

She could hardly remember a time in her life when she had felt so wonderfully happy. Perhaps those early months when she and Vladimir first conspired for their freedom. But that time had been shadowed by doubts. Now there was nothing to keep her from total bliss.

Tonight Karl and his sisters had asked that Sofya, Vladimir and Julia join them for a farewell dinner. Before the end of the first course, the sisters had extracted a promise from Julia to continue the tradition of Sunday visits.

By the time the small party retired to the living room for conversation and coffee, a quiet, distant, melancholic mood was creeping over Sofya.

Vladimir must be telling the other women an entertaining story, for they were laughing, even serious Clara. But off to one side, Karl stood with his hands in his pockets, staring somewhat vacantly at Vladimir.

Not disturbing the congenial group, Sofya gently touched Karl's elbow, and with a nod indicated he was to follow her.

Once the two of them were in Karl's study, Sofya let herself sink into the chair she had occupied so frequently over the last years. Karl stood in front of the desk, leaning against the strong oaken structure, his hands grasping the edge.

"I had to come in here again." Sofya looked around hungrily trying to imprint all the details of this room on her memory. "And I had to tell you again, how grateful I am for your help and friendship."

"I hope you will always think of me as your friend." He was staring at her intently. Perhaps he too wanted to capture images for his memory.

Her eyes were the first to pull away.

"You know, I'd become obsessed with the details of my dissertation paper. Still, I'm very grateful to you for presenting me with such a wonderful problem and for guiding me through to its resolution."

"I loved seeing your enthusiasm, your determination to search an idea to its end, even when you were clearly so exhausted. You are a true scholar."

Sofya smiled. "There is one important detail, however, that escaped my net. I haven't made arrangements for the publication of the paper."

"Don't fret. I'll see it's copied and sent to several professors who will be interested. I'll submit the section on partial differential equations to Crelle's Journal. Publication in the most prestigious mathematical journal in Europe will securely establish your claim to primacy in your findings."

"Thank you. Of course, I'll reimburse you for any expenses. It's just that I'm returning to Russia tomorrow and I fear I won't be able to handle this myself. When I'm in Russia, I become terribly slothful."

"You certainly don't need to apologize for a little bit of slothful behavior. You must renew yourself with a good rest from science."

"As I won't be around to return the favor of promoting quick publication, I'm going to remind you, Karl, that you must not wait so long in submitting your own work."

"So, now the student is scolding the teacher! You have indeed come into your own." Weierstrass laughed, then became serious. "I don't mind so much that my former students use my ideas for their papers. However, I would like them to give me credit, which most of them forget."

"I promise I will never omit recognition of your influence on my future work." She held up her hand as in an oath-taking. "But I want a promise in return."

"That sounds fair."

Sofya leaned toward him. "This is very important to me, Karl. I want you to promise not to take any other woman as a student."

"Dare I ask why?"

"Our meetings are so dear to me. The closeness of our minds, the likeness of our vision, is such a joy, I cannot bear the thought of sharing you with another woman in this way. Call it folly, I've been known to engage in foolish agreements. Call it jealousy, my eternal weakness. Call it a wise career move, I do have a calculating streak. Please, make the promise."

"Of course, I promise," he responded. "You are and always will be my dearest and my only woman confidant. If the university decides to allow women as regular graduate students, something not very likely, I will steer them to another professor."

A long silence passed in which they stared at each other, realizing what mystical vows they had made, almost a mathematical marriage.

Karl broke the spell. "Now, don't think you're getting off so easily, my dear. In turn I want a promise from you."

"What might that be?"

"Not to forget your old teacher and friend. You must write me often. And, you must promise to take a rest from your beloved studies."

"Well, it seems I'm getting quite a bargain, as I would have done what you ask without a promise."

A knock at the door was followed by Clara's voice. "Karl, I know you've no clock in there, but it's past midnight and you've had Sofya to yourself long enough. You must share her with Elise and me. We may not see her for some time."

"I've been rude and selfish, Clara." Karl formally offered Sofya his arm. "It seems I must share you with the others."

☙❧

WHEN THE LAST goodbyes had been said, Weierstrass gently closed the door to his home, and leaned against it.

There would be no more Sunday meetings—except with Julia, and that would be not at all the same.

Karl's sisters were busy in the living room clearing away the remains of the party. The dears had never learned to leave such chores to the maid. He would only be in their way, and he could not bear their happy chatter just now. He headed for his sanctuary, the study.

Karl sat in his great leather chair, stretched his hands out across the big table, and imagined the first time he had seen that beautiful girl sitting across from him. Now there would be no papers spread out between him and the one woman in the world of like mind. Sofya Vasilievna Kovalevskaya, doctor of philosophy in mathematics, awarded *summa cum laude* from the University of Göttingen, was no longer his student. She was his colleague in a distant land with only the promise of letters for companionship.

He was justly proud, he told himself, of his efforts on her behalf. His Sofya had won the distinction of being the first woman to receive a doctorate in mathematics since the days of the Italian Renaissance!

Her paper was a masterpiece. No one could question that.

He was so tired. He rested his head on his outstretched arms, aware of a dampness in his eyes.

"HURRY, SOFYA, we have to be at the station in forty-five minutes if I'm to have time to check all the baggage," Vladimir cheerfully called from the living room of Julia's apartment.

"I'm almost finished," Sofya responded from the room that had once been hers. "Have the porters carry out the trunk and boxes from the living room. Don't let them take that small flowered bag. I'll need that with me."

Vladimir looked questioningly around the room.

"She means these." Julia pointed to the somewhat battered containers. "We packed almost everything last night. She just needs to close up the trunk with her books and mathematical papers. I'll get the porters. See if you can't hurry her up." Julia was gone.

"Can I help?" Vladimir stood at the doorway of what had been Sofya's room.

"Oh, Volodya! Look, I've got all the books and notes and work papers into this last trunk."

"So why isn't it closed?"

"One more little package to go in." She held up a sheaf of copies of the papers she had submitted for her doctorate. "But I couldn't let them go. These papers are my ticket to a life in science."

"I see you've wrapped them with a satin ribbon. Now, tear yourself away from our 'children' and put them into the trunk."

"Of course." Sofya placed the package on top of an assortment of books and papers, then firmly closed the lid.

"I'll help you." Vladimir pulled one leather strap through the latch as Sofya secured the other.

"That's it," Sofya announced joyfully. "I'm done. I'm going home! I'm so happy." She twirled around the room while Vladimir watched.

"Oh, Vladimir, dance with me!" Together they waltzed around the room.

Julia appeared in the doorway with the porters and motioned for them to carry the last trunks down.

Breathlessly Sofya said, "I'm going home, Julia. To the life I've always wanted. Vladimir and I are happy at last. We won't have to worry about money or jobs or being apart. It will be so wonderful! And you'll join us? There is always a place for you with us, our dearest, truest friend."

"Just until I've found a place of my own, thank you." Julia laughed, paused, then added in a doubtful tone, "Assuming all goes well for me in Göttingen."

"I know you'll do brilliantly. Oh, Julia, we've done it. The three of us, all with our doctorates, full-fledged, bona fide scientists. It's a dream come true." Sofya held her arm out to her husband. "Vladimir, tell her. This is a dream come true."

He walked up to the women, putting an arm around each. A warm August breeze was billowing the curtains at the open window. "Ladies, the world awaits us. In fact, it lies at our feet."

Julia's voice was shaky. "If you two don't go soon, you'll miss your train."

"Julia, we're going to miss you." Vladimir sighed, and gave her a brother's kiss on both cheeks. "And you, dear friend, are not to fret about this upcoming examination. You'll do brilliantly."

"You know I'll join you just as soon as I can. Be sure you visit my family and reassure Mama that I'm just fine."

"Consider it done," Sofya said.

Julia looked at the happy couple. "You know, you are both very dear to me." Her voice was soft and filled with emotion. "And if you don't go soon, I think I will burst out crying."

BIBLIOGRAPHY

Bell, E. T. *Men of Mathematics*. Master and Pupil: Weierstrass (1815–1897); Sonya Kowalewski (1850–1891). New York: Simon and Schuster, 1937.

Cooke, Roger. *The Mathematics of Sonya Kovalevskaya*. New York: Springer-Verlag, 1984.

Kennedy, Don H. *Little Sparrow: A Portrait of Sophia Kovalevsky*. Athens, Ohio: Ohio University Press, 1983.

Koblitz, Ann Hibner. *A Convergence of Lives: Sofia Kovalevskaia: Scientist, Writer, Revolutionary*. Boston: Birkhäuser, 1983.

Kochina, P. la. editor. *S. V. Kovalevskaia: Reminiscences and Stories*. On the 125th anniversary of her birth. (In Russian.) 1974. [S. V. Kovalevskaia: Vospominaniia Povesti k. 125-letiiu so dnia rozhdeniia. Nauka. Moskva. 1974.]

Kochina, Pelegeya. *Love and Mathematics: Sofya Kovalevskaya*. Translated from the Russian by Michael Burov. Moscow: Mir Publishers, 1985, revised from the 1981 Russian edition.

Kovalevsky, Sonia and A. C. Leffler (Edgren), Duchessa di Cajanello. *Sonia Kovalevsky: Biography and Autobiography*. I. Memoir by Leffler II. Reminiscences of Childhood in Russia, written by herself. Translated into English by Louise von Cossel. London: Walter Scott, Ltd. Paternoster Square, 1895.

Kovalevsky, Sonya. *Sonya Kovalevsky: Her Recollections of Childhood*. Translated from the Russian by Isabel F. Hapgood. With a biography by Anna Carlotta Leffler, Duchess of Cajanello. Translated from the Swedish by A. M. Cliver Bayley and a biographical note by Lily Wolffsohn. New York: The Century Co., 1895.

Kovalevskaya, Sofya. *Sofya Kovalevskaya: A Russian Childhood*. Translated and introduced by Beatrice Stillman, and with an analysis of Kovalevskaya's mathematics by P. Y. Kochina, USSR Academy of Sciences. New York: Springer-Verlag, 1978.

Shtraikh, S. la. editor. *Reminiscences and Letters*. (In Russian.) Academy of Science, SSSR. 1961. [Vospominaniia i Pis'ma. Akademii Nauk SSSR. S. la. Shtraikh. 1961.]

ABOUT THE AUTHOR

Joan Spicci, a member of the Association for Women in Mathematics, has a bachelor's degree in mathematics from Loyola University of Chicago, and a master's degree in secondary mathematics education from DePaul University. She studied Russian language and history with private instructors and at the University of New Mexico. This, in addition to her mathematical education, made possible the translation of eighty-eight letters of Sofya Kovalevskaya (the first European woman to receive a PhD in mathematics) from Russian to English. She lives in New Mexico with her husband, science fiction and fantasy author Fred Saberhagen. Visit Joan at www.joanspicci.com.

PROPERTY OF:
DAVID O. McKAY LIBRARY
BYU-IDAHO
REXBURG ID 83460-0405